新制多益

全新！TOEIC 聽力題庫解析

Listening

解答本

目錄

本書特色

◆ 完整收錄 10 回聽力測驗模擬試題，比照正式測驗的題型分配及多國發音

本書收錄按照最新出題趨勢編寫的 10 回聽力測驗模擬試題，題型和難易度完整對應新制測驗，聽力題目音檔口音分成美國、加拿大、英國、澳洲式等，分配比例亦如同正式測驗。使你能夠逐步熟悉新制多益測驗的出題模式並熟練快速解題技巧，練就答題反應神經！

◆ 讓你實際測驗時覺得分外熟悉的擬真模擬試題，熟能生巧分數自然提高！

題目不論是太難還是太簡單，對於準備考試都很不利，唯有堅持每月入場應試，隨時根據真實出題趨勢調整模擬試題的難度、深度、廣度、出題傾向與題目型態，只要堅持練習，就能讓你熟悉多益測驗、成績大幅進步！

◆ 解題過程完整說明，讓你避開解題盲點，各種題型都能輕鬆解決！

本書完整分析聽力測驗中的各大題型及相對應的解題策略。解析部分除中英對照翻譯外，均清楚標示題目類型，並按照題型別在詳解中提出最佳解題策略，讓你能在正式測驗碰到類似題目時直接套用，提高解題效率及正確度！

◆ 特別收錄常考單字記憶表，加強記憶最常出現的高頻率單字及片語！

為了讓你更加熟悉經常出現在測驗中的單字和片語，本書特別將每回模擬測驗中的常考單字及片語，整理在解答本 10 回模擬測驗詳解後方的「常考單字記憶表」內，搭配隨書附贈的單字記憶 MP3，更能擴大自己的測驗單字庫、提升字彙實力！

◆ 隨書附上三種 MP3 音檔，滿足你的各種學習需求！

除了按照實際測驗內容，以美、英、澳、加等四國口音錄製的模擬測驗音檔，本書還附上了單題音檔，在複習時可以針對某一特定題目加強練習。另外，本書亦附上了常考單字記憶 MP3 以便複習常考單字記憶表，MP3 會以美、英口音先唸兩次重點單字，再唸一次中文字義，讓你能藉此熟練美英口音差異並加強單字記憶。

◆ 提升效率與效果的各種學習輔助工具，讓你的備考之路更輕鬆！

本書解答本內除詳解外，也附上了中英對照翻譯，再也不須相互對照題目本和解答本，並透過不同顏色標出解題關鍵線索，方便考生抓取解題重點。此外，本書特別收錄按照不同程度設計的學習計畫建議表、目標設定評量表、題型分析＆解題策略、自我檢測表、答案紙、分數換算表，幫助考生提升學習效率、加強成效！

頁面說明

Part 1

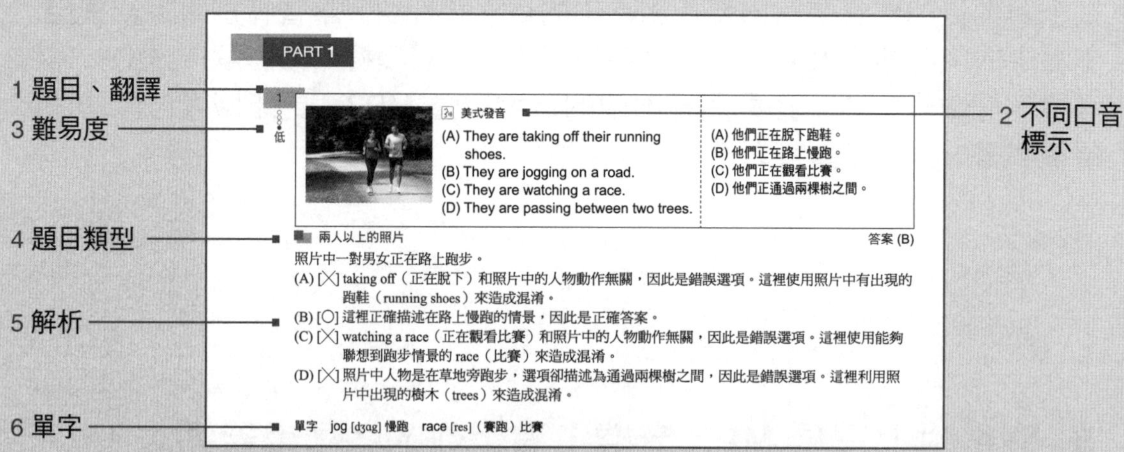

PART 1

1 低

美式發音

(A) They are taking off their running shoes.
(B) They are jogging on a road.
(C) They are watching a race.
(D) They are passing between two trees.

(A) 他們正在脫下跑鞋。
(B) 他們正在路上慢跑。
(C) 他們正在觀看比賽。
(D) 他們正通過兩棵樹之間。

兩人以上的照片　答案 (B)

照片中一對男女正在路上跑步。

(A) [╳] taking off（正在脫下）和照片中的人物動作無關，因此是錯誤選項。這裡使用照片中有出現的跑鞋（running shoes）來造成混淆。
(B) [○] 這裡正確描述在路上慢跑的情景，因此是正確答案。
(C) [╳] watching a race（正在觀看比賽）和照片中的人物動作無關，因此是錯誤選項。這裡使用能夠聯想到跑步情景的 race（比賽）來造成混淆。
(D) [╳] 照片中人物是在草地旁跑步，選項卻描述為通過兩棵樹之間，因此是錯誤選項。這裡利用照片中出現的樹木（trees）來造成混淆。

單字　jog [dʒɑg] 慢跑　race [res]（賽跑）比賽

Part 2

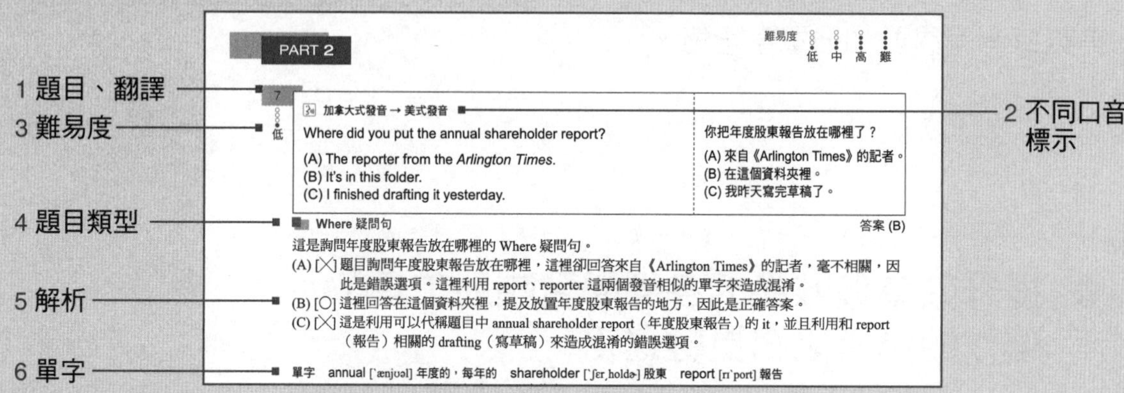

PART 2

難易度 低 中 高 難

7 低

加拿大式發音 → 美式發音

Where did you put the annual shareholder report?

(A) The reporter from the *Arlington Times*.
(B) It's in this folder.
(C) I finished drafting it yesterday.

你把年度股東報告放在哪裡了？

(A) 來自《Arlington Times》的記者。
(B) 在這個資料夾裡。
(C) 我昨天寫完草稿了。

Where 疑問句　答案 (B)

這是詢問年度股東報告放在哪裡的 Where 疑問句。

(A) [╳] 題目詢問年度股東報告放在哪裡，這裡卻回答來自《Arlington Times》的記者，毫不相關，因此是錯誤選項。這裡利用 report、reporter 這兩個發音相似的單字來造成混淆。
(B) [○] 這裡回答在這個資料夾裡，提及放置年度股東報告的地方，因此是正確答案。
(C) [╳] 這是利用可以代稱題目中 annual shareholder report（年度股東報告）的 it，並且利用和 report（報告）相關的 drafting（寫草稿）來造成混淆的錯誤選項。

單字　annual [ˋænjʊəl] 年度的，每年的　shareholder [ˋʃɛr͵holdɚ] 股東　report [rɪˋport] 報告

1. 題目、翻譯

本書收錄了能完整反映新制多益出題傾向的題目。考生在看中文翻譯之前，若能先看一次題目，回想自己為什麼會選出這個答案，再比對一旁的中文翻譯，就能更確實理解題目、掌握文章架構。

2. 不同口音標示

每題皆根據錄音檔中的腔調，標示美國、加拿大、英國、澳洲等不同國家的口音。即便是學過、背過的單字，也可能因為各國口音不同而聽不懂，這個標示將能幫助考生更了解自己對哪種口音的哪個單字或表達方式較不熟悉，方便集中學習。

3. 難易度

每道題目皆經過分析，依據難易度分為「低、中、高、難」四個級別，逐一標示在各題的題號之下，方便考生參考並依照個人英文能力和學習目標專注練習。

4. 題目類型

每一題都特別標示出題目類型，讓考生能夠更快掌握自己容易出錯的題型為何，也方便考生針對特定題型加強複習。

5. 解析

針對各種題型提出最有效、最快速的解題方式，並詳細說明錯誤選項為何不對，同時提供能幫助分辨陷阱選項的解題技巧與說明。

6. 單字

為減少在查看解析前還要先查單字的麻煩，每題皆附上該題出現的重要單字或片語的中文字義和音標。在以英國腔或澳洲腔發音的題目中，有些單字會因口音不同而使得發音不同，書上將同時標註美式、英式發音的音標，以方便考生了解各國口音的差別。

頁面說明

Part 3&4（含 新 新題型）

1 對話或獨白內容、題目、翻譯
2 不同口音標示
4 解題線索
4 解題線索
5 單字
6 題目類型
7 解析
3 難易度
8 換句話說
Questions 71-73 refer to the following telephone message.
第 71-73 題請參考以下電話留言。
英式發音
Marian, it's Haley. 71/72One of my friends invited me to go to the Franklin Music Festival with him on Saturday. 71I said I'd go, and I'd like you to come along too. The festival is going to be held at Carlson Park from noon until 10 P.M. We plan to go at 5:30 because 72our favorite band takes the stage at 6:30 and we'd like to get there an hour earlier to find good seats. Please call or text me whenever you get this message to let me know if you'll be joining us. 73I want to buy tickets this afternoon, since today's the last day to buy them at reduced prices.
Marian，我是 Haley。71/72 我有個朋友邀請我星期六跟他一起去 Franklin 音樂節。71 我說我會去，而且我希望妳也一起來。這場音樂節會從中午開始到晚上 10 點在 Carlson 公園舉行。我們打算 5 點 30 分過去，因為 72 我們最喜歡的樂團會在 6 點 30 分登台，所以我們想要提前一小時到那裡去找好位子。請妳在聽到這則訊息之後打電話或傳訊息給我，告訴我妳會不會和我們一起去。73 我想要在今天下午買票，因為今天是能用優惠價買票的最後一天。
71 What did the speaker agree to do?
(A) Attend an event
(B) Carpool to a meeting
(C) Distribute an itinerary
(D) Organize a festival
71 說話者同意做什麼？
(A) 出席一場活動
(B) 共乘汽車去一場會議
(C) 發送旅遊行程
(D) 籌劃一個節慶
72 What will happen at 6:30 on Saturday?
(A) A park will close.
(B) A band will be interviewed.
(C) A reservation will be made.
(D) A performance will begin.
72 星期六的 6 點 30 分會發生什麼？
(A) 公園會關閉。
(B) 將採訪樂團。
(C) 將進行預約。
(D) 表演會開始。
73 What does the speaker want to do later today?
(A) Exchange a product
(B) Purchase some tickets
(C) Visit a venue
(D) Send some invitations
73 說話者今天晚一點想要做什麼？
(A) 換一件商品
(B) 買一些票
(C) 造訪一個場地
(D) 寄一些邀請函
題目 invite [ɪnˋvaɪt] 邀請 come along 一起去 hold [美 hold 英 həʊld] 使發生；舉行
71 carpool [ˋkɑrˌpul] 共乘汽車 itinerary [aɪˋtɪnəˌrɛrɪ] 旅遊行程 organize [ˋɔrgəˌnaɪz] 籌劃
73 venue [ˋvɛnju] 場地 invitation [ˌɪnvəˋteʃən] 邀請函
71 細節事項相關問題—特定細項 答案 (A)
中
題目詢問說話者同意做什麼事，因此必須注意和題目關鍵字（agree to do）有關的內容。獨白說：「One of my friends invited me to go to the Franklin Music Festival with him on Saturday. I said I'd go」，表示朋友邀自己星期六去音樂節，而自己說會去，因此正確答案是 (A) Attend an event。
72 細節事項相關問題—接下來要做的事 答案 (D)
中
題目詢問星期六的 6 點 30 分時會發生什麼事情，因此要注意和題目關鍵字（6:30 on Saturday）相關的內容。獨白說：「One of my friends invited me to go to the Franklin Music Festival with him on Saturday.」，先說明有一位朋友邀自己星期六去音樂節，接著說：「our favorite band takes the stage at 6:30」，表示最喜歡的樂團會在 6 點 30 分登台，因此正確答案是 (D) A performance will begin.。
換句話說
band takes the stage 樂團登台 → A performance ~ begin 表演開始
73 細節事項相關問題—特定細項 答案 (B)
低
題目詢問說話者今天晚一點想做什麼事情，因此必須注意和題目關鍵字（want to do later today）相關的內容。獨白說：「I want to buy tickets this afternoon」，表示想在今天下午買票，因此正確答案是 (B) Purchase some tickets。

1. 對話或獨白內容、題目、翻譯

本書收錄了能完整反映新制多益出題傾向的題目。考生在看中文翻譯之前，若能先看一次題目，回想自己為什麼會選出這個答案，再比對一旁的中文翻譯，就能更確實理解題目、掌握文章架構。

2. 不同口音標示

每題皆根據錄音檔中的腔調，標示美國、加拿大、英國、澳洲等不同國家的口音。即便是學過、背過的單字，也可能因為各國口音不同而聽不懂，這個標示將能幫助考生更了解自己對哪種口音的哪個單字或表達方式較不熟悉，方便集中學習。

3. 難易度

每道題目皆經過分析，依據難易度分為「低、中、高、難」四個級別，逐一標示在各題的題號之下，方便考生參考並依照個人英文能力和學習目標專注練習。

4. 解題線索

解答本中皆以不同顏色的字體標示出各題的解題線索。建議在看解析之前，先找出對話或獨白中所標示的解題關鍵線索，以練習解題。

5. 單字

為減少在查看解析前還要先查單字的麻煩，每題皆附上該題出現的重要單字或片語的中文字義和音標。在以英國腔或澳洲腔發音的題目中，有些單字會因口音不同而使得發音不同，書上將同時標註美式、英式發音的音標，以方便考生了解各國口音的差別。

6. 題目類型

每一題都特別標示出題目類型，讓考生能夠更快掌握自己容易出錯的題型為何，也方便考生針對特定題型加強複習。

7. 解析

針對各種題型提出最有效、最快速的解題方式，並詳細說明錯誤選項為何不對，同時提供能幫助分辨陷阱選項的解題技巧與說明。

8. 換句話說

將對話或獨白的內容與正確選項之間出現的換句話說，以「對話或獨白內容的表達方式 → 正確選項的表達方式」或「題目的表達方式 → 對話或獨白內容的表達方式」的形式清楚整理出來，讓考生能藉此熟悉 Part 3、4 的出題方式，進而提升分數。

新制多益介紹與測驗注意事項

什麼是多益？

TOEIC 是 Test Of English for International Communication 的縮寫，是針對非英語母語人士，著重於語言基本溝通能力的測驗，目的是評量日常生活與國際商務等方面的實用英語能力。因為是評量日常生活與商業環境中所需的英語能力，所以內容主要包括以下的實用主題：

- 合作開發：研究，產品開發
- 財務會計：借貸，投資，稅務，會計，銀行業務
- 一般事務：契約，協商，行銷，販售
- 技術領域：電器，工業技術，電腦，實驗室
- 事務領域：會議，文書工作
- 物品採購：採購，產品訂購，費用支付
- 飲食：餐廳，聚餐，宴客
- 文化：劇場，體育，郊遊
- 健康：醫療保險，醫院診療，牙科
- 製造：生產線，工廠經營
- 員工：錄用，退休，發薪，升遷，職缺
- 住宅：不動產，搬遷，企業用地

多益測驗的結構

領域	題型	題數	時間	配分
Listening Test 聽力測驗	Part 1 照片描述	6 題（1~6 題）	45 分鐘	495 分
	Part 2 應答問題	25 題（7~31 題）		
	Part 3 簡短對話 新	39 題（32~70 題）		
	Part 4 簡短獨白 新	30 題（71~100 題）		
Reading Test 閱讀測驗	Part 5 單句填空 （文法 / 單字）	30 題（101~130 題）	75 分鐘	495 分
	Part 6 短文填空 新 （文法 / 單字 / 句子）	30 題（131~146 題）		
	Part 7 閱讀文章(理解) 單篇文章綜合題 新 雙篇文章綜合題 多篇文章綜合題 新	54 題 - 29 題（147~175 題） - 10 題（176~185 題） - 15 題（186~200 題）		
總計	7 種題型	200 題	120 分鐘	990 分

1. 報名

- 測驗日期與報名期間，請參見官方網站 www.toeic.com.tw。
- 一般報名期間結束後，如果還有剩餘的名額，會開放追加報名。可追加報名的場次與追加報名期間，請參照官方網站公告。
- 網路報名是最方便的報名方式，只要登入網站，進入報名網頁並填寫資料即可。報名後，可以用信用卡、超商代收等方式繳費。
- 請注意照片檔案必須符合網站中公告的標準，以 jpg 或 gif 格式上傳。

2. 考試當天應該準備的物品

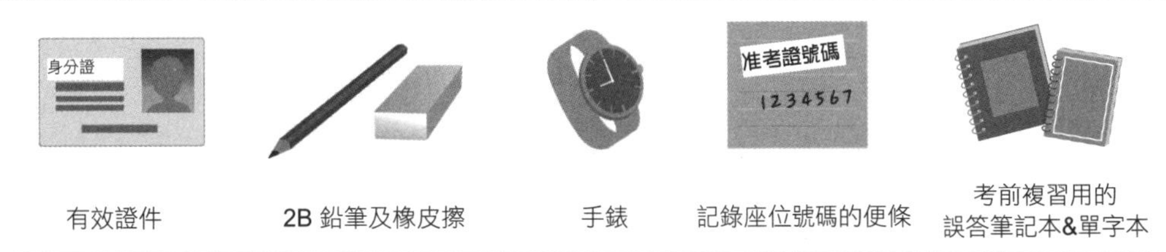

有效證件　2B 鉛筆及橡皮擦　手錶　記錄座位號碼的便條　考前複習用的誤答筆記本&單字本

*有效證件包括身分證正本或有效期限內的護照正本。未滿 16 歲者，可以用有照片的健保 IC 卡代替。因為不寄發准考證，所以要自己記錄座位號碼，依照號碼入座。

3. 測驗注意事項

- 測驗時間開始前必須入場，遲到者不得入場應試，也不接受因為遲到而申請退費。
- 進入試場前，必須將行動電話、手錶等各類電子用品關閉（不得發出聲響）。在監試人員宣布可離開試場前，必須保持關機，否則以違規論，成績不予計分，且不得要求退費或延期。
- 測驗途中不休息。未經許可，不可中途離場或交卷。
- 台灣主辦單位規定，不可以在試題本或其他物品上抄寫題目、答案、劃線或做任何記號，否則視為違規，成績不予計分。

4. 成績查詢

- 測驗結束 15 天後，就可以在官方網站 www.toeic.com.tw 查詢成績。開放查詢成績的期間，請以網站公告為準。
- 紙本成績單大約會在測驗結束的 16 個工作天後寄出。
- 成績單寄發後，就可以在官方網站申請製作多益證書，或者補發成績單。多益證書大約需要 15 個工作天，補發成績單需要 10 個工作天。

各題型與解題策略

Part 1 照片描述（16 題）

・這類型的題目需要針對照片從四個描述中，選出最符合照片內容的選項。

題型

題目	錄音內容
1. 	Number 1. Look at the picture marked number 1 in your test book. (A) He is writing on a sheet of paper. (B) He is reaching for a glass. (C) He is seated near a window. (D) He is opening up a laptop computer.

解析 照片中的男子坐在窗邊，所以 (C) He is seated near a window. 是正確答案。

解題策略

1. 作答前先想像如何描述照片

在聆聽選項前先看照片，並聯想選項中可能會出現的主詞，以及用來描述照片中人物肢體動作或事物狀態的動詞及名詞。在聯想照片描述方式的過程之中，便能夠準確掌握照片內容。如果在測驗音檔的選項中出現了先前聯想到的字詞，就可以更輕鬆聽懂內容並選出正確答案。

2. 要選擇最恰當而非完全一致的照片內容描述

Part 1 要選擇的是最接近、最恰當的照片內容描述，而非與照片內容完全一致的描述。在作答 Part 1 時，必須掌握在 Part 1 經常出現的陷阱選項類型，若能熟悉常見的陷阱選項類型，就能更輕鬆地選出正確答案。

Part 1 常見的陷阱選項類型

・錯誤的人物肢體動作
・提到沒有出現在照片中的人、事、物
・錯誤的人物或物體的狀態及位置
・錯誤描述人物對物體施加的動作
・單從照片無法判斷的事實
・使用容易造成混淆的詞彙

Part 2 應答問題（25 題）

這類型的題目是針對提問或敘述來選擇最適當的回答。

題型

題目	錄音內容
7. Mark your answer on your answer sheet.	Number 7. When is the presentation going to be held? (A) I'm going to discuss sales levels. (B) Sometime on Tuesday. (C) He handled the preparations.

解析 這是利用疑問詞 when 來詢問簡報進行時間的題目，所以指出時間點 Sometime on Tuesday. 的 (B) 是正確答案。

解題策略

1. 絕對不能漏聽題目的第一個單字

Part 2 的題目類型取決於題目句子的開頭，所以絕對不能漏聽第一個單字。在 Part 2 平均會有 11 題以疑問詞開頭的疑問詞疑問句，因此大部分題目只要聽到第一個單字就可以選出正確答案了。而其他類型的題目也一樣能夠透過第一個單字來掌握題型、時態、主詞等與解題相關的資訊。

2. 熟記陷阱選項的類型，善用刪除法來解題

Part 2 中，大致上只會出現幾種固定的陷阱選項類型，因此，只要先熟悉這些陷阱選項的出現模式，就可以在解題時利用刪除法來刪除這些企圖造成混淆的陷阱選項，繼而選出正確答案。

Part 2 常見的陷阱選項類型

・重複題目句子出現過的單字，或利用發音相近的詞彙企圖造成混淆
・利用同義字、多義字或相關詞彙誤導作答
・變換主詞或時態，誤導作答
・以 Yes/No 回答詢問具體資訊的 Wh- 問題

Part 3 簡短對話（39 題）

・聆聽二到三人的簡短對話，並針對相關提問選出正確答案的題型

・題目構成：從 13 段對話中出 39 道題目（一段對話出 3 道題目，部分對話會搭配圖表資料一起出題）

題型（新題型以 新 標示）

題目

32. What are the speakers mainly discussing?
    (A) Finding a venue
    (B) Scheduling a renovation
    (C) Choosing a menu
    (D) Organizing a conference

33. What does the woman offer to do?
    (A) Visit a nearby event hall
    (B) Revise a travel itinerary
    (C) Proceed with a booking
    (D) Contact a facility manager

34. 新 What does the woman mean when she says, "we're all set"?
    (A) Some furniture will be arranged.
    (B) Some memos will be circulated.
    (C) An update will be installed.
    (D) An area will be large enough.

錄音內容

新 Questions 32 through 34 refer to the following conversation.

W: Joseph, I'm worried it'll be too chilly for the outdoor luncheon we've planned for Wednesday.

M: I agree. We'd better book an event hall instead.

W: How about Wolford Hall? I'm looking at its Web site now, and it appears to be available.

M: Oh, that'd be ideal. That place is near our office, so staff won't have to travel far.

W: I can book the hall now, if you want. We need it from 11 A.M. to 2 P.M., right?

M: Yeah. Just make sure it can accommodate 50 people.

W: It says it'll hold up to 70, so we're all set.

M: Perfect. I'll send staff an e-mail with the updated details.

Number 32.
What are the speakers mainly discussing?

Number 33.
What does the woman offer to do?

Number 34.
What does the woman mean when she says, "we're all set"?

解析

32. 題目詢問對話主題。女子說 it'll be too chilly for the outdoor luncheon.，表示天氣會太冷而不適合進行戶外午餐餐會，男子則回答 We'd better book an event hall instead，表示最好改預訂宴會廳，接著兩人繼續討論舉辦宴會的可能場地，因此正確答案為 (A)。

33. 題目詢問女子願意做什麼，女子在對話中說 I can book the hall now，表示她可以現在去預訂宴會廳，因此正確答案是 (C)。

34. 新 題目詢問女子說這句話的意思是什麼。男子說 Just make sure it[hall] can accommodate 50 people，表示只要確定宴會廳能容納 50 個人即可，女子接著說 it'll hold up to 70, so we're all set，表示宴會廳最多可容納 70 個人，因此這個宴會廳的空間夠大、可以使用，故正確答案是 (D)。

各題型與解題策略

解題策略

1. 聽對話之前務必先閱讀題目及選項

① 在播放 Part 3 説明音檔時，請先閱讀第 32 到 34 題的題目和選項。之後就能繼續在播放對話音檔前，先閱讀下一段對話題組的題目及選項。

② 閱讀題目時須先掌握題目類型，再針對此題型決定應特別注意聽對話的哪個部分和哪些內容；若遇到有附上圖表資料的題目，則須一併讀完圖表資料，並掌握其類型與內容。

③ 閱讀選項時，必須先快速區別出各選項之間內容相異的關鍵字。各選項的主詞相異時，句中主詞即為關鍵字，當各選項的主詞相同時，句中的動詞或受詞等則為關鍵字。

2. 一邊聽對話一邊作答

① 以事先閱讀題目和選項時設定的解題策略為依據，在聆聽對話時一邊選出正確答案。

② 若為三人對話，對話音檔開頭會出現「Questions ~ refer to the following conversation with three speakers.」，所以各段對話前的説明須仔細聆聽。

③ 在對話內容播放結束後，必須把握朗讀題目的時間，快速閱讀下一段對話題組的題目和選項，並再次擬定恰當的解題策略。

④ 萬一聽完對話內容還是無法選出正確選項，應立刻選擇你認為最有可能的選項，並直接閱讀下一段對話題組的題目及選項，這是減少答題錯誤率的一個好方法。

3. 一定要仔細聆聽對話的開頭部分

① 有 80% 以上的解題線索均來自對話的開頭部分，所以一定要仔細聆聽對話的開頭部分。

② 詢問對話主題、對話者的職業、對話發生地點等題目，其解題線索大部分都在對話的開頭部分。

③ 若沒聽清楚對話的開頭部分，可能會受對話後半部分出現的特殊表達誤導而答錯，必須特別注意。

Part 4 簡短獨白（30 題）

• 聆聽簡短獨白後，針對相關提問選出正確答案
• 題目構成：從 10 段簡短獨白中出 30 道題目（每段獨白各出 3 道題目，部分獨白會搭配圖表資料一起出題）

題型（新題型以 新 標示）

題目

新

Department	Manager
Accounting	Janet Lee
Sales	Sarah Bedford
Human Resources	David Weber
Marketing	Michael Brenner

92. What is the purpose of the announcement?
(A) To explain a new project
(B) To describe a job opening
(C) To discuss a recent hire
(D) To verify a policy change

93. 新 Look at the graphic. Which department will Shannon Clark manage?
(A) Accounting
(B) Sales
(C) Human Resources
(D) Marketing

94. What will probably happen on September 1?
(A) A job interview
(B) A product launch
(C) A staff gathering
(D) An employee evaluation

錄音內容

Questions 92 through 94 refer to the following announcement and list.

May I have your attention, please? I just received an e-mail from David Weber in human resources regarding a new manager. Shannon Clark will begin working here next month. Ms. Clark has over a decade of experience working for multinational corporations, so she brings a wealth of knowledge to our company. She will be replacing Michael Brenner, who is retiring this month. One of the other department managers . . . um, Janet Lee . . . has arranged a get-together on September 1 to introduce Ms. Clark. Food and beverages will be provided. Please give her a warm welcome.

Number 92.
What is the purpose of the announcement?

Number 93.
Look at the graphic. Which department will Shannon Clark manage?

Number 94.
What will probably happen on September 1?

解析

92. 題目詢問公告的目的。說話者說 I just received an e-mail ~ regarding a new manager. Shannon Clark will begin working here next month，表示剛收到關於新經理 Shannon Clark 將從下個月起任職於此的一封電子郵件，由此可知，正確答案是 (C)。

93. 新 題目詢問 Shannon Clark 將管理哪一個部門。說話者提到 She[Shannon Clark] will be replacing Michael Brenner, who is retiring this month，表示 Shannon Clark 要接替的是將在這個月退休的 Michael Brenner，透過題目提供的表格可知，Michael Brenner 是行銷部的經理，因此正確答案是 (D)。

94. 題目詢問 9 月 1 日可能會發生什麼，說話者說 Janet Lee ~ has arranged a get-together on September 1，表示 Janet Lee 已在 9 月 1 日安排了一個聚會，因此正確答案是 (C)。

各題型與解題策略

解題策略

1. 在聆聽獨白之前務必先閱讀題目及選項

① 在播放 Part 4 說明音檔時，請先閱讀 71 到 73 題的題目和選項。之後就能繼續在播放獨白音檔前，先閱讀下一段獨白題組的題目及選項。

② 閱讀題目時須先掌握題目類型，再針對此題型決定應特別注意聽獨白的哪個部分及哪些內容；若遇到有附上圖表資料的題目，則須一併讀完圖表資料，並掌握其類型與內容。

③ 閱讀選項時，必須先快速區別出各選項之間內容相異的關鍵字。各選項的主詞相異時，句中主詞即為關鍵字，當各選項的主詞相同時，句中的動詞或受詞等則為關鍵字。

2. 一邊聽獨白一邊作答

① 以事先閱讀題目和選項時設定的解題策略為依據，在聆聽獨白時一邊選出正確答案。

② 獨白內容播放結束的同時，三道題目都要答完。

③ 在獨白內容播放結束後，須把握音檔朗讀題目的時間，快速閱讀下一段獨白的題目和選項，並再次擬定恰當的解題策略。

④ 萬一聽完獨白內容仍無法選出正確選項，應立刻選擇你認為最有可能的選項，並直接閱讀下一段獨白題組的題目及選項，這是減少答題錯誤率的一個好方法。

3. 一定要仔細聆聽獨白的開頭部分

① 有 80% 以上的解題線索來自獨白的開頭部分，所以一定要仔細聆聽獨白的開頭。

② 詢問獨白主題、目的、說話者或聽者身分、獨白發生地點等題目，其解題線索大部分都會在獨白開頭的部分出現。

③ 若沒聽清楚獨白的開頭部分，可能會受獨白後半部分出現的特殊表達誤導而答錯，必須特別注意。

個別學習計畫

完成 TEST 01 後，請按分數換算表計算成績，再按照成績挑選適合的學習計畫，並於方框內做標記。在各回完成後，也要記得重新檢視學習計畫。

*完成各回測驗之後，請將成績記錄於題目本前方的「目標達成表」，以確認自己的成績變化。

2 週完成的學習計畫—400 分以上

- 兩週間每天做一回，使用答案紙來模擬實際測驗，再仔細檢討與複習。
- 答錯的題目及難度最高的題目必須再做一次，確定已完全理解。
- 針對答錯的題目，須再次核對正確答案及誤選的選項，並確實理解錯誤選項的錯誤原因。

	Day 1	Day 2	Day3	Day 4	Day 5
Week 1	☐ Test 01 解題&複習	☐ Test 02 解題&複習	☐ Test 03 解題&複習	☐ Test 04 解題&複習	☐ Test 05 解題&複習
Week 2	☐ Test 06 解題&複習	☐ Test 07 解題&複習	☐ Test 08 解題&複習	☐ Test 09 解題&複習	☐ Test 10 解題&複習

3 週完成的學習計畫—300~395 分

- 在三週間，第一、二天均仔細解題及複習一回模擬試題，第三天則針對這兩回模擬試題進行深入學習。
- 答錯的題目及難度最高的題目必須再做一次，確定已完全理解。
- 針對答錯的題目，須再次核對正確答案及誤選的選項，並確實理解錯誤選項的錯誤原因。
- 重新審視解析上標出的題目類型，找出自己最常答錯的題型並特別加強。
- 重新審視對話、獨白中以不同顏色標出的解題線索，再次作答以掌握解題技巧。

	Day 1	Day 2	Day3	Day 4	Day 5
Week 1	☐ Test 01 解題&複習	☐ Test 02 解題&複習	☐ Test 01&02 深入學習	☐ Test 03 解題&複習	☐ Test 04 解題&複習
Week 2	☐ Test 03&04 深入學習	☐ Test 05 解題&複習	☐ Test 06 解題&複習	☐ Test 05&06 深入學習	☐ Test 07 解題&複習
Week 3	☐ Test 08 解題&複習	☐ Test 07&08 深入學習	☐ Test 09 解題&複習	☐ Test 10 解題&複習	☐ Test 09&10 深入學習

4 週完成的學習計畫—295 分以下

- 在四週間，一天解題、一天複習一回模擬試題。
- 答錯的題目及難度最高的題目必須再做一次，確定已完全理解。
- 針對答錯的題目，須再次核對正確答案及誤選的選項，並確實理解錯誤選項的錯誤原因。
- 重新審視解析上標出的題目類型，找出自己最常答錯的題型並特別加強。
- 重新審視對話、獨白中以不同顏色標出的解題線索，再次作答以掌握解題技巧。
- 整理並記住 Part 3 及 Part 4 中出現的換句話說。

	Day 1	Day 2	Day3	Day 4	Day 5
Week 1	☐ Test 01 解題	☐ Test 01 複習	☐ Test 02 解題	☐ Test 02 複習	☐ Test 03 解題
Week 2	☐ Test 03 複習	☐ Test 04 解題	☐ Test 04 複習	☐ Test 05 解題	☐ Test 05 複習
Week 3	☐ Test 06 解題	☐ Test 06 複習	☐ Test 07 解題	☐ Test 07 複習	☐ Test 08 解題
Week 4	☐ Test 08 複習	☐ Test 09 解題	☐ Test 09 複習	☐ Test 10 解題	☐ Test 10 複習

學習計畫的活用方式

搭配其他 HACKERS 多益學習書一起學習，可以更加事半功倍！

400 分以上	300~395 分	295 分以下
《新制多益聽力題庫大全》	《新制多益聽力測驗總整理》	《新制多益聽力課本》

TEST 01

Part 1　原文・翻譯・解析

Part 2　原文・翻譯・解析

Part 3　原文・翻譯・解析 新

Part 4　原文・翻譯・解析 新

MP3 收錄於 TEST 01.mp3

進行深入練習或複習時，可以一邊多聽幾次收錄各國口音的試題 MP3，一邊搭配解答中的中英對照翻譯和解析，以及單字記憶表和多元口音單字記憶MP3，達到事半功倍的效果。

PART 1

1
○○○● 低

🔊 美式發音

(A) They are taking off their running shoes.
(B) They are jogging on a road.
(C) They are watching a race.
(D) They are passing between two trees.

(A) 他們正在脫下跑鞋。
(B) 他們正在路上慢跑。
(C) 他們正在觀看比賽。
(D) 他們正通過兩棵樹之間。

兩人以上的照片 答案 (B)

照片中一對男女正在路上跑步。

(A) [╳] taking off（正在脫下）和照片中的人物動作無關，因此是錯誤選項。這裡使用照片中有出現的跑鞋（running shoes）來造成混淆。

(B) [○] 這裡正確描述在路上慢跑的情景，因此是正確答案。

(C) [╳] watching a race（正在觀看比賽）和照片中的人物動作無關，因此是錯誤選項。這裡使用能夠聯想到跑步情景的 race（比賽）來造成混淆。

(D) [╳] 照片中人物是在草地旁跑步，選項卻描述為通過兩棵樹之間，因此是錯誤選項。這裡利用照片中出現的樹木（trees）來造成混淆。

單字　jog [dʒɑg] 慢跑　race [res]（賽跑）比賽

2
○○●● 中

🔊 澳洲式發音

(A) A woman is getting off the train.
(B) A woman is fastening her seat belt.
(C) A woman is sitting with her legs crossed.
(D) A woman is leaning forward in a chair.

(A) 一名女子正在下火車。
(B) 一名女子正在繫安全帶。
(C) 一名女子正蹺腳坐著。
(D) 一名女子正坐在椅子裡俯身前傾。

單人照片 答案 (C)

照片中一名女子正蹺著腳靠坐在火車座位上。

(A) [╳] 女子正在搭乘火車，選項卻描述為正在下火車，因此是錯誤選項。這裡利用照片的可能拍攝地點「火車（train）」來造成混淆。

(B) [╳] fastening her seat belt（正在繫安全帶）和女子的動作無關，因此是錯誤選項。這裡使用和座位相關的 seat belt（安全帶）來造成混淆，必須多加留意。

(C) [○] 這裡正確描述女子蹺腳坐著的模樣，所以是正確答案。

(D) [╳] 女子向後靠在椅子上，但選項卻描述為俯身前傾（leaning forward），因此是錯誤選項。這裡要注意不要搞混俯身前傾（leaning forward）和向後倚靠（lean against）。

單字　get off 下（火車、飛機等交通工具）　fasten [[美] ˋfæsn̩ [英] ˋfɑ:sən] 扣緊；繫牢　seat belt 安全帶

3
○○●● 中

🔊 英式發音

(A) Some people are distributing documents.
(B) Some people are putting papers into binders.
(C) Some people are gathered around a table.
(D) Some people are making some photocopies.

(A) 一些人正在發放文件。
(B) 一些人正在把紙張放進活頁夾裡。
(C) 一些人聚在桌邊。
(D) 一些人正在影印。

兩人以上的照片 答案 (C)

仔細觀察照片中的人們聚在桌邊的模樣，以及周圍事物的狀態。

(A) [╳] distributing（正在發放）和照片中的人物動作無關，因此是錯誤選項。這裡使用照片中有出現的文件（documents）來造成混淆。

(B) [╳] putting ~ into（正在把～放進）和照片裡的人物動作無關，因此是錯誤選項。這裡使用和照片內容相關的紙張（papers）和活頁夾（binders）來造成混淆。
(C) [〇] 這裡正確描述人們聚在桌邊的模樣，所以是正確答案。
(D) [╳] making some photocopies（正在影印）和照片中的人物動作無關，因此是錯誤選項。這裡使用和照片中出現的文件有關的 photocopies（影印）來造成混淆，必須多加留意。

單字 distribute [dɪˋstrɪbjʊt] 分發，發放 document [㊈ ˋdɑkjəmənt ㊇ ˋdɔkjumənt] 文件
binder [㊈ ˋbaɪndɚ ㊇ ˋbaində]（彙整紙張用的）活頁夾 gather [㊈ ˋgæðɚ ㊇ ˋgæðə]（人等）聚集
make a photocopy 影印

4 中

加拿大式發音

(A) The workers are standing in an aisle.
(B) The workers are assembling a storage shelf.
(C) The workers are entering a warehouse.
(D) The workers are labeling some of the containers.

(A) 工人們正站在走道上。
(B) 工人們正在組裝儲物架。
(C) 工人們正在進入倉庫。
(D) 工人們正在為一些容器貼標籤。

兩人以上的照片 答案 (A)

仔細觀察工人們正站在走道上的模樣和周遭的狀態。
(A) [〇] 選項正確描述工人們正站在走道上的模樣，所以是正確答案。
(B) [╳] assembling（正在組裝）和照片中的人物動作無關，因此是錯誤選項。這裡使用照片中有出現的儲物架（storage shelf）來造成混淆。
(C) [╳] 工人們已經身在倉庫內，但這裡卻描述為正在進入倉庫，因此是錯誤選項。這裡利用照片的可能拍攝地點「倉庫（warehouse）」來造成混淆。
(D) [╳] labeling（正在貼標籤）和工人的動作無關，因此是錯誤選項。這裡使用照片中有出現的容器（containers）來造成混淆。

單字 aisle [aɪl] 通道，走道 assemble [əˋsɛmbl] 組裝 warehouse [ˋwɛrˏhaʊs] 倉庫 label [ˋlebl] 貼標籤；標籤

5 高

美式發音

(A) Safety glasses are being kept in a rack.
(B) The man is looking into a microscope.
(C) The researchers are putting on lab coats.
(D) Some laboratory equipment is on the work surface.

(A) 護目鏡被存放在了架子上。
(B) 男子正在看顯微鏡。
(C) 研究員們正在穿上實驗袍。
(D) 一些實驗器材在工作台上。

兩人以上的照片 答案 (D)

仔細觀察一對男女正在實驗室裡看著螢幕的模樣及周遭事物的狀態。
(A) [╳] 照片中出現了護目鏡（Safety glasses），但不是被存放在架子上（are being kept in a rack），因此是錯誤選項。
(B) [╳] 男子不是正在看顯微鏡（microscope）而是在看螢幕，因此是錯誤選項。這裡使用照片中有出現的顯微鏡（microscope）來造成混淆。
(C) [╳] putting on（正在穿上）和照片中的人物動作無關，因此是錯誤選項。這裡要注意不要搞混表示「穿著」狀態的 wearing，以及表示「正在穿」的 putting on。
(D) [〇] 這裡正確描述一些實驗器材放在工作台上的模樣，所以是正確答案。

單字 rack [ræk] 架子 look into 看～（的裡面） microscope [ˋmaɪkrəˏskop] 顯微鏡
researcher [riˋsɝtʃɚ] 研究員 lab coat 實驗袍

6 ○●●● 高

加拿大式發音

(A) A balcony overlooks a patio.
(B) There are stools arranged in a row.
(C) Stairs lead to the outside of a restaurant.
(D) A dining establishment is filled with customers.

(A) 樓廳俯瞰著露臺。
(B) 有被排成了一排的凳子。
(C) 階梯通往餐廳外面。
(D) 餐廳裡滿是顧客。

事物及風景照片

答案 (B)

仔細觀察室內被排成一排的椅子和周遭事物的狀態。

(A) [╳] 照片中樓廳俯瞰的地方是室內，而不是選項中提到的露臺（patio），因此是錯誤選項。注意不要聽到 A balcony overlooks（樓廳俯瞰）就選擇這個選項。

(B) [○] 這裡正確描述凳子被排成了一排的樣子，所以是正確答案。

(C) [╳] 透過照片無法得知階梯是否通往餐廳外，因此是錯誤選項。注意不要聽到 Stairs（階梯）就選擇這個答案。

(D) [╳] 照片中沒有出現顧客（customers），因此是錯誤選項。注意不要聽到 A dining establishment（餐廳）就選擇這個選項。

單字　overlook [ˌovɚˋlʊk] 俯瞰　patio [ˋpɑtɪˌo] 露臺　stool [stul] 凳子　in a row 一排　lead to 通向～

7 低

加拿大式發音 → 美式發音	
Where did you put the annual shareholder report? (A) The reporter from the *Arlington Times*. (B) It's in this folder. (C) I finished drafting it yesterday.	你把年度股東報告放在哪裡了？ (A) 來自《Arlington Times》的記者。 (B) 在這個資料夾裡。 (C) 我昨天寫完草稿了。

Where 疑問句 答案 (B)

這是詢問年度股東報告放在哪裡的 Where 疑問句。

(A) [╳] 題目詢問年度股東報告放在哪裡，這裡卻回答來自《Arlington Times》的記者，毫不相關，因此是錯誤選項。這裡利用 report、reporter 這兩個發音相似的單字來造成混淆。

(B) [○] 這裡回答在這個資料夾裡，提及放置年度股東報告的地方，因此是正確答案。

(C) [╳] 這是利用可以代稱題目中 annual shareholder report（年度股東報告）的 it，並且利用和 report（報告）相關的 drafting（寫草稿）來造成混淆的錯誤選項。

單字 annual [`ænjʊəl] 年度的，每年的 shareholder [`ʃɛr͵holdɚ] 股東 report [rɪ`port] 報告
reporter [rɪ`portɚ] 記者 draft [dræft] 寫草稿

8 低

英國式發音 → 加拿大式發音	
What is the topic of your presentation? (A) I'll most likely speak at 10 A.M. (B) Most of the presenters have departed. (C) Our new line of products.	你的簡報主題是什麼？ (A) 我最有可能會在早上 10 點發言。 (B) 大部分的發表人都已啟程。 (C) 我們的新系列產品。

What 疑問句 答案 (C)

這是詢問對方簡報主題是什麼的 What 疑問句。

(A) [╳] 題目詢問對方的簡報主題是什麼，這裡卻回答時間，因此是錯誤選項。這裡利用和 presentation（簡報）相關的 speak（發言）來造成混淆。

(B) [╳] 這是利用和 presentation（簡報）相關的 presenters（發表人）來造成混淆的錯誤選項。

(C) [○] 這裡回答「我們的新系列產品」，直接提及簡報主題，因此是正確答案。

單字 topic [[美] `tɑpɪk [英] `tɔpik] 主題 presentation [͵prɛzən`teʃən] 簡報 presenter [prɪ`zɛntɚ] 發表人

9 中

加拿大式發音 → 美式發音	
Did you ever e-mail our manager about the budget? (A) I'm going to deal with that. (B) The CEO missed the luncheon. (C) Every box should be mailed now.	你把預算相關事項用電子郵件寄給我們經理了嗎？ (A) 我正要處理這件事。 (B) 執行長錯過了午餐餐會。 (C) 所有箱子現在都應該寄出了。

助動詞疑問句 答案 (A)

這是確認是否有把預算相關事項用電子郵件寄給經理的助動詞（Do）疑問句。

(A) [○] 這裡回答自己正要處理這件事，間接表示還沒有把預算相關事項用電子郵件寄給經理，因此是正確答案。

(B) [╳] 這是利用和 manager（經理）相關的 CEO（執行長）來造成混淆的錯誤選項。

(C) [╳] 題目詢問是否有把預算相關事項用電子郵件寄給經理，這裡卻回答所有箱子現在都應該寄出了，毫不相關，因此是錯誤選項。這裡利用 ever – Every、e-mail – mailed 等發音相似單字來造成混淆。

單字 manager [`mænɪdʒɚ] 經理，管理者 budget [`bʌdʒɪt] 預算 deal with 處理～
miss [mɪs] 錯過（活動或事項等）；遺漏 luncheon [`lʌntʃən] 午餐餐會 mail [mel] 郵寄

10 ○●●● 高

澳洲式發音 → 英式發音 How do I get to the nearest gas station? (A) Yes, it's open today. (B) Let me get a map. (C) You can fill up the tank.	我該怎麼去最近的加油站？ (A) 是的，它今天有開。 (B) 讓我拿張地圖。 (C) 你可以把油箱加滿。

How 疑問句 答案 (B)

這是詢問要怎麼去最近的加油站的 How 疑問句。這裡必須知道 How 是用來詢問方法的表達。

(A) [╳] 這裡以 Yes 來回答疑問詞疑問句，因此是錯誤選項。這裡使用可以代稱題目中 gas station（加油站）的 it 來造成混淆。

(B) [○] 這裡回答要去拿地圖，間接回應題目提問，因此是正確答案。

(C) [╳] 這是使用可以代稱題目中 I 的 You，且利用可以透過 gas station（加油站）聯想到的動作 fill up the tank（把油箱加滿）來造成混淆的錯誤選項。

單字　get to 去到、抵達　gas station 加油站　open [㊈ `opən ㊇ `əupən] 營業的　fill up 填滿

11 ○○●● 中

加拿大式發音 → 美式發音 Why don't you sign up for a course? (A) I already signed them. (B) For enrolling at Farrell University. (C) I'll think about it.	你何不報名一項課程？ (A) 我已經簽過它們了。 (B) 為了註冊 Farrell 大學。 (C) 我會考慮看看。

提議疑問句 答案 (C)

這是提議對方報名課程的提議疑問句。這裡必須知道 Why don't you 是用來提議的表達。

(A) [╳] 這是利用重複題目中 sign up for（報名～；登記～）的 sign 的另一字義「簽名」來造成混淆的錯誤選項。

(B) [╳] 這是利用與題目中 sign up for（報名～；登記～）意義相似的 enrolling（註冊）及與 course（課程）相關的 University（大學）來造成混淆的錯誤選項。

(C) [○] 這裡回答「會考慮看看」，間接表示還沒決定是否要報名課程，因此是正確答案。

單字　sign up for 報名～；登記～　course [kors] 課程　sign [saɪn] 簽名　enroll [ɪn`rol] 註冊

12 ○○●● 中

美式發音 → 澳洲式發音 We'll be leaving for the beach shortly. (A) Do I have time to use the restroom? (B) A towel and a swimsuit. (C) I believe Bob also left then.	我們很快要出發前往海灘了。 (A) 我還有時間去上個廁所嗎？ (B) 一條毛巾和一件泳衣。 (C) 我相信 Bob 那時也離開了。

陳述句 答案 (A)

這是表示即將前往海灘的客觀事實陳述句。

(A) [○] 這裡反問自己還有沒有時間能去上廁所，對題目陳述做出回應，因此是正確答案。

(B) [╳] 這是利用和 beach（海邊）有關的 towel（毛巾）和 swimsuit（泳衣）來造成混淆的錯誤選項。

(C) [╳] 題目陳述即將前往海灘，這裡回答 Bob 在那時也離開了，與題目陳述毫無相關，因此是錯誤選項。這裡以 left 重複使用題目中的 leaving 來造成混淆。

單字　leave [liv] 離開　shortly [`ʃɔrtlɪ] 很快，馬上　towel [`taʊəl] 毛巾　swimsuit [`swɪmsut] 泳衣

13 ○●●● 高

英式發音 → 澳洲式發音

Who's going to pick up dinner tonight? (A) In 20 minutes. (B) Thanks. The food is very good. (C) We are having it delivered.	誰今晚要去買晚餐？ (A) 20 分鐘後。 (B) 謝謝。食物非常美味。 (C) 我們要叫外送。

Who 疑問句 答案 (C)

這是詢問今晚誰會去買晚餐的 Who 疑問句。

(A) [╳] 題目詢問今晚誰會買晚餐，這裡卻回答時間點，因此是錯誤選項。

(B) [╳] 這是利用和 dinner（晚餐）有關的 food（食物）來造成混淆的錯誤選項。

(C) [○] 這裡回答要叫外送，間接表示沒有人會去買，因此是正確答案。

單字 pick up 購買；拿取 deliver [美 dɪˋlɪvɚ 英 diˋlivə] 運送

14 ○○○● 低

加拿大式發音 → 美式發音

When is the sale at Hayes Department Store ending? (A) It goes until Sunday. (B) The sail has a small tear. (C) Begin when you can.	Hayes 百貨公司的特賣什麼時候結束？ (A) 到週日為止。 (B) 帆上有個小裂縫。 (C) 等你可以再開始。

When 疑問句 答案 (A)

這是詢問百貨公司特賣什麼時候結束的 When 疑問句。

(A) [○] 這裡回答到週日為止，直接回答特賣結束的時間，因此是正確答案。

(B) [╳] 題目詢問百貨公司特賣什麼時候結束，這裡卻回答帆上有小裂縫，毫不相關，因此是錯誤選項。這裡利用發音相似單字 sale – sail 來造成混淆。

(C) [╳] 這是使用和題目中出現的 ending（結束）相反的 Begin（開始）來造成混淆的錯誤選項。

單字 sail [sel] 帆 tear [tɛr] 扯破的洞，撕裂處；撕開 begin [bɪˋgɪn] 開始

15 ○○●● 中

英式發音 → 加拿大式發音

Which wireless keyboard should I get? (A) Yes, I should do that. (B) This one is highly recommended. (C) There's a power outlet over there.	我該買哪款無線鍵盤？ (A) 是的，我該去做那件事。 (B) 非常推薦這款。 (C) 那裡有個插座。

Which 疑問句 答案 (B)

這是詢問要買哪款無線鍵盤的 Which 疑問句。這裡必須聽到 Which wireless keyboard 才有辦法作答。

(A) [╳] 這裡以 Yes 回答疑問詞疑問句，因此是錯誤選項。這裡利用重複題目中出現的 should 來造成混淆。

(B) [○] 這裡針對題目所詢問的無線鍵盤款式做出推薦，因此是正確答案。

(C) [╳] 題目詢問要買哪款無線鍵盤，這裡卻回答那裡有個插座，毫不相關，因此是錯誤選項。注意不要聽到 There's 和 over there 就選擇這個選項。

單字 wireless [美 ˋwaɪrlɪs 英 ˋwaiəlis] 無線的 recommend [ˌrɛkəˋmɛnd] 勸告；推薦 outlet [ˋaʊtˏlɛt] 插座；出口

16 ○○●●● 中

🔊 美式發音 → 澳洲式發音 Why can't we stay at Casa Resort during our trip? (A) Because we plan to send it. (B) You'll need to copy your passport. (C) It is fully booked.	我們在旅行期間為什麼不能住在 Casa 渡假村？ (A) 因為我們計劃要把它寄出。 (B) 你會需要影印你的護照。 (C) 它被訂滿了。

Why 疑問句 答案 (C)

這是詢問旅行期間沒辦法住在 Casa 渡假村原因的 Why 疑問句。

(A) [╳] 題目詢問為什麼旅行期間沒辦法住在 Casa 渡假村，這裡卻回答因為計劃要把它寄出，毫不相關，因此是錯誤選項。注意不要聽到 Because we plan to 就選擇這個選項。

(B) [╳] 這是利用和 trip（旅行）相關的 passport（護照）來造成混淆的錯誤選項。

(C) [○] 這裡回答被訂滿了，提到旅行期間沒辦法住在 Casa 渡假村的原因，因此是正確答案。

單字 stay [ste] 暫住；停留 trip [trɪp] 旅行 plan [plæn] 計劃 passport [[美] ˋpæs͵port [英] ˋpɑːs͵pɔːt] 護照
book [bʊk] 預訂

17 ○●●●● 高

🔊 加拿大式發音 → 英式發音 Are you working or taking time off over the holidays? (A) Try taking the bus. (B) I'll be putting in overtime. (C) Oh, I've never traveled there before.	你假期期間是會工作還是休息？ (A) 試試看搭公車。 (B) 我會申請加班。 (C) 噢，我之前從來沒去過那裡。

選擇疑問句 答案 (B)

這是詢問假期期間是會工作還是休息的選擇疑問句。

(A) [╳] 題目詢問假期期間會工作還是休息，這裡卻回答要試著搭公車，毫不相關，因此是錯誤選項。這裡重複題目中出現的 taking 來造成混淆。

(B) [○] 這裡回答會申請加班，表示選擇在假期期間工作，因此是正確答案。

(C) [╳] 這是利用和 holidays（假期）相關的 traveled（旅行）來造成混淆的錯誤選項。

單字 time off 休息 put in overtime 申請加班 travel [ˋtrævl] 經過，走過；旅行

18 ○●●●● 高

🔊 澳洲式發音 → 英式發音 Should the layout of the bakery be rearranged? (A) Mike has laid out the documents. (B) Across from the bread section. (C) That'd be too difficult.	這間烘焙坊的格局是否應該重新規劃？ (A) Mike 已經把文件擺出來了。 (B) 在麵包區對面。 (C) 這太難了。

助動詞疑問句 答案 (C)

這是詢問烘焙坊的格局是否應重新規劃的助動詞（Should）疑問句。

(A) [╳] 題目詢問烘焙坊的格局是否應重新規劃，這裡卻回答 Mike 已經把文件擺出來了，毫不相關，因此是錯誤選項。這裡利用發音相似單字 layout – laid out 來造成混淆。

(B) [╳] 題目詢問烘焙坊的格局是否應重新規劃，這裡卻回答地點，因此是錯誤選項。這裡利用和 bakery（烘焙坊）相關的 bread（麵包）來造成混淆。

(C) [○] 這裡回答太難了，間接表示自己不想重新規劃，因此是正確答案。

單字 layout [ˋle͵aʊt] 配置，格局 rearrange [͵riəˋrendʒ] 重新布置；重新安排 lay out 展開；擺出
document [[美] ˋdɑkjəmənt [英] ˋdɔkjumənt] 文件 across from 在～對面

19 ○○●● 中

英式發音 → 澳洲式發音 How soon can you scan all of these images? (A) Are you in a hurry? (B) The scanner is on the 6th floor. (C) Sorry for arriving a bit late.	你多快可以把這些圖全都掃描好？ (A) 你很趕嗎？ (B) 掃描器在 6 樓。 (C) 抱歉有點遲到。

How 疑問句

答案 (A)

這是詢問可以多快把全部圖片都掃描好的 How 疑問句。這裡必須知道 How soon 是詢問期間的表達。

(A) [○] 這裡反問對方趕不趕，要求與完成掃描所需時間有關的資訊，因此是正確答案。

(B) [╳] 這是利用發音相似單字 scan – scanner 來造成混淆的錯誤選項。

(C) [╳] 題目詢問可以多快掃描完全部圖片，這裡卻回答「抱歉有點遲到」，毫不相關，因此是錯誤選項。這裡使用和題目的 soon（快，早）意義相反的 late（遲，晚）來造成混淆。

單字　in a hurry 匆忙地；趕緊　arrive [ə`raɪv] 抵達　a bit 一點，少許

20 ○○●● 中

加拿大式發音 → 英式發音 Which is the best airline to take to Orlando, Heights Air or Wide Sky? (A) Personally, I prefer the steak. (B) My airfare was quite cheap. (C) There's not much difference.	去奧蘭多最好的航空公司是 Heights Air 還是 Wide Sky ？ (A) 我個人比較喜歡牛排。 (B) 我的機票滿便宜的。 (C) 都差不多。

選擇疑問句

答案 (C)

這是詢問去奧蘭多最好的航空公司是 Heights Air 還是 Wide Sky 的選擇疑問句。

(A) [╳] 題目詢問去奧蘭多最好的航空公司是 Heights Air 還是 Wide Sky，這裡卻回答個人比較喜歡牛排，毫不相關，因此是錯誤選項。注意不要聽到 Personally, I prefer 就選這個選項。

(B) [╳] 這是利用和 airline（航空公司）相關的 airfare（機票費用）來造成混淆的錯誤選項。

(C) [○] 這裡回答都差不多，表示這兩者皆可選擇，因此是正確答案。

單字　airline [`ɛrˏlaɪn] 航空公司　personally [㊊ `pɝsn̩lɪ ㊇ `pə:sənəli] 個人地　prefer [㊊ prɪ`fɝ ㊇ pri`fə:] 偏好
airfare [㊊ `ɛrfɛr ㊇ `eəfeə] 機票費用　quite [kwaɪt] 相當　difference [`dɪfərəns] 差異

21 ○○●● 中

澳洲式發音 → 美式發音 Who is overseeing marketing for the television show? (A) Either Matilda or Gregory. (B) I saw the forms last night. (C) A person from our group made the map.	電視節目的行銷是誰在監督？ (A) 不是 Matilda 就是 Gregory。 (B) 我昨晚看到了表格。 (C) 我們組裡的一個人做了那份地圖。

Who 疑問句

答案 (A)

這是詢問監督電視節目行銷的人是誰的 Who 疑問句。

(A) [○] 這裡回答不是 Matilda 就是 Gregory，直接回答監督電視節目行銷的可能人選，因此是正確答案。

(B) [╳] 這是利用藉 television show（電視節目）可能會聯想到的動作 saw（看到了）來造成混淆的錯誤選項。

(C) [╳] 題目詢問誰在監督電視節目行銷，這裡卻回答我們組裡的一個人做了那份地圖，毫不相關，因此是錯誤選項。注意不要聽到 A person from our group 就選這個答案。

單字　oversee [㊊ `ovɚ`si ㊇ `əuvə`si:] 監督　either [`iðɚ]（在有兩個可能選項的情形下）不是～就是～

22 高

加拿大式發音 → 英式發音	
Is Stan going to meet his project deadline? (A) A lot of tasks still have to be completed. (B) No, he didn't go there. (C) January 12 of last year.	Stan 能趕上他的專案截止日期嗎？ (A) 還有很多工作必須完成。 (B) 沒有，他沒有去那裡。 (C) 去年的 1 月 12 日。

Be 動詞疑問句 答案 (A)

這是確認 Stan 是否能趕上專案截止日期的 Be 動詞疑問句。

(A) [○] 這裡回答還有很多工作必須完成，間接表示 Stan 趕不上專案截止日期，因此是正確答案。

(B) [╳] 這裡藉由能代稱題目中 Stan 的 he 並將 going 替換成 go 來造成混淆。注意不要聽到 No 就選擇這個答案。

(C) [╳] 這裡使用可以藉 deadline（截止日期）聯想到的日期 January 12（1 月 12 日）來造成混淆，因此是錯誤選項。

單字 meet [mit] 趕上（期限等）；碰面 deadline [`dɛd͵laɪn] 截止期限 task [美 tæsk 英 tɑ:sk] 工作；任務 complete [kəm`plit] 完成

23 高

美式發音 → 英式發音	
Tuition is predicted to increase next semester. (A) The classes were surprisingly challenging. (B) The cost of education is already too high. (C) College faculty and administrators.	學費預計在下學期調漲。 (A) 這些課程意外困難。 (B) 教育費用已經太高了。 (C) 學院教職員及行政人員。

陳述句 答案 (B)

這是表達學費預計在下學期調漲的客觀事實陳述句。

(A) [╳] 這是利用和 Tuition（學費）、semester（學期）相關的 classes（課程）來造成混淆的錯誤選項。

(B) [○] 這裡回答教育費用已經太高了，提出自己的意見，因此是正確答案。

(C) [╳] 這是利用可以透過 Tuition（學費）和 semester（學期）聯想到的教學地點 College（學院）來造成混淆的錯誤選項。

單字 tuition [tju`ɪʃən] 學費 predict [prɪ`dɪkt] 預料，預計 increase [ɪn`kris] 提高，增加 semester [sə`mɛstɚ] 學期 surprisingly [美 sɚ`praɪzɪŋlɪ 英 sə`praiziŋli] 意外地，出乎意料地 challenging [`tʃælɪndʒɪŋ] 困難的，富挑戰性的 faculty [`fækḷtɪ] 教職員 administrator [美 əd`mɪnə͵stretɚ 英 əd`ministreitə] 管理人員；行政人員

24 中

澳洲式發音 → 美式發音	
When will I receive the concert tickets that I purchased online? (A) It'll be held at Davis Hall. (B) You can print them out immediately. (C) The concert should last at least an hour.	我什麼時候會收到線上購買的演唱會門票？ (A) 會在 Davis 廳舉行。 (B) 你可以把它們立刻印出來。 (C) 這場演唱會應該至少會進行一個小時。

When 疑問句 答案 (B)

這是詢問線上購買的演唱會門票什麼時候會收到的 When 疑問句。

(A) [╳] 這是使用可以代稱題目中 concert 的 It 及可以透過 concert（演唱會）聯想到的地點 Davis Hall 來造成混淆的錯誤選項。

(B) [○] 這裡回答可以立刻印出來，提及拿到票的時間，因此是正確答案。

(C) [╳] 題目詢問線上購買的演唱會門票什麼時候會收到，這裡卻回答演唱會至少會進行一個小時，毫不相關，因此是錯誤選項。這裡藉重複題目中出現的 concert 來造成混淆。

單字 receive [rɪ`siv] 收到 purchase [美 `pɝtʃəs 英 `pə:tʃəs] 購買 hold [hold] 舉行；握著 print out 印出 immediately [ɪ`midɪɪtlɪ] 立刻 last [læst] 持續；維持 at least 至少

25 中

美式發音 → 加拿大式發音

Would you like to sit at a table near the window? (A) A more private spot would be great. (B) Put the plate on the table. (C) Please be seated.	你想坐窗戶附近的位子嗎？ (A) 更隱密一點的位子會比較好。 (B) 把盤子放在桌上。 (C) 請入座。

提議疑問句 答案 (A)

這是提議要坐在窗戶附近的提議疑問句。這裡必須知道 Would you like to 是提議的表達。

(A) [◯] 這裡回答更隱密的位子會更好，間接表示拒絕提議，因此是正確答案。

(B) [╳] 題目提議要坐在窗戶附近的座位，這裡卻回答要將盤子放在桌上，毫不相關，因此是錯誤選項。這裡藉重複題目中出現的 table 來造成混淆。

(C) [╳] 這是利用發音相似單字 sit – seated 來造成混淆的錯誤選項。

單字 private [ˋpraɪvɪt] 隱密的；私人的 spot [spɑt] 地方，地點 seat [sit] 使就座；座位

26 中

英式發音 → 澳洲式發音

Pamela has been taking French lessons for her trip, hasn't she? (A) I went to Paris last year. (B) She is fluent in Spanish. (C) That's news to me.	Pamela 為了旅行一直在上法語課，不是嗎？ (A) 我去年去了巴黎。 (B) 她的西班牙語很流利。 (C) 這件事我第一次聽說。

附加問句 答案 (C)

這是確認 Pamela 是否為了旅行一直在上法語課的附加問句。

(A) [╳] 這是利用和 trip（旅行）相關的 went to（前往）、和 French（法語）相關的 Paris（巴黎）來造成混淆的錯誤選項。

(B) [╳] 這是使用可以代稱題目中 Pamela 的 She 及和 French（法語）相關的 Spanish（西班牙語）來造成混淆的錯誤選項。

(C) [◯] 這裡表示自己是第一次聽說，間接表示不知道這件事，因此是正確答案。當要表明對某事不知情時，記得可以用 That's news to me（這件事我第一次聽說）來表達。

單字 take a lesson 上課 French [frɛntʃ] 法語的；法國的 fluent in ～流利

27 高

加拿大式發音 → 美式發音

We've concluded that we need to hire four accountants for tax season. (A) Well, our staff seems to enjoy their gifts. (B) Can we afford to do that? (C) The hiring process for our firm.	我們已經得出結論，我們為了報稅季必須聘用四名會計師。 (A) 這個嘛，我們的員工似乎很喜歡他們的禮物。 (B) 我們負擔得起那樣做嗎？ (C) 我們公司的聘用流程。

陳述句 答案 (B)

這是表達結論是在報稅季期間必須聘用四名會計師的客觀事實陳述句。

(A) [╳] 這是利用和 hire（聘用）有關的 staff（員工）來造成混淆的錯誤選項。

(B) [◯] 這裡反問是否能夠負擔，要求提供更多資訊，因此是正確答案。

(C) [╳] 這是使用和 hire（聘用）相關的 hiring process（聘用流程）及可以使用題目中 we 代稱的 our firm 來造成混淆的錯誤選項。

單字 conclude [kənˋklud] 得出結論 hire [haɪr] 聘僱 accountant [əˋkaʊntənt] 會計師 tax season 報稅季
afford [əˋford] 負擔得起 process [ˋprɑsɛs] 程序，流程

28 ○●●中

澳洲式發音 → 英式發音 Have you heard about our product recall? (A) No, I'll take this item instead. (B) Call him back after the interview. (C) Yes, Ms. Jones informed me this morning.	你聽說我們產品召回的事了嗎？ (A) 不，我改拿這個吧。 (B) 在訪談之後回電給他。 (C) 是的，Jones 小姐今天早上通知我了。

助動詞疑問句 答案 (C)

這是確認是否有聽說產品召回這件事的助動詞（Have）疑問句。

(A) [╳] 這是使用和題目中 product（產品）意義相近的 item（商品）來造成混淆的錯誤選項。注意不要聽到 No 就選擇這個答案。

(B) [╳] 題目詢問是否有聽說產品召回的事，這裡卻回答訪談之後再回電給他，毫不相關，因此是錯誤選項。這裡利用發音相似單字 recall – Call 來造成混淆。

(C) [○] 這裡以 Yes 表示有聽說，並附加說明 Jones 小姐今天早上已經通知過自己了，因此是正確答案。

單字　recall [rɪ`kɔl] 召回；回想　instead [ɪn`stɛd] 做為替代　call back 回電　inform [美 ɪn`fɔrm 英 in`fɔ:m] 通知

29 ●●●●難

美式發音 → 澳洲式發音 Didn't somebody tell the driver to show up here at noon? (A) Someone must have dropped them. (B) Didn't you make the reservation? (C) I'll show you around the new house.	沒有人告訴司機要在中午到這裡來嗎？ (A) 一定有人讓他們下車了。 (B) 你不是預約了嗎？ (C) 我帶你參觀這間新房子。

否定疑問句 答案 (B)

這是確認是否有人告訴司機要在中午到這裡來的否定疑問句。

(A) [╳] 這是使用和題目裡出現的 somebody（某人）意義相同的 Someone（某人），及和 driver（司機）有關的 dropped（下（車等））來造成混淆的錯誤選項。

(B) [○] 這裡反問對方「你不是預約了嗎？」，間接表示自己以為對方已經預約了，因此是正確答案。

(C) [╳] 題目詢問是否有人告訴司機要在中午到這裡來，這裡卻回答要帶對方參觀新房子，毫不相關，因此是錯誤選項。這裡重複題目中出現的 show 來造成混淆。

單字　show up 到來；出現

30 ○●●●高

英式發音 → 加拿大式發音 Maria intends to redecorate her living room. (A) Thanks. I did it myself. (B) I actually like how it looks right now. (C) We made plans for a vacation.	Maria 打算重新裝潢她的客廳。 (A) 謝謝。這我自己做的。 (B) 我其實喜歡它現在看起來的樣子。 (C) 我們做了假期計畫。

陳述句 答案 (B)

這是表達 Maria 打算重新裝潢客廳的客觀事實陳述句。

(A) [╳] 這是使用可以代稱題目中 redecorate ~ living room（重新裝潢客廳）的 did it 來造成混淆的錯誤選項。

(B) [○] 這裡回答自己其實喜歡現在的樣子，提出對陳述內容的意見，因此是正確答案。

(C) [╳] 這是利用和 intends to（打算～）相關的 plans（計畫）來造成混淆的錯誤選項。

單字　intend to 打算～　redecorate [ri`dɛkəˌret] 重新裝潢；重新布置

31 ○●●● 高

美式發音 → 澳洲式發音

The road in front of our office was just repaved, right?

(A) A little over a week ago.
(B) Lyndale Avenue is about a block away.
(C) On the back of the receipt.

我們辦公室前的路才剛重新鋪過，對吧？

(A) 一個禮拜多一點點之前。
(B) Lyndale 大道約在一個街區外。
(C) 在收據的背面。

附加問句 答案 (A)

這是確認辦公室前的路是否才剛重新鋪過的附加問句。

(A) [○] 這裡回答一個禮拜多一點點之前，表示辦公室前的路的確才剛重新鋪過，因此是正確答案。
(B) [╳] 這是利用和 road（道路）相關的 Lyndale Avenue（Lyndale 大道）來造成混淆的錯誤選項。
(C) [╳] 題目詢問辦公室前的路是否才剛重新鋪過，這裡回答在收據的背面，毫不相關，因此是錯誤選項。這裡使用和題目中 front（前面）相反的 back（背面）來造成混淆。

單字 repave [ri`pev] 重新鋪（地面等） avenue [`ævə͵nju] 大街，大道

TEST 1 2 3 4 5 6 7 8 9 10

32
33
34

Questions 32-34 refer to the following conversation.

加拿大式發音 → 美式發音

M: [32]**Who am I supposed to submit this corporate merger article to for review when I'm done drafting it?** It's Friday, and the story is scheduled to be published in our paper's Sunday edition. So, someone will have to approve it by the end of the day.

W: [33]**You can send it to Arnold Smith. Following his promotion last week, he's responsible for all articles published in our weekend edition.**

M: I'll submit it to him this afternoon, then. But first, [34]**could you tell me what you think of the title?** Umm . . . here's a copy of the piece.

第 32-34 題請參考下列對話。

男：[32] 在我寫完這份企業合併報導的草稿之後，我應該要把它交給誰審閱？今天是星期五，而這篇報導預定要刊登在我們報紙的週日版上。所以在今天下班前得有人來通過這篇報導才行。

女：[33] 你可以把它寄給 Arnold Smith。在他上週升職之後，他就負責我們週末版上刊登的所有報導。

男：那我會在今天下午把報導交給他。不過首先，[34] 妳可以告訴我妳覺得這個標題怎麼樣嗎？嗯……這裡有這篇報導的副本。

32 What most likely is the man's occupation?

(A) A salesperson
(B) An accountant
(C) A lawyer
(D) A journalist

32 男子的職業最有可能是什麼？

(A) 業務員
(B) 會計師
(C) 律師
(D) 記者

33 What does the woman say about Arnold Smith?

(A) He was recently promoted.
(B) He reported on some news.
(C) He already revised a file.
(D) He would like some advice.

33 關於 Arnold Smith，女子說了什麼？

(A) 他最近晉升了。
(B) 他報導了一些消息。
(C) 他已經修改了一份檔案。
(D) 他想要一些建議。

34 What does the man ask the woman to do?

(A) Submit a weekly time sheet
(B) Give back a borrowed item
(C) Provide some feedback
(D) Copy some documents

34 男子要求女子做什麼？

(A) 提交一份一週工時表
(B) 繳回一項借用的物品
(C) 提供一些回饋意見
(D) 影印一些文件

題目 be supposed to 應該做～ submit [səb`mɪt] 提交；使服從；使經受 corporate [`kɔrpərɪt] 企業的 merger [mɝdʒɚ] 合併 review [rɪ`vju] 審閱；複審 draft [dræft] 起草；草稿，草圖 story [`storɪ] 報導；故事 publish [`pʌblɪʃ] 刊登（報導等） edition [ɪ`dɪʃən]（發行物的）版；版本 approve [ə`pruv] 批准；核可 promotion [prə`moʃən] 升職

32 accountant [ə`kaʊntənt] 會計師

33 promote [prə`mot] 晉升 report [rɪ`port] 報導 revise [rɪ`vaɪz] 修正；修改

34 time sheet 工時表

32 ○○●● 中 **整體對話相關問題—說話者** 答案 (D)

題目詢問男子的職業，因此要注意聽和身分、職業有關的表達。男子說：「Who am I supposed to submit this corporate merger article to for review when I'm done drafting it?」，詢問自己在寫好企業合併報導的草稿後要交給誰審閱，由此可知男子是記者，因此正確答案是 (D) A journalist。

33 ○○○● 低 **細節事項相關問題—提及** 答案 (A)

題目詢問女子提到了什麼關於 Arnold Smith 的事，因此要注意提到題目關鍵字（Arnold Smith）的前後部分，女子說：「You can send it[article] to Arnold Smith. Following his promotion last week, he's responsible for all articles published in our weekend edition.」，表示可以將報導交給 Arnold Smith，因為 Arnold Smith 在上週升職後就負責週末版上刊登的所有報導，因此正確答案是 (A) He was recently promoted.。

34 ○○●● 中 **細節事項相關問題—要求** 答案 (C)

題目詢問男子要求女子做的事，因此要注意聽男子話中出現要求表達之後的內容。男子對女子說：「could you tell me what you think of the title?」，要求女子針對標題提供她自己的意見，因此正確答案是 (C) Provide some feedback。

35
36
37

Questions 35-37 refer to the following conversation.	第 35-37 題請參考下列對話。
澳洲式發音 → 英式發音	
M: [35]**Thank you for calling Jenkins Automotive Insurance. This is Bernard speaking. What can I do for you?**	男：[35] 感謝您來電 Jenkins 汽車保險。我是 Bernard。有什麼能協助您的？
W: My name is Candace Black, and I'm one of your insurance policy holders. I was just in an accident outside Austin, and [35/36]**I would like my car to be towed to an auto repair shop.** [36]**I don't feel comfortable driving it.**	女：我的名字是 Candace Black，我是你們的保戶之一。我剛在奧斯丁外出了意外，所以 [35/36] 我想要把我的車拖到修車廠。[36] 我不放心開這台車。
M: I completely understand, Ms. Black. A tow truck will be dispatched to your location immediately. But first, [37]**I'd just like to confirm that you've notified the police about the situation.**	男：我完全明白，Black 小姐。我們會立刻派一輛拖吊車到您的所在地點。但首先，[37] 我想確認一下您是否已通知過警方這個狀況了。
W: Yes, I did. In fact, an officer is going to stay here with me until the tow truck arrives.	女：是的，我通知過了。事實上，一位員警會和我一起在這裡等到拖吊車來。
35 Why is the woman calling? (A) To request a service (B) To make an appointment (C) To provide directions (D) To respond to an inquiry	35 女子為什麼打電話？ (A) 要求一項服務 (B) 預約一次會面 (C) 提供路線指引 (D) 回覆一個疑問
36 What does the woman want to avoid doing? (A) Taking a longer route (B) Going to an auto repair shop (C) Operating her vehicle (D) Using public transportation	36 女子想要避免做什麼？ (A) 繞遠路 (B) 去修車廠 (C) 開她的車 (D) 搭乘大眾運輸工具
37 What does the man ask the woman about? (A) Whether she reported an accident (B) Whether she was injured in a collision (C) Whether she arrived at a destination (D) Whether she was notified of a situation	37 男子詢問女子什麼？ (A) 她是否通報了一項事故 (B) 她是否在一次碰撞中受傷 (C) 她是否抵達了一處目的地 (D) 她是否被通知了一個狀況

題目 automotive [美 ˌɔtə`motɪv 英 ˌɔ:tə`məutiv] 汽車的　insurance policy holder 保戶，投保人　tow [美 to 英 təu] 拖
dispatch [dɪ`spætʃ] 派遣　confirm [美 kən`fɝm 英 kən`fə:m] 確認　notify [美 `notəˌfaɪ 英 `nəutifai] 通知；報告
35 direction [də`rɛkʃən] 路線指引；方向
36 route [rut] 道路；路線　vehicle [`viɪkl] 車輛；搭載工具　public transportation 大眾運輸工具
37 report [rɪ`port] 回報，報告　injure [`ɪndʒɚ] 使受傷　collision [kə`lɪʒən] 碰撞

35 ■ **整體對話相關問題—目的**　答案 (A)
中
題目詢問女子打電話的目的，因此必須特別注意對話的開頭。男子說：「Thank you for calling Jenkins Automotive Insurance. ~. What can I do for you?」，表示感謝致電給 Jenkins 汽車保險，並詢問對方需要什麼幫助。女子說：「I would like my car to be towed to an auto repair shop」，表示希望能把車拖去修車廠，由此可知，女子是為了要求服務而打電話，因此正確答案是 (A) To request a service。

36 ■ **細節事項相關問題—特定細項**　答案 (C)
中
題目詢問女子想要避免做什麼，因此要注意和題目關鍵字（avoid doing）相關的內容。女子說：「I would like my car to be towed to an auto repair shop. I don't feel comfortable driving it.」，表示希望將車拖去修車廠，並說自己對於開那輛車感到不放心，因此正確答案是 (C) Operating her vehicle。

37 ■ **細節事項相關問題—特定細項**　答案 (A)
低
題目詢問男子詢問女子什麼，因此要注意男子說的話。男子對女子說：「I'd just like to confirm that you've notified the police about the situation」，表示想要確認女子是否已經告知警察這個情形了，因此正確答案是 (A) Whether she reported an accident。

Questions 38-40 refer to the following conversation.

英式發音 → 加拿大式發音

W: Oh, [38]**I can't believe Pasadena Gallery is going to display my artwork!** Thank you so much.
M: [38]**We take great pride in supporting local artists, and I think your paintings will appeal to our clients. Plus,** [39]**if you go on to achieve success, we can say that your first exhibit was held at our gallery.**
W: Well, I'm very excited. By the way, have you decided on the dates yet?
M: A two-week show would probably work best. I'm thinking about holding it from August 27 to September 10.
W: Ah . . . [40]**Could it start one week earlier—on August 20?** I'm traveling to Berlin to participate in a meet-and-greet event with other aspiring painters on September 8.
M: [40]**That should be fine.**

第 38-40 題請參考下列對話。

女：噢，[38] 真不敢相信 Pasadena 藝廊要展出我的作品！非常感謝你們。
男：[38] 我們對於能夠支持本地藝術家感到非常驕傲，而且我認為妳的畫作會對我們的客戶有吸引力。再加上，[39] 如果妳日後成功了，我們就能說妳的首場展覽是在我們藝廊舉辦的。
女：嗯，我非常興奮。對了，你們已經決定好日期了嗎？
男：雙週展的效果可能是最好的。我在想要從 8 月 27 日辦到 9 月 10 日。
女：啊……[40] 可以提早一週到 8 月 20 日開始嗎？我 9 月 8 日要去柏林參加一場與其他有志成為成功畫家的人一起進行的見面會。
男：[40] 應該沒問題。

38 Where most likely does the man work?
(A) At a theater
(B) At a gallery
(C) At an art school
(D) At a photography studio

38 男子最有可能在什麼地方工作？
(A) 戲院
(B) 藝廊
(C) 藝術學校
(D) 攝影工作室

39 What is implied about the woman?
(A) She has contacted a famous painter.
(B) She has not had an exhibit before.
(C) She has not finished a painting.
(D) She has lived in another country.

39 關於女子，暗示了什麼？
(A) 她已聯繫過一位有名的畫家。
(B) 她之前從來沒有辦過展覽。
(C) 她還沒完成一幅畫作。
(D) 她曾住在另一個國家。

40 When will the show most likely begin?
(A) On August 20
(B) On August 27
(C) On September 8
(D) On September 10

40 展覽最有可能會在什麼時候開始？
(A) 8 月 20 日
(B) 8 月 27 日
(C) 9 月 8 日
(D) 9 月 10 日

題目 display [dɪ`sple] 陳列；展出　artwork [㊕ `ɑrt͵wɝk ㊧ `ɑ:twə:k] 藝術作品　take pride in 對於～感到驕傲　appeal to 對～有吸引力；引起～的興趣　exhibit [ɪg`zɪbɪt] 展覽　meet-and-greet（和群眾面對面的）見面會　aspiring [ə`spaɪrɪŋ] 有抱負的；雄心勃勃的
39 contact [kən`tækt] 聯繫

38 整體對話相關問題—說話者 中　答案 (B)

題目詢問男子的工作地點，因此要注意聽和身分與職業相關的表達。女子說：「I can't believe Pasadena Gallery is going to display my artwork」，表示自己不敢相信 Pasadena 藝廊要展出自己的作品，接著男子說：「We take great pride in supporting local artists, and I think your paintings will appeal to our clients.」，表示他們對於能支持本地藝術家感到驕傲，且相信女子的作品能夠吸引客戶，由此可知，男子的工作地點是藝廊，因此正確答案是 (B) At a gallery。

39 細節事項相關問題—推論 高　答案 (B)

題目詢問對話中暗示了什麼有關女子的事情，因此必須注意和題目關鍵字（woman）相關的內容。男子對女子說：「if you go on to achieve success, we can say that your first exhibit was held at our gallery」，表示如果女子未來成功了，就可以說她的第一場展覽是辦在自己這間藝廊裡，由此可知，女子過去從未辦過展覽，因此正確答案是 (B) She has not had an exhibit before.。

40 細節事項相關問題—特定細項 低　答案 (A)

題目詢問展覽開始的時間點，因此要注意和題目關鍵字（show ~ begin）相關的內容。女子說：「Could it[show] start ~ on August 20?」，詢問是否可以把展覽提早到 8 月 20 日開始，男子之後說：「That should be fine.」，表示沒問題，因此正確答案是 (A) On August 20。

新 41 42 43

Questions 41-43 refer to the following conversation with three speakers.

第 41-43 題請參考下列三人對話。

加拿大式發音 → 美式發音 → 英式發音

M: [41]**What a busy morning. We've received so many complaints today** about the latest update to our company's accounting program.

W1: It's been hard trying to resolve callers' issues . . . Didn't you say you dealt with a really upset customer earlier, Lena?

W2: Yeah. [42]**She was working on a financial report for her company this morning and lost all her data when the program crashed.**

W1: I can understand her frustration, but I'm still not looking forward to answering more calls after lunch.

M: That's for sure. Anyway, speaking of lunch, [43]**how about going to the Italian restaurant across the street? My treat.**

W2: OK. But let's try to return to the office before 1 P.M. I need to finish filing some paperwork.

男： [41] 早上真忙啊。我們今天接到了非常多對於我們公司的會計程式最近一次更新的投訴。

女 1： 要解決打電話來的人的問題一直都很困難……Lena，妳不是說妳之前處理了一個非常生氣的顧客嗎？

女 2： 是啊。[42] 她今天早上在處理她公司的財務報告，結果她所有的資料都在程式當掉時不見了。

女 1： 我可以理解她的沮喪，但我還是不期待在午餐後接到更多電話（的這件事）。

男： 那是當然的。不管怎樣，說到午餐，[43] 去對街的那家義大利餐廳怎麼樣？我請客。

女 2： 好。但我們盡量在下午 1 點前回辦公室吧。我得把一些文書資料歸檔完成。

41 Why have the speakers been busy?

(A) A company has gotten multiple complaints.
(B) Some equipment is being installed.
(C) Some employees are being trained.
(D) A seminar took longer than expected.

41 說話者們為什麼一直很忙？

(A) 一間公司接到了多項投訴。
(B) 正在安裝一些設備。
(C) 正在訓練一些員工。
(D) 一場研討會進行得比預期要久。

42 What does Lena say recently happened?

(A) A team missed a deadline.
(B) A report was submitted.
(C) A shipment was damaged.
(D) A customer lost some data.

42 Lena 說最近發生了什麼？

(A) 一個團隊錯過了截止期限。
(B) 提交了一份報告。
(C) 一批貨物受損。
(D) 一位客戶遺失了一些資料。

43 What does the man offer to do?

(A) Download a file
(B) Pay for a meal
(C) Turn in some paperwork
(D) Call a coworker

43 男子願意做什麼？

(A) 下載一個檔案
(B) 付一頓飯的錢
(C) 繳交一些文書資料
(D) 致電一位同事

題目 complaint [kəm`plent] 抗議；投訴　accounting [ə`kaʊntɪŋ] 會計　resolve [rɪ`zalv] 解決　deal with 處理～
financial [faɪ`nænʃəl] 財務的　crash [kræʃ]（程式等）突然停止運作
frustration [͵frʌs`treʃən]（因無法達成所想而）沮喪，挫敗感　treat [trit] 請客；對待

41 multiple [`mʌltəpl] 多個的　install [ɪn`stɔl] 安裝，設置　train [tren] 訓練

41 ●○○○ 低 **細節事項相關問題—理由** 答案 (A)

題目詢問說話者們忙碌的原因，因此必須注意提到題目關鍵字（busy）的前後部分。男子說：「What a busy morning. We've received so many complaints today」，表示早上很忙碌，並說今天接到了非常多投訴，因此正確答案是 (A) A company has gotten multiple complaints.。

42 ●○○○ 低 **細節事項相關問題—特定細項** 答案 (D)

題目詢問女 2，也就是 Lena 說最近發生了什麼事情，因此要注意女 2 說的話中和題目關鍵字（recently happened）相關的內容。女 2 [Lena] 說：「She[customer] was working on a financial report ~ this morning and lost all her data when the program crashed.」，表示那個顧客今天早上在處理財務報告，結果所有資料都在程式當掉時不見了，因此正確答案是 (D) A customer lost some data.。

43 ●●○○ 中 **細節事項相關問題—提議** 答案 (B)

題目詢問男子願意做的事，因此必須注意聽男子話中提到要為女子做事的部分。男子對女子說：「how about going to the Italian restaurant across the street? My treat.」，表示提議去義大利餐廳吃午餐，並說自己要請客，因此正確答案是 (B) Pay for a meal。

44 45 46 新

Questions 44-46 refer to the following conversation.

澳洲式發音 → 英式發音

M: Can I help the next customer in line?
W: Hello. [44]**I bought these bed sheets at your store last week**, but they're not the correct size for my mattress. So, I'd like to return them.
M: Of course. Did you bring the receipt for the purchase with you?
W: Um, I lost it. [45]**Does that mean that I can't get a refund?**
M: [45/46]**Do you have the same credit card you bought the items with?** I can look up the transaction using the number.
W: [46]**Yes, I have it in my wallet. Uh . . . let me just get it.**

44 What did the woman do last week?
(A) Visited an online store
(B) Requested a refund
(C) Bought some bedding
(D) Replaced a mattress

45 新 What does the man imply when he says, "I can look up the transaction using the number"?
(A) A purchase may be processed.
(B) A product might be available.
(C) A receipt should be located.
(D) A refund can be given.

46 What will the woman most likely do next?
(A) Find a credit card
(B) Go to another store
(C) Check a transaction fee
(D) Compare some merchandise

第 44-46 題請參考下列對話。

男：下一位顧客有什麼需要協助的嗎？
女：哈囉。[44] 我上週在你們店裡買了這些床單，但是它們和我的床墊尺寸不符。所以，我想要把它們退掉。
男：當然。您有帶該筆消費的收據嗎？
女：呃，我弄丟了。[45] 這是說我沒辦法拿到退費了嗎？
男：[45/46] 您有帶您用來購買這些商品的信用卡嗎？我可以用卡號查詢這筆交易。
女：[46] 有，在我的皮夾裡。呃……讓我拿一下。

44 女子上週做了什麼？
(A) 上了一個網路商店
(B) 申請了一筆退費
(C) 購買了一些寢具
(D) 換了一張床墊

45 當男子說：「我可以用卡號查詢這筆交易」，是暗示什麼？
(A) 可能處理過一筆消費了。
(B) 一項產品可能有貨。
(C) 應該要找到一張收據。
(D) 可以給予一筆退費。

46 女子接下來最有可能會做什麼？
(A) 找到一張信用卡
(B) 去另一家店
(C) 確認一筆交易手續費
(D) 比較一些商品

題目 receipt [rɪ`sit] 收據　purchase [美 `pɝtʃəs 英 `pə:tʃəs] 消費　refund [`riˌfʌnd] 退費　look up 查詢
transaction [træn`zækʃən] 交易　wallet [美 `wɑlɪt 英 `wɔlit] 皮夾
44 request [rɪ`kwɛst] 要求給予　bedding [`bɛdɪŋ] 寢具　replace [rɪ`ples] 交換
45 process [`prɑsɛs] 處理　locate [lo`ket] 找出；確定～的地點
46 transaction fee 交易手續費　merchandise [`mɝtʃənˌdaɪz] 商品

44 中 **細節事項相關問題—特定細項** 答案 (C)

題目詢問女子上週做了什麼，因此必須注意提到題目關鍵字（last week）的前後部分。女子說：「I bought these bed sheets at your store last week」，表示上週在男子的店裡買了床單，因此正確答案是 (C) Bought some bedding。

換句話說

bed sheets 床單 → bedding 寢具

新 **45** 高 **細節事項相關問題—掌握意圖** 答案 (D)

題目詢問男子說這句話的意圖，因此要注意提到題目關鍵字（I can look up the transaction using the number）的前後部分。女子說：「Does that mean that I can't get a refund?」，詢問沒有收據是否表示不能退款，男子說：「Do you have the same credit card you bought the items with?」，詢問女子是否有帶購買時使用的信用卡，由此可知，如果有帶購買時使用的信用卡，就可以退款，因此正確答案是 (D) A refund can be given.。

46 低 **細節事項相關問題—接下來要做的事** 答案 (A)

題目詢問女子接下來要做的事，因此要注意對話的最後部分。男子說：「Do you have the same credit card you bought the items with?」，詢問女子是否有帶購買時使用的信用卡，女子說：「Yes, I have it in my wallet. ~ let me just get it.」，表示卡在自己的皮夾內，讓她拿一下，由此可知，女子接下來會找到信用卡，因此正確答案是 (A) Find a credit card。

Questions 47-49 refer to the following conversation.

美式發音 → 澳洲式發音

W: Do you require some assistance?

M: Yes, [47]**I'd like your opinion on which of these ties to get**. Both of them have fashionable patterns, but [47/48]**I'm not sure if the black one will complement this suit I'm buying** for my friend's wedding.

W: Since the suit you've picked is gray, [48]**I think this sky blue tie matches it better**. The black one seems too dark in my opinion.

M: Hmm . . . You're right. Plus, my friend said that light purple will be one of his wedding colors. So, your recommendation will go better with that too. [49]**I'll put it on now just to make sure it suits me**, if that's OK.

第 47-49 題請參考下列對話。

女：您需要一點協助嗎？

男：是的，[47] 我想請妳給我意見看要買哪條領帶。這兩條的花樣都很時髦，但 [47/48] 我不確定黑色那條和這套我要買去參加朋友婚禮的西裝搭不搭。

女：因為你挑好的西裝是灰色的，[48] 所以我想這條天空藍的領帶比較搭。我認為黑色那條似乎太暗了。

男：嗯……妳說得對。而且我朋友說過淺紫色會是他的婚禮主色之一。所以妳推薦的這條也會和那個顏色比較搭。如果可以的話，[49] 我想現在繫上，確定一下它是適合我的。

47 Where most likely is the conversation taking place?

(A) At an event hall
(B) At a fabric factory
(C) At a dry cleaner
(D) At a clothing shop

47 這段對話最有可能發生在哪裡？

(A) 在活動廳
(B) 在織品工廠
(C) 在乾洗店
(D) 在服飾店

48 What does the woman suggest?

(A) Walking over to a counter
(B) Dressing in formal attire
(C) Selecting a different color
(D) Asking for another opinion

48 女子建議什麼？

(A) 走過去到櫃檯
(B) 穿上正式服裝
(C) 選擇不同的顏色
(D) 尋求其他意見

49 What will the man probably do next?

(A) Determine a wedding date
(B) Look over some expenses
(C) Find an associate
(D) Try on an item

49 男子接下來可能會做什麼？

(A) 決定一場婚禮的日期
(B) 查看一些支出
(C) 找到一個同事
(D) 試一個品項

題目 assistance [ə`sɪstəns] 協助 fashionable [`fæʃənəbl̩] 時尚的 pattern [美] `pætɚn [英] `pætən] 花樣；圖案 complement [[美] `kɑmplə͵mɛnt [英] ͵kɔmpli`mənt] 與～相配 suit [sut] 套裝；西裝；適合 match [mætʃ] 適合；和～相配 recommendation [͵rɛkəmɛn`deʃən] 推薦 go with 與～相配 put on 穿上 make sure 確定

48 counter [`kaʊntɚ] 櫃台 dress [drɛs] 穿（衣物） formal attire 正式服裝

49 determine [dɪ`tɝmɪn] 決定 look over 查看，仔細檢查 expense [ɪk`spɛns] 開支；費用 associate [ə`soʃɪɪt] 同事；合夥人 try on 試（衣服等）

47 中 **整體對話相關問題—地點** 答案 (D)

題目詢問對話發生的地點，因此要注意聽和地點有關的表達。男子對女子說：「I'd like your opinion on which of these ties to get」，表示希望女子針對要買哪條領帶給意見，接著說：「I'm not sure if the black one will complement this suit I'm buying」，表示不確定黑色那條和他要買的西裝搭不搭，由此可知，對話發生的地點是在服飾店，因此正確答案是 (D) At a clothing shop。

48 中 **細節事項相關問題—提議** 答案 (C)

題目詢問女子建議什麼，因此要注意聽女子話中出現的建議表達後方的內容。男子說：「I'm not sure if the black one will complement this suit I'm buying」，表示自己不確定黑色那條領帶和要買的西裝是否搭配，接著女子說：「I think this sky blue tie matches it[suit] better」，表示女子認為天空藍那條和西裝比較搭，因此正確答案是 (C) Selecting a different color。

49 低 **細節事項相關問題—接下來要做的事** 答案 (D)

題目詢問男子接下來會做什麼，因此必須注意對話的最後部分。男子說：「I'll put it[tie] on now just to make sure it suits me」，表示為了確定這條領帶適合自己，要立刻試打看看，因此正確答案是 (D) Try on an item。

Questions 50-52 refer to the following conversation.

加拿大式發音 → 美式發音

M: Hi. [50]**I went to singer Farrah Miller's concert** last Thursday at your theater. But I was very disappointed that [50]**there were issues with the sound due to a microphone malfunction**. I want a full refund for my ticket, please.

W: I'm sorry about that, sir. However, we aren't providing refunds because the issue was caused by the band's equipment. [51]**I suggest you make a complaint on Farrah Miller's official Web site.**

M: [51]**I tried that yesterday**, but I haven't heard back yet. [52]**Isn't there anything you can do to compensate me?**

W: Well, we can provide you with a 20 percent discount for a future performance at our venue. [52]**I hope this will make up for the inconvenience you've experienced.**

50 What problem does the man mention?

(A) A concert has been canceled.
(B) A venue was unexpectedly closed.
(C) A show experienced technical difficulties.
(D) A band did not appear as planned.

51 What did the man do yesterday?

(A) Viewed some comments
(B) Visited a ticketing office
(C) Checked schedule changes
(D) Submitted a complaint

52 新 Why does the woman say, "we can provide you with a 20 percent discount"?

(A) To promote a service
(B) To recommend an option
(C) To fulfill a request
(D) To confirm a choice

第 50-52 題請參考下列對話。

男：嗨。上週四 [50] 我在你們劇院看了歌手 Farrah Miller 的演唱會。但是我非常失望 [50] 聲音因為麥克風故障而有問題。我想要全額退票，謝謝。

女：先生，我對此感到抱歉。不過，因為這個問題是樂團設備所造成的，所以我們不會提供退費。[51] 我建議您上 Farrah Miller 的官網提出申訴。

男：[51] 我昨天試著這麼做過了，不過我還沒得到任何回應。[52] 你們沒有辦法做些什麼來補償我嗎？

女：這個嘛，未來在我們場地的演出，我們可以給您八折優惠。[52] 我希望這能彌補您所遭受的不便。

50 男子提到什麼問題？

(A) 演唱會被取消了。
(B) 場地被無預警關閉了。
(C) 演出發生了技術性問題。
(D) 樂團未按照計畫出場。

51 男子昨天做了什麼？

(A) 看了一些評論
(B) 去了一個售票處
(C) 確認了行程變更
(D) 提出了一項申訴

52 女子為什麼說：「我們可以給您八折優惠」？

(A) 為了推廣一項服務
(B) 為了推薦一個選項
(C) 為了滿足一個要求
(D) 為了確認一個選項

題目 issue [`ɪʃju] 問題 malfunction [mæl`fʌŋʃən] 故障；失去功能 compensate [`kɑmpən͵set] 補償 venue [`vɛnju] 場地 make up for 彌補，補償 inconvenience [͵ɪnkən`vinjəns] 不便
50 unexpectedly [͵ʌnɪk`spɛktɪdlɪ] 未預料到地，意外地 technical [`tɛknɪkl̩] 技術性的 as planned 按照計畫的
52 fulfill [fʊl`fɪl] 滿足（願望等） request [rɪ`kwɛst] 請求；要求事項

50 中 **細節事項相關問題—問題點** 答案 (C)

題目詢問男子提到的問題是什麼，因此必須注意聽男子話中出現負面表達之後的內容。男子說：「I went to ~ concert」，表示自己去了演唱會，接著說：「there were issues with the sound due to a microphone malfunction」，表示麥克風故障導致聲音出了問題，因此正確答案是 (C) A show experienced technical difficulties.。

51 低 **細節事項相關問題—特定細項** 答案 (D)

題目詢問男子昨天做了什麼，因此必須注意提到題目關鍵字（yesterday）的前後內容。女子對男子說：「I suggest you make a complaint on Farrah Miller's official Web site.」，表示建議男子上 Farrah Miller 的官方網站提出申訴，接著男子說：「I tried that yesterday」，表示昨天已經試著那麼做了，因此正確答案是 (D) Submitted a complaint。

新 **52** 高 **細節事項相關問題—掌握意圖** 答案 (C)

題目詢問女子的說話意圖，因此要注意提到題目關鍵字（we can provide you with a 20 percent discount）的前後部分內容。男子說：「Isn't there anything you can do to compensate me?」，詢問女子是否能做些什麼來補償自己，女子最後則說：「I hope this will make up for the inconvenience you've experienced.」，表示希望她提出的做法能彌補男子所遭受的不便，由此可知，女子希望能滿足男子的要求，因此正確答案是 (C) To fulfill a request。

53 54 55 新

Questions 53-55 refer to the following conversation with three speakers.	第 53-55 題請參考下列三人對話。
美式發音 → 加拿大式發音 → 澳洲式發音	
W: OK. [53]**Both candidates for the consumer analyst position are qualified. Either would be suitable for the job.**	女：好了。[53] 消費者分析師一職的兩位應徵者都符合資格。他們之中的任何一個都會適合來做這份工作。
M1: I feel that Patricia Spaulding is more versatile, as she's worked on different types of studies. What do you think, Jamie?	男 1：我覺得 Patricia Spaulding 比較全面，因為她曾處理過不同類型的研究。Jamie，你覺得呢？
M2: I agree. She has used several methods to examine consumer trends, and [54]**I'd like her help with some marketing research I'm in charge of now.**	男 2：我同意。她曾用過幾種方法來檢視消費者趨勢，而且 [54] 我想要她在我現在負責的一些行銷研究上提供協助。
M1: Good idea. Also, I thought Ms. Spaulding was more approachable than the other candidate.	男 1：好主意。此外，我認為 Spaulding 小姐比另一位應徵者更友善。
M2: Then let's offer Ms. Spaulding the position. We can notify her today. Stella, could you do that?	男 2：那我們就提供 Spaulding 小姐這個職位吧。我們可以在今天通知她。Stella，可以請妳做這件事嗎？
W: [55]**I'll call her right after this meeting.**	女：[55] 這個會結束後我會立刻打給她。
M2: Thanks. I know she's anxious to hear from us, so let's not keep her waiting.	男 2：謝謝。我知道她急著想要得到我們的回覆，所以不要讓她一直等下去。
53 What are the speakers mainly discussing? (A) Making an applicant list (B) Creating a job advertisement (C) Choosing a candidate (D) Arranging a training session	53 說話者們主要在討論什麼？ (A) 製作應徵者名單 (B) 製作徵才廣告 (C) 選擇應徵者 (D) 安排培訓課程
54 What is Jamie currently working on? (A) A sales report (B) A meeting agenda (C) A consumer survey (D) A marketing study	54 Jamie 現在正在處理什麼？ (A) 銷售報告 (B) 會議議程 (C) 消費者調查 (D) 行銷研究
55 What will the woman probably do after the meeting? (A) Contact an applicant (B) Conduct an interview (C) Edit a posting (D) Listen to a voice mail	55 女子在會後可能會做什麼？ (A) 聯繫一位應徵者 (B) 進行一場面試 (C) 編輯一則貼文 (D) 聽取語音留言

題目 analyst [`ænḷɪst] 分析師　qualified [`kwɑlə͵faɪd] 能勝任的；合格的　versatile [`vɝsətḷ] 多種用途的；多才多藝的
examine [ɪg`zæmɪn] 檢視；細查　trend [trɛnd] 趨勢　in charge of 負責～
approachable [ə`protʃəbḷ] 待人友善的；易親近的　anxious [`æŋkʃəs] 渴望的；焦慮不安的
54 agenda [ə`dʒɛndə] 議程；待辦事項　**55** conduct [kən`dʌkt] 實行；處理　edit [`ɛdɪt] 編輯

53 整體對話相關問題—主題 答案 (C)

中

題目詢問對話主題，因此必須注意對話的開頭部分，並掌握對話整體脈絡。女子說：「Both candidates for the consumer analyst position are qualified. Either would be suitable for the job.」，表示應徵消費者分析師的兩個人都符合資格，其中任何一位都適任，接著說話者們就開始就應徵者進行討論，因此正確答案是 (C) Choosing a candidate。

54 細節事項相關問題—特定細項 答案 (D)

低

題目詢問 Jamie，也就是男 2 現在正在處理什麼，因此必須注意男 2 話中和題目關鍵字（currently working on）相關的內容。男 2 說：「I'd like her[Patricia Spaulding's] help with some marketing research I'm in charge of now」，表示他希望 Patricia Spaulding 能為自己現在負責的行銷研究提供幫助，因此正確答案是 (D) A marketing study。

55 細節事項相關問題—接下來要做的事 答案 (A)

低

題目詢問女子在會議後會做的事情，因此要注意對話中和題目關鍵字（after the meeting）相關的內容。女子說：「I'll call her[Patricia Spaulding] right after this meeting.」，表示自己在會後會立刻打電話給 Patricia Spaulding，因此正確答案是 (A) Contact an applicant。

56
57
58

Questions 56-58 refer to the following conversation.

加拿大式發音 → 英式發音

M: Elaine, I have an idea. [56]**What if our company started subsidizing employee education? We could offer financial support for workers who want to pursue professional courses.**

W: I don't see why not. Many successful corporations invest in staff development. And based on [57]**last Friday's gathering with the board of directors**, our company has enough money in its budget to do the same.

M: So then, how much of the education costs do you think we should cover?

W: [58]**The best way to determine that is to look into the amounts that other similar companies normally provide. Please do some research** and let me know what you find.

56 What does the man suggest?

(A) Reviewing educational materials
(B) Changing degree requirements
(C) Funding professional development
(D) Updating hiring procedures

57 According to the woman, what took place last Friday?

(A) A charity event
(B) A business seminar
(C) A press conference
(D) An executive meeting

58 What does the woman ask the man to do?

(A) Call some directors
(B) Research some amounts
(C) Find a training program
(D) Meet with a financial consultant

第 56-58 題請參考下列對話。

男：Elaine，我有個主意。[56] 要是我們公司開始補助員工教育呢？我們可以為想要上專業課程的員工提供財務上的支援。

女：有何不可。許多成功的企業都會在員工發展上投資。而且根據 [57] **上週五和董事會的聚會**，我們公司有足夠預算一樣這麼做。

男：那麼這樣的話，妳認為我們應該支付多少教育費用？

女：[58] **這件事最好的決定方法是先調查其他類似公司一般提供的金額是多少。請調查一下**，再讓我知道你的調查結果。

56　男子建議什麼？

(A) 審查教材
(B) 變更學位要求條件
(C) 資助專業發展
(D) 更新聘用流程

57　根據女子所說，上週五發生了什麼？

(A) 一場慈善活動
(B) 一場商業研討會
(C) 一場記者會
(D) 一場主管聚會

58　女子要求男子做什麼？

(A) 致電幾位董事
(B) 調查一些金額
(C) 找到一項培訓課程
(D) 與一位財務顧問會面

題目 subsidize [ˋsʌbsəˏdaɪz] 提供補助金　financial [faɪˋnænʃəl] 財務上的；金融的　pursue [pɚˋsu] 進行，從事；追求　invest [ɪnˋvɛst] 投資　gathering [ˋgæðɚɪŋ] 聚會；聚集　board of directors 董事會　determine [美 dɪˋtɝmɪn 英 diˋtə:min] 決定　look into 調查　amount [əˋmaʊnt] 金額

56 degree [dɪˋgri] 學位　requirement [rɪˋkwaɪrmənt] 要求條件　fund [fʌnd] 提供資金

57 executive [ɪgˋzɛkjʊtɪv] 主管；（公司或組織的）領導階層

58 consultant [kənˋsʌltənt] 顧問

56 細節事項相關問題－提議　高　答案 (C)

題目詢問男子的建議內容，因此必須注意聽男子話中出現建議相關表達之後的內容。男子對女子說：「What if our company started subsidizing employee education? We could offer financial support for workers who want to pursue professional courses.」，建議公司資助員工教育，接著說公司可以提供財務上的支援給想要進修的員工，因此正確答案是 (C) Funding professional development。

57 細節事項相關問題－特定細項　中　答案 (D)

題目詢問女子說在上週五發生什麼事，因此必須注意女子所說的話中提到題目關鍵字（last Friday）的前後內容。女子說：「last Friday's gathering with the board of directors」，提到上週五與董事會聚會，因此正確答案是 (D) An executive meeting。

58 細節事項相關問題－要求　中　答案 (B)

題目詢問女子對男子所提出的要求內容，因此必須注意聽在要求表達後方出現的內容。女子對男子說：「The best way ~ is to look into the amounts ~. Please do some research」，表示最好的決定方式是調查其他類似公司所提供的金額是多少，並要求男子去調查金額，因此正確答案是 (B) Research some amounts。

59
60
61

Questions 59-61 refer to the following conversation.

美式發音 → 澳洲式發音

W: Hello. [59]**I'd like to purchase a pressure cooker from your department store** . . . ah . . . the Cookware 550.

M: I can definitely take care of that for you, ma'am. Have you ordered anything over the phone from us before?

W: Yes, I have. There should be an account for Marilyn Tan with a home address at 100 Eastwood Street in Baltimore. However, [60/61]**I'd like the item shipped to my friend's home,** [60]**since it will be a gift for her housewarming party.**

M: Absolutely. [61]**Please just wait a moment while our system loads, and then I'll enter all the necessary information.**

59 Why does the woman place the call?

(A) To verify warranty information
(B) To complain about an error
(C) To ask about a return policy
(D) To place a product order

60 Why does the woman say, "it will be a gift for her housewarming party"?

新

(A) To confirm a delivery time
(B) To ask for a different service
(C) To provide a reason for a request
(D) To express concern about a delay

61 What will the man probably do next?

(A) Shut down a system
(B) Input order details
(C) Meet with shipping personnel
(D) Cancel a previous charge

第 59-61 題請參考下列對話。

女：哈囉。[59] 我想在你們百貨公司買一個壓力鍋……呃……Cookware 550。

男：我當然可以為您處理這件事，小姐。您之前有透過電話向我們訂購過任何東西嗎？

女：有，我曾訂過。應該有個帳號是 Marilyn Tan，住家地址在巴爾的摩市 Eastwood 街 100 號。不過，[60/61] 我想要把這件商品寄到我朋友家，[60] 因為這是要給她的喬遷派對禮物。

男：沒問題。[61] 請稍待片刻，我們系統正在載入，然後我會為您輸入所有必需資料。

59 女子為什麼打這通電話？

(A) 確認保固資訊
(B) 投訴錯誤
(C) 詢問退貨政策
(D) 下訂商品

60 女子為什麼說：「這是要給她的喬遷派對禮物」？

(A) 確認配送時間
(B) 要求不同的服務
(C) 解釋為何提出要求
(D) 針對延誤表達擔心

61 男子接下來可能會做什麼？

(A) 關閉系統
(B) 輸入訂單詳細資料
(C) 與送貨人員碰面
(D) 取消先前的費用

題目 pressure cooker 壓力鍋　take care of 處理～　over the phone 透過電話　account [əˋkaʊnt] 帳號，帳戶　ship [ʃɪp] 運送　housewarming [ˋhaʊsˏwɔrmɪŋ] 喬遷派對

59 warranty [ˋwɔrəntɪ]（品質等的）保固；擔保；保證書　place an order 下訂

61 shut down 關閉　input [ˋɪnˏpʊt]（將資料等）輸入（電腦等）personnel [ˏpɝsn̩ˋɛl]（總稱）員工，人員　charge [tʃɑrdʒ] 收費，費用

59 ○○● 低 **整體對話相關問題—目的** 答案 (D)

題目詢問女子打電話的目的，因此必須注意對話的開頭部分。女子說：「I'd like to purchase a pressure cooker from your department store」，表示想在男子的百貨公司裡買壓力鍋，因此正確答案是 (D) To place a product order。

新 **60** ○●● 中 **細節事項相關問題—掌握意圖** 答案 (C)

題目詢問女子的說話意圖，因此要注意有提到題目關鍵字（it will be a gift for her housewarming party）的前後部分。女子說：「I'd like the item shipped to my friend's home, ~ it will be a gift for her housewarming party」，表示希望商品能寄到朋友家裡，因為那是要給朋友的喬遷派對禮物，由此可知，女子說這句話是為了解釋自己提出這項要求的理由，因此正確答案是 (C) To provide a reason for a request。

61 ○●● 中 **細節事項相關問題—接下來要做的事** 答案 (B)

題目詢問男子接下來要做的事，因此必須注意對話的最後部分。女子說：「I'd like the item shipped to my friend's home」，表示希望把商品寄到自己朋友家裡，後面男子則說：「Please just wait a moment while our system loads, and then I'll enter all the necessary information.」，請對方在系統載入時稍待，並表示自己會在系統載入後輸入所有必需資料，因此正確答案是 (B) Input order details。

換句話說

enter ~ information 輸入資料 → Input ~ details 輸入詳細資料

62 63 64 新

Questions 62-64 refer to the following conversation.

英式發音 → 澳洲式發音

W: [62]**How's the trade fair going for you? My booth has been busy.**
M: Mine too. My company's products are selling well.
W: I wish I had more help. It seems there are more people at the fair this year than usual.
M: A staff member at the registration desk said [63]**there was a 15 percent increase in attendance on the first day this year compared to last year**. However, my company's booth only has two employees working there today . . . umm . . . me and my colleague.
W: So your coworker is all alone at your booth now?
M: Yeah. I'd better get back. [64]**I've promised to assist him with passing out schedules** for the demonstrations we'll be giving this afternoon.

第 62-64 題請參考下列對話。

女：[62] 你們貿易展進行得如何？我的攤位一直很忙。
男：我的也是。我公司的產品賣得很好。
女：我希望我有更多人手。今年來貿易展的人似乎比往常更多。
男：登記處的一個員工說，[63] 今年第一天的出席人數和去年相比增加了百分之十五。然而，今天我公司的攤位只有兩個員工在那裡工作……嗯……我和我同事。
女：所以現在就你同事一個人在你們攤位上嗎？
男：是啊。我最好要回去了。[64] 我答應了要幫他發我們今天下午要進行的展示會的時間表。

62 Where most likely is the conversation taking place?
(A) At a product launch
(B) At a business conference
(C) At a shareholders' meeting
(D) At a trade fair

62 這段對話最有可能發生在哪裡？
(A) 產品發表會
(B) 商務會議
(C) 股東會
(D) 貿易展

63 How is this year's event different from the previous one?
(A) More funding was used.
(B) Registration fees are higher.
(C) More attendees are present.
(D) Additional space was created.

63 今年的活動和去年有何不同？
(A) 運用了更多資金。
(B) 報名費比較貴。
(C) 更多人出席。
(D) 增加了額外的場地。

64 What has the man promised to do?
(A) Take over a work shift
(B) Set up a booth
(C) Replace some equipment
(D) Distribute some documents

64. 男子答應了要做什麼？
(A) 接班
(B) 設立攤位
(C) 更換一些設備
(D) 發放一些文件

題目 registration [ˌrɛdʒɪˋstreʃən] 報名；登記 attendance [əˋtɛndəns] 參加人數；出席
colleague [美 kɑˋlig 英 kɔˋli:g] 同事 coworker [美 ˋkoˏwɝkɚ 英 ˋkəuˏwə:kə] 同事
assist [əˋsɪst] 幫助 pass out 分發 demonstration [ˏdɛmənˋstreʃən]（產品）展示會；實際示範
63 funding [ˋfʌndɪŋ] 資金 attendee [əˋtɛndi] 出席者
64 take over 接手 work shift 輪班工作的班次

62 ■ **整體對話相關問題—地點** 答案 (D)
低
題目詢問對話的發生地點，因此必須注意聽和地點有關的表達。女子對男子說：「How's the trade fair going for you? My booth has been busy.」，詢問貿易展進行得如何，並表示自己的攤位一直很忙，由此可知，對話是發生在貿易展上，因此正確答案是 (D) At a trade fair。

63 ■ **細節事項相關問題—特定細項** 答案 (C)
中
題目詢問今年活動和去年有什麼不同的地方，因此必須注意和題目關鍵字（this year's event different from the previous one）相關的內容。男子說：「there was a 15 percent increase in attendance on the first day this year compared to last year」，表示相較去年，今年第一天的出席人數多了百分之十五，因此正確答案是 (C) More attendees are present.。
換句話說
increase in attendance 出席人數增加 → More attendees are present 更多人出席

64 ■ **細節事項相關問題—特定細項** 答案 (D)
中
題目詢問男子答應要做什麼事情，因此要注意和題目關鍵字（promised to do）相關的內容。男子說：「I've promised to assist him[coworker] with passing out schedules」，表示自己答應了同事會去發展示會的時間表，因此正確答案是 (D) Distribute some documents。

TEST 1 2 3 4 5 6 7 8 9 10

65
66
67

Questions 65-67 refer to the following conversation and menu.

加拿大式發音 → 美式發音

M: Joan, [65]**we need to make arrangements to have a small office party for Angela's birthday next week.**

W: Oh, [65]**thanks for bringing that up . . . I had forgotten about it.** Do you have any ideas?

M: Yes, [66]**I suggest we hold the celebration in the conference room.** But before I buy a cake, I need to know the food budget.

W: [67]**We can spend up to $50 on a cake.** But please make sure it's big enough so that everyone in the office can have a slice—[67]**it should be at least 10 inches**. Whatever you buy, just bring the receipt to Mary in the human resources department, and she'll reimburse you.

新

Holly's Cake Shop Menu

Type	Size	Price
Coconut Cake	8 in	$36
Strawberry Cheesecake	10 in	$54
[67]Carrot Cake	**12 in**	**$46**
Chocolate Cake	14 in	$58

65 Why does the woman thank the man?

(A) He gave her a venue recommendation.
(B) He helped her move to a new office.
(C) He surprised her with a gift.
(D) He reminded her of an occasion.

66 What does the man propose doing?

(A) Using a meeting space
(B) Browsing a sample menu
(C) Choosing a special decoration
(D) Increasing a price limit

67 Look at the graphic. Which cake will the man order?

新
(A) Coconut Cake
(B) Strawberry Cheesecake
(C) Carrot Cake
(D) Chocolate Cake

第 65-67 題請參考下列對話及菜單。

男：Joan，[65] 我們得為下星期 Angela 的生日安排一個小型的辦公室派對。

女：噢，[65] 謝謝你提起這件事……我都忘記了。你有什麼想法嗎？

男：有，[66] 我建議我們把慶祝會辦在會議室裡。不過在我買蛋糕之前，我得先知道食物的預算。

女：[67] 我們最多可以花 50 美金在一個蛋糕上。但請確定蛋糕夠大，能讓辦公室裡的每個人都可以拿到一片—— [67] 應該至少要 10 吋。不管你買什麼，只要把收據拿給人力資源部的 Mary，她就會替你核銷。

Holly 的蛋糕店菜單

種類	尺寸	價格
椰子蛋糕	8 吋	36 美金
草莓起司蛋糕	10 吋	54 美金
[67] 胡蘿蔔蛋糕	12 吋	46 美金
巧克力蛋糕	14 吋	58 美金

65 女子為什麼感謝男子？

(A) 他給了她場地建議。
(B) 他協助她搬到了新辦公室。
(C) 他用禮物給了她驚喜。
(D) 他提醒了她一場活動。

66 男子提議做什麼？

(A) 使用會議場地
(B) 瀏覽菜單打樣
(C) 選擇特殊裝飾
(D) 提高金額限制

67 請看圖表。男子會訂購哪一款蛋糕？

(A) 椰子蛋糕
(B) 草莓起司蛋糕
(C) 胡蘿蔔蛋糕
(D) 巧克力蛋糕

題目 arrangement [ə`rendʒmənt] 安排；準備工作 bring ~ up 提起（話題等） celebration [ˌsɛlə`breʃən] 慶祝活動 budget [`bʌdʒɪt] 預算 make sure 確定，確保 slice [slaɪs]（食物等的）薄片，片 reimburse [ˌriɪm`bɝs] 核銷

65 recommendation [ˌrɛkəmɛn`deʃən] 推薦；建議 remind [rɪ`maɪnd] 使想起；提醒 occasion [ə`keʒən]（特別的）場合；（重大的）活動

66 browse [braʊz] 瀏覽 decoration [ˌdɛkə`reʃən] 裝飾；裝飾品

65 **細節事項相關問題—理由** 答案 (D)

中

題目詢問女子感謝男子的原因，因此必須注意提到題目關鍵字（thank）的前後部分。男子說：「we need to make arrangements to have a small office party for Angela's birthday next week」，表示得要準備下週 Angela 的生日派對了，接著女子就對男子說：「thanks for bringing that up ~. I had forgotten about it」表示感謝男子的提醒，因為她自己忘了這件事，因此正確答案是 (D) He reminded her of an occasion.。

66 **細節事項相關問題—提議** 答案 (A)

中

題目詢問男子建議要做什麼事情，因此必須注意聽男子話中出現要求表達之後的內容。男子說：「I suggest we hold the celebration in the conference room」，建議要把慶祝活動辦在會議室裡，因此正確答案是 (A) Using a meeting space。

換句話說

conference room 會議室 → meeting space 會議場地

新 **67** **細節事項相關問題—圖表資料** 答案 (C)

高

題目詢問男子會訂哪款蛋糕，因此必須確認題目提供的菜單上的資訊，且須注意聽和題目關鍵字（cake ~ order）有關的內容。女子說：「We can spend up to $50 on a cake.」，表示最多可以花 50 美金買蛋糕，接著說：「it should be at least 10 inches」，表示蛋糕至少要 10 吋，由此可知，男子會訂購 50 美金以下、10 吋以上的紅蘿蔔蛋糕，因此正確答案是 (C) Carrot Cake。

68
69
70

[新]

Questions 68-70 refer to the following conversation and subway map.

澳洲式發音 → 英式發音

M: [68]**Welcome to Smooth Beginnings, the nation's top provider of beauty products**. How can I help you?
W: [69]**I'm looking to purchase some moisturizer**. My skin gets a bit dry in the winter. [69]**Where can I find these products?**
M: They're next to the cashier . . . um, just over there.
W: Thanks. By the way, this new store is really nice.
M: I'm glad you like it. We just opened last week. Did you have any trouble finding it?
W: No. I live near the bus terminal, so it was easy to get here by subway.
M: That's right . . . [70]**There are only two stops between the terminal and Norton Station if you take Line 3.**
W: Well, [70]**that line isn't running today because the track is being repaired. But luckily there's another one with the same number of stops. I took that one.**

[新]

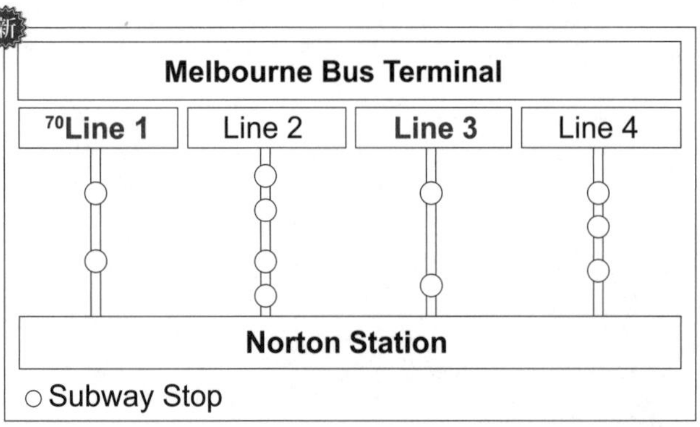

68 Where most likely does the man work?
(A) At a transportation authority
(B) At a travel agency
(C) At an electronics producer
(D) At a cosmetics retailer

69 What does the woman ask about?
(A) The location of an item
(B) The reliability of a service
(C) The time of a delivery
(D) The duration of an event

70 [新] Look at the graphic. Which subway line did the woman take today?
(A) Line 1
(B) Line 2
(C) Line 3
(D) Line 4

第 68-70 題請參考下列對話及地鐵路線圖。

男：[68] 歡迎來到全國第一的美容產品供應商 Smooth Beginnings。您需要什麼呢？
女：[69] 我想要買一些保濕的東西。我的皮膚在冬天變得有點乾燥。[69] 我可以在哪裡找到這些產品呢？
男：它們在收銀台旁邊……嗯，就在那裡。
女：謝謝。對了，這家新的店真不錯。
男：很高興您喜歡。我們上星期剛開幕。您會覺得這裡難找嗎？
女：不會。我住在公車總站附近，所以搭地鐵到這裡很容易。
男：對喔……[70] 如果您搭 3 號線的話，總站到 Norton 站間只有兩站。
女：這個嘛，[70] 那條線今天因為軌道正在維修而沒有營運。不過幸好還有另一條線的停靠站數相同。我搭了那條線。

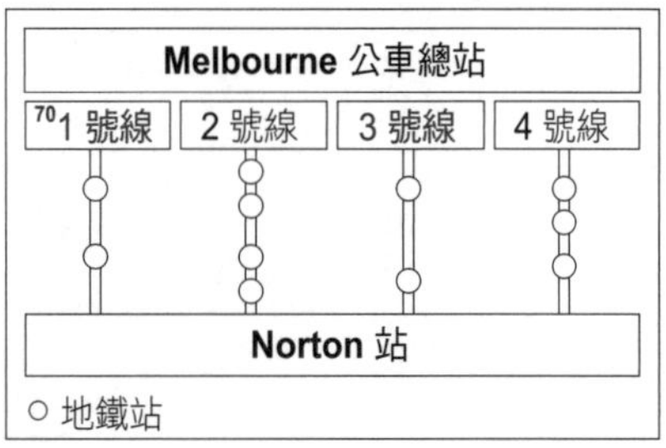

68 男子最有可能在哪裡工作？
(A) 運輸管理機構
(B) 旅行社
(C) 電子產品製造商
(D) 化妝品零售商

69 女子詢問什麼？
(A) 商品的位置
(B) 服務的可靠度
(C) 送貨的時間
(D) 活動時間的長度

70 請看圖表。女子今天搭的地鐵是哪條線？
(A) 1 號線
(B) 2 號線
(C) 3 號線
(D) 4 號線

題目 provider [[美] prə`vaɪdɚ [英] prə`vaidə] 供應商 cashier [[美] kæ`ʃɪr [英] kæ`ʃiə] 收銀員；收銀台 run [rʌn] 行駛；營運 repair [[美] rɪ`pɛr [英] ri`pɛə] 維修 luckily [[美] `lʌkəlɪ [英] `lʌkəli] 幸運地

68 authority [ə`θɔrətɪ] 當局；管理機構 electronics [ɪlɛk`trɑnɪks] 電子產品 producer [prə`djusɚ] 製造商 cosmetic [kɑz`mɛtɪk] 化妝品 retailer [rɪ`telɚ] 零售商

69 reliability [rɪˌlaɪə`bɪlətɪ] 可靠度；可信賴性 duration [djʊ`reʃən]（持續的）時間

68 中 整體對話相關問題—說話者 答案 (D)

題目詢問男子的工作地點，因此必須注意聽和身分、職業相關的表達。男子說：「Welcome to Smooth Beginnings, the nation's top provider of beauty products.」，表示歡迎女子來到全國第一的美容產品供應商 Smooth Beginnings，由此可知，男子的工作地點是化妝品零售商，因此正確答案是 (D) At a cosmetics retailer。

69 低 細節事項相關問題—特定細項 答案 (A)

題目詢問女子提問的內容，因此必須注意聽女子所說的話。女子說：「I'm looking to purchase some moisturizer.」，表示自己想要買保濕的東西，接著問：「Where can I find these products?」，表示她想知道可以在哪裡找到這種商品，因此正確答案是 (A) The location of an item。

新 **70** 高 細節事項相關問題—圖表資料 答案 (A)

題目詢問女子今天搭的地鐵是哪條線，因此必須確認題目提供的地鐵路線相關資訊，並注意和題目關鍵字（subway line）相關的內容。男子說：「There are only two stops between the terminal and Norton Station if you take Line 3.」，表示如果搭 3 號線，公車總站和 Norton 站之間只會停兩站，接著女子說：「that line[line 3] isn't running today ~. But luckily there's another one with the same number of stops. I took that one.」，表示 3 號線今天沒有營運，但很幸運有另一條線的停靠站數和 3 號線一樣，而自己搭了那條線。透過地鐵路線圖可以得知，女子搭了和 3 號線一樣，公車總站和 Norton 站之間只停靠兩站的 1 號線，因此正確答案是 (A) Line 1。

71
72
73

Questions 71-73 refer to the following telephone message.

英式發音

Marian, it's Haley. [71/72]**One of my friends invited me to go to the Franklin Music Festival with him on Saturday.** [71]**I said I'd go**, and I'd like you to come along too. The festival is going to be held at Carlson Park from noon until 10 P.M. We plan to go at 5:30 because [72]**our favorite band takes the stage at 6:30** and we'd like to get there an hour earlier to find good seats. Please call or text me whenever you get this message to let me know if you'll be joining us. [73]**I want to buy tickets this afternoon**, since today's the last day to buy them at reduced prices.

71 What did the speaker agree to do?
(A) Attend an event
(B) Carpool to a meeting
(C) Distribute an itinerary
(D) Organize a festival

72 What will happen at 6:30 on Saturday?
(A) A park will close.
(B) A band will be interviewed.
(C) A reservation will be made.
(D) A performance will begin.

73 What does the speaker want to do later today?
(A) Exchange a product
(B) Purchase some tickets
(C) Visit a venue
(D) Send some invitations

第 71-73 題請參考以下電話留言。

Marian，我是 Haley。[71/72] 我有個朋友邀請我星期六跟他一起去 Franklin 音樂節。[71] 我說我會去，而且我希望妳也一起來。這場音樂節會從中午開始到晚上 10 點在 Carlson 公園舉行。我們打算 5 點 30 分過去，因為 [72] 我們最喜歡的樂團會在 6 點 30 分登台，所以我們想要提前一小時到那裡去找好位子。請妳在聽到這則訊息之後打電話或傳訊息給我，告訴我妳會不會和我們一起去。[73] 我想要在今天下午買票，因為今天是能用優惠價買票的最後一天。

71 說話者同意做什麼？
(A) 出席一場活動
(B) 共乘汽車去一場會議
(C) 發送旅遊行程
(D) 籌劃一個節慶

72 星期六的 6 點 30 分會發生什麼？
(A) 公園會關閉。
(B) 將採訪樂團。
(C) 將進行預約。
(D) 表演會開始。

73 說話者今天晚一點想要做什麼？
(A) 換一件商品
(B) 買一些票
(C) 造訪一個場地
(D) 寄一些邀請函

題目 invite [ɪn`vaɪt] 邀請 come along 一起去 hold [美 hold 英 həuld] 使發生；舉行
71 carpool [`kɑr͵pul] 共乘汽車 itinerary [aɪ`tɪnə͵rɛrɪ] 旅遊行程 organize [`ɔrgə͵naɪz] 籌劃
73 venue [`vɛnju] 場地 invitation [͵ɪnvə`teʃən] 邀請函

71 細節事項相關問題—特定細項 答案 (A)
中
題目詢問說話者同意做什麼事，因此必須注意和題目關鍵字（agree to do）有關的內容。獨白說：「One of my friends invited me to go to the Franklin Music Festival with him on Saturday. I said I'd go」，表示朋友邀自己星期六去音樂節，而自己說會去，因此正確答案是 (A) Attend an event。

72 細節事項相關問題—接下來要做的事 答案 (D)
中
題目詢問星期六的 6 點 30 分時會發生什麼事情，因此要注意和題目關鍵字（6:30 on Saturday）相關的內容。獨白說：「One of my friends invited me to go to the Franklin Music Festival with him on Saturday.」，先說明有一位朋友邀自己星期六去音樂節，接著說：「our favorite band takes the stage at 6:30」，表示最喜歡的樂團會在 6 點 30 分登台，因此正確答案是 (D) A performance will begin.。
換句話說
band takes the stage 樂團登台 → A performance ~ begin 表演開始

73 細節事項相關問題—特定細項 答案 (B)
低
題目詢問說話者今天晚一點想做什麼事情，因此必須注意和題目關鍵字（want to do later today）相關的內容。獨白說：「I want to buy tickets this afternoon」，表示想在今天下午買票，因此正確答案是 (B) Purchase some tickets。

74 75 76

Questions 74-76 refer to the following excerpt from a meeting.

🔊 美式發音

It looks like everyone is here, so let's get started. As most of you know, [74]**our biggest rival . . . um, Dyson Travel . . . now allows customers to create personalized discount travel packages. This is a problem** because it has led to [75]**a significant drop in traffic on our Web site**. The CEO is very concerned and expects us to develop a strategy to deal with the situation quickly. [76]**He suggested that we charge less for our most popular tours. I'm not sure if that'll have any effect, though** . . . Our prices are already low. So, [76]**we should probably come up with some other ways to address this problem.**

74 What is the problem?

(A) A client has made a complaint.
(B) A device does not function.
(C) A discount is no longer available.
(D) A competitor is offering a new service.

75 What does the speaker mention about the Web site?

(A) It includes additional features.
(B) It will be updated regularly.
(C) It was launched yesterday.
(D) It is receiving fewer visitors.

76 新 What does the speaker imply when she says, "Our prices are already low"?

(A) She is upset with a coworker.
(B) She is doubtful about an idea.
(C) She is confused by a situation.
(D) She is concerned about a budget.

第 74-76 題請參考以下會議節錄。

看來大家都到了，那我們就開始吧。如同你們大部分人都知道的，[74] 我們最大的對手……嗯，Dyson 旅遊……現在能讓客人打造個人化的優惠旅遊套裝方案了。因為這造成了 [75] 我們網站的流量明顯下滑，所以這是個問題。執行長感到非常擔心，所以希望我們能快點制定出因應這個情況的策略。[76] 他建議我們降低最受歡迎的旅遊方案的收費。不過我不確定這樣做是否會有什麼效果……我們的價格已經很低了。所以，[76] 我們也許應該想些其他辦法來處理這個問題。

74 問題是什麼？

(A) 客戶提出了申訴。
(B) 器材不能運作。
(C) 沒有折扣了。
(D) 競爭者現在提供了新服務。

75 關於網站，說話者提到什麼？

(A) 有額外的功能。
(B) 會定期更新。
(C) 在昨天啟用了。
(D) 造訪的人減少了。

76 當說話者說：「我們的價格已經很低了」時，她在暗示什麼？

(A) 她對一位同事不滿。
(B) 她對一個想法感到懷疑。
(C) 她對一個情況感到困惑。
(D) 她對一筆預算感到憂心。

題目 personalize [ˋpɝsnəl͵aɪz] 個人化　significant [sɪgˋnɪfəkənt] 顯著的；重大的　develop [dɪˋvɛləp] 開發；制定　strategy [ˋstrætədʒɪ] 策略　come up with 想出～　address [əˋdrɛs] 處理；致詞；地址
75 regularly [ˋrɛgjələlɪ] 定期地　launch [lɔntʃ] 啟動；開始
76 upset with 對～不滿的　doubtful [ˋdaʊtfəl] 不確定的，懷疑的

74 中 細節事項相關問題—特定細項　答案 (D)

題目詢問問題是什麼，因此必須注意有提到題目關鍵字（problem）的前後部分。獨白說：「our biggest rival ~ now allows customers to create personalized discount travel packages. This is a problem」，表示最大的對手現在讓客人能打造個人化的旅遊套裝方案，而這件事是個問題，因此正確答案是 (D) A competitor is offering a new service.。

75 高 細節事項相關問題—提及　答案 (D)

題目詢問說話者提到了什麼與網站有關的事情，因此要注意提到了題目關鍵字（Web site）的前後部分。獨白說：「a significant drop in traffic on our Web site」，提到自己的網站流量明顯下滑了，因此正確答案是 (D) It is receiving fewer visitors.。

換句話說

significant drop in traffic 網站流量明顯下滑 → receiving fewer visitors 造訪的人減少了

新 **76** 高 細節事項相關問題—掌握意圖　答案 (B)

題目詢問說話者意圖，因此必須注意聽題目關鍵字（Our prices are already low）出現的前後部分。獨白說：「He[CEO] suggested that we charge less for our most popular tours. I'm not sure if that'll have any effect, though」，表示雖然執行長建議要降低最受歡迎的旅遊方案的收費，但自己卻不確定這樣做會不會有效果，後面則說：「we should probably come up with some other ways to address this problem」，表示應該想其他方法來處理這個問題，由此可知，說話者對於執行長的想法有所質疑，因此正確答案是 (B) She is doubtful about an idea.。

77
78
79

Questions 77-79 refer to the following advertisement.

加拿大式發音

Is it hard to keep track of all the remote controls for the electronics in your home? Well, [77]**now you can use KepCor's EX3 Universal Remote Control for everything** from audio equipment to kitchen appliances. [78]**The EX3 is simpler to operate than other similar products** thanks to its signal detector, which allows it to easily connect to nearby equipment. Simply press and hold the Scan button near a compatible device to take control of it. Next, select a colored button on the controller to assign to the device. And now, [79]**customers who register their EX3s online will receive a battery charger absolutely free.**

77 What is the speaker advertising?
(A) A speaker system
(B) A kitchen appliance
(C) A device operator
(D) A television set

78 According to the speaker, how is EX3 different from competing products?
(A) It is more durable.
(B) It uses fewer batteries.
(C) It comes in more colors.
(D) It is easier to use.

79 What will customers receive if they register a product online?
(A) A reduced price
(B) A complimentary item
(C) A gift card
(D) An extended warranty

第 77-79 題請參考以下廣告。

很難掌握您家中所有電子產品的遙控器都放在哪裡嗎？這個嘛，[77] 現在您可以使用 KepCor 的 EX3 萬用遙控器來控制從音響設備到廚房電器的一切了。多虧了它能輕易連接附近設備的信號偵測器，[78]EX3 較其他類似產品更易操作。只要在可相容裝置附近按住掃描鍵就能控制該裝置。接下來，在遙控器上選擇一個有顏色的按鍵來對應該裝置。而且現在 [79] 在線上註冊 EX3 的客人都會獲得一個電池充電器，完全免費。

77 說話者在廣告什麼？
(A) 喇叭系統
(B) 廚房電器
(C) 裝置操控器
(D) 電視機

78 根據說話者所說，EX3 和競爭商品之間有何不同？
(A) 更耐用。
(B) 用比較少電池。
(C) 有更多顏色。
(D) 更容易使用。

79 若在線上註冊商品，客人會得到什麼？
(A) 優惠價
(B) 贈品
(C) 禮物卡
(D) 延長保固

題目 keep track of 掌握～的狀態　universal [ˌjunə`vɝsl] 萬用的，通用的　kitchen appliance 廚房電器
operate [`ɑpəˌret] 運作；操作　similar [`sɪmələ] 類似的　detector [dɪ`tɛktə] 偵測器　compatible [kəm`pætəbl] 可相容的
take control of 控制～　assign [ə`saɪn] 派定；指定　register [`rɛdʒɪstə] 註冊　absolutely [`æbsəˌlutlɪ] 絕對地，一定地
78 durable [`djʊrəbl] 耐用的
79 complimentary [ˌkɑmplə`mɛntərɪ] 免費贈送的　warranty [`wɔrəntɪ] 保固

77 整體內容相關問題—主題　答案 (C)
中

題目詢問廣告主題，因此必須注意聽開頭部分。獨白說：「now you can use KepCor's EX3 Universal Remote Control for everything」，表示所有東西都可以用 KepCor 的 EX3 萬用遙控器來操控，接著繼續說明這個遙控器的功能，因此正確答案是 (C) A device operator。

換句話說
Remote Control 遙控器 → device operator 裝置操控器

78 細節事項相關問題—特定細項　答案 (D)
中

題目詢問 EX3 和其他競爭商品的不同之處，因此必須注意和題目關鍵字（EX3 different from competing products）有關的內容。獨白說：「The EX3 is simpler to operate than other similar products」，表示 EX3 相較於其他類似產品更易操作，因此正確答案是 (D) It is easier to use.。

換句話說
is simpler to operate 更易操作 → is easier to use 更容易使用

79 細節事項相關問題—特定細項　答案 (B)
中

題目詢問客人在線上註冊產品所能得到什麼，因此要注意和題目關鍵字（register ~ online）相關的內容。獨白說：「customers who register their EX3s online will receive a battery charger absolutely free」，表示在線上註冊 EX3 的顧客都會免費得到電池充電器，因此正確答案是 (B) A complimentary item。

80
81
82

Questions 80-82 refer to the following telephone message.

澳洲式發音

Hello. I'm calling from The Blue House Restaurant. Yesterday, we received a shipment for [80]**an order I recently made for our restaurant's glassware**. However, [81]**many of the items, like the crystal wine glasses, are in poor shape. Several of them have scratches and stains, but other items are worse**. All of the large blue pitchers are broken. I really can't believe it. [82]**We were supposed to hold our grand opening today, but we couldn't because we didn't have enough glassware**. At this point, I am seriously considering finding another supplier. Please call me at 555-2583 before noon to discuss the solution to this problem.

80 What did the speaker recently do?

(A) Placed a product order
(B) Contacted a new supplier
(C) Called a delivery person
(D) Canceled a purchase

81 新 What does the speaker imply when he says, "I really can't believe it"?

(A) He is shocked by a guest turnout.
(B) He is worried about a late shipment.
(C) He is overwhelmed with requests.
(D) He is disappointed with a service.

82 What is suggested about The Blue House Restaurant's grand opening?

(A) It was delayed.
(B) It began at noon.
(C) It had few attendees.
(D) It included free beverages.

第 80-82 題請參考以下電話留言。

哈囉。我是從 The Blue House 餐廳打來的。昨天我們收到了一批貨，[80] 是我最近為我們餐廳下訂的玻璃器皿。不過，[81] 其中有很多件，像是水晶紅酒杯，狀態都非常糟糕。其中幾件上有刮痕和汙漬，而其他的品項還更糟。所有的藍色大水壺都破了。我真是難以置信。[82] 我們今天原本應該要舉行盛大開幕式，但我們卻因為沒有足夠的玻璃器皿而無法舉行。現在，我正慎重考慮要找其他供應商。請在中午前打 555-2583 給我，討論這個問題的解決方案。

80 說話者最近做了什麼？

(A) 下了一張商品訂單
(B) 聯繫了一家新供應商
(C) 打電話給一位送貨人員
(D) 取消了一筆消費

81 當說話者說：「我真是難以置信」，他在暗示什麼？

(A) 他對來客數感到驚訝。
(B) 他擔心貨物延遲。
(C) 要求多到他難以承受。
(D) 他對服務感到失望。

82 關於 The Blue House 餐廳的盛大開幕式，暗示了什麼？

(A) 延遲了。
(B) 於中午開始。
(C) 出席者很少。
(D) 有免費飲料。

題目 shipment [ˋʃɪpmənt] 運輸的貨物；運送 glassware [美 ˋglæsˏwɛr 英 ˋglɑ:swɛə] 玻璃器皿
poor [美 pʊr 英 puə] 糟糕的 shape [ʃep] 狀態，情況 grand opening 盛大開幕式
supplier [美 səˋplaɪɚ 英 səˋplaiə] 供應商 solution [səˋluʃən] 解決方案
81 turnout [ˋtɝnˏaʊt]（聚會的）到場人數；投票人數 overwhelm [ˏovɚˋhwɛlm] 使難以承受；使不知所措
disappoint [ˏdɪsəˋpɔɪnt] 使失望
82 attendee [əˋtɛndi] 出席者 beverage [ˋbɛvərɪdʒ] 飲料

80 細節事項相關問題—特定細項 答案 (A)
低
題目詢問說話者最近做的事情，因此必須注意獨白中提到題目關鍵字（recently）的前後部分。獨白說：「an order I recently made for our restaurant's glassware」，提到最近替餐廳下訂了玻璃器皿，因此正確答案是 (A) Placed a product order。

新 **81** 細節事項相關問題—掌握意圖 答案 (D)
中
題目詢問說話者說這句話的意圖，因此必須注意提到題目關鍵字（I really can't believe it）的前後部分。獨白說：「many of the items ~ are in poor shape. Several of them have scratches and stains, but other items are worse.」，表示許多品項的狀況很糟，有幾件上面有刮痕和污漬，而其他品項的狀態還更糟，由此可知，說話者對於服務很失望，因此正確答案是 (D) He is disappointed with a service.。

82 細節事項相關問題—推論 答案 (A)
高
題目詢問與 The Blue House 餐廳的盛大開幕式有關的內容，因此必須注意提到題目關鍵字（grand opening）的前後部分。獨白說：「We[The Blue House Restaurant] were supposed to hold our grand opening today, but we couldn't because we didn't have enough glassware.」，表示 The Blue House 餐廳本來要在今天舉行盛大開幕式，但卻因為沒有足夠的玻璃器皿而無法進行，由此可知，店家舉行盛大開幕式的時間延遲了，因此正確答案是 (A) It was delayed.。

83
84
85

Questions 83-85 refer to the following report.

英式發音

Good afternoon. This is Sarah Wilkins from 109.4 FM. [83]**I'm reporting live from the corner of Baker Road and Central Avenue, where the Star Tower is being built.** Traffic along these two major roads was brought to a standstill when a crane collapsed this morning. Although no one was injured, the damaged machinery is blocking both streets completely. Of course, this is causing congestion throughout the area. [84]**If you are planning on heading downtown, visit our Web site first to find out which routes have been affected.** I have Jonathon Grant here—an engineer who works in a nearby office. [85]**He witnessed the accident and has agreed to answer a few questions now.**

83 Where most likely is the speaker?

(A) At a shopping center
(B) In an engineering office
(C) At a construction site
(D) In a radio station

84 What are listeners advised to do?

(A) Postpone a trip
(B) Avoid traveling downtown
(C) Take public transportation
(D) Check traffic conditions

85 What will most likely happen next?

(A) An alternative route will be described.
(B) An interview will be conducted.
(C) An accident location will be identified.
(D) An event schedule will be announced.

第 83-85 題請參考以下報告。

午安。我是 FM 109.4 的 Sarah Wilkins。[83] 我目前在 Baker 路與 Central 大道轉角處，也就是 Star Tower 的興建地點，為您進行實況報導。今天早上起重機的倒塌使這兩條主要道路的交通陷入癱瘓。儘管沒有人受傷，但損壞的機械徹底擋住了這兩條街。當然，這也造成了這整個區域的壅塞。[84] 如果您正打算前往市中心，請先上我們的網站查看有哪些路受到影響。這裡我請到了在附近辦公室工作的工程師 Jonathon Grant。[85] 他目睹了這起意外，並同意現在來回答幾個問題。

83 說話者最有可能在哪裡？

(A) 購物中心
(B) 工程處
(C) 工地
(D) 廣播電臺

84 聽者們被建議做什麼？

(A) 延後旅行
(B) 避免前往市中心
(C) 搭乘大眾運輸工具
(D) 確認交通狀況

85 接下來最有可能會發生什麼？

(A) 詳述替代路線。
(B) 進行採訪。
(C) 確認意外地點。
(D) 宣布活動時間表。

題目 bring ~ to a standstill 使～停滯　collapse [kə`læps] 倒塌　injured [美 `ɪndʒɚd 英 `indʒəd] 受傷的
damaged [`dæmɪdʒd] 受損的　congestion [kən`dʒɛstʃən] 壅塞　head [hɛd] 前往（特定方向或目的地）
witness [美 `wɪtnɪs 英 `witnis] 目睹

83 construction [kən`strʌkʃən] 建設，工程

84 postpone [post`pon] 延期　avoid [ə`vɔɪd] 避免

85 alternative [ɔl`tɝnətɪv] 替代的　conduct [kən`dʌkt] 進行；處理　identify [aɪ`dɛntə͵faɪ] 確認

83 整體內容相關問題—地點　答案 (C)

中

題目詢問說話者的所在地點，因此必須注意聽和地點有關的表達。獨白說：「I'm reporting live from the corner of Baker Road and Central Avenue, where the Star Tower is being built.」，表示說話者目前正在 Baker 路和 Central 大道轉角處，也就是 Star Tower 的興建地點進行實況報導，由此可知，說話者所在的地點是工地，因此正確答案是 (C) At a construction site。

84 細節事項相關問題—提議　答案 (D)

高

題目詢問聽者被建議做什麼，因此要注意聽獨白中後段裡與建議有關的表達。獨白說：「If you are planning on heading downtown, visit our Web site first to find out which routes have been affected.」，表示如果聽者打算前往市中心，請先上他們的網站確認有哪些路受到了影響，因此正確答案是 (D) Check traffic conditions。

換句話說

find out which routes have been affected 查看有哪些路受到影響 → Check traffic conditions 確認交通狀況

85 細節事項相關問題—接下來要做的事　答案 (B)

中

題目詢問接下來最有可能會發生什麼事情，因此要注意聽獨白的最後部分。獨白說：「He[Jonathon Grant] witnessed the accident and has agreed to answer a few questions now.」，表示 Jonathon Grant 目睹了這起意外，並同意來回答幾個問題，由此可知，接下來會進行採訪，因此正確答案是 (B) An interview will be conducted.。

86
87
88

Questions 86-88 refer to the following telephone message.

美式發音

Good morning, Ms. Doliber. My name is Jisoo Lee, and I work at Standard Bank. [86/87]**I want to inform you that we have temporarily suspended your checking account due to suspicious activity**. Specifically, [87]**a cash withdrawal was made at an ATM in Nashville at 12:03 P.M. on July 3 . . . approximately 20 minutes after a purchase was made at a store here in Seattle**. Please contact our security center at 555-0848 to deal with this matter. Before you do this, though, [88]**I recommend that you check your account history for anything else that seems unusual**. You can access this information through our online banking service. Just enter your ID and password as usual, and then you will be provided with further instructions. Thank you.

第 86-88 題請參考以下電話留言。

早安，Doliber 小姐。我的名字是 Jisoo Lee，我在 Standard 銀行工作。[86/87] 我想要通知您，因為出現可疑活動，我們已暫時中止了您的支票帳戶。具體來說，[87]7 月 3 日的中午 12 點 03 分在納什維爾的自動提款機進行了一筆現金提款……大概是在於西雅圖這裡的一家店裡進行一筆消費的 20 分鐘之後。請致電 555-0848 聯絡我們的安全中心以處理這個問題。不過，在您做這件事之前，[88] 我建議您先確認您的帳戶記錄裡是否有其他任何看似不尋常的事項。您可以透過我們的網路銀行服務來取得這項資訊。只要與平常一樣輸入您的使用者名稱及密碼，接著您就會獲得進一步指示。謝謝您。

86 What is the purpose of the call?

(A) To cancel a funds transfer
(B) To verify an online payment
(C) To request an account number
(D) To report a security measure

86 這通電話的目的是什麼？

(A) 取消資金轉帳
(B) 核實線上支付款項
(C) 索取帳戶號碼
(D) 報告安全措施

87 What problem does the speaker mention?

(A) A daily limit was exceeded.
(B) Transactions were made in two cities.
(C) A banking service was unavailable.
(D) Several purchases were made at a store.

87 說話者提到什麼問題？

(A) 超過了每日上限。
(B) 在兩個城市裡進行了交易。
(C) 一項銀行服務無法使用。
(D) 在一間店裡進行了幾筆消費。

88 What does the speaker recommend the listener do?

(A) Examine a record
(B) Make a withdrawal
(C) Visit a center
(D) Change a password

88 說話者建議聽者做什麼？

(A) 檢視一項記錄
(B) 進行一筆提款
(C) 造訪一個中心
(D) 變更一個密碼

題目 temporarily [ˋtɛmpəˏrɛrəlɪ] 暫時地；臨時地　suspend [səˋspɛnd] 暫停；中止　checking account 支票帳戶
suspicious [səˋspɪʃəs] 可疑的　withdrawal [wɪðˋdrɔəl] 提領（現金）　further [ˋfɝðɚ] 進一步的；更遠的
86 verify [ˋvɛrəˏfaɪ] 核實　measure [ˋmɛʒɚ] 措施；手段
87 exceed [ɪkˋsid] 超過　transaction [trænˋzækʃən] 交易　unavailable [ˏʌnəˋveləbl] 無法使用的
88 examine [ɪgˋzæmɪn] 檢視

86 高 **整體內容相關問題─目的** 答案 (D)

題目詢問來電目的，因此必須特別注意獨白的開頭部分。獨白說：「I want to inform you that we have temporarily suspended your checking account due to suspicious activity.」，表示由於帳戶出現了可疑活動，所以已先將帳戶暫停使用了，因此正確答案是 (D) To report a security measure。

87 高 **細節事項相關問題─特定細項** 答案 (B)

題目詢問說話者提到的問題點，因此要注意和題目關鍵字（problem）相關的內容。獨白說：「I want to inform you that we have temporarily suspended your checking account due to suspicious activity.」，表示由於出現可疑活動，所以已先將帳戶暫時中止，接著說：「a cash withdrawal was made at an ATM in Nashville ~ after a purchase was made at a store ~ in Seattle」，表示在西雅圖的一家商店消費後，就到了納什維爾的自動提款機提領現金，由此可知，問題出在交易是發生在兩個不同的城市裡，因此正確答案是 (B) Transactions were made in two cities.。

88 中 **細節事項相關問題─提議** 答案 (A)

題目詢問說話者對聽者提議的事項內容，因此必須注意聽獨白中後半段裡與提議相關的表達。獨白說：「I recommend that you check your account history for anything else that seems unusual」，表示建議聽者要確認帳戶記錄裡是否有其他異狀，因此正確答案是 (A) Examine a record。

89
90
91

Questions 89-91 refer to the following announcement.

澳洲式發音

I have a quick announcement to make. In response to feedback from staff, [89]**management has decided to implement a flextime system.** Employees will be able to start and finish work earlier or later than usual. Note that there are restrictions . . . Staff must still work eight hours daily, and they can't enter the office until 7:30 A.M. Um . . . [90]**security personnel don't arrive at the building until 7:00 A.M.**, and they need time to turn off the alarms. In addition, shifts must end at 8:00 P.M. at the latest. [91]**I'll distribute the updated employee handbook to everyone this afternoon.** It includes a new section with information about this system. Please read through it and then let me know if you have any questions.

89 What is the announcement mainly about?

(A) Employee training
(B) An updated evaluation system
(C) Customer feedback
(D) A new company policy

90 When do security personnel arrive at the building?

(A) At 7:00 A.M.
(B) At 7:30 A.M.
(C) At 8:00 A.M.
(D) At 8:30 A.M.

91 What does the speaker say he will do this afternoon?

(A) Alter a schedule
(B) Revise a manual
(C) Hand out a document
(D) Give a presentation

第 89-91 題請參考以下公告。

我很快宣布一件事。為回應員工提供的回饋意見，[89] 管理階層決定實施彈性工作時間制。員工將可較一般工作時間提早或延後上下班。請注意有幾項限制……員工每日仍需工作八小時，且不能在早上 7 點 30 分之前進入辦公室。嗯……[90] 保全人員要到早上 7 點才會抵達這棟大樓，而他們需要時間來關閉警報。此外，工作時間最晚必須在晚上 8 點結束。[91] 我今天下午會將更新後的員工手冊發給各位。手冊裡有一個關於這個制度資訊的新章節。請仔細閱讀，若有任何問題請讓我知道。

89 這則公告主要與什麼有關？

(A) 員工訓練
(B) 更新後的評估制度
(C) 顧客回饋意見
(D) 新的公司政策

90 保全人員何時抵達這棟大樓？

(A) 早上 7 點
(B) 早上 7 點 30 分
(C) 早上 8 點
(D) 早上 8 點 30 分

91 說話者說他今天下午會做什麼？

(A) 更改行程表
(B) 修改手冊
(C) 發放文件
(D) 發表簡報

題目 implement [(美) `ɪmpləˏmɛnt (英) `implimənt] 施行　flextime [`flɛksˏtaɪm] 彈性工作時間
restriction [rɪ`strɪkʃən] 限制；限制規定　personnel [(美) ˏpɝsn̩`ɛl (英) ˏpə:sə`nel]（總稱）人員
shift [ʃɪft]（輪班的）班次；（輪班的）工作時間　at the latest 最晚　distribute [dɪ`strɪbjʊt] 分發；發放
section [`sɛkʃən] 部分

89 evaluation [ɪˏvælјʊ`eʃən] 評估　policy [`pɑləsɪ] 政策

91 alter [`ɔltɚ] 更改；改變　manual [`mænjʊəl] 說明書；手冊　hand out 發放；分發　document [`dɑkjəmənt] 文件

89 ■ 整體內容相關問題—主題 答案 (D)

中

題目詢問公告主題，因此必須注意聽獨白的開頭部分。獨白說：「management has decided to implement a flextime system」，表示管理階層決定實施彈性工作時間制，並在其後繼續說明這項公司的新政策，因此正確答案是 (D) A new company policy。

90 ■ 細節事項相關問題—特定細項 答案 (A)

低

題目詢問保全抵達公司大樓的時間，因此要注意提到題目關鍵字（security personnel arrive at ~ building）的前後部分。獨白說：「security personnel don't arrive at the building until 7:00 A.M.」，表示保全要到早上 7 點才會抵達，因此正確答案是 (A) At 7:00 A.M.。

91 ■ 細節事項相關問題—接下來要做的事 答案 (C)

中

題目詢問說話者今天下午會做什麼事，因此必須注意提到題目關鍵字（this afternoon）的前後部分。獨白說：「I'll distribute the updated employee handbook to everyone this afternoon.」，表示今天下午會發更新後的員工手冊，因此正確答案是 (C) Hand out a document。

換句話說

distribute ~ employee handbook 發員工手冊 → Hand out a document 發放文件

92
93
94

Questions 92-94 refer to the following announcement and schedule.

加拿大式發音

OK, everyone . . . Auditions for our new sitcom *Morning Coffee* will start tomorrow, so there are a few things I'd like you to be aware of. First, since [92]**I'm directing this show,** [93]**I'll be present at all of the auditions—except for Tuesday morning's. Our screenwriter, Nancy Davis, will unfortunately not be able to make any of the afternoon audition sessions** because of production team meetings scheduled during those times. Also, please note that we've added a role to the show, so there will be an extra session for casting on Thursday. [94]**Information about this new part can be found in the e-mail that I sent out this morning.**

新

	Mon	Tue	[93]Wed	Thu
9 A.M. – 11 A.M.		Session 2	Session 3	
2 P.M. – 4 P.M.	Session 1			Session 4

92 Who most likely is the speaker?

(A) A writer
(B) An actor
(C) A cameraperson
(D) A director

93 新 Look at the graphic. When will the speaker and Nancy Davis attend a session together?

(A) Monday
(B) Tuesday
(C) Wednesday
(D) Thursday

94 What is included in the e-mail sent by the speaker?

(A) Details about a role
(B) Assignments for a team
(C) Requests from a producer
(D) Changes to a script

第 92-94 題請參考以下公告及時間表。

好了，各位……我們新的情境喜劇《Morning Coffee》的試鏡會在明天開始，所以有幾件事我希望各位能注意一下。首先，因為 [92] 我要執導這部戲，[93] 所以我會出席所有的試鏡——除了週二早上的那場。我們的編劇 Nancy Davis 很不巧地將無法出席所有下午場的試鏡，因為製作團隊會議被排定在那些時段進行。另外，請注意我們為這部戲增加了一個角色，所以週四會多一場試鏡來選角。[94] 在我今天早上寄的電子郵件中可以找到這個新角色的相關資訊。

	週一	週二	[93] 週三	週四
上午 9 點一上午 11 點		第二場	第三場	
下午 2 點一下午 4 點	第一場			第四場

92 說話者最有可能是誰？

(A) 作家
(B) 演員
(C) 攝影師
(D) 導演

93 請看圖表。說話者與 Nancy Davis 何時會同場出席？

(A) 週一
(B) 週二
(C) 週三
(D) 週四

94 說話者寄出的電子郵件中有什麼？

(A) 關於一個角色的詳細資訊
(B) 給一個團隊的工作
(C) 來自製作人的要求
(D) 劇本的修改

題目 be aware of 注意～ present [ˋprɛzn̩t] 出席的 session [ˋsɛʃən] 一場；（某活動進行的）一段時間 production [prəˋdʌkʃən]（電影、戲劇等的）製作 role [rol] 角色 part [pɑrt] 角色

94 script [skrɪpt] 劇本；文稿

92 整體內容相關問題—說話者 答案 (D)
低
題目詢問說話者身分，因此要注意聽和身分、職業相關的表達。獨白說：「I'm directing this show」，表示自己要執導這部戲，由此可知，說話者是導演，因此正確答案是 (D) A director。

新 93 細節事項相關問題—圖表資料 答案 (C)
難
題目詢問說話者和 Nancy Davis 一起出席試鏡會的時間是什麼時候，因此必須確認題目提供的時間表上的資訊，並注意和題目關鍵字（speaker and Nancy Davis attend a session together）相關的內容。獨白說：「I'll be present at all of the auditions—except for Tuesday morning's. ~ Nancy Davis, will unfortunately not be able to make any of the afternoon audition sessions」，表示說話者除了週二上午的試鏡之外，其他全都會參加，而 Nancy Davis 則是下午的場次都無法參加，綜合上述並透過時間表可以得知，說話者和 Nancy Davis 會一同出席的是週三那場的試鏡會，因此正確答案是 (C) Wednesday。

94 細節事項相關問題—特定細項 答案 (A)
中
題目詢問說話者寄的電子郵件裡有什麼，因此必須注意和題目關鍵字（included in the e-mail）相關的內容。獨白說：「Information about this new part can be found in the e-mail that I sent out this morning.」，表示新角色的相關資訊可以在今天早上寄的電子郵件中找到，因此正確答案是 (A) Details about a role。

換句話說

Information about ~ new part 新角色的相關資訊 → Details about a role 角色的詳細資訊

Questions 95-97 refer to the following talk and map.

澳洲式發音

Welcome to the Summit Resort. My name is Desmond, and I'll be teaching you some basic snowboarding techniques this morning. [95]**Before we get started, though, you'll watch a brief video about some important safety guidelines.** Then, [96]**everyone has to get suitable gear, including boots, a snowboard, and a helmet. You can rent these items at the shop on the second floor of this building.** Once you have what you need, we'll begin the lesson. [97]**Since Trail A is currently closed due to poor snow conditions, we'll be using the other beginner trail.** All right. Are there any questions at this time?

[新]

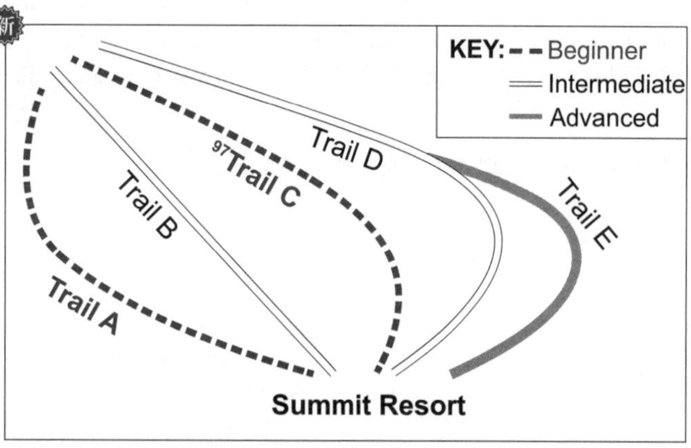

95 What will the listeners do first?

(A) Practice snowboarding techniques
(B) Go to the resort's lobby
(C) Read a safety manual
(D) Watch an instructional video

96 Why should listeners go to the second floor of the building?

(A) To pay for some lessons
(B) To rent a room
(C) To meet a teacher
(D) To get some equipment

97 Look at the graphic. Which trail will the listeners use?

[新]
(A) Trail A
(B) Trail B
(C) Trail C
(D) Trail D

第 95-97 題請參考以下談話及地圖。

歡迎來到 Summit 渡假村。我的名字是 Desmond，今天早上我會教你們一些基本的單板滑雪技巧。[95] 不過，在我們開始前，你們會先看一段關於一些重要安全指導方針的短片。接下來，[96] 大家必須要有適合的裝備，包括靴子、滑雪板及安全帽。你們可以在這棟建築的二樓商店裡租到這些物品。等你們都拿到需要的東西之後，我們就會開始上課。[97] 因為雪道 A 現在因雪況不佳而封閉了，所以我們會使用另一條初學者雪道。好了。目前有什麼問題嗎？

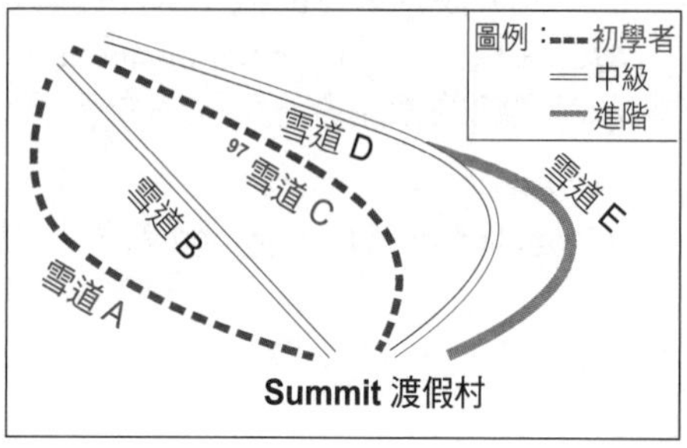

95 聽者們會先做什麼？

(A) 練習單板滑雪技巧
(B) 前往渡假村大廳
(C) 閱讀安全手冊
(D) 觀看教學影片

96 聽者們為什麼要去這棟建築的二樓？

(A) 支付一些課程的費用
(B) 租一間房
(C) 和一個老師碰面
(D) 取得一些裝備

97 請看圖表。聽者們會使用哪一條雪道？

(A) 雪道 A
(B) 雪道 B
(C) 雪道 C
(D) 雪道 D

題目 technique [tɛk`nik] 技巧；技術 brief [brif] 簡短的；短暫的 guideline [`gaɪdˏlaɪn] 指導方針
suitable [`sutəbḷ] 適合的；適當的；恰當的 gear ([美] gɪr [英] giə) 裝備 currently ([美] `kɝəntlɪ [英] `kʌrəntli) 現在
beginner ([美] bɪ`gɪnɚ [英] bi`ginə) 初學者 trail [trel] 路徑；小道
95 instructional [ɪn`strʌkʃənḷ] 教學的
96 equipment [ɪ`kwɪpmənt] 裝備；用具

95 細節事項相關問題—特定細項 答案 (D)

中

題目詢問聽者們會先做什麼，因此必須注意和題目關鍵字（do first）相關的內容。獨白說：「Before we get started, ~ you'll watch a brief video about some important safety guidelines.」，表示在開始上課前會先看一段關於一些重要安全指導方針的影片，因此正確答案是 (D) Watch an instructional video。

96 細節事項相關問題—理由 答案 (D)

中

題目詢問聽者們要去這棟建築二樓的原因，因此要注意提到題目關鍵字（second floor）的前後部分。獨白說：「everyone has to get suitable gear, including boots, a snowboard, and a helmet. You can rent these items at the shop on the second floor of this building.」，表示所有人都要有靴子、滑雪板和安全帽等適合的裝備，接著又說可以到二樓的商店租借這些物品，因此正確答案是 (D) To get some equipment。

換句話說

get suitable gear 有適合的裝備 → get some equipment 取得一些裝備

新 **97** 細節事項相關問題—圖表資料 答案 (C)

中

題目詢問聽者們會用的雪道是哪條，因此作答時必須確認題目提供的地圖資訊，並注意和題目關鍵字（trail ~ use）相關的內容。獨白說：「Since Trail A is currently closed due to poor snow conditions, we'll be using the other beginner trail.」，表示雪道 A 目前因為雪況差而封閉了，所以將使用另一條初學者雪道，透過地圖可以知道，另一條聽者們可以使用的初學者雪道是雪道 C，因此正確答案是 (C) Trail C。

98
99
100

Questions 98-100 refer to the following talk and graph.

英式發音

I hope everyone looked over the quarterly report. If not, I recommend that you do so this afternoon because we have a problem. Only one of the company's software programs met the sales goal of 10,000 units last quarter. [98/99]**We've been asked to create a marketing campaign for the program with the worst sales record,** [99]**and Bryan Swanson's team will do the same for Core Spreadsheet. We don't have to worry about the other program with low sales because it will be discontinued next month.** [100]**I'd like each of you to come up with a specific plan to promote the program assigned to our team,** and we'll discuss them when we meet again on Friday.

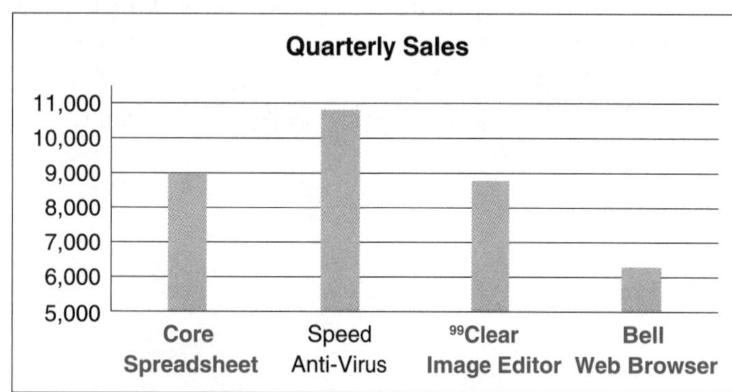

第 98-100 題請參考以下談話及圖表。

我希望大家都看過季報了。如果還沒，我建議大家今天下午看一下，因為我們有麻煩了。上一季公司只有一款軟體程式達成 10,000 套的銷售目標。[98/99] 我們已被要求為銷售記錄最差的程式打造行銷宣傳活動，[99] 而 Bryan Swanson 的團隊則同樣會為 Core Spreadsheet 做規劃。我們不必擔心另一款銷量不佳的程式，因為它會在下個月停產。[100] 我希望你們每個人都想出一個具體計畫來宣傳分派給我們團隊的那款程式，而我們會在週五再次開會討論這些計畫。

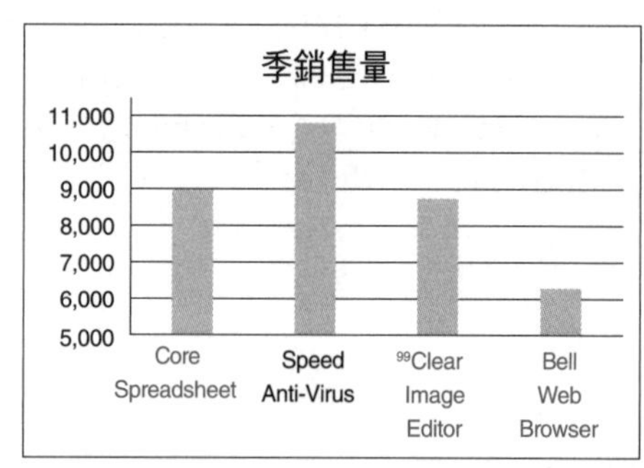

98 What department do the listeners most likely work in?

(A) Sales
(B) Marketing
(C) Accounting
(D) Human resources

98 聽者們最有可能在什麼部門裡工作？

(A) 銷售
(B) 行銷
(C) 會計
(D) 人力資源

99 新 Look at the graphic. Which software product will the company stop selling?

(A) Core Spreadsheet
(B) Speed Anti-Virus
(C) Clear Image Editor
(D) Bell Web Browser

99 請看圖表。公司會停售哪一項軟體產品？

(A) Core Spreadsheet
(B) Speed Anti-Virus
(C) Clear Image Editor
(D) Bell Web Browser

100 What does the speaker ask the listeners to do?

(A) Submit a report
(B) Test a product
(C) Download a program
(D) Prepare a proposal

100 說話者要求聽者們做什麼？

(A) 提交報告
(B) 測試產品
(C) 下載程式
(D) 準備提案

題目 quarterly [美 ˋkwɔrtɚlɪ 英 ˋkwɔ:təli] 季度的　discontinue [ˌdɪskənˋtɪnju] 停止；中斷（生產等）　come up with 想出～　specific [美 spɪˋsɪfɪk 英 spiˋsifik] 具體的　promote [美 prəˋmot 英 prəˋməut] 宣傳
98 accounting [əˋkaʊntɪŋ] 會計
100 prepare [prɪˋpɛr] 準備　proposal [prəˋpozl̩] 提案

98 ■ 整體內容相關問題—聽者 答案 (B)

中

題目詢問聽者們工作的部門是什麼，因此必須注意聽和身分、職業相關的表達。獨白說：「We've been asked to create a marketing campaign for the program with the worst sales record」，表示自己和聽者們被要求為銷售記錄最差的程式打造行銷宣傳活動，由此可知，說話者和聽者們工作的部門是行銷部，因此正確答案是 (B) Marketing。

新 **99** ■ 細節事項相關問題—圖表資料 答案 (C)

難

題目詢問公司要停售哪款軟體產品，因此必須確認題目提供的圖表資料，並注意與題目關鍵字（software product ~ company stop selling）相關的內容。獨白說：「We've been asked to create a marketing campaign for the program with the worst sales record, and Bryan Swanson's team will do the same for Core Spreadsheet. We don't have to worry about the other program with low sales because it will be discontinued next month.」，表示自己及聽者們被要求為銷售記錄最差的程式打造行銷宣傳活動，Bryan Swanson 的團隊則會負責 Core Spreadsheet 的規劃，而另一個銷量差的產品將在下個月停產，因此不用擔心它。透過圖表可以知道，公司要停售的軟體程式是未達銷售目標、且未被分派給行銷團隊做行銷宣傳活動規劃的產品，就是 Clear Image Editor，因此正確答案是 (C) Clear Image Editor。

100 ■ 細節事項相關問題—要求 答案 (D)

中

題目詢問說話者要求聽者做什麼，因此要注意聽獨白後半段中出現的要求相關表達。獨白說：「I'd like each of you to come up with a specific plan to promote the program assigned to our team」，表示希望聽者們都想出具體計畫來宣傳分派給自己團隊的程式，因此正確答案是 (D) Prepare a proposal。

換句話說

come up with a ~ plan 想出計畫 → Prepare a proposal 準備提案

TEST 02

Part 1 原文・翻譯・解析

Part 2 原文・翻譯・解析

Part 3 原文・翻譯・解析 新

Part 4 原文・翻譯・解析 新

MP3 收錄於 TEST 02.mp3。

進行深入練習或複習時，可以一邊多聽幾次收錄各國口音的試題 MP3，一邊搭配解答中的中英對照翻譯和解析，以及單字記憶表和多元口音單字記憶 MP3，達到事半功倍的效果。

PART 1

1 中

加拿大式發音

(A) She is decorating a bookshelf.
(B) She is replacing a light bulb.
(C) She is covering a sofa in plastic.
(D) She is taking a lamp out of a box.

(A) 她正在裝飾書架。
(B) 她正在換燈泡。
(C) 她正在把沙發用塑膠蓋起來。
(D) 她正在把檯燈從箱子裡拿出來。

單人照片 答案 (D)

仔細觀察一名女子拿著檯燈的模樣及周遭事物的狀態。

(A) [╳] decorating（正在裝飾）和女子的動作無關，因此是錯誤選項。這裡使用照片中出現的書架（bookshelf）來造成混淆。

(B) [╳] 透過照片無法得知女子是否正在換燈泡，因此是錯誤選項。這裡使用可透過女子拿著檯燈的樣子而聯想到的 replacing a light bulb（正在換燈泡）來造成混淆。

(C) [╳] 照片中的沙發已被塑膠覆蓋著，這裡卻說女子正在把沙發用塑膠蓋起來，因此是錯誤選項。注意不要聽到 sofa（沙發）和 plastic（塑膠）就選擇這個答案。

(D) [○] 這裡正確描述女子正在把檯燈從箱子裡拿出來的模樣 ，所以是正確答案。

單字　decorate [ˋdɛkəˏret] 裝飾；布置　replace [rɪˋples] 替換　light bulb 燈泡　cover [ˋkʌvɚ] 覆蓋

2 低

英式發音

(A) They are buying train tickets.
(B) They are emptying their backpacks.
(C) They are facing the windows.
(D) They are pushing against a door.

(A) 他們正在買火車票。
(B) 他們正在清空他們的後背包。
(C) 他們正面向窗戶。
(D) 他們正在推門。

兩人以上的照片 答案 (C)

照片中有一對男女背著後背包，站在火車上往外望。

(A) [╳] buying（正在買）和照片中的人物動作無關，因此是錯誤選項。這裡使用和照片的可能拍攝地點有關的 train tickets（火車票）來造成混淆。

(B) [╳] emptying（正在清空）和照片中的人物動作無關，因此是錯誤選項。這裡使用照片中出現的後背包（backpacks）來造成混淆。

(C) [○] 這裡正確描述兩個人面向窗戶站著的模樣，因此是正確答案。

(D) [╳] pushing（正在推）和照片中的人物動作無關，因此是錯誤選項。這裡使用照片中出現的門（door）來造成混淆。

單字　empty [ˋɛmptɪ] 清空　backpack [ˋbækˏpæk] 後背包　face [fes] 面向；面對　push [pʊʃ] 推

3 中

加拿大式發音

(A) The woman is using an appliance.
(B) The woman is carrying a water bottle.
(C) The woman is drinking from a mug.
(D) The woman is setting a carpet on the floor.

(A) 女子正在使用設備。
(B) 女子正拿著水瓶。
(C) 女子正在喝馬克杯裡的東西。
(D) 女子正在地板上鋪地毯。

單人照片 答案 (A)

照片中出現一名女子蹲在飲水機前倒水。

(A) [○] 這裡正確描述女子正在使用設備的模樣，所以是正確答案。注意這裡以 appliance（設備）來表示飲水機。

(B) [╳] carrying（拿著）和女子的動作無關，因此是錯誤選項。這裡使用可能會從飲水機聯想到的水瓶（water bottle）來造成混淆。

(C) [╳] drinking（正在喝）和女子的動作無關，因此是錯誤選項。這裡使用照片中出現的馬克杯（mug）來造成混淆。

(D) [╳] setting（正在鋪）和女子的動作無關，因此是錯誤選項。注意不要聽到 a carpet on the floor（地板上的地毯）就選擇這個答案。

單字 appliance [əˋplaɪəns]（尤指電器）設備，裝置 carry [ˋkærɪ] 拿；搬運 set [sɛt] 放置；設置

4 中

美式發音

(A) Some shoppers are exchanging bags.
(B) Some shoppers are pointing at a pillar.
(C) Some shoppers are passing a display.
(D) Some shoppers are trying on clothing.

(A) 一些購物者正在交換袋子。
(B) 一些購物者正指著柱子。
(C) 一些購物者正經過陳列品。
(D) 一些購物者正在試穿衣服。

兩人以上的照片 答案 (C)

照片中有兩個人拿著購物袋，正經過旁邊陳列著的物品。

(A) [╳] 照片中的人拿著袋子，但選項卻描述為正在交換（exchanging），因此是錯誤選項。

(B) [╳] pointing at（正指著）和照片中的人物動作無關，因此是錯誤選項。這裡使用照片中出現的柱子（pillar）來造成混淆。

(C) [○] 這裡正確描述購物者正經過旁邊陳列品的模樣，所以是正確答案。

(D) [╳] trying on（正在試穿）和照片中的人物動作無關，因此是錯誤選項。這裡使用照片中出現的衣物（clothing）來造成混淆。

單字 shopper [ˋʃɑpɚ] 購物者 exchange [ɪksˋtʃendʒ] 交換 pillar [ˋpɪlɚ] 柱子 pass [pæs] 經過
display [dɪˋsple] 展示品；展示 try on 試穿 clothing [ˋkloðɪŋ] 衣物

5 高

澳洲式發音

(A) A man is lifting a bowl off the ground.
(B) A vendor is filling containers.
(C) Vases are being stacked in a corner.
(D) Some pottery is being made by hand.

(A) 一名男子正把一個碗從地上拿起來。
(B) 一個小販正在把容器填滿。
(C) 正在把花瓶堆放在一個角落裡。
(D) 正在用手製作一些陶器。

單人照片 答案 (D)

照片中的一名男子正用手在製作陶瓷。

(A) [╳] lifting（正在拿起）和男子的動作無關，因此是錯誤選項。這裡使用照片中有出現的碗（bowl）來造成混淆。

(B) [╳] filling（正在填滿）和男子的動作無關，因此是錯誤選項。這裡使用照片中有出現的 containers（容器）來造成混淆。

(C) [╳] 照片中雖然有看起來像花瓶的陶器，但沒有正在堆放（are being stacked）的動作，因此是錯誤選項。

(D) [○] 這裡正確描述正在用手製作一些陶器的模樣 ，所以是正確答案。

單字 lift [lɪft] 提起；舉起 bowl [㊈ bol ㊊ bəul] 碗 ground [graʊnd] 地面
vendor [㊈ ˋvɛndɚ ㊊ ˋvendə] 小販；供應商 fill [fɪl] 填滿 container [㊈ kənˋtenɚ ㊊ kənˋteinə] 容器；貨櫃
vase [㊈ ves ㊊ vɑːz]（裝飾用的）瓶；花瓶 stack [stæk] 累積 corner [㊈ ˋkɔrnɚ ㊊ ˋkɔːnə] 角落
pottery [㊈ ˋpɑtərɪ ㊊ ˋpɔtəri] 陶器

6

●●●●●

難

[🔊] 英式發音

(A) A narrow pathway ends at an open field.
(B) Pedestrians are walking across a street.
(C) There is an unoccupied bench in a park.
(D) A section of the lawn is being mowed.

(A) 窄路的盡頭是空曠的田野。
(B) 行人正在穿越街道。
(C) 公園裡有一張空著的長椅。
(D) 正在修剪部分草坪。

兩人以上的照片

答案 (C)

仔細觀察照片中一對男女正在散步的樣子並注意周遭整體景象。

(A) [╳] 透過照片無法確認路的盡頭是否為空曠的田野（open field），因此是錯誤選項。這裡使用照片中出現的路（pathway）來造成混淆。

(B) [╳] 行人並非正在穿越街道，而是正沿著路走，因此是錯誤選項。注意不要聽到 Pedestrians are walking（行人正在行走）就選擇這個答案。

(C) [○] 這裡正確描述公園裡的長椅空著的狀態 ，所以是正確答案。

(D) [╳] 照片中出現了草坪，但沒有正在修剪（is being mowed）草坪的動作，因此是錯誤選項。

單字 pathway [`pæθ͵we] 路；小徑　pedestrian [pə`dɛstrɪən] 行人
unoccupied [[美] ʌn`ɑkjə͵paɪd [英] `ʌn`ɔkjupaid] 沒人占用的；空著的
mow [[美] mo [英] məu] 割（草、穀物等）；修剪（草地等）

7
低

加拿大式發音 → 美式發音

When will the clients arrive?	客戶何時會抵達？
(A) They most likely will.	(A) 他們很有可能會。
(B) The building lobby.	(B) 建築物的大廳。
(C) No later than 3 o'clock.	(C) 最晚 3 點。

When 疑問句 答案 (C)

這是詢問客戶何時會抵達的 When 疑問句。

(A) [╳] 這是藉著能代稱題目中出現的 clients（客戶）的 They，且重複使用 will 來造成混淆的錯誤選項。

(B) [╳] 題目詢問客戶何時抵達，這裡卻回答地點，因此是錯誤選項。這裡利用可用來回答 Where 疑問句的選項內容來回答題目的 When 疑問句，企圖造成混淆，小心不要聽成 Where will the clients arrive（客戶會抵達哪裡），而選擇這個選項。

(C) [○] 這裡回答最晚 3 點，提到客戶的抵達時間，因此是正確答案。

單字 client [`klaɪənt] 客戶 no later than 最晚～；不晚於～

8
中

英式發音 → 澳洲式發音

Which of these shirts do you think I should buy?	你認為我應該買哪一件襯衫？
(A) You should wrap them.	(A) 你應該把它們包起來。
(B) My preference is the brown one.	(B) 我比較喜歡棕色那件。
(C) Yes, it's the perfect size.	(C) 是的，尺寸剛剛好。

Which 疑問句 答案 (B)

這是詢問該買哪一件襯衫的 Which 疑問句。這裡必須聽到 Which of these shirts 才能順利作答。

(A) [╳] 這是使用能代稱題目中 I 的 You，及能代稱 shirts（襯衫）的 them 來造成混淆的錯誤選項。

(B) [○] 這裡表達了自己對襯衫顏色的偏好，建議對方應該要買棕色的那件，因此是正確答案。

(C) [╳] 這裡以 Yes 來回答疑問詞疑問句，因此是錯誤選項。這裡利用和 shirts（襯衫）有關的 size（尺寸）來造成混淆。

單字 wrap [ræp] 包，裹 preference [`prɛfərəns] 偏好

9
中

美式發音 → 加拿大式發音

Will my transportation costs be reimbursed?	我的交通費會被核銷嗎？
(A) We stopped in Venice.	(A) 我們在威尼斯停留。
(B) If you hand in the receipts.	(B) 如果你繳交收據的話。
(C) I'll look in my purse.	(C) 我會在我的包包裡找找。

助動詞疑問句 答案 (B)

這是確認是否會核銷自己的交通費的助動詞（Will）疑問句。

(A) [╳] 這是利用可能會從 transportation（交通）聯想到的地點「Venice（威尼斯）」來造成混淆的錯誤選項。

(B) [○] 這裡回答「如果你繳交收據的話」，間接表示會核銷對方的交通費，因此是正確答案。

(C) [╳] 這是利用可能會從 transportation costs（交通費）聯想到的 purse（包包）來造成混淆的錯誤選項。

單字 reimburse [ˌriɪm`bɝs] 核銷；償付 hand in 繳交 receipt [rɪ`sit] 收據

10 ○○●● 中

🔊 澳洲式發音 → 英式發音	
Do you know who was named the new lead engineer? (A) I can't recall the restaurant's name. (B) Someone was recruited from outside the firm. (C) Mr. Vans placed the order.	你知道是誰被提名為新的首席工程師嗎？ (A) 我想不起來那間餐廳的名字了。 (B) 某個從公司外部招募進來的人。 (C) Vans 先生下了那張訂單。

包含疑問詞的一般疑問句 答案 (B)

這是詢問被提名為新的首席工程師的人是誰的包含 who 的一般疑問句。

(A) [╳] 這是利用 name 的名詞意義「名字」，重複題目中的 named（被提名）來造成混淆的錯誤選項。注意不要聽到 I can't recall 就選擇這個答案。

(B) [○] 這裡回答是某個從公司外部招募進來的人，提到新的首席工程師人選，因此是正確答案。

(C) [╳] 題目詢問新的首席工程師是誰，這裡卻回答 Vans 先生下了那張訂單，因此是錯誤選項。這裡利用人名 Mr. Vans 來造成混淆。

單字 name [nem] 命名；提名；名字 recall [rɪ`kɔl] 回憶，回想 recruit [rɪ`krut] 招募；聘用
outside [`aʊt`saɪd] 在外面 place an order 下一張訂單

11 ○○●● 中

🔊 加拿大式發音 → 美式發音	
How did your meeting with the investment adviser turn out? (A) That's what I'd recommend. (B) It was canceled at the last minute. (C) The meat is in the refrigerator.	你和投資顧問的會面結果怎麼樣了？ (A) 那是我會推薦的。 (B) 它在最後一刻取消了。 (C) 肉在冰箱裡。

How 疑問句 答案 (B)

這是詢問和投資顧問之間的會面進行得如何的 How 疑問句。

(A) [╳] 這是利用和 adviser（顧問）有關的 recommend（推薦）來造成混淆的錯誤選項。

(B) [○] 這裡回答在最後一刻取消了，間接表示沒有和投資顧問進行會面，因此是正確答案。

(C) [╳] 題目詢問和投資顧問之間的會面進行得如何，這裡卻回答肉在冰箱裡，毫不相關，因此是錯誤選項。這裡利用發音相似單字 meeting – meat 來造成混淆。

單字 investment [ɪn`vɛstmənt] 投資 adviser [əd`vaɪzɚ] 顧問 turn out 結果～
recommend [͵rɛkə`mɛnd] 推薦；建議 at the last minute 在最後一刻 refrigerator [rɪ`frɪdʒə͵retɚ] 冰箱

12 ○○○● 低

🔊 澳洲式發音 → 英式發音	
Where should I visit with my family? (A) That's right. We spent a weekend there. (B) A clerk at Midwestern Travel Agency. (C) The Cayman Islands are popular.	我該和我的家人去哪裡呢？ (A) 沒錯。我們在那裡待了一個週末。 (B) 一個 Midwestern 旅行社的員工。 (C) 開曼群島很受歡迎。

Where 疑問句 答案 (C)

這是詢問要和家人一起去哪裡的 Where 疑問句。

(A) [╳] 這裡使用意思與 Yes 相同的 That's right 來回答疑問詞疑問句，且題目中沒有可對應 there 的對象，因此是錯誤選項。

(B) [╳] 這是使用可以透過 visit（造訪）聯想到的 Travel Agency（旅行社）來造成混淆的錯誤選項。

(C) [○] 這裡回答開曼群島很受歡迎，提到可以和家人一起去的地點，因此是正確答案。

單字 visit [`vɪzɪt] 造訪；參觀 clerk [美] klɝk [英] klɑ:k] 員工 popular [[美] `pɑpjəlɚ [英] `pɔpjulə] 受歡迎的

13 ○○●● 中

🔊 美式發音 → 加拿大式發音

Who volunteered for our community service event?

(A) Thanks for offering your time.
(B) The event was a major success.
(C) Why don't you ask our boss about that?

誰自願去做我們的社區服務活動？

(A) 謝謝你願意花時間。
(B) 這項活動非常成功。
(C) 你為什麼不去問老闆這件事呢？

■ **Who 疑問句** 答案 (C)

這是詢問誰自願去做社區服務活動的 Who 疑問句。

(A) [╳] 這是利用和 volunteered（自願去做）有關的 offering ~ time（願意花時間）來造成混淆的錯誤選項。

(B) [╳] 題目詢問誰自願去做社區服務活動，這裡卻回答該活動很成功，毫不相關，因此是錯誤選項。這裡透過重複題目中出現的 event 來造成混淆。

(C) [○] 這裡以反問來間接表示自己不知道，因此是正確答案。

單字 volunteer [ˌvalənˋtɪr] 自願去做　community service 社區服務　major [ˋmedʒɚ] 重大的
success [səkˋsɛs] 成功　boss [bɔs] 老闆；長官

14 ○○●● 中

🔊 澳洲式發音 → 英式發音

A taxi is coming for me at 7 A.M.

(A) Sure, taxes are due on April 15th.
(B) You'll have to be up very early, then.
(C) Sometime this morning.

計程車會在早上 7 點來接我。

(A) 當然，稅金應在 4 月 15 日以前支付。
(B) 那你就得非常早起床了。
(C) 今天早上的某個時間。

■ **陳述句** 答案 (B)

這是表達計程車會在早上 7 點來接自己的客觀事實陳述句。

(A) [╳] 題目表達計程車會在早上 7 點來接自己，這裡卻回答稅金應在 4 月 15 日以前支付，毫不相關，因此是錯誤選項。這裡使用發音相似單字 taxi – taxes 來造成混淆。

(B) [○] 這裡回答對方得非常早起床，提出自己對此陳述內容的想法，因此是正確答案。

(C) [╳] 這是利用和 7 A.M.（早上 7 點）相關的 morning（早上）來造成混淆的錯誤選項。

單字 tax [tæks] 稅金　due [[美] dju [英] dju:]（錢等）應支付的；到期的

15 ○○●● 中

🔊 美式發音 → 澳洲式發音

Who's responsible for promoting the technology expo?

(A) The response was very positive.
(B) Mr. Graves hasn't selected anyone yet.
(C) That seems like a reasonable deadline.

誰負責宣傳科技博覽會？

(A) 反應非常正面。
(B) Graves 先生還沒有選定任何人。
(C) 那似乎是個合理的截止期限。

■ **Who 疑問句** 答案 (B)

這是詢問誰負責宣傳科技博覽會的 Who 疑問句。

(A) [╳] 這是利用發音相似單字 responsible – response 來造成混淆的錯誤選項。

(B) [○] 這裡回答 Graves 先生還沒選定任何人，間接表示還沒決定是誰負責宣傳科技博覽會，因此是正確答案。

(C) [╳] 題目詢問是誰負責宣傳科技博覽會，這裡卻回答那似乎是合理的截止期限，毫不相關，因此是錯誤選項。這裡使用發音相似單字 responsible – reasonable 來造成混淆。

單字 promote [prəˋmot] 宣傳　expo [ˌɛkspo] 博覽會　reasonable [ˋriznəbl̩] 適當的；合理的

16 ○●●● 中

🔊 英式發音 → 澳洲式發音 I have an appointment with Mr. Khan in 10 minutes. (A) Yes, he's been expecting you. (B) I've been appointed team leader. (C) We were too busy at the time.	我和 Khan 先生約了 10 分鐘後會面。 (A) 是的，他已經在等你了。 (B) 我已被指派為組長了。 (C) 我們那時太忙了。

陳述句 答案 (A)

這是表達自己和 Khan 先生約了 10 分鐘後會面的客觀事實陳述句。

(A) [○] 這裡以 Yes 來表示自己知道對方約了 10 分鐘後和 Khan 先生會面，並附加說明 Khan 先生已經在等待對方了，因此是正確答案。

(B) [╳] 題目表達自己約了 10 分鐘後和 Khan 先生會面，這裡卻回答被指派為組長，毫不相關，因此是錯誤選項。這裡利用發音相似單字 appointment – appointed 來造成混淆。

(C) [╳] 這是利用和 in 10 minutes（10 分鐘後）相關的 at the time（那時）來造成混淆的錯誤選項。

單字 appointment [ə`pɔɪntmənt]（會面等的）約定 expect [ɪk`spɛkt] 等待（約好的對象）；期待
appoint [ə`pɔɪnt] 指派，任命

17 ○●●● 高

🔊 加拿大式發音 → 英式發音 Why are there only three candidates for our job opening? (A) Oh, Drake has the other résumés. (B) No, I haven't found a job yet. (C) We will open another location.	我們開的職缺為什麼只有三個應徵者？ (A) 噢，Drake 有其他的履歷表。 (B) 沒有，我還沒找到工作。 (C) 我們會開另一家分店。

Why 疑問句 答案 (A)

這是詢問為什麼只有三個應徵者的 Why 疑問句。

(A) [○] 這裡回答 Drake 有其他的履歷表，間接表示除了三個應徵者外還有其他人應徵，因此是正確答案。

(B) [╳] 這裡以 No 來回答疑問詞疑問句，因此是錯誤選項。這裡利用和 job opening（職缺）有關的 found a job（找工作）來造成混淆。

(C) [╳] 這是使用可以藉由 job opening（職缺）聯想到的雇用原因 open another location（開另一家分店）來造成混淆的錯誤選項。

單字 candidate [`kændədet] 應徵者；候選人 résumé [[美] ˌrɛzjʊ`me [英] ˌrezju:`mei] 履歷表

18 ○●●● 高

🔊 英式發音 → 澳洲式發音 This evening's press conference has been rescheduled. (A) When our collection was announced. (B) You have to push this button. (C) I wonder why there's a delay.	今晚的記者會已經改期了。 (A) 宣布我們新系列商品的時候。 (B) 你得按這個按鈕。 (C) 我好奇為什麼會延期。

陳述句 答案 (C)

這是表達今晚的記者會已經改期的客觀事實陳述句。

(A) [╳] 這是利用和 press conference（記者會）相關的 announced（宣布）來造成混淆的錯誤選項。

(B) [╳] 題目說的是今晚的記者會已經改期，這裡卻回答對方必須按這個按紐，毫不相關，因此是錯誤選項。這裡使用和題目中 press（媒體）的另一字義「按壓」意思相同的 push 來造成混淆。

(C) [○] 這裡回答好奇為什麼會延期，提出自己對題目陳述內容的意見，因此是正確答案。

單字 press conference 記者會 reschedule [[美] ri`skɛdʒʊl [英] ri:`ʃedju:l] 重新排定時間
collection [kə`lɛkʃən]（服飾等的）新系列商品；收藏品 announce [ə`naʊns] 宣布；公告
wonder [[美] `wʌndɚ [英] `wʌndə] 好奇；納悶 delay [dɪ`le] 延期；延誤

19 ●●●● 難

美式發音 → 加拿大式發音 Don't we have an insufficient number of brochures? (A) My team won't be attending the seminar. (B) I designed some of them myself. (C) This lighting is insufficient.	我們的小冊子數量不是不夠嗎？ (A) 我的團隊不會參加這場研討會。 (B) 其中的一些是我自己設計的。 (C) 照明不足。

否定疑問句 答案 (A)

這是確認小冊子數量是否不足的否定疑問句。

(A) [○] 這裡說明自己團隊不會參加研討會，間接表示沒有小冊子數量不足的這件事，因此是正確答案。

(B) [╳] 這是利用和 brochures（小冊子）有關的 designed（設計），以及可以代稱 brochures（小冊子）的 them 來造成混淆的錯誤選項。

(C) [╳] 題目確認小冊子數量是否不足，這裡卻回答照明不足，毫不相關，因此是錯誤選項。這裡透過重複題目中出現的 insufficient 來造成混淆。

單字 insufficient [ˌɪnsəˋfɪʃənt] 不足的；不充分的 brochure [broˋʃʊr] 小冊子 design [dɪˋzaɪn] 設計 lighting [ˋlaɪtɪŋ] 照明

20 ●●○○ 中

英式發音 → 美式發音 Why don't we ask if the flight attendant has headphones? (A) We don't want to go to that convention. (B) An economy class seat. (C) I don't need any right now.	我們何不問問看空服員有沒有耳機？ (A) 我們不想去那場大會。 (B) 一個經濟艙座位。 (C) 我現在不需要。

提議疑問句 答案 (C)

這是提議去問空服員有沒有耳機的提議疑問句。這裡必須知道 Why don't we 是表示提議的表達。

(A) [╳] 題目提議去詢問空服員有沒有耳機，這裡卻回答不想去大會，毫不相關，因此是錯誤選項。注意不要聽到 We don't want 就選擇這個答案。

(B) [╳] 這是利用和題目中 flight attendant（空服員）裡表示「飛機航班」的 flight 有關的 economy class seat（經濟艙座位）來造成混淆的錯誤選項。

(C) [○] 這裡回答自己現在不需要，間接拒絕提議，因此是正確答案。

單字 flight attendant 空服員 economy class（客機的）經濟艙

21 ●●●○ 高

加拿大式發音 → 澳洲式發音 Aren't special permits required in order to park here? (A) Yes, those changes are necessary. (B) The outing was held at Hawthorne Park. (C) This lot is open to the public.	要在這裡停車不是需要特別許可證嗎？ (A) 是的，那些更動是必要的。 (B) 那場郊遊辦在了 Hawthorne 公園。 (C) 這片空地是對外開放的。

否定疑問句 答案 (C)

這是確認是否需要特別許可證才能在這裡停車的否定疑問句。

(A) [╳] 這是利用和 required（需要）相關的 necessary（必要的）來造成混淆的錯誤選項。注意不要聽到 Yes 就選擇這個答案。

(B) [╳] 題目詢問是否需要特別許可證才能在這裡停車，這裡卻回答郊遊辦在了公園，毫不相關，因此是錯誤選項。這裡利用題目中 park（停車）的名詞意義「公園」來造成混淆。

(C) [○] 這裡回答空地是對外開放的，間接表示不需要特別許可證，因此是正確答案。

單字 permit [ˋpɝmɪt] 許可（證） necessary [ˋnɛsəˌsɛrɪ] 不可避免的；必需的 outing [ˋaʊtɪŋ] 郊遊 lot [lɑt]（有特定用處的）一塊地

22 ○○● 低

美式發音 → 加拿大式發音

What organization are we partnering with? (A) It's been nice working with you. (B) Actually, I organized the party. (C) An environmental research institute.	我們要和什麼組織合作？ (A) 很高興和您合作。 (B) 事實上，我策劃了那場派對。 (C) 一個環境研究機構。

What 疑問句 答案 (C)

這是詢問要和什麼組織合作的 What 疑問句。這題一定要聽到 What organization 才能順利作答。

(A) [╳] 這是利用和 partnering with（和～合作）相關聯的 working with（和～合作）來造成混淆的錯誤選項。

(B) [╳] 這是利用 organization – organized、partnering – party 這兩組發音相似單字來造成混淆的錯誤選項。

(C) [〇] 這裡回答環境研究機構，提到合作的組織，因此是正確答案。

單字 organization [ˌɔrgənəˋzeʃən] 組織，機構 partner with 和～合作 organize [ˋɔrgəˌnaɪz] 籌備；組織 environmental [ɪnˌvaɪrənˋmɛntḷ] 環境的 institute [ˋɪnstətjut] 機構；學院

23 ○●● 中

澳洲式發音 → 美式發音

When was an inspection last conducted at your establishment? (A) Just over a month ago, I believe. (B) The inspector left the message. (C) I looked at it closely.	上次在你們機構進行視察是什麼時候？ (A) 就在一個多月前吧，我想。 (B) 視察人員留下了這則訊息。 (C) 我仔細看過它了。

When 疑問句 答案 (A)

這是詢問上次在對方機構進行視察是什麼時候的 When 疑問句。

(A) [〇] 這裡回答就在一個多月前，提到上次進行視察的時間點，因此是正確答案。

(B) [╳] 題目詢問上次在對方機構進行視察是什麼時候，這裡卻回答視察人員留下了訊息，毫不相關，因此是錯誤選項。這裡利用發音相似單字 inspection – inspector 來造成混淆。

(C) [╳] 這是利用可以從 inspection（視察）聯想到的行為 looked at ~ closely（仔細看）來造成混淆的錯誤選項。

單字 inspection [ɪnˋspɛkʃən] 視察 establishment [ɪsˋtæblɪʃmənt] 機構，設施

24 ●●● 高

美式發音 → 澳洲式發音

How does going out for dinner next week sound to you? (A) I usually bring my lunch to work. (B) Let me check my schedule. (C) I had a great time.	你覺得下星期去外面吃晚餐怎麼樣？ (A) 我通常會帶午餐去上班。 (B) 讓我看看我的行程表。 (C) 我玩得很愉快。

提議疑問句 答案 (B)

這是向對方提議下星期去外面吃晚餐的提議疑問句。這裡必須知道 How does ~ sound 是表示提議的表達。

(A) [╳] 這是利用和 dinner（晚餐）有關的 lunch（午餐）來造成混淆的錯誤選項。

(B) [〇] 這裡回答要看看行程表，間接表示不一定會答應，因此是正確答案。

(C) [╳] 這是利用和 going out for dinner（去外面吃晚餐）有關的 a great time（很愉快）來造成混淆的錯誤選項。

25 中

🔊 英式發音 → 加拿大式發音

A celebrity spokesperson has finally been selected for the company.

(A) Well, each person should get one.
(B) I was told this place is famous.
(C) Yes, Joseph mentioned that earlier.

公司終於選定了一位名人代言人。
(A) 這個嘛，每個人都應該拿到一個。
(B) 我聽說這個地方很有名。
(C) 沒錯，Joseph 之前有提過。

陳述句 答案 (C)

這是表達公司終於選定了名人代言人的客觀事實陳述句。

(A) [╳] 題目說公司終於選定了名人代言人，這裡卻回答每個人都應該拿到一個，毫不相關，因此是錯誤選項。這裡利用發音相似單字 spokesperson – person 來造成混淆。

(B) [╳] 這是利用和 celebrity（名人）相關的 famous（有名的）來造成混淆的錯誤選項。

(C) [○] 這裡以 Yes 來表達自己知道公司終於選定了名人代言人，並附加說明表示 Joseph 之前有提過這件事，因此是正確答案。

單字 celebrity [səˋlɛbrətɪ] 名人；明星 spokesperson [美] ˋspoks͵pɝsn̩ [英] ˋspəuks͵pə:sn̩] 發言人；代言人
mention [ˋmɛnʃən] 說起，提及

26 中

🔊 英式發音 → 澳洲式發音

Have Sam and Janie registered for the accounting workshop?

(A) These are the proper forms.
(B) One of the accounts is low on money.
(C) They'll do so after lunch.

Sam 和 Janie 已經報名會計工作坊了嗎？
(A) 這些是正確的表單。
(B) 其中一個帳戶的錢快要沒有了。
(C) 他們午餐後會去做這件事。

助動詞疑問句 答案 (C)

這是確認 Sam 和 Janie 是否已經報名會計工作坊的助動詞（Have）疑問句。

(A) [╳] 這是利用和 registered for（報名～）相關的 forms（表單）來造成混淆的錯誤選項。

(B) [╳] 題目想要確認 Sam 和 Janie 是否已經報名會計工作坊，這裡卻回答其中一個帳戶的錢快要沒有了，毫不相關，因此是錯誤選項。這裡利用發音相似單字 accounting – accounts 來造成混淆。

(C) [○] 這裡回答他們午餐後會去做這件事，間接表示 Sam 和 Janie 還沒報名，因此是正確答案。

單字 register for 報名～ accounting [əˋkaʊntɪŋ] 會計 proper [[美] ˋprɑpɚ [英] ˋprɔpə] 適當的；正確的
form [[美] fɔrm [英] fɔ:m] 表格；表單 account [əˋkaʊnt] 帳戶 low on ～快要沒有了

27 低

🔊 加拿大式發音 → 英式發音

Was Jones Industries or Peters Manufacturing contracted to produce our shoe line?

(A) Our contract expires soon.
(B) Clients waited in line for several hours.
(C) A different one was chosen.

承包生產我們鞋子系列商品的是 Jones 工業還是 Peters 製造？
(A) 我們的合約很快要到期了。
(B) 客戶排隊等了幾個小時。
(C) 選擇了其他家。

選擇疑問句 答案 (C)

這是詢問承包生產鞋子系列商品的廠商是哪家的選擇疑問句。

(A) [╳] 這是透過表示「合約」之意的名詞 contract 來重複使用題目中出現的 contracted（承包）來造成混淆的錯誤選項。

(B) [╳] 題目詢問承包生產鞋子系列商品的廠商是哪家，這裡卻回答客戶排隊等了幾個小時，毫不相關，因此是錯誤選項。這裡利用題目中 line 的另一字義「隊伍」來造成混淆。

(C) [○] 這裡回答選擇了其他家，表示承包生產的廠商並非題目提供的兩個選項之一，而是第三方，因此是正確答案。

單字 contract [kənˋtrækt] 承包；締約 produce [prəˋdjus] 生產；製造 expire [[美] ɪkˋspaɪr [英] iksˋpaiə] 到期
wait in line 排隊等待 choose [tʃuz] 選擇，挑選

28 ○●●● 高

🔊 澳洲式發音 → 美式發音 Curtis is joining us for a picnic on Saturday, right? (A) The weather was nice on Sunday. (B) Did you bring some snacks? (C) That's why we planned it for the morning.	Curtis 星期六會和我們一起野餐，對吧？ (A) 星期日那時的天氣很好。 (B) 你有帶些點心嗎？ (C) 那就是為什麼我們安排在早上。

■ **附加問句** 答案 (C)

這是確認 Curtis 星期六是否會一起去野餐的附加問句。

(A) [×] 這是利用和 Saturday（星期六）有關的 Sunday（星期日）來造成混淆的錯誤選項。

(B) [×] 這是利用和 picnic（野餐）有關的 snacks（點心）來造成混淆的錯誤選項。

(C) [○] 這裡回答那就是安排在早上的原因，間接表示 Curtis 星期六會一起去野餐，所以才把野餐安排在早上，因此是正確答案。

單字　join [dʒɔɪn] 和～一起；加入　bring [brɪŋ] 帶來　snack [snæk] 點心；輕食

29 ○○●● 中

🔊 英式發音 → 加拿大式發音 Are you going to forward the memo to personnel, or should I do that? (A) It's up to you. (B) The entire human resources division. (C) It discusses the new leave policy.	你會把那份備忘錄轉寄給人事部嗎？還是應該我去寄？ (A) 看你決定。 (B) 整個人力資源部門。 (C) 它詳述了新的休假政策。

■ **選擇疑問句** 答案 (A)

這是詢問是對方會轉寄備忘錄，還是應該自己去寄的選擇疑問句。

(A) [○] 這裡回答由對方決定，表示會依對方意見來進行，因此是正確答案。

(B) [×] 這是利用和 personnel（人事部）相關的 division（部門）來造成混淆的錯誤選項。

(C) [×] 這裡使用可以代稱題目中 memo（備忘錄）的 It，並利用能透過 memo（備忘錄）內容來聯想到的 new leave policy（新的休假政策）來造成混淆，因此是錯誤選項。

單字　forward [[美] `fɔrwɚd [英] `fɔ:wəd] 轉寄；傳達　entire [ɪn`taɪr] 全部的，整個的　discuss [dɪ`skʌs] 討論；詳述
policy [`pɑləsɪ] 政策；手段

30 ○●●● 高

🔊 澳洲式發音 → 美式發音 What could be the cause of our company's recent drop in sales? (A) Because I dropped a platter. (B) Shoppers' buying habits are changing. (C) The sails were torn by the strong winds.	我們公司最近銷售額下滑的原因可能是什麼？ (A) 因為我弄掉了一個盤子。 (B) 購買者的購買習慣正在改變。 (C) 帆被強風扯破了

■ **What 疑問句** 答案 (B)

這是詢問公司最近銷售額下滑的原因是什麼的 What 疑問句。這裡必須知道 What could be the cause 是用來詢問理由的表達。

(A) [×] 這裡將題目中的 drop（下滑）改以動詞「dropped」來重複使用，企圖造成混淆。注意不要聽到 Because 就選擇這個選項。

(B) [○] 這裡回答購買者的購買習慣正在改變，提到公司最近銷售額下滑的原因，因此是正確答案。

(C) [×] 題目詢問公司最近銷售額下滑的原因是什麼，這裡卻回答帆被強風扯破了，毫不相關，因此是錯誤選項。這裡利用發音相似單字 sales – sails 來造成混淆。

單字　cause [kɔz] 理由，原因　drop [[美] drɑp [英] drɔp] 下滑；掉落　platter [`plætɚ]（大而淺的）盤子
sail [sel] 帆　tear [tɛr] 撕裂；扯破

31 ○●●● 高

加拿大式發音 → 美式發音 The business center is scheduled to be remodeled this fall. (A) I heard the project could cost millions. (B) Here's the spring catalog. (C) We already sent her the outline.	商務中心預定在今年秋天進行整修。 (A) 我聽說這項計畫可能會花上幾百萬。 (B) 這是春季型錄。 (C) 我們已經寄給她大綱了

陳述句

答案 (A)

這是表達商務中心預定在今年秋天進行整修的客觀事實陳述句。

(A) [○] 這裡回答聽說該計畫可能會花上幾百萬，提供附加資訊，因此是正確答案。

(B) [╳] 這是利用和 fall（秋天）相關的 spring（春天）來造成混淆的錯誤選項。

(C) [╳] 題目說商務中心預定在今年秋天進行整修，這裡卻回答自己已經寄給她大綱了，毫不相關，因此是錯誤選項。這裡利用發音相似單字 center – sent her 來造成混淆。

單字　remodel [riˋmɑdl] 整修；改建　cost [kɔst] 花費　outline [ˋaʊtˏlaɪn] 大綱；概要

32
33
34

Questions 32-34 refer to the following conversation.

🔊 英式發音 → 加拿大式發音

W: [32]**A representative of the state government just contacted me regarding our recent funding proposal. Our request was approved, so the community center is going to be the recipient of a technology grant worth** $75,000.

M: Wonderful! Now [33]**we can finally afford to replace the outdated electronics in our computer lab with more modern equipment.** People in the community are going to be very pleased with the news.

W: That's right. However, [34]**there are limitations on how the grant money can be spent. So, we'll have to read over the documents carefully** before buying computers or other devices.

32 What will the community center receive?

(A) Donations from a company
(B) Computers from local charities
(C) Funds from the government
(D) Equipment from a university

33 What are the speakers planning to do?

(A) Upgrade old devices
(B) Move to a larger building
(C) Order additional books
(D) Run an educational workshop

34 Why must the speakers review some documents?

(A) To compare some prices
(B) To identify some donors
(C) To determine some restrictions
(D) To research some venues

第 32-34 題請參考下列對話。

女：[32] 一位州政府的代表剛剛就我們最近的資金提案和我聯絡。我們的申請被批准了，所以社區中心將會獲得一筆價值 75,000 美金的科技補助金。

男：太棒了！現在 [33] 我們終於能負擔得起把我們電腦教室裡的老舊電子產品換成較現代化的設備了。社區裡的人會非常開心聽到這個消息的。

女：沒錯。不過，[34] 能怎麼花這筆補助金是有限制的。所以，在買電腦或其他設備之前，我們得先仔細看過那些文件。

32 社區中心將獲得什麼？

(A) 來自一間公司的捐款
(B) 來自當地慈善機構的電腦
(C) 來自政府的資金
(D) 來自一所大學的設備

33 說話者們打算做什麼？

(A) 升級老舊設備
(B) 搬到更大的建築物
(C) 訂購更多書
(D) 舉辦教育工作坊

34 說話者們為什麼必須檢視一些文件？

(A) 比較一些價格
(B) 辨認一些捐款人
(C) 確定一些限制
(D) 調查一些場地

題目 funding [`fʌndɪŋ] 資金　proposal [[美] prə`pozḷ [英] prə`pəuzəl] 提案　approve [ə`pruv] 批准；認可
grant [[美] grænt [英] grɑ:nt] 補助金　afford to（經濟上）負擔得起～　outdated [ˌaʊt`detɪd] 老舊的；過時的
limitation [[美] ˌlɪmə`teʃən [英] ˌlimi`teiʃən] 限制

32 charity [`tʃærətɪ] 慈善機構

34 restriction [rɪ`strɪkʃən] 限制；限制規定　venue [`vɛnju] 場地

32 ○○●● 中 細節事項相關問題—特定細項 答案 (C)

題目詢問社區中心將獲得什麼，因此必須注意和題目關鍵字（community center receive）相關的內容。女子說：「A representative of the state government just contacted me regarding our recent funding proposal. Our request was approved, so the community center is going to be the recipient of a technology grant」，表示州政府的人剛剛就資金提案聯絡了說話者，並表示申請已被批准了，因此社區中心將獲得一筆補助金，因此正確答案是 (C) Funds from the government。

33 ○○●● 中 細節事項相關問題—特定細項 答案 (A)

題目詢問說話者計畫要做什麼，因此要注意和題目關鍵字（planning to do）相關的內容。男子說：「we can finally afford to replace the outdated electronics in our computer lab with more modern equipment」，表示終於能夠把電腦教室的老舊電子產品換成比較現代化的設備了，因此正確答案是 (A) Upgrade old devices。

換句話說

replace the outdated electronics ~ with more modern equipment 把老舊電子產品換成較現代化的設備
→ Upgrade old devices 升級老舊設備

34 ○○●● 中 細節事項相關問題—理由 答案 (C)

題目詢問說話者必須檢視文件的原因，因此必須注意和題目關鍵字（review some documents）相關的內容。女子說：「there are limitations on how the grant money can be spent. So, we'll have to read over the documents carefully」，表示因為補助金的使用有限制，所以必須先仔細看過文件。因此正確答案是 (C) To determine some restrictions。

35 36 37 新

Questions 35-37 refer to the following conversation.

第 35-37 題請參考下列對話。

美式發音 → 加拿大式發音

W: Good morning, Mr. Abdul. This is Alicia Ponds calling from Davenport Architecture. We received your résumé and cover letter in regard to our associate architect position. And [35]**we would like to invite you in for an interview this Thursday**. Are you available in the morning?

M: Thank you for contacting me. I already have an appointment scheduled then, but [36]**I'm free that afternoon or at any time before 12 P.M. on Friday.**

W: [36]**Thursday afternoon at 2 P.M. will be fine.**

M: I'll mark it in my calendar. [37]**Is there anything else I should bring?** Like a reference letter?

W: [37]**I'd appreciate an example of a blueprint that you created** for a previous employer. Other than that, I have everything I need.

女：早安，Abdul 先生。我是從 Davenport 建築打來的 Alicia Ponds。關於我們助理建築師一職，我們收到了您的履歷表及求職信。因此 [35] **我們想要邀請您這星期四前來面試**。您那天早上有時間嗎？

男：謝謝您與我聯絡。我那個時間已經有排事情了，但 [36] **我那天下午或星期五中午 12 點前的任何時間都有空。**

女：[36] **星期四下午 2 點可以。**

男：我會把這件事標在我的行事曆上。[37] **我還有需要帶什麼東西嗎？**像是推薦信？

女：[37] **若有您為之前的雇主所製作的藍圖範本，我會很感激。**除了這個之外，需要的東西我都有了。

35 Why did the woman contact the man?

(A) To verify a delivery time
(B) To inquire about job duties
(C) To arrange an interview
(D) To confirm a contract detail

35 女子為何聯絡男子？

(A) 確認送貨時間
(B) 詢問工作職責
(C) 安排一場面試
(D) 確認合約細節

36 When will the speakers most likely meet?

(A) On Thursday morning
(B) On Thursday afternoon
(C) On Friday morning
(D) On Friday afternoon

36 說話者最有可能會在何時碰面？

(A) 星期四早上
(B) 星期四下午
(C) 星期五早上
(D) 星期五下午

37 What will the man most likely bring for the woman?

(A) A résumé
(B) A work sample
(C) An application form
(D) A reference letter

37 男子最有可能會為女子帶來什麼？

(A) 履歷表
(B) 作品範本
(C) 申請表
(D) 推薦信

題目 cover letter 求職信 in regard to 關於～ available [əˋveləbl] 有時間的 mark [mɑrk] 標記；標明 reference letter 推薦信 appreciate [əˋpriʃɪˏet] 欣賞；評鑑；感激 blueprint [ˋbluˋprɪnt] 藍圖

35 verify [ˋvɛrəˏfaɪ] 確認；核實 inquire [ɪnˋkwaɪr] 詢問 job duty 工作職責 arrange [əˋrendʒ] 安排

35 低 整體對話相關問題—目的 答案 (C)

題目詢問女子為什麼要聯絡男子，因此必須注意對話的開頭部分。女子對男子說：「we would like to invite you in for an interview this Thursday」，表示希望邀請男子在星期四前來面試，因此正確答案是 (C) To arrange an interview。

36 低 細節事項相關問題—特定細項 答案 (B)

題目詢問說話者們碰面的時間，因此必須注意和題目關鍵字（meet）相關的內容。男子說：「I'm free that[Thursday] afternoon or at any time before 12 P.M. on Friday」，表示星期四下午或星期五中午 12 點前都有空，接著女子說：「Thursday afternoon at 2 P.M. will be fine.」，表示星期四下午兩點可以，因此正確答案是 (B) On Thursday afternoon。

37 中 細節事項相關問題—特定細項 答案 (B)

題目詢問男子會為女子帶來什麼，因此必須注意提及題目關鍵字（bring）的前後部分。男子對女子說：「Is there anything else I should bring?」，詢問還有沒有其他需要帶的東西，女子說：「I'd appreciate an example of a blueprint that you created」，表示想要男子之前做過的藍圖範本，因此正確答案是 (B) A work sample。

換句話說

example of a blueprint 藍圖範本 → work sample 作品範本

38 39 40

Questions 38-40 refer to the following conversation.

🔊 英式發音 → 澳洲式發音

W: Do you know why our investor Mr. Herman hasn't gotten in touch with me yet? He was supposed to call at around 9:00 A.M. today, which is when his flight was scheduled to arrive. But it's 9:45 now, and I haven't heard from him.

M: I just received a message from his secretary indicating that [38]**his flight was delayed in Detroit**. Apparently, [38]**his departure was postponed by an hour due to a severe blizzard**. His flight should arrive shortly, however.

W: Oh, I see. In that case, [39]**we'll have to hold off starting the presentation on product development until this afternoon, as Mr. Herman is flying in to listen to it.**

M: Yes, that looks unavoidable at this point. [40]**I'll notify the research team.**

38 What does the man say about Detroit?

(A) It experienced bad weather.
(B) It has a newly built airport.
(C) It is only an hour away.
(D) It is hosting a major event.

39 According to the woman, why is Mr. Herman coming to the office?

(A) To train some personnel
(B) To discuss travel arrangements
(C) To make an announcement
(D) To observe a presentation

40 What will the man probably do next?

(A) Take a lunch break
(B) Begin a meeting
(C) Pass on some information
(D) Share some sales reports

第 38-40 題請參考下列對話。

女：你知道為什麼我們的投資人 Herman 先生還沒有和我聯絡嗎？他原本應該要在今天早上 9 點左右打電話的，那是他班機預定抵達的時間。但現在是 9 點 45 分了，我卻還沒有接到他的聯絡。

男：我剛接到他祕書傳來的訊息，說 [38] 他的班機在底特律延誤了。顯然，[38] 他因為劇烈的暴風雪而延後了一小時起飛。不過，他的班機應該很快就會到了。

女：噢，我知道了。如果是這樣，[39] 我們就得把產品開發簡報延後到今天下午再開始了，因為 Herman 先生是飛來要聽這個簡報的。

男：是的，現在這看來無法避免了。[40] 我會通知研究團隊。

38 關於底特律，男子說什麼？

(A) 經歷了壞天氣。
(B) 有新建的機場。
(C) 只要一小時的路程就到。
(D) 正在主辦大型活動。

39 根據女子所說，Herman 先生為何要前來這個辦公室？

(A) 訓練一些員工
(B) 討論旅行安排
(C) 宣布一件事
(D) 觀看一場簡報

40 男子接下來可能會做什麼？

(A) 午休
(B) 開始開會
(C) 傳遞一些資訊
(D) 分享一些銷售報告

題目 get in touch with 與～聯絡　apparently [ə`pærəntlɪ] 顯然地　severe [美 sə`vɪr 英 si`viə] 嚴重的；劇烈的
blizzard [美 `blɪzɚd 英 `blizəd] 暴風雪　hold off 延期；推遲　unavoidable [ˌʌnə`vɔɪdəbl] 無法避免的
38 host [host] 主辦　**40** pass on 傳遞～；接著進行～

38 細節事項相關問題—提及　答案 (A)

●●○ 中

題目詢問男子提到什麼有關底特律的事，因此要注意提到題目關鍵字（Detroit）的前後部分。男子說：「his [Mr. Herman's] flight was delayed in Detroit」，表示 Herman 先生的班機在底特律延誤，接著說：「his departure was postponed by an hour due to a severe blizzard」，表示飛機因為劇烈的暴風雪而延後了一小時起飛，因此正確答案是 (A) It experienced bad weather.。

換句話說

severe blizzard 劇烈的暴風雪 → bad weather 壞天氣

39 細節事項相關問題—理由　答案 (D)

●○○ 低

題目詢問女子說 Herman 先生來辦公室的原因是什麼，因此必須注意女子話中與題目關鍵字（Mr. Herman coming to the office）相關的內容。女子說：「we'll have to hold off starting the presentation ~, as Mr. Herman is flying in to listen to it」，表示 Herman 先生飛過來是為了要聽簡報，所以應該把簡報延後。因此正確答案是 (D) To observe a presentation。

40 細節事項相關問題—接下來要做的事　答案 (C)

●●○ 中

題目詢問男子接下來可能會做什麼，因此要注意對話的最後部分。男子說：「I'll notify the research team.」，表示自己會通知研究團隊，因此正確答案是 (C) Pass on some information。

TEST 1 2 3 4 5 6 7 8 9 10

41 42 43 新

Questions 41-43 refer to the following conversation.

美式發音 → 加拿大式發音

W: Pardon me. Is there an ATM I can use other than the one by the bank's entrance? [41] **Quite a few people are in line to use that one.**

M: Unfortunately, the only other one in the building is undergoing regular maintenance. It won't be accessible for about an hour.

W: Hmm . . . I'm in a bit of a rush. [42] **I need to withdraw cash before I fly to Vancouver for a business trip.**

M: Well, the teller at the end of the counter is helping another customer, but that shouldn't take too long. [43] **You can get cash from her once she's available.** I'm sure you'll find that option faster than using the machine.

W: Yeah, you're probably right. Thanks for the suggestion.

第 41-43 題請參考下列對話。

女：不好意思。除了銀行門口旁的那台之外，還有其他我可以用的自動提款機嗎？[41] 那台有太多人排隊要用了。

男：很不巧，這棟大樓裡唯一的另一台提款機正在定期維護中。大概還要一個小時才能用。

女：嗯……我有點趕。[42] 我得在飛去溫哥華出差前先領錢。

男：這個嘛，櫃檯最底的那個櫃員正在協助另一位顧客，但那應該不會花上太久時間。[43] 等她一忙完，您就可以找她領錢。我保證您會發現，這樣做比去用那台機器來得快。

女：是啊，你應該是對的。謝謝你的建議。

41 What problem does the woman mention?

(A) A line has formed at a device.
(B) A machine has been damaged.
(C) A bank has closed for construction.
(D) A fee has been increased.

41 女子提到什麼問題？

(A) 一台設備前有人排隊。
(B) 一台機器遭到毀損。
(C) 一家銀行因施工而關閉。
(D) 一項費用增加了。

42 新 What does the woman mean when she says, “I'm in a bit of a rush”?

(A) She needs to return to the office.
(B) She does not want to miss a train.
(C) She has to catch a flight soon.
(D) She is late for a social gathering.

42 當女子說：「我有點趕」，意思是什麼？

(A) 她得回辦公室。
(B) 她不想錯過列車。
(C) 她很快得去趕飛機。
(D) 她參加社交聚會遲到了

43 What does the man suggest the woman do?

(A) Make a formal complaint
(B) Travel to another branch
(C) Postpone a trip
(D) Speak with an employee

43 男子建議女子做什麼？

(A) 提出正式申訴
(B) 前往另一間分行
(C) 延後一趟旅程
(D) 和一位員工說話

題目 entrance [\`ɛntrəns] 入口 undergo [ˌʌndɚ\`go] 接受（治療、手術等）；經歷 regular [\`rɛgjəlɚ] 定期的；正常的 maintenance [\`mentənəns] 維護；維持 accessible [æk\`sɛsəbl̩] 可使用的；可接觸的 withdraw [wɪð\`drɔ] 提領（錢） business trip 出差 teller [\`tɛlɚ]（銀行窗口的）櫃員

41 damaged [\`dæmɪdʒd] 受損的 construction [kən\`strʌkʃən] 建設；工程

42 social gathering 社交聚會

43 formal [\`fɔrml̩] 正式的 complaint [kəm\`plent] 申訴

41 ■ **細節事項相關問題—問題點** 答案 (A)

中

題目詢問女子提到的問題是什麼，因此必須注意聽女子話中在負面表達之後出現的內容。女子說：「Quite a few people are in line to use that one[ATM].」，表示有很多人在為了使用提款機排隊，因此正確答案是 (A) A line has formed at a device.。

新 **42** ■ **細節事項相關問題—掌握意圖** 答案 (C)

中

題目詢問女子的說話意圖，因此要注意提到題目引用句（I'm in a bit of a rush）的前後部分。女子說：「I need to withdraw cash before I fly to Vancouver for a business trip.」，表示在她飛去溫哥華出差前必須先領錢，由此可知女子很快要去趕飛機，因此正確答案是 (C) She has to catch a flight soon.。

43 ■ **細節事項相關問題—提議** 答案 (D)

中

題目詢問男子建議女子做什麼，因此要注意聽男子話中出現提議表達之後的內容。男子對女子說：「You can get cash from her[teller] once she's available.」，表示一旦櫃員有空，女子就可以去跟她領錢，因此正確答案是 (D) Speak with an employee。

Questions 44-46 refer to the following conversation.

美式發音 → 澳洲式發音

W: Hello. This is Wendy Rahn from Silver Fork Engineering. I'm calling about some of the air conditioning units in our office building. [44]**Three of them are extremely loud and have been distracting our employees.** [45]**Could you please send a technician to look at them tomorrow?**

M: I'm sorry. But all of our technicians are booked through Thursday. With the hot weather, we've been repairing a lot of air conditioners lately. However, one is available this Friday. Would it be acceptable for him to stop by on that day instead?

W: That would work. [46]**We're holding a staff picnic on Friday**, so there won't be anyone here to get in the repairperson's way. The building manager can give him access to our office.

44 According to the woman, what has caused a distraction?

(A) Excessive heat
(B) Building construction
(C) Untidy offices
(D) Noisy appliances

45 What does the woman ask the man to do?

(A) Replace some equipment
(B) Send a technician
(C) Clean an office space
(D) Change an appointment date

46 What is probably going to take place on Friday?

(A) A company outing
(B) A retirement party
(C) A technical seminar
(D) A grand opening

第 44-46 題請參考下列對話。

女： 哈囉。我是 Silver Fork 工程的 Wendy Rahn。我打來是想說與我們辦公大樓裡的一些空調裝置有關的事。[44] 它們之中有三台非常大聲，一直使我們的員工無法專心。[45] 可以請您明天派位技術人員過來看看它們嗎？

男： 我很抱歉。但我們所有技術人員到週四都約滿了。因為天氣炎熱，我們最近一直有很多空調要修。不過，有一位技術人員這週五有空。他改在那天過去可以嗎？

女： 可以。[46] 我們週五要舉行員工野餐，所以這裡不會有任何人妨礙維修人員。大樓管理人可以讓他進我們辦公室。

44 根據女子所說，造成無法專心的是什麼？

(A) 酷熱
(B) 大樓工程
(C) 雜亂的辦公室
(D) 發出噪音的設備

45 女子要求男子做什麼？

(A) 更換一些設備
(B) 派遣一位技術人員
(C) 清理一個辦公空間
(D) 更改一個會面日期

46 週五可能會舉行什麼？

(A) 公司郊遊
(B) 退休派對
(C) 技術研討會
(D) 盛大開幕式

題目 distract [dɪ`strækt] 使（注意力）不集中，使無法專心 lately [`letlɪ] 最近 acceptable [ək`sɛptəbl] 不錯的；可接受的 get in the way 妨礙

44 untidy [ʌn`taɪdɪ] 雜亂的 appliance [ə`plaɪəns] 設備

46 outing [`aʊtɪŋ] 郊遊 retirement [rɪ`taɪrmənt] 退休；引退

44 細節事項相關問題—特定細項 答案 (D)

中

題目詢問女子說會造成無法專心的是什麼，因此必須注意女子所說的話中和題目關鍵字（distraction）有關的內容。女子說：「Three of them[air conditioning units] are extremely loud and have been distracting our employees.」，表示有三台空調的聲音非常大，使員工無法專心工作，因此正確答案是 (D) Noisy appliances。

45 細節事項相關問題—要求 答案 (B)

低

題目詢問女子要求男子做什麼，因此要注意聽女子話中出現要求表達之後的內容。女子對男子說：「Could you please send a technician to look at them[air conditioning units] tomorrow?」，要求男子明天派技術人員前來看看空調，因此正確答案是 (B) Send a technician。

46 細節事項相關問題—接下來要做的事 答案 (A)

中

題目詢問週五會舉行什麼，因此要注意提到題目關鍵字（Friday）的前後部分。女子說：「We're holding a staff picnic on Friday」，表示週五要舉行員工野餐，因此正確答案是 (A) A company outing。

換句話說

staff picnic 員工野餐 → company outing 公司郊遊

Questions 47-49 refer to the following conversation.

🔊 加拿大式發音 → 英式發音

M: Good morning. I work at Spector Industries, and we want to convert a vacant lot on our property into a garden with a seating area. [47] **Could your landscaping company handle a job of that scale?**

W: Absolutely. Although our firm mostly does residential work, [48] **we have commercial clients too. In fact, just last summer we did a large landscaping project for the Seward Grocery Store**, which is located three blocks from your facility.

M: Oh, really? I pass by that building daily, and I'm always impressed with how nice its front lawn looks.

W: We certainly appreciate the compliment. Now, [49] **why don't you tell me more about the work you'd like done?**

47 Where does the woman work?

(A) At a consultancy
(B) At a real estate company
(C) At a grocery store
(D) At a landscaping firm

48 What does the woman say her company did last summer?

(A) Took on a commercial job
(B) Expanded to other cities
(C) Relocated its headquarters
(D) Raised its prices

49 What does the woman ask for?

(A) Property locations
(B) Budget amounts
(C) Price comparisons
(D) Project details

第 47-49 題請參考下列對話。

男：早安。我是 Spector 工業的員工，我們想要把我們土地上的一塊空地改成附有座位區的花園。[47] 你們景觀設計公司可以承接這種規模的工作嗎？

女：當然可以。儘管我們公司做的多半是住宅工程，但 [48] 我們也有商業客戶。事實上，我們去年夏天才為 Seward 雜貨店做了大型的景觀設計工程，它位在離您公司三個街區的地方。

男：噢，真的嗎？我每天都會經過那棟建築物，而且我一直都對它前面的草坪看起來有多漂亮感到印象深刻。

女：我們真的很感謝您的稱讚。那麼，[49] 您何不多告訴我一點與您想做的工程有關的事呢？

47 女子在哪裡工作？

(A) 顧問公司
(B) 不動產公司
(C) 雜貨店
(D) 景觀設計公司

48 女子說她公司去年夏天做了什麼？

(A) 承接了一件商業案
(B) 擴展到了其他城市
(C) 總公司搬遷了
(D) 漲價了

49 女子要求什麼？

(A) 土地地點
(B) 預算金額
(C) 價格比較
(D) 工程細節資訊

題目 convert [kən`vɝt] 轉變　lot [lɑt]（有特定用處的）一塊地　property [`prɑpɚtɪ] 地產，不動產
landscaping [`lændskepɪŋ] 景觀設計　scale [skel] 規模　residential [[美] ˌrɛzə`dɛnʃəl [英] ˌrezi`denʃəl] 居住用的；住宅的
commercial [[美] kə`mɝʃəl [英] kə`mə:ʃəl] 商務的；商用的
47 consultancy [kən`sʌltənsɪ] 顧問公司　real estate 不動產
48 take on 承擔；接受（工作等）headquarters [`hɛd`kwɔrtɚz] 總公司
49 comparison [kəm`pærəsn] 比較

47 ■ **整體對話相關問題—說話者** 答案 (D)

低

題目詢問女子的工作地點，因此要注意聽和身分、職業相關的表達。男子對女子說：「Could your landscaping company handle a job of that scale?」，詢問女子的景觀設計公司是否可以處理這種規模的工作，因此正確答案是 (D) At a landscaping firm。

48 ■ **細節事項相關問題—特定細項** 答案 (A)

低

題目詢問女子說她公司去年夏天做了什麼，因此必須注意提到題目關鍵字（last summer）的前後部分。女子說：「we have commercial clients too. In fact, just last summer we did a large landscaping project for the Seward Grocery Store」，表示她公司其實也有商業客戶，而且去年夏天幫 Seward 雜貨店做了景觀設計工程，因此正確答案是 (A) Took on a commercial job。

49 ■ **細節事項相關問題—要求** 答案 (D)

中

題目詢問女子要求什麼，因此要注意聽女子話中出現要求表達之後的內容。女子對男子說：「why don't you tell me more about the work you'd like done?」，要求男子告訴自己更多與工程相關的事，由此可知女子想知道更多工程相關的細節資訊，因此正確答案是 (D) Project details。

新

50 51 52

Questions 50-52 refer to the following conversation with three speakers.

美式發音 → 加拿大式發音 → 澳洲式發音

W: Hello. [50/51]**I've come to pick up medicine prescribed to me by Dr. Vasquez.** My name is Marcia Chow.
M1: Certainly. [51]**Here you are.** Can I help you with anything else today?
W: Yes. Do you know if it is possible to get a free flu shot at the medical clinic next door?
M1: It costs $30, I believe.
W: I see. And [51]**where exactly should I go to get the shot?** I've never been inside the clinic before.
M1: I'm not sure. Ah . . . [51]**I can ask my supervisor, though. One moment, please. Daniel**, this customer is interested in getting a flu vaccination at the clinic. [52]**Where exactly should she go?**
M2: [52]**Just head to the eighth floor—the area for family medicine.** You can't miss it.

第 50-52 題請參考下列三人對話。

女： 哈囉。[50/51] 我來拿 Vasquez 醫生開給我的藥。我的名字是 Marcia Chow。
男 1： 好的。[51] 這給妳。我今天還有什麼能為妳做的嗎？
女： 有的。你知道有沒有可能可以在隔壁診所打免費的流感疫苗呢？
男 1： 我想這要花 30 美金。
女： 我知道了。那 [51] 我確切應該要去哪裡打呢？我之前從來沒有進去過那間診所。
男 1： 我不確定。呃……[51] 不過我可以問我主管。請稍等。Daniel，這位客人想要去那間診所打流感疫苗。[52] 她確切應該要去哪裡？
男 2： [51] 直接到八樓——家庭醫學那區。妳一定找得到。

50 What is the purpose of the woman's visit?
(A) To view some test results
(B) To schedule an appointment
(C) To get some medication
(D) To pick up a building map

50 女子的造訪目的是什麼？
(A) 看一些檢驗結果
(B) 排定會面時間
(C) 拿一些藥
(D) 拿大樓的地圖

51 Who most likely are the men?
(A) Pharmacists
(B) Doctors
(C) Medical researchers
(D) Clinic directors

51 男子們最有可能是誰？
(A) 藥師
(B) 醫生
(C) 醫學研究員
(D) 診所主任

52 What information does Daniel provide?
(A) The location for a shot
(B) The name of a business
(C) The cost of an examination
(D) The number of a room

52 Daniel 提供了什麼資訊？
(A) 打針的地點
(B) 公司的名稱
(C) 檢驗的花費
(D) 房間的號碼

題目 prescribe [prɪ`skraɪb] 開～處方 flu shot 流感疫苗 supervisor [ˌsupɚ`vaɪzɚ] 上司，主管 vaccination [ˌvæksn`eʃən] 疫苗接種
50 medication [ˌmɛdɪ`keʃən] 藥物 **51** pharmacist [`fɑrməsɪst] 藥師 **52** examination [ɪgˌzæmə`neʃən] 檢驗；調查

50 整體對話相關問題─目的 答案 (C)
低
題目詢問女子的造訪目的，因此必須注意對話的開頭部分。女子說：「I've come to pick up medicine prescribed to me by Dr. Vasquez.」，表示來拿 Vasquez 醫生開給自己的藥，因此正確答案是 (C) To get some medication。

51 整體對話相關問題─說話者 答案 (A)
高
題目詢問對話中兩男子的身分，因此要注意聽和身分、職業相關的表達。女子說：「I've come to pick up medicine prescribed to me by Dr. Vasquez.」，表示來拿 Vasquez 醫生開給自己的藥，接著男 1 說：「Here you are.」，表示男 1 把藥拿給了女子，在對話中後段，女子說：「where exactly should I go to get the shot?」，詢問要去哪裡打疫苗，男 1 說：「I can ask my supervisor ~. Daniel」，表示可以幫忙女子詢問自己的上司 Daniel，並叫了男 2[Daniel]。由此可知，兩位男子都是藥師，因此正確答案是 (A) Pharmacists。

52 細節事項相關問題─特定細項 答案 (A)
中
題目詢問男 2，也就是 Daniel 提供了什麼資訊，因此要注意聽男 2 話中和題目關鍵字（information）相關的內容。男 1 對男 2 [Daniel] 說：「Where exactly should she[customer] go?」，詢問客人確切要去哪裡，男 2 說：「Just head to the eighth floor—the area for family medicine.」，表示女子應該直接到八樓的家庭醫學那一區，因此正確答案是 (A) The location for a shot。

53
54
55

Questions 53-55 refer to the following conversation.	第 53-55 題請參考下列對話。
英式發音 → 澳洲式發音	
W: Calvin, do you have a portable storage device that I can borrow? I need to move the file for the marketing presentation I'm giving at the staff meeting to my laptop.	女：Calvin，你有能借我的可攜式儲存裝置嗎？我得把我要在員工會議上發表的行銷簡報檔案移到我的筆記型電腦裡。
M: I've got one in my drawer. Now . . . um . . . [53] **isn't that the meeting taking place three days from now?**	男：我抽屜裡有一個。是說……嗯……[53] 那個會不是三天後才要開嗎？
W: [53] **It's two days away.** But [54] **I'd like to rehearse in advance, since I'll be presenting in front of our department head.**	女：[53] 是再過兩天要開。但 [54] 因為我要在我們部門主管前做簡報，所以我想事先演練一下。
M: That makes sense. Well, if you want, I can join you in the conference room to watch your presentation. [55] **I'll give you my feedback on it so that you'll be better prepared for any questions that might come up.**	男：很有道理。嗯，如果妳想的話，我可以和妳一起去會議室看妳做簡報。[55] 我可以就妳的簡報給妳一些回饋意見，這樣妳就可以對所有可能會出現的問題做更好的準備。
53 When will a meeting take place? (A) In one day (B) In two days (C) In three days (D) In four days	53 會議什麼時候會開？ (A) 一天後 (B) 兩天後 (C) 三天後 (D) 四天後
54 What does the woman want to do? (A) Speak with a department head (B) Set a project timeline (C) Practice giving a presentation (D) Attend a technology conference	54 女子想要做什麼？ (A) 和部門主管談話 (B) 訂計畫時間表 (C) 練習發表簡報 (D) 參加科技會議
55 新 What does the man mean when he says, "I can join you in the conference room"? (A) He will finish a task soon. (B) He will offer some comments. (C) He has agreed to a time change. (D) He has booked a meeting space.	55 當男子說：「我可以和妳一起去會議室」，意思是什麼？ (A) 他很快會完成一項任務。 (B) 他會提供一些意見。 (C) 他同意了一項時間更動。 (D) 他訂了一個會議場地。

題目 portable [美 `portəbḷ 英 `pɔ:təbl] 可攜帶的　storage [`storɪdʒ] 儲存，保管　device [dɪ`vaɪs] 設備，裝置
rehearse [美 rɪ`hɝs 英 ri`hə:s] 演練，排練　make sense 合理；講得通　come up 被提及；出現

53 細節事項相關問題—特定細項　答案 (B)
低
題目詢問開會時間，因此必須注意和題目關鍵字（meeting take place）相關的內容。男子說：「isn't that the meeting taking place three days from now?」，向女子確認會議是否是在三天後舉行，女子回答：「It's two days away.」，表示是兩天後要開會，因此正確答案是 (B) In two days。

54 細節事項相關問題—特定細項　答案 (C)
低
題目詢問女子想做什麼，因此要注意和題目關鍵字（woman want to do）相關的內容。女子說：「I'd like to rehearse in advance, since I'll be presenting in front of our department head」，表示因為自己要在部門主管前進行簡報，所以想要事先演練，因此正確答案是 (C) Practice giving a presentation。

新 **55** 細節事項相關問題—掌握意圖　答案 (B)
中
題目詢問男子的說話意圖，因此要注意在題目引用句（I can join you in the conference room）之前和之後的部分。男子說：「I'll give you my feedback on it[presentation] so that you'll be better prepared for any questions that might come up.」，表示願意給女子一些回饋意見，幫忙女子為所有可能會出現的問題做好準備，由此可知，男子會提供一些意見，因此正確答案是 (B) He will offer some comments.。

56
57
58

Questions 56-58 refer to the following conversation.	第 56-58 題請參考下列對話。
加拿大式發音 → 美式發音	
M: As you can see, [56] **the apartment we're in comes with two bedrooms, a bathroom, living room, and modern kitchen.** Additionally, the Chicago skyline can be seen from the bedroom. Rent is $1,900 a month. If you're interested in filling out an application, I have one right here.	男：如您所見，[56] 我們所在的這間公寓備有兩間臥室、一間浴室、客廳及現代化的廚房。此外，從臥室可以看到芝加哥的天際線。租金是一個月 1,900 美金。如果您有興趣填寫申請表，我這裡就有一份。
W: The apartment is very impressive. But [57] **I have another showing tomorrow, which I'd like to follow through with before making a decision on where to live.**	女：這間公寓十分令人印象深刻。但 [57] 我明天還有另一間要看，我想要看完它再決定要住在哪裡。
M: Of course. Just be aware that [58] **another potential tenant saw the unit this morning.** Although she has yet to submit an application, she assured me that she was going to do so soon. Whoever turns one in first will be given priority.	男：當然。只是要請您注意，[58] 今天早上有另一位可能會租的人來看過這間公寓。儘管她還沒繳交申請表，但她跟我保證她很快就會交。先繳交申請表的人將會有優先權。
56 Where most likely are the speakers? (A) In a building lobby (B) At a real estate office (C) At a construction site (D) In a residential unit	56 說話者們最有可能在哪裡？ (A) 大樓的大廳 (B) 不動產營業處 (C) 工地 (D) 住宅單位
57 Why does the woman want to wait to make up her mind? (A) She needs to determine a budget. (B) She has to consult a friend. (C) She will look at another space. (D) She is unsure about contract terms.	57 為什麼女子想要晚一點再決定？ (A) 她需要決定預算。 (B) 她得去詢問朋友意見。 (C) 她會去看另一個地方。 (D) 她對合約條件有疑慮。
58 What happened earlier today? (A) An open house event was advertised. (B) A vacant apartment was visited. (C) A property was professionally cleaned. (D) A down payment was made.	58 今天稍早發生了什麼？ (A) 廣告了一個開放看屋的活動。 (B) 有人造訪了一間閒置的公寓。 (C) 專業清理了一筆物業。 (D) 支付了一筆頭期款。

題目 come with 備有～，附有～ skyline [ˋskaɪˏlaɪn] 天際線 potential [pəˋtɛnʃəl] 潛在的；可能的 tenant [ˋtɛnənt] 承租人 unit [ˋjunɪt]（公寓大樓等的）一個單位 assure [əˋʃʊr] 向～保證，擔保 priority [praɪˋɔrətɪ] 優先權；優先

56 real estate 不動產 residential [ˏrɛzəˋdɛnʃəl] 居住的；住宅的

57 determine [dɪˋtɝmɪn] 決定；確定；判定 budget [ˋbʌdʒɪt] 預算，（預計支出的）費用
consult [kənˋsʌlt] 向～尋求意見 term [tɝm]（談判、合約等的）條件，條款

58 open house（用來出租或買賣的）開放看屋 advertise [ˋædvɚˏtaɪz] 廣告 vacant [ˋvekənt] 空著的；閒置的
property [ˋprɑpɚtɪ] 不動產，物業 down payment（分期付款的）頭期款

56 整體對話相關問題—地點 答案 (D)
高

題目詢問對話發生的地點，因此要注意聽與地點有關的表達。男子說：「the apartment we're in comes with two bedrooms, a bathroom, living room, and modern kitchen」，表示說話者們目前所在的公寓有兩間臥室、一間浴室、客廳及現代化的廚房，由此可知，說話者們現在身處住宅單位裡，因此正確答案是 (D) In a residential unit。

57 細節事項相關問題—理由 答案 (C)
高

題目詢問女子想要晚一點再決定的原因，因此要注意和題目關鍵字（wait to make up her mind）相關的內容。女子說：「I have another showing tomorrow, which I'd like to follow through with before making a decision on where to live」，表示明天還有一間房子要看，且在看完那間房前還不想做決定，因此正確答案是 (C) She will look at another space.。

58 細節事項相關問題—特定細項 答案 (B)
低

題目詢問今天稍早發生了什麼，因此要注意和題目關鍵字（earlier today）相關的內容。男子說：「another potential tenant saw the unit this morning」，表示有其他可能會租的人在今天早上來看過這間公寓了，因此正確答案是 (B) A vacant apartment was visited.。

TEST 1 2 3 4 5 6 7 8 9 10

Questions 59-61 refer to the following conversation.

🔊 澳洲式發音 → 英式發音

M: [59]**How are negotiations going with TruCare Medical Supplies? Did the president of TruCare say whether the company agrees to our acquisition terms regarding the retention of personnel?**

W: Yes. He agreed that none of our existing employees will be dismissed immediately. However, [60]**all staff will be subject to a six-month evaluation following the purchase to determine whether they will receive contract extensions.**

M: Hmm . . . Well, at least everyone will have a chance to maintain their jobs. Have financial figures been discussed at all?

W: As of now, [61]**we're being offered $45 million, which our analysts tell me is a bit low. I need your approval to ask the company to pay $48 million instead.**

第 59-61 題請參考下列對話。

男：[59] 和 TruCare 醫療用品之間的協商進行得怎麼樣？TruCare 的總裁有說他們公司是否同意我們與員工留任有關的收購條件嗎？

女：有。他同意我們現有員工之中沒有人會被立即解雇。不過，[60] 全部員工在收購之後都必須接受六個月的評估以決定他們是否會得到續聘。

男：嗯……這個嘛，至少所有人都會有機會保住工作。有討論到什麼財務數字嗎？

女：目前為止，[61] 對我們的開價是 4500 萬美金，我們的分析師跟我說這有點低。我需要你的批准來要求他們公司改付 4800 萬美金。

59 What is the conversation mainly about?

(A) The reason for evaluations
(B) The details of a negotiation
(C) The success of an investment
(D) The cost of operations

59 這段對話主要與什麼有關？

(A) 評估的理由
(B) 談判的細節資訊
(C) 投資的成功
(D) 營運的成本

60 What is mentioned about staff?

(A) They will receive salary increases.
(B) They will learn specialized skills.
(C) They will transfer to a new division.
(D) They will undergo an assessment.

60 關於員工，提到了什麼？

(A) 會獲得加薪。
(B) 會學習專業技能。
(C) 會轉調到新部門。
(D) 會接受評估。

61 Why does the woman require the man's approval?

(A) She needs to conduct an analysis.
(B) She plans to post a memo.
(C) She wants to submit another offer.
(D) She wishes to agree to a deal.

61 為什麼女子需要男子的批准？

(A) 她需要進行一項分析。
(B) 她打算張貼一則備忘錄。
(C) 她想要提交另一個開價。
(D) 她想要達成一筆交易。

題目 negotiation [[美] nɪˌgoʃɪ`eʃən [英] niˌgəuʃi`eiʃən] 協商　acquisition [ˌækwə`zɪʃən] 收購；獲得
term [[美] tɝm [英] tə:m]（合約、協商等的）條件　retention [rɪ`tɛnʃən] 保持；保留
personnel [[美] ˌpɝsn`ɛl [英] ˌpə:sə`nel]（總稱）員工，人員　dismiss [dɪs`mɪs] 解雇　be subject to 遭受～；須經～
evaluation [ɪˌvæljʊ`eʃən] 評估　purchase [[美] `pɝtʃəs [英] `pə:tʃəs] 購買；消費
determine [[美] dɪ`tɝmɪn [英] di`tə:min] 決定　analyst [`ænḷɪst] 分析師　approval [ə`pruvḷ] 批准；核可；同意

60 specialized [`spɛʃəlˌaɪzd] 專業的　transfer [træns`fɝ] 調動；轉換　undergo [ˌʌndɚ`go] 經歷；接受（檢查等）
assessment [ə`sɛsmənt] 評估

61 deal [dil] 交易

59 整體對話相關問題—主題 答案 (B)

高

題目詢問對話主題，因此必須注意對話的開頭部分。男子說：「How are negotiations going with TruCare Medical Supplies? Did the president of TruCare say whether the company agrees to our acquisition terms regarding the retention of personnel?」，詢問與 TruCare 醫療用品之間的協商進行得如何，以及 TruCare 的總裁是否同意與員工留任有關的收購條件，接著說話者們繼續談論與協商內容相關的細節資訊，因此正確答案是 (B) The details of a negotiation。

60 細節事項相關問題—提及 答案 (D)

高

題目詢問提到了什麼與員工有關的內容，因此要注意提到題目關鍵字（staff）的前後部分。女子說：「all staff will be subject to a six-month evaluation ~ to determine whether they will receive contract extensions」，表示所有員工都將必須接受六個月的評估來決定是否能夠得到續聘，因此正確答案是 (D) They will undergo an assessment.。

61 細節事項相關問題—理由 答案 (C)

中

題目詢問女子為什麼需要男子的批准，因此必須注意和題目關鍵字（require the man's approval）相關的內容。女子說：「we're being offered $45 million ~. I need your approval to ask the company to pay $48 million instead.」，表示目前得到的出價是 4500 萬美金，但需要男子的批准來要求對方公司改付 4800 萬美金，因此正確答案是 (C) She wants to submit another offer.。

Questions 62-64 refer to the following conversation and floor plan.

第 62-64 題請參考下列對話及樓層平面圖。

美式發音 → 澳洲式發音

W: Roger, we have to get the auditorium lobby ready before people arrive for [62]**tonight's debut performance of the play *Going for Broke*.**

M: Right, I've got the actors' photographs framed for display. What else is there to do?

W: [63]**Can you set up some tables where programs can be handed out?**

M: Sure. There are a few in the basement. I'll ask Jacob to help me carry them up here. His shift starts in 15 minutes.

W: OK. And finally, [64]**we need a spot where fans can take photos with the cast after the show.**

M: [64]**Let's put it where it was last year . . . in the area to the left when you enter the building, just before you reach the refreshment stand.**

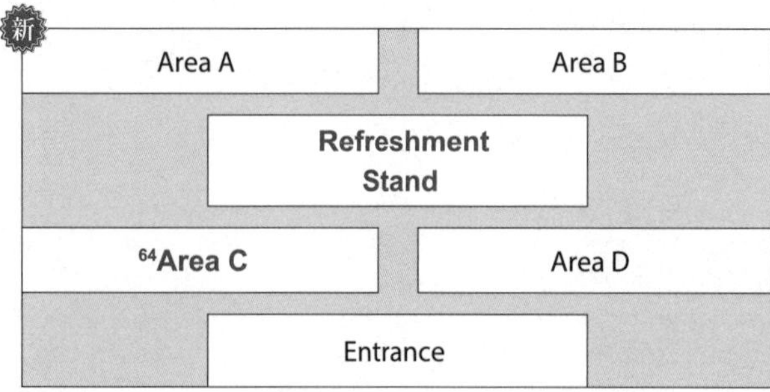

女：Roger，我們得在 [62] 今晚首演的戲《Going for Broke》的觀眾到場前把劇院大廳準備好。

男：沒錯，我已經把演員的照片裱框展示了。還有什麼事要做嗎？

女：[63] 你可以擺放一些用來發節目表的桌子嗎？

男：當然。地下室裡有一些桌子。我會請 Jacob 幫我把它們搬上來這裡。他的班在 15 分鐘後開始。

女：好。還有最後，[64] 我們需要一個地方讓粉絲們能在演出後和演員們合照。

男：[64] 我們把它設在和去年一樣的地方吧……進入大樓後的左邊那一區，就在要到茶點攤之前的地方。

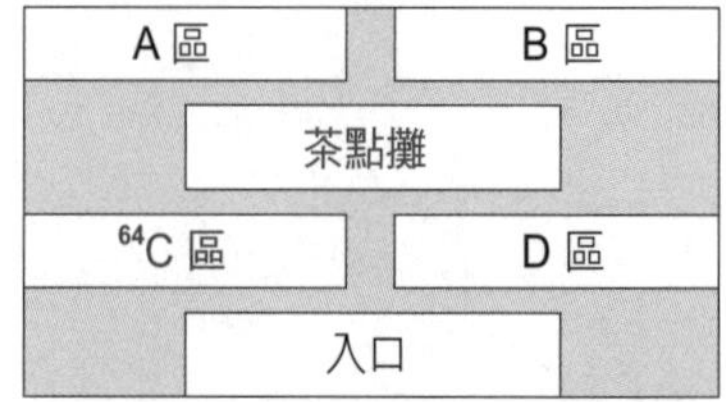

62 What type of event is happening tonight?

(A) A performance rehearsal
(B) An awards ceremony
(C) A movie screening
(D) A play opening

62 今晚要進行哪種活動？

(A) 表演彩排
(B) 頒獎典禮
(C) 電影放映
(D) 戲劇首演

63 What does the woman ask the man to do?

(A) Arrange some furniture
(B) Work a late shift
(C) Hang up some frames
(D) Greet incoming guests

63 女子要求男子做什麼？

(A) 擺放一些家具
(B) 上晚班
(C) 掛起一些相框
(D) 接待來賓

64 新 Look at the graphic. Where most likely will photos be taken?

(A) In Area A
(B) In Area B
(C) In Area C
(D) In Area D

64 請看圖表。最有可能會在哪裡拍照？

(A) A 區
(B) B 區
(C) C 區
(D) D 區

題目 auditorium [ˌɔdəˋtorɪəm] 劇院；禮堂 debut [deɪˋbju] 初次登台 frame [frem] 裱框；相框 display [dɪˋsple] 展示；展覽品 set up 擺放；設置 program [ˋprogræm] 節目表，行程計畫表 hand out 分發，發下 basement [ˋbesmənt] 地下室 shift [ʃɪft]（輪班制工作的）一班 cast [kæst]（電影、戲劇或演出的）演員陣容 refreshment [rɪˋfrɛʃmənt] 茶點 stand [stænd] 貨攤；攤位

62 screening [ˋskrinɪŋ] 放映 opening [ˋopənɪŋ]（戲劇的）首演；開頭

63 arrange [əˋrendʒ] 擺放；排列；安排 hang up 懸掛（在牆上等） greet [grit] 接待；問候 incoming [ˋɪnˌkʌmɪŋ] 即將到來的；進來的

62 細節事項相關問題—特定細項 答案 (D)

中

題目詢問今天晚上進行的活動類型，因此要注意提到題目關鍵字（tonight）的前後部分。女子說：「tonight's debut performance of the play *Going for Broke*」，提到今晚有一齣戲《Going for Broke》要進行首演，因此正確答案是 (D) A play opening。

換句話說

debut performance of the play 戲的首演 → play opening 戲劇首演

63 細節事項相關問題—要求 答案 (A)

中

題目詢問女子要求男子做什麼，因此要注意聽女子話中出現要求表達之後的內容。女子說：「Can you set up some tables where programs can be handed out?」，要求男子擺放要用來發節目表的桌子，因此正確答案是 (A) Arrange some furniture。

換句話說

set up some tables 擺放一些桌子 → Arrange some furniture 擺放一些家具

新 64 細節事項相關問題—圖表資料 答案 (C)

中

題目詢問可能的拍照地點，因此要注意和題目關鍵字（photos ~ taken）相關的內容。女子說：「we need a spot where fans can take photos with the cast after the show」，表示需要一個地方讓粉絲們能在演出後和演員們合照，接著男子說：「Let's put it[spot] ~ in the area to the left when you enter the building, just before you reach the refreshment stand.」，表示可以把拍照地點設置在進入大樓後的左邊那一區，就在要到茶點攤之前的地方，透過平面圖可以確認，將會進行拍照的地點是 C 區，因此正確答案是 (C) In Area C。

65 66 67 [新]

Questions 65-67 refer to the following conversation and coupon.

第 65-67 題請參考下列對話及優惠券。

加拿大式發音 → 英式發音

M: Excuse me. [65]**I'd like to buy a pad to make my bike's seat more comfortable. Do you have the Explorer XS Cushion in stock?**

W: Yes, it's right here. And you're in luck. [66]**The product has a retail price of $56, but it's currently marked down by 10 percent.**

M: That's great. Plus, I've got this coupon to use.

W: Hmm . . . Unfortunately, it won't be valid for this purchase.

M: Oh, I see what you mean. Well, I'll still take the pad. I need it as I'm going biking this weekend.

W: OK. [67]**If you're finished shopping, I can show you the way to the cashier area.**

M: [67]**Yes, this is all I'm looking for today.**

男：不好意思。[65] 我想要買一個墊子讓我的自行車座椅更舒服點。你們有 Explorer XS Cushion 的現貨嗎？

女：有的，就在這裡。而且你運氣很好。[66] 這款商品的零售價格是 56 美金，但它現在打九折。

男：太棒了。另外，我還有這張優惠券可以用。

女：嗯……不幸的是，這張優惠券不能用在這筆消費上。

男：噢，我懂妳的意思了。嗯，我還是要買這個墊子。我這個週末去騎自行車的時候需要它。

女：好的。[67] 如果你已經買完了，我可以帶你去結帳區。

男：[67] 是的，我今天要買的只有這個。

[新]

Pacific Sports Supplies

[66]20% off any purchase over $100

Valid until July 31
At all branches in California
May be combined with other discounts

Pacific 運動用品

[66] 任一消費超過 100 美金可享八折

7 月 31 日以前
於加州所有門市適用
可與其他折扣合併使用

65 What does the man ask about?

(A) The popularity of some merchandise
(B) The durability of a component
(C) The weight of some equipment
(D) The availability of an accessory

65 男子詢問什麼？

(A) 一些商品的受歡迎度
(B) 一個零件的耐用度
(C) 一些設備的重量
(D) 一個配件的可得性

66 [新] Look at the graphic. Why is the man unable to use the coupon?

(A) An expiration date has already passed.
(B) A branch is not participating in a promotion.
(C) A product is currently on sale.
(D) A purchase amount is too low.

66 請看圖表。男子為何無法使用這張優惠券？

(A) 已經過期了。
(B) 分店沒有參加促銷活動。
(C) 產品正在特價。
(D) 消費金額太低。

67 What will the woman probably do next?

(A) Provide gear recommendations
(B) Restock a bike display
(C) Lead a customer to a checkout
(D) Process a request for a refund

67 女子接下來可能會做什麼？

(A) 推薦裝備
(B) 補自行車顯示器的貨
(C) 帶一位顧客去結帳台
(D) 處理一筆退款的要求

題目 pad [pæd]（座椅的）墊子　in stock 有庫存的　retail [`ritel] 零售的　currently [`kɝəntlɪ] 現在，目前
mark down 調降價格　valid [`vælɪd] 有效的；站得住腳的　purchase [美] `pɝtʃəs [英] `pə:tʃəs] 購買；消費

65 merchandise [`mɝtʃən͵daɪz] 貨物，商品　durability [͵djʊrə`bɪlətɪ] 耐用度；耐久性
component [kəm`ponənt] 零件；（機器、設備等的）構成要素　weight [wet] 重量
availability [ə͵velə`bɪlətɪ] 可得性；可用性　accessory [æk`sɛsərɪ] 附件；配件

66 expiration date 截止日期　participate in 參加～　promotion [prə`moʃən] 促銷活動；宣傳；升職　on sale 特價

67 gear [gɪr] 裝備　recommendation [͵rɛkəmɛn`deʃən] 推薦　restock [ri`stɑk] 補貨　checkout [`tʃɛk͵aʊt] 結帳台
process [`prɑsɛs] 處理　request [rɪ`kwɛst] 要求　refund [`ri͵fʌnd] 退款

65 ■ 細節事項相關問題—特定細項 答案 (D)

中

題目詢問男子詢問什麼，因此必須注意聽男子說的話。男子說：「I'd like to buy a pad to make my bike's seat more comfortable. Do you have the Explorer XS Cushion in stock?」，表示想買讓自行車座椅更舒適的墊子，並詢問 Explorer XS Cushion 這件商品是否有現貨，因此正確答案是 (D) The availability of an accessory。

新 66 ■ 細節事項相關問題—圖表資料 答案 (D)

難

題目詢問男子不能使用優惠券的原因，因此必須確認題目提供的優惠券上的資訊，並注意和題目關鍵字（unable to use）相關的內容。女子說：「The product has a retail price of $56, but it's currently marked down by 10 percent.」，表示產品零售價是 56 美金，現在打九折，透過優惠券上面寫的內容可知，消費要超過 100 美金才能使用優惠券，但這個墊子的價格低於 100 美金，因此正確答案是 (D) A purchase amount is too low.。

67 ■ 細節事項相關問題—接下來要做的事 答案 (C)

中

題目詢問女子接下來可能會做的事，因此必須注意對話的最後部分。女子對男子說：「If you're finished shopping, I can show you the way to the cashier area.」，表示如果已經買完了，那她可以帶男子去結帳區，而男子回答：「Yes, this is all I'm looking for today.」，表示他今天要買的只有這個，由此可知，女子接下來將帶男子去結帳區，因此正確答案是 (C) Lead a customer to a checkout。

68 69 70 新

Questions 68-70 refer to the following conversation and flight schedule.

第 68-70 題請參考下列對話及航班時刻表。

澳洲式發音 → 美式發音

M: Let's hurry, Kelsey. [68]**I'm concerned we won't catch our connecting flight to our destination.**

W: Wait—look here. [70]**This screen says our flight has been delayed.**

M: Yeah, you're right. In that case, [69]**I'd like to find a spot in this terminal that provides Wi-Fi. I need to download the lecture notes from the sales conference we attended in Cincinnati.**

W: Just so you know, there's a charge to use the airport's Internet service.

M: Really? I'd rather not pay a fee. Well, [70]**I should still have time to review the notes before our noon meeting today in Portland.**

W: Yeah. Ms. Anderson probably won't ask us much about the conference anyway. She'll be more interested in whether we secured any sales contracts on our trip.

男：我們要快一點，Kelsey。[68] 我擔心我們會趕不上飛往目的地的中轉航班。

女：等等——看這裡。[70] 這個螢幕上說我們的班機延誤了。

男：對耶，妳說得沒錯。這樣的話，[69] 我想要在這座航廈裡找個有無線網路的地方。我得下載我們在辛辛那提參加的那場銷售會議的講座筆記。

女：提醒你一下，使用機場網路服務是要收費的。

男：真的嗎？我不太想付費。嗯，[70] 在我們今天在波特蘭開午間會議之前，我應該還有時間複習這些筆記。

女：是啊，反正 Anderson 小姐可能不會問我們很多跟這場會議有關的事。她會對我們這次出差是否有拿到任何銷售合約更感興趣。

新

Flight	Destination	Status	Updated Arrival Time
AB701	Phoenix	On Time	9:00 A.M.
[70]**UR770**	**Portland**	**Delayed**	10:30 A.M.
WX803	Cincinnati	Delayed	12:00 P.M.
ZP890	Portland	On Time	3:30 P.M.
TA900	Dallas	Delayed	6:00 P.M.

航班	目的地	狀態	最新抵達時間
AB701	鳳凰城	準點	早上 9 點
[70]UR770	波特蘭	延誤	早上 10 點 30 分
WX803	辛辛那提	延誤	中午 12 點
ZP890	波特蘭	準點	下午 3 點 30 分
TA900	達拉斯	延誤	下午 6 點

68 Why is the man worried?

(A) A ticket was not printed.
(B) An airport is located far away.
(C) A flight might be missed.
(D) A terminal has been blocked off.

68 男子為什麼擔心？

(A) 沒有把一張票券印出來。
(B) 一座機場位在很遙遠的地方。
(C) 可能會錯過一架航班。
(D) 一座航廈已被封閉。

69 What does the man want to do?

(A) Listen to a lecture on a laptop
(B) Access the Internet
(C) Check in at a gate
(D) Inform a supervisor of an arrival time

69 男子想要做什麼？

(A) 在筆記型電腦上聽講座
(B) 使用網路
(C) 在登機門報到
(D) 告知主管抵達時間

70 Look at the graphic. Which flight will the speakers take?

新

(A) UR770
(B) WX803
(C) ZP890
(D) TA900

70 請看圖表。說話者會搭哪一架航班？

(A) UR770
(B) WX803
(C) ZP890
(D) TA900

題目 delay [dɪˋle] 延遲；延誤 lecture note 講座筆記 attend [əˋtɛnd] 參加 charge [tʃɑrdʒ] 費用；索價 review [rɪˋvju] 重新檢視；複習 secure [sɪˋkjʊr] 確保；獲得 contract [ˋkɑntrækt] 合約

68 block off 封閉（道路等）；封鎖（出入口等）

69 access [ˋæksɛs] 存取（電腦裡的資料）；使用 check in（搭飛機或入住旅館時）報到 inform [ɪnˋfɔrm] 告知 supervisor [ˌsupəˋvaɪzə] 主管，管理者

68 ■ 細節事項相關問題—問題點　答案 (C)

低

題目詢問男子感到擔心的原因，因此必須注意男子話中出現負面表達之後的內容。男子說：「I'm concerned we won't catch our connecting flight to our destination.」，表示擔心會趕不上飛往目的地的中轉航班，因此正確答案是 (C) A flight might be missed.。

69 ■ 細節事項相關問題—特定細項　答案 (B)

中

題目詢問男子想做什麼，因此必須注意和題目關鍵字（man want to do）相關的內容。男子說：「I'd like to find a spot in this terminal that provides Wi-Fi. I need to download the lecture notes from the sales conference we attended in Cincinnati.」，表示想在航廈裡找個有無線網路的地方，並接著說自己得下載在辛辛那提參加的那場銷售會議的講座筆記，因此正確答案是 (B) Access the Internet。

新 70 ■ 細節事項相關問題—圖表資料　答案 (A)

難

題目詢問說話者們會搭哪架航班，因此必須確認題目提供的航班時刻表，並注意和題目關鍵字（flight ~ speakers take）相關的內容。女子說：「This screen says our flight has been delayed.」，表示說話者們預計要搭的航班已經延誤了，之後男子說：「I should ~ have time to review the notes before our noon meeting today in Portland」，表示應該有時間在今天中午於波特蘭開會前複習筆記，透過圖表可知，延誤的航班中，前往波特蘭的 UR770 是說話者們要搭的航班，因此正確答案是 (A) UR770。

71
72
73

Questions 71-73 refer to the following recorded message.

美式發音

Hello, Mr. Richter. This is Deloris Burke from Anytime Optical. As a friendly reminder, you have a 3:30 P.M. appointment on Saturday, January 13. Also, [71]**we moved our main office . . . It's now on Clyde Boulevard**, right next door to the Devon Art Gallery. To avoid any complications during your visit, [72]**we ask that you have your current pair of glasses and a copy of your latest prescription on hand.** Our optometrist will need to look at them both before conducting your eye examination. [73]**Please arrive at least 15 minutes early, as you'll need to fill out a couple of brief forms.**

71 What was changed recently?

(A) The name of a company
(B) The time of an appointment
(C) The cost of a service
(D) The location of a business

72 What is the listener asked to do?

(A) Request new glasses
(B) Contact a physician
(C) Arrange an examination
(D) Bring a document

73 Why should the listener show up early?

(A) To talk with a specialist
(B) To pay an outstanding bill
(C) To complete some paperwork
(D) To take a short test

第 71-73 題請參考下列錄音訊息。

哈囉，Richter 先生。我是 Anytime 光學的 Deloris Burke。友善提醒，您在 1 月 13 日星期六下午 3 點 30 分有預約。此外，[71] 我們的總部搬家了……現在在 Clyde 大道上，就在 Devon 藝廊的隔壁。為免您在造訪期間碰上任何困難，[72] 我們希望您把您目前一副眼鏡及最新一份處方箋帶在手邊。我們的驗光師在為您檢查眼睛之前需要先查看它們。[73] 請提早至少 15 分鐘抵達，因為您會需要填寫兩份簡表。

71 最近改變了什麼？

(A) 公司名稱
(B) 預約時間
(C) 服務收費
(D) 公司位置

72 聽者被要求做什麼？

(A) 索取新眼鏡
(B) 聯絡醫師
(C) 安排檢查
(D) 攜帶文件

73 聽者為何應該提早到？

(A) 要和專家談話
(B) 要支付未結清的帳單
(C) 要完成一些文書資料
(D) 要接受簡短的測試

題目 prescription [prɪˋskrɪpʃən] 處方箋　on hand 在手邊，在身邊　optometrist [ɑpˋtɑmətrɪst] 驗光師
examination [ɪgˌzæməˋneʃən] 檢查；檢視
72 physician [fɪˋzɪʃən]（內科）醫師
73 specialist [ˋspɛʃəlɪst] 專家　outstanding [ˋaʊtˋstændɪŋ] 未結清的；未解決的　complete [kəmˋplit] 完成
paperwork [ˋpepɚˌwɝk] 文書資料；文書工作

71 **細節事項相關問題—特定細項** 　答案 (D)
低

題目詢問最近改變了什麼，因此要注意和題目關鍵字（changed recently）相關的內容。獨白說：「we moved our main office ~. It's now on Clyde Boulevard」，表示總部搬家了，現在總部位在 Clyde 大道上，由此可知，最近公司的位置改變了，因此正確答案是 (D) The location of a business。

72 **細節事項相關問題—要求** 　答案 (D)
中

題目詢問聽者被要求做什麼，因此要注意聽獨白中後半段裡與要求相關的表達。獨白說：「we ask that you have ~ a copy of your latest prescription on hand」，表示要求聽者攜帶最新一份處方箋，因此正確答案是 (D) Bring a document。

73 **細節事項相關問題—理由** 　答案 (C)
中

題目詢問聽者應該要提早抵達的原因，因此必須注意提到題目關鍵字（early）的前後部分。獨白說：「Please arrive at least 15 minutes early, as you'll need to fill out a couple of brief forms.」，表示聽者至少要提前 15 分鐘抵達，因為到時會需要填寫兩份簡表，因此正確答案是 (C) To complete some paperwork。

換句話說

fill out ~ forms 填寫表格 → complete ~ paperwork 完成文書資料

74
75
76

Questions 74-76 refer to the following broadcast.

澳洲式發音

And now for an entertainment update . . . The musical *City Streets* will run from March 27 to April 4 at the Conway Theater. [74]**This is the first production at the theater since it was purchased by Eastwood Entertainment earlier this year.** In a press conference this morning, [75]**a company representative confirmed that the original cast members would be featured, including actor Gerald Frey**. Of course, tickets will go quickly, as [75]**many people will want to take advantage of this opportunity to see him on stage**. The theater will begin selling tickets on February 20, and prices are expected to range from $35 to $65. And for those of you who aren't aware, the theater was renovated last month, so be sure to [76]**look at the updated seating map on its Web site.**

第 74-76 題請參考下列廣播。

然後現在是最新娛樂消息……音樂劇《City Streets》將於 3 月 27 日至 4 月 4 日在 Conway 劇院演出。[74] 這是自今年稍早被 Eastwood 娛樂買下後，第一部在這間劇院上演的作品。在今天早上的一場記者會中，[75] 一位公司代表證實將由原班底演員主演，包括演員 Gerald Frey。當然，門票會賣得很快，因為 [75] 很多人都會想要利用這個機會看他登台演出。劇院將於 2 月 20 日開始售票，售價預期會在 35 美金到 65 美金之間。此外提醒沒注意到的聽眾們，這間劇院在上個月整修了，所以一定要 [76] 上它網站看看最新的座位圖。

74 What is mentioned about the Eastwood Entertainment?
(A) It is planning a fundraiser.
(B) It has recently relocated.
(C) It will hire a new manager.
(D) It purchased a venue.

74 關於 Eastwood 娛樂，提到了什麼？
(A) 正在規劃募款活動。
(B) 最近搬遷了。
(C) 會聘用一位新的經理。
(D) 買了一個場地。

75 新 What does the speaker imply when he says, "tickets will go quickly"?
(A) A theater has few seats.
(B) A deal is ending.
(C) A price is reasonable.
(D) An actor is famous.

75 當說話者說：「門票會賣得很快」，是暗示什麼？
(A) 劇院的座位很少。
(B) 交易要結束了。
(C) 售價很合理。
(D) 演員很有名。

76 What does the speaker recommend that listeners do?
(A) View an online map
(B) Purchase a discounted ticket
(C) Attend a press conference
(D) Call a local theater

76 說話者建議聽者們做什麼？
(A) 看一張網路上的圖
(B) 買一張折扣後的票
(C) 參加一場記者會
(D) 打電話給一家當地的劇院

題目 run [rʌn] 持續進行　production [prəˋdʌkʃən]（戲劇、電影等）作品；製造；生產　press conference 記者會
confirm [美 kənˋfɝm 英 kənˋfə:m] 確認；證實　cast [美 kæst 英 kɑ:st] 演出陣容
feature [美 fitʃɚ 英 fi:tʃə]（電影等）由～主演；以～為特色　take advantage of 利用～　range from ~ to 在～之間
74 fundraiser [ˋfʌndˏrezɚ] 募款活動　venue [ˋvɛnju]（演唱會、運動競賽、演講等的）場地

74 細節事項相關問題—提及 中　答案 (D)

題目詢問提到什麼有關 Eastwood 娛樂的事，因此必須注意提到題目關鍵字（Eastwood Entertainment）的前後部分。獨白說：「This[musical *City Streets*] is the first production at the theater since it was purchased by Eastwood Entertainment earlier this year.」，表示音樂劇《City Streets》是這間劇院在被 Eastwood 娛樂買下後上演的第一部作品，由此可知，Eastwood 娛樂購買了場地，因此正確答案是 (D) It purchased a venue.。

新 **75** 細節事項相關問題—掌握意圖 高　答案 (D)

題目詢問說話者意圖，因此要注意題目引用句（tickets will go quickly）的前後部分。獨白說：「a company representative confirmed that the original cast members would be featured, including actor Gerald Frey」，表示這部劇會由包含演員 Gerald Frey 在內的原班底主演，之後說：「many people will want to take advantage of this opportunity to see him[actor Gerald Frey] on stage」，表示很多人會想藉此機會看 Gerald Frey 登台，由此可知這位演員很有名，因此答案是 (D) An actor is famous.。

76 細節事項相關問題—提議 低　答案 (A)

題目詢問說話者建議聽者們要做什麼，因此要注意聽出現在獨白後半段與提議表達相關的內容。獨白說：「look at the updated seating map on its Web site」，表示建議聽眾要去網站上看最新的座位圖，因此正確答案是 (A) View an online map。

77
78
79

Questions 77-79 refer to the following introduction.

英式發音

I'd like to begin by introducing myself. My name is Catherine Coulson, and [77]**I'm the consultant who has been hired to advise your team on marketing techniques**. As far as my credentials go, I worked in the field of market research for two decades before [78]**branching out on my own to found Prime Advertising Services five years ago**. Throughout my career, I've consulted for dozens of the country's largest companies with much success. [79]**Over the next two weeks, I'm going to collaborate with you all to create a series of online advertisements** to ensure your firm's brand recognition among consumers. Together, I think we can greatly improve your company's standing in the market.

77 Who is the speaker?

(A) A research assistant
(B) A corporate advisor
(C) A product engineer
(D) A Web site designer

78 What did the speaker do five years ago?

(A) Started a new company
(B) Created a social media platform
(C) Oversaw a business merger
(D) Accepted a job at an agency

79 What will happen over the next two weeks?

(A) Discounts will be offered.
(B) A survey will be conducted.
(C) A campaign will be developed.
(D) Evaluations will be performed.

第 77-79 題請參考下列介紹。

我想從介紹我自己開始。我的名字是 Catherine Coulson，[77] 我是受聘來就你們團隊在行銷技巧上提供建議的顧問。在我的資歷介紹方面，在 [78] 我五年前自立門戶創立 Prime 廣告服務之前，我在市場調查領域裡工作了二十年。在我整個職業生涯之中，我曾為數十間國內最大的公司提供諮詢且成效顯著。[79] 在接下來的兩星期，我將與你們大家合作打造一系列的線上廣告，以確保你們公司在消費者間的品牌辨識度。大家一起，我相信我們能大大提升你們公司在市場中的地位。

77 說話者是誰？

(A) 研究助理
(B) 企業顧問
(C) 產品工程師
(D) 網站設計師

78 說話者在五年前做了什麼？

(A) 創立一間新公司
(B) 創造一個社群媒體平台
(C) 監督一次企業合併
(D) 接受一份代理機構的工作

79 在接下來的兩星期會發生什麼？

(A) 會提供折扣。
(B) 會進行調查。
(C) 會制訂宣傳活動。
(D) 會進行評估。

題目 credential [krɪ`dɛnʃəl] 資格證書；資歷　branch out 開始發展（新工作或新業務等）　found [faʊnd] 建立
dozen [`dʌzn̩] 數十；一打　collaborate [kə`læbə͵ret] 合作　ensure (美) ɪn`ʃʊr (英) in`ʃuə] 確保
brand recognition 品牌辨識度

78 platform [`plæt͵fɔrm]（電腦或智慧型手機可用的系統或軟體程式）平台　oversee [`ovə`si] 監督　merger [mɝdʒɚ] 合併

77 整體內容相關問題—說話者　中　答案 (B)

題目詢問說話者的身分，因此要注意聽和身分、職業相關的表達。獨白說：「I'm the consultant who has been hired to advise your team on marketing techniques」，表示自己受聘來擔任行銷技巧上的顧問，由此可知，說話者是位企業顧問，因此正確答案是 (B) A corporate advisor。

換句話說

consultant 顧問 → advisor 顧問

78 細節事項相關問題—特定細項　高　答案 (A)

題目詢問說話者在五年前做了什麼，因此必須注意提到題目關鍵字（five years ago）的前後部分。獨白說：「branching out on my own to found Prime Advertising Services five years ago」，表示五年前自立門戶，創立了 Prime 廣告服務，因此正確答案是 (A) Started a new company。

79 細節事項相關問題—接下來要做的事　高　答案 (C)

題目詢問接下來的兩星期會發生什麼，因此要注意提到題目關鍵字（next two weeks）的前後部分：「Over the next two weeks, I'm going to collaborate with you all to create a series of online advertisements」，表示接下來的兩星期會和大家合作打造一系列的線上廣告，因此正確答案是 (C) A campaign will be developed.。

換句話說

create a series of online advertisements 打造一系列的線上廣告 → A campaign ~ be developed 制訂宣傳活動

Questions 80-82 refer to the following advertisement.

加拿大式發音

[80]**At Recycled Tech, we specialize in the sale of used electronics.** We sell laptops, tablets, desktop computers, and much more, all of which are available at up to 60 percent off their original retail prices! Although you may be accustomed to purchasing new items, all of our products come with a one-year warranty, so you can buy with confidence! And in addition to great prices, [81]**we hold a drawing every month to give a free tablet to one lucky customer.** [82]**All you need to do to enter the drawing is to make a purchase of at least $100.** Both in-store and online purchases qualify for this offer, so be sure to shop at Recycled Tech today!

80 What type of business is being advertised?

(A) An electronics retailer
(B) A waste disposal company
(C) An appliance repair shop
(D) A computer manufacturer

81 According to the speaker, what happens each month?

(A) A device is put on sale.
(B) An exhibit is held.
(C) An item is given away.
(D) A donation is made.

82 How can listeners take part in a drawing?

(A) By becoming a member
(B) By making an online profile
(C) By using a coupon
(D) By spending a certain amount

第 80-82 題請參考下列廣告。

[80] 在 Recycled Tech，我們專門銷售二手電子產品。我們販售筆記型電腦、平板電腦、桌上型電腦及其他更多品項，全都能用原零售價四折起買到！儘管您可能慣於購買全新商品，但我們所有商品都附有一年保固，所以您可以放心購買！而且除了價格優惠以外，[81] 我們每個月都舉辦一次抽獎，送一台免費的平板電腦給一位幸運的客人。[82] 只要消費 100 美金以上就能參加抽獎。不論是店內或線上消費都符合這個抽獎的資格，所以今天一定要來 Recycled Tech 購物喔！

80 在廣告的是哪種公司？

(A) 電子產品零售商
(B) 廢棄物處理公司
(C) 器材維修行
(D) 電腦製造商

81 根據說話者所說，每個月會發生什麼？

(A) 一件裝置特價。
(B) 舉辦一個展覽。
(C) 贈送一項商品。
(D) 捐出一筆錢。

82 聽者們可以如何參加抽獎？

(A) 成為會員
(B) 建立線上簡介
(C) 使用優惠券
(D) 消費一定金額

題目 specialize [ˋspɛʃəlˌaɪz] 專門做 be accustomed to 慣於～ come with 附有～ warranty [ˋwɔrəntɪ] 保固；保證書 confidence [ˋkɑnfədəns] 信任；確信，把握 drawing [ˋdrɔɪŋ] 抽籤
80 waste [west] 廢棄物 disposal [dɪˋspozl̩] 處理
81 give away 贈送～
82 take part in 參與～ amount [əˋmaʊnt] 數額

80 低 整體內容相關問題—主題 答案 (A)

題目詢問廣告主題，因此必須注意聽獨白的開頭部分。獨白說：「At Recycled Tech, we specialize in the sale of used electronics.」，表示 Recycled Tech 專門販售二手電子產品，由此可知，在廣告的是電子產品零售商，因此正確答案是 (A) An electronics retailer。

81 中 細節事項相關問題—特定細項 答案 (C)

題目詢問每個月會發生什麼，因此要注意和題目關鍵字（each month）相關的內容。獨白說：「we hold a drawing every month to give a free tablet to one lucky customer」，表示每個月都會舉辦抽獎，送一位幸運的客人免費的平板電腦，因此正確答案是 (C) An item is given away.。

82 中 細節事項相關問題—方法 答案 (D)

題目詢問參加抽獎的方法，因此要注意提到題目關鍵字（drawing）的前後部分。獨白說：「All you need to do to enter the drawing is to make a purchase of at least $100.」，表示消費 100 美金以上就能參加抽獎，因此正確答案是 (D) By spending a certain amount。

換句話說

make a purchase of at least $100 消費 100 美金以上 → spending a certain amount 消費一定金額

83
84
85

Questions 83-85 refer to the following talk.	第 83-85 題請參考下列談話。
美式發音	
Western College will be holding a job fair on Saturday, September 14, for its students. The event will be an excellent way for [83]**a small investment company like ours** to reach out to potential future employees. That's why [84]**I'd like to have at least two staff members operate a booth at the event.** [85]**Informational pamphlets have already been made and printed.** So, [84]**those who volunteer would only be responsible for attending the event, answering attendees' questions, and passing out materials.** If this sounds like something you'd be willing to do, please let me know by the end of the week so that I can make the necessary arrangements.	Western 學院將於 9 月 14 日星期六為學生舉辦一場就業博覽會。這活動對 [83] 像我們這種小型投資公司來說，是接觸可能的未來員工的絕佳方法。這也就是為什麼 [84] 我希望至少有兩名員工去這個活動上擺一個攤位。[85] 說明用的小冊子已經印製好了。所以 [84] 自願去參加的人只需要負責出席活動、回答參加者的問題及發放資料。如果這聽起來像是你會願意去做的事，請在這週末前讓我知道，以便我進行必要的安排。
83 Where most likely does the speaker work? (A) At a university (B) At a print shop (C) At a financial firm (D) At an advertising agency	83 說話者最有可能在哪裡工作？ (A) 大學 (B) 影印店 (C) 金融公司 (D) 廣告代理商
84 Why are volunteers needed? (A) To plan a job fair for students (B) To rent an informational booth (C) To post flyers around a city (D) To represent a business at an event	84 為什麼需要自願者？ (A) 要為學生規劃就業博覽會 (B) 要租說明用的攤位 (C) 要在市內各處張貼傳單 (D) 要在活動中代表公司
85 According to the speaker, what has already been done? (A) A legal professional was contacted. (B) Some handouts were prepared. (C) Applications were collected. (D) Some questions were answered.	85 根據說話者所說，什麼已經完成了？ (A) 聯繫了一位法律專業人士。 (B) 準備了一些印刷品。 (C) 收集了申請書。 (D) 回答了一些問題。

題目 fair [fɛr] 集會 potential [pəˋtɛnʃəl] 潛在的；可能的 pass out 分發；分配 arrangement [əˋrendʒmənt] 安排；排列
83 agency [ˋedʒənsɪ] 代理商；代理機構

83 中 **整體內容相關問題—說話者** 答案 (C)

題目詢問說話者的工作地點，因此要注意聽和身分、職業相關的表達。獨白說：「a small investment company like ours」，提到「像我們這種小型投資公司」，由此可知，說話者在金融公司裡工作，因此正確答案是 (C) At a financial firm。

84 高 **細節事項相關問題—理由** 答案 (D)

題目詢問需要自願者的原因，因此必須注意和題目關鍵字（volunteers needed）相關的內容。獨白說：「I'd like to have at least two staff members operate a booth at the event」，表示希望至少有兩名員工去擺攤，接著說：「those who volunteer would only be responsible for attending the event, answering attendees' questions, and passing out materials」，表示自願者只需要負責出席活動、回答參加者的問題及發放資料，因此正確答案是 (D) To represent a business at an event。

85 中 **細節事項相關問題—特定細項** 答案 (B)

題目詢問已經完成了什麼，因此要注意獨白中和題目關鍵字（already ~ done）相關的內容。獨白說：「Informational pamphlets have already been made and printed.」，表示說明用的小冊子已經印製完成，因此正確答案是 (B) Some handouts were prepared。

換句話說

Informational pamphlets have ~ been made and printed 說明用的小冊子已經印製好了
→ handouts were prepared 準備了一些印刷品

86
87
88

Questions 86-88 refer to the following excerpt from a meeting.

加拿大式發音

Just a quick note about the training session on next Tuesday… [86]**I know you've all been busy this week creating the newest version of our anti-virus application**, but [87]**you should still attend the session. It's going to be crucial**. In fact, I'm even willing to give you an extra day to finish up your project, if necessary. The company has hired a renowned expert on Internet security to conduct this workshop, and I'm certain he will have a lot of useful information to share. [88]**You should sign up this morning**, though. Some of the other team leaders mentioned that they were going to encourage their staff members to participate as well. I don't want you to lose out on this opportunity.

第 86-88 題請參考下列會議節錄。

簡單說一下和下週二培訓課程有關的事……[86] 我知道你們大家這週全都在忙著製作我們最新版本的防毒應用程式，但 [87] 你們仍應參加這次課程。這件事相當重要。事實上，若有必要，我甚至願意多給你們一天時間來完成你們的專案。公司聘請了知名的網路安全專家來進行這次的工作坊，我相信他會有很多有用的資訊可以分享。不過，[88] 你們應該要在今天早上報名。其他有幾位組長也提到他們會鼓勵他們的組員參加。我不希望你們錯過這次的機會。

86 What are the listeners working on this week?

(A) Designing an electronic device
(B) Preparing for a trade show
(C) Organizing a corporate workshop
(D) Developing a software program

86 聽者們這週在處理什麼？

(A) 設計一款電子設備
(B) 準備一場貿易展
(C) 籌備一場企業工作坊
(D) 開發一款軟體程式

87 新 What does the speaker imply when he says, "I'm even willing to give you an extra day to finish up your project"?

(A) A machine still needs to be fixed.
(B) A team has too few personnel.
(C) A training session is important.
(D) A lot of problems have been found.

87 說話者說：「我甚至願意多給你們一天時間來完成你們的專案」，是暗示什麼？

(A) 還是必須把一台機器修好。
(B) 一個團隊的人手太少。
(C) 一個培訓課程很重要。
(D) 已經發現了很多問題。

88 What does the speaker recommend?

(A) Registering for an event
(B) Meeting with superiors
(C) Reviewing a program
(D) Conducting a study

88 說話者建議什麼？

(A) 報名一場活動
(B) 和上級會面
(C) 檢視一個程式
(D) 進行一項研究

題目 be willing to 願意做～；樂於～ necessary [ˋnɛsə͵sɛrɪ] 必需的；必要的 renowned [rɪˋnaʊnd] 有名的；有名聲的 expert [ˋɛkspɝt] 專家 conduct [kənˋdʌkt] 引導；帶領；實施 certain [ˋsɝtən] 確信的；有把握的 useful [ˋjusfəl] 有用的 participate [pɑrˋtɪsə͵pet] 參加 lose out 錯失

86 trade show 貿易展 corporate [ˋkɔrpərɪt] 企業的，公司的 develop [dɪˋvɛləp] 開發；制定

87 personnel [͵pɝsn̩ˋɛl]（總稱）員工，人員

86 中 **細節事項相關問題—特定細項** 答案 (D)

題目詢問聽者們本週在處理什麼，因此要注意提到題目關鍵字（this week）的前後部分：「I know you've all been busy this week creating the newest version of our anti-virus application」，表示自己知道大家這週都在忙著製作最新版本的防毒應用程式，由此可知，聽者們本週都在開發軟體程式，因此正確答案是 (D) Developing a software program。

換句話說

creating the ~ application 製作應用程式 → Developing a software program 開發軟體程式

新 **87** 中 **細節事項相關問題—掌握意圖** 答案 (C)

題目詢問說話者意圖，因此要注意提到題目引用句（I'm even willing to give you an extra day to finish up your project）的前後部分。獨白說：「you should ~ attend the session. It's going to be crucial.」，表示聽者們應該去參加課程，這件事相當重要，由此可知，培訓課程很重要，因此正確答案是 (C) A training session is important.。

88 低 **細節事項相關問題—提議** 答案 (A)

題目詢問說話者建議什麼，因此要注意聽獨白後半部裡有出現提議相關表達的句子。獨白說：「You should sign up this morning」，表示聽者們應該要在今天早上報名工作坊，因此正確答案是 (A) Registering for an event。

TEST 1 2 3 4 5 6 7 8 9 10

89 90 91

Questions 89-91 refer to the following telephone message.

第 89-91 題請參考下列電話留言。

美式發音

Hello, this is Olga Nabokov. I live at 4209 Grand Avenue, and [89]**I'm calling because I'm very unhappy with the lawn care service your company recently provided.** My front lawn has more weeds than usual this year, so I arranged for one of your employees to spray a chemical on it last Sunday. [90]**I was told that the substance he used would kill the weeds within a few days of its application, but a week has passed without any noticeable change.** I think he needs to visit my home again. [91]**Please call me at 555-0583 to discuss a date and time.** I would prefer next Saturday afternoon, if possible. Thank you.

哈囉。我是 Olga Nabokov。我住在 Grand 大道 4209 號，[89] 我打來是因為我對於你們公司最近提供的草坪養護服務非常不滿意。我家前面的草坪今年長了比往常更多的雜草，所以我上星期日請你們一位員工來噴灑化學藥劑。[90] 他告訴我他用的這種物質會在施用後的幾天內殺死那些雜草，但一個禮拜過去了卻沒有什麼明顯的改變。我覺得他必須再來我家一趟。[91] 請打 555-0583 給我來討論日期和時間。如果可能的話，我比較希望在下星期六下午。謝謝你。

89 What is the purpose of the call?

(A) To cancel a payment
(B) To change a service
(C) To confirm an address
(D) To make a complaint

89 這通電話的目的是什麼？

(A) 取消付款
(B) 更改服務
(C) 確認地址
(D) 提出申訴

90 新 What does the speaker mean when she says, "I think he needs to visit my home again"?

(A) A package was not delivered.
(B) A worker was not available.
(C) A treatment was not effective.
(D) A task was not agreed upon.

90 當說話者說：「我覺得他必須再來我家一趟」，意思是什麼？

(A) 一個包裹沒有送達。
(B) 一位員工沒有空。
(C) 一項處置沒有效果。
(D) 一件任務未取得一致意見。

91 What does the speaker want to discuss?

(A) An application process
(B) A refund policy
(C) A future appointment
(D) A discount amount

91 說話者想要討論什麼？

(A) 一項申請的程序
(B) 一項退款的政策
(C) 一次未來的約定
(D) 一筆折扣的金額

題目 weed [wid] 雜草 spray [spre] 噴灑 chemical [ˋkɛmɪkl] 化學製品；化學藥劑 substance [ˋsʌbstəns] 物質；實質 application [ˌæpləˋkeʃən] 施用；申請 noticeable [ˋnotɪsəbl̩] 明顯的；值得注意的 prefer [prɪˋfɝ] 較喜歡，偏好

89 payment [ˋpemənt] 支付；支付款項 complaint [kəmˋplent] 抱怨；申訴

90 package [ˋpækɪdʒ] 包裹 treatment [ˋtritmənt] 處置；（施用藥品等手段的）治療 effective [ɪˋfɛktɪv] 有效的

91 refund [ˋriˌfʌnd] 退款 appointment [əˋpɔɪntmənt]（正式的）會面；（會面的）約定 amount [əˋmaʊnt] 總額；數量

89 整體內容相關問題—目的 答案 (D)

低

題目詢問來電目的，因此必須注意獨白的開頭部分。獨白說：「I'm calling because I'm very unhappy with the lawn care service your company recently provided」，表示自己是因為非常不滿意對方公司所提供的草坪養護服務，才會打這通電話，由此可知，說話者是為了申訴而打電話，因此正確答案是 (D) To make a complaint。

新 **90** 細節事項相關問題—掌握意圖 答案 (C)

高

題目詢問說話者意圖，因此要注意提到題目引用句（I think he needs to visit my home again）的前後部分。獨白說：「I was told that the substance he[one of your employees] used would kill the weeds within a few days of its application, but a week has passed without any noticeable change.」，表示該公司員工說他用的這種物質，會在施用後的幾天內殺死那些雜草，但結果過了一個禮拜也沒有什麼明顯變化，由此可知，該公司員工對於雜草的處置無效，因此正確答案是 (C) A treatment was not effective.。

91 細節事項相關問題—特定細項 答案 (C)

低

題目詢問說話者想討論什麼，因此要注意提到題目關鍵字（discuss）的前後部分。獨白說：「Please call me ~ to discuss a date and time.」，表示希望對方打電話給自己來討論日期和時間，因此正確答案是 (C) A future appointment。

92
93
94

Questions 92-94 refer to the following instructions.

英式發音

Good morning, and [92]**thanks for attending this one-day seminar on import and export laws** here in the United Kingdom. If you look at the program that was handed out earlier, you'll see that the seminar is going to be broken down into three main sections. [93]**During the first part of the meeting, I am going to give a lecture, in which I will discuss the most recent changes to the country's laws.** Following that, we will focus on a handful of well-known case studies that highlight breaches of those regulations. Finally, we will conclude by holding an open forum. At that point, [94]**you all will be given an opportunity to pose questions related to your specific industries.**

92 What is the topic of the seminar?

(A) Labor laws
(B) Trade regulations
(C) Investment strategies
(D) Overseas markets

93 What will most likely happen first?

(A) A case study will be reviewed.
(B) Guests will divide into groups.
(C) Programs will be handed out.
(D) A talk will be given.

94 According to the speaker, what will listeners be able to do?

(A) Work on independent exercises
(B) Inquire about their fields
(C) Take a brief break for lunch
(D) Turn in forms after the session

第 92-94 題請參考下列指示。

早安，[92] 感謝出席這場針對英國這裡的進出口法令的一日研討會。若您看到先前發放的課程表，您就會發現這次的研討會將分成三大部分。[93] 在這次會議的第一部分，我會進行一場講座，其中我會討論到本國最新的法令變更。在此之後，我們會專注於幾件重點在於違反了這些規定的知名個案研究。最後，我們會用進行公開討論來收尾。屆時 [94] 大家都會有機會能提出與您所屬特定產業有關的疑問。

92 研討會主題是什麼？

(A) 勞工法令
(B) 貿易規範
(C) 投資策略
(D) 海外市場

93 最有可能會先發生什麼？

(A) 檢視一個個案研究。
(B) 賓客會分成小組。
(C) 會發放課程表。
(D) 會進行一場演說。

94 根據說話者所說，聽者們將能做什麼？

(A) 進行獨自練習
(B) 詢問有關他們領域的事
(C) 短暫休息吃午餐
(D) 在會後繳交表格

題目 import [[美] `ɪmport [英] `impɔːt] 進口　export [[美] `ɛksport [英] `ekspɔːt] 出口
program [[美] `progræm [英] `prəugræm]（課程、節目等的）時間表；行程表　a handful of（數量不多的）幾個～
case [kes] 案例　breach [britʃ] 違反；破壞　open forum 公開討論會，公開論壇

94 independent [ˌɪndɪ`pɛndənt] 獨立的；獨自的　session [`sɛʃən] 集會；會議

92 細節事項相關問題—特定細項　答案 (B)

高

題目詢問研討會主題，因此要注意和題目關鍵字（topic of the seminar）相關的內容。獨白說：「thanks for attending this one-day seminar on import and export laws」，表示感謝出席這場針對進出口法令的一日研討會，因此正確答案是 (B) Trade regulations。

換句話說

import and export laws 進出口法令 → Trade regulations 貿易規範

93 細節事項相關問題—特定細項　答案 (D)

低

題目詢問最有可能會先發生什麼，因此要注意和題目關鍵字（happen first）相關的內容。獨白說：「During the first part of the meeting, I am going to give a lecture, in which I will discuss the most recent changes to the country's laws.」，表示在會議的第一部分會進行一場討論最新法令變更的講座，因此正確答案是 (D) A talk will be given.。

94 細節事項相關問題—特定細項　答案 (B)

中

題目詢問聽者們將可以做什麼，因此要注意聽和題目關鍵字（listeners be able to do）相關的內容。獨白說：「you all will be given an opportunity to pose questions related to your specific industries」，表示大家都會有機會能提出與所屬特定產業有關的疑問，因此正確答案是 (B) Inquire about their fields。

95
96
97

Questions 95-97 refer to the following talk and chart.

第 95-97 題請參考下列談話與圖表。

澳洲式發音

For those of you who don't know me, my name is Lucas Scott. **[95]I'm in charge of collecting and analyzing data about consumer trends. [96]I've been asked to discuss the results of the survey that I e-mailed to customers on our mailing list last Wednesday.** Um, we requested their opinions on our current line of products. Many were impressed with the design of our newest shoes . . . the Hornet Pumps. They said they plan to buy them even though they are more expensive than our other items. However, **[97]we got some negative feedback on our second-best-selling athletic shoes.** A number of customers indicated that they felt they weren't durable enough. Now . . . please turn your attention to the screen behind me to see my slideshow.

向不認識我的人介紹一下，我的名字是 Lucas Scott。[95] 我負責收集與分析有關消費者趨勢的數據。[96] 我被要求詳細說明我在上個星期三，以電子郵件寄給在我們郵寄名單上的顧客的那份調查的結果。嗯，我們要求他們就我們現有的系列產品提供意見。很多人對我們的最新鞋款……The Hornet Pumps 的設計感到印象深刻。他們表示，即使這款鞋比我們其他品項還要貴，他們還是打算要買。然而，[97] 我們在我們賣得第二好的運動鞋上收到了一些負面的回饋意見。一些客人表示他們覺得這款鞋不夠耐穿。現在……請把注意力轉向我身後的螢幕來看看我的投影片。

新

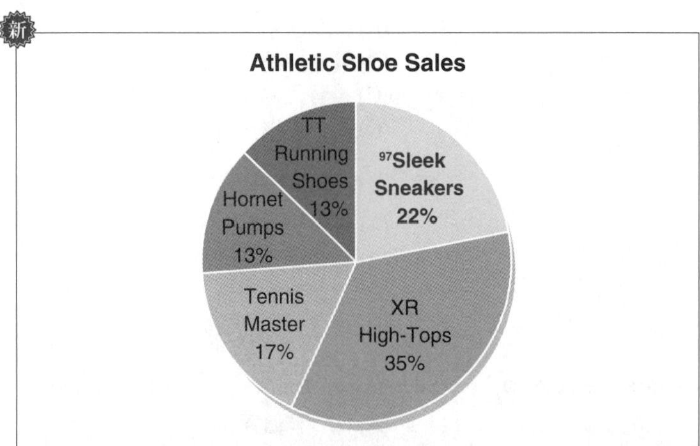

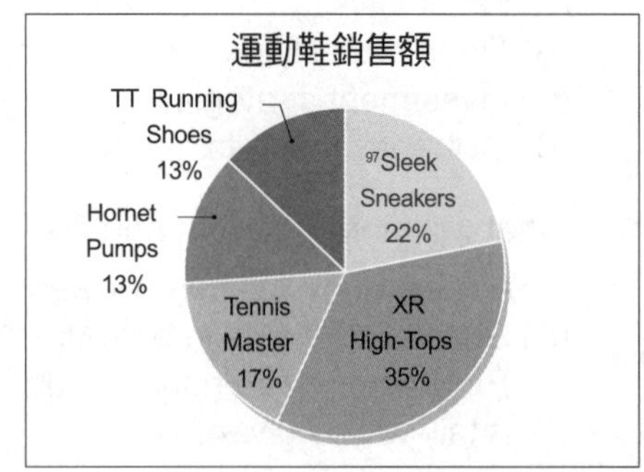

95 Who most likely is the speaker?

(A) A product designer
(B) A company spokesperson
(C) A research analyst
(D) A corporate lawyer

95 說話者最有可能是誰？

(A) 產品設計師
(B) 公司發言人
(C) 研究分析師
(D) 企業律師

96 What did the speaker do last week?

(A) Held an informal meeting
(B) Distributed questionnaires
(C) Responded to queries
(D) Tested merchandise

96 說話者上星期做了什麼？

(A) 舉行了非正式的會議
(B) 發送了問卷
(C) 回應了疑問
(D) 測試了商品

97 新 Look at the graphic. Which product are customers dissatisfied with?

(A) XR High-Tops
(B) Sleek Sneakers
(C) Tennis Master
(D) Hornet Pumps

97 請看圖表。顧客對哪個產品不滿意？

(A) XR High-Tops
(B) Sleek Sneakers
(C) Tennis Master
(D) Hornet Pumps

題目 analyze [ˋænḷ͵aɪz] 分析　impressed [ɪmˋprɛst] 感到印象深刻的；感到欽佩的　expensive [ɪkˋspɛnsɪv] 昂貴的
indicate [ˋɪndə͵ket] 表明；指出　durable [美 ˋdjʊrəbḷ 英 ˋdjurəbl] 耐用的；持久的

95 spokesperson [ˋspoks͵pɝsṇ] 發言人；代言人　analyst [ˋænḷɪst] 分析師

96 informal [ɪnˋfɔrmḷ] 非正式的　questionnaire [͵kwɛstʃənˋɛr] 問卷；意見調查表　query [ˋkwɪrɪ] 疑問
merchandise [ˋmɝtʃən͵daɪz] 商品，貨物

95 低 **整體內容相關問題—說話者** 答案 (C)

題目詢問說話者身分，因此要注意聽和身分、職業相關的表達。獨白說：「I'm in charge of collecting and analyzing data about consumer trends.」，表示自己負責收集與分析有關消費者趨勢的數據，因此正確答案是 (C) A research analyst。

96 中 **細節事項相關問題—特定細項** 答案 (B)

題目詢問說話者上星期做了什麼，因此必須注意和題目關鍵字（last week）相關的內容。獨白說：「I've been asked to discuss the results of the survey that I e-mailed to customers on our mailing list last Wednesday.」，表示自己被要求詳細說明有關上個星期三，以電子郵件寄給顧客的那份調查的結果，因此正確答案是 (B) Distributed questionnaires。

新 97 中 **細節事項相關問題—圖表資料** 答案 (B)

題目詢問顧客對哪個產品不滿意，因此在作答時須確認題目提供的圖表資料，並注意和題目關鍵字（customers dissatisfied with）相關的內容。獨白說：「we got some negative feedback on our second-best-selling athletic shoes」，表示在賣得第二好的運動鞋上收到了一些負面的回饋意見，透過圖表可知，顧客是對於賣得第二好的 Sleek Sneakers 不滿意，因此正確答案是 (B) Sleek Sneakers。

98
99
100

Questions 98-100 refer to the following talk and table.

英式發音

Welcome to the Sahara Wildlife Reserve. When [98]**your professor contacted us about arranging a special tour for his class members**, we were happy to accommodate his request. Today, I'll be showing you around the facility and introducing you to our director and some of the other people who work here . . . like the biologists and medical staff. The reserve currently covers an area of 500 acres, but [99]**an additional 100 acres will be . . . um . . . added to it later this fall**. We need all this space because we care for 200 animals from 60 different species. [100]**The first inhabitant that you're going to see arrived here 10 days ago. It is our only animal under six months old.** Her enclosure is just this way.

Animal Name	Species	Age
Mocha	[100]**Sand fox**	**5 months**
Ginger	Jackal	10 months
Omar	Hyena	6 years
Pebble	Ostrich	28 years

98 Who most likely are the listeners?

(A) Guest lecturers
(B) Government inspectors
(C) New employees
(D) University students

99 What is mentioned about the Sahara Wildlife Reserve?

(A) It relies entirely on donations.
(B) It will be expanded this year.
(C) It offers internship opportunities.
(D) It cannot take in any more animals.

100 Look at the graphic. What will the listeners see first?

(A) A sand fox
(B) A jackal
(C) A hyena
(D) An ostrich

第 98-100 題請參考下列談話與表格。

歡迎來到 Sahara 野生動植物保留區。當 [98] 你們教授與我們聯絡，說要為他班上的同學們安排一場特別導覽時，我們開心地答應了他的請求。今天我會帶你們參觀這座設施，並把你們介紹給我們主任和其他一些在這裡工作的人……像是生物學家和醫療人員。這個保留區目前占地 500 英畝，不過 [99] 今年秋天晚一點的時候將會增加……嗯……額外的 100 英畝。我們需要這一整個地方是因為我們照顧了由 60 個不同物種所組成的 200 隻動物。[100] 各位即將看到的第一隻棲息在這裡的動物，在 10 天前抵達了這裡。牠是我們唯一年齡在六個月以下的動物。往這邊走就是她的圍場。

動物名	物種	年齡
Mocha	[100] 沙狐	5 個月
Ginger	胡狼	10 個月
Omar	鬣狗	6 歲
Pebble	鴕鳥	28 歲

98 聽者們最有可能是誰？

(A) 客座講者
(B) 政府稽查人員
(C) 新進員工
(D) 大學生

99 關於 Sahara 野生動植物保留區，提到了什麼？

(A) 它完全仰賴捐款。
(B) 它今年將會被擴大。
(C) 它提供實習機會。
(D) 它無法收留更多動物了。

100 請看圖表。聽者們會先看到什麼？

(A) 一隻沙狐
(B) 一隻胡狼
(C) 一隻鬣狗
(D) 一隻鴕鳥

題目 wildlife [ˋwaɪldˏlaɪf] 野生動植物 reserve [美 rɪˋzɝv 英 riˋzəːv] 保留區；保存 professor [美 prəˋfɛsɚ 英 prəˋfesə] 教授
accommodate [美 əˋkɑməˏdet 英 əˋkɔmədeit] 為～提供所需；答應～的請託；容納 facility [fəˋsɪlətɪ] 設施
biologist [美 baɪˋɑlədʒɪst 英 baiˋɔlədʒist] 生物學家 medical [ˋmɛdɪkl] 醫療的 species [ˋspiʃiz] 物種
inhabitant [美 ɪnˋhæbətənt 英 inˋhæbitənt] 棲息動物；（某地區的）居住者
enclosure [美 ɪnˋkloʒɚ 英 inˋkləuʒə] 圈地；圍場
98 inspector [ɪnˋspɛktɚ] 稽查人員，視察人員
99 rely on 依賴～ donation [doˋneʃən] 捐款；捐獻

98 ■ 整體內容相關問題—聽者 答案 (D)

低

題目詢問聽者身分，因此要注意聽和身分、職業相關的表達。獨白說：「your professor contacted us about arranging a special tour for his class members」，表示自己接獲聽者們的教授聯繫，希望能為他班上的同學們安排一場特別導覽，由此可知，聽者們是大學生，因此正確答案是 (D) University students。

99 ■ 細節事項相關問題—提及 答案 (B)

中

題目詢問提到了什麼與 Sahara 野生動植物保留區有關的事，因此必須注意和題目關鍵字（Sahara Wildlife Reserve）相關的內容。獨白說：「an additional 100 acres will be ~ added to it[Sahara Wildlife Reserve] later this fall」，表示今年秋天晚一點的時候將會增加額外的 100 英畝，因此正確答案是 (B) It will be expanded this year.。

換句話說

additional 100 acres will be ~ added 將增加額外的 100 英畝 → will be expanded 將會被擴大

新 **100** ■ 細節事項相關問題—圖表資料 答案 (A)

中

題目詢問聽者們會先看到什麼，因此必須確認題目提供的圖表資料內容，並注意聽和題目關鍵字（see first）相關的內容。獨白說：「The first inhabitant that you're going to see arrived here 10 days ago. It is our only animal under six months old.」，表示即將看到的第一隻動物在 10 天前抵達了這裡，且是唯一年齡在六個月以下的動物，透過表格可以知道，最先看到的動物會是 5 個月大的沙狐，因此正確答案是 (A) A sand fox。

TEST 1 2 3 4 5 6 7 8 9 10

TEST 03

Part 1 原文・翻譯・解析

Part 2 原文・翻譯・解析

Part 3 原文・翻譯・解析 新

Part 4 原文・翻譯・解析 新

MP3 收錄於 TEST 03.mp3。

進行深入練習或複習時，可以一邊多聽幾次收錄各國口音的試題 MP3，一邊搭配解答中的中英對照翻譯和解析，以及單字記憶表和多元口音單字記憶 MP3，達到事半功倍的效果。

1
○○●
低

加拿大式發音

(A) The man is holding a power drill.
(B) The man is picking up one of the boards.
(C) The man is packing some tools.
(D) The man is cutting a piece of wood.

(A) 男子正拿著一支電鑽。
(B) 男子正在拿起其中一塊板子。
(C) 男子正在收拾一些工具。
(D) 男子正在切一塊木頭。

單人照片

答案 (A)

照片中一名男子拿著電鑽站在木板前。

(A) [○] 這裡正確描述男子拿著電鑽的模樣，所以是正確答案。
(B) [╳] picking up（正在拿起）和男子的動作無關，因此是錯誤選項。這裡使用照片中有出現的板子（boards）來造成混淆。
(C) [╳] packing（收拾）和男子的動作無關，因此是錯誤選項。這裡使用照片中有出現的工具（tools）來造成混淆。
(D) [╳] cutting（正在切）和男子的動作無關，因此是錯誤選項。這裡使用照片中有出現的一塊木頭（a piece of wood）來造成混淆。

單字　power drill 電鑽　pick up 拿起　board [bord] 板子　pack [pæk] 收拾；打包

2
○○●
低

英式發音

(A) They're placing their feet on a rug.
(B) They're installing an electronic device.
(C) They're watching television from a couch.
(D) They're repositioning some cushions.

(A) 他們正把腳放在地毯上。
(B) 他們正在安裝一項電子設備。
(C) 他們正在沙發上看著電視。
(D) 他們正在把一些靠墊換位置。

兩人以上的照片

答案 (C)

照片中一對男女正坐在沙發上看著電視。

(A) [╳] 照片中的人把腳放在沙發上，但這裡卻描述成放在地毯（rug）上，因此是錯誤選項。place 表示將某物放到某地，必須特別記住。
(B) [╳] installing（正在安裝）和照片中的人物動作無關，因此是錯誤選項。這裡使用和照片中出現的電視相關的 electronic device（電子設備）來造成混淆，必須特別留意。
(C) [○] 這裡正確描述一對男女坐在沙發上看著電視的模樣，所以是正確答案。
(D) [╳] repositioning（正在把～換位置）和照片中的人物動作無關，因此是錯誤選項。這裡使用照片中有出現的靠墊（cushions）來造成混淆。

單字　place [ples] 放置　rug [rʌg] 地毯　install [ɪn`stɔl] 安裝，設置　electronic device 電子設備
couch [kaʊtʃ] 沙發；躺椅　reposition [ˌripə`zɪʃən] 變換位置（到其他地點）；換～的位置

3
○●●
中

美式發音

(A) One woman is hanging up a gown.
(B) One woman is taking a measurement.
(C) A tailor is greeting some customers.
(D) A dress is being altered on a sewing machine.

(A) 有名女子正在掛起一件禮服。
(B) 有名女子正在測量尺寸。
(C) 一位裁縫正在接待一些客人。
(D) 正在一台縫紉機上修改一件禮服。

兩人以上的照片

答案 (B)

照片中一名女子正拿著尺在測量另一名女子的尺寸。

(A) [╳] 照片中的女子不是在掛起（hanging up）一件禮服，因此是錯誤選項。這裡使用照片中有出現的禮服（gown）來造成混淆。

(B) [○] 這裡正確描述一名女子正在測量尺寸的模樣，所以是正確答案。
(C) [╳] greeting（正在接待）和裁縫的動作無關，因此是錯誤選項。這裡使用照片中出現的裁縫（tailor）來造成混淆。
(D) [╳] 照片中沒有出現縫紉機（sewing machine），雖然照片中出現了禮服，但並非正在被修改（is being altered），因此是錯誤選項。

單字 hang up 懸掛 gown [gaʊn] 禮服；長袍 take a measurement 測量尺寸 tailor [`telɚ] 裁縫
greet [grit] 接待；打招呼 alter [`ɔltɚ] 修改；改變 sewing machine 縫紉機

4 ○●●● 高

加拿大式發音

(A) Trees are lined up alongside a building.
(B) Some cars are exiting a parking lot.
(C) The windows of a building are being cleaned.
(D) A banner is posted on a structure.

(A) 樹木沿著一棟建築物排列。
(B) 一些車輛正在離開停車場。
(C) 正在清潔一棟建築物的窗戶。
(D) 一張橫幅被張貼在一棟建築物上。

事物及風景照片 答案 (D)

仔細確認照片中建築物上張貼著橫幅的樣子及周遭環境。
(A) [╳] 樹木（Trees）並非沿著建築物排列，沿著建築物排列的是車輛，因此是錯誤選項。
(B) [╳] 照片中沒有正在離開停車場（exiting a parking lot）的車，因此是錯誤選項。注意不要聽到 Some cars（一些車輛）和 parking lot（停車場）就選擇這個答案。
(C) [╳] 照片中雖有窗戶，但並非正在被清潔（are being cleaned），因此是錯誤選項。注意不要聽到 The windows of a building（一棟建築物的窗戶）就選這個答案。
(D) [○] 這裡正確描述橫幅張貼在建築物上的樣子，所以是正確答案。這裡必須記得 structure 可以用來表示建築。

單字 line up 排列成行 parking lot 停車場 banner [`bænɚ] 橫幅；旗幟 structure [`strʌktʃɚ] 建築物

5 ○●●● 高

澳洲式發音

(A) Merchandise is being handed to a woman.
(B) Some bottles are being wrapped in paper.
(C) A store employee is putting up a sign.
(D) Meat is being removed from a display case.

(A) 正在把商品交給一名女子。
(B) 正在把一些瓶子包進紙張裡。
(C) 一名店員正在放上一個標示。
(D) 正在把肉從展示櫃裡移走。

兩人以上的照片 答案 (A)

仔細觀察一名女子正從店員手中接過物品的模樣和周遭事物的狀態。
(A) [○] 這裡正確描述店員正在把商品交給女子的樣子，所以是正確答案。
(B) [╳] 照片中出現了瓶子，但不是正在被包起來（are being wrapped），因此是錯誤選項。注意不要聽到 Some bottles（一些瓶子）就選擇這個答案。
(C) [╳] 照片中沒有正在放上標示（putting up a sign）的店員，因此是錯誤選項。
(D) [╳] 照片中出現了肉，但並非正在把肉移走（is being removed），因此是錯誤選項。注意不要聽到 Meat（肉）和 display case（展示櫃）就選擇這個答案。

單字 hand [hænd] 交給 wrap [ræp] 包；裹 put up 放上；設置 remove [rɪ`muv] 移除；移開
display case 展示櫃

6 ○○●● 中

英式發音

(A) A railroad track emerges from a tunnel.
(B) A train has arrived at a platform.
(C) A group of people has collected at a bus stop.
(D) A ticket agent is checking passes.

(A) 一列鐵軌從一條隧道中出現。
(B) 一列火車抵達了一個月台。
(C) 一群人已經聚集在一個公車站牌了。
(D) 一位售票員正在查票。

兩人以上的照片 答案 (B)

仔細觀察照片中火車正在進站的模樣，以及周遭事物的狀態。

(A) [╳] 透過照片無法確認隧道（tunnel）的存在與否，因此是錯誤選項。這裡使用照片中出現的鐵軌（railroad track）來造成混淆。

(B) [○] 這裡正確描述火車抵達月台的樣子，所以是正確答案。

(C) [╳] 人們聚集的地點是火車月台，而非選項描述的公車站牌（bus stop），因此是錯誤選項。注意不要聽到 A group of people has collected（一群人已經聚集）就選擇這個答案。

(D) [╳] 透過照片無法確認售票員（ticket agent）的存在與否，因此是錯誤選項。這裡使用和照片拍攝地點有關的 checking passes（正在查票）來造成混淆。

單字　railroad track 鐵軌　emerge [美 ɪ`mɝdʒ 英 i`məːdʒ] 出現；顯露
platform [美 `plætˌfɔrm 英 `plætˌfɔːm] 月台　collect [kə`lɛkt] 聚集

7 低

[audio] 美式發音 → 澳洲式發音

When are you heading to the medical convention?

(A) We've got a booth on the third floor.
(B) I'm departing on June 14.
(C) About twenty minutes from downtown.

你何時要前往醫學大會？

(A) 我們在三樓有一個攤位了。
(B) 我會在 6 月 14 日出發。
(C) 離市中心大概二十分鐘。

When 疑問句 答案 (B)

這是詢問何時要前往醫學大會的 When 疑問句。

(A) [╳] 這是利用和 convention（大會）相關的 booth（攤位）來造成混淆的錯誤選項。
(B) [○] 這裡提到 6 月 14 日出發，也就是要前往醫學大會的時間點，因此是正確答案。
(C) [╳] 題目詢問何時前往醫學大會，這裡卻回答前往市中心的所需時間，因此是錯誤選項。

單字 head [hɛd] 朝向；前往 medical [`mɛdɪkl̩] 醫學的；醫療的 depart [[美] dɪ`pɑrt [英] di`pɑ:t] 離開；出發
downtown [ˌdaʊn`taʊn] 市中心；城市裡的商業區

8 中

[audio] 加拿大式發音 → 美式發音

Who manages our corporate acquisitions?

(A) If everyone cooperates.
(B) He managed to arrive on time.
(C) That's the director's responsibility.

誰在處理我們的企業收購？

(A) 如果所有人都合作的話。
(B) 他設法準時抵達了。
(C) 那是董事的責任。

Who 疑問句 答案 (C)

這是詢問誰在處理企業收購的 Who 疑問句。

(A) [╳] 題目詢問誰在處理企業收購，這裡卻回答如果所有人都合作的話，毫不相關，因此是錯誤選項。這裡利用發音相似單字 corporate – cooperates 來造成混淆。
(B) [╳] 題目中沒有出現可用 He 代稱的對象，因此是錯誤選項。這裡藉著表達「設法達成」之意的 managed 來重複使用題目中的 manages（處理）以造成混淆。
(C) [○] 這裡回答那是董事的責任，提及處理企業收購的人，因此是正確答案。

單字 manage [`mænɪdʒ] 處理；設法達成 corporate [`kɔrpərɪt] 企業的，公司的
acquisition [ˌækwə`zɪʃən] 收購；取得 cooperate [ko`ɑpəˌret] 合作，協力 director [də`rɛktɚ] 董事；主管
responsibility [rɪˌspɑnsə`bɪlətɪ] 責任；義務

9 低

[audio] 英式發音 → 澳洲式發音

Currently, a train ticket to Barcelona costs 40 Euros.

(A) I'll take one, please.
(B) Luggage is stored separately.
(C) The exchange rate in Europe.

目前一張到巴塞隆納的火車票要 40 歐元。

(A) 我要一張，謝謝。
(B) 行李是分開存放的。
(C) 在歐洲的匯率。

陳述句 答案 (A)

這是表達目前一張到巴塞隆納的火車票要 40 歐元的客觀事實陳述句。

(A) [○] 這裡說要一張，表示自己願意付 40 歐元買去巴塞隆納的火車票，因此是正確答案。
(B) [╳] 這是利用和 train（火車）相關的 Luggage（行李）來造成混淆的錯誤選項。
(C) [╳] 這是利用和 Euros（歐元）相關的 exchange rate（匯率）、Europe（歐洲）來造成混淆的錯誤選項。

單字 currently [[美] `kɝəntlɪ [英] `kʌrəntli] 現在，目前 cost [[美] kɔst [英] kɔst] 要價～；花費 luggage [`lʌgɪdʒ] 行李
store [[美] stor [英] stɔ:] 保管；存放；商店 separately [`sɛpərɪtlɪ] 分別地 exchange rate 匯率

10 ○○●● 中

美式發音 → 加拿大式發音 Is Klein Avenue closed down throughout the weekend? (A) No, I don't own a truck any longer. (B) Throughout the main hallway. (C) Yes, a section has to be repaved.	Klein 大道這整個週末都封閉嗎？ (A) 不，我不再擁有卡車了。 (B) 遍布整個主廊道。 (C) 是的，有一區必須重鋪。

Be 動詞疑問句 答案 (C)

這是確認 Klein 大道是否整個週末都會封閉的 Be 動詞疑問句。

(A) [╳] 這是透過可藉著 Klein Avenue（Klein 大道）而聯想到的交通相關詞彙 truck（卡車）來造成混淆的錯誤選項。注意不要聽到 No 就選擇這個選項。

(B) [╳] 題目詢問 Klein 大道是否整個週末都會封閉，這裡卻回答遍布整個主廊道，毫不相關，因此是錯誤選項。這裡將題目中出現的 throughout（從頭到尾～）改以「遍布～」之意重複使用，企圖造成混淆。

(C) [○] 這裡以 Yes 來表示 Klein 大道這整個週末都會封閉，並附加說明「有一區必須重鋪」的資訊，因此是正確答案。

單字 close down 封閉 throughout [θru`aʊt] 遍布～；從頭到尾～ not ~ any longer 不再～ own [on] 擁有 hallway [`hɔl͵we] 走道，廊道 section [`sɛkʃən] 區；部分 repave [ri`pev] 重鋪

11 ○○○● 低

英式發音 → 澳洲式發音 Would you care to check your coat? (A) Yes, it's my boat. (B) Thanks, but I'm OK. (C) Write the check to Drew Howard.	您想要寄放您的大衣嗎？ (A) 是的，它是我的船。 (B) 謝謝，但不用了。 (C) 開支票給 Drew Howard。

提議疑問句 答案 (B)

這是詢問是否要寄放大衣的提議疑問句。這裡必須知道 Would you care to 是用來表示提議的表達。

(A) [╳] 這是利用發音相似單字 coat – boat 來造成混淆的錯誤選項。注意不要聽到 Yes 就選擇這個答案。

(B) [○] 這裡說「謝謝，但不用了」，表示拒絕提議，因此是正確答案。

(C) [╳] 題目詢問是否要寄放大衣，這裡卻回答開支票給 Drew Howard，毫不相關，因此是錯誤選項。這裡將題目中出現的 check（寄放）以名詞「支票」之義重複使用，企圖造成混淆。

單字 check [tʃɛk] 寄放；檢查；支票

12 ○○○● 低

英式發音 → 加拿大式發音 How often does your firm conduct quality control tests? (A) Every January and July. (B) There are three more spots. (C) I suggest using the remote control.	你公司多久進行一次品質管制測試？ (A) 每年的一月和七月。 (B) 還有三個地方。 (C) 我建議使用遙控器。

How 疑問句 答案 (A)

這是詢問公司進行品質管制測試頻率的 How 疑問句。這裡必須知道 How often 是詢問頻率。

(A) [○] 這裡回答每年的一月和七月，提到公司進行品質管制測試的頻率，因此是正確答案。

(B) [╳] 這是利用能夠表示頻率的數字 three，再加上能藉著 conduct ~ tests（進行測試）而聯想到的測試地點 spots（地方）來造成混淆的錯誤選項。

(C) [╳] 題目詢問公司進行品質管制測試的頻率，這裡卻回答建議使用遙控器，毫不相關，因此是錯誤選項。這裡企圖以重複使用題目中出現的 control 來造成混淆。

單字 conduct [kən`dʌkt] 實施，進行 quality control 品質管制 spot [spɑt] 地方；場所 suggest [sə`dʒɛst] 建議；暗示 remote control 遙控器

13 中

🔊 澳洲式發音 → 美式發音 Doesn't the bank have a smartphone application? (A) The bank has a location nearby. (B) You can download it for free. (C) A cover letter must be submitted with it.	這家銀行不是有智慧型手機的應用程式嗎？ (A) 這家銀行在附近有一間分行。 (B) 你可以免費下載它。 (C) 一定要一併提交一封求職信。

否定疑問句 答案 (B)

這是詢問銀行是否有智慧型手機的應用程式的否定疑問句。

(A) [╳] 題目詢問銀行是否有智慧型手機的應用程式，這裡卻回答該銀行在附近有一間分行，毫不相關，因此是錯誤選項。這裡將題目中出現的 bank have 以 bank has 的形式來重複使用，企圖造成混淆。

(B) [○] 這裡回答可以免費下載，間接表示銀行有智慧型手機的應用程式，因此是正確答案。

(C) [╳] 這是利用與題目中 application（應用程式）的另外一個意思「申請書」相關的 cover letter（求職信）和 submitted（提交）來造成混淆的錯誤選項。

單字 application [[美] ˌæpləˋkeʃən [英] ˌæpliˋkeiʃən] 應用程式；申請書 nearby [ˋnɪrˌbaɪ] 在附近
download [ˋdaʊnˌlod] 下載 cover letter 求職信 submit [səbˋmɪt] 提交

14 中

🔊 英式發音 → 加拿大式發音 Where should we go to eat dinner following the screening? (A) Probably around 8 P.M. (B) I don't know where deliveries go. (C) I was thinking of having Latin food.	電影結束後，我們該去哪裡吃晚餐？ (A) 大概在晚上 8 點。 (B) 我不知道貨送到哪裡了。 (C) 我之前在想要吃拉丁菜。

Where 疑問句 答案 (C)

這是詢問電影結束後要去哪裡吃晚餐的 Where 疑問句。

(A) [╳] 題目詢問電影結束後要去哪裡吃晚餐，這裡卻回答了時間點，因此是錯誤選項。

(B) [╳] 這是藉由重複使用題目中出現的 Where 和 go 來造成混淆的錯誤選項。注意不要聽到 I don't know where 就選擇這個答案。

(C) [○] 這裡回答之前在想要吃拉丁菜，間接提到要去的地點，因此是正確答案。

單字 following [[美] ˋfɑləwɪŋ [英] ˋfɔləuiŋ] 在～之後 screening [ˋskrinɪŋ]（電影等）放映；篩選
probably [ˋprɑbəblɪ] 也許；大概 delivery [dɪˋlɪvərɪ] 遞送的貨物或信件

15 低

🔊 美式發音 → 加拿大式發音 Why were you late for the consultation yesterday? (A) There was heavy traffic on the highway. (B) Don't worry. She'll be on time. (C) By at least fifteen minutes or so.	你昨天諮商為什麼遲到了？ (A) 當時公路上塞車。 (B) 別擔心。她會準時到的。 (C) 差至少十五分鐘左右。

Why 疑問句 答案 (A)

這是詢問昨天諮商為什麼遲到的 Why 疑問句。

(A) [○] 這裡回答公路上塞車，提到昨天遲到的原因，因此是正確答案。

(B) [╳] 題目詢問昨天諮商為什麼遲到，這裡卻回答「別擔心。她會準時到的」，毫不相關，因此是錯誤選項。這裡利用和題目中 late（遲的）意義相反的 on time（準時）來造成混淆。

(C) [╳] 這是透過能從 late（遲的）聯想到的延遲時間 fifteen minutes or so（十五分鐘左右）來造成混淆的是錯誤選項。

單字 consultation [ˌkɑnsəlˋteʃən] 諮商；診察 heavy traffic 交通繁忙；塞車 highway [ˋhaɪˌwe] 公路；幹道
or so 大概～，～左右

16 中

🔊 澳洲式發音 → 英式發音

Should we rent a car while we're in Morocco or rely on cabs?

(A) He's very reliable.
(B) I'd rather have a vehicle.
(C) I bought one while living in New York.

我們在摩洛哥的時候應該要租輛車還是要靠計程車？

(A) 他非常可靠。
(B) 我比較想要有台車。
(C) 我住在紐約時買了一個。

選擇疑問句 答案 (B)

這是詢問在摩洛哥期間要租車還是要靠計程車的選擇疑問句。

(A) [╳] 題目詢問在摩洛哥期間要租車還是要靠計程車，這裡卻回答他非常可靠，毫不相關，因此是錯誤選項。這裡利用發音相似單字 rely – reliable 來造成混淆。

(B) [○] 這裡說比較想要有台車，間接表示要選擇租車，因此是正確答案。

(C) [╳] 這是藉由能代稱題目中 car（車）的 one，並重複使用 while 企圖造成混淆的錯誤選項。

單字 rent [rɛnt] 租用；出租 rely on 依靠～ cab [kæb] 計程車 reliable [rɪˋlaɪəbl̩] 值得信賴的；可靠的
would rather 寧可～；比較想要～ vehicle [[美] ˋviɪkl̩ [英] ˋvi:ikl] 車輛；搭載工具

17 高

🔊 美式發音 → 加拿大式發音

Which spare bookcase do you want moved into your office?

(A) Whichever binder isn't being used.
(B) A few movers just showed up.
(C) The one with lots of shelves.

你想要把哪一個空書櫃搬進你的辦公室裡？

(A) 只要是沒在用的活頁夾都可以。
(B) 幾位搬家工人才剛到。
(C) 有很多層架的那一個。

Which 疑問句 答案 (C)

這是詢問要把哪一個空書櫃搬進辦公室裡的 Which 疑問句。這裡一定要聽到 Which spare bookcase 才能順利作答。

(A) [╳] 這是利用發音相似單字 Which – Whichever，並使用與 bookcase（書櫃）有關的 binder（活頁夾）來造成混淆的錯誤選項。

(B) [╳] 題目詢問要把哪一個空書櫃搬進辦公室裡，這裡卻回答幾位搬家工人才剛到，毫不相關，因此是錯誤選項。這裡利用發音相似單字 moved – movers 來造成混淆。

(C) [○] 這裡回答有很多層架的那一個，提到要搬進辦公室裡的書櫃特徵，因此是正確答案。

單字 spare [spɛr] 閒置的；剩下的 bookcase [ˋbʊkˏkes] 書架；書櫃
binder [ˋbaɪndɚ]（用來整理紙類文書的）活頁夾 mover [ˋmuvɚ] 搬家工人；搬家公司
show up 出現；到場 shelf [ʃɛlf]（書櫃等的）層架

18 高

🔊 澳洲式發音 → 美式發音

Does this pair of jeans come in black as well?

(A) Every pair of sunglasses.
(B) Only blue ones are available.
(C) Come over after work.

這件牛仔褲也有黑色的嗎？

(A) 每副太陽眼鏡。
(B) 只有藍色的有貨。
(C) 下班後過來一趟。

助動詞疑問句 答案 (B)

這是確認牛仔褲是否也有黑色款的助動詞（Do）疑問句。

(A) [╳] 題目確認牛仔褲是否也有黑色款，這裡卻回答每副太陽眼鏡，毫不相關，因此是錯誤選項。這裡藉著重複題目中出現的 pair of 來造成混淆。

(B) [○] 這裡回答只有藍色的有貨，間接回答沒有黑色款的，因此是正確答案。

(C) [╳] 這是藉重複題目中出現的 come 來造成混淆的錯誤選項。

單字 come in（商品等）有貨；可以買到 available [əˋveləbl̩] 可以買到的；可使用的

19 中

英式發音 → 加拿大式發音

Benson Lawn Care has excellent customer service. (A) What a great company logo! (B) I've read about it on the Internet. (C) At the customer service desk.	Benson 草坪養護公司有非常棒的顧客服務。 (A) 這個公司商標很棒！ (B) 我曾在網路上看到過這件事。 (C) 在顧客服務櫃台。

陳述句 答案 (B)

這是表示 Benson 草坪養護公司有非常棒的顧客服務的陳述句。

(A) [╳] 這裡使用和題目中 excellent（非常棒的）意思相同的 great（很棒的）來造成混淆。注意不要聽到 What a great company 就選擇這個答案。

(B) [○] 這裡回答曾在網路上看到過這件事，間接表達自己知道 Benson 草坪養護公司有非常棒的顧客服務，因此是正確答案。

(C) [╳] 題目陳述 Benson 草坪養護公司有非常棒的顧客服務，這裡卻回答在顧客服務櫃台，毫不相關，因此是錯誤選項。這裡透過重複題目中出現的 customer service 來造成混淆。

單字 excellent [`ɛksḷənt] 非常棒的、卓越的

20 中

澳洲式發音 → 美式發音

How far from your house is Sharper Mall? (A) Well, I'd like to go shopping. (B) From noon until 1 o'clock. (C) Let me check a map quickly.	你家到 Sharper 購物中心有多遠？ (A) 這個嘛，我想要去購物。 (B) 從中午到 1 點鐘。 (C) 讓我很快查一下地圖。

How 疑問句 答案 (C)

這是詢問 Sharper 購物中心離對方家多遠的 How 疑問句。這裡必須知道 How far 是詢問距離的表達。

(A) [╳] 這是利用與 Mall（購物中心）有關的 go shopping（去購物）來造成混淆的錯誤選項。

(B) [╳] 題目詢問 Sharper 購物中心離對方家多遠，這裡卻回答了一段期間，因此是錯誤選項。這裡透過重複題目中出現的 from 來造成混淆。

(C) [○] 這裡說要很快查一下地圖，間接回答了問題，因此是正確答案。

單字 check [tʃɛk] 確認；檢查 quickly [`kwɪklɪ] 快速地

21 高

加拿大式發音 → 美式發音

When do you expect to hire a permanent assistant? (A) It'll be permanently installed. (B) I'm waiting for approval. (C) The help is much appreciated.	你預計什麼時候要聘一位正職助理？ (A) 這會是永久性安裝。 (B) 我正在等待批准。 (C) 非常感謝協助。

When 疑問句 答案 (B)

這是詢問對方預計什麼時候要聘正職助理的 When 疑問句。

(A) [╳] 題目詢問對方預計什麼時候要聘正職助理，這裡卻回答會是永久性安裝，毫不相關，因此是錯誤選項。這裡利用發音相似單字 permanent – permanently 來造成混淆。

(B) [○] 這裡表示自己正在等待批准，間接回答了問題，因此是正確答案。

(C) [╳] 這是使用和題目中 assistant（助理）的另一字義「幫手」有關的 help（協助）來造成混淆的錯誤選項。

單字 expect [ɪk`spɛkt] 預計；盼望 permanent [`pɝmənənt] 永久的；固定性的 assistant [ə`sɪstənt] 幫手，助理 install [ɪn`stɔl] 安裝 approval [ə`pruvḷ] 批准；承認 appreciate [ə`priʃɪˌet] 感謝，感激

22 ○●●● 中

英式發音 → 澳洲式發音	
The mayor is giving a speech today in the town square.	市長今天要在鎮上的廣場進行演說。
(A) I'm glad you decided to give a lecture. (B) I heard it'll cover education funding. (C) If I have enough time.	(A) 我很開心你決定去演講了。 (B) 我聽說會談到教育資金。 (C) 如果我有足夠時間的話。

陳述句 答案 (B)

這是表達市長今天要在鎮上的廣場進行演說的客觀事實陳述句。

(A) [╳] 這是利用與 giving a speech（進行演說）有關的 give a lecture（去演講）來造成混淆的錯誤選項。

(B) [○] 這裡回答自己聽說會談到教育資金，提到其他關於這場演說的資訊，因此是正確答案。

(C) [╳] 題目陳述市長今天要在鎮上的廣場進行演說，但這裡卻以回答「你要參加嗎？」提問的答案來回應，因此是錯誤選項。

單字 mayor [美 `meɚ 英 `mɛə] 市長 give a speech 進行演說 square [美 skwɛr 英 skwɛə] 廣場
decide [dɪ`saɪd] 決定 give a lecture 去演講；進行講座 cover [美 `kʌvɚ 英 `kʌvə] 覆蓋；包括
funding [`fʌndɪŋ] 提供資金；資金

23 ●●●● 難

澳洲式發音 → 英式發音	
Who created the notice that's hanging in the front window?	掛在前面窗戶上的那個告示是誰做的？
(A) A sign was put up there? (B) I registered to receive e-mail notifications. (C) We can hang them next to the door.	(A) 那上面有掛告示？ (B) 我為了收到電子郵件通知而註冊了。 (C) 我們可以把它們掛在門邊。

Who 疑問句 答案 (A)

這是詢問是誰做了掛在前面窗戶上的那個告示的 Who 疑問句。

(A) [○] 這裡反問「那上面有掛告示？」，間接表示自己不知道那裡有掛告示，因此是正確答案。

(B) [╳] 題目詢問誰做了掛在前面窗戶上的那個告示，這裡卻回答自己為了收到電子郵件通知而註冊了，毫不相關，因此是錯誤選項。這裡使用和題目中 notice（告示）的另一字義「通知」意義相近的 notifications（通知）來造成混淆。

(C) [╳] 這裡以 hang 重複使用題目中出現的 hanging，並利用與 window（窗戶）相關的 door（門）來造成混淆。

單字 create [krɪ`et] 製造；創造 notice [`notɪs] 告示；通知 hang [hæŋ] 懸掛 sign [saɪn] 告示牌；標示
put up 設置；建造 register [美 `rɛdʒɪstɚ 英 `redʒistə] 登記；註冊
notification [美 ˌnotəfə`keʃən 英 ˌnəutifi`keiʃən] 通知；通知書

24 ○●●● 高

英式發音 → 加拿大式發音	
Why haven't you unpacked your belongings yet?	你為什麼還沒把你的東西打開拿出來？
(A) Because the price tag was removed. (B) I was meeting with a colleague. (C) No, we haven't done it yet.	(A) 因為標價被拿掉了。 (B) 我之前在和一位同事見面。 (C) 不，我們還沒有做那件事。

Why 疑問句 答案 (B)

這是詢問為什麼還沒把東西打開拿出來的 Why 疑問句。

(A) [╳] 題目詢問為什麼還沒把東西打開拿出來，這裡卻回答標價被拿掉了，毫不相關，因此是錯誤選項。注意不要聽到 Because 就選擇這個選項。

(B) [○] 這裡回答之前在和一位同事見面，提到還沒把東西打開拿出來的原因，因此是正確答案。

(C) [╳] 這裡用 No 回答疑問詞疑問句，因此是錯誤選項。這裡透過重複題目中出現的 haven't 和 yet 以造成混淆。

單字 unpack [ʌn`pæk] 打開（行李或包裹等）把東西拿出來
belongings [美 bə`lɔŋɪŋz 英 bi`lɔːŋinz] 隨身物品；擁有物 remove [rɪ`muv] 移開；去除
colleague [kɑ`lig] 同事

25 中

🔊 美式發音 → 澳洲式發音

Has the singer Jeff Bloom agreed to perform at our charity event?

(A) Cash donations are preferred.
(B) Some musicians were playing along the street.
(C) It appears that he can participate.

歌手 Jeff Bloom 同意要在我們的慈善活動上表演了嗎？

(A) 現金捐款較佳。
(B) 一些音樂家當時在沿街演奏。
(C) 看來他可以參加。

助動詞疑問句 答案 (C)

這是確認歌手 Jeff Bloom 是否同意要在慈善活動上表演的助動詞（Have）疑問句。

(A) [╳] 這是利用和 charity（慈善）相關的 donations（捐款）來造成混淆的錯誤選項。

(B) [╳] 這裡使用和 singer（歌手）相關的 musicians（音樂家）及與 perform（表演）相關的 playing（演奏）來造成混淆。

(C) [◯] 這裡回答看來他可以參加，表示歌手 Jeff Bloom 同意在慈善活動上表演，因此是正確答案。

單字 perform [pɚ`fɔrm] 表演 charity [`tʃærətɪ] 慈善 donation [[美] do`neʃən [英] dəu`neiʃən] 捐款；捐獻
prefer [[美] prɪ`fɝ [英] pri`fəː] 偏好 appear [[美] ə`pɪr [英] ə`piə] 看來，似乎
participate [[美] pɑr`tɪsə͵pet [英] pɑː`tisipeit] 參與

26 高

🔊 加拿大式發音 → 美式發音

The heat in the office can be turned down, can't it?

(A) I'm not sure who can adjust it.
(B) Yes, both of these sheets.
(C) The rack is a bit too high.

辦公室的暖氣可以轉小，不是嗎？

(A) 我不確定誰可以調整它。
(B) 是的，這兩張單子都是。
(C) 這個架子有點太高了。

附加問句 答案 (A)

這是確認辦公室的暖氣是否可以轉小的附加問句。

(A) [◯] 這裡回答不確定誰可以調整，間接表示自己對此不清楚，因此是正確答案。

(B) [╳] 這是利用發音相似單字 heat – sheets 來造成混淆的錯誤選項。注意不要聽到 Yes 就選擇這個答案。

(C) [╳] 這是利用和 turned down（轉小）有關的 high（高的）來造成混淆的錯誤選項。

單字 turn down 轉小（溫度、聲音等） adjust [ə`dʒʌst] 調整 sheet [ʃit]（紙張）一張；床單；表單
rack [ræk] 架子

27 中

🔊 澳洲式發音 → 英式發音

We need to send out the wedding invitations for Ms. Lang and her fiancé.

(A) The ceremony is in Hall A.
(B) No, Mr. Cho is not invited.
(C) I totally forgot about that.

我們得為 Lang 小姐和她的未婚夫把喜帖寄出去。

(A) 典禮是在 A 廳。
(B) 不，Cho 先生沒有受邀。
(C) 我完全忘了這件事。

陳述句 答案 (C)

這是表達得為 Lang 小姐和她的未婚夫把喜帖寄出去的客觀事實陳述句。

(A) [╳] 這是利用和 wedding（婚禮）有關的 ceremony（典禮）來造成混淆的錯誤選項。

(B) [╳] 題目說得為 Lang 小姐和她的未婚夫把喜帖寄出去，這裡卻回答 Cho 先生沒被邀請，毫不相關，因此是錯誤選項。這裡利用發音相似單字 invitations – invited 來造成混淆。

(C) [◯] 這裡說自己完全忘了這件事，表示自己不記得要寄喜帖，因此是正確答案。

單字 send out 寄出 invitation [͵ɪnvə`teʃən] 邀請函；邀請 fiancé [[美] ͵fiən`se [英] fi`ɑːnsei] 未婚夫
ceremony [[美] `sɛrə͵monɪ [英] `seriməni] 典禮，儀式 totally [[美] `totḷɪ [英] `təutəli] 完全地
forget [[美] fɚ`gɛt [英] fə`get] 忘記

28 ○●●● 高

🗣 英式發音 → 加拿大式發音 What's the problem with the flyers we printed for the seminar? (A) There is a stack of printer paper over there. (B) Everything seems fine. (C) I'm flying into Madrid for the seminar.	我們為研討會印的傳單有什麼問題嗎？ (A) 那裡有一疊影印紙。 (B) 一切看起來都很好。 (C) 我要飛到馬德里參加研討會。

■ What 疑問句 答案 (B)

這是詢問為研討會印的傳單有什麼問題的 What 疑問句。

(A) [╳] 這是利用發音相似單字 printed – printer 以及和 flyers（傳單）有關的 paper（紙張）來造成混淆的錯誤選項。

(B) [○] 這裡回答一切看起來都很好，間接表示為研討會印的傳單沒有什麼問題，因此是正確答案。

(C) [╳] 這裡利用發音相似單字 flyers – flying 及重複使用題目中出現的 seminar 來造成混淆。

單字 flyer [[美] `flaɪɚ [英] `flaiə] 傳單 stack [stæk] 堆疊；一堆，一疊

29 ○○●● 中

🗣 加拿大式發音 → 美式發音 Do you think we should buy a new refrigerator? (A) Our current one still works well. (B) Across from the break room. (C) No, I think they're next to the stoves.	你覺得我們應該買新的冰箱嗎？ (A) 我們現在這台還很好用。 (B) 在休息室對面。 (C) 不，我想它們在爐子旁邊。

■ 助動詞疑問句 答案 (A)

這是確認是否應該要買新冰箱的助動詞（Do）疑問句。

(A) [○] 這裡回答現在的還很好用，間接表示不需要買新冰箱，因此是正確答案。

(B) [╳] 這是利用從 refrigerator（冰箱）聯想到的可能使用地點 break room（休息室）來造成混淆的錯誤選項。

(C) [╳] 這是利用和 refrigerator（冰箱）相關的 stoves（爐子）來造成混淆的錯誤選項。注意不要聽到 No, I think 就選擇這個答案。

單字 current [`kɝənt] 現在的，當前的 break room 休息室 stove [stov] 爐子

30 ○●●● 高

🗣 澳洲式發音 → 美式發音 Should I order a filing cabinet with a single drawer or one with three? (A) Extra storage is always helpful. (B) In the top drawer. (C) Most of the documents are in there.	我應該訂有一個抽屜的檔案櫃，還是該訂有三個抽屜的？ (A) 額外的儲藏空間永遠都有用。 (B) 在最上面的抽屜裡。 (C) 大部分的文件都在那裡。

■ 選擇疑問句 答案 (A)

這是詢問應該訂有一個抽屜的檔案櫃，還是訂有三個抽屜那款的選擇疑問句。

(A) [○] 這裡回答額外的儲藏空間永遠都有用，間接表示應該要訂有三個抽屜的檔案櫃，因此是正確答案。

(B) [╳] 題目詢問應該訂有一個抽屜的檔案櫃，還是該訂有三個抽屜的，這裡卻回答在最上面的抽屜裡，毫不相關，因此是錯誤選項。這裡藉重複使用題目中出現的 drawer 來造成混淆。

(C) [╳] 這是利用和 filing cabinet（檔案櫃）有關的 documents（文件），以及可以代稱題目中 filing cabinet（檔案櫃）的 there 來造成混淆的錯誤選項。

單字 order [[美] `ɔrdɚ [英] `ɔ:də] 訂購 filing cabinet 檔案櫃 single [`sɪŋgl̩] 一個的；個別的
drawer [[美] `drɔɚ [英] `drɔ:ə] 抽屜 extra [`ɛkstrə] 額外的；外加的 helpful [`hɛlpfəl] 有用的，有幫助的
document [`dɑkjəmənt] 文件；公文

31 ○●●●● 高

英式發音 → 澳洲式發音 While Peter is editing the slide show, we should rehearse the rest of the presentation. (A) Why don't you go first? (B) Everyone found it relaxing. (C) The editor likes the manuscript.	在 Peter 編輯投影片的時候，我們應該要演練這場簡報剩下的部分。 (A) 你要不要先開始？ (B) 大家都覺得這很令人放鬆。 (C) 編輯喜歡這份原稿。

陳述句 答案 (A)

這是提議要在 Peter 編輯投影片時，演練簡報其它部分的陳述句。

(A) [○] 這裡反問對方要不要先開始，間接表示同意，因此是正確答案。

(B) [╳] 這是使用可以代稱題目中 presentation（簡報）的 it，並使用與題目中 rest（剩餘部分）的另一字義「休息」有關的 relaxing（令人放鬆的）來造成混淆的錯誤選項。

(C) [╳] 這是使用發音相似單字 editing – editor 及與 presentation（簡報）相關的 manuscript（原稿）來造成混淆的錯誤選項。

單字 edit [`ɛdɪt] 編輯；校訂 rehearse [美 rɪ`hɝs 英 ri`həːs] 排練，演練 rest [rɛst] 剩餘部分；休息
presentation [ˌprɛzn̩`teʃən] 簡報；發表 relaxing [rɪ`læksɪŋ] 令人放鬆的；輕鬆愉悅的
editor [美 `ɛdɪtɚ 英 `editə] 編輯；（報章雜誌的）主編；校訂者
manuscript [美 `mænjəˌskrɪpt 英 `mænjuskript] 原稿；手稿

TEST 1 2 3 4 5 6 7 8 9 10

32 33 34

Questions 32-34 refer to the following conversation.

美式發音 → 加拿大式發音

W: Ted, [32]**have you booked accommodations for the speakers presenting at the environmental conference on January 12 that our company is organizing?**

M: I was planning to reserve rooms for all eight speakers at the Drake Inn. It's the same hotel we used when we arranged the trade show last month. But nothing is confirmed yet. Why?

W: Well, [33]**the Silkwood Hotel is offering a 15 percent discount on all deluxe suites booked next week.** [34]**The details about the deal are included in the newsletter that the hotel sent out by e-mail yesterday.**

M: [34]**Could you forward the message to me?** I'll check it out.

32 Who most likely are the speakers?

(A) Travel agents
(B) Event planners
(C) Advertising executives
(D) Environmental researchers

33 What is mentioned about the Silkwood Hotel?

(A) It launched a new service.
(B) It has renovated its suites.
(C) It is hosting a conference.
(D) It will hold a promotion.

34 What does the man ask the woman to do?

(A) Call a company
(B) Make a reservation
(C) Revise a newsletter
(D) Send an e-mail

第 32-34 題請參考下列對話。

女： Ted，[32] 你已經替 1 月 12 日要在我們公司籌辦的環境會議上報告的講者們訂好住宿了嗎？

男： 我本來打算替全部八位講者都在 Drake 旅店訂房。這家旅館和我們上個月在籌備貿易展時訂的是同一家。但一切都還沒有確定。怎麼了嗎？

女： 這個嘛，[33] Silkwood 飯店正在提供下週預訂豪華套房全都打八五折的優惠。[34] 這個方案的細節資訊在昨天這間飯店用電子郵件寄來的電子報裡有。

男： [34] 妳可以把那封信轉寄給我嗎？我會研究一下。

32 說話者們最有可能是誰？

(A) 旅行社專員
(B) 活動規劃人員
(C) 廣告業務主管
(D) 環境研究員

33 關於 Silkwood 飯店，提到了什麼？

(A) 推出了一項新服務。
(B) 整修了它的套房。
(C) 正在舉辦一場會議。
(D) 將舉辦一項促銷活動。

34 男子要求女子做什麼？

(A) 打電話給一間公司
(B) 進行一項預約
(C) 修改一份業務通訊
(D) 寄出一封電子郵件

題目 book [bʊk] 預訂　accommodation [əˌkɑmə`deʃən] 住宿；住宿設施　present [prɪ`zɛnt] 報告；發表　environmental [ɪnˌvaɪrən`mɛntl] 環境的　conference [`kɑnfərəns] 會談；會議　organize [`ɔrgəˌnaɪz] 籌辦；組織　reserve [rɪ`zɝv] 預約　confirm [kən`fɝm] 確定；證實　discount [`dɪskaʊnt] 折價；折扣優惠　deluxe [dɪ`lʌks] 豪華的　deal [dil] 交易；方案　newsletter [`njuz`lɛtɚ] 業務通訊　forward [`fɔrwɚd] 轉發（信件等）；傳遞　check out 了解～的情況；查看～

32 advertising [`ædvɚˌtaɪzɪŋ] 廣告業；（總稱）廣告　executive [ɪg`zɛkjʊtɪv] 執行者；業務主管

33 launch [lɔntʃ] 推出；著手進行　renovate [`rɛnəˌvet] 整修；翻新　host [host] 舉辦　promotion [prə`moʃən] 促銷活動；宣傳

32 ○○●● 中 **整體對話相關問題—說話者** 答案 (B)

題目詢問說話者的身分，因此必須注意聽對話中和身分、職業相關的表達。女子說：「have you booked accommodations for the speakers presenting at the environmental conference ~ that our company is organizing?」，詢問是否已為公司籌辦的環境會議的講者們訂好住宿了，由此可知，說話者是活動規劃人員，因此正確答案是 (B) Event planners。

33 ○○●● 中 **細節事項相關問題—提及** 答案 (D)

題目詢問提到 Silkwood 飯店的什麼，因此必須注意提到題目關鍵字（Silkwood Hotel）的前後部分。女子說：「the Silkwood Hotel is offering a 15 percent discount on all deluxe suites booked next week」，表示 Silkwood 飯店正在提供下週預訂豪華套房全都打八五折的優惠，因此正確答案是 (D) It will hold a promotion.。

34 ○○○● 低 **細節事項相關問題—要求** 答案 (D)

題目詢問男子要求女子做什麼，因此要注意聽男子話中與要求相關的表達內容。女子說：「The details about the deal are included in the newsletter that the hotel sent out by e-mail yesterday.」，表示這個方案的相關細節資訊，可以在這間飯店昨天寄來的電子郵件裡找到，接著男子對女子說：「Could you forward the message to me?」，要求女子把那封信轉寄給自己，因此正確答案是 (D) Send an e-mail。

35 36 37 新

Questions 35-37 refer to the following conversation.

英式發音 → 澳洲式發音

W: Our competitor is launching a free delivery service next month. To stay competitive, [35]**we should consider eliminating the fee to deliver furniture from our store to customers' homes as well**. What do you think?

M: Hmm . . . [36]**I'm concerned we'd need to buy additional delivery trucks.** More customers would use that service if there were no charge.

W: Well, we could just lease them instead. That would require less initial investment.

M: I like your suggestion. Do you believe we should prepare a cost projection report before we discuss the idea with our supervisor?

W: Yes, let's do that. [37]**Can I get my tablet back from you?** I lent it to you yesterday, and it contains the report template we'll need.

35 Where most likely do the speakers work?

(A) At a car rental agency
(B) At a home electronics shop
(C) At a furniture retailer
(D) At a courier company

36 Why is the man worried?

(A) More vehicles may be required.
(B) Customers have submitted complaints.
(C) Branches might be closed.
(D) Total sales have dropped.

37 What does the woman ask for?

(A) An electronic device
(B) A truck key
(C) An order form
(D) A business card

第 35-37 題請參考下列對話。

女：我們的競爭對手下個月要推免運服務。為了保有競爭力，[35] 我們也應該考慮不收把家具從我們店送到顧客家裡的運費。你覺得怎麼樣？

男：嗯……[36] 我擔心我們會需要買更多貨車。如果不收費的話，會有更多顧客使用這項服務。

女：這個嘛，我們可以就改用租的。這樣需要的初期投資會比較少。

男：我喜歡妳的建議。妳認為我們在和主管討論這個想法之前，應該要先準備一份成本估計報告嗎？

女：是的，我們來做吧。[37] 我可以跟你拿回我的平板電腦嗎？我昨天把它借給你了，它裡面有我們會用到的報告範本。

35 說話者們最有可能在哪裡工作？

(A) 租車行
(B) 家電行
(C) 家具零售商
(D) 快遞公司

36 男子為何感到擔心？

(A) 可能會需要更多車輛。
(B) 顧客提出了申訴。
(C) 分店可能會關閉。
(D) 整體銷售額下降了。

37 女子要求取得什麼？

(A) 電子設備
(B) 卡車鑰匙
(C) 訂購單
(D) 名片

題目 competitor [美 kəm`pɛtətɚ 英 kəm`petitə] 競爭者　launch [lɔntʃ] 推出；著手開始
competitive [美 kəm`pɛtətɪv 英 kəm`petitiv] 有競爭力的；競爭的　eliminate [美 ɪ`lɪmə͵net 英 i`limineit] 消除；淘汰
lease [lis] 租用　initial [ɪ`nɪʃəl] 初期的　investment [ɪn`vɛstmənt] 投資；投資額　projection [prə`dʒɛkʃən] 預測；估計
template [美 `tɛmplɪt 英 `templit] 範本，樣板

35 home electronics 家電產品　courier company 快遞公司

35 整體對話相關問題—說話者　答案 (C)

低

題目詢問說話者的工作地點，因此要注意聽和身分、職業相關的表達。女子說：「we should consider eliminating the fee to deliver furniture from our store to customers' homes as well」，表示他們應該考慮不收取家具的運費，由此可知，說話者們在家具零售商裡工作，因此正確答案是 (C) At a furniture retailer。

36 細節事項相關問題—問題點　答案 (A)

中

題目詢問男子感到擔心的原因，因此必須注意聽男子話中出現負面表達之後的內容。男子說：「I'm concerned we'd need to buy additional delivery trucks.」，表示擔心會需要買更多貨車，因此正確答案是 (A) More vehicles may be required.。

37 細節事項相關問題—要求　答案 (A)

低

題目詢問女子要求取得什麼，因此要注意聽女子話中出現要求表達之後的內容。女子對男子說：「Can I get my tablet back from you?」，詢問是否能從男子那裡拿回自己的平板電腦，因此正確答案是 (A) An electronic device。

38
39
40

Questions 38-40 refer to the following conversation.

美式發音 → 澳洲式發音

W: Now, [38]**we can take a look at the compiled feedback from the recent diner questionnaire and see if we can find some useful information to help improve our restaurant.**

M: Well, it looks like a majority of guests made positive comments about our facility's decor and layout. However, there are several complaints about the attitudes of some of our serving staff.

W: I see. [39]**I think it's best we hold a training session to remind employees about our standards of service when dealing with customers.**

M: That's a thought. [40]**I can even share some great tips from the conference on the food service industry that I attended last week.**

38 What is the conversation mainly about?

(A) A company dinner
(B) A guest list
(C) A remodeling project
(D) A customer survey

39 What does the woman recommend?

(A) Speaking to a manager
(B) Training some staff
(C) Changing some rules
(D) Attending a conference

40 What did the man do last week?

(A) Sampled a food selection
(B) Hired a new chef
(C) Participated in an event
(D) Modified an agenda

第 38-40 題請參考下列對話。

女：現在，[38] 我們可以來看一下從最近對來用餐的人所做的問卷中收集到的回饋意見，然後看看我們是否能得到一些有用的資訊來幫助改善我們的餐廳。

男：嗯，看樣子大部分賓客對我們餐廳的裝潢和配置都給了正面意見。不過，有幾則針對我們某些服務人員態度的投訴。

女：我知道了。[39] 我認為我們最好舉辦一次培訓課程，提醒員工我們在應對顧客時的服務規範。

男：好主意。[40] 我甚至可以分享從我上週參加的那場食品服務產業會議所得來的一些很棒的訣竅。

38 這段對話主要與什麼有關？

(A) 公司晚宴
(B) 來賓名單
(C) 整修計畫
(D) 顧客調查

39 女子建議什麼？

(A) 和經理談談
(B) 訓練一些員工
(C) 改變一些規則
(D) 參加一場會議

40 男子上週做了什麼？

(A) 試吃了選出的食物
(B) 聘了新主廚
(C) 參加了活動
(D) 修改了議程

題目 compile [kəm`paɪl] 收集（資料等）；匯編　feedback [`fid͵bæk] 回饋意見　diner [`daɪnɚ] 用餐的人　questionnaire [͵kwɛstʃən`ɛr]（調查情況用的）問卷；意見調查表　improve [ɪm`pruv] 改善；提升　majority [美 mə`dʒɔrətɪ 英 mə`dʒɔ:riti] 大多數　facility [fə`sɪlətɪ]（有特定用途的）設施，場地　decor [美 de`kɔr 英 dei`kɔ:]（室內）裝潢　layout [`le͵aʊt] 配置；版面設計　remind [rɪ`maɪnd] 提醒　standard [`stændɚd] 標準；規範　deal with 處理～；應對～

40 sample [`sæmpl̩] 試吃；樣品　modify [`mɑdə͵faɪ] 修改　agenda [ə`dʒɛndə] 議程；待議事項

38 ■ 整體對話相關問題—主題　答案 (D)

中

題目詢問對話主題，因此必須注意對話開頭的部分。女子說：「we can take a look at the compiled feedback from the recent diner questionnaire and see if we can find some useful information to help improve our restaurant」，表示要來看一下最近來用餐的人所做的問卷，看看是否能從中得到一些有用的回饋意見，藉這些資訊來幫助改善餐廳，接下來對話就開始說明問卷的調查結果，因此正確答案是 (D) A customer survey。

39 ■ 細節事項相關問題—提議　答案 (B)

低

題目詢問女子建議什麼，因此要注意聽女子話中出現提議表達之後的內容。女子說：「I think it's best we hold a training session to remind employees about our standards of service when dealing with customers.」，表示自己認為最好要辦一場培訓課程，提醒員工在應對顧客時的服務規範，因此正確答案是 (B) Training some staff。

40 ■ 細節事項相關問題—特定細項　答案 (C)

低

題目詢問男子上週做了什麼，因此要注意提到題目關鍵字（last week）的前後部分。男子說：「I can even share some great tips from the conference ~ that I attended last week.」，表示自己可以分享在上週參加會議時得到的一些很棒的訣竅，因此正確答案是 (C) Participated in an event。

Questions 41-43 refer to the following conversation.

🔊 英式發音 → 加拿大式發音

W: Good morning, Jerry. I have a quick question for you. [41]**Was your water bill higher than usual this month? Mine was, and I can't figure out why.** I thought there might be a problem affecting everyone in the building.

M: No. It's possible that there's an issue with your pipe system. You should have someone inspect it.

W: That's a good idea. [42]**I'll need to find someone who will give me a fair price**, though. It could be a big job.

M: [43]**The plumber who I hired to work on my bathroom was very professional. Here—I'll give you his phone number.**

41 What problem does the woman mention?

(A) A worker is not available.
(B) An inspection was rescheduled.
(C) A bill has not arrived.
(D) A charge was higher than expected.

42 [新] What does the woman imply when she says, "It could be a big job"?

(A) She is concerned about cost.
(B) She would like to get another opinion.
(C) She will hire an assistant.
(D) She thinks a project should be postponed.

43 What will the man probably do next?

(A) Replace a broken pipe
(B) Provide contact information
(C) Look for a cheaper alternative
(D) Order additional tools

第 41-43 題請參考下列對話。

女：早安，Jerry。我有個小問題想問你。[41] 你這個月的水費帳單有比平常高嗎？我的比平常高，但我想不通為什麼會這樣。我認為可能發生了某個影響到了這棟大樓裡所有人的問題。

男：沒有。可能是妳的管道系統有問題。妳應該要請人來檢查。

女：這是個好主意。不過 [42] 我得找個開價公道的人。這可能會是個大工程。

男：[43] 我請來處理我浴室的那位水管工人非常專業。這個——我給妳他的電話號碼。

41 女子提到什麼問題？

(A) 一位工人沒空。
(B) 一次視察改期了。
(C) 還沒收到一份帳單。
(D) 一筆費用比預期的要高。

42 當女子說：「這可能會是個大工程」時，是暗示什麼？

(A) 她擔心費用。
(B) 她想要得到另一個意見。
(C) 她會聘一位助理。
(D) 她認為一項計畫應該要延後。

43 男子接下來可能會做什麼？

(A) 替換壞掉的管道
(B) 提供聯絡資訊
(C) 尋找更便宜的替代方案
(D) 訂購額外的工具

題目 figure out 理解；想出　affect [ə`fɛkt] 影響　inspect [ɪn`spɛkt] 檢查　fair [[美] fɛr [英] fɛə] 公正的；公道的　plumber [`plʌmɚ] 水管工人　professional [prə`fɛʃənl̩] 專業的
41 reschedule [ri`skɛdʒʊl] 重新安排時間
42 assistant [ə`sɪstənt] 助理　postpone [post`pon] 使延期；延遲
43 replace [rɪ`ples] 替換　alternative [ɔl`tɝnətɪv] 替代方案　additional [ə`dɪʃənl̩] 額外的

41 ■ **細節事項相關問題—問題點** 答案 (D)
中
題目詢問女子提到的問題點，因此要注意聽女子話中出現負面表達之後的內容。女子對男子說：「Was your water bill higher than usual this month? Mine was, and I can't figure out why.」，詢問對方這個月的水費是否比平常高，並表示自己的水費比平常高，但想不通為什麼會這樣，因此正確答案是 (D) A charge was higher than expected.。

[新] **42** ■ **細節事項相關問題—掌握意圖** 答案 (A)
中
題目詢問女子的說話意圖，因此要注意題目引用句（It could be a big job）的前後部分。女子在前面一句說：「I'll need to find someone who will give me a fair price」，表示要找開價公道的人，由此可知，女子在擔心費用，因此正確答案是 (A) She is concerned about cost.。

43 ■ **細節事項相關問題—接下來要做的事** 答案 (B)
低
題目詢問男子接下來可能會做什麼，因此要注意對話的最後部分。男子說：「The plumber who I hired to work on my bathroom was very professional. Here—I'll give you his phone number.」，表示自己請來處理浴室的水管工人非常專業，接著說要給女子這位工人的電話號碼，因此正確答案是 (B) Provide contact information。

換句話說
phone number 電話號碼 → contact information 聯絡資訊

44 45 46 [新]

Questions 44-46 refer to the following conversation with three speakers.

第 44-46 題請參考下列三人對話。

🔊 澳洲式發音 → 美式發音 → 英式發音

M: Excuse me, Ms. Hill. [44]**Do you have a few minutes to talk about the new brochure for our fitness center?**
W1: We need your approval before we have it printed.
W2: I've got some time now. I was just looking through it. To be honest, it still needs some work.
M: What do you think needs to be addressed?
W2: [45]**It should include more details about the improvements we made to our facilities last month.** Specifically, our weight-lifting rooms were all expanded, and skylights were installed above the indoor pool.
W1: Oh, thank you for pointing that out. We should've been more specific.
M: I agree. [46]**I can call the firm we contracted to design the brochure after lunch and request the changes.**

男： 不好意思，Hill 小姐。[44] 您有一點時間可以談談我們健身中心新的小冊子的事嗎？
女 1： 我們在送印前需要您的批准。
女 2： 我現在有一些時間。我剛剛才把它掃過一遍。老實說，它還需要再做一些處理。
男： 您認為需要處理什麼呢？
女 2： [45] 它裡面應該要有更多關於我們上個月對設施進行的改善措施的細節資訊。具體來說，我們的舉重室全都擴大了，室內游泳池的上方也安裝了天窗。
女 1： 噢，謝謝您指出了這件事。我們應該要更具體的。
男： 我同意。[46] 我可以在午餐後打給我們承辦設計小冊子的廠商並要求修改。

44 What is the conversation mainly about?
(A) A printing error
(B) A construction project
(C) A business pamphlet
(D) An employee transfer

44 這段對話主要與什麼有關？
(A) 印刷錯誤
(B) 工程計畫
(C) 公司小冊子
(D) 員工轉調

45 What happened last month?
(A) Customer refunds were processed.
(B) A new location was opened.
(C) An agreement was signed.
(D) Some facilities were renovated.

45 上個月發生了什麼？
(A) 處理了顧客退款。
(B) 開了一個新據點。
(C) 簽了一份合約。
(D) 整修了一些設施。

46 What does the man offer to do?
(A) Distribute some brochures
(B) Inspect a building
(C) Interview a designer
(D) Contact another company

46 男子願意做什麼？
(A) 分發一些小冊子
(B) 檢查一棟建築物
(C) 採訪一位設計師
(D) 聯絡另一間公司

題目 brochure [[美] broˋʃʊr [英] brəuˋʃjuə] 小冊子 approval [əˋpruvḷ] 批准 look through 快速瀏覽一遍
address [əˋdrɛs] 處理（問題等） skylight [ˋskaɪˏlaɪt]（屋頂、天花板等上的）天窗 install [ɪnˋstɔl] 安裝，設置
point out [kənˋtrækt] 指出，提到 contract [kənˋtrækt] 承包；承辦
45 process [ˋprɑsɛs] 處理 renovate [ˋrɛnəˏvet] 翻新；整修
46 distribute [dɪˋstrɪbjʊt] 分發 inspect [ɪnˋspɛkt] 檢查

44 整體對話相關問題—主題 答案 (C)
中
題目詢問對話主題，因此必須注意對話開頭，並掌握整體對話脈絡。男子對女 2 說：「Do you have a few minutes to talk about the new brochure for our fitness center?」，詢問對方是否有時間能談與健身中心新的小冊子有關的事，接著繼續提到關於小冊子的其他資訊，因此正確答案是 (C) A business pamphlet。

45 細節事項相關問題—特定細項 答案 (D)
中
題目詢問上個月發生了什麼事，因此要注意提到題目關鍵字（last month）的前後部分。女 2 說：「It[brochure] should include more details about the improvements we made to our facilities last month.」，表示小冊子裡面應該要有更多與上個月設施改善相關的細節資訊，由此可知，上個月整修了一些設施，因此正確答案是 (D) Some facilities were renovated.。

46 細節事項相關問題—提議 答案 (D)
低
題目詢問男子願意做什麼，因此要注意聽男子話中有提到要為女子做事的內容。男子說：「I can call the firm we contracted to design the brochure after lunch and request the changes.」，表示午餐後可以打給承辦公司並要求修改設計，因此正確答案是 (D) Contact another company。

47
48
49

Questions 47-49 refer to the following conversation.	第 47-49 題請參考下列對話。
美式發音 → 加拿大式發音	
W: Liwei, [47]**a few of our junior copywriters approached me about getting raises this year. Do you think it's possible?**	女：Liwei，[47] 幾位我們的資淺文案師來找我談今年加薪的事情。你覺得有可能加薪嗎？
M: Unfortunately, our labor costs have increased dramatically of late. I don't think we can afford to award raises at this time.	男：不幸的是，我們的人事成本最近大幅增加了。我不認為我們在這個時候能給得起加薪。
W: But [48]**they've done such a wonderful job on all of our magazine issues over the past year.** It seems like the right thing to do. [48]**Can't we appeal to upper management about their request?**	女：但是 [48] 他們過去一年間在我們雜誌的所有刊號上都表現得非常出色。似乎應該要這麼做才對。[48] 我們不能把他們的要求提給高層嗎？
M: [49]**Let's bring it up when we meet with department heads this Thursday** . . . But I don't think it will go well, since management has been emphasizing how high our labor expenses are at the moment.	男：[49] 我們這週四和部長們開會時提出來好了……但我不認為會有好結果，因為管理階層一直在強調我們的人事成本現在有多高。
47 What does the woman ask the man about? (A) A deadline extension (B) A project's progress (C) A staff request (D) A meeting's location	47 女子詢問男子什麼？ (A) 延長截止期限 (B) 計畫的進展 (C) 員工的要求 (D) 會議地點
48 新 Why does the woman say, "It seems like the right thing to do"? (A) To approve an employee transfer (B) To recommend hosting a celebration (C) To show support for higher salaries (D) To promote a potential candidate	48 女子為什麼說：「似乎應該要這麼做才對」？ (A) 為批准員工轉調 (B) 為建議舉辦慶祝活動 (C) 為展現對較高薪資的支持 (D) 為推銷可能的人選
49 What does the man suggest? (A) Postponing a client appointment (B) Mentioning a proposal at a gathering (C) Finishing presentation materials (D) Rearranging seats for a conference	49 男子建議什麼？ (A) 推遲一場和客戶的會面 (B) 在聚會中提及一項提議 (C) 完成簡報資料 (D) 重新安排會議的座位

題目 junior [ˋdʒunjɚ] 年輕的；資淺的　approach [əˋprotʃ] 找～談論；接近　raise [rez]（費用等的）提升；加薪
labor cost 人事費用　dramatically [drəˋmætɪkl̩ɪ] 劇烈地；大幅地　of late 最近　afford [əˋford] 負擔得起
issue [ˋɪʃjʊ] 發行（刊物等）；（報刊等的）期號　appeal to 向～請求；向～求助　upper [ˋʌpɚ] 上面的
management [ˋmænɪdʒmənt] 管理階層　bring up 提出（話題等）　**48** potential [pəˋtɛnʃəl] 潛在的；有可能性的
49 gathering [ˋgæðərɪŋ] 聚會，集會　material [məˋtɪrɪəl] 資料；素材　rearrange [ˌriəˋrendʒ] 重新安排

47 高 **細節事項相關問題—特定細項** 答案 (C)

題目詢問女子詢問男子什麼，因此必須注意聽女子所說的話。女子對男子說：「a few of our junior copywriters approached me about getting raises this year. Do you think it's possible?」，表示幾位資淺文案師來找自己談今年加薪的事，女子接著詢問男子加薪這件事有沒有可能，因此正確答案是 (C) A staff request。

新 **48** 高 **細節事項相關問題—掌握意圖** 答案 (C)

題目詢問女子的說話意圖，因此要注意聽題目引用句（It seems like the right thing to do）的前後部分。女子說：「they[junior copywriters]'ve done such a wonderful job on all of our magazine issues over the past year」，表示資淺文案師們過去一年間在所有刊號上都表現得非常出色，後面則說：「Can't we appeal to upper management about their request[getting raises]?」，詢問是否可以把他們的加薪要求提給高層，由此可知，女子支持加薪這件事，因此正確答案是 (C) To show support for higher salaries。

49 中 **細節事項相關問題—提議** 答案 (B)

題目詢問男子建議什麼，因此要注意聽男子話中出現提議表達之後的內容。男子對女子說：「Let's bring it[request] up when we meet with department heads this Thursday」，提議這週四和部長們開會時提出這件事，因此正確答案是 (B) Mentioning a proposal at a gathering。

50
51
52

Questions 50-52 refer to the following conversation.

英式發音 → 加拿大式發音

W: Thanks for returning my call so quickly, Derrick. [50]**There's a problem with the projector in our boardroom. Someone knocked it off the table, and now it doesn't work properly.**

M: Oh, no. We bought that less than a month ago. Plus, [51]**I'll need it when I give a presentation to the board of directors this afternoon.**

W: That's why I'm contacting you. Fortunately, it turns on, but it's making a buzzing sound.

M: Well, at least it's operating. You know, [52]**I just heard that the IT department doesn't have many requests to deal with today**. Maybe I can get someone to look at it quickly and confirm that it's fine.

50 What is the problem?

(A) A purchase was not approved.
(B) A delivery will arrive late.
(C) A device is malfunctioning.
(D) A proposal was rejected.

51 What is scheduled to happen in the afternoon?

(A) An employee orientation
(B) An executive meeting
(C) A technology seminar
(D) A product demonstration

52 What does the man imply about the IT department?

(A) It will hire additional staff.
(B) It is not currently busy.
(C) It moved to a new office.
(D) It has a new department head.

第 50-52 題請參考下列對話。

女：謝謝你這麼快回我電話，Derrick。[50] 我們會議室裡的投影機有問題。有人把它從桌上撞了下來，結果現在它沒辦法正常運作了。

男：噢，不。那台我們才買不到一個月。而且 [51] 我今天下午對董事會做簡報時會需要它。

女：這就是為什麼我要聯絡你。幸運的是，它打得開，只是會發出嗡嗡聲。

男：嗯，至少它有在運作。是說，[52] 我剛聽說資訊科技部今天要處理的要求不多。說不定我可以趕快找到人去看一下，確認它沒有問題。

50 問題是什麼？

(A) 一筆採購沒被批准。
(B) 一批貨會晚到。
(C) 一項設備故障中。
(D) 一項提議被拒絕了。

51 下午預定會發生什麼？

(A) 員工說明會
(B) 主管會議
(C) 科技研討會
(D) 產品展示會

52 關於資訊科技部，男子暗示什麼？

(A) 將聘用更多員工。
(B) 現在不忙。
(C) 搬到了新的辦公室。
(D) 有新的部門主管。

TEST 1 2 3 4 5 6 7 8 9 10

題目 projector [美 prə`dʒɛktɚ 英 prə`dʒektə] 投影機　boardroom [美 `bord͵rum 英 `bɔ:dru:m] 會議室
knock ~ off 撞掉；撞倒　turn on 打開（電燈等）　buzzing [bʌzɪŋ] 嗡嗡聲　operate [`ɑpə͵ret] 操作；運作
50 approve [ə`pruv] 批准；承認　malfunction [mæl`fʌŋkʃən]（機器等的）故障　reject [rɪ`dʒɛkt] 拒絕
51 executive [ɪg`zɛkjʊtɪv] 主管；執行者　demonstration [͵dɛmən`streʃən] 示範；展示會

50 細節事項相關問題—問題點　答案 (C)
中
題目詢問問題是什麼，因此要注意聽對話中出現負面表達之後的內容。女子說：「There's a problem with the projector in our boardroom. Someone knocked it off the table, and now it doesn't work properly.」，表示會議室裡的投影機有問題，因為有人把它從桌上撞掉了，所以它現在不能正常運作，因此正確答案是 (C) A device is malfunctioning.。

51 細節事項相關問題—特定細項　答案 (B)
中
題目詢問下午預定會發生什麼，因此要注意提到題目關鍵字（afternoon）的前後部分。男子說：「I'll need it[projector] when I give a presentation to the board of directors this afternoon」，表示今天下午自己對董事會做簡報時會需要投影機，因此正確答案是 (B) An executive meeting。

52 細節事項相關問題—推論　答案 (B)
高
題目詢問男子暗示什麼與資訊科技部有關的事，因此必須注意提到題目關鍵字（IT department）的前後部分。男子說：「I just heard that the IT department doesn't have many requests to deal with today」，表示自己剛剛聽說資訊科技部今天要處理的要求不多，因此正確答案是 (B) It is not currently busy.。

53
54
55

Questions 53-55 refer to the following conversation.	第 53-55 題請參考下列對話。
美式發音 → 澳洲式發音	
W: When will we be getting more units of the L7? [53]**We've been sold out of that smartphone model all week, but customers keep coming in to buy it.**	女：我們什麼時候會拿到更多台 L7？[53] 我們已經缺這款智慧型手機的貨缺了一整個禮拜了，但還是一直有客人過來要買它。
M: It's hard to say. The phone is extremely popular across the country, so most stores are out of stock. Plus, [54]**the product manufacturer hasn't indicated when our next inventory order will be shipped out**. However, you can offer to put shoppers who want the item on a waiting list.	男：這很難說。這款手機在全國各地都非常受歡迎，所以大部分店家都沒貨。再加上，[54] 產品製造商沒有說清楚我們訂的下一批貨物清單上的東西什麼時候會出貨。不過，妳可以提議把想要買這款手機的客人加進等候名單裡。
W: OK. By the way, [55]**we've had high customer traffic in the store, so I think we need another staff member to work weekday evenings.**	女：好。對了，[55] 我們店裡的來客數一直很多，所以我認為我們平日晚上需要多一個員工工作。
M: Good point. I'll post a notice in the break room to see if any of our employees are looking for extra hours.	男：好主意。我會在休息室裡貼一張公告，看看我們的員工之中，有沒有人正想要多上點班的。
53 According to the woman, what do some customers want to buy? (A) A portable charger (B) A room furnishing (C) A mobile phone (D) A remote controller	53 根據女子所說，一些客人想要買什麼？ (A) 攜帶式充電器 (B) 房內家具 (C) 行動電話 (D) 遙控器
54 What is the man uncertain about? (A) Why a product is unavailable (B) Where an item is located (C) How much a device costs (D) When a shipment will arrive	54 男子不確定什麼？ (A) 一件產品為什麼買不到 (B) 一件商品的所在位置 (C) 一項設備的花費多少 (D) 一批貨什麼時候會到
55 What does the woman suggest? (A) Assigning another worker to a shift (B) Offering customers a discount (C) Contacting a product manufacturer (D) Rewarding some staff members	55 女子建議什麼？ (A) 多指派一位員工上一個時段的班 (B) 提供客人折扣 (C) 聯絡產品製造商 (D) 獎勵一些員工

題目 sell out 售完　extremely [ɪkˋstrimlɪ] 非常，極其　across the country 全國各地　out of stock 沒有庫存的；缺貨的　manufacturer [美 ˌmænjəˋfæktʃərɚ 英 ˌmænjuˋfæktʃərə] 製造商　indicate [ˋɪndəˌket] 指明；表達　inventory [美 ˋɪnvənˌtorɪ 英 ˋinvəntri] 貨物清單；存貨　ship out 發貨；（搭船）離開　traffic [ˋtræfɪk]（客人的）來往量　break room 休息室

53 portable [ˋportəbl] 攜帶式的　charger [ˋtʃɑrdʒɚ] 充電器　furnishing [ˋfɝnɪʃɪŋ] 家具；室內陳設　remote [rɪˋmot] 遠距的

54 uncertain [ʌnˋsɝtn̩] 不確定的　unavailable [ˌʌnəˋveləbl] 買不到的；無法得到的　shipment [ˋʃɪpmənt] 運送；運送的貨物　**55** assign [əˋsaɪn] 指派　shift [ʃɪft] 輪班；（輪班的）工作時間

53 細節事項相關問題—特定細項 答案 (C)

低

題目詢問女子說客人想買什麼，因此必須注意聽女子話中和題目關鍵字（customers want to buy）相關的內容。女子說：「We've been sold out of that smartphone model all week, but customers keep coming in to buy it.」，表示這款智慧型手機已經缺貨一整個禮拜了，但還是一直有客人過來要買它，因此正確答案是 (C) A mobile phone。

54 細節事項相關問題—特定細項 答案 (D)

中

題目詢問男子不確定什麼，因此要注意和題目關鍵字（uncertain）相關的內容。男子說：「the product manufacturer hasn't indicated when our next inventory order will be shipped out」，表示產品製造商沒有說清楚訂的下一批商品什麼時候會出貨，因此正確答案是 (D) When a shipment will arrive。

55 細節事項相關問題—提議 答案 (A)

中

題目詢問女子建議什麼，因此要注意聽女子話中出現提議表達之後的內容。女子說：「we've had high customer traffic in the store, so I think we need another staff member to work weekday evenings」，表示因為店內來客數眾多，所以自己認為平日晚上應該要多一個員工工作，因此正確答案是 (A) Assigning another worker to a shift。

56
57
58

Questions 56-58 refer to the following conversation.

英式發音 → 加拿大式發音

W: Excuse me. [56]**Isn't the museum featuring a special exhibit about space exploration for the next few weeks? I heard a commercial on the radio that made it sound quite interesting.**

M: That's correct. The exhibit is called *Deep Universe*, and it includes several interactive displays. [57]**The most popular is a collection of instruments from an actual space shuttle. Um, these were lent to us by the National Space Agency.**

W: Wow! I'd like to check that out. [58]**Is access to the exhibit included in the regular entrance fee?**

M: I'm afraid not. [58]**It will be an extra $15 per person.**

56 How did the woman find out about the event at the museum?

(A) By listening to the radio
(B) By watching television
(C) By reading a magazine
(D) By talking to a friend

57 According to the man, what did the National Space Agency do?

(A) Purchased some instruments
(B) Conducted a study
(C) Designed a display
(D) Provided some items

58 What costs an extra fee?

(A) Participating in a guided tour
(B) Accessing a temporary exhibit
(C) Attending a lecture series
(D) Viewing a documentary film

第 56-58 題請參考下列對話。

女：不好意思。[56] 這間博物館不是在接下來的幾週要特別展出一個與太空探索有關的特展嗎？我在廣播裡聽到了一則廣告，從廣告上聽起來這展覽相當有趣。

男：是這樣沒錯。這場展覽叫做《Deep Universe》，其中包含了幾個互動式展覽。[57] 最受歡迎的是一堆來自一架真實太空梭的設備。嗯，這些是由國家太空署出借給我們的。

女：哇！我想去看看那個。[58] 一般入場費裡有包含參觀這場展覽嗎？

男：恐怕沒有。[58] 每人會多 15 美金。

56 關於這場在博物館的活動，女子是如何得知的？

(A) 聽廣播
(B) 看電視
(C) 看雜誌
(D) 和朋友聊天

57 根據男子所說，國家太空署做了什麼？

(A) 購買一些設備
(B) 進行一項研究
(C) 設計一場展覽
(D) 提供一些物件

58 什麼要額外收費？

(A) 參加導覽行程
(B) 參觀臨時展
(C) 出席系列講座
(D) 看紀錄片

題目 feature [美 fitʃɚ 英 fiːtʃə] 特載；以～做為號召　exhibit [ɪg`zɪbɪt] 展覽　space exploration 太空探索
commercial [美 kə`mɝʃəl 英 kə`məːʃəl] 商業廣告　interactive [ˌɪntɚ`æktɪv] 互動的；交互作用的
display [dɪ`sple] 展覽，陳列　collection [kə`lɛkʃən] 收藏品；一堆（東西）　instrument [`ɪnstrəmənt] 儀器；設備
space shuttle 太空梭　check out 去～看看；了解～的情況　access [`æksɛs] 進入的權利；接近；進入

57 conduct [kən`dʌkt] 實施；進行　design [dɪ`zaɪn] 設計

58 temporary [`tɛmpəˌrɛrɪ] 臨時的

56 細節事項相關問題—方法　答案 (A)

低

題目詢問女子得知博物館這場活動的方法，因此要注意與題目關鍵字（find out about the event at the museum）相關的內容。女子說：「Isn't the museum featuring a special exhibit about space exploration for the next few weeks? I heard a commercial on the radio that made it sound quite interesting.」，確認博物館在接下來的幾週是不是要特別展出一個與太空探索有關的特展，並接著說自己在廣播上聽到了廣告，覺得這場展覽聽起來很有趣，因此正確答案是 (A) By listening to the radio。

57 細節事項相關問題—特定細項　答案 (D)

高

題目詢問男子說國家太空署做了什麼，因此要注意聽男子話中提到題目關鍵字（National Space Agency）的前後部分。男子說：「The most popular is a collection of instruments from an actual space shuttle. ~ these were lent to us by the National Space Agency.」，表示最受歡迎的是一堆來自一架真實太空梭的設備，並接著說這些是國家太空署出借的，因此正確答案是 (D) Provided some items。

58 細節事項相關問題—特定細項　答案 (B)

低

題目詢問要額外收費的是什麼，因此要注意與題目關鍵字（extra fee）相關的內容。女子說：「Is access to the exhibit[special exhibit] included in the regular entrance fee?」，詢問參觀特展的費用是否包含在一般入場費裡，男子說：「It will be an extra $15 per person.」，表示每人會需要多付 15 美金，因此正確答案是 (B) Accessing a temporary exhibit。

59 60 61 新

Questions 59-61 refer to the following conversation.	第 59-61 題請參考下列對話。
澳洲式發音 → 美式發音	
M: [59]**I just want to see how your department is progressing with preparations for our annual clearance sale**, which starts this Friday.	男：[59] 我只是想看一下你們部門針對我們在這週五開始的年度清倉特賣所做的準備工作進展如何。
W: There's a slight problem. Some display racks were broken when our staff moved them from the front of the store on Tuesday. Do we have any extras in the back room?	女：有個小問題。一些展示架在我們員工週二把它們從店門口搬開的時候壞掉了。我們裡面還有多的嗎？
M: Unfortunately not. [60]**We'll have to place a rush order for more racks because we need them to arrive on Thursday.**	男：不巧沒有了。[60] 我們得要下一筆急單訂更多架子，因為我們需要它們在週四到。
W: But the store manager has to approve such orders, right? I'm on my way to his office now anyway, so I'll submit a formal request for him to sign off on.	女：不過店經理必須批准這種訂單，對吧？反正我現在正要去他的辦公室，所以我會交一張正式申請給他批准。
M: Thanks. In the meantime, [61]**I'll double-check if we have sufficient shopping bags underneath every cash register.**	男：謝謝。在此同時，[61] 我會再確認一次我們所有收銀台底下是否都有足夠的購物袋。
59 What does the man ask the woman about? (A) The location of merchandise (B) Preparations for an event (C) The progress of construction work (D) Plans for a staff meeting	59 男子詢問女子什麼？ (A) 商品的位置 (B) 活動的準備工作 (C) 施工的進度 (D) 員工會議的計畫
60 According to the man, when do the extra racks need to arrive? (A) On Tuesday (B) On Wednesday (C) On Thursday (D) On Friday	60 根據男子所說，額外的架子需要在什麼時候到？ (A) 週二 (B) 週三 (C) 週四 (D) 週五
61 What does the man say he will do? (A) Sweep the aisles (B) Verify supply levels (C) Confirm a discount amount (D) Locate delivered packages	61 男子說他會做什麼？ (A) 清掃走廊 (B) 確認備品量 (C) 確認折扣金額 (D) 找出送到的包裹

題目 clearance sale 清倉特賣　display rack 展示架　place an order 下訂　rush [rʌʃ] 急迫的
on one's way to 在去～的途中　formal [`fɔrml] 正式的　sign off on 批准～　double-check 再次確認，再次檢查
sufficient [sə`fɪʃənt] 充分的　cash register 收銀台

59 merchandise [`mɝtʃən͵daɪz] 商品

61 sweep [swip] 清掃；掃除　aisle [aɪl] 走道，通道　verify [`vɛrə͵faɪ] 確認　supply [sə`plaɪ] 備品；補給品

59 細節事項相關問題—特定細項　答案 (B)

中

題目詢問男子向女子詢問什麼，因此必須注意聽男子說的話。男子說：「I just want to see how your department is progressing with preparations for our annual clearance sale」，表示想看看女子所在的部門針對年度清倉特賣所做的準備工作進展如何，因此正確答案是 (B) Preparations for an event。

60 細節事項相關問題—特定細項　答案 (C)

低

題目詢問男子說額外的架子要在什麼時候到，因此要注意聽男子話中與題目關鍵字（extra racks need to arrive）相關的內容。男子說：「We'll have to place a rush order for more racks because we need them to arrive on Thursday.」，表示因為需要額外的架子在週四抵達，因此必須下一筆急單，因此正確答案是 (C) On Thursday。

61 細節事項相關問題—接下來要做的事　答案 (B)

高

題目詢問男子說他會做什麼，因此必須注意聽男子話中提到與題目關鍵字（will do）相關的內容。男子說：「I'll double-check if we have sufficient shopping bags underneath every cash register」，表示自己會再次確認收銀台下方是否都有足夠的購物袋，因此正確答案是 (B) Verify supply levels。

62 63 64

Questions 62-64 refer to the following conversation.

加拿大式發音 → 英式發音

M: Hi. This is Kirk from TeleCorp. [62]**I received the voice mail you left with us earlier this morning** about adding more hard drives to the computer server you ordered. I can do it, but [63]**the cost will be higher.** And I'll have to change the contract.

W: [63]**That's what I figured. How much more will it be?**

M: Well . . . The cost will be about $500 higher than my previous quote.

W: OK. That's fine. Will the change to my order affect the installation date?

M: No, I'll come next Monday, as originally scheduled. [64]**It'll take about one hour longer than anticipated, though. That means I'll finish on Tuesday at 12 P.M. instead of 11 A.M.**

第 62-64 題請參考下列對話。

男：嗨。我是 TeleCorp 的 Kirk。[62] 我接到了您今天早上留給我們的語音訊息，提到想在您訂購的電腦伺服器上加上更多硬碟。這我可以做到，但 [63] 費用會提高，且我也必須修改合約。

女：[63] 我想也是這樣。費用會提高多少呢？

男：這個嘛……費用會比我之前的報價多大概 500 美金。

女：好。這沒關係。我修改訂單會影響到安裝日期嗎？

男：不會。我下星期一會按原定時間過去。[64] 不過，安裝會比原本預期的多花一個小時左右。這也就是說，我會在星期二的中午 12 點完工，而不是在早上 11 點。

62 According to the man, what did the woman do earlier today?

(A) Recorded a message
(B) Stopped by a reception desk
(C) Received a parcel
(D) Canceled an order

62 根據男子所說，女子今天稍早做了什麼？

(A) 錄了一段訊息
(B) 去了一下接待櫃檯
(C) 收了一件包裹
(D) 取消一筆訂單

63 新 What does the woman mean when she says, "That's what I figured"?

(A) She noticed an error.
(B) She confirmed a delay.
(C) She anticipated a cost increase.
(D) She identified staffing needs.

63 當女子說：「我想也是這樣」，意思是什麼？

(A) 她注意到了一個錯誤。
(B) 她確認了一項延誤。
(C) 她預期到了一筆費用的增加。
(D) 她確認了人力需求。

64 When did the man originally plan to finish the work?

(A) At 10 A.M.
(B) At 11 A.M.
(C) At 12 P.M.
(D) At 1 P.M.

64 男子原本計畫在什麼時候完工？

(A) 早上 10 點
(B) 早上 11 點
(C) 中午 12 點
(D) 下午 1 點

題目 contract [ˋkɑntrækt] 合約　figure [美 ˋfɪgjɚ 英 ˋfɪgə] 估計；料到　quote [kwot] 報價　affect [əˋfɛkt] 影響　installation [͵ɪnstəˋleʃən] 安裝　originally [əˋrɪdʒən!ɪ] 原本　anticipate [ænˋtɪsə͵pet] 預想

63 notice [ˋnotɪs] 注意到　delay [dɪˋle] 延遲　identify [aɪˋdɛntə͵faɪ] 確認

62 ■ 細節事項相關問題—特定細項　答案 (A)

中

題目詢問男子說女子今天稍早做了什麼，因此必須注意聽男子話中與題目關鍵字（woman ~ earlier today）相關的內容。男子說：「I received the voice mail you left with us earlier this morning」，表示收到女子今天早上留的語音訊息，因此正確答案是 (A) Recorded a message。

新 **63** ■ 細節事項相關問題—掌握意圖　答案 (C)

中

題目詢問女子的說話意圖，因此要注意題目引用句（That's what I figured）的前後部分。男子說：「the cost will be higher」，表示費用會提高，接著女子說：「That's what I figured. How much more will it be?」，表示自己也是這麼想的，並接著詢問費用會提高多少，由此可知，女子之前就預想到費用會提高，因此正確答案是 (C) She anticipated a cost increase.。

64 ■ 細節事項相關問題—特定細項　答案 (B)

中

題目詢問男子原定要在什麼時候完工，因此要注意與題目關鍵字（originally plan to finish the work）有關的內容。男子說：「It'll take about one hour longer than anticipated ~. That means I'll finish ~ at 12 P.M. instead of 11 A.M.」，表示會比原本預期的多花上一小時，所以完工時間會由原本的早上 11 點改為中午 12 點，由此可知，男子的原定完工時間是早上 11 點，因此正確答案是 (B) At 11 A.M.。

65 66 67 新

Questions 65-67 refer to the following conversation and receipt.

第 65-67 題請參考下列對話及收據。

澳洲式發音 → 美式發音

M: Paula, [65]**is your dress ready for the charity fund-raiser we're attending tomorrow evening?**

W: It's still at the dry cleaners, since it needed to be shortened a few inches. I'll pick it up tomorrow morning.

M: You go to Bedford Dry Cleaners, don't you? [66]**I'm thinking about switching to that one, as my current dry cleaner will shut down in June.**

W: Well, Bedford's customer service is exceptional, and they even have monthly discounts. Ah . . . [67]**in May, they're providing 10 percent off work on all leather items.**

M: That sounds great. Maybe I'll come with you tomorrow and drop off some of my button-down shirts.

男：Paula，[65] 妳要穿去我們明天晚上參加的那場慈善募款活動的洋裝準備好了嗎？

女：因為還要把它改短幾吋，所以還在乾洗店裡。我明天早上會去拿。

男：你是去 Bedford 乾洗店，不是嗎？[66] 我在想要換去那家，因為我現在去的乾洗店要在六月歇業了。

女：嗯，Bedford 的顧客服務很棒，而且他們甚至有每月折扣。啊……[67] 在五月，他們對所有皮製品都打九折。

男：這聽起來很棒。也許我明天會和妳一起去，送一些我的正式襯衫過去。

新

Bedford Dry Cleaners

Customer: Paula Steinman

Drop-off Date: **May 22**

Item	Service	Charge
Jean jacket	Add buttons	$5
Silk dress	Shorten	$15
Leather skirt	[67]**Clean**	$20
Silk shirt	Press	$10
Total Paid		$50

Bedford 乾洗店

顧客：Paula Steinman

送件日期：5 月 22 日

品項	服務	費用
牛仔外套	加鈕扣	5 美金
絲質洋裝	改短	15 美金
皮裙	[67]清潔	20 美金
絲質襯衫	熨平	10 美金
總支付金額		50 美金

65 What event will the speakers attend tomorrow night?
(A) A grand opening sale
(B) A fashion show
(C) A fund-raising event
(D) A trade fair

65 說話者們明天晚上會參加什麼活動？
(A) 盛大開幕的特賣會
(B) 時裝秀
(C) 募款活動
(D) 貿易展

66 Why does the man want to switch dry cleaners?
(A) A garment was damaged.
(B) A business is going to close.
(C) A promotion has expired.
(D) A location is more convenient.

66 男子為何想要換乾洗店？
(A) 一件衣服受損了。
(B) 一家公司要關門了。
(C) 一項促銷活動到期了。
(D) 一間據點比較方便。

67 新 Look at the graphic. Which service qualifies for a discount?
(A) Adding buttons
(B) Shortening
(C) Cleaning
(D) Pressing

67 請看圖表。哪項服務符合折扣資格？
(A) 加鈕扣
(B) 改短
(C) 清潔
(D) 熨平

題目 charity [`tʃærətɪ] 慈善　fund-raiser 募款活動　shorten [`ʃɔrtn̩] 減少；縮短　pick up 拿取～　switch [swɪtʃ] 改變；轉換　current (美) `kɝənt (英) `kʌrənt] 現在的　shut down（店家）歇業　exceptional [ɪk`sɛpʃənl] 優秀的　leather [`lɛðɚ] 皮革製的　drop off 把～帶到～

66 garment [`gɑrmənt] 衣服　damaged [`dæmɪdʒd] 受損的　promotion [prə`moʃən] 促銷活動　expire [ɪk`spaɪr] 到期；（期限）截止　convenient [kən`vinjənt] 接近而便利的；方便的

67 qualify for 符合～的資格　press [prɛs] 熨燙（衣服等）

65 低 細節事項相關問題—特定細項 答案 (C)

題目詢問說話者們明天晚上要參加的活動是什麼，因此必須注意與題目關鍵字（attend tomorrow night）相關的內容。男子對女子說：「is your dress ready for the charity fund-raiser we're attending tomorrow evening?」，詢問女子要穿去參加明天晚上那場慈善募款活動的洋裝是否已經準備好了，因此正確答案是 (C) A fund-raising event。

換句話說

charity fund-raiser 慈善募款活動 → fund-raising event 募款活動

66 中 細節事項相關問題—理由 答案 (B)

題目詢問男子想要換乾洗店的原因，因此要注意與題目關鍵字（switch dry cleaners）相關的內容。男子說：「I'm thinking about switching to that one[Bedford Dry Cleaners], as my current dry cleaner will shut down in June.」，表示自己現在去的乾洗店六月要歇業了，因此正在想要換成 Bedford 乾洗店，因此正確答案是 (B) A business is going to close.。

新 67 中 細節事項相關問題—圖表資料 答案 (C)

題目詢問符合折扣資格的服務是哪一項，因此必須注意題目提供的收據資訊及與題目關鍵字（service qualifies for a discount）相關的內容。女子說：「in May, they[Bedford Dry Cleaners]'re providing 10 percent off work on all leather items」，表示 Bedford 乾洗店在五月對所有皮製品都打九折，由此可知，5 月 22 日送件的皮裙符合折扣資格，因此正確答案是 (C) Cleaning。

新

68 69 70

Questions 68-70 refer to the following conversation and notice.

加拿大式發音 → 英式發音

M: Welcome to the Hartford Public Library.
W: Hi. I'd like to borrow this book. I have my library card right here.
M: OK. And just to let you know, we've increased the loan period. [68]**You can borrow books for up to three weeks now.**
W: Great. Um, [69]**I also want to check out some new books that were supposed to arrive on August 13**, but they aren't on the shelves.
M: I know the two you're referring to. [69]**The guidebook will be available on August 23. There's a typo on the notice. But the other one was damaged in transit, and the replacement won't arrive until September.**
W: Hmm . . . [70]**Can you recommend another book on that topic?**
M: Sure. [70]**I'll check our system for a similar title.**

第 68-70 題請參考下列對話及公告。

男：歡迎光臨 Hartford 公共圖書館。
女：嗨。我想要借這本書。我的圖書證在這裡。
男：好的。另外跟您說一下，我們已經把借閱期延長了。[68] 現在您借書最多可借三個星期。
女：太好了。嗯，[69] 我還想要借一些應該要在 8 月 13 日到館的新書，但它們不在架上。
男：我知道您在說的那兩本書。[69] 那本旅遊指南會在 8 月 23 日開放借閱。通知上有個地方打錯了。但另一本在運送途中受損了，而用來替換的那本要到九月才會到館。
女：嗯……[70] 可以請你就這個主題推薦其他書嗎？
男：當然。[70] 我來查查我們系統裡類似的書名。

新

Hartford Public Library
New Books (August)

Field	Title	Available from
Language	*Beginner Japanese*	August 7
Home	*Storage and You*	August 7
History	[69]***The History of London***	**August 13**
Travel	***A Guide to Marseilles***	**August 13**

Hartford 公共圖書館
新書（8 月）

領域	書名	開放借閱時間
語言	*Beginner Japanese*	8 月 7 日
家庭	*Storage and You*	8 月 7 日
歷史	[69]*The History of London*	8 月 13 日
旅遊	*A Guide to Marseilles*	8 月 13 日

68 According to the man, what is the maximum loan period?
(A) One week
(B) Two weeks
(C) Three weeks
(D) Four weeks

68 根據男子所說，借閱期最長是多久？
(A) 一週
(B) 兩週
(C) 三週
(D) 四週

69 Look at the graphic. Which book will arrive in September?
新
(A) *Beginner Japanese*
(B) *Storage and You*
(C) *The History of London*
(D) *A Guide to Marseilles*

69 請看圖表。哪一本書會在九月到館？
(A) *Beginner Japanese*
(B) *Storage and You*
(C) *The History of London*
(D) *A Guide to Marseilles*

70 What will the man most likely do next?
(A) Update a library account
(B) Search for a publication
(C) Order a replacement book
(D) Speak with a supervisor

70 男子接下來最有可能會做什麼？
(A) 更新圖書館帳號
(B) 搜尋一本出版品
(C) 訂購用來替換的書
(D) 和主管談談

題目 loan [lon] 借出　check out 借出（書等）　shelf [ʃɛlf]（書架等的）架子　refer to 談論，提及
guidebook [ˋgaɪd͵bʊk] 旅遊指南　available [əˋveləbl] 可用的　typo [ˋtaɪpo] 打字錯誤　in transit 運送途中
replacement [rɪˋplesmənt] 替代物；替換
70 search for 搜尋～，搜索～　publication [͵pʌblɪˋkeʃən] 出版品；刊物

68 低 **細節事項相關問題—程度** 答案 (C)

題目詢問借閱期最長是多久，因此要注意與題目關鍵字（maximum loan period）相關的內容。男子說：「You can borrow books for up to three weeks now.」，表示現在最多可以借上三週，因此正確答案是 (C) Three weeks。

新 **69** 難 **細節事項相關問題—圖表資料** 答案 (C)

題目詢問九月會到館的是哪本書，因此必須確認題目提供的公告資訊，並注意和題目關鍵字（book ~ arrive in September）相關的內容。女子說：「I also want to check out some new books that were supposed to arrive on August 13」，表示自己想借一些應該要在 8 月 13 日到館的新書，接著男子說：「The guidebook will be available on August 23. ~ the other one was damaged in transit, and the replacement won't arrive until September.」，表示旅遊指南會在 8 月 23 日開放借閱，另一本則是在運送途中受損了，而用來替換的書要到九月才會到館，由此可知，在 8 月 13 日開放借閱的不是旅遊書，而是歷史書《The History of London》，但它因為運送途中受損而須替換，而用來替換的那本要九月才會到館，因此正確答案是 (C) *The History of London*。

70 中 **細節事項相關問題—接下來要做的事** 答案 (B)

題目詢問男子接下來可能會做什麼，因此要注意對話的最後部分。女子說：「Can you recommend another book ~?」，詢問男子是否能推薦其他書，男子說：「I'll check our system for a similar title.」，表示要從系統裡去查類似的書名，因此正確答案是 (B) Search for a publication。

換句話說

check ~ system for a similar title 從系統裡去查類似的書名 → Search for a publication 搜尋一本出版品

71
72
73

Questions 71-73 refer to the following announcement.

英式發音

Attention, all Quickstone Corporation employees. [71]**Next week, from June 9 to 13, all staff members are encouraged to make donations of clothing, books, and toys.** These will be given to the Victoria Community Center to be distributed to needy families. Large plastic boxes will be placed in the lobby of our office building for workers to put items into. [72]**Four volunteers from our company are also needed to help deliver the containers to the center on Monday, June 16,** at 5 P.M. [73]**Those interested should call Marcy Dwyer in the human resources department at extension 700 before the end of the day.** We look forward to great participation in this charitable effort on behalf of our organization.

第 71-73 題請參考下列公告。

Quickstone Corporation 全體員工請注意。[71] 下星期，從 6 月 9 日到 13 日，歡迎所有員工捐贈衣物、書籍及玩具。這些東西將會交給 Victoria 社區中心發送給有需要的家庭。我們辦公大樓的大廳裡將會放置大型塑膠箱讓員工們可以把東西放進去。[72] 還需要我們公司四個自願的人協助，把這些箱子在 6 月 16 日星期一的下午 5 點運到那間中心。[73] 有興趣的人請在今天下班前打分機 700 給人力資源部的 Marcy Dwyer。我們期待各位能代表本公司熱烈參與這次的慈善活動。

71 What can employees do next week?
(A) Sign up for a contest
(B) Donate some items
(C) Make various crafts
(D) Decorate a lobby

71 員工們下週可以做什麼？
(A) 報名一場比賽
(B) 捐贈一些物品
(C) 製作各式各樣的工藝品
(D) 裝飾大廳

72 When will employees most likely visit the community center?
(A) On June 9
(B) On June 12
(C) On June 13
(D) On June 16

72 員工們最有可能會在什麼時候去那間社區中心？
(A) 6 月 9 日
(B) 6 月 12 日
(C) 6 月 13 日
(D) 6 月 16 日

73 What should some listeners do before the end of the day?
(A) Contact a coworker
(B) Pick up a product
(C) Participate in a workshop
(D) Request a deadline extension

73 某些聽者在下班前應該要做什麼？
(A) 聯絡一位同事
(B) 領取一件產品
(C) 參加一場工作坊
(D) 申請延長截止期限

題目 make a donation 捐贈　distribute [dɪ`strɪbjʊt] 分發　needy [`nidɪ]（經濟上）有需要的；貧窮的
interested [美 `ɪntərɪstɪd 英 `intəristid] 感興趣的　extension [ɪk`stɛnʃən] 分機；延長　look forward to 期待～
participation [美 pɑr͵tɪsə`peʃən 英 pɑː͵tisi`peiʃən] 參與　charitable [美 `tʃærətəbl̩ 英 `tʃæritəbl] 慈善的
on behalf of 代表～　organization [美 ͵ɔrgənə`zeʃən 英 ͵ɔːgənai`zeiʃən] 組織；團體
71 donate [`donet] 捐贈　various [`vɛrɪəs] 各式各樣的　craft [kræft] 工藝品

71 細節事項相關問題—特定細項 答案 (B)
中
題目詢問員工們下星期能做什麼，因此要注意提到題目關鍵字（next week）的前後部分。獨白說：「Next week, ~, all staff members are encouraged to make donations of clothing, books, and toys.」，表示歡迎所有員工捐贈衣物、書籍及玩具，因此正確答案是 (B) Donate some items。
換句話說
make donations of clothing, books, and toys 捐贈衣物、書籍及玩具 → Donate some items 捐贈一些物品

72 細節事項相關問題—特定細項 答案 (D)
低
題目詢問員工們去那間社區中心的時間點，因此要注意和題目關鍵字（visit the community center）相關的內容。獨白說：「Four volunteers from our company are also needed to help deliver the containers to the center on Monday, June 16」，表示 6 月 16 日星期一需要四名公司裡自願的人幫忙把東西運到社區中心，由此可知，員工們在 6 月 16 日會去社區中心，因此正確答案是 (D) On June 16。

73 細節事項相關問題—特定細項 答案 (A)
低
題目詢問某些聽者在今天下班前應該要做什麼，因此要注意提到題目關鍵字（before the end of the day）的前後部分。獨白說：「Those interested should call Marcy Dwyer in the human resources department ~ before the end of the day.」，表示有興趣的人應該要在下班前打給人力資源部的 Marcy Dwyer，因此正確答案是 (A) Contact a coworker。

74 75 76

Questions 74-76 refer to the following telephone message.

加拿大式發音

This message is for Amy Yang. My name is Floyd Lamar, and I'm an employee at the Center Street DVD Shop. [74]**You rented *The Brothers O'Brien* five days ago, which makes it two days past due.** Please return it as soon as possible. We will be closed from December 24 to 26 for the holidays, so [75]**you should use the return bin near the entrance during that period.** Of course, you will have to pay a late fee. [76]**You currently owe $10, and this will increase by $5 per day until we receive the DVD. So, you should act quickly.** If you have any questions, call 555-8039.

74 What is the speaker mainly discussing?

(A) A damaged product
(B) An overdue rental
(C) A new return policy
(D) An online reservation

75 What does the speaker recommend the listener do on the holidays?

(A) Use the side entrance of a building
(B) Call an information hotline
(C) Place an item in a container
(D) Go to the shop in the morning

76 Why should the listener act quickly?

(A) A schedule has been changed.
(B) A complaint has been made.
(C) A service will be canceled.
(D) An amount will increase.

第 74-76 題請參考下列電話留言。

這是給 Amy Yang 的留言。我的名字是 Floyd Lamar，我是 Center 街 DVD 店的員工。[74] 您在五天前租了《The Brothers O'Brien》，現在已經過期兩天了。請盡速歸還。因為我們在 12 月 24 到 26 日放假不營業，所以[75] 您在這段期間須使用在入口附近的歸還箱。當然，您將必須支付一筆逾期罰款。[76] 您目前積欠 10 美金，而在我們拿到那片 DVD 之前，這筆欠款每天會增加 5 美金。因此，您應盡快處理。如有任何問題，請致電 555-8039。

74 說話者主要在說什麼？

(A) 一件受損的產品
(B) 一件過期的出租品
(C) 一項新的歸還政策
(D) 一筆線上預約

75 說話者建議聽者在假期期間做什麼？

(A) 使用大樓側的入口
(B) 致電服務熱線
(C) 將一個物件放進容器裡
(D) 在早上去那間店

76 為何聽者應盡快處理？

(A) 一張時間表被更動了。
(B) 一項申訴被提出了。
(C) 一項服務將被取消。
(D) 一筆金額將會增加。

題目 period [ˋpɪrɪəd] 時期　late fee 逾期罰款　owe [o] 積欠（債務等）
74 damaged [ˋdæmɪdʒd] 受損的　overdue [ˋovɚˋdju] 逾期的　policy [ˋpɑləsɪ] 方針，政策　reservation [ˌrɛzɚˋveʃən] 預約
75 hotline [ˋhɑtlaɪn] 熱線
76 amount [əˋmaʊnt] 金額；總額

74 整體內容相關問題—主題　　答案 (B)

中

題目詢問電話留言的主題，因此必須特別注意聽獨白的開頭部分。獨白說：「You rented *The Brothers O'Brien* five days ago, which makes it two days past due.」，表示聽者在五天前租了《The Brothers O'Brien》，而且已過期兩天，接著繼續說明與出租品過期相關的內容，因此正確答案是 (B) An overdue rental。

75 細節事項相關問題—提議　　答案 (C)

中

題目詢問說話者建議聽者在假期期間做什麼，因此要注意聽獨白中後半部裡出現提議相關表達的句子。獨白說：「you should use the return bin near the entrance during that period[holidays]」，表示聽者在這段假期期間須使用在入口附近的歸還箱，因此正確答案是 (C) Place an item in a container。

76 細節事項相關問題—理由　　答案 (D)

低

題目詢問聽者應盡快處理這件事的原因是什麼，因此要注意提到題目關鍵字（act quickly）的前後部分：「You currently owe $10, and this will increase by $5 per day until we receive the DVD. So, you should act quickly.」，表示聽者目前積欠了 10 美金，而在說話者拿到 DVD 之前，每天欠款都會增加 5 美金，因此聽者應盡快處理，因此正確答案是 (D) An amount will increase.。

77
78
79

Questions 77-79 refer to the following talk.	第 77-79 題請參考下列談話。
澳洲式發音	
Everyone, we've reached our final stop . . . Patterson Beach. This is where the famous scene from the movie *Paradise* was shot. [77]**If you look to your left, you'll see the dock where Mark Campbell and Alyssa Perth performed their wedding scene.** We'll spend about an hour here. [78]**I know I originally told you 30 minutes, but we're running a bit ahead today.** So feel free to take as many pictures as you like and enjoy the sunshine. Afterwards, we will visit an outdoor crafts market near the beach before heading back to the resort. Oh . . . [79]**you shouldn't remove your shoes when you are on the beach** because the sand is full of sharp shells and rocks. OK, please follow me.	各位，我們已經抵達了我們的終點站……Patterson 海灘。這裡是電影《Paradise》裡知名場景的拍攝地點。[77] 如果你們往自己的左邊看去，你們會看到那座 Mark Campbell 與 Alyssa Perth 演出他們婚禮那幕的碼頭。我們會在這裡待大概一個小時。[78] 我知道我原本是跟你們說 30 分鐘，不過我們今天進度有點超前。所以歡迎你們盡情拍照並享受陽光。接下來，我們會在返回度假村之前，先去海灘附近的戶外工藝品市集。噢……[79] 你們在海灘上的時候不要把鞋子脫掉，因為沙子裡充斥著尖銳的貝殼和石頭。好了，請跟我來。
77 Who most likely is Mark Campbell? (A) An actor (B) A tour guide (C) A resort manager (D) A photographer	77 Mark Campbell 最有可能是誰？ (A) 演員 (B) 導遊 (C) 度假村經理 (D) 攝影師
78 新 Why does the speaker say, "We'll spend about an hour here"? (A) To request that listeners be patient (B) To encourage participation in a performance (C) To notify listeners of a schedule change (D) To confirm that a plan will be followed	78 為什麼說話者說：「我們會在這裡待大概一個小時」？ (A) 要求聽者們要有耐心 (B) 鼓勵參加一場演出 (C) 告知聽者們一項行程變更 (D) 確認會按一項計畫進行
79 What are listeners instructed to do? (A) Keep their shoes on (B) Avoid touching a display (C) Secure their belongings (D) Use protective gear	79 聽者們被指示做什麼？ (A) 一直穿著鞋子 (B) 避免碰觸展品 (C) 保管好他們的隨身物品 (D) 使用防護裝備

題目 scene [sin]（戲劇、電影的）場景 shoot [ʃut] 拍攝；射擊 dock [美 dɑk 英 dɔk] 碼頭
perform [美 pɚˋfɔrm 英 pəˋfɔ:m] 演出；實行 head [hɛd] 前往；駛向 remove [rɪˋmuv] 去除；脫掉
follow [美 ˋfɑlo 英 ˋfɔləu] 跟隨；按照

78 patient [ˋpeʃənt] 有耐心的

79 avoid [əˋvɔɪd] 避免 secure [sɪˋkjʊr] 保管；確保；安全的 protective [prəˋtɛktɪv] 防護的；保護用的 gear [gɪr] 裝備

77 細節事項相關問題—特定細項 答案 (A)

中

題目詢問 Mark Campbell 的身分，因此要注意聽和題目所詢問對象（Mark Campbell）的身分、職業相關的表達。獨白說：「If you look to your left, you'll see the dock where Mark Campbell ~ performed ~ wedding scene.」，表示如果聽者們朝他們自己的左邊看去，就會看到 Mark Campbell 演出婚禮那幕的碼頭，由此可知，Mark Campbell 是演員，因此正確答案是 (A) An actor。

新 **78** 細節事項相關問題—掌握意圖 答案 (C)

高

題目詢問說話者的說話意圖，因此要注意題目引用句（We'll spend about an hour here）的前後部分。獨白說：「I know I originally told you 30 minutes, but we're running a bit ahead today.」，表示雖然自己原本說的是會待 30 分鐘，不過今天的進度超前了，由此可知，說話者是想告知聽者們行程和原定計畫不同了，因此正確答案是 (C) To notify listeners of a schedule change。

79 細節事項相關問題—特定細項 答案 (A)

低

題目詢問聽者們被指示做什麼，因此要注意和題目關鍵字（instructed to do）相關的內容。獨白說：「you shouldn't remove your shoes when you are on the beach」，告知聽者們不要在海灘上脫鞋，因此正確答案是 (A) Keep their shoes on。

80
81
82

Questions 80-82 refer to the following broadcast.

美式發音

In tonight's *Around Town* segment, we're going to look at a recently completed construction project here in San Bernardino. [80]**Burke Industries opened its City Springs Mall yesterday.** This 200,000 square meter facility contains more than 275 stores and restaurants. It is expected to generate annual sales of approximately $20,000 per square meter. Of course, [81]**the city government will collect more taxes as a result.** The mall will also create at least 5,000 new jobs, which is important because [82]**high unemployment has been a problem in the area since Analytic Systems moved its factory abroad last year.** We will now take a short commercial break. When we return, a representative from Burke Industries will join us to answer some questions.

第 80-82 題請參考下列廣播。

在今晚的《Around Town》單元，我們要來看看最近在聖伯納迪諾這裡完工的一項建案。[80]Burke 工業的 City Springs 購物中心在昨天開幕。這座占地 200,000 平方公尺的設施裡擁有超過 275 家商店及餐廳。預期每平方公尺將產出約 20,000 美金的年度銷售額。當然，[81] 市政府會因此而收到更多稅金。這間購物中心也會創造至少 5,000 份新工作，這件事很重要，因為 [82] 自從去年 Analytic Systems 將其工廠移往海外，高失業率就一直是這一區的問題。我們現在要進一小段廣告休息一下。等我們回來之後，Burke 工業的一位代表將會加入我們來回答一些問題。

80 What happened yesterday?

(A) A retail facility began operations.
(B) A construction site was chosen.
(C) An economic report was released.
(D) A company merger took place.

81 What does the speaker say about the city government?

(A) It will request repayment of a debt.
(B) It will receive additional revenue.
(C) It will take control of a property.
(D) It will manage a renovation project.

82 What is suggested about Analytic Systems?

(A) It will increase its payroll taxes.
(B) It will purchase another factory.
(C) Its relocation caused many job losses.
(D) Its closure was due to financial problems.

80 昨天發生了什麼事？

(A) 零售設施開始營運。
(B) 選定了工程地點。
(C) 發布了經濟報告。
(D) 進行了公司合併。

81 關於市政府，說話者說什麼？

(A) 它會要求清償債務。
(B) 它會獲得額外稅收。
(C) 它會掌控一處物業。
(D) 它會處理一項整修計畫。

82 關於 Analytic Systems，暗示了什麼？

(A) 它會增加工資稅。
(B) 它會再買一間工廠。
(C) 它的遷址導致許多人失業。
(D) 它的歇業是因為財務問題。

題目 segment [ˋsɛgmənt]（電視節目等的）單元 construction [kənˋstrʌkʃən] 建設；建造 square meter 平方公尺 generate [ˋdʒɛnəˏret] 產出 annual [ˋænjʊəl] 年度的 approximately [əˋprɑksəmɪtlɪ] 大約 tax [tæks] 稅；稅金 unemployment [ˏʌnɪmˋplɔɪmənt] 失業率；失業（狀態） abroad [əˋbrɔd] 往海外 commercial [kəˋmɝʃəl]（電視或廣播節目裡的）商業廣告 representative [rɛprɪˋzɛntətɪv] 代表；代表人員

80 operation [ˏɑpəˋreʃən] 營運；運轉

81 repayment [rɪˋpemənt] 償還 debt [dɛt] 債務 revenue [ˋrɛvəˏnju] 稅收；收益 take control of 控制～ property [ˋprɑpɚtɪ] 物業；不動產

82 payroll tax 工資稅 closure [ˋkloʒɚ] 歇業；關閉

80 細節事項相關問題—特定細項 答案 (A)

中

題目詢問昨天發生了什麼，因此要注意提到題目關鍵字（yesterday）的前後部分。獨白說：「Burke Industries opened its City Springs Mall yesterday.」，表示 Burke 工業的 City Springs 購物中心昨天開幕，因此正確答案是 (A) A retail facility began operations.。

81 細節事項相關問題—提及 答案 (B)

高

題目詢問說話者說了什麼有關市政府的事，因此要注意提到題目關鍵字（city government）的前後部分。獨白說：「the city government will collect more taxes as a result」，表示市政府會因此收到更多稅金，因此正確答案是 (B) It will receive additional revenue.。

82 細節事項相關問題—推論 答案 (C)

難

題目詢問關於 Analytic Systems 暗示了什麼，因此要注意提到題目關鍵字（Analytic Systems）的前後部分。獨白說：「high unemployment has been a problem in the area since Analytic Systems moved its factory abroad last year」，表示自從 Analytic Systems 去年將工廠搬到海外，高失業率就一直是這一區的問題，由此可知，Analytic Systems 的遷址造成了很多人失業，因此正確答案是 (C) Its relocation caused many job losses.。

83 84 85

Questions 83-85 refer to the following telephone message.

澳洲式發音

Good morning, Ms. Harris. This is Michael Banner returning your call. [83]**I'm delighted that you've chosen us for your daughter's graduation party at your home next month. As to your question, we offer a wide range of dishes** that are compatible with your dietary restrictions. Um, [84]**we have provided food for several vegan events in the past, including a vegan barbeque!** A real triumph . . . [84]**I wasn't sure we were going to be able to prepare suitable food for that event.** Anyway, [85]**I'll e-mail you some questions about your event and budget this afternoon.** Please respond by Friday so that I can start planning the menu and prepare some sample dishes for you to taste.

83 Who most likely is the speaker?

(A) A caterer
(B) A hotel manager
(C) A decorator
(D) A conference organizer

84 What does the man mean when he says, "A real triumph"?

新

(A) A company has won an award.
(B) A task was difficult to complete.
(C) A request was unexpected.
(D) An event was well attended.

85 What will the man do later in the day?

(A) Prepare a budget
(B) Answer some questions
(C) E-mail a client
(D) Send some samples

第 83-85 題請參考下列電話留言。

早安，Harris 小姐。我是要回您電話的 Michael Banner。[83] 我很高興您選擇了我們負責下個月在您府上為您女兒舉辦的畢業派對。關於您的疑問，我們提供了各式各樣可配合您飲食禁忌的菜色。嗯，[84] 我們過去曾為幾場全素的活動提供食物，包括一場全素的燒烤！真是一大成功……[84] 我當時並不確定我們是否能為那場活動籌備適合的食物。總之，[85] 我今天下午會用電子郵件寄給您一些有關您活動及預算的問題。請在星期五前回覆，以便我開始規劃菜單並準備一些給您試菜的菜色。

83 說話者最有可能是誰？

(A) 外燴業者
(B) 飯店經理
(C) 裝潢師傅
(D) 會議籌辦人

84 當男子說：「真是一大成功」，意思是什麼？

(A) 一間公司贏得了一個獎項。
(B) 一項任務很難完成。
(C) 一項要求在意料之外。
(D) 一個活動出席踴躍。

85 男子這天稍晚會做什麼？

(A) 準備一份預算案
(B) 回答一些問題
(C) 寄電子郵件給客戶
(D) 寄一些樣本

題目 delighted [dɪ`laɪtɪd] 高興的　graduation [ˌgrædʒʊ`eʃən] 畢業　a wide range of 各式各樣的；範圍廣泛的
dish [dɪʃ] 菜餚；盤碟　compatible [kəm`pætəbl] 適合的；相容的　dietary [(美) `daɪəˌtɛrɪ (英) `daiəteri] 飲食的
restriction [rɪ`strɪkʃən] 限制　vegan [(美) `vigən (英) `vigən] 全素食的；全素主義者　triumph [`traɪəmf] 大成功，勝利
respond [(美) rɪ`spɑnd (英) ri`spɔnd] 回應；回答　taste [test] 試吃；味道

83 整體內容相關問題—說話者 答案 (A)

中

題目詢問說話者的身分，因此必須注意聽獨白中和身分、職業相關的表達。獨白說：「I'm delighted that you've chosen us for your daughter's graduation party ~. ~ we offer a wide range of dishes」，表示很高興聽者請自己公司負責下個月的畢業派對，隨後談及與提供食物相關的內容，由此可知，說話者是外燴業者，因此正確答案是 (A) A caterer。

新 **84 細節事項相關問題—掌握意圖** 答案 (B)

高

題目詢問說話者的說話意圖，因此要注意題目引用句（A real triumph）的前後部分。獨白說：「we have provided food for several vegan events in the past, including a vegan barbeque!」，表示過去曾為幾場全素的活動提供食物，接著說：「I wasn't sure we were going to be able to prepare suitable food for that event.」，表示當時並不確定是否能為那場活動籌備適合的食物，由此可知，這項工作在執行上具有一定難度，因此正確答案是 (B) A task was difficult to complete.。

85 細節事項相關問題—接下來要做的事 答案 (C)

低

題目詢問男子晚點會做什麼，因此要注意和題目關鍵字（later in the day）相關的內容。獨白說：「I'll e-mail you some questions about your event and budget this afternoon」，表示自己今天下午會寄電子郵件詢問與活動及預算有關的問題，因此正確答案是 (C) E-mail a client。

86
87
88

Questions 86-88 refer to the following announcement.	第 86-88 題請參考下列公告。
英式發音	
Welcome to the Museum of Science. [86]**We are pleased to announce that an audio tour is now available. To use this service, request a media player and headphones** at the main information booth. [87]**As you move through the museum, sensors on the device will detect nearby exhibits, causing the appropriate recorded messages to be played.** Please note that temporary exhibitions are not covered by the tour, including the one on the history of photography that runs until October 25. [88]**If you would like more information about this exhibition, simply pick up a brochure from the rack next to the main entrance.** It includes detailed descriptions of the items on display. Thank you.	歡迎來到科學博物館。[86] 我們很高興宣布現在可以使用語音導覽了。要使用這項服務，請在主服務台索取媒體播放機及耳機。[87] 當您於博物館中移動時，裝置上的感應器會偵測附近展品，讓相應的錄音訊息得以播放。請注意臨時展品不涵蓋於此導覽內，包括展出到 10 月 25 日的攝影歷史展內的那件展品。[88] 若您想取得與這項展品有關的更多資訊，只要從正門旁的架子上拿一本小冊子即可。它裡面對於展示中的那些品項有著詳細的描述。謝謝您。
86 What is the purpose of the announcement? (A) To promote a product (B) To announce a regulation (C) To describe an event (D) To introduce a service	86 這段公告的目的是什麼？ (A) 宣傳一件產品 (B) 宣布一項規定 (C) 描述一個活動 (D) 介紹一項服務
87 What does the speaker mention about the device? (A) It can be used in many museums. (B) It plays content automatically. (C) It must be reserved in advance. (D) It has several language settings.	87 關於這個裝置，說話者提到什麼？ (A) 可以在許多博物館中使用。 (B) 會自動播放內容。 (C) 必須事先預約。 (D) 有數種語言設定。
88 According to the speaker, how can listeners get information about a temporary exhibition? (A) By speaking to an employee (B) By visiting a booth (C) By joining a group (D) By reading a pamphlet	88 根據說話者所說，聽者們可以如何取得與一件臨時展品有關的資訊？ (A) 和一位員工說話 (B) 造訪一個攤位 (C) 加入一個團體 (D) 閱讀一本小冊子

題目 available [ə`veləbḷ] 可使用的　sensor [美 `sɛnsɚ 英 `sensə] 感應器　detect [dɪ`tɛkt] 偵測；察覺
exhibit [ɪg`zɪbɪt] 展示品　appropriate [美 ə`proprɪˌet 英 ə`prəupriət] 適當的；相稱的
brochure [美 bro`ʃʊr 英 brəu`ʃjuə] 小冊子　rack [ræk] 架子　description [dɪ`skrɪpʃən] 描述
86 promote [prə`mot] 宣傳
87 automatically [ˌɔtə`mætɪkḷɪ] 自動地　in advance 事先
88 join [dʒɔɪn] 加入

86 **整體內容相關問題—目的** 答案 (D)
中
題目詢問這段公告的目的，因此必須注意聽獨白開頭的部分。獨白說：「We are pleased to announce that an audio tour is now available. To use this service, request a media player and headphones」，表示很高興宣布現在可以使用語音導覽了，且索取媒體播放機及耳機就能使用這項服務，接著又繼續介紹更多和這項服務有關的資訊，因此正確答案是 (D) To introduce a service。

87 **細節事項相關問題—提及** 答案 (B)
高
題目詢問說話者提到什麼與這個裝置有關的事，因此要注意提到題目關鍵字（device）的前後部分。獨白說：「As you move through the museum, sensors on the device will detect nearby exhibits, causing the appropriate recorded messages to be played.」，表示當人們在博物館內移動時，裝置會偵測附近展品，讓相應的錄音訊息得以播放，由此可知，這個裝置會自動播放內容，因此正確答案是 (B) It plays content automatically.。

88 **細節事項相關問題—方法** 答案 (D)
中
題目詢問聽者們能獲得臨時展品相關資訊的方法，因此必須注意聽和題目關鍵字（get information about a temporary exhibition）相關的內容。獨白說：「If you would like more information about this exhibition[temporary exhibition], simply pick up a brochure from the rack next to the main entrance.」，表示如果想獲得更多關於臨時展品的資訊，只要從正門旁的架子上拿一本小冊子即可，因此正確答案是 (D) By reading a pamphlet。

89

90

91

Questions 89-91 refer to the following advertisement.

美式發音

[89]Internet access should be affordable for everyone. That's why Emerson Digital is offering a special package for people living in Creston. For just $14.99 per month, you'll enjoy upload and download speeds comparable to those of more expensive packages offered by other companies. And you can try it at no risk. **[90]If you are a resident of the region, you qualify for a free, one-week evaluation period. [91]Just visit our office at 1432 Pine Street to register today. Be advised that you will have to show an identification card that includes your current address to sign up.** Don't miss out on this great offer!

89 What is being advertised?

(A) A television package
(B) An insurance policy
(C) An Internet service
(D) An electronic device

90 What do residents qualify for?

(A) A gift certificate
(B) A software upgrade
(C) A discounted rate
(D) A complimentary trial

91 What should listeners bring to the office?

(A) A copy of a receipt
(B) A credit card
(C) A registration form
(D) A piece of identification

第 89-91 題請參考下列廣告。

[89] 使用網路的權利應該要是所有人都能夠負擔的。這就是為什麼 Emerson Digital 現正針對住在 Creston 的人提供特別套裝方案。每月只要 14.99 美金，您就享有可與其他公司所提供的那些較為昂貴的套裝方案相比擬的上傳及下載速度。且您可以放心試試看。[90] 若您是這區的居民，您就符合取得為期一週的免費試用期的資格。[91] 今天就到我們在 Pine 街 1432 號的辦公室登記吧。請注意，您將必須出示上面有現居地址的身分證來進行登記。不要錯過這項絕佳優惠！

89 在廣告什麼？

(A) 電視套裝方案
(B) 保單
(C) 網路服務
(D) 電子裝置

90 居民符合什麼的資格？

(A) 禮券
(B) 軟體升級
(C) 折扣價
(D) 免費試用

91 聽者們應該帶什麼去辦公室？

(A) 收據影本
(B) 信用卡
(C) 登記表
(D) 身份證件

題目 affordable [əˋfɔrdəbḷ]（價格）可負擔的；實惠的　comparable [ˋkɑmpərəbḷ] 可比擬的；比得上的
risk [rɪsk] 風險；危險　resident [ˋrɛzədənt] 居民　region [ˋridʒən] 地區　qualify [ˋkwɑləˏfaɪ] 符合～的資格
evaluation [ɪˏvæljʊˋeʃən] 評估　period [ˋpɪrɪəd] 期間　register [ˋrɛdʒɪstɚ] 登記，註冊　advise [ədˋvaɪz] 告知
identification card 身分證　miss out on 錯過～

89 insurance policy 保單，保險契約　electronic [ɪlɛkˋtrɑnɪk] 電子的

90 gift certificate 禮券　rate [ret] 費用，價格　complimentary [ˏkɑmpləˋmɛntərɪ] 免費（贈送）的　trial [ˋtraɪəl] 試用

91 receipt [rɪˋsit] 收據

89 整體內容相關問題—主題 答案 (C)
低

題目詢問廣告的主題是什麼，因此要注意聽獨白的開頭部分。獨白說：「Internet access should be affordable for everyone. That's why Emerson Digital is offering a special package」，表示使用網路的權利應該是要人人都負擔得起，而這就是 Emerson Digital 提供特別套裝方案的原因，由此可知，這是網路服務的廣告，因此正確答案是 (C) An Internet service。

90 細節事項相關問題—特定細項 答案 (D)
高

題目詢問身為居民會符合什麼的資格，因此必須注意和題目關鍵字（residents qualify for）有關的內容。獨白說：「If you are a resident of the region, you qualify for a free, one-week evaluation period.」，表示如果是這區的居民，就符合取得為期一週的免費試用期的資格，因此正確答案是 (D) A complimentary trial。

換句話說

free ~ evaluation period 免費試用期 → complimentary trial 免費試用

91 細節事項相關問題—特定細項 答案 (D)
低

題目詢問聽者們應該帶什麼去辦公室，因此要注意和題目關鍵字（bring to the office）相關的內容。獨白說：「Just visit our office ~ to register today. Be advised that you will have to show an identification card ~ to sign up.」，表示聽者們今天就可以去公司辦公室登記，登記時將必須出示身分證，由此可知，聽者們應該要把身分證帶去辦公室，因此正確答案是 (D) A piece of identification。

92
93
94

Questions 92-94 refer to the following talk and table.

澳洲式發音

Just a couple of things to keep in mind this week. [92]**Our distribution center has a new floor manager**, Brett Jensen. He's been hired to manage the evening shift, so his hours will be from 3 to 11 P.M. [93]**If one of you is willing to show him around the facility later this afternoon, that'd be great.** Also, beginning tomorrow, we'll be receiving a number of shipments from suppliers. While the schedule posted next to the loading dock is mostly right, there's one piece of outdated information. [94]**The shipment of microwaves is going to arrive a day later—on May 15.** The dishwashers and dryers scheduled to get here earlier in the week should arrive as planned, though.

新

Delivery Schedule		
Date	**Company**	**Shipment Contents**
May 12	Lloyd Ferris	Dishwashers
May 13	Monroe Industries	Dryers
May 14	[94]**Abdul & Sons**	**Microwaves**
May 15	Stone Incorporated	Refrigerators

92 Where do the listeners work?

(A) At a retail store
(B) At a distribution center
(C) At a testing facility
(D) At a manufacturing plant

93 What does the speaker ask one of the listeners to do?

(A) Give an employee a tour
(B) Post a notice near an exit
(C) Print out a new schedule
(D) Record some notes

94 新 Look at the graphic. Which company has postponed its delivery?

(A) Lloyd Ferris
(B) Monroe Industries
(C) Abdul & Sons
(D) Stone Incorporated

第 92-94 題請參考下列談話及表格。

本週只有幾件事要特別注意。[92] 我們的配送中心來了一位新樓管 Brett Jensen。他被請來管理晚班，因此他的上班時間會是從下午 3 點到晚上 11 點。[93] 如果你們之中有人今天下午稍晚願意帶他參觀這座設施的話，那就太好了。此外，從明天開始，我們會從供應商那裡收到一些貨。雖然貼在裝卸碼頭旁的那張時間表大致上是正確的，但有一條資訊需要更新。[94] 微波爐那批貨將會晚一天抵達——在 5 月 15 日。不過在本週稍早排定要送到這裡的洗碗機及烘乾機應該會按計畫送達。

運送時間表		
日期	公司	貨物內容
5 月 12 日	Lloyd Ferris	洗碗機
5 月 13 日	Monroe Industries	烘乾機
5 月 14 日	[94]Abdul & Sons	微波爐
5 月 15 日	Stone Incorporated	冰箱

92 聽者們在哪裡工作？

(A) 零售商店
(B) 配送中心
(C) 檢測設施
(D) 製造工廠

93 說話者要求其中一位聽者做什麼？

(A) 帶一位員工參觀
(B) 在出口附近張貼告示
(C) 印出新的時間表
(D) 做一些記錄

94 請看圖表。哪間公司延後送貨？

(A) Lloyd Ferris
(B) Monroe Industries
(C) Abdul & Sons
(D) Stone Incorporated

題目 distribution [美 ˏdɪstrəˋbjuʃən 英 ˏdistriˋbju:ʃən] 分配；分發　floor [美 flor 英 flɔ:] 樓層
shift [ʃɪft] 輪班；（輪班的）工作時間　show ~ around 帶～參觀　a number of 一些～
shipment [ˋʃɪpmənt] 運輸的貨物；運輸　supplier [美 səˋplaɪɚ 英 səˋplaiə] 供給業者，供應商
post [美 post 英 pəust] 張貼　loading dock 裝卸碼頭；卸貨平台　outdated [ˏaʊtˋdetɪd] 過時的；老舊的
92 testing [ˋtɛstɪŋ] 測試；檢測

92 ■ 整體內容相關問題—聽者 答案 (B)

低

題目詢問聽者們的工作地點，因此要注意聽和身分、職業相關的表達。獨白說：「Our distribution center has a new floor manager」，表示配送中心來了新樓管，由此可知，聽者們的工作地點是配送中心，因此正確答案是 (B) At a distribution center。

93 ■ 細節事項相關問題—要求 答案 (A)

中

題目詢問說話者要求其中一位聽者做什麼，因此要注意聽獨白中半段有出現提議相關表達的句子。獨白說：「If one of you is willing to show him[new floor manager] around the facility later this afternoon, that'd be great.」，表示希望有人今天下午稍晚願意帶新樓管參觀這座設施，因此正確答案是 (A) Give an employee a tour。

新 94 ■ 細節事項相關問題—圖表資料 答案 (C)

中

題目詢問延後送貨的是哪間公司，因此必須確認題目提供的圖表資訊，並注意和題目關鍵字（postponed ~ delivery）有關的內容。獨白說：「The shipment of microwaves is going to arrive a day later—on May 15.」，表示微波爐那批貨會晚一天在 5 月 15 日抵達，透過圖表可以得知，延後送貨的是運送微波爐的 Abdul & Sons，因此正確答案是 (C) Abdul & Sons。

95
96
97

Questions 95-97 refer to the following telephone message and sign.

第 95-97 題請參考下列電話留言及告示牌。

美式發音

Hello, Mr. Peters. It's Caley Francis from the Baldwin Performing Arts Center. [95]**I wanted to let you know that you have won two free tickets for the ballet *Bold Winter*.** If you are not interested in seeing this performance, call me back immediately at 555-0939. [96]**I'll switch these tickets with those for another production.** To claim your prize, [97]**you need to visit our administration office at 1201 Harbor Street** . . . um, one block away from our main building on Field Street. Parking is limited, so I recommend that you take public transportation. The office is within walking distance of the Oakridge Subway Station.

哈囉，Peters 先生。我是 Baldwin 表演藝術中心的 Caley Francis。[95] 我想要通知您，您已贏得了兩張芭蕾表演《Bold Winter》的免費門票。如果您沒有興趣看這場表演，請立即撥打 555-0939 回電給我。[96] 我會把這兩張票換成其他演出的票。為領取您的獎品，[97] 您必須前往我們位於 Harbor 街 1201 號的行政辦公室……嗯，離我們在 Field 街的總部大樓一個街區的距離。停車位有限，因此我建議您搭乘大眾運輸工具。從 Oakridge 地鐵站走路就可以到這間辦公室。

新

Oakridge Subway Station

←	[97]**Exit 10 Harbor Street**	Exit 11 Field Street	→
	Exit 12 Bridge Street	Exit 13 Oak Street	

Oakridge 地鐵站
[97] 出口 10
Harbor 街
出口 11
Field 街
出口 12
Bridge 街
出口 13
Oak 街

95 Why is the speaker calling?

(A) To announce an art gallery opening
(B) To explain a membership program
(C) To notify a prize winner
(D) To request an outstanding payment

95 説話者為何致電？

(A) 宣布一間藝廊開幕
(B) 説明一項會員計畫
(C) 通知一位得獎者
(D) 索取一筆未清償的款項

96 What does the speaker offer to do?

(A) Exchange some tickets
(B) Cancel a fee
(C) Provide a refund
(D) Reserve some seats

96 説話者願意做什麼？

(A) 換一些票券
(B) 取消一筆費用
(C) 提供一筆退款
(D) 保留一些座位

97 新 Look at the graphic. Which exit is closest to the administration office?

(A) Exit 10
(B) Exit 11
(C) Exit 12
(D) Exit 13

97 請看圖表。哪一個出口離行政辦公室最近？

(A) 出口 10
(B) 出口 11
(C) 出口 12
(D) 出口 13

題目 production [prəˋdʌkʃən]（戲劇、藝術、電影等的）作品　claim [klem] 領取；主張
administration [ədˏmɪnəˋstreʃən] 行政　limited [ˋlɪmɪtɪd] 有限的；受限的　public transportation 大眾運輸工具
95 outstanding [ˋaʊtˋstændɪŋ] 未清償的；傑出的　payment [ˋpemənt]（支付）款項

95 整體內容相關問題—目的 答案 (C)

中

題目詢問致電的目的，因此必須注意聽獨白的開頭部分。獨白說：「I wanted to let you know that you have won two free tickets for the ballet ~.」，告知聽者贏得了兩張芭蕾表演的免費門票，因此正確答案是 (C) To notify a prize winner。

96 細節事項相關問題—提議 答案 (A)

中

題目詢問說話者願意做什麼，因此要注意聽獨白的中段部分裡，與說話者表示要做的事情有關的內容。獨白說：「I'll switch these tickets[free tickets] with those for another production.」，表示會將這兩張票換成其他作品的票，因此正確答案是 (A) Exchange some tickets。

新 **97** 細節事項相關問題—圖表資料 答案 (A)

低

題目詢問離行政辦公室最近的出口是哪個，因此必須確認題目提供的告示牌上的資訊，並注意和題目關鍵字（exit ~ closest to the administration office）相關的內容。獨白說：「you need to visit our administration office at ~ Harbor Street」，說明聽者必須前往位在 Harbor 街的行政辦公室，透過告示牌可以得知，通往 Harbor 街的出口 10 離行政辦公室最近，因此正確答案是 (A) Exit 10。

98
99
100

Questions 98-100 refer to the following excerpt from a meeting and map.

加拿大式發音

All right, I want to talk about the party we're planning for our interns. [98]**They were a great help during the product launch we hosted last month**, and I think an informal dinner on Friday will be a good way to thank them. [99]**I know some of you are planning to make your team members work late that night on the Coleman Industries project, but let's push it back to next week.** I don't want anyone to miss out on this chance to socialize together. Since everyone seemed to enjoy the restaurant we chose for Mr. Sanderson's retirement party, [100]**let's hold the dinner there. Um, the one next to the parking lot on Gray Road . . . right across from Shea Pub.** OK. That's all for now.

新

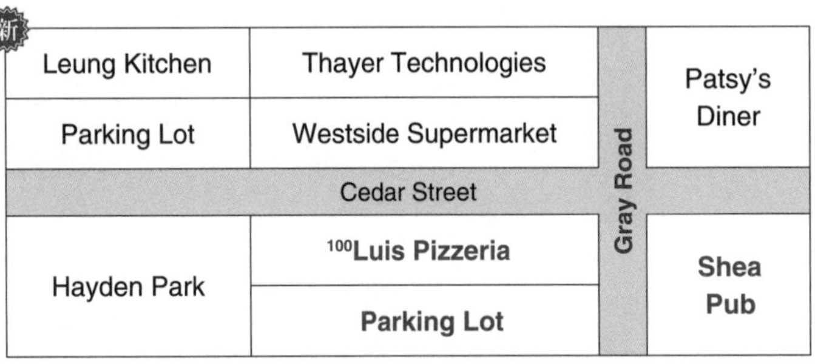

Leung Kitchen	Thayer Technologies	Gray Road	Patsy's Diner
Parking Lot	Westside Supermarket		
Cedar Street			
Hayden Park	[100]**Luis Pizzeria**		**Shea Pub**
	Parking Lot		

98 According to the speaker, what did the interns do?

(A) Assisted with a company event
(B) Participated in off-site training
(C) Organized a surprise party
(D) Created a financial report

99 What are the listeners told to do?

(A) Cancel a team meeting
(B) Submit a project plan
(C) Conduct intern evaluations
(D) Reschedule overtime work

100 Look at the graphic. Where does the speaker suggest going?
新

(A) Leung Kitchen
(B) Patsy's Diner
(C) Luis Pizzeria
(D) Shea Pub

第 98-100 題請參考下列會議節錄及地圖。

好了，我想談談我們正計畫要為實習生舉辦的派對。[98] 他們在我們上個月主辦的產品發表會上幫了大忙，所以我想在週五吃一頓輕鬆的晚餐會是個對他們表達感謝的好方法。[99] 我知道你們有些人打算要讓你們的組員在那天晚上加班處理 Coleman 工業的專案，不過我們把這件事延後到下週吧。我不希望有人錯過這次彼此交流的機會。因為大家看起來都很喜歡我們之前為 Sanderson 先生的退休派對所選擇的那間餐廳，[100] 所以我們就在那裡吃晚餐吧。嗯，在 Gray 路上那個停車場的隔壁那間……就在 Shea 酒吧的對面。好。目前就先這樣。

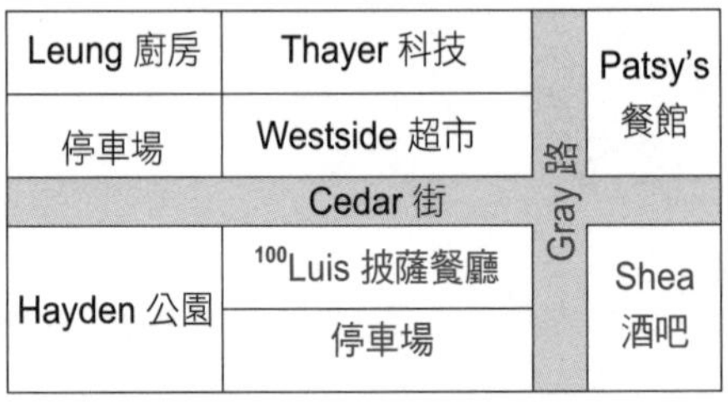

Leung 廚房	Thayer 科技	Gray 路	Patsy's 餐館
停車場	Westside 超市		
Cedar 街			
Hayden 公園	[100]Luis 披薩餐廳		Shea 酒吧
	停車場		

98 根據說話者所說，實習生們做了什麼？

(A) 協助一場公司活動
(B) 參加了外部培訓
(C) 籌辦了一場驚喜派對
(D) 製作了一份財務報告

99 聽者們被要求做什麼？

(A) 取消一次小組會議
(B) 提交一份專案計畫
(C) 進行實習生評估
(D) 重新安排加班時間

100 請看圖表。說話者建議去哪裡？

(A) Leung 廚房
(B) Patsy 的餐館
(C) Luis 披薩餐廳
(D) Shea 酒吧

題目 product launch 產品發表會 host [host] 主辦；主持 dinner [ˋdɪnɚ] 晚餐；晚宴 push back 延後（時間、日期等） socialize [ˋsoʃəˏlaɪz] 交流；交際 retirement [rɪˋtaɪrmənt] 退休 next to 在～的隔壁 across from 在～的對面

98 assist [əˋsɪst] 協助

99 conduct [kənˋdʌkt] 實行 evaluation [ɪˏvæljʊˋeʃən] 評估

98 ■ 細節事項相關問題—特定細項 答案 (A)

中

題目詢問實習生們做了什麼，因此要注意聽和題目關鍵字（interns do）相關的內容。獨白說：「They[interns] were a great help during the product launch we hosted last month」，表示實習生們在上個月公司的產品發表會上幫了大忙，因此正確答案是 (A) Assisted with a company event。

換句話說

product launch 產品發表會 → company event 公司活動

99 ■ 細節事項相關問題—要求 答案 (D)

高

題目詢問聽者們被要求做什麼，因此要注意聽獨白中半段裡用到要求相關表達的句子。獨白說：「I know some of you are planning to make your team members work late that night ~, but let's push it back to next week.」，表示自己知道有些人計畫讓組員加班處理專案，不過說話者希望能把加班這件事延到下週，因此正確答案是 (D) Reschedule overtime work。

新 100 ■ 細節事項相關問題—圖表資料 答案 (C)

高

題目詢問說話者建議要去的地點是哪裡，因此必須確認題目提供的地圖資訊，並注意和題目關鍵字（speaker suggest going）相關的內容。獨白說：「let's hold the dinner there. ~ the one next to the parking lot on Gray Road ~ right across from Shea Pub.」，表示那間餐廳在 Gray 路上那個停車場的隔壁、Shea 酒吧的對面，從圖中可以得知，在 Gray 路上那個停車場的旁邊、Shea 酒吧對面的是 Luis 披薩餐廳，因此正確答案是 (C) Luis Pizzeria。

TEST 04

Part 1　原文・翻譯・解析

Part 2　原文・翻譯・解析

Part 3　原文・翻譯・解析 新

Part 4　原文・翻譯・解析 新

MP3 收錄於 TEST 04.mp3。

進行深入練習或複習時，可以一邊多聽幾次收錄各國口音的試題 MP3，一邊搭配解答中的中英對照翻譯和解析，以及單字記憶表和多元口音單字記憶 MP3，達到事半功倍的效果。

PART 1

1
○○●
低

澳洲式發音

(A) A woman is getting out of a seat.
(B) A woman is closing a compartment.
(C) A woman is reaching for a suitcase.
(D) A woman is drawing a curtain.

(A) 一名女子正在離開座位。
(B) 一名女子正在關上置物格。
(C) 一名女子正把手伸向行李箱。
(D) 一名女子正在拉窗簾。

單人照片 答案 (C)

照片中一名女子正把手伸向行李架上的行李箱。

(A) [╳] getting out of（正從～離開）和女子的動作無關，因此是錯誤選項。這裡使用照片中出現的座位（seat）來造成混淆。

(B) [╳] closing（正在關）和女子的動作無關，因此是錯誤選項。這裡使用會聯想到行李的置物格（compartment）來造成混淆。

(C) [○] 這裡正確描述一名女子把手伸向行李架上的行李箱，所以是正確答案。這裡必須知道 reach for 是把手伸向某物的意思。

(D) [╳] drawing a curtain（拉窗簾）和女子的動作無關，因此是錯誤選項。這裡使用照片中有出現的窗簾（curtain）來造成混淆。

單字 get out of 離開～ compartment [美 kəm`pɑrtmənt 英 kəm`pɑ:tmənt]（設備、容器等為特別目的而劃分出來的）隔間，格 reach for 把手伸向～ draw [drɔ] 拉

2
○○●
中

加拿大式發音

(A) A wheel is being taken off a car.
(B) A mechanic is hammering on metal.
(C) A man is pumping fuel into a vehicle.
(D) A man is wearing safety gear.

(A) 正把一個輪子從車上拿下。
(B) 一名技師正在錘打金屬。
(C) 一名男子正在把燃料灌進車裡。
(D) 一名男子穿戴著安全裝備。

單人照片 答案 (D)

仔細觀察照片中穿戴著安全裝備修理汽車的男子，以及周遭事物的狀態。

(A) [╳] 照片中的輪子已經脫離車體了，這裡卻使用現在進行式被動語態（is being taken off）描述成正在被拿下，因此是錯誤選項。

(B) [╳] hammering（正在錘打）和男子的動作無關，因此是錯誤選項。這裡透過可以從修理汽車而聯想到的 hammering on metal（正在錘打金屬）來造成混淆。

(C) [╳] pumping fuel（正在灌燃料）和男子的動作無關，因此是錯誤選項。這裡使用照片中出現的車（vehicle）來造成混淆。

(D) [○] 這裡正確描述穿戴著安全裝備的男子模樣，所以是正確答案。另外，注意不要將穿戴好安全裝備的 wearing 和正在穿上的動詞 putting on 搞混。

單字 take off 脫去；除去 mechanic [mə`kænɪk] 技師；維修人員 hammer [`hæmɚ]（用鎚子）敲擊，錘打 pump [pʌmp] 灌入 fuel [`fjʊəl] 燃料

3
○○●
中

英式發音

(A) The woman is vacuuming a floor.
(B) The woman is walking into a house.
(C) The woman is approaching an entrance.
(D) The woman is bending over a chair.

(A) 女子正在用吸塵器吸地板。
(B) 女子正在走進房子裡。
(C) 女子正在靠近入口。
(D) 女子正彎腰彎向椅子。

■ 單人照片　答案 (A)

仔細確認一名女子拿著吸塵器打掃屋內的模樣。

(A) [○] 這裡正確描述女子使用吸塵器打掃屋內的模樣，所以是正確答案。

(B) [╳] walking into a house（正在走進一間房子）和女子的動作無關，因此是錯誤選項。這裡利用拍照地點——房子（house）來造成混淆。

(C) [╳] approaching an entrance（正在靠近入口）和女子的動作無關，因此是錯誤選項。這裡利用照片中出現的入口（entrance）來造成混淆。

(D) [╳] 女子是朝著吸塵器彎腰，但這裡卻描述成向椅子彎腰，因此是錯誤選項。

單字　vacuum [美 `vækjʊəm 英 `vækjuəm] 用吸塵器吸；吸塵器　approach [美 ə`protʃ 英 ə`prəutʃ] 接近　bend [bɛnd] 彎曲（身體等）

4 高

美式發音

(A) A man is giving an item to a waitress.
(B) A woman is touching some jewelry on her wrist.
(C) Water is being poured in a glass.
(D) Food is being served to some diners.

(A) 一名男子正在把一個東西給女服務生。
(B) 一名女子正摸著她手腕上的一些珠寶。
(C) 正在把水倒進玻璃杯裡。
(D) 正在上菜給一些用餐的人。

■ 兩人以上的照片　答案 (D)

仔細觀察照片中人們坐在餐廳，而一名女子正在上菜的模樣，以及周遭事物的狀態。

(A) [╳] 照片中正在拿東西給別人的不是男子，而是女服務生，因此是錯誤選項。

(B) [╳] 照片中沒有正在摸手腕上珠寶的女子，因此是錯誤選項。注意不要聽到 jewelry on her wrist（她手腕上的珠寶）就選擇這個選項。

(C) [╳] 照片中沒有出現正在把水倒進玻璃杯裡的動作，因此是錯誤選項。

(D) [○] 這裡正確描述正在上菜給用餐的人的動作，所以是正確答案。

單字　wrist [rɪst] 手腕　pour [por] 倒（液體等）　serve [sɝv] 上（食物、飲料等）　diner [`daɪnɚ] 用餐的人

5 中

加拿大式發音

(A) A drawing is being placed on a stand.
(B) A man is exhibiting artwork in a gallery.
(C) An umbrella has been opened above a canvas.
(D) A man is wiping his hands with a cloth.

(A) 正在把一幅圖畫放在架子上。
(B) 一名男子正在藝廊裡展出藝術品。
(C) 一把傘被打開了放在畫布上方。
(D) 一名男子正在用布擦手。

■ 單人照片　答案 (C)

仔細觀察照片中一名男子在戶外畫畫的模樣，以及周遭事物的位置和狀態。

(A) [╳] 照片中的畫已經放在架子上了，這裡卻使用現在進行式被動語態（is being placed）表示正在放，因此是錯誤選項。

(B) [╳] exhibiting（正在展出）和男子的動作無關，且照片拍攝地點並非藝廊（gallery），因此是錯誤選項。這裡使用與照片中出現的圖畫有關的 artwork（藝術品）來造成混淆，必須特別注意。

(C) [○] 這裡正確描述一把傘被打開了放在畫布上方，所以是正確答案。

(D) [╳] wiping（正在擦）和男子的動作無關，因此是錯誤選項。這裡使用照片中出現的布（cloth）來造成混淆。

單字　drawing [`drɔɪŋ] 圖畫　artwork [`ɑrt͵wɝk] 藝術品　canvas [`kænvəs] 帆布；（油畫的）畫布　wipe [waɪp] 擦拭　cloth [klɔθ] 布；織品；衣料

6
高

美式發音

(A) Words have been written on a whiteboard.
(B) A plant has been situated in a hallway.
(C) Monitors have been set up on the desks.
(D) The blinds have been shut in an office.

(A) 字被寫在了白板上。
(B) 一株植物被放在走廊上了。
(C) 螢幕被架設在桌上了。
(D) 一間辦公室裡的百葉窗被拉上了。

事物及風景照片

答案 (C)

仔細觀察照片中辦公室的物品位置和狀態。

(A) [╳] 照片中的白板上沒有寫字，因此是錯誤選項。這裡使用照片中出現的白板（whiteboard）來造成混淆。

(B) [╳] 植物位在辦公室內，這裡卻描述為在走廊（hallway）上，因此是錯誤選項。注意不要聽到 A plant has been situated（一株植物被放在了）就選擇這個選項。

(C) [○] 這裡正確描述螢幕被架設在桌子上的景象，所以是正確答案。

(D) [╳] 照片中的百葉窗是打開的狀態，但這裡卻描述成拉上，因此是錯誤選項。這裡利用照片拍攝地點的辦公室（office）來造成混淆。

單字　plant [plænt] 植物　situate [ˋsɪtʃʊˏet] 使位於　hallway [ˋhɔlˏwe] 走廊；通道　set up 架設，設置
shut [ʃʌt] 關上；封閉

7 低

澳洲式發音 → 英式發音	
How do you feel about this article?	你覺得這篇報導如何？
(A) To review the editorial.	(A) 為了審閱這篇社論。
(B) I think so too.	(B) 我也這麼認為。
(C) It is extremely impressive.	(C) 它非常令人印象深刻。

How 疑問句 答案 (C)

這是詢問對報導想法的 How 疑問句。這裡必須知道 How do you feel about 是用來詢問意見的表達。

(A) [╳] 這是利用和 article（報導）有關的 editorial（社論）來造成混淆的錯誤選項。

(B) [╳] 這是使用可以對應題目中 you 的 I，並且以和 feel（覺得）意思相近的 think（思考）來造成混淆的錯誤選項。

(C) [○] 這裡回答非常令人印象深刻，提到對報導的想法，因此是正確答案。

單字　feel [fil] 覺得；感覺　review [rɪ`vju] 審閱；重新檢視　editorial [美 ˌɛdə`tɔrɪəl 英 ˌedi`tɔːriəl]（報刊等的）社論　extremely [ɪk`strimlɪ] 非常，極度　impressive [ɪm`prɛsɪv] 令人印象深刻的

8 低

美式發音 → 澳洲式發音	
What movie are you going to see?	你要去看什麼電影？
(A) At the cinema on Camus Drive.	(A) 在 Camus 路上的電影院。
(B) I bought the tickets already.	(B) 我已經買票了。
(C) The one starring Claire Holt.	(C) Claire Holt 主演的那一部。

What 疑問句 答案 (C)

這是詢問要看什麼電影的 What 疑問句。這裡一定要聽到 What movie 才能順利作答。

(A) [╳] 題目詢問要看什麼電影，這裡卻回答地點，因此是錯誤選項。這裡利用和 movie（電影）有關的 cinema（電影院）來造成混淆。

(B) [╳] 這是利用和 movie（電影）相關的 tickets（票）來造成混淆的錯誤選項。

(C) [○] 這裡回答由 Claire Holt 主演的那部，提到要看的電影，因此是正確答案。

單字　cinema [`sɪnəmə] 電影院；電影　star [美 stɑr 英 stɑː] 由～主演

9 中

加拿大式發音 → 英式發音	
Have you read through the manual yet?	你看完那本手冊了嗎？
(A) I found out through my secretary.	(A) 我從我祕書那裡知道的。
(B) Yes, you can take it.	(B) 看完了，你可以把它拿走。
(C) It appears to be automatic.	(C) 這看起來像是自動的。

助動詞疑問句 答案 (B)

這是確認是否已將說明書看完的助動詞（Have）疑問句。

(A) [╳] 這是使用可以對應題目中 you 的 I，並且將題目中的 read through（看完）的 through 改以介系詞「透過」之意來重複使用，企圖造成混淆的錯誤選項。

(B) [○] 這裡以 Yes 表示已將說明書看完，並說對方可以拿走，提供更多資訊，因此是正確答案。

(C) [╳] 這是使用和題目中 manual（說明書）的另一字義「手動的」相反的 automatic（自動的）來造成混淆的錯誤選項。

單字　read through 從頭到尾看一遍；快速看過（以找出錯誤）　manual [`mænjʊəl] 手冊；手動的　appear [美 ə`pɪr 英 ə`piə] 似乎，看起來好像　automatic [ˌɔtə`mætɪk] 自動的

10 ○○○● 低

🔊 英式發音 → 加拿大式發音	
Can we have our glasses of wine refilled? (A) No, I don't wear glasses. (B) I didn't see who spilled it. (C) Sure, right away.	可以幫我們把玻璃杯裡的紅酒重新加滿嗎？ (A) 沒有，我沒有戴眼鏡。 (B) 我沒看到是誰打翻的。 (C) 當然，馬上來。

助動詞疑問句 答案 (C)

這是確認是否可以請對方幫忙把酒加滿的助動詞（Can）疑問句。

(A) [╳] 這是以題目中 glasses（玻璃杯）的另一字義「眼鏡」來造成混淆的錯誤選項。注意不要聽到 No 就選擇這個選項。

(B) [╳] 這是利用可以代稱題目中 wine（紅酒）的 it，再加上發音相似單字 refilled – spilled 來造成混淆的錯誤選項。

(C) [○] 這裡以 Sure 表達可以再次把紅酒倒滿，並說現在立刻就做，因此是正確答案。

單字 refill [`rifɪl] 再裝滿 spill [spɪl] 使溢出；使濺出

11 ○○●● 中

🔊 澳洲式發音 → 美式發音	
When did you last have a chance to communicate with Mr. Lin? (A) Friday works for me too. (B) I ran into him today. (C) We discussed our workflow.	你上次有機會跟 Lin 先生交流是什麼時候？ (A) 星期五我也可以。 (B) 我今天偶然碰到他了。 (C) 我們討論了我們的工作流程。

When 疑問句 答案 (B)

這是詢問上次有機會跟 Lin 先生交流是什麼時候的 When 疑問句。

(A) [╳] 題目詢問上次有機會跟 Lin 先生交流是什麼時候，這裡卻回答自己星期五也可以，毫不相關，因此是錯誤選項。注意不要聽到 Friday 就選擇這個答案。

(B) [○] 這裡回答今天偶然碰到他，間接表示今天有和 Lin 先生交流的機會，因此是正確答案。

(C) [╳] 這是使用可以對應 you 和 Mr. Lin 的 We，並且使用和 communicate（交流）相關的 discussed（討論了）來造成混淆的錯誤選項。

單字 communicate [美] kə`mjunə͵ket [英] kə`mju:nikeit] 交流；溝通 run into 偶然碰到
workflow [`wɝk͵flo] 工作流程

12 ○○●● 中

🔊 英式發音 → 加拿大式發音	
How can we increase our sales volume this quarter? (A) Try to lower the seat. (B) I agree. It's very loud. (C) By hiring more telemarketers.	我們要如何提升這一季的銷售量？ (A) 把座椅調低試試。 (B) 我同意。它的聲音非常大。 (C) 透過聘用更多的電話推銷人員。

How 疑問句 答案 (C)

這是詢問要如何提升這一季銷售量的 How 疑問句。這裡必須知道 How 是用來詢問方法的表達。

(A) [╳] 這是藉著與題目中 increase（增加）意義相反的 lower（降低）來造成混淆的錯誤選項。注意不要聽到 Try to 就選擇這個選項。

(B) [╳] 這裡利用與 Yes 意思相同的 I agree 來回答疑問詞疑問句，因此是錯誤選項。這裡使用與題目中 volume（總量）的另一字義「音量」相關的 loud（大聲的），企圖造成混淆。

(C) [○] 這裡回答透過聘用更多的電話推銷人員，提到提升銷售量的方法，因此是正確答案。

單字 volume [[美] `vɑljəm [英] `vɔljum] 總量；音量 lower [`loɚ] 降下；降低

13 ●●● 難

加拿大式發音 → 美式發音	
Your café offers a vegetarian soup, doesn't it? (A) You must be thinking of another place. (B) Could I have a cup of coffee? (C) All soups are made fresh daily.	你們咖啡廳有供應素湯，不是嗎？ (A) 你一定是想成另一家了。 (B) 可以給我來杯咖啡嗎？ (C) 所有湯都是每天新鮮製作的。

附加問句 答案 (A)

這是確認對方咖啡廳是否有供應素湯的附加問句。

(A) [○] 這裡回答一定是想成另一家了，間接表示自己咖啡廳裡不提供素湯，因此是正確答案。

(B) [╳] 這是使用和 café（咖啡廳）有關的 coffee（咖啡）來造成混淆的錯誤選項。

(C) [╳] 題目詢問對方咖啡廳是否提供素湯，這裡卻回答所有湯都是每天新鮮製作的，毫不相關，因此是錯誤選項。這裡以 soups 來重複使用題目中的 soup，企圖造成混淆。

單字 offer [`ɔfɚ] 供應 vegetarian [ˌvɛdʒə`tɛrɪən] 素食的；素食主義者的

14 ●●○ 中

英式發音 → 加拿大式發音	
There are several interns starting next Thursday. (A) The Internet isn't currently working. (B) Please make sure their work areas are ready. (C) Why is the inspection beginning so late?	下星期四開始會有幾個實習生。 (A) 網路現在不能用。 (B) 請確定他們的工作區都準備好了。 (C) 為什麼視察開始得這麼晚？

陳述句 答案 (B)

這是表達下星期四開始會有幾個實習生的客觀事實陳述句。

(A) [╳] 題目說下星期四開始會有幾個實習生，這裡卻回答網路現在不能用，毫不相關，因此是錯誤選項。這裡利用發音相似單字 interns – Internet 來造成混淆。

(B) [○] 這裡回答要確定他們的工作區都準備好了，表示要在實習生到來之前先做好準備工作，因此是正確答案。

(C) [╳] 這是利用和題目中 starting（開始）意義相近的 beginning（開始）來造成混淆的錯誤選項。

單字 work [wɝk] 工作；運作 inspection [ɪn`spɛkʃən] 視察

15 ●●● 高

澳洲式發音 → 美式發音	
Are the safety measures clear, or should I further explain them? (A) I understand them perfectly. (B) Someone should clear out the lockers. (C) I took the room's measurements.	安全措施都清楚了嗎？還是我該再多做說明？ (A) 我完全理解它們了。 (B) 應該要有人去清空置物櫃。 (C) 我量了這個房間的大小。

選擇疑問句 答案 (A)

這是詢問是否已經清楚安全措施，或還需要再多做說明的選擇疑問句。

(A) [○] 這裡回答完全理解，間接表示已經清楚安全措施了，因此是正確答案。

(B) [╳] 題目詢問是否已經清楚安全措施，或還需要再多做說明，這裡卻回答應該要有人去清空置物櫃，毫不相關，因此是錯誤選項。這裡以表「清空」之意的動詞片語 clear out 來重複使用題目中的 clear（清楚的），企圖造成混淆。

(C) [╳] 這是利用發音相似單字 measures – measurements 來造成混淆的錯誤選項。

單字 measure [美 `mɛʒɚ 英 `meʒə] 措施；手段 clear [美 klɪr 英 kliə] 清楚的；易懂的
further [美 `fɝðɚ 英 `fə:ðə] 進一步地 explain [ɪk`splen] 說明
perfectly [`pɝfɪktlɪ] 正確地；完全地；完美地 clear out 清空 take a measurement 測量

16 高

🔊 加拿大式發音 → 澳洲式發音

How about I drive you to the amusement park?

(A) Oh, about three or four times.
(B) Aren't you riding with other friends?
(C) I thought it was a lot of fun.

我開車載你去遊樂園怎麼樣？

(A) 噢，大概三或四次吧。
(B) 你不是要和其他朋友一起搭車嗎？
(C) 我覺得那非常好玩。

提供疑問句 答案 (B)

這是表示要開車載對方去遊樂園的提供疑問句。這裡必須知道 How about 是表示提供的表達。

(A) [╳] 題目說要開車載對方去遊樂園，這裡卻回答大概三或四次，毫不相關，因此是錯誤選項。這裡藉重複使用題目中出現的 about 以造成混淆。

(B) [○] 這裡藉反問來確認說話者是否要和其他朋友一起搭車，要求更多資訊，因此是正確答案。

(C) [╳] 這是利用和 amusement park（遊樂園）相關的 fun（樂趣）來造成混淆的錯誤選項。

單字 drive [draɪv] 開車載送 amusement park 遊樂園 ride [raɪd] 搭（車等）

17 高

🔊 加拿大式發音 → 英式發音

What am I supposed to do with these packages?

(A) Yes, I suppose so.
(B) They belong in Sandy Dawson's office.
(C) The parcel arrived yesterday.

我應該怎麼處理這些包裹？

(A) 是的，我想是這樣。
(B) 它們應該要放在 Sandy Dawson 的辦公室。
(C) 包裹昨天到了。

What 疑問句 答案 (B)

這是詢問要怎麼處理包裹的 What 疑問句。

(A) [╳] 這裡以 Yes 來回答疑問詞疑問句，因此是錯誤選項。這裡用表「猜想」之意的 suppose 重複使用題目中出現的 supposed（應該要）以造成混淆。

(B) [○] 這裡回答它們應該要放在 Sandy Dawson 的辦公室，間接表示應該要把這些包裹送去 Sandy Dawson 的辦公室，因此是正確答案。

(C) [╳] 這是以和題目中 packages（包裹）意思相近的 parcel（包裹）來造成混淆的錯誤選項。

單字 be supposed to 應該要～ package [`pækɪdʒ] 包裹 belong in 應該在～
parcel [[美] `pɑrsḷ [英] `pɑ:sl] 包裹

18 中

🔊 英式發音 → 澳洲式發音

Who should be put in charge of creating our spring collection?

(A) The fashion show is this coming summer.
(B) Most of the clothing is too big for me.
(C) I suggest bringing in an outside designer.

應該要讓誰來負責製作我們的春季新裝？

(A) 時裝展在接下來的這個夏天。
(B) 這些衣服大部分對我來說都太大了。
(C) 我建議外聘一位設計師。

Who 疑問句 答案 (C)

這是詢問應該要讓誰負責製作春季新裝的 Who 疑問句。

(A) [╳] 這是使用和 spring（春天）有關的 summer（夏天）以及和 collection（新裝）相關的 fashion show（時裝展）來造成混淆的錯誤選項。

(B) [╳] 這是以和 collection（新裝）相關的 clothing（衣服）來造成混淆的錯誤選項。

(C) [○] 這裡提議外聘一位設計師，針對應該要讓誰負責製作春季新裝提供建議，因此是正確答案。

單字 collection [kə`lɛkʃən]（為特定季節設計的一系列衣物等的）新裝；收藏品 bring in 把～帶入
outside [`aʊt`saɪd] 外部的

19 中

🔊 美式發音 → 加拿大式發音

Won't the staff be meeting later in the week?

(A) They're slightly understaffed.
(B) Mr. Gimple didn't make it.
(C) I'll ask about that this afternoon.

員工們在這週晚一點不是要開會嗎？

(A) 他們有點人手不足。
(B) Gimple 先生沒有及時趕到。
(C) 我今天下午會問問看這件事。

否定疑問句 答案 (C)

這是詢問員工們在這週晚一點是不是要開會的否定疑問句。

(A) [╳] 題目詢問員工們在這週晚一點是不是要開會，這裡卻回答有點人手不足，毫不相關，因此是錯誤選項。這裡使用發音相似單字 staff – understaffed 來造成混淆。

(B) [╳] 這是使用和 meeting（開會）相關的 make it（趕上）來造成混淆的錯誤選項。

(C) [○] 這裡回答今天下午會問問看，間接表示自己不知道是否要開會，因此是正確答案。

單字 slightly [ˋslaɪtlɪ] 輕微地 understaffed [ˏʌndɚˋstæft] 人手不足的 make it 及時趕到；達成

20 高

🔊 澳洲式發音 → 美式發音

Where will the second restroom be built?

(A) The architect has the floor plans.
(B) Some building supplies.
(C) It should be finished by tomorrow.

第二間廁所會蓋在哪裡？

(A) 建築師有樓層平面圖。
(B) 一些建築用品。
(C) 應該明天以前會完成。

Where 疑問句 答案 (A)

這是詢問第二間廁所會蓋在哪裡的 Where 疑問句。

(A) [○] 這裡回答建築師有樓層平面圖，間接表示自己不知道，因此是正確答案。

(B) [╳] 這是利用和 built（蓋）相關的 building（建築）來造成混淆的錯誤選項。

(C) [╳] 題目詢問第二間廁所會蓋在哪裡，這裡卻回答明天以前會完成，毫不相關，因此是錯誤選項。這裡利用可回答 When 疑問句的選項內容來回答題目的 Where 疑問句，企圖造成混淆，注意不要誤聽成 When will the second restroom be built（什麼時候會蓋第二間廁所），而選擇這個選項。

單字 second [ˋsɛkənd] 第二的 architect [ˋɑrkəˏtɛkt] 建築師 floor plan 樓層平面圖 building supplies 建築用品

21 高

🔊 英式發音 → 加拿大式發音

We're getting many customer complaints lately.

(A) We've gone through customs.
(B) So I've heard.
(C) There wasn't much rain today.

我們最近接到很多客訴。

(A) 我們已經通過海關了。
(B) 我聽說是這樣。
(C) 今天沒下什麼雨。

陳述句 答案 (B)

這是提到最近接到很多客訴的陳述句。

(A) [╳] 這是藉著重複使用題目中出現的 We，並以發音相似單字 customer – customs 來造成混淆的錯誤選項。

(B) [○] 這裡回答聽說是這樣，表示自己也知道這件事，因此是正確答案。

(C) [╳] 這是使用和題目中 many（許多的）意思相同的 much（許多的），並以和 lately（最近）有關的 today（今天）來造成混淆的錯誤選項。

單字 complaint [kəmˋplent] 抱怨，不滿 lately [ˋletlɪ] 最近 go through 通過 customs [ˋkʌstəmz] 海關

22 ●●●○ 高

🔊 澳洲式發音 → 英式發音

Do patients typically check in at the reception desk?

(A) We appreciate her patience.
(B) That desk is quite nice.
(C) Unless they're instructed otherwise.

病人一般是在接待櫃檯報到嗎？

(A) 我們感謝她的耐心。
(B) 那張桌子相當不錯。
(C) 除非他們有收到其他指示。

助動詞疑問句 答案 (C)

這是確認病人一般是否是在接待櫃檯報到的助動詞（Do）疑問句。

(A) [╳] 題目詢問病人一般是否是在接待櫃檯報到，這裡卻回答對於她的耐心表達感謝，毫不相關，因此是錯誤選項。這裡利用發音相似單字 patients – patience 來造成混淆。

(B) [╳] 這是藉由重複題目中出現的 desk 來造成混淆的錯誤選項。

(C) [○] 這裡回答除非他們有收到其他指示，間接表示病人一般的確是在接待櫃檯報到，因此是正確答案。

單字 patient [ˋpeʃənt] 病人；有耐心的 typically [ˋtɪpɪkl̩ɪ] 普通地，一般地 check in 報到
reception desk 接待櫃台 appreciate [əˋpriʃɪˏet] 感謝 unless [ʌnˋlɛs] 除非
otherwise [ˋʌðɚˏwaɪz] 不同地；以其他方式

23 ●●○○ 中

🔊 美式發音 → 澳洲式發音

The modified surveys were e-mailed to consumers, weren't they?

(A) That's what I was told.
(B) Questions about the company.
(C) Here is my e-mail address.

修改過的調查表已經用電子郵件寄給消費者了，不是嗎？

(A) 我是這麼被告知的。
(B) 有關這間公司的問題。
(C) 這是我的電子郵件地址。

附加問句 答案 (A)

這是確認修改過的調查表是否已經用電子郵件寄給消費者了的附加問句。

(A) [○] 這裡回答自己是這麼被告知的，表示修改過的調查表已經用電子郵件寄給消費者了，因此是正確答案。

(B) [╳] 這是使用和 surveys（調查表）相關的 Questions（問題）來造成混淆的錯誤選項。

(C) [╳] 題目詢問修改過的調查表是否已經用電子郵件寄給消費者了，這裡卻回答這是自己的電子郵件地址，毫不相關，因此是錯誤選項。這裡以表「電子郵件」之意的名詞 e-mail 來重複使用題目中的 e-mailed（用電子郵件寄），企圖造成混淆。

單字 modify [ˋmɑdəˏfaɪ] 修改，更改 survey [ˋsɝve]（意見）調查表 consumer [kənˋsjumɚ] 消費者

24 ●●●○ 高

🔊 英式發音 → 加拿大式發音

Who is the more qualified candidate, Jordan Fink or Erin Manifold?

(A) During the next interview.
(B) Their résumés are comparable.
(C) The quality of this item is poor.

誰是比較適任的應徵者？Jordan Fink 還是 Erin Manifold？

(A) 在下一次面試期間。
(B) 他們的履歷不相上下。
(C) 這個物件的品質不好。

選擇疑問句 答案 (B)

這是詢問 Jordan Fink 和 Erin Manifold 之間誰更適任的選擇疑問句。

(A) [╳] 這是利用和 candidate（應徵者）相關的 interview（面試）來造成混淆的錯誤選項。

(B) [○] 這裡回答他們的履歷不相上下，不在兩人之間做出選擇，因此是正確答案。

(C) [╳] 題目詢問 Jordan Fink 和 Erin Manifold 之間誰更適任，這裡卻回答這個物件的品質不好，毫不相關，因此是錯誤選項。這裡使用發音相似單字 qualified – quality 來造成混淆。

單字 qualified [[美] ˋkwɑləˏfaɪd [英] ˋkwɔlifaid] 適任的；符合資格的 candidate [ˋkændədet] 應徵者
interview [ˋɪntɚˏvju] 面試 résumé [ˏrɛzjʊˋme] 履歷表 comparable [ˋkɑmpərəbl] 不相上下的；可比較的

25 ○●●● 中

澳洲式發音 → 英式發音	
I'm confused about how to prepare for the product launch. (A) Follow these directions. (B) It was attended by the press. (C) I don't understand the novel either.	我對於要如何為產品發表會做準備感到困惑。 (A) 按照這些指示。 (B) 媒體來參加了。 (C) 我也不懂這本小說。

陳述句 答案 (A)

這是表達對於要如何為產品發表會做準備感到困惑的陳述句。

(A) [○] 這裡回答按照這些指示，提到解決困惑的方法，因此是正確答案。

(B) [╳] 這是使用可以代稱題目中 product launch（產品發表會）的 It 及與 launch（發表會）有關的 attended（出席）和 press（媒體）來造成混淆的錯誤選項。

(C) [╳] 題目說對於要如何為產品發表會做準備感到困惑，這裡卻說自己也不懂這本小說，毫不相關，因此是錯誤選項。注意不要聽到 I don't understand ~ either 就選擇這個選項。

單字 confused [kən`fjuzd] 混亂的；感到困惑的 prepare [㊣ prɪ`pɛr ㊕ pri`pɛə] 準備
launch [lɔntʃ] 發表會；發表；開始 follow [㊣ `fɑlo ㊕ `fɔləu] 按照；跟隨
direction [də`rɛkʃən] 指示；指導 attend [ə`tɛnd] 出席，參加 press [prɛs] 媒體；新聞界

26 ○●●● 中

加拿大式發音 → 美式發音	
Why did you ask Kurt to organize the building tour? (A) You can register near the entrance. (B) Guided tours are free. (C) He's led them in the past.	你為什麼要求 Kurt 來籌辦這場建物遊覽？ (A) 你可以在靠近入口處登記。 (B) 導覽行程是免費的。 (C) 他以前曾主辦過。

Why 疑問句 答案 (C)

這是詢問為什麼要求 Kurt 來籌辦這場建物遊覽的 Why 疑問句。

(A) [╳] 這是利用和 tour（遊覽）相關的 register（登記）來造成混淆的錯誤選項。

(B) [╳] 題目詢問為什麼要求 Kurt 來籌辦這場建物遊覽，這裡卻回答導覽行程是免費的，毫不相關，因此是錯誤選項。這裡利用 tours 來重複題目中出現的 tour 以造成混淆。

(C) [○] 這裡回答他以前曾主辦過，提到要求他籌辦的原因，因此是正確答案。

單字 organize [`ɔrgə͵naɪz] 籌辦；組織 register [`rɛdʒɪstɚ] 登記 entrance [`ɛntrəns] 入口
guided [gaɪdɪd] 有嚮導的 lead [lid] 領導；帶領

27 ○●●● 高

英式發音 → 澳洲式發音	
Where does the firm intend to open another branch? (A) It hasn't been trimmed. (B) A few possibilities are being considered. (C) The president is from San Francisco.	公司打算在哪裡開另一間分公司？ (A) 這還沒有被修剪過。 (B) 正在考慮幾個可能的選項。 (C) 總裁來自舊金山。

Where 疑問句 答案 (B)

這是詢問公司打算在哪裡開另一間分公司的 Where 疑問句。

(A) [╳] 這是使用和題目中 branch（分公司）的另一字義「樹枝」有關的 trimmed（被修剪過）來造成混淆的錯誤選項。

(B) [○] 這裡回答正在考慮幾個可能的選項，間接表示還沒決定地點，因此是正確答案。

(C) [╳] 題目詢問公司打算在哪裡開另一間分公司，這裡卻回答總裁來自舊金山，毫不相關，因此是錯誤選項。這裡利用地點 San Francisco（舊金山）來造成混淆。

單字 intend to 打算～ branch [㊣ bræntʃ ㊕ brɑ:ntʃ] 分公司；樹枝 trim [trɪm] 修剪
possibility [㊣ ͵pɑsə`bɪlətɪ ㊕ ͵pɔsə`biliti] 可能性；可能的選項 consider [㊣ kən`sɪdɚ ㊕ kən`sidə] 考慮
president [㊣ `prɛzədənt ㊕ `prezidənt] 總裁；主席

28 ○●●● 高

☊ 加拿大式發音 → 美式發音 One more person must be named to the executive council. (A) I got great advice from my attorney. (B) Can anyone be appointed? (C) You must make the booking in advance.	必須再指名一個人去行政會議。 (A) 我從我律師那裡得到了很好的建議。 (B) 有人可以指派嗎？ (C) 你必須提前預訂。

陳述句 答案 (B)

這是提到必須再指名一個人去行政會議的陳述句。

(A) [╳] 這是利用和 council（會議）相關的 advice（建議）來造成混淆的錯誤選項。

(B) [○] 題目說必須再指名一個人去行政會議，這裡反問「有人可以指派嗎？」，要求取得更多資訊，因此是正確答案。

(C) [╳] 這裡回答必須提前預訂，毫不相關，因此是錯誤選項。這裡藉重複題目中出現的 must 來造成混淆。

單字 name [nem] 指名；選擇 executive [ɪg`zɛkjʊtɪv] 行政上的 council [`kaʊnsl] 會議；理事會
advice [əd`vaɪs] 建議，勸告 attorney [ə`tɝnɪ] 律師 appoint [ə`pɔɪnt] 指派，任命 booking [`bʊkɪŋ] 預訂
in advance 提前

29 ○●●● 中

☊ 美式發音 → 英式發音 Doesn't your photography studio specialize in portraits? (A) All of the pictures have been framed. (B) We perform a wide array of services. (C) Our studio is in Las Vegas.	你們攝影工作室不是專做人物攝影嗎？ (A) 所有的照片都已經裱框了。 (B) 我們各式各樣的服務都做。 (C) 我們的工作室在拉斯維加斯。

否定疑問句 答案 (B)

這是確認對方的攝影工作室是否專做人物攝影的否定疑問句。

(A) [╳] 這是利用和 photography（攝影）相關的 pictures（照片）來造成混淆的錯誤選項。

(B) [○] 這裡回答各式各樣的服務都做，間接表示除了人物攝影，也提供其他服務，因此是正確答案。

(C) [╳] 題目想確認對方的攝影工作室是否專做人物攝影，這裡卻回答工作室在拉斯維加斯，毫不相關，因此是錯誤選項。這裡透過重複題目中出現的 studio 來造成混淆。

單字 photography [fə`tɑgrəfɪ] 攝影 specialize in 專門做～ portrait [`portret] 人物寫真；肖像
frame [frem] 裱框 a wide array of 各式各樣的

30 ○●●● 中

☊ 澳洲式發音 → 美式發音 Why haven't any of these posters been placed in the storefront? (A) Beside the information booth. (B) OK, but contact the store first. (C) I was wondering the same thing.	為什麼這些海報一張都沒貼在店門口？ (A) 在服務台旁邊。 (B) 好，但先聯絡那家店。 (C) 我也在納悶這件事。

Why 疑問句 答案 (C)

這是詢問為什麼沒有把海報貼在店門口的 Why 疑問句。

(A) [╳] 題目詢問為什麼沒有把海報貼在店門口，這裡卻回答地點，毫不相關，因此是錯誤選項。這裡使用可以透過 placed（放置）聯想到的位置相關表達 Beside（在～旁邊）來造成混淆。

(B) [╳] 這裡以和 Yes 意思相同的 OK 來回答疑問詞疑問句，因此是錯誤選項。這裡利用發音相似單字 storefront – store first 來造成混淆。

(C) [○] 這裡回答自己也在納悶這件事，間接表示不知道，因此是正確答案。

單字 place [ples] 放置；擺放 storefront [[美] `stor͵frʌnt [英] `stɔ:frʌnt] 店鋪面向馬路的那個部分
contact [`kɑntækt] 聯絡 wonder [`wʌndɚ] 納悶；覺得奇怪

31 ○●●● 高

加拿大式發音 → 英式發音 Are you interested in going for a short walk before our lunch break ends? (A) As long as we have enough time. (B) No, I've been there once. (C) A brief meal with coworkers.	在我們午休結束之前，你想要去散個步嗎？ (A) 只要我們有足夠的時間。 (B) 不，我曾去過那裡一次。 (C) 和同事吃頓便飯。

Be 動詞疑問句

答案 (A)

這是和對方確認是否想在午休結束前去散步的 Be 動詞疑問句。

(A) [○] 這裡回答只要有足夠的時間，間接表示午休結束前願意去散步，因此是正確答案。

(B) [╳] 這裡使用可以代稱題目中 you 的 I，並且利用和題目中 going（去）有關的 I've been（我曾去過）來造成混淆。注意不要聽到 No 就選擇這個答案。

(C) [╳] 這是利用和 lunch（午餐）相關的 meal（餐點）來造成混淆的錯誤選項。

單字　go for a walk 去散步　as long as 只要～　coworker [美 ˋkoˏwɝkɚ 英 ˋkəuˏwəːkə] 同事

TEST 1 2 3 4 5 6 7 8 9 10

32
33
34

Questions 32-34 refer to the following conversation.

🔊 澳洲式發音 → 美式發音

M: Selina, is your phone working? [32]**I just tried to make a call, but there's a busy signal when I pick up my receiver.**

W: I have the same problem. I contacted Mr. Bradford, the technical manager, and he said that the entire fourth floor has been affected. [33]**His team is fixing the phone lines now**, but it looks like we'll have to rely on our mobile devices to call clients until the matter is resolved.

M: Hmm . . . That's going to be an issue because I'm supposed to participate in a conference call in 15 minutes.

W: I see. Well, maybe [34]**you should head to the third floor and use a phone in the meeting room there.**

第 32-34 題請參考下列對話。

男：Selina，妳的電話能用嗎？[32] 我剛想要打電話，但我拿起話筒的時候就出現了忙音。

女：我遇到了同樣的問題。我聯絡了技術經理 Bradford 先生，他說整個四樓都受到了影響。[33] 他們團隊現在正在修理電話線路，不過看來在這件事解決之前，我們都得靠自己的行動裝置來打給客戶了。

男：嗯……這樣會是個問題，因為我應該要在 15 分鐘後參加一場電話會議的。

女：我知道了。嗯，或許 [34] 你該去三樓用那裡會議室的電話。

32 What is the conversation mainly about?

(A) A new telephone system
(B) A technical issue
(C) A departmental meeting
(D) A building renovation

32. 這段對話主要與什麼有關？

(A) 一個新的電話系統
(B) 一個技術問題
(C) 一場部門會議
(D) 一次大樓整修

33 What is Mr. Bradford's team doing?

(A) Fixing an Intranet system
(B) Bringing in more materials
(C) Repairing some telephone lines
(D) Establishing a wireless connection

33. Bradford 先生的團隊正在做什麼？

(A) 修理內部網路系統
(B) 帶進更多素材
(C) 修理一些電話線路
(D) 設置無線連線

34 What does the woman suggest?

(A) Working on a different floor
(B) Unplugging a machine from the wall
(C) Notifying customers about an error
(D) Purchasing a piece of equipment

34. 女子建議什麼？

(A) 在不同樓層工作
(B) 把一台機器的插頭從牆上拔掉
(C) 通知顧客一項錯誤
(D) 購買一件設備

題目 busy signal 忙音　receiver [[美] rɪ`sivɚ [英] ri`si:və] 話筒；接收者　rely on 依靠～　resolve [rɪ`zɑlv] 解決
32 renovation [͵rɛnə`veʃən] 整修；翻新
33 fix [fɪks] 修理　repair [rɪ`pɛr] 修理　establish [ə`stæblɪʃ] 設置
34 unplug [͵ʌn`plʌg] 拔（電器的）插頭　notify [`notə͵faɪ] 通知

32 中 **整體對話相關問題－主題** 答案 (B)

題目詢問對話主題，因此要注意對話的開頭部分。男子說：「I just tried to make a call, but there's a busy signal when I pick up my receiver.」，表示自己剛剛想要打電話，拿起話筒時卻聽到了忙音，後續對話接著說明與電話線路故障相關的內容，因此正確答案是 (B) A technical issue。

33 低 **細節事項相關問題－特定細項** 答案 (C)

題目詢問 Bradford 先生的團隊現在正在做什麼，因此要注意和題目關鍵字（Mr. Bradford's team doing）相關的內容。女子說：「His[Mr. Bradford's] team is fixing the phone lines now」，表示 Bradford 先生的團隊正在修理電話線路，因此正確答案是 (C) Repairing some telephone lines。

換句話說

fixing the phone lines 正在修理電話線路 → Repairing some telephone lines 修理一些電話線路

34 低 **細節事項相關問題－提議** 答案 (A)

題目詢問女子建議什麼，因此要注意聽女子話中和提議相關的表達。女子說：「you should head to the third floor and use a phone in the meeting room there」，建議男子到三樓去用那裡會議室的電話，因此正確答案是 (A) Working on a different floor。

35 36 37

Questions 35-37 refer to the following conversation.

加拿大式發音 → 英式發音

M: [35]**My family and I will be visiting the ruins of Tikal in a few hours for a guided tour.** However, I forgot to arrange a ride to the site. I heard another guest talking about a shuttle service provided by the resort and would like to know more about it.

W: That's right. [36]**We have our own vehicles that take visitors to destinations in the area.** Plus, [36]**there is no charge for the service for those staying at our accommodation.**

M: Is it possible for us to take a shuttle at 1 P.M.? We need to be at the site around 1:30 P.M.

W: [37]**Hold on. Let me just make sure that there is a shuttle departing at that time.**

35 What does the man's family plan to do?

(A) Book a table at a restaurant
(B) Find some accommodations
(C) Travel to another country
(D) Visit a tourist attraction

36 What is provided for free to guests?

(A) Meals
(B) Internet access
(C) Transportation
(D) Guidebooks

37 Why does the woman ask the man to wait?

(A) She needs to help someone else.
(B) She needs to verify something.
(C) She wants to provide a brochure.
(D) She wants to print passes to a site.

第 35-37 題請參考下列對話。

男：[35] 我家人和我在幾個小時後就要去 Tikal 遺跡參加導覽行程了。但我忘了要安排去那個地方的車。我聽到其他客人在說由度假村提供的接駁服務，所以我想再多了解一下這項服務。

女：沒錯。[36] 我們有自己的車可以載遊客前往那一區裡的目的地。此外，[36] 住我們住宿設施的遊客可以免費使用這項服務。

男：我們有可能可以在下午 1 點搭乘接駁車嗎？我們必須在下午 1 點 30 分左右抵達那個地方。

女：[37] 請稍等。讓我確認一下那個時候會有接駁車發車。

35. 男子的家人計畫做什麼？

(A) 在餐廳預訂一桌
(B) 找一些住宿設施
(C) 前往其他國家
(D) 造訪一個觀光景點

36. 免費提供什麼給客人？

(A) 餐點
(B) 網路使用權
(C) 運輸工具
(D) 旅遊指南

37. 女子為何要求男子等待？

(A) 她必須協助其他人。
(B) 她必須確認某事。
(C) 她想要提供一本小冊子。
(D) 她想要印去一個地方的通行證。

題目 ruin [`rʊɪn] 遺跡；廢墟　arrange [ə`rendʒ] 安排　ride [raɪd] 車輛；交通工具　site [saɪt] 地點；場所
vehicle [美 `viɪkl] 英 `vi:ikl] 車輛；搭載工具　destination [美 ˌdɛstə`neʃən 英 ˌdesti`neiʃən] 目的地
accommodation [美 əˌkɑmə`deʃən 英 əˌkɔmə`deiʃn] 住宿；住宿設施　depart [美 dɪ`pɑrt 英 di`pɑ:t] 離開；啟程
36 transportation [ˌtrænspɚ`teʃən] 運輸工具
37 verify [`vɛrəˌfaɪ] 確認；核實　brochure [bro`ʃʊr] 小冊子

35 細節事項相關問題－特定細項　答案 (D)
中

題目詢問男子的家人計畫做什麼，因此要注意和題目關鍵字（man's family plan to do）相關的內容。男子說：「My family and I will be visiting the ruins of Tikal in a few hours for a guided tour.」，表示自己和家人在幾個小時後要參加 Tikal 遺跡的導覽行程，因此正確答案是 (D) Visit a tourist attraction。

36 細節事項相關問題－特定細項　答案 (C)
中

題目詢問免費提供給客人什麼，因此要注意和題目關鍵字（free to guests）相關的內容。女子說：「We have our own vehicles that take visitors to destinations in the area.」，表示自己度假村有車可以載遊客到目的地，接著說：「there is no charge for the service for those staying at our accommodation」，表示住在自己的住宿設施裡的客人可以免費使用該服務，因此正確答案是 (C) Transportation。

37 細節事項相關問題－理由　答案 (B)
中

題目詢問女子要求男子等候的原因，因此要注意和題目關鍵字（wait）相關的內容。女子對男子說：「Hold on. Let me just make sure that there is a shuttle departing at that time.」，要求對方等自己確認該時間會有接駁車發車，因此正確答案是 (B) She needs to verify something.。

38 39 40 新

Questions 38-40 refer to the following conversation.	第 38-40 題請參考下列對話。
美式發音 → 加拿大式發音	
W: This is *Classical Chat* on 104.5 FM. [38]**My guest today is Rupert Harvey, a cellist in the Fordham Symphony Orchestra. Welcome, Mr. Harvey.**	女：這裡是 FM 104.5 的《Classical Chat》。[38] 我今天的來賓是 Fordham 交響樂團的大提琴家 Rupert Harvey。歡迎 Harvey 先生。
M: [38]**Thank you.** I'm a big fan of your show.	男：[38] 謝謝妳。我是妳節目的大粉絲。
W: I'm glad to have you here. So, your orchestra is planning to hold a concert on March 20, correct?	女：我很高興能請到你來這裡。對了，你們交響樂團計畫要在 3 月 20 日舉辦一場音樂會，對嗎？
M: Yes. And the proceeds from this performance will go to the Carter Institute. Um, [39]**this organization provides financial support to a variety of groups in the city that offer music programs for children.**	男：是的。而且這次演出的收益都會交給 Carter 機構。嗯，[39] 這間機構對市內提供兒童音樂課程的各種團體提供財務支援。
W: Great. We'll get into that in more detail in a few minutes. But first, we have a special treat for listeners! [40]**Mr. Harvey will give a live performance right now.**	女：太棒了。我們等一下會就這件事再詳細討論。但首先，我們為聽眾們準備了特別福利！[40]Harvey 先生現在將會進行現場演奏。

38 Who most likely is the man?
(A) A performer
(B) An event planner
(C) An instructor
(D) A radio host

38. 男子最有可能是誰？
(A) 表演者
(B) 活動企劃人員
(C) 講師
(D) 廣播主持人

39 What is mentioned about the Carter Institute?
(A) It organizes lessons for musicians.
(B) It receives support from the city.
(C) It holds performances for children.
(D) It gives funds to local groups.

39. 關於 Carter 機構，提到了什麼？
(A) 它籌辦給音樂家的課程。
(B) 它獲得市府支持。
(C) 它為兒童舉辦表演。
(D) 它給當地團體資金。

40 新 What does the woman mean when she says, "we have a special treat for listeners"?
(A) A ticket will be given away.
(B) A special guest will be introduced.
(C) An interview will be held.
(D) A musical piece will be played.

40. 當女子說：「我們為聽眾們準備了特別福利」時，意思是什麼？
(A) 將送出一張票。
(B) 將介紹一位特別來賓。
(C) 將進行一場採訪。
(D) 將演奏一首樂曲。

題目 proceeds [ˋprosidz] 收益 organization [ˏɔrgənəˋzeʃən] 組織，機構 a variety of 各種～；各式各樣的
39 organize [ˋɔrgəˏnaɪz] 籌辦；組織
40 give away 送出；分發 introduce [ˏɪntrəˋdjus] 介紹 piece [pis]（藝術類的）作品；曲子

38 整體對話相關問題－說話者 (中) 答案 (A)

題目詢問男子的身分，因此要注意聽和身分、職業相關的表達。女子說：「My guest today is Rupert Harvey, a cellist ~. Welcome, Mr. Harvey.」，表示自己今天的來賓是大提琴家 Rupert Harvey，並說歡迎 Harvey 先生，接著男子說：「Thank you.」，表示感謝，由此可知，男子是個表演者，因此正確答案是 (A) A performer。

39 細節事項相關問題－提及 (高) 答案 (D)

題目詢問提到了什麼關於 Carter 機構的事，因此要注意提到題目關鍵字（Carter Institute）的前後部分。男子說：「this organization[Carter Institute] provides financial support to a variety of groups in the city that offer music programs for children」，表示 Carter 機構對市內提供兒童音樂課程的各種團體提供財務支援，因此正確答案是 (D) It gives funds to local groups.。

新 **40** 細節事項相關問題－掌握意圖 (中) 答案 (D)

題目詢問女子的說話意圖，因此要注意題目引用句（we have a special treat for listeners）的前後部分。女子說：「Mr. Harvey will give a live performance right now.」，表示 Harvey 先生現在將進行表演，由此可知，Harvey 先生將演奏一首樂曲，因此正確答案是 (D) A musical piece will be played.。

Questions 41-43 refer to the following conversation.

英式發音 → 澳洲式發音

W: Hi, Mr. Young. This is Fatima from *Carolina Monthly*. [41]**I've been assigned to take your picture for the article we're writing about you, and I'm wondering when you'd be free to meet with me.**

M: I'll be available tomorrow at 3 P.M., Fatima. Where do you want to get together?

W: Since the article focuses on your architectural work, perhaps [42]**we could meet at the construction site of the latest building you designed, the Grand Theater.** I'd like to photograph you in front of the partially finished structure.

M: That sounds good. By the way, [43]**once the building is completed next month, I'll be happy to bring you back and let you capture images of the interior as well.**

41 What are the speakers mainly discussing?

(A) A press conference
(B) An architect position
(C) A photo shoot
(D) A magazine subscription

42 What does the woman propose?

(A) Meeting at a construction site
(B) Rescheduling an appointment
(C) Contacting a theater owner
(D) Revising an article

43 What does the man say the woman can do?

(A) Return to a venue at a later date
(B) Bring a copy of a publication
(C) Exhibit some images at a gallery
(D) Print out some blueprints

第 41-43 題請參考下列對話。

女：嗨，Young 先生。我是《Carolina Monthly》的 Fatima。[41] 我被指派為我們要寫的那篇關於您的報導拍攝您的照片，所以我想知道您什麼時候會有時間與我見面。

男：我明天下午 3 點有空，Fatima。妳想要在哪裡碰面？

女：因為這篇報導著重在您的建築作品上，也許 [42] 我們可以在您最新設計的建築物 Grand Theater 的工地碰面。我想要為您在已部分完工的建築物前拍照。

男：這聽起來不錯。順道一提，[43] 等這座建築物下個月一完工，我會很樂意帶妳回來，讓妳也能拍攝這座建築物內部的照片。

41. 說話者們主要在討論什麼？

(A) 記者會
(B) 建築師職位
(C) 拍照
(D) 雜誌訂閱

42. 女子提議什麼？

(A) 在工地碰面
(B) 重新安排會面時間
(C) 聯絡劇院老闆
(D) 修改報導

43. 男子說女子可以做什麼？

(A) 在之後的日子回到一個場地
(B) 帶一本出版品
(C) 在一間藝廊展出一些圖片
(D) 印出一些藍圖

題目 assign [ə`saɪn] 指派；選派　architectural [[美] ˌɑrkə`tɛktʃərəl [英] ˌɑ:ki`tektʃərəl] 建築的
capture [[美] `kæptʃɚ [英] `kæptʃə]（以照片或文字）刻劃；拍攝　interior [[美] ɪn`tɪrɪɚ [英] in`tiəriə] 內部；室內

41 subscription [səb`skrɪpʃən] 訂閱

43 venue [`vɛnju]（事件等的）發生地點；場地　publication [ˌpʌblɪ`keʃən] 出版品　blueprint [`blu`prɪnt] 藍圖

41 ■ **整體對話相關問題－主題**　答案 (C)

中

題目詢問對話主題，因此要注意對話的開頭部分。女子說：「I've been assigned to take your picture ~, and I'm wondering when you'd be free to meet with me.」，表示自己要替對方拍照，並想知道對方有空見面的時間，接下來並繼續說明與拍照相關的內容，因此正確答案是 (C) A photo shoot。

42 ■ **細節事項相關問題－提議**　答案 (A)

低

題目詢問女子提議什麼，因此要注意聽女子話中和提議相關的表達。女子說：「we could meet at the construction site of the latest building you designed, the Grand Theater」，提議在男子最新設計的建築物 Grand Theater 的工地碰面，因此正確答案是 (A) Meeting at a construction site。

43 ■ **細節事項相關問題－特定細項**　答案 (A)

高

題目詢問男子說女子可以做什麼，因此要注意和題目關鍵字（woman can do）相關的內容。男子說：「once the building is completed next month, I'll be happy to bring you back and let you capture images of the interior as well」，表示很樂意在該建築物下個月完工後，帶女子回去拍攝建築物的內部，因此正確答案是 (A) Return to a venue at a later date。

44
45
46

Questions 44-46 refer to the following conversation.

美式發音 → 加拿大式發音

W: I'm dissatisfied with Gordon Distribution Services. Our retail outlet has received incorrect shipments of goods from them on multiple occasions over the previous six months. For instance, just [44]**last Tuesday we received a dozen pairs of Eclipse basketball shoes**, which is fewer than I requested. Plus, the company has yet to address my complaints.

M: Considering the ongoing troubles that we're experiencing with that company, [45]**I think it would be best for us to partner with another firm.**

W: In that case, I'll reach out to other reputable distributors that provide services in the Madison area. Ah . . . but before I do that, [46]**can you help me hang up some signs about our membership program changes throughout the store?**

44 According to the woman, what happened last Tuesday?

(A) A professional contract expired.
(B) A shipment of goods arrived.
(C) A complaint was submitted online.
(D) A customer exchanged an item.

45 How does the man want to deal with the problem?

(A) By renewing an agreement
(B) By demanding a full refund
(C) By starting a new business relationship
(D) By asking for a membership discount

46 What does the woman request the man do?

(A) Display some signs
(B) Organize a storage area
(C) Edit a service catalog
(D) Deliver some merchandise

第 44-46 題請參考下列對話。

女：我對於 Gordon 配送服務很不滿意。在過去的六個月期間，我們的零售通路已經多次收到他們送錯的貨物了。舉例來說，就在 [44] 上星期二我們收到了一打的 Eclipse 籃球鞋，這比我要求的要少。而且，這間公司到現在還沒處理我的投訴。

男：考慮到我們現在在這間公司上所遇到的麻煩，[45] 我想我們最好和其他公司合作。

女：這樣的話，我會聯絡其他有信譽且有在 Madison 區提供服務的配送業者。啊……但在我做這件事之前，[46] 你可以幫我把關於我們會員計畫更動的一些標示掛在店裡的各處嗎？

44. 根據女子所說，上星期二發生了什麼？

(A) 一份專業合約到期了。
(B) 一批貨送達了。
(C) 線上提交了一筆申訴。
(D) 一位顧客更換了一個品項。

45. 男子想要如何處理這個問題？

(A) 續約
(B) 要求全額退費
(C) 開始新的商業關係
(D) 要求取得會員折扣

46. 女子要求男子做什麼？

(A) 陳列一些標示
(B) 規劃儲藏區域
(C) 編輯服務型錄
(D) 運送一些商品

題目 dissatisfied [dɪs`sætɪs͵faɪd] 不滿意的　shipment [`ʃɪpmənt] 運輸；運輸的貨物　address [ə`drɛs] 處理　complaint [kəm`plent] 抱怨；申訴　partner [`pɑrtnɚ] 與～合作；與～成為夥伴　reputable [`rɛpjətəbl] 聲譽良好的　hang up 懸掛

44 expire [ɪk`spaɪr] 到期；屆滿

45 renew [rɪ`nju] 更新；（契約等）展期　agreement [ə`grimənt] 合約，協議；同意　demand [dɪ`mænd] 要求　full refund 全額退費

44 中　細節事項相關問題－特定細項　答案 (B)

題目詢問女子說上星期二發生了什麼，因此要確認女子話中提到題目關鍵字（last Tuesday）的前後部分。女子說：「last Tuesday we received a dozen pairs of Eclipse basketball shoes」，表示上星期二收到了一打的 Eclipse 籃球鞋，因此正確答案是 (B) A shipment of goods arrived.。

45 高　細節事項相關問題－方法　答案 (C)

題目詢問男子想要如何處理問題，因此要注意和題目關鍵字（deal with the problem）相關的內容。男子說：「I think it would be best for us to partner with another firm」，表示自己認為最好要改和其他公司合作，因此正確答案是 (C) By starting a new business relationship。

換句話說

partner with another firm 和其他公司合作 → starting a new business relationship 開始新的商業關係

46 低　細節事項相關問題－要求　答案 (A)

題目詢問女子要求男子做什麼，因此要注意聽女子話中出現要求表達之後的內容。女子對男子說：「can you help me hang up some signs about our membership program changes throughout the store?」，要求男子幫忙把關於會員計畫更動的一些標示掛在店裡的各處，因此正確答案是 (A) Display some signs。

47
48
49

Questions 47-49 refer to the following conversation.

澳洲式發音 → 英式發音

M: [47]**I've taken a look at your slideshow for the marketing presentation we will give to Upturn Incorporated** in November. I have some feedback on it that I would like to discuss with you.

W: Certainly. Let me just open the file on my computer quickly so that we can review it together. OK, what part do you want to talk about?

M: I think [48]**you should add more content to the sixth slide** about the results of our market research. Specifically, you can note that we've included rainforest images in the billboards because Upturn's target market responds positively to images of nature.

W: Sure. [49]**I'll also put emphasis on how many people on our team responded more positively to red text than black text.** That seems worth noting as well.

第 47-49 題請參考下列對話。

男：[47] 我看了一下妳為我們要在十一月向 Upturn 公司報告所做的行銷簡報投影片。我有一些針對它的意見想要和妳討論。

女：當然。我很快開一下我電腦裡的檔案，這樣我們就能一起再看一次。好了，你想要討論的是哪一個部分？

男：我認為 [48] 妳應該在第六張投影片加進更多與我們市場調查結果有關的內容。具體來說，妳可以提到我們在廣告看板上放了雨林的圖像，因為 Upturn 公司的目標市場對於自然圖像的反應很正面。

女：沒問題。[49] 我也會強調我們團隊中有多少人對紅字比對黑字的反應更正面。這似乎也值得提一下。

47 What is the conversation mainly about?

(A) Expenses for a billboard design
(B) The length of a marketing campaign
(C) Materials for a business presentation
(D) The results of a periodic evaluation

48 What does the man suggest the woman do?

(A) Replace some images
(B) Delegate duties to workers
(C) Perform market research
(D) Include more information

49 What will the woman emphasize?

(A) The types of products being released
(B) The reaction of people to different colors
(C) The cost of organizing a focus group
(D) The success of a television commercial

47. 這段對話主要與什麼有關？

(A) 廣告看板設計的費用
(B) 行銷宣傳活動的長度
(C) 商業簡報的素材
(D) 定期評估的結果

48. 男子建議女子做什麼？

(A) 更換一些圖像
(B) 委派員工職務
(C) 做市場調查
(D) 加進更多資訊

49. 女子會強調什麼？

(A) 要發行的產品類型
(B) 人們對不同顏色的反應
(C) 組織焦點團體的費用
(D) 一支電視廣告的成功

題目 note [[美] not [英] nəut] 提到 rainforest [\`renˏfɑrɪst] 雨林 billboard [[美] \`bɪlˏbord [英] \`bilˏbɔ:d] 廣告看板 put emphasis on 強調～

47 expense [ɪk\`spɛns] 費用 periodic [ˏpɪrɪ\`ɑdɪk] 定期的 evaluation [ɪˏvæljʊ\`eʃən] 評估

48 delegate [\`dɛləˏget] 委派（某人）做；授權 duty [\`djutɪ] 職務；義務

49 release [rɪ\`lis] 發行，釋出 commercial [kə\`mɝʃəl]（電視或廣播中的）商業廣告

47 ■ 整體對話相關問題－主題 答案 (C)

中

題目詢問對話主題，因此要注意對話的開始部分。男子說：「I've taken a look at your slideshow for the marketing presentation we will give to Upturn Incorporated」，表示自己已經看過了要向 Upturn 公司報告的行銷簡報投影片，對話接著繼續談論簡報內容，因此正確答案是 (C) Materials for a business presentation。

48 ■ 細節事項相關問題－提議 答案 (D)

低

題目詢問男子對女子建議什麼，因此要注意聽男子話中和提議相關的表達。男子對女子說：「you should add more content to the sixth slide」，建議女子在第六張投影片加進更多內容，因此正確答案是 (D) Include more information。

49 ■ 細節事項相關問題－特定細項 答案 (B)

中

題目詢問女子會強調什麼，因此要注意和題目關鍵字（emphasize）相關的內容。女子說：「I'll ~ put emphasis on how many people on our team responded more positively to red text than black text.」，表示她會強調團隊中有多少人對紅字的反應比對黑字要好，因此正確答案是 (B) The reaction of people to different colors。

新

50 51 52

Questions 50-52 refer to the following conversation with three speakers.

第 50-52 題請參考下列三人對話。

美式發音 → 澳洲式發音 → 英式發音

W1: [51]**Tim, Laura . . . Have you had a chance to speak with Mr. Kang from Seaward Financial yet?** [50]**He needs help finding employees for the new office** his company is opening in San Diego.
M: Oh, yes. [51]**He stopped by this morning.**
W2: Right. [51]**We explained how our firm can manage the recruiting process**, and he seemed very interested.
W1: Great. So, he's decided to hire us, then?
W2: Uh, not exactly. While the meeting went smoothly, he still hasn't made up his mind. [52]**I think we need to explain more clearly how much time and money he'll save by paying us to do the work.**
M: [52]**I agree.** It's the only way we'll be able to convince him to become a client.

女 1： [51]Tim、Laura……你們已經有機會和 Seaward 金融的 Kang 先生談過了嗎？[50] 他需要有人幫他公司要在聖地牙哥開設的新辦事處找員工。
男： 噢，對。[51] 他今天早上有來。
女 2： 沒錯。[51] 我們說明了我們公司能夠如何處理招募程序，而他看起來非常感興趣。
女 1： 太好了。那麼，他已經決定要請我們了，是嗎？
女 2： 呃，不完全是。雖然會議進行得很順利，但他還沒有下定決心。[52] 我認為我們得更加清楚地說明，他付錢給我們處理這件事可以讓他省下多少時間和金錢。
男： [52] 我同意。這是我們能夠說服他成為客戶的唯一方法。

50 Where do the speakers most likely work?
(A) At a financial institution
(B) At a staffing agency
(C) At an office supply store
(D) At a graphic design firm

50. 說話者們最有可能在哪裡工作？
(A) 金融機構
(B) 人力仲介公司
(C) 辦公用品店
(D) 平面設計公司

51 What did Tim and Laura do this morning?
(A) Met with a potential client
(B) Attended a staff meeting
(C) Made travel arrangements
(D) Conducted job interviews

51. Tim 與 Laura 今天早上做了什麼？
(A) 和潛在客戶見面
(B) 參加員工會議
(C) 安排旅行
(D) 進行工作面試

52 What do Tim and Laura recommend?
(A) Reviewing a contract
(B) Visiting some companies
(C) Explaining some benefits
(D) Changing a process

52. Tim 與 Laura 建議什麼？
(A) 檢視一份合約
(B) 拜訪一些公司
(C) 說明一些好處
(D) 變更一個程序

題目 recruit [rɪˋkrut] 聘僱；招募 make up one's mind（某人）下定決心 convince [kənˋvɪns] 說服；使確信

50 整體對話相關問題－說話者 答案 (B)

中

題目詢問說話者的工作地點，因此要注意聽和身分、職業相關的表達。女 1 對男子和女 2 說：「He[Mr. Kang] needs help finding employees for the new office」，表示 Kang 先生想為新辦事處找員工，接著對話繼續談論有關處理招募程序的事，由此可知，說話者們在人力仲介公司工作，因此正確答案是 (B) At a staffing agency。

51 細節事項相關問題－特定細項 答案 (A)

中

題目詢問男子 Tim 和女 2 的 Laura 今天早上做了什麼，因此要注意提到題目關鍵字（this morning）的前後部分。女 1 對男子和女 2 說：「Tim, Laura ~. Have you had a chance to speak with Mr. Kang ~?」，詢問他們是否有機會和 Kang 先生談過了，男子說：「He stopped by this morning.」，表示 Kang 先生今天早上有來，女 2 說：「We explained how our firm can manage the recruiting process」，表示自己和男子一起說明了公司能夠如何處理招募程序，因此正確答案是 (A) Met with a potential client。

52 細節事項相關問題－提議 答案 (C)

中

題目詢問男子 Tim 和女 2 的 Laura 建議什麼，因此要注意聽男子 Tim 和女 2 的 Laura 話中出現提議表達之後的內容。女 2 說：「I think we need to explain more clearly how much time and money he[Mr. Kang]'ll save by paying us to do the work.」，表示認為得更加清楚地向 Kang 先生說明，付錢請自己公司來處理這件事可以讓他省下多少時間和金錢，接著男子說：「I agree.」，表示同意，因此正確答案是 (C) Explaining some benefits。

53
54
55

Questions 53-55 refer to the following conversation.	第 53-55 題請參考下列對話。
澳洲式發音 → 美式發音	
M: Inez, did you hear that a new employee will start working for us next Monday? His name is Danny Williams.	男：Inez，妳聽說下星期一開始會有一個新員工來上班了嗎？他的名字是 Danny Williams。
W: I did. [53]**A representative from the IT team—Joowon Kim—called this morning and said he will set up a computer** for him tomorrow afternoon.	女：我聽說了。[53] 有一個資訊科技組的人，Joowon Kim 今天早上打來說他明天下午會幫他裝電腦。
M: Great, but [54]**Danny will also need access to CashFind—our company's online financial research application.** He'll use it for the budget analysis project. [54]**You should make sure this is arranged before he starts.**	男：太好了，不過 [54]Danny 也會需要取得我們公司的線上金融研究應用程式 CashFind 的使用權利。他在做預算分析專案時會用到它。[54] 妳應該要確保這件事會在他開始上班前處理好。
W: Oh . . . I didn't realize that. [55]**I'll e-mail the Web services team requesting a CashFind password now.**	女：噢……我沒想到這件事。[55] 我會現在寄電子郵件給網路服務組索取 CashFind 的密碼。
53 Who most likely is Joowon Kim? (A) A technician (B) A Web designer (C) A company intern (D) An accountant	53. Joowon Kim 最有可能是誰？ (A) 技術人員 (B) 網頁設計師 (C) 公司實習生 (D) 會計
54 新 Why does the man say, "He'll use it for the budget analysis project"? (A) To extend an assignment deadline (B) To inform a manager of a change (C) To advocate for more training (D) To emphasize the necessity of a task	54. 男子為什麼說：「他在做預算分析專案時會用到它」？ (A) 為了延長一項任務的截止期限 (B) 為了通知經理一項變更 (C) 為了主張有更多培訓 (D) 為了強調一項任務的必要性
55 What will the woman probably do next? (A) Log on to a system (B) Contact another team (C) Read a financial report (D) Revise a service request	55. 女子接下來可能會做什麼？ (A) 登入一個系統 (B) 聯絡另一組 (C) 閱讀一份財務報告 (D) 修改一項服務申請

題目 set up 設置（機器等） access [ˋæksɛs] 使用的權利 financial [faɪˋnænʃəl] 金融的；財務的 budget [ˋbʌdʒɪt] 預算 analysis [əˋnæləsɪs] 分析

54 extend [ɪkˋstɛnd] 延長 assignment [əˋsaɪnmənt]（經分派的）任務；作業 inform [ɪnˋfɔrm] 告知 advocate for 主張～；擁護～ emphasize [ˋɛmfə͵saɪz] 強調 necessity [nəˋsɛsətɪ] 必要性；必需品

53 **細節事項相關問題－特定細項** 答案 (A)

中

題目詢問 Joowon Kim 的身分，因此要注意聽和提問對象（Joowon Kim）身分、職業相關的表達。女子說：「A representative from the IT team—Joowon Kim ~ will set up a computer」，表示資訊科技組的人 Joowon Kim 會來裝電腦，因此正確答案是 (A) A technician。

換句話說

representative from the !T team 資訊科技組的人 → technician 技術人員

新 **54** **細節事項相關問題－掌握意圖** 答案 (D)

高

題目詢問男子的說話意圖，因此要注意題目引用句（He'll use it for the budget analysis project）的前後部分。男子先說：「Danny will also need access to CashFind—our company's online financial research application」，表示 Danny 會需要取得應用程式 CashFind 的使用權利，後面說：「You should make sure this is arranged before he starts.」，要求女子確保這件事會在新人開始上班前處理好，由此可知，男子是想強調完成一項任務的必要性，因此正確答案是 (D) To emphasize the necessity of a task。

55 **細節事項相關問題－接下來要做的事** 答案 (B)

低

題目詢問女子接下來會做什麼，因此要注意對話的最後部分。女子說：「I'll e-mail the Web services team requesting a CashFind password now.」，表示會現在寄電子郵件給網路服務組索取 CashFind 的密碼，因此正確答案是 (B) Contact another team。

56
57
58

Questions 56-58 refer to the following conversation.

英式發音 → 加拿大式發音

W: [56]**I just found out about the new inventory tracking software** that was installed on our computers on Tuesday. But [56]**its functions are a bit unusual, so I'm having some trouble**. Have you figured out how to properly use it?

M: For the most part. [57]**Reading the user manual has been helpful. I recommend you do the same.** A digital copy of it was e-mailed to everyone a few days ago.

W: Oh, really? [58]**I never received the message.** Can you forward it to me so I can look it over?

M: Certainly. However, it's odd that you weren't included in the original e-mail. [58]**You should inform our manager about that** to ensure you're a part of future group messages and important announcements.

第 56-58 題請參考下列對話。

女：[56] 我剛剛才發現星期二的時候安裝在我們電腦上的新庫存追蹤軟體。不過 [56] 它的功能和平常用的有點不同，所以我碰到了一些困難。你已經搞懂要怎麼正確使用它了嗎？

男：大部分搞懂了。[57] 看使用者手冊一直都很有用。我建議妳也這麼做。電子版在幾天前用電子郵件寄給大家了。

女：噢，真的嗎？[58] 我從來沒有收到過這封信。你可以把它轉寄給我，讓我可以仔細看看嗎？

男：當然。不過，原始的電子郵件裡沒有妳真是奇怪。[58] 妳應該跟我們經理說這件事，確保未來的群組信和重要公告都會把妳包含在內。

56 What problem does the woman mention?

(A) She forgot to update an application.
(B) A machine stopped functioning.
(C) She is unfamiliar with a program.
(D) An inventory level is too low.

57 What does the man suggest?

(A) Referring to a handbook
(B) E-mailing some colleagues
(C) Consulting with an advisor
(D) Copying some manuals

58 According to the man, what should the woman talk to the manager about?

(A) Acquiring additional computer parts
(B) Customizing some new software
(C) Errors in an important file
(D) Complications with a messaging system

56. 女子提到什麼問題？

(A) 她忘了更新一個應用程式。
(B) 一台機器停止運作了。
(C) 她對一個程式不熟悉。
(D) 一項庫存的數量太少。

57. 男子建議什麼？

(A) 參考一本手冊
(B) 寄電子郵件給一些同事
(C) 找一位顧問諮詢
(D) 影印一些手冊

58. 根據男子所說，女子應該和經理說什麼？

(A) 購買額外的電腦零件
(B) 客製化一些新軟體
(C) 一個重要檔案裡的錯誤
(D) 傳訊系統的問題

題目 inventory [㊊ `ɪnvən͵torɪ ㊇ `invəntri] 存貨；庫存清單　tracking [trækɪŋ] 追蹤；跟蹤　install [ɪn`stɔl] 設置，安裝
function [`fʌŋkʃən] 功能　figure out 理解；搞懂　properly [㊊ `prɑpɚlɪ ㊇ `prɔpəli] 恰當地；正確地
forward [㊊ `fɔrwɚd ㊇ `fɔ:wəd] 傳送；轉發　look over 仔細查看　odd [ɑd] 奇怪的
57 refer to 參考～　handbook [`hænd͵bʊk] 手冊　consult [kən`sʌlt] 諮詢　advisor [əd`vaɪzɚ] 顧問
58 part [pɑrt] 零件　customize [`kʌstəm͵aɪz] 客製化　complication [͵kɑmplə`keʃən]（造成情況變複雜的）困難；問題

56 細節事項相關問題－問題點 答案 (C)

中
題目詢問女子提到什麼問題，因此要注意聽女子話中出現負面表達的內容。女子說：「I just found out about the new inventory tracking software」，表示自己剛剛才發現新的庫存追蹤軟體，接著說：「its functions are a bit unusual, so I'm having some trouble」，表示它的功能和平常用的有點不同，所以使用上碰到了一些困難，因此正確答案是 (C) She is unfamiliar with a program.。

57 細節事項相關問題－提議 答案 (A)

中
題目詢問男子建議什麼，因此要注意聽男子話中和提議相關的表達。男子說：「Reading the user manual has been helpful. I recommend you do the same.」，表示看使用者手冊一直都很有用，並建議女子也這麼做，因此正確答案是 (A) Referring to a handbook。

58 細節事項相關問題－特定細項 答案 (D)

高
題目詢問男子說女子應該跟經理說什麼，因此要注意男子話中和題目關鍵字（talk to the manager about）相關的內容。女子說：「I never received the message.」，表示自己從未收到信，後面男子則說：「You should inform our manager about that」，表示女子應該和經理說這件事，因此正確答案是 (D) Complications with a messaging system。

59
60
61

Questions 59-61 refer to the following conversation.

澳洲式發音 → 美式發音

M: Hello, Melanie. This is John Peters calling from the payroll department. [59]**I want to let you know that I noticed an error on last month's time sheets for one of your employees.**

W: Is that so? I made sure to double-check all of the sheets against my team's schedule before approving them. Which employee are you referring to?

M: Teresa Ford. Although she is a part-time employee, she entered 120 hours for the month of January. That's about 40 more hours than she normally works.

W: [60]**I actually increased her hours to 30 per week** last month, and that situation will continue moving forward. I already informed the head of human resources about it, but [61]**I'll call him right now and ask him to update the information in your database** today.

59 Why is the man calling the woman?

(A) To discuss a potential inaccuracy
(B) To report a computer glitch
(C) To switch a payment method
(D) To announce staff replacements

60 What does the woman say about Teresa Ford?

(A) She was transferred to another department.
(B) She has been assigned additional hours.
(C) She is using the wrong time sheets.
(D) She needs to submit some documents.

61 What will the woman probably do next?

(A) Take a call from a customer
(B) Update employee payroll records
(C) Submit a request to a coworker
(D) Analyze some sales data

第 59-61 題請參考下列對話。

男：哈囉，Melanie。我是從薪資管理部打來的 John Peters。[59] 我想要通知妳，我發現妳其中一個員工上個月的工時表上有錯。

女：是這樣嗎？我在批准之前都一定會重複對照檢查我們團隊的所有行程表和工時表。你說的是哪一個員工呢？

男：Teresa Ford。她是兼職人員，可是她卻在一月登錄了 120 個小時。這比她正常的工作時間多了大約 40 個小時。

女：[60] 我其實上個月把她的時數增加到每週 30 小時了，而這個情況會繼續維持下去。我已經通知過人力資源部的主管這件事了，但 [61] 我現在會打給他，請他今天更新你們資料庫裡的資訊。

59. 男子為何打電話給女子？

(A) 討論可能的錯誤
(B) 回報電腦的小故障
(C) 變更支付方式
(D) 宣布更換人手

60. 關於 Teresa Ford，女子說什麼？

(A) 她被調到另一個部門了。
(B) 她被分派到了額外的時數。
(C) 她在用的工時表是錯的。
(D) 她需要提交一些文件。

61. 女子接下來可能會做什麼？

(A) 接聽來自一位顧客的電話
(B) 更新員工的薪資記錄
(C) 向同事提出一項要求
(D) 分析一些銷售資料

題目 payroll department 薪資管理部　time sheet 工時表　double-check 重複檢查　against [ə`gɛnst] 對照　enter [美 `ɛntɚ 英 `entə] 輸入；登錄

59 inaccuracy [ɪn`ækjərəsɪ] 錯誤；不精確　glitch [glɪtʃ] 小故障

59 ■ **整體對話相關問題－目的** 答案 (A)
○●●● 高

題目詢問男子為什麼要打電話給女子，因此要注意對話的開頭。男子對女子說：「I want to let you know that I noticed an error on last month's time sheets for one of your employees.」，表示自己發現女子的其中一個員工上個月的工時表上有錯，由此可知，男子是為了要和女子討論一個可能的錯誤而打電話給她，因此正確答案是 (A) To discuss a potential inaccuracy。

60 ■ **細節事項相關問題－提及** 答案 (B)
○○●● 中

題目詢問女子提到什麼與 Teresa Ford 有關的事情，因此要注意和題目關鍵字（Teresa Ford）相關的內容。女子說：「I ~ increased her[Teresa Ford's] hours to 30 per week」，表示她將 Teresa Ford 的時數增加到了每週 30 小時，因此正確答案是 (B) She has been assigned additional hours.。

61 ■ **細節事項相關問題－接下來要做的事** 答案 (C)
○●●● 高

題目詢問女子接下來會做什麼，因此要注意對話的最後部分。女子說：「I'll call him[head of human resources] right now and ask him to update the information in your database」，表示自己現在會打給人力資源部的主管，請他今天更新資料庫裡的資訊，因此正確答案是 (C) Submit a request to a coworker。

62
63
64

Questions 62-64 refer to the following conversation and table.

美式發音 → 澳洲式發音

W: Eastside Cable. How may I help you?
M: Hi. This is Jeremy Monroe. [62]**A worker is supposed to install a new cable box at my property today, but I can't remember the appointment time.**
W: Just a minute . . . Um, he'll be there at 2 P.M.
M: Thanks. I also want to change my TV package. I'm viewing your online brochure now.
W: OK . . . Well, [63]**for this month only, Package A is offered at a discount.**
M: But [63]**that doesn't include the service I'm most interested in. I prefer Package B.**
W: I see. Well, [64]**you're certainly free to upgrade to that one, but you'll have to pay the standard rate.**

第 62-64 題請參考下列對話與表格。

女：Eastside Cable。有什麼我能協助您的嗎？
男：嗨。我是 Jeremy Monroe。[62] 今天應該會有個工人要到我家安裝新的機上盒，但我不記得約好的時間了。
女：稍等一下……嗯，他下午 2 點會到。
男：謝謝。我還想要更改我的電視頻道套餐方案。我現在正在看你們的線上說明冊。
女：好的……嗯，[63]A 套餐方案有折扣，只限這個月。
男：但是 [63] 它裡面沒有我最感興趣的那項服務。我比較喜歡 B 套餐方案。
女：我知道了。嗯，[64] 您當然可以升級成那個套餐方案，但您將須支付標準費用。

Eastside Cable

	Service			
	Premium Sports Channels	[63]**Game Downloads**	Premium Movie Channels	Video Recording
Package A	√		√	√
Package B		√		√
Package C	√	√	√	

Eastside Cable

	服務			
	精選體育頻道	[63] 遊戲下載	精選電影頻道	錄影
A 套餐方案	√		√	√
B 套餐方案		√		√
C 套餐方案	√	√	√	

62 What did the man forget?

(A) An activation code
(B) A product pamphlet
(C) A fee payment
(D) A visit time

62. 男子忘了什麼？

(A) 啟動碼
(B) 產品的小冊子
(C) 費用支付
(D) 造訪時間

63 Look at the graphic. Which service is the man most interested in?

(A) Premium Sports Channels
(B) Game Downloads
(C) Premium Movie Channels
(D) Video Recording

63. 請看圖表。男子最感興趣的是哪一項服務？

(A) 精選體育頻道
(B) 遊戲下載
(C) 精選電影頻道
(D) 錄影

64 According to the woman, what is the man unable to receive?

(A) A gift with purchase
(B) A company brochure
(C) A piece of equipment
(D) A reduced price

64. 根據女子所說，男子無法得到什麼？

(A) 消費贈禮
(B) 公司的說明冊
(C) 一件設備
(D) 折扣價

題目 property [美 ˋprɑpɚtɪ 英 ˋprɔpəti] 不動產；財產　brochure [美 broˋʃʊr 英 brəuˋʃjuə]（說明或廣告用的）小冊子　rate [ret] 費用

62 activation [ˌæktəˋveʃən] 啟動　code [kod] 代碼；密碼　pamphlet [ˋpæmflɪt]（說明或廣告用的）小冊子　payment [ˋpemənt] 支付；支付款項

62 細節事項相關問題－特定細項 答案 (D)

中

題目詢問男子忘了什麼，因此要注意和題目關鍵字（forget）相關的內容。男子說：「A worker is supposed to install a new cable box at my property today, but I can't remember the appointment time.」，表示今天應該會有工人要到自己家裡安裝新的機上盒，但他不記得約好的時間，因此正確答案是 (D) A visit time。

新 63 細節事項相關問題－圖表資料 答案 (B)

難

題目詢問男子最感興趣的是什麼服務，因此必須確認題目提供的圖表，並注意題目關鍵字（service ~ most interested in）的前後部分。女子說：「for this month only, Package A is offered at a discount」，表示 A 套餐方案在這個月有折扣，而男子回答：「that doesn't include the service I'm most interested in. I prefer Package B.」，表示 A 套餐方案裡沒有自己最感興趣的服務，所以自己比較喜歡 B 套餐方案，透過圖表可知，A 套餐方案裡沒有、但 B 套餐方案裡有的是遊戲下載，因此正確答案是 (B) Game Downloads。

64 細節事項相關問題－特定細項 答案 (D)

高

題目詢問女子說男子無法得到什麼，因此必須確認女子話中和題目關鍵字（unable to receive）相關的內容。女子說：「you're ~ free to upgrade to that one[Package B], but you'll have to pay the standard rate」，表示男子可以升級成 B 套餐方案，不過將須支付標準費用，因此正確答案是 (D) A reduced price。

65
66
67

新

Questions 65-67 refer to the following conversation and instruction manual.

英式發音 → 加拿大式發音

W: Hi, Billy. What are you doing?
M: I'm trying to assemble this table. Um, [65]**our manager told me to set up another one in this conference room.**
W: Is it very complicated?
M: The instructions are pretty straightforward. [66]**I've used all the bolts to attach the legs to the tabletop. However, one of the remaining parts seems to be missing.**
W: That must be frustrating. Have you contacted the company you ordered it from?
M: [67]**I called them this morning, but their customer service department was busy dealing with other issues. I'm going to try them again during my lunch hour.**

第 65-67 題請參考下列對話與說明書。

女：嗨，Billy。你在做什麼？
男：我正試著要把這張桌子組裝起來。嗯，[65] 我們經理要我在這間會議室裡再設置一張桌子。
女：它很複雜嗎？
男：這個說明滿好懂的。[66] 我已經用全部的螺栓把桌腳和桌面接起來了。不過，剩下的零件之中似乎有一個不見了。
女：這一定很令人洩氣。你聯絡過你訂這張桌子的公司了嗎？
男：[67] 我今天早上打給他們了，但他們的客服部門當時正忙著處理其他問題。我打算在我午休期間再打一次給他們看看。

新

Perez Office Table

Parts Included:

Part A: **Tabletop**(1)
Part B: **Legs**(2)
[66]**Part C**: Support bases (2)
Part D: **Bolts**(8)

Perez 辦公桌
零件包含：
A 零件：桌面 (1)
B 零件：桌腳 (2)
66C 零件：支撐底座 (2)
D 零件：螺栓 (8)

65 Where does the conversation most likely take place?

(A) In a meeting room
(B) In an employee lounge
(C) In a furniture store
(D) In a warehouse

65. 這段對話最有可能發生在哪裡？

(A) 會議室
(B) 員工休息室
(C) 家具店
(D) 倉庫

66 Look at the graphic. Which part is missing?

(A) Part A
(B) Part B
(C) Part C
(D) Part D

66. 請看圖表。哪一個零件不見了？

(A) A 零件
(B) B 零件
(C) C 零件
(D) D 零件

67 What will the man probably do during his lunch break?

(A) Call a business
(B) Move some tables
(C) Look over a manual
(D) Find additional tools

67. 男子在他的午休期間可能會做什麼？

(A) 打電話給一間公司
(B) 移動一些桌子
(C) 查看一本手冊
(D) 尋找額外的工具

題目 assemble [ə`sɛmbl] 組裝　complicated [(美) `kɑmplə͵ketɪd (英) `kɔmplikeitid] 複雜的
instruction [ɪn`strʌkʃən]（講解使用或操作方法的）說明（書）　straightforward [͵stret`fɔrwɚd] 簡單的；易懂的
remaining [rɪ`menɪŋ] 剩下的　missing [`mɪsɪŋ] 缺失的；不見的
frustrating [(美) `frʌstretɪŋ (英) `frʌstreitiŋ] 令人挫折的；令人洩氣的
contact [(美) kən`tækt (英) kən`tækt] 聯絡　deal with 處理～
65 warehouse [`wɛr͵haʊs] 倉庫
67 business [`bɪznɪs] 公司　look over 查看　manual [`mænjʊəl]（說明或介紹用的）手冊
additional [ə`dɪʃənl] 額外的；添加的

65 ○○● 低 **整體對話相關問題－地點** 答案 (A)

題目詢問對話的發生地點，因此要注意聽和地點相關的表達。男子說：「our manager told me to set up another one[table] in this conference room」，表示經理要求在這間會議室裡多設置一張桌子，由此可知，對話地點在會議室，因此正確答案是 (A) In a meeting room。

新 66 ○●●● 高 **細節事項相關問題－圖表資料** 答案 (C)

題目詢問不見的是哪個零件，因此必須確認題目提供的說明書，並注意題目關鍵字（part ~ missing）的前後部分。男子說：「I've used all the bolts to attach the legs to the tabletop. However, one of the remaining parts seems to be missing.」，表示自己已經用全部的螺栓把桌腳和桌面接起來了，但剩下的零件之中有一個不見了，透過說明書可以得知，剩下的是 C 零件，因此正確答案是 (C) Part C。

67 ○○● 低 **細節事項相關問題－接下來要做的事** 答案 (A)

題目詢問男子在他的午休期間可能會做什麼，因此要注意和題目關鍵字（during ~ lunch break）相關的內容。男子說：「I called them[company] this morning, but their customer service department was busy ~. I'm going to try them again during my lunch hour.」，表示今天早上打了電話給那間公司，但他們的客服部門正在忙著處理別的事，所以男子打算在自己的午休期間再打給那間公司看看，因此正確答案是 (A) Call a business。

新

68
69
70

Questions 68-70 refer to the following conversation and graph.

美式發音 → 澳洲式發音

W: [68]**I'm sorry I couldn't attend our product launch event, George. Speaking with our vice president took longer than expected.**

M: That's OK. What did Mr. Darner need to talk to you about?

W: He's concerned about our most expensive oven model. [69]**Sales have dropped for three consecutive months since a competitor put out a similar product.**

M: Ah, [69]**you mean the one released by Saber Electronics in July?**

W: [69]**Right. Mr. Darner wants me to present some ideas for increasing our model's sales** to the board of directors next Thursday.

M: That's a big responsibility. [70]**If you need any assistance with collecting data, I can help you out.**

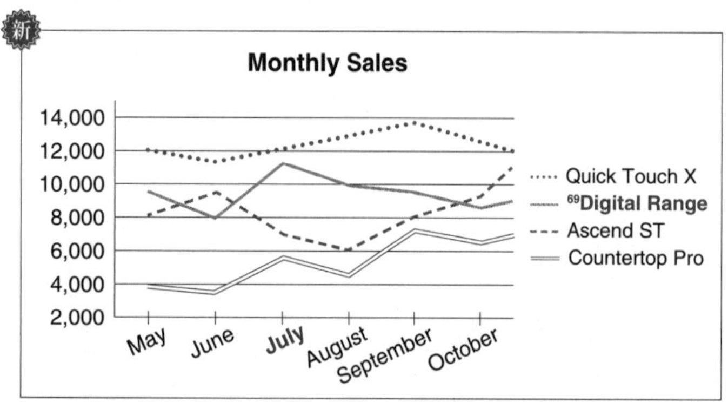

第 68-70 題請參考下列對話與圖表。

女：[68] 我很抱歉沒能參加我們的產品發表活動，George。和副總裁談話花了比預期要久的時間。

男：沒關係。Darner 先生需要和妳談什麼？

女：他在擔心我們最貴的那款烤箱。[69] 自從競爭對手推出了類似產品，銷售量已經連三個月下滑了。

男：啊，[69] 妳是說 Saber 電子在七月推出的那款嗎？

女：[69] 沒錯。Darner 先生要我在下週四就提高我們那款的銷售量向董事會提出一些構想。

男：這件事責任重大。[70] 如果妳在收集資料上需要任何協助，我可以幫忙妳。

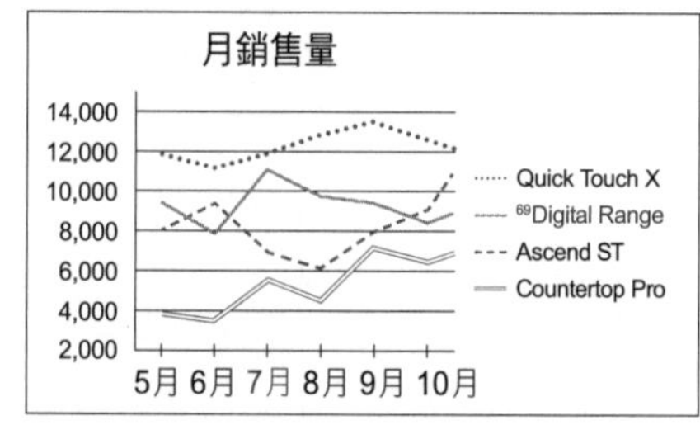

68 Why did the woman miss the event?

(A) She was welcoming new employees.
(B) She was leading a department workshop.
(C) She was talking to an executive.
(D) She was meeting with a client.

69 Look at the graphic. Which model will the woman give a presentation on?

新

(A) Quick Touch X
(B) Digital Range
(C) Ascend ST
(D) Countertop Pro

70 What does the man offer to do?

(A) Organize an investor event
(B) Gather some information
(C) Help with a marketing campaign
(D) Edit a sales report

68. 女子為何錯過了活動？

(A) 她在迎接新員工。
(B) 她在主持部門工作坊。
(C) 她在和主管談話。
(D) 她在和客戶開會。

69. 請看圖表。女子會針對哪一款做簡報？

(A) Quick Touch X
(B) Digital Range
(C) Ascend ST
(D) Countertop Pro

70. 男子願意做什麼？

(A) 籌辦一場投資人活動
(B) 收集一些資料
(C) 協助一次行銷宣傳活動
(D) 編輯一份銷售報告

題目 vice president 副總裁　concerned [kən`sɝnd] 憂慮的，擔心的　consecutive [kən`sɛkjʊtɪv] 連續的　competitor [kəm`pɛtətɚ] 競爭對手　put out 發表（商品等）　release [rɪ`lis] 推出　board of directors 董事會　responsibility [(美) rɪˏspɑnsə`bɪlətɪ (英) riˏspɔnsə`biliti] 責任；職責　assistance [ə`sɪstəns] 協助

68 welcome [`wɛlkəm] 迎接，歡迎　lead [lid] 領導　executive [ɪg`zɛkjʊtɪv] 主管

70 organize [`ɔrgəˏnaɪz] 籌辦　investor [ɪn`vɛstɚ] 投資者

68 ■ **細節事項相關問題－理由** 答案 (C)

中

題目詢問女子錯過活動的原因，因此要注意和題目關鍵字（miss the event）相關的內容。女子說：「I'm sorry I couldn't attend our product launch event ~. Speaking with our vice president took longer than expected.」，先對於自己沒能參加產品發表活動表示抱歉，再說明沒能參加活動，是因為和副總裁間的談話花了比預期要長的時間，因此正確答案是 (C) She was talking to an executive.。

換句話說

vice president 副總裁 → executive 主管

69 ■ **細節事項相關問題－圖表資料** 答案 (B)

難

題目詢問女子會針對哪一款產品做簡報，因此必須確認題目提供的圖表，並注意和題目關鍵字（model ~ give a presentation on）相關的內容。女子說：「Sales have dropped for three consecutive months since a competitor put out a similar product.」，表示從競爭對手推出類似產品後，銷售量就連三個月下滑，接著男子說：「you mean the one[product] released by Saber Electronics in July?」，向女子確認她說的是不是 Saber 電子在七月推出的產品。女子說：「Right. Mr. Darner wants me to present some ideas for increasing our model's sales」，女子先表示的確是那款，再提到 Darner 先生要自己就提升公司這款的銷售量提出一些構想。透過圖表可知，在七月競爭對手推出類似產品後，銷售量就連三個月下滑的是 Digital Range，因此女子會針對 Digital Range 做簡報，正確答案是 (B) Digital Range。

70 ■ **細節事項相關問題－提議** 答案 (B)

中

題目詢問男子願意做什麼，因此要注意聽男子話中提到要為女子做事的部分。男子對女子說：「If you need any assistance with collecting data, I can help you out.」，表示如果女子在收集資料上需要協助，自己可以幫忙，因此正確答案是 (B) Gather some information。

換句話說

collecting data 收集資料 → Gather ~ information 收集資料

71
72
73

Questions 71-73 refer to the following announcement.

加拿大式發音

May I have your attention, please? [71]**There is a red Jupiter four-door sedan in parking lot 4D that is currently blocking the hospital's east exit.** Its license plate number is DTG103. [71]**We ask the owner to please move the car immediately.** Also, [72]**as a reminder, vehicles should never be left in the hospital's emergency areas.** [73]**To identify these, look for red and yellow stripes on the pavement.** Anyone who parks their vehicle in one of these areas will be subject to a fine of up to $500 in accordance with state laws. We appreciate your cooperation.

第 71-73 題請參考下列公告。

請大家注意一下。[71] 現在停車場 4D 上有一台紅色 Jupiter 四門轎車擋到了醫院的東邊出口。車牌號碼是 DTG103。[71] 請車主立即移車。此外，[72] 在此提醒，車輛切勿停放於醫院急診區內。[73] 要辨識急診區，請注意路面上的紅黃條紋。任何將車輛停放於這些區域內的人都將根據州法被處以最高 500 美金的罰鍰。我們感謝您的配合。

71 Who most likely is the speaker?
(A) A delivery person
(B) A tow truck driver
(C) A hospital employee
(D) A city worker

71. 說話者最有可能是誰？
(A) 送貨員
(B) 拖吊車駕駛
(C) 醫院員工
(D) 市府員工

72 What does the speaker remind listeners to do?
(A) Use marked entrances and exits
(B) Consult with medical officials
(C) Contact emergency personnel
(D) Avoid parking in certain zones

72. 說話者提醒聽者們做什麼？
(A) 使用有標示的出入口
(B) 諮詢醫務人員
(C) 聯繫急救人員
(D) 避免在某些區域內停車

73 According to the speaker, what should listeners look for?
(A) Detour signs
(B) Colored lines
(C) Lighted displays
(D) Traffic cones

73. 根據說話者所說，聽者們應該注意什麼？
(A) 繞道標誌
(B) 有顏色的線
(C) 亮著的顯示器
(D) 交通錐

題目 license plate number 車牌號碼　identify [aɪˋdɛntəˏfaɪ] 辨識　pavement [ˋpevmənt] 路面　be subject to 須受～　fine [faɪn] 罰金；罰鍰　in accordance with 根據～　cooperation [koˏɑpəˋreʃən] 合作，協力

71 tow truck 拖吊車

73 detour [ˋditʊr] 繞道

71 整體對話相關問題－說話者　　答案 (C)

中

題目詢問說話者身分，因此要注意聽和身分、職業相關的表達。獨白說：「There is a red Jupiter four-door sedan ~ that is currently blocking the hospital's east exit.」，表示有一台紅色 Jupiter 四門轎車擋到了醫院的東邊出口，接著說：「We ask the owner to please move the car immediately.」，表示要求車主立即移車，由此可知，說話者是在醫院工作的員工，因此正確答案是 (C) A hospital employee。

72 細節事項相關問題－特定細項　　答案 (D)

中

題目詢問說話者提醒聽者們做什麼，因此要注意和題目關鍵字（remind listeners to do）相關的內容。獨白說：「as a reminder, vehicles should never be left in the hospital's emergency areas」，提醒聽者們切勿把車輛停放於醫院急診區內，因此正確答案是 (D) Avoid parking in certain zones。

換句話說

vehicles should never be left in the ~ emergency areas 車輛切勿停放於急診區內

→ Avoid parking in certain zones 避免在某些區域內停車

73 細節事項相關問題－特定細項　　答案 (B)

低

題目詢問說話者說聽者們應該要注意什麼，因此必須注意提到題目關鍵字（look for）的前後部分。獨白說：「To identify these[emergency areas], look for red and yellow stripes on the pavement.」，表示要辨識急診區，就要注意路面上的紅黃條紋，因此正確答案是 (B) Colored lines。

74 75 76

Questions 74-76 refer to the following telephone message.

美式發音

Hi, Minho. This is Katy. I just finished giving the presentation to our client in Philadelphia. It went well, but there's a massive snowstorm here, so [74]**my return flight to Houston will depart much later than scheduled. This means that I won't get back this evening.** Would you mind making the presentation to Techworth at 3 P.M. today? [75]**You helped create the application they're interested in last year**, so the presentation's contents should be very familiar to you. I e-mailed you the necessary files a few minutes ago. Could you confirm that you received them and can cover for me? [76]**If you need any help with this assignment, contact my assistant**, Beth Richards. She can be reached at extension 345. Thanks.

第 74-76 題請參考下列電話留言。

嗨，Minho。我是 Katy。我剛在費城結束對我們客戶的簡報。簡報進行得很順利，但這裡發生了嚴重的暴風雪，所以 [74] 我飛回休士頓的班機會比原定時間晚很多起飛。這也就是說，我今天晚上不會回去。你願意在今天下午 3 點去對 Techworth 做簡報嗎？ [75] 你去年協助製作了他們感興趣的那款應用程式，所以這份簡報的內容對你來說應該非常熟悉。我幾分鐘前用電子郵件把必要的檔案寄給你了。能否請你確認你是否已收到了檔案且可替我做簡報呢？ [76] 如果你在這件工作上需要任何協助，請聯絡我的助理 Beth Richards。可以打分機 345 聯絡她。謝謝。

74 新 Why does the speaker say, "there's a massive snowstorm here"?

(A) To express concern about a delivery
(B) To request help with booking a flight
(C) To indicate uncertainty about a decision
(D) To provide the reason for a delay

75 According to the speaker, what did the listener do last year?

(A) He helped develop a program.
(B) He hired a programmer.
(C) He gave a presentation to a client.
(D) He transferred to another branch.

76 What does the speaker suggest the listener do?

(A) Reschedule a meeting
(B) Speak with an assistant
(C) Cancel a trip
(D) E-mail a file

74. 說話者為什麼說：「這裡發生了嚴重的暴風」？

(A) 表達對於交貨的憂慮
(B) 要求協助預訂班機
(C) 表明一項決定的不確定性
(D) 提供造成延遲的理由

75. 根據說話者所說，聽者去年做了什麼？

(A) 他協助開發了一個程式。
(B) 他聘請了一位程式設計師。
(C) 他向一位客戶做了簡報。
(D) 他調到了另一間分公司。

76. 說話者建議聽者做什麼？

(A) 重新安排會議時間
(B) 和一位助理說話
(C) 取消一趟旅行
(D) 以電子郵件寄送一個檔案

題目 client [ˋklaɪənt] 客戶 massive [ˋmæsɪv] 巨大的；嚴重的 content [ˋkɑntɛnt] 內容 familiar [fəˋmɪljɚ] 熟悉的 cover for 頂替～
74 book [bʊk] 預訂 uncertainty [ʌnˋsɝtn̩tɪ] 不確定性
75 develop [dɪˋvɛləp] 開發

新 **74** 細節事項相關問題－掌握意圖 中 答案 (D)

題目詢問說話者意圖，因此要注意題目引用句（there's a massive snowstorm here）的前後部分。獨白說：「my return flight to Houston will depart much later than scheduled. This means that I won't get back this evening.」，表示返回休士頓的班機會比原定時間晚很多起飛，也就是說今晚無法回去，由此可知，說話者想要為自己的延遲提供理由，因此正確答案是 (D) To provide the reason for a delay。

75 細節事項相關問題－特定細項 中 答案 (A)

題目詢問聽者去年做了什麼，因此要注意提到題目關鍵字 （last year）的前後部分。獨白說：「You helped create the application they[Techworth]'re interested in last year」，表示聽者在去年協助製作了 Techworth 公司感興趣的那款應用程式，因此正確答案是 (A) He helped develop a program.。

換句話說

create the application 製作應用程式 → develop a program 開發程式

76 細節事項相關問題－提議 低 答案 (B)

題目詢問說話者建議聽者做什麼，因此要注意聽獨白中後半部分出現提議相關表達的句子。獨白說：「If you need any help with this assignment, contact my assistant」，表示如果聽者需要與這項工作有關的協助，請聯繫自己的助理，因此正確答案是 (B) Speak with an assistant。

77 78 79

Questions 77-79 refer to the following excerpt from a meeting.	第 77-79 題請參考下列會議節錄。
加拿大式發音	
[77]**Over the month of August, we will be painting and remodeling parts of our office.** This work will take place on the third floor, and it may be a bit noisy. That's why [78]**personnel from our division are going to use temporary workstations on the fourth floor**. Since the construction is scheduled to begin in a couple of weeks, preparations have already been made, with desks having been set up on the designated floor. However, [79]**staff members' work computers won't be relocated until the final week of this month**. I understand that these temporary changes will be an inconvenience, but I trust that everyone will try to make the best of the situation.	[77] 在八月這個月，我們部分辦公室將進行粉刷和整修。這項工程會在三樓進行，而且可能會有點吵。這也就是為什麼 [78] 我們部門的員工將會使用在四樓的臨時工作站。因為這項工程排定在兩個星期後開始，所以準備工作已經做好了，並已在指定樓層設置了桌子。不過，[79] 員工工作用的電腦要到這個月的最後一週才會放到新的位置。我知道這些暫時性的變動會造成困擾，不過我相信大家都會努力為這個情況做最好的安排。
77 According to the speaker, what will happen in August? (A) Some computers will be purchased. (B) A division will be expanded. (C) A building will be renovated. (D) Some workers will be trained.	77. 根據說話者所說，八月會發生什麼？ (A) 會採購一些電腦。 (B) 會擴大一個部門。 (C) 會整修一棟大樓。 (D) 會訓練一些員工。
78 What is located on the fourth floor? (A) Temporary workstations (B) Executive offices (C) Construction tools (D) New conference rooms	78. 什麼位在四樓？ (A) 臨時工作站 (B) 主管辦公室 (C) 工程工具 (D) 新的會議室
79 What will most likely be done toward the end of this month? (A) Desks will be set up. (B) Equipment will be moved. (C) Staff will go on leave. (D) Painters will finish a job.	79. 這個月快結束時，最有可能會完成什麼？ (A) 會設置桌子。 (B) 會移動設備。 (C) 員工會休假。 (D) 油漆工人會完成工作。

題目 personnel [ˌpɝsn̩ˋɛl]（總稱）員工，人員 temporary [ˋtɛmpəˌrɛrɪ] 臨時的 workstation [ˋwɝkˌsteʃən] 工作站 construction [kənˋstrʌkʃən] 工程；建設 designate [ˋdɛzɪgˌnet] 指定；指名 relocate [riˋloket] 重新安置；遷移 inconvenience [ˌɪnkənˋvinjəns] 不方便；困擾 make the best of 充分善用（不好的條件等）

79 toward [təˋwɔrd] 朝向；接近 equipment [ɪˋkwɪpmənt] 設備；用具

77 細節事項相關問題－接下來要做的事 答案 (C)

中

題目詢問八月會發生什麼，因此要注意提到題目關鍵字（August）的前後部分。獨白說：「Over the month of August, we will be painting and remodeling parts of our office.」，表示八月期間部分辦公室會進行粉刷與整修，因此正確答案是 (C) A building will be renovated.。

78 細節事項相關問題－特定細項 答案 (A)

低

題目詢問是什麼位於四樓，因此要注意提到題目關鍵字（fourth floor）的前後部分。獨白說：「personnel ~ are going to use temporary workstations on the fourth floor」，表示員工將使用在四樓的臨時工作站，因此正確答案是 (A) Temporary workstations。

79 細節事項相關問題－特定細項 答案 (B)

中

題目詢問這個月快結束時可能會發生什麼，因此要注意和題目關鍵字（the end of this month）相關的內容。獨白說：「staff members' work computers won't be relocated until the final week of this month」，表示員工工作用的電腦將會在這個月的最後一週被放到新的位置，因此正確答案是 (B) Equipment will be moved.。

80
81
82

Questions 80-82 refer to the following telephone message.

英式發音

Hello, Ms. Olsen. [80]**I'm calling from Vine Express to let you know that we're holding a package for you. One of our employees tried to deliver the item to your house three times**, but you were not home on any of those occasions. Because the parcel needs to be signed for, [81]**you'll have to pick it up at our sorting facility** at 896 West Pine Drive between 9 A.M. and 5 P.M. [82]**If you don't retrieve the package within seven days, it will be returned to the sender.** For more information about the item, please feel free to call us at 555-9172. Thank you.

第 80-82 題請參考下列電話留言。

哈囉，Olsen 小姐。[80] 我這裡是 Vine 快遞，打電話來是想要通知您，我們這裡現在有一件您的包裹。我們其中一位員工已試著把這件包裹送到您家三次了，但這三次您都不在家。因為這件包裹需要簽收，[81] 您將必須在早上 9 點到下午 5 點間，到我們位於 West Pine 路 896 號的分揀站領取這件包裹。[82] 如果您沒有在七天內來取回，則這件包裹將會被退回給寄件人。若想取得更多與此包裹相關的資訊，歡迎打 555-9172 給我們。謝謝您。

80 Where most likely does the speaker work?
(A) At a real estate firm
(B) At a retail outlet
(C) At a travel agency
(D) At a delivery company

80. 說話者最有可能在哪裡工作？
(A) 在一間不動產公司
(B) 在一間零售通路
(C) 在一家旅行社
(D) 在一間貨運公司

81 What does the speaker instruct the listener to do?
(A) Provide an electronic signature
(B) Return a parcel
(C) Visit a facility
(D) Confirm an address

81. 說話者指示聽者做什麼？
(A) 提供一個電子簽名
(B) 退回一個包裹
(C) 造訪一間設施
(D) 確認一個地址

82 What does the speaker say might happen after seven days?
(A) A message will be sent out.
(B) A request will be processed.
(C) A tracking number will expire.
(D) A package will be shipped back.

82. 說話者說七天後可能會發生什麼？
(A) 會送出一則訊息。
(B) 會處理一項要求。
(C) 一個追蹤碼會到期。
(D) 一件包裹會被送回。

題目 parcel [美 `pɑrsl 英 `pɑ:sl] 包裹　sorting [美 sɔrtɪŋ 英 sɔ:tiŋ] 分類；挑選　retrieve [rɪ`triv] 取回；重新得到
80 real estate 不動產
81 signature [`sɪgnətʃɚ] 簽名
82 process [`prɑsɛs] 處理　tracking [trækɪŋ] 追蹤　expire [ɪk`spaɪr] 到期

80 整體內容相關問題－說話者　答案 (D)
中
題目詢問說話者的工作地點，因此要注意聽和身分、職業相關的表達。獨白說：「I'm calling from Vine Express to let you know that we're holding a package for you. One of our employees tried to deliver the item to your house three times」，表示自己公司這裡現在有聽者的包裹，並說公司員工已試著送去聽者家三次，由此可知，說話者在貨運公司工作，因此正確答案是 (D) At a delivery company。

81 細節事項相關問題－特定細項　答案 (C)
低
題目詢問說話者指示聽者去做什麼，因此必須注意和題目關鍵字（instruct ~ to do）相關的內容。獨白說：「you'll have to pick it[parcel] up at our sorting facility」，要求聽者前往分揀站領取包裹，因此正確答案是 (C) Visit a facility。

82 細節事項相關問題－特定細項　答案 (D)
中
題目詢問說話者說在七天後可能會發生什麼，因此要注意提到題目關鍵字 （seven days）的前後部分。獨白說：「If you don't retrieve the package within seven days, it will be returned to the sender.」，表示聽者如果沒有在七天內來取回包裹，則會將這件包裹退回給寄件人，因此正確答案是 (D) A package will be shipped back.。

換句話說
be returned 退回 → be shipped back 送回

83
84
85

Questions 83-85 refer to the following excerpt from a meeting.	第 83-85 題請參考下列會議節錄。
英式發音	
As we discussed in our last meeting, [83]**the employee who will receive the gift certificate for having the most sales will be announced today**. But before I do this, [84]**I'd like to congratulate everyone on the sales team. After calculating your sales from last month** and comparing them to those from the previous month, we found that they'd all increased. [85]**Several of you boosted your sales by more than 50 percent**, but, um . . . that still wasn't good enough. [85]**Our winner actually doubled her monthly sales by signing a service contract with a hotel chain.** I'd like to now ask Christine McKesson to come up and accept her reward.	如同我們在上次會議中討論的，[83] 今天將宣布因銷售額最高而將獲得禮券的員工。但在我宣布之前，[84] 我想先恭喜銷售團隊的全體同仁。在計算過你們上個月的銷售額，並與前一個月的銷售額相比較之後，我們發現全部人的銷售額都提升了。[85] 你們之中有幾個人的銷售額成長了超過百分之五十，不過，嗯……這樣還是不夠好。[85] 我們的贏家藉著和一間連鎖飯店簽下服務合約而讓她的本月銷售額實際上翻倍了。現在我想要請 Christine McKesson 上來領取她的獎勵。
83 What is the speaker mainly discussing? (A) A company expansion (B) A performance incentive (C) An upcoming promotion (D) A budget increase	83. 說話者主要在談論什麼？ (A) 公司擴張 (B) 績效獎勵 (C) 即將進行的升職 (D) 預算增加
84 Who is the speaker most likely addressing? (A) Corporate executives (B) Event organizers (C) Hotel personnel (D) Sales professionals	84. 說話者最有可能在對誰說話？ (A) 公司主管 (B) 活動籌辦人 (C) 飯店人員 (D) 銷售專業人員
85 新 What does the speaker mean when she says, "that still wasn't good enough"? (A) An employee achieved better results. (B) A task was not completed on schedule. (C) A contract will have to be revised. (D) A team must participate in a program.	85. 當說話者說：「這樣還是不夠好」時，意思是什麼？ (A) 一名員工達到了更好的成果。 (B) 一項任務沒有照預定時間完成。 (C) 將必須修改一份合約。 (D) 一個團隊必須參與一項計畫。

題目 gift certificate 禮券 previous [ˋpriviəs] 先前的 boost [bust] 使成長；增加 still [stɪl] 仍然；儘管如此 double [ˋdʌbl̩] 使成兩倍

83 expansion [ɪkˋspænʃən] 擴張 performance [pɚˋfɔrməns] 績效；性能；表演 incentive [ɪnˋsɛntɪv] 獎勵；動機 budget [ˋbʌdʒɪt] 預算

85 result [rɪˋzʌlt] 成果；結果 revise [rɪˋvaɪz] 修改，修正 participate [pɑrˋtɪsə͵pet] 參與

83 **整體內容相關問題－主題** 答案 (B)

中

題目詢問說話者在談論的主題是什麼，因此要注意聽獨白的開頭部分。獨白說：「the employee who will receive the gift certificate for having the most sales will be announced today」，表示今天將公布銷售額最高、能獲得禮券的員工是誰，並接著提到與獲得實質獎勵有關的內容，因此正確答案是 (B) A performance incentive。

84 **整體內容相關問題－聽者** 答案 (D)

低

題目詢問聽者的身分，因此要注意聽和身分、職業相關的表達。獨白說：「I'd like to congratulate everyone on the sales team. ~ calculating your sales from last month」，表示想對銷售團隊全體人員表達祝賀，並提及計算了聽者們上個月的銷售額，由此可知，說話者說話的對象是專門從事銷售的銷售專業人員，因此正確答案是 (D) Sales professionals。

換句話說

everyone on the sales team 銷售團隊的全體同仁 → Sales professionals 銷售專業人員

新 **85** **細節事項相關問題－掌握意圖** 答案 (A)

高

題目詢問說話者意圖，因此要注意題目引用句（that still wasn't good enough）的前後部分。獨白說：「Several of you boosted your sales by more than 50 percent」，表示團隊裡有幾個人的銷售額成長了超過 50%，接著說：「Our winner actually doubled her monthly sales by signing a service contract with a hotel chain.」，表示贏得獎勵的人因為和連鎖飯店簽下了合約而讓月銷售額翻倍，由此可知，有一位員工達到了更好的銷售額，因此正確答案是 (A) An employee achieved better results.。

86
87
88

Questions 86-88 refer to the following radio broadcast.	第 86-88 題請參考下列電台廣播。
加拿大式發音	
In business news, local firm [86]**Digital Solutions has announced plans to release the latest version of its mobile phone application**, SpeakVid. The application allows users to record, edit, and share short video messages. [87]**It has become hugely popular, resulting in a sharp rise in the developer's stock prices.** The upgrade is anticipated among consumers and investors alike. The general public is excited for the application's updated interface, while business analysts predict that the upgrade will expand the firm's market base. SpeakVid has attracted national media coverage already, and [88]**experts believe that interest will increase next month when the new version of the application comes out.**	在商業新聞，本地公司 [86]Digital Solutions 已宣布計畫釋出其手機應用程式 SpeakVid 的最新版本。此應用程式可以讓使用者錄製、編輯並分享簡短的影像訊息。[87] 它變得十分受歡迎，也使得開發商的股價勁揚。在消費者及投資人之間均對此次升級感到期待。一般大眾對於此應用程式的最新介面感到興奮，而商業分析師預期此次升級將會擴大這間公司的市場基礎。SpeakVid 已吸引了國內媒體來報導，而 [88] 專家認為下個月當這個應用程式的新版本推出時，媒體的興趣也會增加。
86 What type of business most likely is Digital Solutions? (A) An online retailer (B) A software developer (C) A graphic design company (D) A recording studio	86. Digital Solutions 最有可能是什麼類型的公司？ (A) 線上零售業者 (B) 軟體開發商 (C) 平面設計公司 (D) 錄音室
87 Why has the firm's stock value risen? (A) Its product has been very successful. (B) Its operations have moved overseas. (C) It was awarded a major contract. (D) It has teamed up with another business.	87. 這間公司的股價為何上揚了？ (A) 它的產品非常成功。 (B) 它的事業已移往海外。 (C) 它獲得了一份重大合約。 (D) 它與其它公司合作了。
88 What does the speaker say will happen next month? (A) A device will be distributed to stores. (B) A merger will be formalized. (C) An application will be released. (D) A cell phone will be reviewed.	88. 說話者說下個月會發生什麼？ (A) 一款設備會被分送到店裡。 (B) 一項合併會正式確定。 (C) 將釋出一款應用程式。 (D) 將評論一支手機。

題目 edit [`ɛdɪt] 編輯　result in 導致～（結果）　sharp [ʃɑrp] 劇烈的；尖銳的　stock price 股價　interface [`ɪntɚ͵fes] 介面　coverage [`kʌvərɪdʒ]（新聞等的）報導；（處理或涉及的）涵蓋範圍

87 operation [͵ɑpə`reʃən] 事業，活動；營運　team up 合作

88 merger [mɝdʒɚ] 合併　formalize [`fɔrml͵aɪz] 正式確定　review [rɪ`vju] 評論；重新審視

86 ■ 細節事項相關問題－特定細項　答案 (B)

中

題目詢問 Digital Solutions 是什麼類型的公司，因此要注意提到題目關鍵字（Digital Solutions）的前後部分。獨白說：「Digital Solutions has announced plans to release the latest version of its mobile phone application」，表示 Digital Solutions 已宣布計畫釋出其最新版本的手機應用程式，由此可知，Digital Solutions 是軟體開發商，因此正確答案是 (B) A software developer。

87 ■ 細節事項相關問題－理由　答案 (A)

中

題目詢問這間公司股價上揚的原因，因此要注意和題目關鍵字（stock value risen）相關的內容。獨白說：「It[application] has become hugely popular, resulting in a sharp rise in the developer's stock prices.」，表示這款應用程式很受歡迎，造成開發商的股價勁揚，因此正確答案是 (A) Its product has been very successful.。

88 ■ 細節事項相關問題－接下來要做的事　答案 (C)

低

題目詢問說話者說下個月會發生什麼，因此要注意提到題目關鍵字（next month）的前後部分。獨白說：「experts believe that interest will increase next month when the new version of the application comes out」，提到專家認為當下個月新版應用程式釋出時，媒體的興趣也會增加，由此可知，新版應用程式會在下個月釋出，因此正確答案是 (C) An application will be released.。

89
90
91

Questions 89-91 refer to the following announcement.

🔊 澳洲式發音

I've got an announcement for all IT staff members. I know you've had many requests for technical assistance from other departments. There were more problems than expected following [89]**our recent merger with Fairfield Financial**. I'm happy to inform you, though, that [90]**new staff members have been hired for our team** . . . um, five in total. Once [90]**they start working in October**, your workload should be significantly reduced. But [91]**keep in mind that we still need to update the customer database software this month**. The marketing team isn't able to access some records, so [91]**it needs to be done as soon as possible**. This means that you'll be working long hours over the next few weeks, but the end is in sight.

第 89-91 題請參考下列公告。

我有一件事要對所有資訊科技部的同仁宣布。我知道你們已經接到了很多來自其他部門的技術協助申請。在 [89] 我們最近與 Fairfield 金融合併之後，發生了比預期更多的問題。不過，我很高興告訴你們，[90] 公司已經為我們團隊聘請了新員工……嗯，總共五位。一旦 [90] 他們在十月開始工作，你們的工作量應該會大幅減少。不過 [91] 請記得，我們這個月仍得更新顧客資料庫軟體。因為行銷團隊無法存取一些記錄，所以 [91] 這件事需要盡快完成。這表示你們在接下來的幾週都將長時間工作，不過已經看得到終點了。

89 According to the speaker, what did the company recently do?

(A) Launched a new service
(B) Closed some offices
(C) Joined with another firm
(D) Changed some policies

89. 根據說話者所說，這間公司最近做了什麼？

(A) 開辦了一項新服務
(B) 關閉了一些辦公室
(C) 和另一間公司結合了
(D) 變更了一些政策

90 What will probably happen in October?

(A) Personnel will begin working.
(B) A team will be assembled.
(C) A department will be shut down.
(D) Employees will create a database.

90. 十月可能會發生什麼？

(A) 員工將開始工作。
(B) 會組成一個團隊。
(C) 會關閉一個部門。
(D) 員工將建立一個資料庫。

91 新 What does the speaker imply when he says, "The marketing team isn't able to access some records"?

(A) A task will be reassigned.
(B) A job should not be postponed.
(C) A supervisor should be notified.
(D) A project will be canceled.

91. 當說話者說：「行銷團隊無法存取一些記錄」時，是暗示什麼？

(A) 一項任務會被重新分派。
(B) 一件工作不應推遲。
(C) 一位主管應該被通知。
(D) 一項專案會被取消。

題目 technical [`tɛknɪkl] 技術的　assistance [ə`sɪstəns] 支援，協助　merger [㊥ mɝdʒɚ ㊕ mə:dʒə] 合併
workload [㊥ `wɝk͵lod ㊕ `wə:k͵ləud] 工作量　significantly [sɪg`nɪfəkəntlɪ] 顯著地；大幅地　keep in mind 記得
access [`æksɛs] 存取（資料等）

89 launch [lɔntʃ] 開辦　join [dʒɔɪn] 結合；連結　firm [fɝm] 公司

90 personnel [͵pɝsn̩`ɛl]（總稱）員工，人員　assemble [ə`sɛmbl] 組合；召集　shut down 關閉

91 postpone [post`pon] 推遲　supervisor [͵supɚ`vaɪzɚ] 監督者；主管　notify [`notə͵faɪ] 通知

89 ■ **細節事項相關問題－特定細項** 答案 (C)

中

題目詢問公司最近做了什麼，因此要注意和題目關鍵字（company recently do）相關的內容。獨白說：「our recent merger with Fairfield Financial」，提到最近和 Fairfield 金融合併，由此可知，公司最近和另一間公司結合了，因此正確答案是 (C) Joined with another firm。

90 ■ **細節事項相關問題－接下來要做的事** 答案 (A)

低

題目詢問十月可能會發生什麼，因此要注意提到題目關鍵字（October）的前後部分。獨白說：「new staff members have been hired for our team」，表示公司已為自己團隊雇用了新員工，接著說：「they start working in October」，表示新員工們會從十月開始工作，因此正確答案是 (A) Personnel will begin working.。

新 **91** ■ **細節事項相關問題－掌握意圖** 答案 (B)

高

題目詢問說話者的說話意圖，因此要注意題目引用句（The marketing team isn't able to access some records）的前後部分。獨白說：「keep in mind that we still need to update the customer database software this month」，表示要記得這個月仍得更新顧客資料庫軟體，引用句之後則說：「it needs to be done as soon as possible」，表示這件事需要盡快完成，由此可知，更新顧客資料庫軟體的這項工作不應推遲，因此正確答案是 (B) A job should not be postponed.。

92 93 94

Questions 92-94 refer to the following telephone message.

美式發音

I'm calling on behalf of Music Central in Newark, New Jersey. I apologize for this last-minute change, but [92]**I need to update the order that my store put in yesterday** for a bulk shipment of electronics. As of now, the order is for 20 portable Kentmoore speakers, 25 wireless Conquest microphones, and 25 Pure Sound noise-canceling headphones. However, [93]**we need 10 more Kentmoore speakers than were originally requested**. If it's not too late to add items to our order, please do so and bill us for the additional costs. Also, [94]**I'd appreciate it if you could e-mail me an updated invoice at purchasing@soundequip.com this afternoon**.

第 92-94 題請參考下列電話留言。

我是代表在紐澤西州紐華克市的 Music Central 打電話來的。我很抱歉在最後一刻才要改，但 [92] 我必須更新我們店昨天下的那筆電子產品大宗貨物的訂單。目前為止，這筆訂單裡有 20 個可攜式 Kentmoore 喇叭、25 個無線 Conquest 麥克風及 25 個 Pure Sound 降噪耳罩式耳機。但是，[93] 我們需要比原本要求的再多 10 個 Kentmoore 喇叭。如果還來得及把這些品項加進我們的訂單裡，請把它們加進去，然後向我們請這筆多出來的費用。此外，[94] 如果你們能在今天下午將更新後的發貨單用電子郵件寄到 purchasing@soundequip.com 的話，我會非常感謝。

92 Why is the speaker calling?

(A) To ask about an incorrect invoice
(B) To change an earlier order
(C) To thank a company for its services
(D) To get information about a speaker

93 What does Music Central need?

(A) Extra microphones
(B) A partial refund
(C) Additional speakers
(D) An extended warranty

94 What is the listener asked to do this afternoon?

(A) Send a revised statement
(B) Print a company catalog
(C) Fill out a registration form
(D) Ship a sample product

92. 說話者為何打電話？

(A) 詢問與一張錯誤的發票有關的事
(B) 變更稍早的訂單
(C) 感謝一間公司提供服務
(D) 取得與一個喇叭有關的資訊

93. Music Central 需要什麼？

(A) 額外的麥克風
(B) 部份退款
(C) 額外的喇叭
(D) 延長保固

94. 聽者今天下午被要求做什麼？

(A) 寄出改過的明細表
(B) 列印公司型錄
(C) 填寫報名表
(D) 運送產品的樣品

題目 last-minute 在最後一刻的　put in an order 下訂　bulk [bʌlk] 大量的，大批的
portable [`portəb!] 可攜帶的；手提的　bill [bɪl] 請款　invoice [`ɪnvɔɪs] 發票；發貨單
92 incorrect [ˌɪnkə`rɛkt] 不正確的
93 partial [`pɑrʃəl] 部分的　warranty [`wɔrəntɪ] 保固；保證（書）
94 statement [`stetmənt] 明細表；聲明　registration form 報名表

92 整體內容相關問題－目的　答案 (B)

低

題目詢問打電話的目的，因此要注意聽獨白開頭的部分。獨白說：「I need to update the order that my store put in yesterday」，表示要更新昨天下的訂單，由此可知，說話者是為了變更訂單而打電話，因此正確答案是 (B) To change an earlier order。

93 細節事項相關問題－特定細項　答案 (C)

低

題目詢問 Music Central 需要什麼，因此要注意和題目關鍵字（Music Central need）相關的內容。獨白說：「we[Music Central] need 10 more Kentmoore speakers than were originally requested」，表示需要比原本要求的再多 10 個 Kentmoore 喇叭，因此正確答案是 (C) Additional speakers。

94 細節事項相關問題－要求　答案 (A)

中

題目詢問聽者被要求在今天下午做什麼，因此要注意提到題目關鍵字（this afternoon）的前後部分。獨白說：「I'd appreciate it if you could e-mail me an updated invoice ~ this afternoon」，表示希望聽者能在今天下午將更新後的發貨單用電子郵件寄出，因此正確答案是 (A) Send a revised statement。

換句話說

e-mail ~ an updated invoice 將更新後的發貨單用電子郵件寄出 → Send a revised statement 寄出改過的明細表

95
96
97

Questions 95-97 refer to the following announcement and a survey.

第 95-97 題請參考下列公告與調查表。

澳洲式發音

Thank you for participating in this focus group. [95]**The designer of the product . . . uh, Greg Henderson . . . wanted to welcome you personally, but he's dealing with a problem at our factory.** Anyway, the goal today is to get your feedback on our newest product, the Flow S60. We are confident that there is a strong demand for it. [96]**In a recent survey about upcoming purchases, a large percentage of respondents indicated that they plan to buy this type of device soon. Next to air conditioners, it was the most popular choice.** However, we're concerned that our model may be difficult to operate. So to start, [97]**please give your opinion about the most recent draft of the user instructions. I'll hand this document out now . . .**

謝謝你們參與這個焦點團體。[95] 這項產品的設計者……呃，Greg Henderson……原本想要親自歡迎各位，但他正在我們工廠中處理一個問題。不管怎樣，今天的目標是取得你們對於我們的最新產品 Flow S60 的回饋意見。我們有信心對這項產品的需求會很強烈。[96] 在近期一項與即將進行的消費有關的調查之中，有很大百分比的受訪者指出他們計畫很快要買這個類型的裝置。繼冷氣之後，它是最受歡迎的選擇。不過，我們擔心我們這款可能會不好操作。所以一開始，[97] 請針對最新的使用者說明的草稿提供你們的意見。我現在會把這份文件發下去……

新

Survey Results	
Air Conditioner	**34%**
[96]Air Purifier	**26%**
Electric Fan	22%
Space Heater	18%

調查結果	
冷氣	34%
[96] 空氣清淨機	26%
電扇	22%
小型暖氣機	18%

95 Why is Greg Henderson unavailable?
(A) He is participating in a focus group.
(B) He is attending a design conference.
(C) He is visiting a production plant.
(D) He is inspecting a research facility.

95. Greg Henderson 為何沒有空？
(A) 他正在參與一個焦點團體。
(B) 他正在參加一場設計會議。
(C) 他正在巡視生產工廠。
(D) 他正在視察一個研究設施。

96 Look at the graphic. What type of device is the Flow S60?
新
(A) An air conditioner
(B) An air purifier
(C) An electric fan
(D) A space heater

96. 請看圖表。Flow S60 是什麼類型的裝置？
(A) 冷氣
(B) 空氣清淨機
(C) 電扇
(D) 小型暖氣機

97 What will the speaker distribute?
(A) Manuals
(B) Application forms
(C) Promotional brochures
(D) Questionnaires

97. 說話者將分發什麼？
(A) 使用手冊
(B) 申請表
(C) 宣傳小冊子
(D) 問卷

題目 focus group 焦點團體（對於要測試的商品提供意見的消費者團體）
confident [㊇ `kɑnfədənt ㊈ `kɔnfidənt] 確信的；有信心的 demand [㊇ dɪ`mænd ㊈ di`mɑ:nd] 需求
percentage [㊇ pɚ`sɛntɪdʒ ㊈ pə`sentidʒ] 百分比 respondent [㊇ rɪ`spɑndənt ㊈ ri`spɔndənt] 應答者
indicate [`ɪndə͵ket] 指出；表明 next to 繼～之後；在～旁邊 operate [㊇ `ɑpə͵ret ㊈ `ɔpəreit] 操作
draft [㊇ dræft ㊈ dræft] 草稿，草圖 instruction [ɪn`strʌkʃən]（講解使用或操作方法的）說明（書）
96 purifier [`pjʊrə͵faɪɚ] 淨化器 electric fan 電風扇
97 manual [`mænjʊəl] 使用手冊 brochure [bro`ʃʊr] 小冊子

95 細節事項相關問題－理由 答案 (C)

中

題目詢問 Greg Henderson 為什麼沒有空，因此要注意和題目關鍵字（Greg Henderson unavailable）相關的內容。獨白說：「The designer of the product ~ Greg Henderson ~ wanted to welcome you personally, but he's dealing with a problem at our factory.」，表示產品設計者 Greg Henderson 原本想要親自歡迎聽者們，但他正在工廠中處理問題，因此正確答案是 (C) He is visiting a production plant.。

換句話說

dealing with a problem at ~ factory 正在工廠中處理問題 → visiting a production plant 正在巡視生產工廠

新 96 細節事項相關問題－圖表資料 答案 (B)

中

題目詢問 Flow S60 是什麼類型的裝置，因此必須確認題目提供的調查結果，並注意獨白中出現題目關鍵字（Flow S60）的前後部分。獨白說：「In a recent survey about upcoming purchases, a large percentage of respondents indicated that they plan to buy this type of device[Flow S60] soon. Next to air conditioners, it was the most popular choice.」，表示在近期的調查之中，有很大百分比的受訪者說他們很快會買這種類型的裝置，且這類裝置是繼冷氣之後最受歡迎的選擇。透過題目提供的調查結果可知，繼冷氣之後最受歡迎的是空氣清淨機，因此正確答案是 (B) An air purifier。

97 細節事項相關問題－特定細項 答案 (A)

中

題目詢問說話者將分發什麼，因此要注意和題目關鍵字（distribute）相關的內容。獨白說：「please give your opinion about the most recent draft of the user instructions. I'll hand this document out now」，表示希望聽者就最新的使用者說明的草稿提供意見，並說接下來要把該文件發下去，因此正確答案是 (A) Manuals。

換句話說

distribute 分發 → hand ~ out 分發

98
99
100

Questions 98-100 refer to the following advertisement and map.

第 98-100 題請參考下列廣告與路線圖。

美式發音

Looking for a quick and affordable way to see the sights in Boston? Then hop on the Bean Bus! Our bus stops at historical sites throughout the city. [98]**To purchase a ticket, drop by our company's information booth in the lobby of the Stanford Hotel.** Tickets usually cost $20, but [99]**we will be offering a 10 percent discount during the month of May** to celebrate our company's fifth anniversary. For route information, visit www.beanbus.com. [100]**Please note that the bus will not stop at the site between Boston Harbor and Bunker Hill from June 25 until July 15** due to ongoing road construction in the area. Explore Boston with the Bean Bus today!

在找又快又便宜在波士頓觀光的方法嗎？那麼就跳上 Bean 巴士吧！我們的巴士會停靠市內各處的歷史景點。[98] 若需購票，請到我們公司在 Stanford 飯店大廳裡的服務台。票價一般是 20 美金，不過 [99] 我們在五月這個月會提供九折優惠，以慶祝我們公司的五週年。請上 www.beanbus.com 取得路線資訊。[100] 請注意，巴士在 6 月 25 日到 7 月 15 日間不會停靠於波士頓港和邦克山之間的景點，因為該區正在進行道路工程。今天就和 Bean 巴士一起探索波士頓！

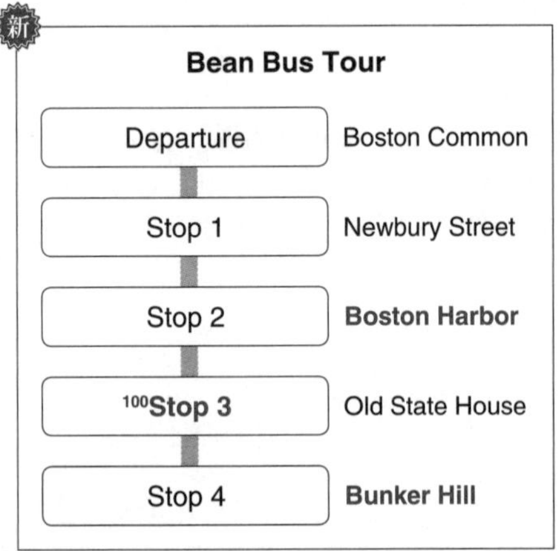

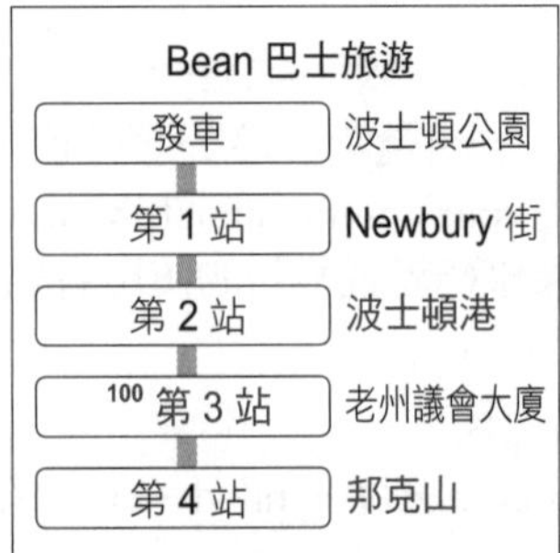

98 What does the speaker mention about the information booth?

(A) It opened five years ago.
(B) It will begin selling souvenirs.
(C) It has few employees.
(D) It is located in a hotel.

98. 關於服務台，說話者提到什麼？

(A) 它在五年前開了。
(B) 它會開始販售紀念品。
(C) 它的員工很少。
(D) 它位在飯店裡。

99 Which month will the company offer a discount?

(A) April
(B) May
(C) June
(D) July

99. 這間公司會在哪個月提供折扣？

(A) 四月
(B) 五月
(C) 六月
(D) 七月

100 新 Look at the graphic. Which stop will be temporarily inaccessible?

(A) Stop 1
(B) Stop 2
(C) Stop 3
(D) Stop 4

100. 請看圖表。哪一站會暫時不能去？

(A) 第 1 站
(B) 第 2 站
(C) 第 3 站
(D) 第 4 站

題目 affordable [ə`fɔrdəbḷ]（價格）實惠的；負擔得起的 hop [hɑp]（輕快地）跳上（交通工具） historical site 歷史景點 route [rut] 路線；路 ongoing [`ɑn͵goɪŋ] 進行中的

98 souvenir [`suvə͵nɪr] 紀念品 located [`loketɪd] 位於的

100 temporarily [`tɛmpə͵rɛrəlɪ] 暫時地 inaccessible [͵ɪnæk`sɛsəbḷ] 無法去的

98 ○○● 低 **細節事項相關問題－提及** 答案 (D)

題目詢問說話者提到什麼與服務台有關的事，因此必須注意聽提到題目關鍵字（information booth）的前後部分。獨白說：「To purchase a ticket, drop by our company's information booth in the lobby of the Stanford Hotel.」，表示請要買票的人到位在 Stanford 飯店大廳的該公司服務台買票，因此正確答案是 (D) It is located in a hotel.。

99 ○○● 低 **細節事項相關問題－特定細項** 答案 (B)

題目詢問說話者說會在哪個月打折，因此要注意提到題目關鍵字（month ~ offer a discount）的前後部分。獨白說：「we will be offering a 10 percent discount during the month of May」，表示五月這個月會打九折，因此正確答案是 (B) May。

新 100 ○●● 中 **細節事項相關問題－圖表資料** 答案 (C)

題目詢問暫時不能去的是哪一站，因此必須確認題目提供的路線圖，並注意與題目關鍵字（stop ~ temporarily inaccessible）相關的內容。獨白說：「Please note that the bus will not stop at the site between Boston Harbor and Bunker Hill from June 25 until July 15」，表示在 6 月 25 日到 7 月 15 日間，不會停靠於波士頓港和邦克山之間的景點。透過路線圖可知，暫時不會停靠的是在波士頓港和邦克山之間的老州議會大廈，也就是第 3 站，因此正確答案是 (C) Stop 3。

TEST 05

Part 1 原文・翻譯・解析

Part 2 原文・翻譯・解析

Part 3 原文・翻譯・解析 新

Part 4 原文・翻譯・解析 新

MP3 收錄於 TEST 05.mp3。

進行深入練習或複習時，可以一邊多聽幾次收錄各國口音的試題 MP3，一邊搭配解答中的中英對照翻譯和解析，以及單字記憶表和多元口音單字記憶 MP3，達到事半功倍的效果。

PART 1

1 ○○○● 低

🔊 美式發音

(A) A man is adjusting his helmet.
(B) A man is staring at a coworker.
(C) They are changing some screens.
(D) They are typing on some keyboards.

(A) 一名男子正在調整他的安全帽。
(B) 一名男子正盯著一位同事。
(C) 他們正在更換一些螢幕。
(D) 他們正在一些鍵盤上打字。

兩人以上的照片 答案 (B)

照片中有兩名戴著安全帽的男子在控制室中。

(A) [╳] 照片中沒有正在調整安全帽（adjusting his helmet）的男子，因此是錯誤選項。這裡使用照片中有出現的安全帽（helmet）來造成混淆。

(B) [○] 這裡正確描述一名男子正盯著同事的樣子，所以是正確答案。

(C) [╳] changing some screens（正在更換一些螢幕）和男子的動作無關，因此是錯誤選項。這裡使用照片中有出現的螢幕（screens）來造成混淆。

(D) [╳] typing（正在打字）和男子的動作無關，且透過照片無法確認鍵盤（keyboards）的存在，因此是錯誤選項。

單字　adjust [əˋdʒʌst] 調整　coworker [ˋkoˏwɝkɚ] 同事

2 ○●●● 高

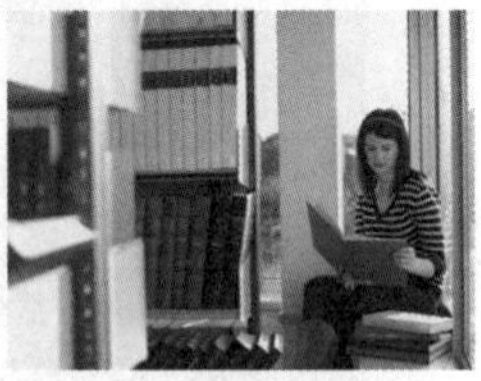

🔊 澳洲式發音

(A) She is reviewing the content of a book.
(B) She is stacking reading material on a windowsill.
(C) She is crossing her arms over her chest.
(D) She is turning the page of a publication.

(A) 她正在檢視一本書的內容。
(B) 她正在把閱讀材料堆放在窗台上。
(C) 她正雙手抱胸。
(D) 她正在翻一本出版品。

單人照片 答案 (A)

照片中有一名女子正坐在窗邊看書。

(A) [○] 這裡正確描述女子正在檢視書本內容的樣子，所以是正確答案。

(B) [╳] 窗台上已經堆著書，但這裡的描述是正在堆放，因此是錯誤選項。這裡必須知道 windowsill 是窗台的意思。

(C) [╳] 女子沒有雙手抱胸，而是蹺著腳，因此是錯誤選項。注意不要聽到 She is crossing her ~（她交叉著她的～）就選擇這個答案。這裡必須知道可以利用現在進行式（is crossing）來描述人的狀態。

(D) [╳] 這裡透過能藉女子正在看書的模樣而聯想到的 turning the page of a publication（正在翻一本出版品）來造成混淆，因此是錯誤選項。

單字　stack [stæk] 堆疊；堆放　windowsill [美] ˋwɪndoˏsɪl [英] ˋwindəusil] 窗台　cross one's arms 交叉雙臂
chest [tʃɛst] 胸膛　publication [[美] ˏpʌblɪˋkeʃən [英] ˏpʌbliˋkeiʃən] 出版品；出版

3 ○○●● 中

🔊 加拿大式發音

(A) He is taking off an apron.
(B) He is inspecting baked goods.
(C) He is pulling a tray from an oven.
(D) He is leaning against some equipment.

(A) 他正在脫下圍裙。
(B) 他正在查看烘焙品。
(C) 他正從烤箱裡拉出托盤。
(D) 他正靠著某件設備。

■ 單人照片 答案 (B)

照片中有一名男子正在烤箱前看著麵包。

(A) [╳] taking off（正在脫下）和男子的動作無關，因此是錯誤選項。這裡使用照片中有出現的圍裙（apron）來造成混淆。

(B) [○] 這裡正確描述男子正在查看烘焙品（麵包）的模樣，因此是正確答案。

(C) [╳] 男子從烤箱中拿出的是麵包，但這裡卻描述成拉出托盤（tray），因此是錯誤選項。注意不要聽到 He is pulling ~（男子正在拉～）就選擇這個答案。

(D) [╳] 男子是把身體彎向這個設備，但這裡卻描述成靠著（leaning against），因此是錯誤選項。

單字 inspect [ɪn`spɛkt] 查看；檢視 tray [tre] 托盤 lean against 倚靠～

4 高

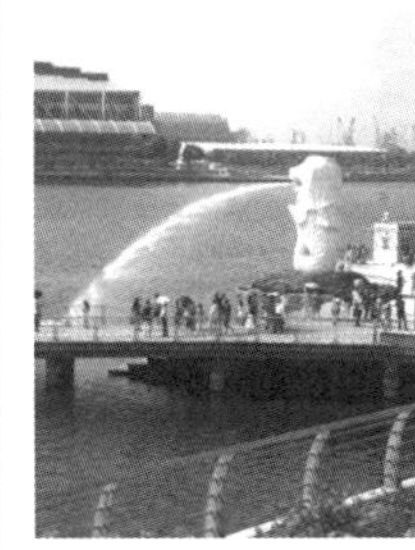

英式發音

(A) A passenger boat is docked in a harbor.
(B) A handrail borders a series of steps.
(C) Some people are riding bicycles on a wharf.
(D) Water is being sprayed from a statue.

(A) 一艘客船正停在港口裡。
(B) 一列階梯旁有扶手圍著。
(C) 一些人正在碼頭上騎腳踏車。
(D) 水正從雕像裡噴出來。

■ 兩人以上的照片 答案 (D)

仔細確認眾人待在水邊的模樣和周遭景物的狀態。

(A) [╳] 透過照片無法確認所在地點是否是港口（harbor），也無法確認客船（passenger boat）是否存在，因此是錯誤選項。

(B) [╳] 透過照片無法確認階梯（steps）是否存在，因此是錯誤選項。注意不要聽到 A handrail borders（欄杆／扶手圍著）就選擇這個答案。

(C) [╳] 照片中沒有正在騎腳踏車（riding bicycles）的人，且無法確認照片拍攝地點是碼頭（wharf），因此是錯誤選項。

(D) [○] 這裡正確描述水正從雕像裡噴出來，所以是正確答案。

單字 passenger boat 客船 dock [㊥dɑk ㊧dɔk]（船等）停靠 harbor [㊥`hɑrbɚ ㊧`hɑ:bə] 港口 handrail [`hænd͵rel] 欄杆；扶手 border [㊥`bɔrdɚ ㊧`bɔ:də] 圍繞；沿著 wharf [㊥hwɔrf ㊧hwɔ:f] 碼頭 spray [spre] 噴灑

5 中

加拿大式發音

(A) Various containers are sitting on a cart.
(B) Some fruit is set out on a blanket.
(C) Ingredients have been placed in jars.
(D) A loaf of bread has been cut in half.

(A) 各式容器在推車上。
(B) 一些水果被擺在毯子上。
(C) 材料已被擺進了罐子裡。
(D) 一條麵包已被切成了兩半。

■ 事物及風景照片 答案 (C)

仔細觀察照片中台面上放著許多食材的樣子。

(A) [╳] 容器不在推車（cart）上，而是在台面上，因此是錯誤選項。注意不要聽到 Various containers are sitting on ~（各種容器在～）就選擇這個答案。

(B) [╳] 照片中沒有毯子（blanket），因此是錯誤選項。注意不要聽到 Some fruit is set out on ~（一些水果被擺在～上）就選擇這個答案。

(C) [○] 這裡正確描述材料已被擺在罐子裡的樣子，所以是正確答案。

(D) [╳] 麵包完整地放在台面上，這裡卻描述為已被切成兩半（been cut in half），因此是錯誤選項。

單字 container [kən`tenɚ] 容器；貨櫃 set out 擺放 ingredient [ɪn`gridɪənt] 材料 jar [dʒɑr] 罐；瓶

6 ○●●●● 高

🔊 英式發音

(A) Some vehicles are parked in a lot.
(B) A truck is driving along a highway.
(C) A portion of the pavement has been damaged.
(D) Some lines are being painted on a road.

(A) 一些車輛停在一塊地上。
(B) 一台卡車正沿著公路行駛。
(C) 一部分的路面已被破壞了。
(D) 正在一條路上畫一些線。

事物及風景照片 答案 (A)

仔細觀察照片中路旁停著一些車的模樣，以及周遭事物的狀態。

(A) [○] 這裡正確描述路旁停著一些車子的樣子，所以是正確答案。

(B) [╳] 照片中的卡車停在路邊，這裡卻描述成正在行駛，且照片拍攝地點不是公路（highway），因此是錯誤選項。

(C) [╳] 透過照片無法確認路面是否已被破壞，因此是錯誤選項。

(D) [╳] 照片中的路面上已經畫好線了，這裡卻以現在進行式被動語態（are being painted）描述成正在畫，因此是錯誤選項。

單字 vehicle [[美] \`viɪkḷ [英] \`vi:ikl] 車輛；搭載工具 park [[美] pɑrk [英] pɑ:k] 停放（車輛等）
lot [[美] lɑt [英] lɔt]（有特定用途的）一塊地 highway [\`haɪˌwe] 公路 portion [[美] \`porʃən [英] \`pɔ:ʃən] 部分
pavement [\`pevmənt] 鋪設過的地面，路面；人行道 damage [\`dæmɪdʒ] 損壞；毀損 paint [pent] 畫；漆

7 低

🔊 美式發音 → 澳洲式發音	
Who is waiting for you in your office?	誰在你辦公室裡等你？
(A) Mr. Sanders took the file.	(A) Sanders 先生拿了那個檔案。
(B) To wait in line.	(B) 為了排隊等待。
(C) A friend from college.	(C) 一個大學朋友。

Who 疑問句 答案 (C)

這是詢問誰在辦公室裡等待對方的 Who 疑問句。

(A) [╳] 題目詢問誰在辦公室裡等待，這裡卻回答 Sanders 先生拿了那個檔案，毫不相關，因此是錯誤選項。這裡利用人名 Sanders 來造成混淆。

(B) [╳] 題目詢問誰在辦公室裡等待，這裡卻回答目的，因此是錯誤選項。這裡以 wait 來重複使用題目中出現的 waiting，藉此造成混淆。

(C) [○] 這裡回答一個大學朋友，提到在辦公室等自己的人，因此是正確答案。

單字 take [tek] 拿走 wait in line 排隊等待 college [[美] `kɑlɪdʒ [英] `kɔlidʒ] 大學；學院

8 低

🔊 英式發音 → 加拿大式發音	
Will you be able to contact me later?	你晚點可以和我聯絡嗎？
(A) My assistant can go with them.	(A) 我的助理可以和他們一起去。
(B) Yes, I'll do so at three.	(B) 可以，我會在三點聯絡。
(C) No, I don't see the waiter.	(C) 不行，我沒看到那個服務生。

助動詞疑問句 答案 (B)

這是詢問對方晚點能否聯絡自己的助動詞（Will）疑問句。

(A) [╳] 題目詢問對方晚點能否聯絡自己，這裡卻回答自己的助理可以和他們一起去，毫不相關，因此是錯誤選項。這裡使用和題目 be able to（能夠～）意思相同的 can（能夠～）來造成混淆。

(B) [○] 這裡以 Yes 表示可以，並說會在三點聯絡，提供附加資訊，因此是正確答案。

(C) [╳] 這裡使用可以代稱題目中 you 的 I，並利用發音相似單字 later – waiter 來造成混淆。注意不要聽到 No 就選擇這個答案。

單字 contact [[美] kən`tækt [英] kən`tækt] 聯絡 assistant [ə`sɪstənt] 助理

9 低

🔊 澳洲式發音 → 美式發音	
Where would you like to sit for the concert?	你演唱會想要坐哪裡？
(A) In the back row.	(A) 後排。
(B) A local band performed.	(B) 一個當地樂團演出了。
(C) No, I probably wouldn't.	(C) 不，我可能不會。

Where 疑問句 答案 (A)

這是詢問演唱會想要坐哪裡的 Where 疑問句。

(A) [○] 這裡回答後排，提到演唱會想坐的位置，因此是正確答案。

(B) [╳] 這是利用和 concert（演唱會）相關的 band（樂團）和 performed（演出）來造成混淆的錯誤選項。

(C) [╳] 這裡以 No 來回答疑問詞疑問句，因此是錯誤選項。這裡利用與題目的 Where would you 發音相似的 Would you 來造成混淆，注意不要因為聽成 Would you like to sit for the concert?（你想去演唱會嗎？）而選擇這個選項。

單字 row [ro] 列，排 local [`lokḷ] 當地的 perform [pɚ`fɔrm] 演出 probably [`prɑbəblɪ] 也許

10
●●○ 中

英式發音 → 澳洲式發音

You live on the east side of town, don't you?

(A) The eastern highway is blocked off.
(B) I did for a few years.
(C) I lost the key to the house.

你住在小鎮的東邊，不是嗎？

(A) 東邊的公路封閉了。
(B) 我之前住了幾年。
(C) 我把那間房子的鑰匙搞丟了。

附加問句 答案 (B)

這是確認對方是否住在小鎮的東邊的附加問句。

(A) [╳] 題目詢問對方是否住在小鎮的東邊，這裡卻回答東邊的公路封閉了，毫不相關，因此是錯誤選項。這裡利用與題目中 east（東的）意義相近的 eastern（東邊的）來造成混淆。

(B) [〇] 這裡回答之前住了幾年，間接表示自己現在不住在小鎮的東邊，因此是正確答案。

(C) [╳] 這是使用能夠從 live（居住）聯想到的與家相關的表達 key to the house（那間房子的鑰匙）來造成混淆的錯誤選項。

單字 highway [ˋhaɪˏwe] 公路；幹道 block off 封閉

11
●●● 高

加拿大式發音 → 美式發音

Should we renew our lease or relocate the boutique?

(A) Not according to our rental agreement.
(B) It's a fashionable store.
(C) I want to stay in this space.

我們應該要續租還是重新找地方開這間精品店？

(A) 根據我們的租約不是這樣。
(B) 這是一間時髦的店。
(C) 我想要留在這裡。

選擇疑問句 答案 (C)

這是詢問要續租還是要搬遷的選擇疑問句。

(A) [╳] 這是利用和 lease（租約）相關的 rental agreement（租約）來造成混淆的錯誤選項。

(B) [╳] 這是利用和 boutique（精品店）相關的 fashionable store（時髦的店）來造成混淆的錯誤選項。

(C) [〇] 這裡回答想要留在這裡，間接表示希望續租，因此是正確答案。

單字 renew [rɪˋnju]（合約等）展期；更新 lease [lis] 租約；租賃 relocate [riˋloket] 搬遷；重新安置
boutique [buˋtik] 精品店 rental [ˋrɛntl] 租賃；租金 fashionable [ˋfæʃənəbl] 時髦的

12
●●○ 中

英式發音 → 加拿大式發音

Which of those bags is yours?

(A) Use the overhead compartment.
(B) Mine is in the closet.
(C) You'll need a luggage voucher.

這些包包中哪個是你的？

(A) 使用上方行李架。
(B) 我的在櫃子裡。
(C) 你會需要行李憑證。

Which 疑問句 答案 (B)

這是詢問對方的包包是哪一個的 Which 疑問句。這裡一定要聽到 Which of those bags 才能順利作答。

(A) [╳] 題目詢問對方的包包是哪一個，這裡卻回答使用上方行李架，毫不相關，因此是錯誤選項。這裡使用能夠從 bags（包包）聯想到的放置地點 overhead compartment（上方行李架）來造成混淆。

(B) [〇] 這裡回答自己的在櫃子裡，間接表示這些包包之中沒有自己的，因此是正確答案。

(C) [╳] 這是利用和 bags（包包）有關的 luggage（行李）來造成混淆的錯誤選項。

單字 compartment [kəmˋpɑrtmənt]（為特定目的而劃分的）隔間 voucher [ˋvaʊtʃɚ] 憑證；票券；保證人

13 高

美式發音 → 澳洲式發音

What day is your dentist appointment on?	你的牙醫約診在哪一天？
(A) For a regular check-up.	(A) 為了做定期健康檢查。
(B) I wrote it down in my calendar.	(B) 我把它寫在了我的行事曆上。
(C) He is only available during the day.	(C) 他只有白天有空。

What 疑問句 答案 (B)

這是詢問對方的牙醫約診是在哪一天的 What 疑問句。這裡一定要聽到 What day 才能順利作答。

(A) [╳] 這是利用和 dentist appointment（牙醫約診）相關的 regular check-up（定期健康檢查）來造成混淆的錯誤選項。

(B) [○] 這裡回答寫在了行事曆上，間接表示要看行事曆才會知道，因此是正確答案。

(C) [╳] 題目中沒有可以 He 可代稱的對象，因此是錯誤選項。這裡使用可以透過 appointment（預約會面）聯想到的時間相關表達 available（有空的），並且利用題目中 day（一天）的另一字義「白天」來造成混淆。

單字 day [de] 一天；白天 dentist [`dɛntɪst] 牙醫 appointment [ə`pɔɪntmənt] 會面；（會面的）約定
regular [[美] `rɛgjəlɚ [英] `regjulə] 定期的；規則的 calendar [[美] `kæləndɚ [英] `kælində] 行事曆；日曆
available [ə`veləbl̩] 有空的，可取得聯繫的

14 中

加拿大式發音 → 美式發音

Am I allowed to bring a beverage into the theater?	我可以帶飲料進劇院嗎？
(A) It's not permitted.	(A) 這不被允許。
(B) We are sitting close to the stage.	(B) 我們坐得離舞臺很近。
(C) I'll get some coffee.	(C) 我會去拿一點咖啡。

Be 動詞疑問句 答案 (A)

這是詢問能否帶飲料進劇院的 Be 動詞疑問句。

(A) [○] 這裡回答不被允許，表示不能帶飲料進劇院，因此是正確答案。

(B) [╳] 這是利用和 theater（劇院）有關的 stage（舞台）來造成混淆的錯誤選項。

(C) [╳] 這是利用和 beverage（飲料）有關的 coffee（咖啡）來造成混淆的錯誤選項。

單字 allow [ə`laʊ] 容許；允許 beverage [`bɛvərɪdʒ] 飲料 permit [pɚ`mɪt] 允許 stage [stedʒ] 舞台

15 中

澳洲式發音 → 英式發音

Which employees need to attend tomorrow's training?	哪些員工需要參加明天的訓練？
(A) Only people from the accounting department.	(A) 只有會計部的人。
(B) At an employment agency.	(B) 在一個就業服務處。
(C) I'm happy to oversee it.	(C) 我很樂意監督它。

Which 疑問句 答案 (A)

這是詢問哪些員工需要參加明天的訓練的 Which 疑問句。這裡一定要聽到 Which employees 才能順利作答。

(A) [○] 這裡回答只有會計部的人，提到要參加訓練的對象，因此是正確答案。

(B) [╳] 題目詢問哪些員工需要參加明天的訓練，這裡卻回答地點，因此是錯誤選項。這裡利用發音相似單字 employees – employment 來造成混淆。

(C) [╳] 這是利用可以用來代稱 training（訓練）的 it，並利用和 training（訓練）有關的 oversee（監督）來造成混淆的錯誤選項。

單字 training [`trenɪŋ] 訓練，培訓 accounting [ə`kaʊntɪŋ] 會計 employment [ɪm`plɔɪmənt] 受僱
oversee [[美] `ovɚ`si [英] `əuvə`si:] 監督

16 ○○●●中

加拿大式發音 → 英式發音

Could you change the bulb for this lamp?	你可以替這盞檯燈換燈泡嗎？
(A) Sure, you can turn the TV on. (B) Yes, but not immediately. (C) All of the records we modified.	(A) 當然，你可以把電視打開。 (B) 可以，但不是馬上。 (C) 我們修改過的所有記錄。

要求疑問句 答案 (B)

這是要求對方換燈泡的要求疑問句。這裡必須知道 Could you 是要求的表達。

(A) [╳] 這是利用和 lamp（檯燈）相關的 turn ~ on（打開）來造成混淆的錯誤選項。注意不要聽到 Sure 就選擇這個答案。

(B) [○] 這裡以 Yes 表示同意要求，並附加說明表示不是馬上去換，因此是正確答案。

(C) [╳] 這是利用和題目中 change（更換）意思相近的 modified（修改）來造成混淆的錯誤選項。

單字 bulb [bʌlb] 燈泡 lamp [læmp] 檯燈 turn on 打開～ immediately [ɪˋmidɪɪtlɪ] 馬上，立刻
record [美 ˋrɛkɚd 英 ˋrekɔrd] 記錄 modify [美 ˋmɑdəˌfaɪ 英 ˋmɔdifai] 修改

17 ○●●●高

澳洲式發音 → 美式發音

How do you suggest improving this manuscript?	你建議要如何改善這份原稿？
(A) The author made a public appearance. (B) Let's shorten it by 25 percent. (C) Well, Novak recommends Midway Bistro.	(A) 作者公開現身了。 (B) 我們把它縮短 25% 吧。 (C) 這個嘛，Novak 推薦 Midway 餐酒館。

How 疑問句 答案 (B)

這是詢問對方建議要如何改善原稿的 How 疑問句。這裡必須知道 How do you suggest 是在向對方詢問意見。

(A) [╳] 這是利用和 manuscript（原稿）相關的 author（作者）來造成混淆的錯誤選項。

(B) [○] 這裡回答縮短 25%，提出改善方式，因此是正確答案。

(C) [╳] 題目詢問對方建議要如何改善原稿，這裡卻回答 Novak 推薦 Midway 餐酒館，毫不相關，因此是錯誤選項。這裡利用和題目 suggest（建議）意思相近的 recommends（推薦）來造成混淆。

單字 suggest [səˋdʒɛst] 建議 improve [ɪmˋpruv] 改善，改進
manuscript [美 ˋmænjəˌskrɪpt 英 ˋmænjuskript] 原稿；手稿 public appearance 公開現身
shorten [ˋʃɔrtn̩] 縮短；減少 recommend [ˌrɛkəˋmɛnd] 推薦；建議

18 ○○●●中

加拿大式發音 → 英式發音

When was the projector in the conference room fixed?	會議室裡的投影機是什麼時候修好的？
(A) I will arrange a conference call. (B) They repaired it a week ago. (C) Details of the project are posted on the wall.	(A) 我會安排一場電話會議。 (B) 他們在一週前修的。 (C) 這個專案的細節資訊張貼在牆上了。

When 疑問句 答案 (B)

這是詢問會議室裡的投影機是在何時修好的 When 疑問句。

(A) [╳] 題目詢問會議室裡的投影機是什麼時候修好的，這裡卻回答自己會安排電話會議，毫不相關，因此是錯誤選項。這裡透過重複使用題目中出現的 conference 來造成混淆。

(B) [○] 這裡回答在一週前修的，表示會議室裡的投影機是在一週前修好的，因此是正確答案。

(C) [╳] 這是利用發音相似單字 projector – project 來造成混淆的錯誤選項。

單字 arrange [əˋrendʒ] 安排 conference call 電話會議 repair [美 rɪˋpɛr 英 riˋpɛə] 維修
post [美 post 英 pəust] 張貼

19 中

🔊 美式發音 → 加拿大式發音	
Do you want to stop by the history museum?	你想順道去歷史博物館嗎？
(A) So long as it's free.	(A) 只要它是免費的。
(B) When we stopped by the campus.	(B) 當我們順路去那個校園的時候。
(C) The Aztec exhibit was the highlight.	(C) 阿茲特克展是主打。

助動詞疑問句 答案 (A)

這是詢問對方是否想順道去歷史博物館的助動詞（Do）疑問句。

(A) [○] 這裡回答只要它是免費的，間接表示免費的話就願意去博物館，因此是正確答案。

(B) [╳] 題目詢問是否想去博物館，這裡卻回答當順路去那個校園的時候，毫不相關，因此是錯誤選項。這裡以 stopped by 來重複題目中出現的 stop by，企圖造成混淆。

(C) [╳] 這是利用和 museum（博物館）相關的 exhibit（展覽）來造成混淆的錯誤選項。

單字 stop by 順道前往；短暫停留 so long as 只要～ campus [ˋkæmpəs]（大學等的）校園
exhibit [ɪgˋzɪbɪt] 展覽；展示 highlight [ˋhaɪˏlaɪt] 最重要（或最精采）的部分

20 中

🔊 英式發音 → 澳洲式發音	
When does the hotel restaurant normally open?	飯店餐廳通常什麼時候開？
(A) Breakfast is served beginning at 6 A.M.	(A) 早餐在早上 6 點開始供應。
(B) Are you open to driving?	(B) 你有意願開車嗎？
(C) I think the buffet is quite good.	(C) 我覺得自助餐很不錯。

When 疑問句 答案 (A)

這是詢問飯店餐廳通常何時營業的 When 疑問句。

(A) [○] 這裡回答早餐在早上 6 點開始供應，間接表示餐廳在早上 6 點開始營業，因此是正確答案。

(B) [╳] 題目詢問飯店餐廳通常何時營業，這裡卻反問對方是否有意願開車，毫不相關，因此是錯誤選項。這裡將題目中的 open（開始營業）以形容詞的另一字義「願意接受（想法或態度）的」來重複使用，企圖造成混淆。

(C) [╳] 這是利用和 restaurant（餐廳）相關的 buffet（自助餐）來造成混淆的錯誤選項。

單字 normally [㊤ ˋnɔrmḷɪ ㊥ ˋnɔːməli] 通常，一般 be open to 對～願意接受

21 高

🔊 加拿大式發音 → 美式發音	
Why haven't we received any of the new monitors?	為什麼我們還沒收到任何新螢幕？
(A) I'll check on the order's status.	(A) 我會去確認訂單狀態。
(B) My manager received similar instructions.	(B) 我的經理接到了類似的指示。
(C) They have touchscreens as well.	(C) 他們也有觸控式螢幕。

Why 疑問句 答案 (A)

這是詢問為什麼還沒收到任何新螢幕的 Why 疑問句。

(A) [○] 這裡回答會去確認訂單狀態，間接表示自己不知道，因此是正確答案。

(B) [╳] 題目詢問為什麼還沒收到任何新螢幕，這裡卻回答自己的經理收到了類似的指示，毫不相關，因此是錯誤選項。這裡透過重複使用題目中出現的 received 來造成混淆。

(C) [╳] 這是使用可以代稱題目中 monitors（螢幕）的 They，並利用和 monitors（螢幕）相關的 touchscreens（觸控式螢幕）來造成混淆的錯誤選項。

單字 receive [rɪˋsiv] 接到，收到 check on 確認（是否有異常） status [ˋstetəs]（進行的）狀態
similar [ˋsɪmələ] 類似的 instruction [ɪnˋstrʌkʃən] 指示

22 ●●●○ 高

澳洲式發音 → 美式發音 Our firm is having a new logo designed. (A) Yes, I often buy that brand. (B) Hopefully, it will be appealing. (C) Ken has resigned from his position.	我們公司正請人在設計新的標誌。 (A) 是的，我常買那個牌子。 (B) 但願它會很吸引人。 (C) Ken 已辭去了他的職務。

陳述句 答案 (B)

這是表達公司正請人在設計新標誌的客觀事實陳述句。

(A) [╳] 這是利用和 logo（標誌）相關的 brand（品牌）來造成混淆的錯誤選項。

(B) [○] 這裡回答但願它會很吸引人，提出關於設計標誌這件事的意見，因此是正確答案。

(C) [╳] 題目說公司正請人在設計新標誌，這裡卻回答 Ken 已辭職了，毫不相關，因此是錯誤選項。這裡使用發音相似單字 designed – resigned 來造成混淆。

單字 hopefully [`hopfəlɪ] 但願；懷抱希望地 appealing [ə`pilɪŋ] 吸引人的 resign [rɪ`zaɪn] 辭去 position [pə`zɪʃən] 職位，職務

23 ●●●○ 高

英式發音 → 加拿大式發音 Didn't Alan already proofread the newsletter that will be shared with gym members? (A) We typically e-mail it out once per month. (B) Read the proposal whenever you can. (C) The draft is still being completed.	Alan 不是已經校對過會和健身房會員們分享的業務通訊了嗎？ (A) 我們一般每個月會用電子郵件寄出一次。 (B) 等你可以的時候，請看這份提案。 (C) 草稿還正在做。

否定疑問句 答案 (C)

這是詢問 Alan 是否已經校對過會和健身房會員們分享的業務通訊的否定疑問句。

(A) [╳] 題目詢問 Alan 是否已經校對過會和健身房會員們分享的業務通訊，這裡卻回答一般每個月會用電子郵件寄出一次，毫不相關，因此是錯誤選項。這裡使用可以代稱題目中 newsletter（業務通訊）的 it 來造成混淆。

(B) [╳] 這是利用和 newsletter（業務通訊）相關的 Read（看）來造成混淆的錯誤選項。

(C) [○] 這裡回答草稿還正在做，間接表示 Alan 尚未校對過會和健身房會員們分享的業務通訊，因此是正確答案。

單字 proofread [`pruf͵rid] 校對 newsletter [美 `njuz`lɛtɚ 英 `nju:z`letə] 業務通訊；商業通訊 typically [`tɪpɪklɪ] 一般，通常 proposal [prə`pozl] 提案 draft [dræft] 草稿，草圖 complete [kəm`plit] 完成；填寫（表格等）

24 ●●●○ 高

美式發音 → 澳洲式發音 Payroll mistakes should be reported to Ms. Colt, right? (A) Yes, take a souvenir. (B) We were paid yesterday. (C) No, Mr. Yang handles them.	薪資明細有錯應該要回報給 Colt 小姐，對吧？ (A) 是的，拿個紀念品。 (B) 我們昨天拿到錢了。 (C) 不是，這種事是 Yang 先生在處理。

附加問句 答案 (C)

這是詢問薪資明細有錯是否是向 Colt 小姐回報的附加問句。

(A) [╳] 這是利用可以用來回答附加問句的 Yes 及發音相似單字 mistakes – take 來造成混淆的錯誤選項。

(B) [╳] 這是利用和 Payroll（薪資明細）有關的 paid（支付金錢）來造成混淆的錯誤選項。

(C) [○] 這裡以 No 來表示薪資明細有錯不是向 Colt 小姐回報，並說這種事是 Yang 先生在處理，提供附加資訊，因此是正確答案。

單字 payroll [`pe͵rol] 薪資明細 mistake [mɪ`stek] 錯誤 report [rɪ`port] 回報；報告 souvenir [美 `suvə͵nɪr 英 `su:vəniə] 紀念品 handle [`hændl] 處理

25 高

澳洲式發音 → 英式發音

The CEO has decided to step down in late October.	執行長已決定要在十月底卸任。
(A) An executive officer. (B) You've made the right decision. (C) He'll be difficult to replace.	(A) 一位執行主管。 (B) 你做了正確的決定。 (C) 要取代他很難。

陳述句 答案 (C)

這是表達執行長已決定要在十月底卸任的客觀事實陳述句。

(A) [╳] 題目陳述執行長已決定要在十月底卸任，這裡卻回答人物身分，因此是錯誤選項。這裡使用和 CEO（執行長）相關的 executive officer（執行主管）來造成混淆。

(B) [╳] 這是利用發音相似單字 decided – decision 來造成混淆的錯誤選項。這裡透過可能會誤想成 He has 的 You've 來造成混淆，注意不要把這個選項誤想成是 He has made the right decision（他做了正確的決定）而選擇這個答案。

(C) [○] 這裡回答要取代他很難，提出自己對此陳述內容的意見，因此是正確答案。

單字 step down 退位；卸任 executive officer 行政主管 replace [rɪˋples] 取代（其他人或事物）

26 高

加拿大式發音 → 英式發音

Are you still in Atlanta, or has your train left the station?	你還在亞特蘭大嗎？還是你的火車已經離站了？
(A) I'm heading to Denver now. (B) I think I'll go to Atlanta for vacation. (C) Really? My friend is from there.	(A) 我現在正前往丹佛。 (B) 我想我會去亞特蘭大度假。 (C) 真的嗎？我朋友是那裡人。

選擇疑問句 答案 (A)

這是詢問對方是還在亞特蘭大，還是已搭乘火車離站的選擇疑問句。

(A) [○] 這裡回答自己現在正前往丹佛，表示已搭乘火車離站，因此是正確答案。

(B) [╳] 這是企圖以重複題目中出現的亞特蘭大來造成混淆的錯誤選項。

(C) [╳] 題目詢問對方是還在亞特蘭大，還是已搭乘火車離站，這裡卻回答自己的朋友是那裡人，毫不相關，因此是錯誤選項。這裡使用可以代稱題目中出現的亞特蘭大的 there 來造成混淆。

單字 head [hɛd] 前往；朝向 vacation [veˋkeʃən] 度假

27 高

美式發音 → 加拿大式發音

Some of the shelves by the registers look low on merchandise.	收銀機旁的一些架子上看起來快沒貨了。
(A) Yes, from our warehouse in Ohio. (B) Shelves will be installed soon. (C) They'll be stocked now that we have more goods.	(A) 是的，來自我們在俄亥俄州的倉庫。 (B) 架子很快會裝上。 (C) 既然我們現在有比較多貨，會把它們補上的。

陳述句 答案 (C)

這是描述收銀機旁的一些架子上看起來快沒貨了的陳述句。

(A) [╳] 這是使用能夠從 merchandise（商品）聯想到的貨物存放地點 warehouse（倉庫）來造成混淆的錯誤選項。

(B) [╳] 題目提到收銀機旁的一些架子上看起來快沒貨了，這裡卻回答架子很快會裝上，毫不相關，因此是錯誤選項。這裡藉由重複使用題目中出現的 shelves 來造成混淆。

(C) [○] 這裡回答會把貨補上，提出問題的解決方法，因此是正確答案。

單字 register [ˋrɛdʒɪstɚ] 收銀機 low on ～幾乎耗盡 merchandise [ˋmɝtʃən͵daɪz] 貨物，商品
warehouse [ˋwɛr͵haʊs] 倉庫 stock [stɑk] 把（貨架等）填滿；儲備（貨物等）

28

○○●● 中

🔊 澳洲式發音 → 英式發音

Are you able to troubleshoot computer problems?

(A) That depends on the issue.
(B) You've been no trouble at all.
(C) The laptops are for business use only.

你可以解決電腦的問題嗎？

(A) 這取決於問題是什麼。
(B) 你完全沒有造成麻煩。
(C) 這台筆記型電腦僅供業務使用。

Be 動詞疑問句 答案 (A)

這是詢問是否能解決電腦問題的 Be 動詞疑問句。

(A) [○] 這裡回答取決於問題是什麼，表示要看電腦發生的是什麼問題，才能知道自己是否能解決，因此是正確答案。

(B) [╳] 題目詢問是否能解決電腦的問題，這裡卻回答對方完全沒有造成麻煩，毫不相關，因此是錯誤選項。這裡使用發音相似單字 troubleshoot – trouble 來造成混淆。

(C) [╳] 這是利用和 computer（電腦）相關的 laptops（筆記型電腦）來造成混淆的錯誤選項。

單字 troubleshoot [ˋtrʌbḷˏʃut] 分析並解決問題　depend on 取決於～
trouble [ˋtrʌbḷ] 麻煩，困擾；造成麻煩　for business use 供業務使用

29

○○●● 中

🔊 澳洲式發音 → 美式發音

Why did the diners return these appetizers to the kitchen?

(A) Do you provide full refunds?
(B) My favorite dish is the mushroom pasta.
(C) Some of the chicken seems undercooked.

為什麼用餐客人把這些開胃菜退回廚房了？

(A) 你們提供全額退款嗎？
(B) 我最喜歡的菜是蘑菇義大利麵。
(C) 有些雞肉看起來好像沒煮熟。

Why 疑問句 答案 (C)

這是詢問為什麼用餐客人把開胃菜退回了廚房的 Why 疑問句。

(A) [╳] 題目詢問為什麼用餐客人把開胃菜退回了廚房，這裡卻反問是否提供全額退款，毫不相關，因此是錯誤選項。這裡使用和題目中 return（退回）的另一字義「退貨」有關的 refunds（退款）來造成混淆。

(B) [╳] 這是利用和 appetizers（開胃菜）有關的 dish（菜餚）、mushroom pasta（蘑菇義大利麵）來造成混淆的錯誤選項。

(C) [○] 這裡回答有些雞肉看起來好像沒煮熟，提到客人將開胃菜退回廚房的原因，因此是正確答案。

單字 appetizer [[美] ˋæpəˏtaɪzɚ [英] ˋæpitaizə] 開胃菜　seem [sim] 看起來好像
undercooked [ˋʌndɚˏkʊkt]（食物）沒有煮熟的

30

○●●● 高

🔊 加拿大式發音 → 英式發音

Where can I find a copy of the annual budget?

(A) You should talk to someone in the finance team.
(B) It was completed in April.
(C) We brought in over $20 million last year.

我在哪裡可以找到年度預算案的副本？

(A) 你應該去問問財務團隊的人。
(B) 它在四月完成了。
(C) 我們去年帶進了超過兩千萬美金。

Where 疑問句 答案 (A)

這是詢問可以在哪裡找到年度預算案副本的 Where 疑問句。

(A) [○] 這裡回答應該去問問財務團隊的人，提及能找到年度預算案副本的可能方法，因此是正確答案。

(B) [╳] 題目詢問可以在哪裡找到年度預算案副本，這裡卻回答在四月完成了，毫不相關，因此是錯誤選項。這裡使用可以代稱 a copy of the annual budget（年度預算案的副本）的 It 來造成混淆。

(C) [╳] 這是使用能夠從 budget（預算案）聯想到的金額相關表達 $20 million（兩千萬美金）來造成混淆的錯誤選項。

單字 annual [ˋænjʊəl] 每年的；年度的　budget [ˋbʌdʒɪt] 預算；預算案　finance [faɪˋnæns] 財務；財政
complete [kəmˋplit] 完成　bring in 帶進（利潤等）

31 ●●●● 難

美式發音 → 澳洲式發音 But I thought Ms. Stein had to postpone her flight to Mexico City. (A) Airport shuttles leave every hour. (B) That was before her plans were updated. (C) Actually, the function went longer than expected.	但我以為 Stein 小姐得延後她飛往墨西哥市的班機。 (A) 機場接駁車每小時發車。 (B) 那是在她的計畫更新之前。 (C) 其實，這場宴會進行得比預期要久。

陳述句　　答案 (B)

這是表示自己以為 Stein 小姐得延後她飛往墨西哥市班機的陳述句。

(A) [╳] 這是利用和 flight（班機）相關的 Airport（機場）來造成混淆的錯誤選項。

(B) [◯] 這裡回答那是在她的計畫更新之前，表示現在 Stein 小姐不用延後班機了，因此是正確答案。

(C) [╳] 這是利用和 postpone（延後）相關的 longer than expected（比預期要久）來造成混淆的錯誤選項。

單字　postpone [post`pon] 延後，延期　update [ʌp`det] 更新；為～提供最新消息
function [`fʌŋkʃən] 宴會；聚會　expect [ɪk`spɛkt] 預期

TEST 1 2 3 4 5 6 7 8 9 10

32
33
34

Questions 32-34 refer to the following conversation.	第 32-34 題請參考下列對話。
加拿大式發音 → 英式發音	
M: I'm calling from Data-Trend Enterprises. [32]**We have a client flying in from Shanghai tomorrow morning and would like a driver from your chauffeur service to pick her up from the airport.**	男：我這裡是 Data-Trend 企業。[32] 我們有一位客戶明天早上會從上海飛來這裡，所以想要請你們私人司機服務的一位司機到機場去接她。
W: I can arrange that for you. May I have her name, flight number, and arrival time?	女：我可以為您安排。可以給我她的名字、班機編號及抵達時間嗎？
M: Her name is Tina Ming, and she'll be arriving on Flight DF304 at 10:20 A.M. Also, [33]**could she be taken to the Palm Hotel before being brought to our office?** She'll need to drop off her luggage.	男：她的名字是 Tina Ming，她會搭乘編號 DF304 的班機在早上 10 點 20 分抵達。此外，[33] 在載她到我們辦公室之前，可以先送她到 Palm 飯店嗎？她需要放行李。
W: No problem. [34]**I'll add the pickup to our schedule**, and one of our employees will be at the airport in the morning to get her.	女：沒問題。[34] 我會把這趟接送加進我們的行程表，然後我們會有一位員工在早上到機場去接她。
32 Why is the man calling? (A) To purchase a ticket (B) To hire a car service (C) To change a reservation (D) To confirm a flight time	32. 男子為何打電話？ (A) 為了購買票券 (B) 為了租用汽車服務 (C) 為了變更預約 (D) 為了確認班機時間
33 Where will Ms. Ming most likely go first upon arrival? (A) To an office (B) To a train station (C) To a hotel (D) To a rental agency	33. Ming 小姐在一抵達之後，最有可能會先去哪裡？ (A) 辦公室 (B) 火車站 (C) 飯店 (D) 租賃公司
34 What does the woman say she will do? (A) Update a timetable (B) Sign an agreement (C) Return a vehicle (D) Wait in an airport	34. 女子說她會做什麼？ (A) 更新行程表 (B) 簽署合約 (C) 歸還車輛 (D) 在機場等候

題目 chauffeur [`ʃofɚ] 私人司機　arrange [ə`rendʒ] 安排　drop off 帶（到某地點）放下
33 rental [`rɛntḷ] 租賃
34 timetable [`taɪm͵tebl] 行程表　agreement [ə`grimənt] 合約　vehicle [`viɪkḷ] 車輛；搭載工具

32 中 **整體對話相關問題－目的** 答案 (B)

題目詢問男子打電話的目的，因此要注意對話開頭的內容。男子說：「We have a client flying in from Shanghai tomorrow morning and would like a driver from your chauffeur service to pick her up from the airport.」，表示明天早上有客戶要從上海飛來這裡，所以想要有一位司機到機場接她，因此正確答案是 (B) To hire a car service。

33 中 **細節事項相關問題－特定細項** 答案 (C)

題目詢問 Ming 小姐在抵達後最可能會先去哪裡，因此要注意和題目關鍵字（Ms. Ming ~ go first）相關的內容。男子對女子說：「could she[Ms. Ming] be taken to the Palm Hotel before being brought to our office?」，希望司機在載 Ming 小姐到他們辦公室之前，先送她去 Palm 飯店，因此正確答案是 (C) To a hotel。

34 高 **細節事項相關問題－接下來要做的事** 答案 (A)

題目詢問女子說她會做什麼，因此要注意和題目關鍵字（will do）相關的內容。女子說：「I'll add the pickup to our schedule」，表示會將這趟接送加進行程表，因此正確答案是 (A) Update a timetable。

換句話說

add the pickup to ~ schedule 把這趟接送加進行程表 → Update a timetable 更新行程表

35 36 37

Questions 35-37 refer to the following conversation.

美式發音 → 加拿大式發音

W: Hello. My name is Leslie Carver from Dannis Incorporated. [35]**My department will be having a luncheon on July 2 at noon. I'd like you to deliver food and drinks** to the eighth-floor conference room for approximately 50 people on that day.

M: OK, Ms. Carver. Do you expect any attendees with special dietary requirements?

W: Yes, actually. [36]**I noticed on your online menu that you have vegetarian sandwiches**, so could I please order 10 of those? For the remaining sandwiches, I think a combination of the chicken salad and roast beef ones would work. Also, [37]**do you offer drinks without any sugar?**

35 What are the speakers mainly discussing?

(A) Local restaurants
(B) Food rates
(C) Event catering
(D) Diet programs

36 What does the woman mention about the menu?

(A) It includes a vegetarian selection.
(B) It was recently revised.
(C) It indicates discounts for group orders.
(D) It shows new drink varieties.

37 What does the woman ask the man about?

(A) Meal prices
(B) Venue choices
(C) Delivery times
(D) Beverage options

第 35-37 題請參考下列對話。

女：哈囉。我是 Dannis 公司的 Leslie Carver。[35] 我的部門要在 7 月 2 日中午舉行一場午餐餐會。我想請你們在那天送大約五十人份的食物和飲料到八樓的會議室。

男：好的，Carver 小姐。妳預期會有任何有特殊飲食要求的出席者嗎？

女：其實有。[36] 我注意到你們的線上菜單上有素食三明治，那能請幫我訂十個嗎？至於剩下的三明治，我想雞肉沙拉三明治和烤牛肉三明治的組合應該可以。還有，[37] 你們有提供無糖飲料嗎？

35. 說話者們主要在討論什麼？

(A) 當地餐廳
(B) 食物價格
(C) 活動外燴
(D) 飲食計畫

36. 關於菜單，女子提到什麼？

(A) 裡面有素食的選擇。
(B) 最近被修改過。
(C) 指出團訂有打折。
(D) 列出了新的飲料種類。

37. 女子詢問男子什麼？

(A) 餐點價格
(B) 場地選擇
(C) 送貨時間
(D) 飲料選擇

題目 department [dɪ`pɑrtmənt] 部門　luncheon [`lʌntʃən] 午餐餐會　deliver [dɪ`lɪvɚ] 運送　attendee [ə`tɛndi] 出席者　dietary [`daɪəˏtɛrɪ] 飲食的　requirement [rɪ`kwaɪrmənt] 要求；必要條件　vegetarian [ˏvɛdʒə`tɛrɪən] 素食的　remaining [rɪ`menɪŋ] 剩下的，剩餘的　combination [ˏkɑmbə`neʃən] 組合；混合

35 catering [`ketərɪŋ] 提供飲食的服務；外燴

36 selection [sə`lɛkʃən] 選擇；可供選擇的東西　indicate [`ɪndəˏket] 指出　variety [və`raɪətɪ] 種類；各種

37 venue [`vɛnju] 場地

35 整體對話相關問題－主題　答案 (C)

中

題目詢問對話主題，因此要注意對話的開頭，並掌握整體對話脈絡。女子說：「My department will be having a luncheon on July 2 at noon. I'd like you to deliver food and drinks」，表示自己部門要在 7 月 2 日中午舉行一場午餐餐會，希望能請男子的公司送食物和飲料過來，接著談論有關這場活動的食物和飲料選擇，因此正確答案是 (C) Event catering。

36 細節事項相關問題－提及　答案 (A)

中

題目詢問女子提到什麼與菜單有關的事，因此要確認女子話中提到題目關鍵字（menu）的前後部分。女子說：「I noticed on your online menu that you have vegetarian sandwiches」，表示注意到男子公司的線上菜單上有素食三明治，因此正確答案是 (A) It includes a vegetarian selection.。

37 細節事項相關問題－特定細項　答案 (D)

低

題目詢問女子向男子詢問什麼，因此要注意聽女子說的話。女子對男子說：「do you offer drinks without any sugar?」，詢問男子的公司是否有提供無糖飲料，因此正確答案是 (D) Beverage options。

換句話說

drinks 飲料 → Beverage 飲料

38 39 40

Questions 38-40 refer to the following conversation.

澳洲式發音 → 美式發音

M: Good afternoon. My name is Frank Peters, and [38]**I have my yearly physical examination today with Dr. Murray.** My appointment is at 10:45 A.M.

W: Hello, Mr. Peters. [38]**Please wait while I pull up your records.** Also, [39]**did you by chance bring your health insurance card today?** If so, please place it on the counter.

M: Yes, I have it right here. But may I ask what you need it for? Isn't my insurance information already on file?

W: [40]**All the state hospitals recently adopted a new record-sharing system that will keep patients like you from having to register personal information at each facility.** I just want to confirm that your medical records are in order following the upgrade.

38 Who most likely is the woman?

(A) A clinic patient
(B) A personal assistant
(C) A receptionist
(D) A pharmacist

39 What does the woman ask for?

(A) An insurance card
(B) A driver's license
(C) A registration form
(D) A medicine prescription

40 According to the woman, what is a benefit of the new system?

(A) Patients will be notified.
(B) Records will be protected.
(C) Information will be shared.
(D) Software will be upgraded.

第 38-40 題請參考下列對話。

男：午安。我的名字是 Frank Peters，[38] 我今天和 Murray 醫生約了做年度健康檢查。我的預約是早上 10 點 45 分。

女：哈囉，Peters 先生，[38] 請稍等我把您的病歷調出來。另外，[39] 您今天是否剛好有帶健保卡呢？如果有的話，請把它放在櫃檯上。

男：有，我這裡有。但我能問一下妳為什麼需要它嗎？我的保險資料不是都已經在檔案裡了嗎？

女：[40] 所有的州立醫院最近都採用了新的病歷共享系統，讓像您這樣的病患不必在個別設施中登記個人資料。我只是想要確認您的就醫記錄在這次升級後都已就緒。

38. 女子最有可能是誰？

(A) 診所病患
(B) 個人助理
(C) 接待人員
(D) 藥師

39. 女子要求取得什麼？

(A) 保險卡
(B) 駕照
(C) 報名表
(D) 用藥處方箋

40. 根據女子所說，新系統的好處是什麼？

(A) 會通知患者。
(B) 會保護記錄。
(C) 會共享資訊。
(D) 會升級軟體。

題目 physical examination 健康檢查　by chance 剛好，偶然　adopt [ə`dɑpt] 採用　register [`rɛdʒɪstɚ] 登記，註冊　in order 就緒

38 pharmacist [`fɑrməsɪst] 藥師

39 prescription [prɪ`skrɪpʃən] 處方箋

40 notify [`notə͵faɪ] 通知，告知

38 整體對話相關問題－說話者 　答案 (C)

高

題目詢問女子的身分，因此要注意聽和身分、職業相關的表達。男子說：「I have my yearly physical examination today with Dr. Murray」，表示自己今天和 Murray 醫生約了做年度健康檢查，接著女子說：「Please wait while I pull up your records.」，表示請對方稍等讓她把資料調出來，由此可知，女子是負責接待的人，因此正確答案是 (C) A receptionist。

39 細節事項相關問題－要求 　答案 (A)

低

題目詢問女子要求取得什麼，因此必須注意聽女子話中出現要求表達的內容。女子說：「did you ~ bring your health insurance card today?」，詢問男子是否有帶健保卡，因此正確答案是 (A) An insurance card。

40 細節事項相關問題－特定細項 　答案 (C)

高

題目詢問女子提到什麼新系統的好處，因此要確認女子話中和題目關鍵字（new system）相關的內容。女子說：「All the state hospitals recently adopted a new record-sharing system that will keep patients ~ from having to register personal information at each facility.」，表示所有的州立醫院最近都採用了新的病歷共享系統，而這個系統可以讓病患不必在個別設施中登記個人資料，因此正確答案是 (C) Information will be shared.。

TEST 1 2 3 4 5 6 7 8 9 10

新

41 42 43

Questions 41-43 refer to the following conversation.

加拿大式發音 → 英式發音

M: Good morning, Ms. Willard. This is Hiro Kusanagi from Décor Max. I visited your booth at the Virginia Crafts Exhibition, and I was impressed with the wooden picture frames you make. [41]**Would you be willing to sell them at my store on a commission basis?**

W: I'd be very interested, Mr. Kusanagi. [42]**Why don't I bring some samples to your store later this week?**

M: Great. We can talk about prices and other details then as well. Um, [43]**how many frames can you produce each month?**

W: About 40 . . . But I could make more if I hired a couple of assistants for my workshop.

M: That probably won't be necessary right away. But we can talk more about that when we meet.

41 What is the purpose of the call?

(A) To arrange a workshop tour
(B) To order some decorative items
(C) To reserve an exhibition booth
(D) To propose a business deal

42 What does the woman offer to do?

(A) Visit a store
(B) Mail some samples
(C) Reduce some prices
(D) Hang up a frame

43 What does the man ask about?

(A) A production capacity
(B) The size of a workforce
(C) A manufacturing process
(D) The names of some assistants

第 41-43 題請參考下列對話。

男：早安，Willard 小姐。我是 Décor Max 的 Hiro Kusanagi。我在維吉尼亞工藝展上去過您的攤位，而我對您製作的木質相框感到印象深刻。[41] 您有意願以抽成的方式把它們放在我店裡賣嗎？

女：我非常有興趣，Kusanagi 先生。[42] 要不要我這週晚一點帶些樣品去你的店裡？

男：太好了。那我們也可以討論一下價格和其他細節。嗯，[43] 您每個月能產出多少個相框？

女：大概 40 個……但如果我為我的工作坊請兩個助手，那我就能做更多個。

男：這可能現在還不需要。不過這等我們見面時可以再談一下。

41. 這通電話的目的是什麼？

(A) 安排參觀工作坊
(B) 訂購一些裝飾品
(C) 預訂展覽攤位
(D) 提出商業交易

42. 女子願意做什麼？

(A) 造訪一間店
(B) 郵寄一些樣品
(C) 降低一些價格
(D) 掛起一個相框

43. 男子詢問什麼？

(A) 生產量能
(B) 人力多寡
(C) 製造程序
(D) 一些助手的名字

題目 craft [kræft] 工藝　exhibition [ˌɛksəˋbɪʃən] 展覽　impressed [ɪmˋprɛst] 感到印象深刻的　commission [kəˋmɪʃən] 佣金　sample [美 ˋsæmpḷ 英 ˋsæmpl] 樣品　assistant [əˋsɪstənt] 助手，助理　workshop [美 ˋwɝkˌʃɑp 英 ˋwəːkʃɔp] 工作坊

41 arrange [əˋrendʒ] 安排　decorative [ˋdɛkərətɪv] 裝飾性的　propose [prəˋpoz] 提議；提出

42 mail [mel] 郵寄

43 capacity [kəˋpæsətɪ] 能力　workforce [ˋwɝkˌfors]（特定企業、組織等的全部）員工；勞動力

41 難　**整體對話相關問題－目的**　答案 (D)

題目詢問這通電話的目的是什麼，因此必須注意對話開頭的內容。男子說：「Would you be willing to sell them[wooden picture frames] at my store on a commission basis?」，詢問女子是否有意願以抽成的方式把相框放在自己店裡賣，因此正確答案是 (D) To propose a business deal。

42 中　**細節事項相關問題－提議**　答案 (A)

題目詢問女子願意做什麼，因此要注意聽女子話中有提到要為男子做什麼的部分。女子對男子說：「Why don't I bring some samples to your store later this week?」，表示自己這週晚一點可以帶樣品去男子的店裡，因此正確答案是 (A) Visit a store。

43 高　**細節事項相關問題－特定細項**　答案 (A)

題目詢問男子的詢問內容是什麼，因此要注意聽男子所說的話。男子說：「how many frames can you produce each month?」，詢問女子每個月可以產出多少個相框，因此正確答案是 (A) A production capacity。

44
45
46

Questions 44-46 refer to the following conversation.

英式發音 → 澳洲式發音

W: Alonso, are you done creating the blueprints for the Morissey Building? [44]**Our supervisor wants to review them in our meeting at 4:00 P.M.**

M: Not yet. [45]**I'm still working on the presentation slideshow for the seminar I'm leading tomorrow on finding architectural inspiration. It's been taking me longer than anticipated.**

W: Hmm . . . I gave a similar presentation to new hires last year. [46]**How about I finish the slideshow so that you can focus on the blueprints?**

M: I'll e-mail you the presentation materials in a minute. Let me just wrap up the design for this slide and save the file to my computer. [46]**I really appreciate your assistance.**

第 44-46 題請參考下列對話。

女： Alonso，你完成 Morissey 大樓的藍圖了嗎？[44] 我們主管想要在我們下午 4 點的會議上檢討它們。

男： 還沒。[45] 我還在處理我明天要主持的那場關於尋找建築靈感的研討會要用的簡報投影片。這花了我比預期更久的時間。

女： 嗯……我去年對新進員工做過類似的簡報。[46] 要不要我來完成這個投影片，好讓你能專注在那份藍圖上？

男： 我會馬上把簡報材料用電子郵件寄給妳。讓我把這張投影片的設計弄完，再把檔案存進我的電腦裡就好。[46] 我真的很感謝妳的幫忙。

44 According to the woman, what does the supervisor want to do?

(A) Search for an architect
(B) Change a meeting time
(C) Look over some plans
(D) Evaluate some staff

45 What problem does the man mention?

(A) A task is taking too long.
(B) A new hire is going to be late.
(C) A building has been closed down.
(D) A customer has made a complaint.

46 新 Why does the man say, "I'll e-mail you the presentation materials in a minute"?

(A) To agree to take on an assignment
(B) To show interest in a project
(C) To accept an offer of help
(D) To express concern about a situation

44. 根據女子所說，主管想要做什麼？

(A) 尋找建築師
(B) 更改會議時間
(C) 檢視一些圖紙
(D) 評估一些員工

45. 男子提到什麼問題？

(A) 一項工作花了太久時間。
(B) 一位新進員工會遲到。
(C) 一棟大樓已經封閉了。
(D) 一位顧客已經提出了申訴。

46. 男子為什麼說：「我會馬上把簡報材料用電子郵件寄給妳」？

(A) 為同意承接一項任務
(B) 為對一個計畫表示興趣
(C) 為接受一項協助的提議
(D) 為對一個情況表示憂慮

題目 blueprint [`blu`prɪnt] 藍圖；設計圖　architectural [美 ˌɑrkə`tɛktʃərəl 英 ˌɑːki`tektʃərəl] 建築的　inspiration [美 ˌɪnspə`reʃən 英 ˌinspə`reiʃən] 靈感　anticipate [æn`tɪsəˌpet] 預期　new hire 新進人員　wrap up 完成

45 close down 封閉　complaint [kəm`plent] 申訴；抱怨

46 take on 承接　concern [kən`sɝn] 憂慮

44 ■ 細節事項相關問題－特定細項 中　答案 (C)

題目詢問女子說主管想做什麼，因此必須確認女子話中和題目關鍵字（supervisor want to do）相關的內容。女子說：「Our supervisor wants to review them[blueprints] in our meeting at 4:00 P.M.」，表示主管想要在下午的會議上檢討藍圖，因此正確答案是 (C) Look over some plans。

45 ■ 細節事項相關問題－問題點 中　答案 (A)

題目詢問男子提到什麼問題，因此必須注意聽男子話中出現負面表達的內容。男子說：「I'm still working on the presentation slideshow for the seminar ~. It's been taking me longer than anticipated.」，表示自己還在做研討會要用的簡報投影片，而這件事比預期的更花時間，因此正確答案是 (A) A task is taking too long.。

新 46 ■ 細節事項相關問題－掌握意圖 高　答案 (C)

題目詢問男子的說話意圖，因此要注意題目引用句（I'll e-mail you the presentation materials in a minute）的前後部分。女子說：「How about I finish the slideshow so that you can focus on the blueprints?」，提議自己來完成投影片，讓男子能專注於藍圖上，而後男子說：「I ~ appreciate your assistance.」，表示感謝女子的幫忙，由此可知，男子接受女子提供協助的提議，因此正確答案是 (C) To accept an offer of help。

新

47 48 49

Questions 47-49 refer to the following conversation with three speakers.

[🔊] 加拿大式發音 → 美式發音 → 澳洲式發音

M1: Yumi and Brian, [47]**will Hall A in our museum have enough room for the Egyptian art exhibition?**

W: Maybe. There aren't many pieces to display, right?

M2: Just two dozen. But [48]**they're all large, so we need a big space . . . I recommend Hall C instead.** Is it available?

M1: It will be. Korean tapestries are there now, but our director said to take them down on August 1.

W: Umm . . . [49]**I'm a little worried, since that only gives us three days to set up the necessary pieces.**

M2: How about printing the labels for the Egyptian works beforehand? Then we could just move everything into the hall prior to the event.

W: OK. I'll grab the artwork list for us to reference now.

第 47-49 題請參考下列三人對話。

男 1：Yumi 和 Brian，[47] 我們博物館的 A 廳有足夠空間給埃及藝術展嗎？

女：可能有。要展出的物件沒有很多，對嗎？

男 2：就兩打。但 [48] 它們全都很大，所以我們需要一個大場地……我建議改用 C 廳。它能用嗎？

男 1：之後可以。韓國掛毯現在在那裡，不過我們館長說過要在 8 月 1 日把它們拿下來。

女：嗯……[49] 我有點擔心，因為這樣就只給了我們三天來設置那些必要物件。

男 2：要不要事先印好這些埃及作品的標籤？那我們就只要在活動前把所有東西都搬進展廳就好。

女：好。我現在去拿藝術品清單來給我們參考。

47 What are the speakers mainly discussing?

(A) A museum closing
(B) A historical site
(C) A remodeled venue
(D) A future exhibition

47. 說話者們主要在討論什麼？

(A) 一間博物館休館
(B) 一個歷史景點
(C) 一個整修過的場地
(D) 未來的一場展覽

48 What does Brian imply about Hall C?

(A) It is currently vacant.
(B) It will be expanded soon.
(C) It is bigger than another area.
(D) It will be used for a convention.

48. 關於 C 廳，Brian 暗示什麼？

(A) 現在是空著的。
(B) 很快會擴大。
(C) 比另一個場地要大。
(D) 會被用來舉辦大會。

49 Why is the woman concerned?

(A) A project deadline is unclear.
(B) A display has too few items.
(C) A space has to be enlarged.
(D) A schedule might be tight.

49. 女子為什麼擔心？

(A) 計畫的截止期限不明。
(B) 展覽的物件太少。
(C) 必須擴大場地。
(D) 時間表可能會很緊湊。

題目 room [rum] 空間；位置　exhibition [ˌɛksə`bɪʃən] 展覽　display [dɪ`sple] 展示　dozen [`dʌzn̩] 一打，12 個
tapestry [`tæpɪstrɪ] 掛毯　take ~ down 將～拿下來；拆除（建物等）　set up 設置
beforehand [[美] bɪ`forˌhænd [英] bi`fɔ:hænd] 事先　artwork [`ɑrtˌwɝk] 藝術品　reference [`rɛfərəns] 做為參考；提及
48 currently [`kɝəntlɪ] 現在　vacant [`vekənt] 空著的　expand [ɪk`spænd] 使擴張
49 enlarge [ɪn`lɑrdʒ] 擴大　tight [taɪt]（沒有餘裕時間而）緊湊的

47 ■ 整體對話相關問題－主題　　答案 (D)

低

題目詢問對話主題，因此要注意對話的開頭，並掌握整體對話的脈絡。男 1 說：「will Hall A in our museum have enough room for the Egyptian art exhibition?」，詢問博物館 A 廳是否有足夠空間給埃及藝術展用，接著繼續談論與未來的這項展覽有關的內容，因此正確答案是 (D) A future exhibition。

48 ■ 細節事項相關問題－推論　　答案 (C)

高

題目詢問男 2 的 Brian 暗示了什麼與 C 廳有關的內容，因此要確認男 2 所說的話裡出現題目關鍵字（Hall C）的前後部分。男 2[Brian] 說：「they[pieces]'re all large, so we need a big space ~. I recommend Hall C instead.」，表示因為要展出的物件都很大，所以需要大場地，並建議改用 C 廳，由此可知，C 廳比另一個場地要大，因此正確答案是 (C) It is bigger than another area.。

49 ■ 細節事項相關問題－問題點　　答案 (D)

中

題目詢問女子擔心什麼，因此必須注意聽女子話中出現負面表達之後的內容。女子說：「I'm a little worried, since that only gives us three days to set up the necessary pieces.」，表示自己對於只給三天來擺設物件感到有點擔心，因此正確答案是 (D) A schedule might be tight.。

50
51
52

Questions 50-52 refer to the following conversation.

澳洲式發音 → 英式發音

M: Good afternoon. This is Carlos Tran, and I'm a representative from the Riverside Business Institute. [50]**I was hoping to reach Ms. Brenda Ling in regard to the advanced accounting course she completed last week.**

W: [50]**This is Ms. Ling.** What can I do for you?

M: I'm contacting the participants who went through the course to gather feedback. The responses we receive will help our organization to improve its services and curriculum in the future. [51]**Could you spare a moment to answer some questions?** It won't take up much of your time.

W: I'm actually quite busy at the moment. [52]**I'll have some free time in the afternoon, however. Please call me back after 2 P.M.**

50 What did the woman do last week?

(A) Finished taking a class
(B) Completed an accounting report
(C) Attended a ceremony
(D) Taught a business course

51 What does the man ask the woman to do?

(A) Seek out an advisor
(B) Check some messages
(C) Rearrange a schedule
(D) Respond to some questions

52 What will the man probably do after 2 P.M.?

(A) Get in touch with the woman again
(B) Distribute handouts to participants
(C) Visit an administrator's office
(D) Submit a curriculum outline

第 50-52 題請參考下列對話。

男：午安。我是 Carlos Tran，Riverside 商業學院的代表。[50] 我想找 Brenda Ling 小姐談談與她上星期上完的進階會計課程有關的事。

女：[50] 我是 Ling 小姐。有什麼我可以為您做的嗎？

男：我正在聯絡上過這個課程的參加者來收集回饋意見。我們收到的回應將有助於我們學院在未來改善服務及課程。[51] 您能空出一點時間來回答一些問題嗎？不會花您太多時間的。

女：我現在其實很忙。[52] 不過我下午會有一些空閒時間。請在下午 2 點以後再打給我。

50. 女子上星期做了什麼？

(A) 上完了一門課
(B) 完成了一份會計報告
(C) 參加了一個典禮
(D) 教了一堂商業課程

51. 男子要求女子做什麼？

(A) 找一位顧問
(B) 確認一些訊息
(C) 重新安排一份時間表
(D) 回答一些問題

52. 男子在下午 2 點後可能會做什麼？

(A) 再次和女子聯繫
(B) 把講義發給參加者
(C) 造訪管理員辦公室
(D) 提交課程大綱

題目 institute [美 `ɪnstətjut 英 `institju:t] 學院；協會　advanced [美 əd`vænst 英 əd`vɑ:nst] 進階的；高級的；先進的
participant [美 pɑr`tɪsəpənt 英 pɑ:`tisipənt] 參加者　gather [美 `gæðɚ 英 `gæðə] 收集；使聚集
curriculum [kə`rɪkjələm] 課程　spare [美 spɛr 英 spɛə] 空出（時間等）

51 advisor [əd`vaɪzɚ] 顧問　rearrange [ˌriə`rendʒ] 重新安排（時間、地點等）

52 get in touch with 和～聯繫　administrator [əd`mɪnəˌstretɚ] 管理人員；行政人員

50 細節事項相關問題－特定細項　答案 (A)

中

題目詢問女子上星期做了什麼，因此要注意提到題目關鍵字（last week）的前後部分。男子說：「I was hoping to reach Ms. Brenda Ling in regard to the ~ course she completed last week.」，表示想找 Brenda Ling 小姐談和上週上完的課有關的事，接著女子說：「This is Ms. Ling.」，表示自己就是 Ling 小姐，由此可知，女子上星期把課上完了，因此正確答案是 (A) Finished taking a class。

51 細節事項相關問題－要求　答案 (D)

低

題目詢問男子要求女子做什麼，因此要注意聽男子話中出現要求表達之後的內容。男子對女子說：「Could you spare a moment to answer some questions?」，詢問女子是否能空出一點時間來回答一些問題，因此正確答案是 (D) Respond to some questions。

換句話說

answer some questions 回答一些問題 → Respond to some questions 回答一些問題

52 細節事項相關問題－接下來要做的事　答案 (A)

中

題目詢問男子在下午 2 點以後可能會做什麼，因此要注意提到題目關鍵字（after 2 P.M.）的前後部分。女子說：「I'll have some free time in the afternoon ~. Please call me back after 2 P.M.」，表示自己下午有空閒時間，並要求男子在兩點以後再打，因此正確答案是 (A) Get in touch with the woman again。

新

53 54 55

Questions 53-55 refer to the following conversation.	第 53-55 題請參考下列對話。
美式發音 → 加拿大式發音	
W: Hi, there. [53]**It's my first time selling my fruits and vegetables at this farmer's market.** I noticed that your booth is popular. [54]**How do you attract so many customers?**	女：嗨，你好。[53] 這是我第一次在這個農夫市集裡賣我的水果和蔬菜。我注意到你的攤位很受歡迎。[54] 你是怎麼吸引到這麼多顧客的呢？
M: [54]**I upload pictures of my products online.** My blog gets a lot of visitors, and [54]**many of them decide to stop by my stall.** How about trying something similar?	男：[54] 我把我產品的照片上傳到了網路上。我的部落格有很多人看，而且 [54] 他們之中有很多人決定要來我攤位逛逛。妳要不要做做看類似的事情？
W: That's a great idea. Thanks for the advice. Also, do you know if vendors can get a discount at other sellers' stands?	女：這主意真棒。謝謝你的建議。還有，你知道攤販能不能在其他賣家的攤位上拿到折扣嗎？
M: I'm not sure. [55]**You should ask the market's organizer** about that. Oh! There he is now, talking to the owner of Diana's Juice Bar.	男：我不確定。[55] 妳應該去問市集的籌辦人這件事。噢！他現在在那裡，正在和 Diana's 果汁吧的攤主說話。
W: OK. [55]**I'll do that right now.**	女：好。[55] 我現在立刻去問。
53 Who most likely is the woman? (A) A supermarket manager (B) A restaurant owner (C) A produce vendor (D) A market analyst	53. 女子最有可能是誰？ (A) 超市經理 (B) 餐廳老闆 (C) 農產品攤販 (D) 市場分析師
54 新 What does the man mean when he says, "My blog gets a lot of visitors"? (A) A Web site needs to be updated. (B) An information source is accurate. (C) An online discount is available. (D) An advertising method is effective.	54. 當男子說：「我的部落格有很多人看」，意思是什麼？ (A) 需要更新一個網站。 (B) 一個資料來源是正確的。 (C) 可以使用一個線上折扣。 (D) 一種廣告方法有效。
55 What will the woman probably do next? (A) Request a product sample (B) Sell some merchandise (C) Look over some research (D) Speak to an event organizer	55. 女子接下來可能會做什麼？ (A) 索取一個產品樣本 (B) 販售一些商品 (C) 查看一些研究 (D) 和活動籌辦人說話

題目 attract [ə`trækt] 吸引　stop by 順路造訪；短暫停留　stall [stɔl] 攤位　vendor [`vɛndɚ] 攤販　seller [`sɛlɚ] 賣家　stand [stænd] 攤位
53 produce [`prɑdjus] 農產品　analyst [`ænlɪst] 分析師
54 source [sors] 來源　accurate [`ækjərɪt] 精確的；正確的　available [ə`veləbl̩] 可使用的
55 sample [`sæmpl̩] 樣本；品嘗　look over 查看

53 整體對話相關問題－說話者　中　答案 (C)

題目詢問女子的身分，因此要注意聽和身分、職業相關的表達。女子說：「It's my first time selling my fruits and vegetables at this farmer's market.」，表示自己是第一次在這個農夫市集裡賣水果和蔬菜，由此可知，女子是農產品攤販，因此正確答案是 (C) A produce vendor。

新 **54** 細節事項相關問題－掌握意圖　高　答案 (D)

題目詢問男子的說話意圖，因此要注意題目引用句（My blog gets a lot of visitors）的前後部分。女子對男子說：「How do you attract so many customers?」，詢問男子如何能吸引到這麼多客人，男子說：「I upload pictures of my products online.」，表示自己把產品的照片上傳到了網路上，接著說：「many of them[visitors] decide to stop by my stall」，表示有很多人決定到男子的攤位上逛逛，由此可知，男子的意思是自己這種廣告方法有效，因此正確答案是 (D) An advertising method is effective.。

55 細節事項相關問題－接下來要做的事　低　答案 (D)

題目詢問女子接下來可能會做的事，因此必須注意對話的最後部分。男子對女子說：「You should ask the market's organizer」，表示她應該去問市集的籌辦人，接著女子說：「I'll do that right now.」，表示自己會立刻去問，因此正確答案是 (D) Speak to an event organizer。

56
57
58

Questions 56-58 refer to the following conversation.

加拿大式發音 → 美式發音

M: Hi. My name is Cody Tate, and I'm calling from the Bryant Park Activities Center. 56**I'd like to talk to you about the neighborhood event you've volunteered to work at tomorrow.**

W: Oh . . . 56**I assume you're referring to the Bryant Town Carnival.**

M: That's correct. According to our records, 57**you've agreed to set up game booths at the carnival.** 58**Would you be able to work at the ticket booth for a few hours once the event begins as well? The person who was assigned that responsibility has fallen ill, so we need someone to fill in for her.**

W: Yes, of course. However, I can only stay until about 5 P.M., as I have another engagement later in the day.

第 56-58 題請參考下列對話。

男：嗨。我的名字是 Cody Tate，我這裡是 Bryant 公園活動中心。56 我想和妳談談與妳明天自願要幫忙的社區活動有關的事。

女：噢……56 我想你是在說 Bryant 鎮嘉年華會。

男：沒錯。根據我們的記錄，57 妳已經答應要在嘉年華會上設置遊戲攤位了。58 妳能在活動開始後也去售票攤位顧幾個小時嗎？原本被分配到這項任務的人生病了，所以我們需要有人頂替她。

女：當然可以。不過，我只能待到下午 5 點左右，因為我那天晚一點還有另一個約。

56 What is scheduled to take place tomorrow?

(A) A trade fair
(B) A private party
(C) A corporate event
(D) A community festival

56. 明天預定會舉行什麼？

(A) 一場貿易展
(B) 一個私人派對
(C) 一個企業活動
(D) 一個社區慶典

57 According to the man, what has the woman agreed to do?

(A) Pass out programs to guests
(B) Arrive in the afternoon
(C) Set up some booths
(D) Manage ticket sales

57. 根據男子所說，女子已經答應要做什麼了？

(A) 把節目表發給賓客
(B) 在下午抵達
(C) 設置一些攤位
(D) 處理售票

58 What does the man ask the woman to do?

(A) Contribute to a charity
(B) Replace another worker
(C) Revise some records
(D) Coordinate with a supervisor

58. 男子要求女子做什麼？

(A) 對慈善事業做出貢獻
(B) 替代另一位工作人員
(C) 修改一些記錄
(D) 和主管協調

題目 volunteer [ˌvɑlənˋtɪr] 自願做；自願提供　refer to 指稱～　set up 設置　assign [əˋsaɪn] 分派（工作、任務等）；指派　fill in for 頂替～　engagement [ɪnˋgedʒmənt] 約會

57 pass out 分發　manage [ˋmænɪdʒ] 處理

58 contribute [kənˋtrɪbjut] 貢獻；捐款　charity [ˋtʃærətɪ] 慈善事業　coordinate [koˋɔrdnet] 協調

56 細節事項相關問題－特定細項　答案 (D)

中

題目詢問明天預定會舉行什麼，因此要注意提到題目關鍵字（tomorrow）的前後部分。男子說：「I'd like to talk to you about the neighborhood event you've volunteered to work at tomorrow.」，表示想和對方談談與明天進行的社區活動有關的事，接著女子說：「I assume you're referring to the Bryant Town Carnival.」，表示男子在說的是 Bryant 鎮嘉年華會，由此可知，明天有社區慶典，因此正確答案是 (D) A community festival。

57 細節事項相關問題－特定細項　答案 (C)

低

題目詢問男子說女子已經答應要做什麼，因此必須確認男子話中和題目關鍵字（agreed to do）相關的內容。男子說：「you've agreed to set up game booths at the carnival」，表示女子已經答應要在嘉年華會上設置遊戲攤位，因此正確答案是 (C) Set up some booths。

58 細節事項相關問題－要求　答案 (B)

中

題目詢問男子要求女子做什麼，因此要注意聽男子話中出現要求表達之後的內容。男子說：「Would you be able to work at the ticket booth for a few hours once the event begins as well? The person who was assigned that responsibility has fallen ill, so we need someone to fill in for her.」，詢問女子是否能在活動開始之後也去售票攤位顧幾個小時，因為原本被分配到這項任務的人生病了，所以需要有人頂替那個人，因此正確答案是 (B) Replace another worker。

59 60 61 新

Questions 59-61 refer to the following conversation with three speakers.	第 59-61 題請參考下列三人對話。
澳洲式發音 → 加拿大式發音 → 英式發音	
M1: [59]**Maybe we could hang this painting behind our spa's reception desk.**	男 1： [59] 或許我們可以把這幅畫掛在我們水療館的接待櫃台後面。
M2: I like the relaxing beach scene.	男 2： 我喜歡這個悠閒的海灘景色。
M1: Yeah. Plus, the blue colors match the spa's interior. But first, we should ask Monica's opinion. Hey, Monica. [60]**How about buying this painting for our lobby?**	男 1： 對啊。而且這個藍色和水療館裡面很搭。不過首先，我們應該要問問 Monica 的意見。嘿，Monica。[60] 要不要買這幅畫放在我們大廳？
W: Don't we have something like that near the entrance?	女： 我們在入口附近不是有跟那類似的東西了嗎？
M1: You mean the one with the sailboats?	男 1： 妳是說有帆船的那幅嗎？
M2: [60]**I hadn't thought of that. We wouldn't want two related works close together.**	男 2： [60] 我之前沒想到那個。我們不會想要把兩件同類型的作品放在一起的。
W: [61]**What about buying artwork from a Web site** instead of at a gallery? There will be more choices online.	女： [61] 要不要從網站上買藝術品，而不要在藝廊買呢？網路上會有更多選擇。
M2: Oh! Have you two heard of Crafty.com? It sells reasonably priced works from less popular artists.	男 2： 噢！你們兩個有聽過 Crafty.com 嗎？它在賣價格合理、由比較沒那麼受歡迎的藝術家所做的作品。
W: We can browse that site when we return from our lunch break.	女： 等我們午休結束回來，我們可以看看那個網站。

59 Where do the speakers most likely work?
(A) At a gallery
(B) At a spa
(C) At a design studio
(D) At a retail outlet

59. 說話者們最有可能在哪裡工作？
(A) 藝廊
(B) 水療館
(C) 設計工作室
(D) 零售通路

60 新 Why does the woman say, "Don't we have something like that near the entrance"?
(A) To propose a solution
(B) To confirm a location
(C) To offer encouragement
(D) To disagree with a suggestion

60. 為什麼女子說：「我們在入口附近不是有跟那類似的東西了嗎」？
(A) 提出一個解決方案
(B) 確認一個地點
(C) 提供鼓勵
(D) 不同意一項建議

61 What does the woman suggest?
(A) Looking for artwork online
(B) Picking up a catalog
(C) Taking an extended break
(D) Going to a popular attraction

61. 女子建議什麼？
(A) 在網路上找藝術品
(B) 拿一份型錄
(C) 延長休息時間
(D) 去一個熱門景點

題目 relaxing [rɪˋlæksɪŋ] 悠閒的 match [mætʃ] 和～相配 sailboat [美 ˋselˌbot 英 ˋseilbəut] 帆船
60 confirm [kənˋfɝm] 確認 **61** attraction [əˋtrækʃən] 景點

59 整體對話相關問題－說話者 低 答案 (B)

題目詢問說話者們的工作地點，因此要注意聽和身分、職業相關的表達。男 1 說：「Maybe we could hang this painting behind our spa's reception desk.」，表示可以把這幅畫掛在他們水療館的接待櫃台後面，由此可知，說話者們在水療館工作，因此正確答案是 (B) At a spa。

新 **60** 細節事項相關問題－掌握意圖 中 答案 (D)

題目詢問女子的說話意圖，因此要注意題目引用句（Don't we have something like that near the entrance）的前後部分。前面男 1 說：「How about buying this painting for our lobby?」，提議買這幅畫放在大廳裡，後面男 2 說：「I hadn't thought of that. We wouldn't want two related works close together.」，表示之前沒有想到那個，且不想把兩幅同類型的作品放在一起，由此可知，女子不同意要買那幅畫的建議，因此正確答案是 (D) To disagree with a suggestion。

61 細節事項相關問題－提議 中 答案 (A)

題目詢問女子建議什麼，因此必須注意聽女子話中出現的提議相關表達。女子說：「What about buying artwork from a Web site」，建議在網站上買藝術品，因此正確答案是 (A) Looking for artwork online。

62
63
64

Questions 62-64 refer to the following conversation.

澳洲式發音 → 美式發音

M: It's Liam O'Reilly from the Cypress Mall branch. [62]**I'm assisting a customer who is interested in renting a van that can seat a minimum of eight people. Do you happen to have any available?** Unfortunately, the two we have on our lot are reserved for use later today.

W: Let me check the database. Ah . . . yes, [62]**it appears we have three that would be appropriate.** [63]**Why don't I ask a staff member to drive one to your location right away?** It shouldn't take more than 15 minutes or so.

M: That's great. I'm sure the customer won't mind waiting. [64]**Please tell the employee to inform me upon reaching the facility.** Thanks.

62 What type of business do the speakers probably work for?

(A) A taxi service
(B) A vehicle rental agency
(C) A shipping company
(D) An automotive dealership

63 What does the woman propose?

(A) Asking a worker to make a delivery
(B) Meeting a customer at a main office
(C) Changing some travel arrangements
(D) Contacting a different location

64 What does the man request?

(A) A notification upon arrival
(B) A ride to another facility
(C) A prepayment for a reservation
(D) A duplicate of an agreement

第 62-64 題請參考下列對話。

男：我是 Cypress 購物中心分行的 Liam O'Reilly。[62] 我正在協助一位客人，他想租一輛至少能坐八人的廂型車。你們有任何剛好能租的嗎？很不巧，我們停車場裡有的那兩輛今天晚一點都被預訂要用了。

女：讓我查查資料庫。啊……有，[62] 看起來我們有三輛適合的。[63] 要不要我請一位員工立刻把一輛開去你們那裡？應該不會花超過 15 分鐘左右。

男：太好了。我確定這位客人不會介意要等。[64] 請跟那位員工說一到中心就通知我。謝謝。

62. 說話者們可能在什麼類型的公司裡工作？

(A) 計程車服務
(B) 租車行
(C) 貨運公司
(D) 汽車經銷商

63. 女子提議什麼？

(A) 請一位員工送過去
(B) 在總公司和一位客人見面
(C) 更改一些旅行安排
(D) 聯絡另外的據點

64. 男子要求什麼？

(A) 抵達時通知
(B) 搭車到其他設施
(C) 為預約先付款
(D) 合約的副本

題目 assist [əˋsɪst] 幫助　van [væn] 廂型車　seat [sit] 容納～人　minimum [ˋmɪnəməm] 最少的；最低限度的
lot [[美] lɑt [英] lɔt]（有特定用途的）一塊地；場地　appropriate [əˋproprɪˌet] 適合的；恰當的
inform [[美] ɪnˋfɔrm [英] inˋfɔ:m] 通知

62 automotive [ˌɔtəˋmotɪv] 汽車的　dealership [ˋdiləˌʃɪp] 經銷商　**63** arrangement [əˋrendʒmənt] 安排；準備工作

64 notification [ˌnotəfəˋkeʃən] 通知；告示　prepayment [priˋpemənt] 預付；提前支付　duplicate [ˋdjupləkɪt] 副本

62 整體對話相關問題－說話者　答案 (B)

中

題目詢問說話者們在什麼類型的公司裡工作，因此要注意聽和身分、職業相關的表達。男子說：「I'm assisting a customer who is interested in renting a van ~. Do you happen to have any available?」，表示自己正在協助想租車的客人，並詢問對方是否有車可出租，女子說：「it appears we have three that would be appropriate」，表示看起來有三輛是適合出租的，由此可知，說話者們是在租車行裡工作，因此正確答案是 (B) A vehicle rental agency。

63 細節事項相關問題－提議　答案 (A)

中

題目詢問女子提議什麼，因此要注意聽女子話中出現的提議相關表達。女子說：「Why don't I ask a staff member to drive one[van] to your location right away?」，提議要請一位員工立刻把車開去男子的所在地點，因此正確答案是 (A) Asking a worker to make a delivery。

64 細節事項相關問題－要求　答案 (A)

中

題目詢問男子要求什麼，因此要注意聽男子話中出現要求表達之後的內容。男子說：「Please tell the employee to inform me upon reaching the facility.」，表示要請員工在抵達時通知自己，因此正確答案是 (A) A notification upon arrival。

換句話說

inform ~ upon reaching 一到達就通知 → A notification upon arrival 抵達時通知

新

Questions 65-67 refer to the following conversation and map.

加拿大式發音 → 英式發音

M: Excuse me. [65]**Where is the observation deck for the harbor located?**

W: [65]**Just walk toward Starfish Beach after you exit this visitor center. The deck is on the corner.** Ah . . . and it's fortunate you came today. [66]**The boardwalk will be filled with people tomorrow because of a kite-flying competition.**

M: Good to know. By the way, I'll be able to see Dune Island from the deck, right?

W: Yes. New viewing machines were just installed there, and the weather is clear today.

M: Great! Also, [67]**I'm curious how much the parking fee for the nearby lot is.**

W: The regular price is $20 per day. But [67]**local residents only pay $15 because they get a 25 percent discount.**

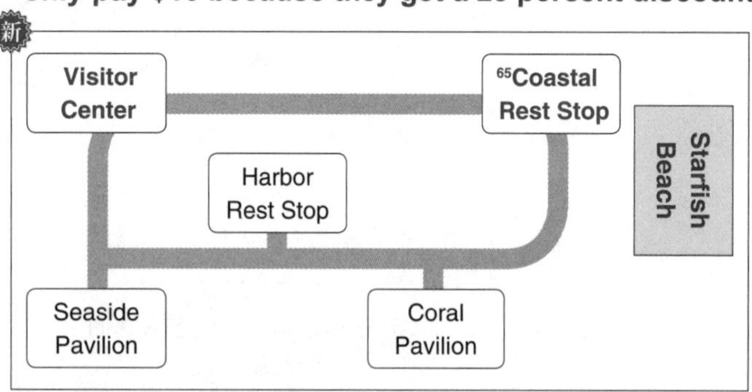

65 Look at the graphic. Where is the observation deck located?

新

(A) In Seaside Pavilion
(B) In Coastal Rest Stop
(C) In Harbor Rest Stop
(D) In Coral Pavilion

66 What does the woman say about the boardwalk?

(A) It will be crowded tomorrow.
(B) It will undergo renovations.
(C) It is far from a parking lot.
(D) It was damaged by poor weather.

67 How much of a parking fee discount is offered to local residents?

(A) 10 percent
(B) 15 percent
(C) 20 percent
(D) 25 percent

第 65-67 題請參考下列對話及地圖。

男：不好意思。[65] 這個港口的觀景台在哪裡呢？

女：[65] 你出了這個遊客中心後，就朝 Starfish 海灘走。那個觀景台在轉角處。啊……而且你很幸運是今天來。[66] 木棧道上明天會擠滿人，因為有放風箏比賽。

男：真不錯。對了，我可以從台上看到 Dune 島，對吧？

女：可以。那裡剛安裝了新的觀賞裝置，而且今天的天氣很晴朗。

男：太棒了！還有，[67] 我想知道附近停車場的停車費用是多少。

女：正常費用是每天 20 美金。但是 [67] 當地居民只要付 15 美金，因為他們有七五折的折扣。

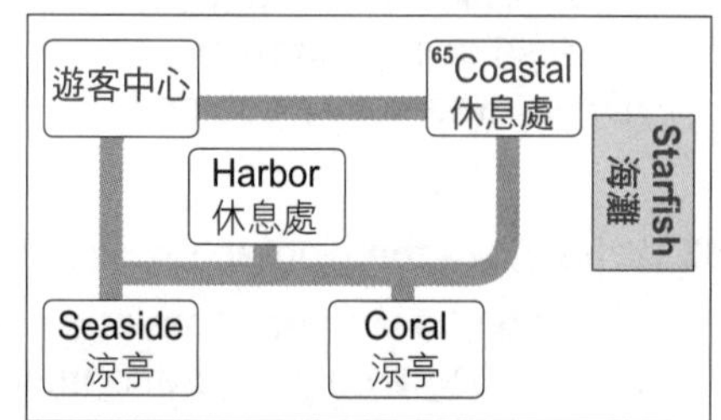

65. 請看圖表。觀景台在哪裡？

(A) 在 Seaside 涼亭
(B) 在 Coastal 休息處
(C) 在 Harbor 休息處
(D) 在 Coral 涼亭

66. 關於木棧道，女子說什麼？

(A) 明天會很擁擠。
(B) 會進行整修。
(C) 離停車場很遠。
(D) 因為爛天氣而壞了。

67. 給當地居民的停車費折扣是多少？

(A) 九折
(B) 八五折
(C) 八折
(D) 七五折

題目 observation deck 觀景台 harbor [ˋhɑrbɚ] 港口 exit [ˋɛksɪt] 出去 fortunate [美 ˋfɔrtʃənɪt 英 ˋfɔ:tʃənit] 幸運的 boardwalk [美 ˋbord͵wɔk 英 ˋbɔ:dwɔ:k]（在海邊等地的）木棧道 be filled with 充滿～ kite-flying 放風箏 competition [美 ͵kɑmpəˋtɪʃən 英 ͵kɔmpiˋtiʃən] 比賽 install [ɪnˋstɔl] 安裝 nearby [ˋnɪr͵baɪ] 附近的 resident [美 ˋrɛzədənt 英 ˋrezidənt] 居民

66 crowded [ˋkraʊdɪd] 擁擠的 undergo [͵ʌndɚˋgo] 進行 renovation [͵rɛnəˋveʃən] 整修；翻新

新 **65** ○●●● 高 ■ **新細節事項相關問題－圖表資料** 答案 (B)

題目詢問觀景台的位置在哪裡，因此必須確認題目提供的地圖，並注意和題目關鍵字（observation deck located）有關的前後部分。男子說：「Where is the observation deck for the harbor located?」，詢問港口觀景台的位置在哪裡，女子說：「Just walk toward Starfish Beach after you exit this visitor center. The deck is on the corner.」，表示在出了遊客中心後，往 Starfish 海灘的方向走，就會在轉角處找到觀景台。透過地圖可知，觀景台位於 Coastal 休息處，因此正確答案是 (B) In Coastal Rest Stop。

66 ○○●● 中 ■ **細節事項相關問題－提及** 答案 (A)

題目詢問女子說了什麼與木棧道有關的事，因此必須確認女子話中提到題目關鍵字（boardwalk）的前後部分。女子說：「The boardwalk will be filled with people tomorrow because of a kite-flying competition.」，表示因為明天有放風箏比賽，所以到時木棧道上會擠滿人，因此正確答案是 (A) It will be crowded tomorrow.。

換句話說

be filled with people 會擠滿人 → be crowded 擁擠

67 ○○○● 低 ■ **細節事項相關問題－程度** 答案 (D)

題目詢問當地居民可以得到多少停車費折扣，因此要注意和題目關鍵字（parking fee discount ~ to local residents）相關的內容。男子說：「I'm curious how much the parking fee for the nearby lot is」，表示想知道附近停車場的停車費用是多少，接著女子說：「local residents only pay $15 because they get a 25 percent discount」，表示當地居民有七五折的折扣，所以只要付 15 美金就可以了，因此正確答案是 (D) 25 percent。

68
69
70

Questions 68-70 refer to the following conversation and schedule.

美式發音 → 澳洲式發音

W: [68]**Did you see this section of the carpet? There's a rather large stain here.**
M: Oh! What a mess! Maybe something was spilled during the year-end party that occurred earlier this afternoon. I'm worried because [69]**our clients from Downview Legal Associates are arriving for a meeting at 3 P.M.**
W: We should use Conference Room D instead, seeing as it's unoccupied right now.
M: All right. [70]**I'll gather up our presentation handouts and bring them** there. While I do that, please call the building maintenance team. They should deal with the stain in Conference Room C as soon as possible, since Janice Chung will conduct an interview there later this afternoon.

新

Conference Room C Schedule

Meeting Time	Booked By
10 A.M. – 11 A.M.	Scott White
1 P.M. – 2 P.M.	Vera Gonzalez
3 P.M. – 4 P.M.	[69]**Brad Derby**
4 P.M. – 5 P.M.	Janice Chung

68 What problem does the woman mention?
(A) A meeting space is fully booked.
(B) A mark has been made on a rug.
(C) An applicant is running behind schedule.
(D) A light fixture has been damaged.

69 新 Look at the graphic. Who booked the room for a client meeting?
(A) Scott White
(B) Vera Gonzalez
(C) Brad Derby
(D) Janice Chung

70 What will the man probably do next?
(A) Collect some documents
(B) Contact a colleague
(C) Attend an interview
(D) Download some information

第 68-70 題請參考下列對話及時間表。

女：[68] 你有看到地毯上這一塊嗎？有個滿大的汙漬在這裡。
男：噢！真髒！也許在今天下午稍早舉辦的尾牙派對上有什麼東西打翻了。我覺得很擔心，因為 [69] 我們來自 Downview 律師事務所的客戶會在下午 3 點來開會。
女：我們應該改用 D 會議室，它現在看起來沒有人在用。
男：好吧。[70] 我會把我們的簡報資料收拾好帶去那裡。在我做這件事的時候，請打電話給大樓的維護團隊。他們應該要盡快處理 C 會議室裡的汙漬，因為 Janice Chung 今天下午晚一點會在那裡進行面試。

C 會議室時間表

會議時間	預約者
上午 10 點到 11 點	Scott White
下午 1 點到 2 點	Vera Gonzalez
下午 3 點到 4 點	[69]Brad Derby
下午 4 點到 5 點	Janice Chung

68. 女子提到什麼問題？
(A) 一個會議場地的預約已滿。
(B) 一塊汙漬被弄在了地毯上。
(C) 一位應徵者比預定時間晚到。
(D) 一個燈具被破壞了。

69. 請看圖表。誰為了和客戶開會而預約了這個場地？
(A) Scott White
(B) Vera Gonzalez
(C) Brad Derby
(D) Janice Chung

70. 男子接下來可能會做什麼？
(A) 收集一些文件
(B) 聯絡一位同事
(C) 參加一場面試
(D) 下載一些資訊

題目 section [ˋsɛkʃən] 區塊；部分 stain [sten] 汙漬 mess [mɛs] 髒亂的東西；亂七八糟的狀態 spill [spɪl]（液體等）濺出 year-end 年終的 unoccupied [ʌnˋɑkjə͵paɪd] 無人使用的 gather up 收拾 handout [ˋhændaʊt]（印製的）資料；講義 maintenance [ˋmentənəns] 養護；維持 deal with 處理～
68 mark [mɑrk] 汙漬；痕跡 rug [rʌg] 地毯 light fixture 燈具 damaged [ˋdæmɪdʒd] 受損的
70 collect [kəˋlɛkt] 收集 contact [kənˋtækt] 聯絡 colleague [ˋkɑlig] 同事 attend [əˋtɛnd] 參加

68 細節事項相關問題－問題點　答案 (B)

中

題目詢問女子提到什麼問題，因此必須注意聽女子話中出現負面表達之後的內容。女子說：「Did you see this section of the carpet? There's a rather large stain here.」，詢問男子是否有看到地毯上有一塊滿大的汙漬，因此正確答案是 (B) A mark has been made on a rug.。

換句話說

stain 汙漬 → mark 汙漬

新 69 細節事項相關問題－圖表資料　答案 (C)

高

題目詢問是誰為了和客戶開會而預約了這個場地，因此必須確認題目提供的時間表上的資訊，並注意和題目關鍵字（booked ~ for a client meeting）相關的內容。男子說：「our clients ~ are arriving for a meeting at 3 P.M.」，表示客戶會在下午 3 點來開會，透過時間表可知，為了和客戶開會而預約了場地的人是 Brad Derby，因此正確答案是 (C) Brad Derby。

70 細節事項相關問題－接下來要做的事　答案 (A)

中

題目詢問男子接下來可能會做什麼，因此必須注意對話的最後部分。男子說：「I'll gather up our presentation handouts and bring them」，表示自己會把簡報資料收拾好帶去，因此正確答案是 (A) Collect some documents。

71
72
73

Questions 71-73 refer to the following telephone message.

美式發音

Good morning, Ms. Chancy. I work at Source Incorporated, and [71]**I'm calling to inform you about a credit card that our company just released** called the Gold Rewards Card. [72]**It offers a unique benefits package that caters to the spending habits of each customer. These benefits include 10 percent off at 20 major retail chains.** Moreover, points accumulated through card purchases may be transferred to any of the five most popular frequent-flyer programs.[73]**If you want to take advantage of this amazing opportunity, just fill out an application form at www.sourceinc.com!**

71 Where does the speaker most likely work?

(A) At a financial institution
(B) At a recruitment firm
(C) At a sportswear retailer
(D) At a chain restaurant

72 How much of a discount can some customers receive?

(A) 5 percent
(B) 10 percent
(C) 15 percent
(D) 20 percent

73 What is the listener instructed to do?

(A) Call a hotline
(B) Complete an online form
(C) Reset an old code
(D) Learn about a point system

第 71-73 題請參考下列電話留言。

早安，Chancy 小姐。我在 Source 公司工作，而 [71] 我打來是想要向您介紹我們公司剛發行的一張叫做 Gold Rewards 卡的信用卡。[72] 它會配合每位客人的消費習慣提供獨一無二的優惠套裝方案。這些優惠包括可以在 20 個大型連鎖零售商店裡打九折。此外，透過信用卡消費所累積的點數可以轉移到最受歡迎的五個飛行常客計畫中的任一計畫。[73] 若您想要利用這個絕佳的機會，就到 www.sourceinc.om 填寫申請表吧！

71. 說話者最有可能在哪裡工作？

(A) 金融機構
(B) 人力公司
(C) 運動服飾零售商
(D) 連鎖餐廳

72. 某些客人能夠得到多少折扣？

(A) 九五折
(B) 九折
(C) 八五折
(D) 八折

73. 聽者被指示做什麼？

(A) 打熱線電話
(B) 填好線上表單
(C) 重新設定舊密碼
(D) 了解點數制度

題目 benefit [ˋbɛnəfɪt] 利益，好處　cater [ˋketɚ] 迎合，配合（需求）；提供飲食　accumulate [əˋkjumjəˏlet] 累積　frequent-flyer program 飛行常客計畫　take advantage of 利用～

71 recruitment [rɪˋkrutmənt] 招募

73 hotline [ˋhɑtlaɪn] 熱線電話

71 整體對話相關問題－說話者　答案 (A)

中

題目詢問說話者的工作地點，因此要注意聽和身分、職業相關的表達。獨白說：「I'm calling to inform you about a credit card that our company just released」，表示自己來電是想要介紹公司剛發行的信用卡，由此可知，說話者是在金融機構內工作，因此正確答案是 (A) At a financial institution。

72 細節事項相關問題－程度　答案 (B)

低

題目詢問某些客人能夠獲得多少優惠，因此必須注意和題目關鍵字（discount）相關的內容。獨白說：「It[Gold Rewards Card] offers a unique benefits package that caters to the spending habits of each customer. These benefits include 10 percent off at 20 major retail chains.」，表示 Gold Rewards 卡會配合每位客人的消費習慣來提供優惠套裝方案，而這些優惠包括可以在 20 個大型連鎖零售商店裡打九折，因此正確答案是 (B) 10 percent。

73 細節事項相關問題－特定細項　答案 (B)

中

題目詢問聽者被指示做什麼，因此要注意和題目關鍵字（instructed to do）相關的內容。獨白說：「If you want to take advantage of this amazing opportunity, just fill out an application form at www.sourceinc.com!」，表示如果想要利用這個絕佳的機會，就到網站上填寫申請表，因此正確答案是 (B) Complete an online form。

74 75 76

Questions 74-76 refer to the following speech.

英式發音

[74]**Please join me in welcoming Jason Chao to the stage, as he is being given the Employee of the Year Award.** Mr. Chao was named one of our marketing firm's supervisors late last year, and he's really shown his worth to the company since then. [75]**He was responsible for all of the marketing activities we implemented for Tiger Cars, including some of our most successful magazine advertisements to date.** Because of that campaign, [76]**we have attracted several new clients and have consequently seen our profits rise in recent months.** So, let's give a big round of applause for Mr. Chao.

第 74-76 題請參考下列致詞。

[74] 請和我一起歡迎 Jason Chao 上台，因為他將獲頒年度最佳員工獎。Chao 先生在去年底被任命為我們行銷公司的主管之一，而他自那時起便真正展現了他對公司的價值。[75] 他負責我們為 Tiger Cars 所施行的所有行銷活動，其中包含一些我們到目前為止最成功的雜誌廣告。因為那次的宣傳活動，[76] 我們吸引到了幾位新客戶，並因此在最近幾個月看到我們的利潤有所提升。那麼，讓我們熱烈掌聲歡迎 Chao 先生。

74 What is the purpose of the speech?
(A) To introduce an employee
(B) To provide instructions
(C) To open a conference
(D) To promote a new car

74. 這段致詞的目的是什麼？
(A) 介紹員工
(B) 提供指示
(C) 為會議開場
(D) 宣傳新車

75 According to the speaker, what was Mr. Chao in charge of?
(A) Writing a magazine article
(B) Communicating with clients
(C) Meeting monthly sales targets
(D) Running an advertising campaign

75. 根據說話者所說，Chao 先生之前負責了什麼？
(A) 撰寫雜誌報導
(B) 和客戶溝通
(C) 達成月銷售目標
(D) 管理廣告宣傳活動

76 What has the company done recently?
(A) Cut its production costs
(B) Opened a new branch
(C) Increased its earnings
(D) Launched a publication

76. 這間公司最近完成了什麼？
(A) 削減生產成本
(B) 開設新的分公司
(C) 提升利潤
(D) 發行刊物

題目 worth [美 wɝθ 英 wə:θ] 價值　implement [美 \`ɪmpləˌmɛnt 英 \`impliment] 實施，施行　attract [ə\`trækt] 吸引　consequently [美 \`kɑnsəˌkwɛntlɪ 英 \`kɔnsikwentli] 結果，因此　profit [美 \`prɑfɪt 英 \`prɔfit] 利益；利潤　applause [ə\`plɔz] 鼓掌

75 meet [mit] 達成（目標等）　target [\`tɑrgɪt] 目標　run [rʌn] 經營；管理

76 earning [\`ɝnɪŋ] 收入；利潤　publication [ˌpʌblɪ\`keʃən] 刊物；出版品

74 整體內容相關問題－目的　答案 (A)
中
題目詢問這段致詞的目的是什麼，因此要注意聽這段獨白的開頭部分。獨白說：「Please join me in welcoming Jason Chao to the stage, as he is being given the Employee of the Year Award.」，表示歡迎將獲頒年度最佳員工獎的 Jason Chao 上台，並接著介紹他，因此正確答案是 (A) To introduce an employee。

75 細節事項相關問題－特定細項　答案 (D)
中
題目詢問 Chao 先生之前負責了什麼，因此要注意和題目關鍵字（Mr. Chao in charge of）相關的內容。獨白說：「He [Mr. Chao] was responsible for all of the marketing activities ~ for Tiger Cars, including some of our most successful magazine advertisements to date.」，表示 Chao 先生負責為 Tiger Cars 所施行的所有行銷活動，其中包含一些到目前為止最成功的雜誌廣告，因此正確答案是 (D) Running an advertising campaign。

76 細節事項相關問題－特定細項　答案 (C)
中
題目詢問這間公司最近完成了什麼，因此要注意和題目關鍵字（company done recently）相關的內容。獨白說：「we[company] have ~ seen our profits rise in recent months」，表示公司利潤在最近幾個月提升了，因此正確答案是 (C) Increased its earnings。

換句話說
have ~ seen ~ profits rise 看到利潤有所提升 → Increased ~ earnings 提升利潤

TEST 1 2 3 4 5 6 7 8 9 10

77
78
79

Questions 77-79 refer to the following announcement.

澳洲式發音

Holmstead Bookstore is excited to announce that the final installment in author Marianne Lane's popular series of fantasy novels, *Wicked Witches*, will be released on November 10. [77]**To celebrate, our Westport branch will give away tickets to the book signing event** being held there on November 30. These will be given to the first 300 customers who purchase her novel at that branch. If you are interested in this opportunity, be sure to get there early on the 10th. [78]**Ms. Lane has a lot of fans who will be thrilled about this chance to meet her.** For more information regarding this and other Holmstead offers, [79]**I recommend downloading our mobile application.**

77 What is the announcement mainly about?
(A) A store opening
(B) A membership upgrade
(C) A monthly sale
(D) An event promotion

78 What does the speaker say people will be excited to do?
(A) Attend a screening
(B) Sign up for a newsletter
(C) Watch a performance
(D) Meet an author

79 What does the speaker suggest listeners do?
(A) Purchase a pass
(B) Download a program
(C) Check an online schedule
(D) Bring a valid ID card

第 77-79 題請參考下列公告。

Holmstead 書店很高興宣布，作家 Marianne Lane 很受歡迎的奇幻小說《Wicked Witches》系列的最後一集將在 11 月 10 日發行。[77] 為表慶祝，我們的 Westport 分店將送出 11 月 30 日辦在那裡的簽書會門票。這些門票將會送給前 300 位在該分店購買她小說的客人。如果您對這個機會有興趣，請務必在 10 日那天提早抵達那裡。[78]Lane 小姐擁有很多會對這個能與她見面的機會感到興奮的粉絲。要了解更多有關本活動及其他 Holmstead 優惠的資訊，我推薦您下載我們的行動應用程式。

77. 這則公告主要與什麼有關？
(A) 商店開張
(B) 會員資格升級
(C) 每月特賣
(D) 活動宣傳

78. 說話者說人們會對於要去做什麼感到很興奮？
(A) 出席電影放映
(B) 登記取得業務通訊
(C) 觀賞表演
(D) 與作家見面

79. 說話者建議聽者們做什麼？
(A) 購買通行證
(B) 下載程式
(C) 查詢線上時間表
(D) 帶有效的身分證

題目 installment [ɪn`stɔlmənt]（連載中或系列中的）一集，一篇　author [㊈ `ɔθɚ ㊇ `ɔ:θə] 作家
branch [㊈ bræntʃ ㊇ brɑ:ntʃ] 分店，分公司　give away 贈送　opportunity [㊈ ˌɑpɚ`tjunətɪ ㊇ ˌɔpə`tju:niti] 機會
regarding [㊈ rɪ`gɑrdɪŋ ㊇ ri`gɑ:diŋ] 關於～　offer [㊈ `ɔfɚ ㊇ `ɔ:fə] 優惠；提供
78 screening [`skrinɪŋ]（電影等）放映　newsletter [`njuz`lɛtɚ] 業務通訊　performance [pɚ`fɔrməns] 表演
79 pass [pæs] 入場證；通行證　valid [`vælɪd] 有效的

77 整體內容相關問題－主題　答案 (D)
中

題目詢問公告的主題，因此要注意聽獨白的開頭部分。獨白說：「To celebrate, our Westport branch will give away tickets to the book signing event」，表示 Westport 分店為了慶祝而要送出簽書會門票，接著提到活動的相關內容，因此正確答案是 (D) An event promotion。

78 細節事項相關問題－特定細項　答案 (D)
低

題目詢問人們會對於要去做什麼感到很興奮，因此要注意和題目關鍵字（excited to do）相關的內容。獨白說：「Ms. Lane[author] has a lot of fans who will be thrilled about this chance to meet her.」，表示 Lane 小姐的很多粉絲會很興奮能有和她見面的機會，因此正確答案是 (D) Meet an author。

79 細節事項相關問題－提議　答案 (B)
低

題目詢問說話者建議聽者們做什麼，因此要注意聽獨白後半部出現提議相關表達的句子。獨白說：「I recommend downloading our mobile application」，建議聽者們去下載行動應用程式，因此正確答案是 (B) Download a program。

換句話說
downloading ~ mobile application 下載行動應用程式 → Download a program 下載程式

80 81 82

Questions 80-82 refer to the following excerpt from a meeting.	第 80-82 題請參考下列會議節錄。
美式發音	
I have some important news. This spring, our firm will be partnering with the watch design company Elevated Time. [80]**We've been commissioned to produce the company's newest line of high-end watches.** Elevated Time sells its watches in over 50 countries, so [81]**this will be our most profitable contract yet. It is a major opportunity for a growing firm like ours**, and we need to do our best to make sure things go well. [82]**If the company is pleased with our final products, I'm quite positive that we'll be able to secure future work with them.**	我有一些重要的消息。這個春天，我們公司將會與手錶設計公司 Elevated Time 合作。[80] 我們已被委託生產該公司最新的高檔手錶系列產品。Elevated Time 在超過 50 個國家中販售他們的手錶，因此 [81] 這會是我們到目前為止獲利最高的合約。這對於像我們這樣在成長中的公司來說是個重要的機會，所以我們必須盡全力確保一切順利進行。[82] 如果這間公司對我們的成品感到滿意，那我相當有自信我們將能拿到他們未來的工作。
80 What industry does the speaker most likely work in? (A) Manufacturing (B) Construction (C) Advertising (D) Distribution	80. 說話者最有可能在什麼產業內工作？ (A) 製造 (B) 建築 (C) 廣告 (D) 分銷
81 新 Why does the speaker say, "Elevated Time sells its watches in over 50 countries"? (A) To motivate some volunteers (B) To emphasize the growth of a company (C) To encourage registration (D) To highlight the significance of a deal	81. 說話者為什麼說：「Elevated Time 在超過 50 個國家中販售他們的手錶」？ (A) 為了激勵一些志工 (B) 為了強調一間公司的成長 (C) 為了鼓勵登記 (D) 為了強調一筆交易的重要性
82 What does the speaker expect to do? (A) Make an upcoming deadline (B) Expand a factory (C) Continue a business relationship (D) Develop a successful design	82. 說話者預期要做什麼？ (A) 訂一個即將到來的截止日期 (B) 擴大一間工廠 (C) 持續一段業務關係 (D) 開發一個成功的設計

題目 partner [ˋpɑrtnɚ] 與～合作；與～成為夥伴 commission [kəˋmɪʃən] 委託；委託製作 high-end 高檔的
positive [ˋpɑzətɪv] 有自信的

80 distribution [ˌdɪstrəˋbjuʃən] 分發；分銷

81 motivate [ˋmotəˌvet] 激勵；賦予動機 emphasize [ˋɛmfəˌsaɪz] 強調 highlight [ˋhaɪˌlaɪt] 強調

80 中 **整體內容相關問題－說話者** 答案 (A)

題目詢問說話者在什麼產業裡工作，因此要注意聽和身分、職業相關的表達。獨白說：「We've been commissioned to produce the ~ newest line of high-end watches.」，表示自己公司被委託生產最新的高檔手錶系列產品，由此可知，說話者在製造業工作，因此正確答案是 (A) Manufacturing。

新 **81** 高 **細節事項相關問題－掌握意圖** 答案 (D)

題目詢問說話者的說話意圖，因此要注意題目引用句（Elevated Time sells its watches in over 50 countries）的前後部分。獨白說：「this will be our most profitable contract yet. It is a major opportunity for a growing firm like ours」，表示這是到目前為止獲利最高的合約，且這張合約對於自己正在成長中的公司來說是個重要的機會，由此可知，說話者說這句話是想要強調這筆交易的重要性，因此正確答案是 (D) To highlight the significance of a deal。

82 高 **細節事項相關問題－特定細項** 答案 (C)

題目詢問說話者預期要做什麼，因此要注意和題目關鍵字（expect to do）相關的內容。獨白說：「If the company [Elevated Time] is pleased with our final products, I'm quite positive that we'll be able to secure future work with them.」，表示如果 Elevated Time 滿意成品，那麼說話者就相當有自信自己的公司在未來能拿到他們的工作，由此可知，說話者預期要和 Elevated Time 持續一段業務關係，因此正確答案是 (C) Continue a business relationship。

換句話說

secure future work with 拿到未來的工作 → Continue a business relationship 持續一段業務關係

TEST 1 2 3 4 5 6 7 8 9 10

83

84

85

Questions 83-85 refer to the following speech.

加拿大式發音

I want to begin by saying [83]**it's been an honor to spend the final two decades of my career working in the public sector here at the State Consumer Protection Agency.** As the legal department administrator, [84]**I oversaw the creation of numerous laws** that helped protect the rights and safety of consumers. That's something I'm very proud of, and I'll always cherish my time here. Although I look forward to spending more time with my family, I will miss working with such a skilled group of people. Finally, [85]**let me express my gratitude to all of you for organizing this party. I had no idea that one was being planned.** Thank you.

83 Who most likely is the speaker?

(A) A political candidate
(B) A journalist
(C) A private attorney
(D) A government employee

84 What was the speaker responsible for?

(A) Overseeing an expansion
(B) Creating regulations
(C) Managing a special budget
(D) Carrying out research

85 What does the speaker say about the party?

(A) He expected more guests.
(B) He did not know about it.
(C) He planned to invite his family.
(D) He was involved in organizing it.

第 83-85 題請參考下列致詞。

我想先說，[83] 很榮幸我職業生涯的最後二十年能在州立消費者保護局這個公部門這裡的工作中度過。身為法務部門的行政官，[84] 我監督過許多協助保護消費者權利及安全的法規設立。這是令我感到非常驕傲的事，而我會永遠珍惜我在這裡的時光。儘管我期待能花更多時間陪伴家人，但我會懷念與這麼一個專業團隊一起工作的這件事。最後，[85] 讓我對籌辦這場派對的你們大家表達我的感謝。我之前完全不知道有在計畫要辦派對。謝謝你們。

83. 說話者最有可能是誰？

(A) 政治候選人
(B) 記者
(C) 私人律師
(D) 政府雇員

84. 說話者之前負責什麼？

(A) 監督擴建
(B) 設立法規
(C) 管理特殊預算
(D) 進行研究

85. 關於這場派對，說話者說什麼？

(A) 他之前預期會有更多賓客。
(B) 他之前不知道這件事。
(C) 他之前計畫邀請他的家人。
(D) 他有參與籌辦這場派對。

題目 state [stet] 國家；州　legal department 法務部門　administrator [əd`mɪnə͵stretɚ] 管理人；行政官員　oversee [`ovɚ`si] 監督　cherish [`tʃɛrɪʃ] 珍惜

83 attorney [ə`tɝnɪ] 律師；法定代理人

83 整體內容相關問題－說話者　答案 (D)

高

題目詢問說話者身分，因此要注意聽和身分、職業相關的表達。獨白說：「it's been an honor to spend the final two decades of my career working in the public sector here at the State Consumer Protection Agency」，表示很榮幸自己職業生涯的最後二十年能在州立消費者保護局這個公部門裡度過，由此可知，說話者是在政府機構裡工作的政府雇員，因此正確答案是 (D) A government employee。

84 細節事項相關問題－特定細項　答案 (B)

中

題目詢問說話者之前負責什麼，因此必須注意和題目關鍵字（responsible for）相關的內容。獨白說：「I oversaw the creation of numerous laws」，表示自己監督過許多法規的設立，因此正確答案是 (B) Creating regulations。

85 細節事項相關問題－提及　答案 (B)

中

題目詢問說話者提到什麼與這場派對有關的事，因此要注意提到題目關鍵字 （party）的前後部分。獨白說：「let me express my gratitude to all of you for organizing this party. I had no idea that one was being planned.」，表示想要感謝籌辦這場派對的所有人，並說自己事前完全不知道有要辦這個派對，因此正確答案是 (B) He did not know about it.。

86
87
88

Questions 86-88 refer to the following talk.

英式發音

Thank you for volunteering at our community center's basketball tournament. I have a few last-minute things to discuss with you before the event begins. First of all, [86]**two volunteers should stay outside this gymnasium** to direct traffic. While you are doing this, [87]**please make sure that visitors do not park near the rear entrance.** That area must be kept clear for emergency vehicles. [88]**Once the event is over, all of you should help the janitorial staff by picking up any garbage left by attendees.** OK . . . that's it for now. I'll let you know if I need your assistance with anything else.

86 Where most likely are the listeners?

(A) At a university
(B) At an outdoor market
(C) At a sports facility
(D) At a community park

87 Why does the speaker say, "That area must be kept clear for emergency vehicles"?

新

(A) To explain a request
(B) To correct a misstatement
(C) To make a complaint
(D) To suggest an alternative

88 What are listeners asked to do after the event?

(A) Clean up a venue
(B) Assist attendees
(C) Speak with a staff member
(D) Direct traffic

第 86-88 題請參考下列談話。

謝謝你們來擔任我們社區中心籃球錦標賽的志工。在活動開始前，我有最後幾件事要與各位討論。首先，[86] 應該要有兩位志工待在這座體育館外指揮交通。你們在做這件事的時候，[87] 請確保來賓不要把車停在靠近後門的地方。那塊區域必須保持暢通給緊急車輛用。[88] 活動一結束，你們所有人都應該協助管理人員撿拾參加者們留下的任何垃圾。好……現在就先這樣。如果我還有任何事需要你們幫忙，我會讓你們知道。

86. 聽者們最有可能在哪裡？

(A) 大學
(B) 露天市場
(C) 運動設施
(D) 社區公園

87. 為什麼說話者說：「那塊區域必須保持暢通給緊急車輛用」？

(A) 為解釋一個要求
(B) 為糾正一個錯誤陳述
(C) 為提出一項申訴
(D) 為建議一個替代方案

88. 聽者們被要求在活動後做什麼？

(A) 清理一個場地
(B) 協助參加者
(C) 和一位員工談話
(D) 指揮交通

題目 tournament [美 `tɝnəmənt 英 `tuənəmənt] 比賽；錦標賽 gymnasium [dʒɪm`nezɪəm] 體育館
janitorial staff（大樓等場地的）管理人員 assistance [ə`sɪstəns] 幫助
87 alternative [ɔl`tɝnətɪv]（供選擇的）替代方案
88 venue [`vɛnju]（活動或事件等進行的）場地

86 整體內容相關問題－地點 答案 (C)

中

題目詢問聽者們的所在地點，因此要注意聽獨白中出現地點表達之後的內容。獨白說：「two volunteers should stay outside this gymnasium」，表示應該要有兩位志工待在這座體育館外，由此可知，聽者們身在體育館，也就是運動設施之中，因此正確答案是 (C) At a sports facility。

換句話說

gymnasium 體育館 → sports facility 運動設施

新 87 細節事項相關問題－掌握意圖 答案 (A)

高

題目詢問說話者的說話意圖，因此要注意題目引用句（That area must be kept clear for emergency vehicles）的前後部分。獨白說：「please make sure that visitors do not park near the rear entrance」，表示要確保來賓不要把車停在靠近後門的地方，由此可知，說話者是想要解釋提出這項要求的原因，因此正確答案是 (A) To explain a request。

88 細節事項相關問題－要求 答案 (A)

中

題目詢問聽者們被要求在活動後做什麼，因此要注意聽獨白後半部出現要求相關表達的句子。獨白說：「Once the event is over, all of you should help the janitorial staff by picking up any garbage left by attendees.」，表示活動一結束，所有人都應該協助管理人員撿拾參加者們留下的垃圾，因此正確答案是 (A) Clean up a venue。

89
90
91

Questions 89-91 refer to the following radio broadcast.

澳洲式發音

Welcome to *This Week in Brooklyn* on Central Radio 96.1 FM. On Tuesday, the latest phase of a redevelopment project in the Bentham neighborhood was completed. Over the last three months, [89]**an old toy factory has been renovated to provide studios for artists. The space is going to open its doors this Friday**, with painters, writers, musicians, and other artists holding a party for the grand opening event. The developer of the site—who also [90]**converted the old Wentworth Warehouse into apartments**—hopes that it will serve to further improve the area. [91]**Now, we'll have a brief talk with one of the construction company's board members**, Steven Godering.

第 89-91 題請參考下列電台廣播。

歡迎收聽 FM 96.1 Central 電台的《This Week in Brooklyn》。在星期二，Bentham 區重開發案的最後階段完工了。在過去的三個月間，[89] 一間老舊的玩具工廠已被翻新為供藝術家使用的工作室。這個場地將在本週五開幕，與畫家、作家、音樂家及其他藝術家一同舉辦一場盛大開幕的活動派對。此處的開發商——也是 [90] 將老舊的 Wentworth 倉庫改建成公寓的開發商——希望這個場地會有助於這個地區的進一步提升。[91] 現在，我們將和建設公司董事會成員之一的 Steven Godering 進行簡短對談。

89 According to the speaker, what will be opening this week?

(A) A toy shop
(B) A radio station
(C) An artist workspace
(D) An apartment building

89. 根據說話者所說，本週什麼會開幕？

(A) 玩具店
(B) 廣播電台
(C) 藝術家的工作空間
(D) 公寓大樓

90 What is mentioned about Wentworth Warehouse?

(A) It was converted into housing.
(B) It was purchased at a discount.
(C) It was demolished recently.
(D) It was moved to another area.

90. 關於 Wentworth 倉庫，提到了什麼？

(A) 它被改建成了住宅。
(B) 它以折扣價被買下。
(C) 它最近被拆除了。
(D) 它被搬到另外一個區域了。

91 What will listeners probably hear next?

(A) A song
(B) An advertisement
(C) A news report
(D) An interview

91. 聽者們接下來可能會聽到什麼？

(A) 一首歌
(B) 一則廣告
(C) 一篇新聞報導
(D) 一段訪談

題目 phase [fez] 階段，時期 convert [美 kən`vɝt 英 kən`vɜ:t] **轉變，變換**
improve [美 ɪm`pruv 英 ɪm`pru:v] 改善；提升 brief [brif] 簡短的 board member **董事會成員**
90 housing [`haʊzɪŋ] 住宅 demolish [dɪ`mɑlɪʃ] 拆除

89 ■ 細節事項相關問題－特定細項 答案 (C)

中

題目詢問什麼會在本週開幕，因此要注意和題目關鍵字（opening this week）相關的內容。獨白說：「an old toy factory has been renovated to provide studios for artists. The space is going to open its doors this Friday」，表示玩具工廠已被翻新成了供藝術家使用的工作室，且這個場地會在本週五開幕，因此正確答案是 (C) An artist workspace。

90 ■ 細節事項相關問題－提及 答案 (A)

中

題目詢問提到了什麼與 Wentworth 倉庫有關的事情，因此必須注意聽提到題目關鍵字（Wentworth Warehouse）的前後部分。獨白說：「converted the old Wentworth Warehouse into apartments」，表示老舊的 Wentworth 倉庫被改建成了公寓，因此正確答案是 (A) It was converted into housing.。

91 ■ 細節事項相關問題－特定細項 答案 (D)

低

題目詢問聽者們接下來可能會聽到什麼，因此必須注意聽獨白的最後部分。獨白說：「Now, we'll have a brief talk with one of the construction company's board members」，表示現在將和建設公司的董事會成員進行簡短對談，由此可知，聽者們接下來會聽到訪談，因此正確答案是 (D) An interview。

92
93
94

Questions 92-94 refer to the following telephone message and building directory.

英式發音

Kenny, it's Nina Emerson. [92]**I'm calling about our conversation yesterday afternoon** concerning the firm's incoming recruits. [93]**You asked if I'd be willing to take charge of their orientation session** next Friday. I just remembered that I'll be out of town for a convention that day, so I can't assist you. However, [93]**Victoria Styles has directed training workshops in the past, and she's offered to help out**. I suggest talking with her in person sometime today. Just note that her office is no longer on the third floor . . . [94]**She moved to the top floor when she transferred to another department.** As for your comments about the Greenway Project, we'll have to discuss that when I get back.

第 92-94 題請參考下列電話留言及樓層指南。

Kenny，我是 Nina Emerson。[92] 我打來是想講和我們昨天下午談到的與即將要來公司的新人有關的事。[93] 你那時問我是否願意負責他們下星期五的新進人員訓練。我剛剛想起來，我那天要出城去參加一場會議，所以我無法協助你。不過，[93] Victoria Styles 以前曾主持過培訓工作坊，而且她願意幫忙。我建議你今天找時間親自和她談談。只是要注意她的辦公室已經不在三樓了……[94] 她調到另一個部門時搬去了最高的那層樓。至於你對 Greenway 專案的意見，等我回來我們得談談。

新

Landville Plaza Directory

Floor	Department
1	Finance
2	Sales
3	Human Resources
4	Customer Service
5	[94]**Research and Development**

Landville Plaza 樓層指南

樓層	部門
1	財務
2	銷售
3	人力資源
4	顧客服務
5	[94] 研發

92 According to the speaker, what did the listener do yesterday?

(A) Held interviews with applicants
(B) Departed for a gathering
(C) Talked to a colleague
(D) Transferred to a new division

92. 根據說話者所說，聽者昨天做了什麼？

(A) 面試應徵者
(B) 出發去一個聚會
(C) 和一位同事說話
(D) 調到一個新部門

93 What is Victoria Styles willing to do?

(A) Lead an orientation session
(B) Accept a promotion
(C) Make some travel arrangements
(D) Reach out to a customer

93. Victoria Styles 願意做什麼？

(A) 主持新進人員訓練
(B) 接受升職
(C) 做一些旅行安排
(D) 聯絡一位顧客

94 新 Look at the graphic. What department does Victoria Styles work in?

(A) Finance
(B) Human Resources
(C) Customer Service
(D) Research and Development

94. 請看圖表。Victoria Styles 在什麼部門裡工作？

(A) 財務
(B) 人力資源
(C) 顧客服務
(D) 研發

題目 incoming [ˋɪnˏkʌmɪŋ] 即將到來的；進來的 recruit [rɪˋkrut] 新成員 take charge of 負責～ help out 幫助～解決困難
comment [美 ˋkɑmɛnt 英 ˋkɔment] 意見，評論
92 division [dəˋvɪʒən] 部門
93 lead [lid] 領導；主持

92 ■ 細節事項相關問題－特定細項 答案 (C)
低

題目詢問聽者昨天做了什麼，因此要注意和題目關鍵字（listener do yesterday）相關的內容。獨白說：「I'm calling about our conversation yesterday afternoon」，表示說話者打來是想講和聽者昨天下午談到的有關的事，由此可知，聽者和說話者昨天有說過話，因此正確答案是 (C) Talked to a colleague。

93 ■ 細節事項相關問題－特定細項 答案 (A)
中

題目詢問 Victoria Styles 願意做什麼，因此要注意提到題目關鍵字（Victoria Styles）的前後部分。獨白說：「You asked if I'd be willing to take charge of their[recruits'] orientation session」，表示對方詢問自己是否有意願負責新員工的新進人員訓練，後面則提到：「Victoria Styles has directed training workshops in the past, and she's offered to help out」，表示 Victoria Styles 以前曾主持過培訓工作坊，且她願意幫忙，因此正確答案是 (A) Lead an orientation session。

新 94 ■ 細節事項相關問題－圖表資料 答案 (D)
中

題目詢問 Victoria Styles 在什麼部門工作，因此必須確認題目提供的樓層指南，並注意和題目關鍵字（department ~ Victoria Styles work in）相關的內容。獨白說：「She[Victoria Styles] moved to the top floor when she transferred to another department.」，表示 Victoria Styles 調到另一個部門時搬去了最高樓層，由此可知，Victoria Styles 工作的部門是最高那層樓的研發部，因此正確答案是 (D) Research and Development。

95
96
97

Questions 95-97 refer to the following announcement and ticket.

美式發音

May I have your attention, please? [95]**Passengers bound for Hartsville may begin boarding the vessel at 3:10 P.M.** For those of you traveling to Bridgeport, [96]**there will be a delay,** unfortunately. Your ship is expected to arrive here at 3:30, which means that you won't be able to board until 4:00. [96]**A car that was disembarking at the last stop had some engine trouble**, and a tow truck had to be called to remove it from the ship. We apologize for the inconvenience. Finally, the ferry for Harrisburg will depart on schedule at 4:10. [97]**Please remember to review the pamphlet with information about emergency procedures** after you board the vessel. You will find it on your seat. Thank you.

新

EASTERN FERRY LINE

ADULT
SINGLE FARE

[95]Destination: Hartsville
Ship Name: Atlantic Star

Ticket No. E12304

95 Look at the graphic. When will the ticket holder be permitted to board the vessel?

新

(A) At 3:10 P.M.
(B) At 3:30 P.M.
(C) At 4:00 P.M.
(D) At 4:10 P.M.

96 What is the cause of the delay?

(A) A vehicle broke down.
(B) A tow truck is unavailable.
(C) A ship must be inspected.
(D) A ferry has been overbooked.

97 What are listeners asked to do?

(A) Reserve a seat
(B) Read a document
(C) Exchange a ticket
(D) Check a schedule

第 95-97 題請參考下列公告及票券。

請大家注意一下我這裡可以嗎？[95] 前往 Hartsville 的乘客可以在下午 3 點 10 分開始登船。至於你們之中那些要前往 Bridgeport 的人，則不幸 [96] 會有所延誤。你們的船預期會在 3 點 30 分抵達這裡，這意味著你們在 4 點前都無法登船。[96] 一輛原本要在前一站下船的車的引擎出了一些問題，所以不得不打電話請拖吊車來把它從船上拖下去。我們為此不便致上歉意。最後，前往 Harrisburg 的渡輪會按預定在 4 點 10 分出發。[97] 請記得在登船後仔細查看上面有緊急程序相關資訊的小冊子。你們可以在自己的座位上找到它。謝謝你們。

EASTERN 渡輪公司

成人
單程票

[95] 目的地：Hartsville
船名：Atlantic Star

票號 E12304

95. 請看圖表。持票者何時會被允許登船？

(A) 下午 3 點 10 分
(B) 下午 3 點 30 分
(C) 下午 4 點
(D) 下午 4 點 10 分

96. 延誤的原因是什麼？

(A) 車輛故障。
(B) 沒有拖吊車可用。
(C) 必須檢查船隻。
(D) 渡輪超賣了。

97. 聽者們被要求做什麼？

(A) 預約座位
(B) 閱讀文件
(C) 換票
(D) 確認時間表

題目 bound for 前往～　board [bord] 登上（車、船或飛機等交通工具）　vessel [ˋvɛsl̩] 船
travel [ˋtrævl̩] 移動（到另一地點）；旅行　disembark [ˌdɪsɪmˋbɑrk] 下（車、船或飛機等交通工具）
inconvenience [ˌɪnkənˋvinjəns] 不便　emergency procedure 緊急程序

96 break down 故障　inspect [ɪnˋspɛkt] 檢查　overbook [ˌovɚˋbʊk] 超賣（機位、客房等）

新 95 ●●● 高 細節事項相關問題－圖表資料 答案 (A)

題目詢問持票者何時可以登船，因此必須確認題目提供的票券資訊，並注意和題目關鍵字（ticket holder ~ board the vessel）相關的內容。獨白說：「Passengers bound for Hartsville may begin boarding the vessel at 3:10 P.M.」，表示前往 Hartsville 的乘客可以在下午 3 點 10 分開始登船，因此目的地是 Hartsville 的這位持票者可以在下午 3 點 10 分開始登船，因此正確答案是 (A) At 3:10 P.M.。

96 ●●○ 中 細節事項相關問題－理由 答案 (A)

題目詢問延誤的原因，因此要注意獨白中提到題目關鍵字（delay）的前後部分。獨白說：「there will be a delay」，表示會有所延誤，接著說：「A car that was disembarking at the last stop had some engine trouble」，表示發生延誤，是因為要在前一站下船的一輛車的引擎出了一些問題，因此正確答案是 (A) A vehicle broke down。

換句話說

A car ~ had some engine trouble 一輛車的引擎出了一些問題 → A vehicle broke down 車輛故障

97 ●●○ 中 細節事項相關問題－要求 答案 (B)

題目詢問聽者們被要求做什麼，因此要注意聽獨白後半段裡出現要求相關表達的句子。獨白說：「Please remember to review the pamphlet with information about emergency procedures」，要求乘客在登船後仔細查看小冊子，因此正確答案是 (B) Read a document。

換句話說

review the pamphlet 查看小冊子 → Read a document 閱讀文件

98

99

100

Questions 98-100 refer to the following excerpt from a meeting and table.

加拿大式發音

First of all, [98]**thank you for developing the new solar panel so quickly. I didn't expect the prototype to be ready for another two weeks.** And it looks like this panel will be a significant improvement over our existing model. Assuming it functions as expected, we should see a 15 percent increase in power generation. Which brings me to the next stage of the project . . . [99]**The initial test of the panel will be conducted next week.** The forecast calls for rain on Monday, and [99]**Tuesday is a national holiday, so we'll do it on the next clear day.** My assistant—[100]**Charlotte Cruz—confirmed with the maintenance department this morning** that we'll be able to gain access to the building's roof to set up our equipment. Any questions?

新

Monday	Tuesday	Wednesday	[99]Thursday	Friday
(rain)	(sun)	(rain)	(sun)	(sun)

第 98-100 題請參考下列會議節錄及表格。

首先，[98] 謝謝你們這麼快開發出了新的太陽能板。我原本以為這個原型要再兩週才會做好。而且看起來這款板子大幅改良了我們現有的那款。假設它按預期那樣發揮作用，那我們應該會看到發電量有百分之十五的提升。這將能讓我進入這項計畫的下一階段……[99] 這款板子的初步測試會在下週進行。氣象預報說週一會下雨，而 [99] 週二是國定假日，所以我們會在下個晴天做這件事。我的助理——[100]Charlotte Cruz——今天早上和維修部門確認過，我們將可以進到這棟大樓的樓頂架設我們的裝備。有什麼問題嗎？

週一	週二	週三	[99] 週四	週五
(雨)	(晴)	(雨)	(晴)	(晴)

98 Why does the speaker thank the listeners?

(A) A feature was added to a product.
(B) A model received positive reviews.
(C) A report contained accurate data.
(D) A task was finished ahead of schedule.

99 Look at the graphic. When will the test most likely be conducted?

新

(A) On Tuesday
(B) On Wednesday
(C) On Thursday
(D) On Friday

100 What did Charlotte Cruz do this morning?

(A) Confirmed a reservation
(B) Contacted another department
(C) Inspected a site
(D) Set up some equipment

98. 說話者為什麼感謝聽者們？

(A) 產品增加了功能。
(B) 款式得到了正面的評論。
(C) 報告裡有精確的數據了。
(D) 任務早於預定時間完成了。

99. 請看圖表。測試最有可能會在什麼時候進行？

(A) 週二
(B) 週三
(C) 週四
(D) 週五

100. Charlotte Cruz 今天早上做了什麼？

(A) 確認預約
(B) 聯絡另一個部門
(C) 檢查一個地點
(D) 架設一些設備

題目 solar panel 太陽能板　prototype [ˋprotəˏtaɪp] 樣品；原型　significant [sɪgˋnɪfəkənt] 大幅的；顯著的　existing [ɪgˋzɪstɪŋ] 現有的；現行的　power generation 發電　initial [ɪˋnɪʃəl] 最初的　call for 預報未來可能的天氣狀況　national holiday 國定假日　set up 架設

98 accurate [ˋækjərɪt] 精確的　ahead of schedule 早於預定時間或行程

98 細節事項相關問題－理由 答案 (D)

中

題目詢問說話者感謝聽者們的理由，因此必須注意提到題目關鍵字（thank）的前後部分。獨白說：「thank you for developing the new solar panel so quickly. I didn't expect the prototype to be ready for another two weeks.」，表示感謝聽者們這麼快就把新的太陽能板開發出來了，並表示自己原本以為要再兩週才會做好，因此正確答案是 (D) A task was finished ahead of schedule.。

新 99 細節事項相關問題－圖表資料 答案 (C)

高

題目詢問最有可能在什麼時候進行測試，因此要確認題目提供的圖表資訊，並注意提到題目關鍵字（test ~ conducted）的前後部分。獨白說：「The initial test of the panel will be conducted next week.」，表示下週會初步測試太陽能板，接著說：「Tuesday is a national holiday, so we'll do it on the next clear day」，提到因為週二是國定假日，所以會在週二之後的下一個晴天進行測試。透過圖表可知，週二之後的下一個晴天是週四，所以會在週四進行測試，正確答案是 (C) On Thursday。

100 細節事項相關問題－特定細項 答案 (B)

高

題目詢問 Charlotte Cruz 今天早上做了什麼，因此要注意和題目關鍵字（Charlotte Cruz do this morning）相關的內容。獨白說：「Charlotte Cruz ~ confirmed with the maintenance department this morning」，表示 Charlotte Cruz 今天早上和維修部門確認過了，由此可知，Charlotte Cruz 今天早上聯絡了維修部門，因此正確答案是 (B) Contacted another department。

TEST 06

Part 1 原文・翻譯・解析

Part 2 原文・翻譯・解析

Part 3 原文・翻譯・解析 新

Part 4 原文・翻譯・解析 新

MP3 收錄於 TEST 06.mp3。

進行深入練習或複習時，可以一邊多聽幾次收錄各國口音的試題 MP3，一邊搭配解答中的中英對照翻譯和解析，以及單字記憶表和多元口音單字記憶 MP3，達到事半功倍的效果。

1
○○●●
中

美式發音

(A) The man's gripping a railing.
(B) The man's digging dirt out of a vase.
(C) The man's kneeling down.
(D) The man's watering some plants.

(A) 男子正抓著欄杆。
(B) 男子正在把土從花瓶裡挖出來。
(C) 男子正跪著。
(D) 男子正在替一些植物澆水。

單人照片

答案 (C)

照片中的男子正蹲著在處理植物。

(A) [╳] 男子並非抓著欄杆（railing），而是抓著植物，因此是錯誤選項。注意不要聽到 The man's gripping（男子正抓著）就選擇這個選項。
(B) [╳] digging（正在挖）和男子的動作無關，因此是錯誤選項。這裡使用照片中有出現的花瓶（vase）來造成混淆。
(C) [○] 這裡正確描述男子跪著的樣子，因此是正確答案。這裡必須知道 kneel down 是跪著的意思。
(D) [╳] watering（正在澆水）和男子的動作無關，因此是錯誤選項。這裡利用照片中有出現的植物（plants）來造成混淆。

單字 grip [grɪp] 抓 railing [ˋrelɪŋ] 欄杆 dig [dɪg] 挖 vase [ves] 花瓶 kneel down 跪下 water [ˋwɔtɚ] 澆水

2
○○●●
中

加拿大式發音

(A) A woman is hiking up a hill.
(B) They are standing under a branch.
(C) A man is tightening a strap.
(D) They are raising their arms.

(A) 一名女子正在爬上山坡。
(B) 他們正站在樹枝下方。
(C) 一名男子正在把帶子綁緊。
(D) 他們正舉著手臂。

兩人以上的照片

答案 (D)

照片中有一對在山坡上的男女正舉著手臂查看周圍景觀。

(A) [╳] 照片中沒有正在爬上山坡（hiking up a hill）的女子，因此是錯誤選項。這裡使用照片拍攝地點「山坡（hill）」來造成混淆。
(B) [╳] 照片中的男女站在離樹木有一段距離的地方，這裡卻描述成在樹枝下方，因此是錯誤選項。注意不要聽到 They are standing（他們站著）就選擇這個選項。
(C) [╳] 照片中沒有在把帶子綁緊（tightening a strap）的男子，因此是錯誤選項。這裡使用照片中出現的背包帶子（strap）來造成混淆。
(D) [○] 這裡正確描述一對男女舉著手臂的樣子，所以是正確答案。

單字 hike [haɪk] 向上走；健行 hill [hɪl] 山坡，小山 branch [bræntʃ] 樹枝 tighten [ˋtaɪtn̩] 使變緊
strap [stræp] 帶子 raise [rez] 舉起；提高

3
○○○●
低

澳洲式發音

(A) He is loading a trunk with baggage.
(B) He is replacing a tire.
(C) He is opening a car door.
(D) He is unzipping a backpack.

(A) 他正在把行李裝進後車廂裡。
(B) 他正在換輪胎。
(C) 他正在開車門。
(D) 他正在拉開後背包的拉鍊。

單人照片

答案 (A)

照片中有一名男子正在把行李放進後車廂裡。

(A) [○] 這裡正確描述男子正在把行李放進後車廂裡的樣子，所以是正確答案。
(B) [╳] replacing（正在換）和男子的動作無關，因此是錯誤選項。這裡使用照片中有出現的輪胎（tire）來造成混淆。

(C) [╳] opening（正在開）和男子的動作無關，因此是錯誤選項。這裡使用照片中有出現的車門（car door）來造成混淆。

(D) [╳] unzipping（正在拉開拉鍊）和男子的動作無關，因此是錯誤選項。這裡使用照片中有出現的後背包（backpack）來造成混淆。

單字　load [美 lod 英 ləud] 裝載（行李等）　baggage [`bægɪdʒ] 行李　replace [rɪ`ples] 替換
unzip [ʌn`zɪp] 拉開拉鍊

4 高

英式發音

(A) The woman is stocking some jewelry.
(B) Folded garments are stacked in piles.
(C) A salesperson is showing customers an item.
(D) Some apparel is being ironed.

(A) 女子正在補一些珠寶的貨。
(B) 摺好的衣物被堆成一疊一疊的。
(C) 一位銷售人員正在向客人們展示一件商品。
(D) 正在熨平一些衣物。

單人照片　答案 (B)

仔細觀察照片中一名女子站在服飾店裡的樣子以及周遭事物的狀態。

(A) [╳] stocking（正在補貨）和女子的動作無關，因此是錯誤選項。這裡使用和照片拍攝地點相關的 jewelry（珠寶）來造成混淆。

(B) [〇] 這裡正確描述衣物被堆成一疊一疊的模樣，所以是正確答案。這裡必須知道 garment 是「衣物」的意思。

(C) [╳] 照片中只有一個人，但這裡卻以 customers（客人們）來描述，因此是錯誤選項。

(D) [╳] 照片中出現了衣物，但沒有被正在被熨平（is being ironed）的衣物，因此是錯誤選項。注意不要聽到 Some apparel（一些衣物）就選擇這個答案。

單字　stock [美 stɑk 英 stɔk] 把（商品等）填滿　garment [美 `gɑrmənt 英 `gɑ:mənt] 衣物　stack [stæk] 堆放
pile [paɪl] 疊；堆　apparel [ə`pærəl] 衣物

5 中

澳洲式發音

(A) Some seats are occupied in a courtyard.
(B) Chairs are positioned under umbrellas.
(C) Some leaves have fallen onto a patio.
(D) Steps lead into a swimming pool.

(A) 庭院裡的一些座位被占用了。
(B) 椅子被放在傘下了。
(C) 一些葉子掉在了露台上。
(D) 階梯通往游泳池。

事物及風景照片　答案 (B)

這是在戶外拍攝的照片，且可以看到有椅子和陽傘。

(A) [╳] 照片中所有椅子都空著，但這裡卻描述成被占用（occupied）了，因此是錯誤選項。

(B) [〇] 這裡正確描述椅子在傘下的樣子，所以是正確答案。這裡必須知道可以用來表達「陽傘」的 umbrella。

(C) [╳] 照片中的葉子在樹上，但這裡卻描述成掉在露台上（fallen onto a patio），因此是錯誤選項。

(D) [╳] 照片中沒有出現游泳池（swimming pool），因此是錯誤選項。這裡使用照片中有出現的階梯（Steps）來造成混淆。

單字　occupy [美 `ɑkjə͵paɪ 英 `ɔkju͵pai] 占用；占據　courtyard [美 `kort`jɑrd 英 `kɔ:t`jɑ:d] 庭院
position [pə`zɪʃən] 放置（在適當位置）

6 ●●●● 難

美式發音

(A) Carts are being pushed down a path.
(B) Cyclists are biking on a racetrack.
(C) Buildings border a street.
(D) A signboard has been attached to a gate.

(A) 正在延著一條路推手推車。
(B) 自行車手正在賽道上騎自行車。
(C) 建築物在街道兩旁。
(D) 一個招牌被裝在大門上了。

兩人以上的照片 答案 (C)

仔細觀察照片中兩側建築物之間的道路和人，以及周遭事物的狀態。

(A) [╳] 照片中沒有手推車（Carts），因此是錯誤選項。這裡使用照片拍攝地點的「路（path）」來造成混淆。

(B) [╳] 照片中沒有賽道（racetrack），因此是錯誤選項。注意不要聽到 Cyclists are biking（自行車手正在騎自行車）就選擇這個答案。

(C) [○] 這裡正確描述建築物在街道兩旁的樣子，所以是正確答案。這裡必須知道 border 是描述「形成～的邊」的意思。

(D) [╳] 招牌不在大門（gate）上，而是在建築物的牆上，因此是錯誤選項。注意不要聽到 A signboard has been attached to（一個招牌被裝在）就選擇這個答案。

單字 path [pæθ] 道路；小徑 racetrack [ˋrestræk] 賽道 border [ˋbɔrdɚ] 形成～的邊 attach to 裝在～

7 低

英式發音 → 澳洲式發音

Whose eyeglasses are these? (A) A new prescription. (B) Classes are held weekly. (C) They look like Mira's.	這是誰的眼鏡？ (A) 一張新的處方箋。 (B) 課程每週舉行。 (C) 它們看起來是 Mira 的。

Who 疑問句 答案 (C)

這是詢問是誰的眼鏡的 Who（Whose）疑問句。

(A) [╳] 這是使用容易從 eyeglasses（眼鏡）聯想到的視力相關單字 prescription（處方箋）來造成混淆的錯誤選項。

(B) [╳] 題目詢問是誰的眼鏡，這裡卻回答課程每週舉行，毫不相關，因此是錯誤選項。這裡使用發音相似單字 eyeglasses – Classes 來造成混淆。

(C) [○] 這裡回答看起來是 Mira 的，提到眼鏡的主人，因此是正確答案。

單字 prescription [prɪˋskrɪpʃən] 處方箋 weekly [ˋwiklɪ] 每週

8 高

美式發音 → 加拿大式發音

When will Unit 23 be vacated? (A) A lease for a rental space. (B) The tenant moved out yesterday. (C) In that apartment complex.	23 室什麼時候會被清空？ (A) 一個出租空間的租約。 (B) 房客昨天搬出去了。 (C) 在那個公寓社區內。

When 疑問句 答案 (B)

這是詢問 23 室何時會被清空的 When 疑問句。

(A) [╳] 這是利用和 Unit 23（23 室）相關的 rental space（出租空間）來造成混淆的錯誤選項。

(B) [○] 這裡回答房客昨天搬出去了，表示 23 室已經清空，因此是正確答案。

(C) [╳] 題目詢問 23 室何時會被清空，這裡卻回答地點，因此是錯誤選項。這裡利用和 Unit 23（23 室）相關的 apartment complex（公寓社區）來造成混淆。

單字 vacate [ˋveket] 清空 lease [lis] 租約 rental [ˋrɛntl] 供出租的 tenant [ˋtɛnənt] 房客；承租人 complex [ˋkɑmplɛks]（建築物等的）複合體

9 低

加拿大式發音 → 美式發音

Where can I find a restaurant nearby? (A) Washburn Café is at the end of the block. (B) Just for a quick bite to eat. (C) I was able to find my license.	我可以在附近哪裡找到餐廳？ (A) Washburn 咖啡廳在這個街區底端。 (B) 只是要簡單吃點東西。 (C) 我當時可以找到我的執照。

Where 疑問句 答案 (A)

這是詢問可以在附近哪裡找到餐廳的 Where 疑問句。

(A) [○] 這裡回答 Washburn 咖啡廳在這個街區底端，提到餐廳所在位置，因此是正確答案。

(B) [╳] 這是利用和 restaurant（餐廳）相關的 eat（吃）來造成混淆的錯誤選項。

(C) [╳] 題目詢問可以在附近哪裡找到餐廳，這裡卻回答可以找到自己的執照，毫不相關，因此是錯誤選項。這裡利用重複使用題目中出現的 find 來造成混淆。

單字 café [kəˋfe] 咖啡廳；簡餐店 bite [baɪt] 能快速食用的小份量食物 license [ˋlaɪsns] 執照；許可證

10 ○○● 低

澳洲式發音 → 英式發音	
You work at Riley Industries, don't you?	你在 Riley 工業工作，不是嗎？
(A) That's correct. (B) Her shift will be starting soon. (C) No, I don't have those tools.	(A) 沒錯。 (B) 她的班很快要開始了。 (C) 不，我沒有那些工具。

附加問句 答案 (A)

這是確認對方是否在 Riley 工業工作的附加問句。

(A) [○] 這裡回答沒錯，表示自己的確在 Riley 工業工作，因此是正確答案。

(B) [╳] 題目中沒有可以用 Her 代稱的對象，這是利用與 work（工作）相關的 shift（輪班工作時間）來造成混淆的錯誤選項。

(C) [╳] 題目詢問對方是否在 Riley 工業工作，這裡卻回答自己沒有那些工具，毫不相關，因此是錯誤選項。注意不要聽到 No, I don't 就選擇這個選項。

單字　shift [ʃɪft] 輪班工作時間　tool [tul] 工具

11 ○○● 低

澳洲式發音 → 美式發音	
Who told you about this art festival?	是誰和你說這個藝術節的？
(A) One of my coworkers. (B) It runs pretty late. (C) My art teacher is from Spain.	(A) 我的一位同事。 (B) 它進行到很晚。 (C) 我的藝術老師來自西班牙。

Who 疑問句 答案 (A)

這是詢問是誰和對方提及藝術節的 Who 疑問句。

(A) [○] 這裡回答是自己的一位同事，提到提及藝術節的人，因此是正確答案。

(B) [╳] 這是使用可以代稱題目中 art festival（藝術節）的 It，並利用能夠從 festival（節慶）聯想到的時間相關表達 runs pretty late（進行到很晚）來造成混淆的錯誤選項。

(C) [╳] 這是藉由重複使用題目中出現的 art 來造成混淆的錯誤選項。注意不要聽到 My art teacher 就選擇這個選項。

單字　coworker [ˋkoˏwɝkɚ] 同事　run [rʌn] 進行

12 ○●● 中

美式發音 → 加拿大式發音	
Where will actress Marie Lawson be signing autographs?	女演員 Marie Lawson 會在哪裡進行簽名？
(A) She appeared in a television drama. (B) You can write your name here. (C) At the Guthrie Theater.	(A) 她在一齣電視劇裡現身了。 (B) 你可以把你的名字寫在這裡。 (C) 在 Guthrie 劇院。

Where 疑問句 答案 (C)

這是詢問女演員 Marie Lawson 會在哪裡進行簽名的 Where 疑問句。

(A) [╳] 這是利用可以代稱題目中 Marie Lawson 的 She 並以與 actress（女演員）相關的 television drama（電視劇）來造成混淆的錯誤選項。

(B) [╳] 這是利用與 signing（簽名）相關的 write ~ name（寫名字）來造成混淆的錯誤選項。

(C) [○] 這裡回答在 Guthrie 劇院，提到 Marie Lawson 要進行簽名的地點，因此是正確答案。

單字　sign [saɪn] 簽名　autograph [ˋɔtəˏgræf]（名人的）親筆簽名　appear [əˋpɪr] 出現；演出

13 中

🔊 加拿大式發音 → 英式發音

Will you place an event program on each chair?

(A) Dr. Delahanty's sitting in this row.
(B) The event was in Rome.
(C) I can do it in a minute.

你可以在每張椅子上都放上活動節目表嗎？

(A) Delahanty 博士會坐在這一排。
(B) 這個活動當時在羅馬。
(C) 我可以立刻去做。

要求疑問句 答案 (C)

這是要求對方在每張椅子上都放上活動節目表的要求疑問句。這裡必須知道 Will you 是要求的表達。

(A) [╳] 這是利用與 chair（椅子）相關的 sitting（坐下）來造成混淆的錯誤選項。

(B) [╳] 這是藉重複使用題目中出現的 event，並以與題目中 place（放置）的另一字義「地點」相關的 Rome（羅馬）來造成混淆的錯誤選項。

(C) [○] 這裡回答可以立刻去做，表示接受對方提出的要求，因此是正確答案。

單字　program [ˋprogræm] 節目表　row [[美] ro [英] rəu]（一排）座位　in a minute 立刻

14 中

🔊 美式發音 → 澳洲式發音

Has Mr. Harrison forwarded you the memo about holiday bonuses?

(A) No, he never asked about the costumes.
(B) I just received it.
(C) It'll be shut down over the holidays.

Harrison 先生已經把與假期獎金有關的備忘錄轉寄給你了嗎？

(A) 不，他從沒問過關於這些服裝的事情。
(B) 我剛收到了。
(C) 它在假期期間會關閉。

助動詞疑問句 答案 (B)

這是詢問 Harrison 先生是否已經把與假期獎金有關的備忘錄轉寄給對方的助動詞（Have）疑問句。

(A) [╳] 這是利用可代稱題目中 Harrison 先生的 he，並使用和題目中 holiday（假期）的另一字義「節日」相關的 costumes（服裝）來造成混淆的錯誤選項。注意不要聽到 No, he never 就選擇這個選項。

(B) [○] 這裡回答剛收到，表示 Harrison 先生已經把備忘錄轉寄給自己了，因此是正確答案。

(C) [╳] 題目詢問 Harrison 先生是否已經把與假期獎金有關的備忘錄轉寄給對方，這裡卻回答它在假期期間會關閉，毫不相關，因此是錯誤選項。這裡以 holidays 來重複使用題目中出現的 holiday，企圖造成混淆。

單字　forward [ˋfɔrwɚd] 轉寄；傳送　bonus [ˋbonəs] 獎金；額外津貼
costume [[美] ˋkɑstjum [英] ˋkɔstju:m] 服裝；戲服　shut down 關閉

15 中

🔊 加拿大式發音 → 英式發音

The speech was very informative, don't you think so?

(A) I'm giving one at 5 P.M.
(B) When will it most likely start?
(C) The lecturer was quite knowledgeable.

這場演講非常有用，你不覺得嗎？

(A) 我要在下午 5 點進行一場。
(B) 它最有可能會在什麼時候開始？
(C) 講師的知識相當豐富。

附加問句 答案 (C)

這是針對自己覺得這場演講非常有用的意見尋求對方同意的附加問句。

(A) [╳] 這是利用可以代稱題目中 you 的 I 及可代稱 speech（演講）的 one 來造成混淆的錯誤選項。

(B) [╳] 題目詢問對方是否覺得這場演講很有用，這裡卻反問最有可能會在什麼時候開始，提及未來的時間點，因此是錯誤選項。這裡使用可以代稱題目中 speech（演講）的 it 來造成混淆。

(C) [○] 這裡回答講師的知識相當豐富，間接表示這場演講很有用，因此是正確答案。

單字　informative [ɪnˋfɔrmətɪv] 有用的；有教育意義的　lecturer [[美] ˋlɛktʃərɚ [英] ˋlektʃərə] 講者；講師
knowledgeable [[美] ˋnɑlɪdʒəbḷ [英] ˋnɔlidʒəbl] 知識淵博的；有見識的

16 中

🔊 美式發音 → 加拿大式發音 Is Crystal Spa still in business? (A) Some of these business cards. (B) We're here until June 24. (C) You'll have to check its Web site.	Crystal 水療館還在營業嗎？ (A) 這些名片中的一些。 (B) 我們會在這裡到 6 月 24 日。 (C) 你得要去它的網站上確認。

Be 動詞疑問句 答案 (C)

這是詢問 Crystal 水療館是否還在營業的 Be 動詞疑問句。

(A) [╳] 題目詢問 Crystal 水療館是否還在營業，這裡卻回答這些名片中的一些，毫不相關，因此是錯誤選項。這裡藉重複題目中出現的 business 企圖造成混淆。

(B) [╳] 這是使用能夠從 in business（營業中的）聯想到的機構營業相關表達 until June 24（到 6 月 24 日）來造成混淆的錯誤選項。

(C) [○] 這裡回答得要去網站上確認，間接表示自己不知道，因此是正確答案。

單字　business card 名片

17 中

🔊 澳洲式發音 → 英式發音 This budget report seems to have some numerical errors. (A) He works at a pharmaceutical company. (B) Can you point them out to me? (C) I'm having a problem with my phone.	這份預算報告似乎有一些數字上的錯誤。 (A) 他在藥廠工作。 (B) 你可以幫我把它們指出來嗎？ (C) 我的電話有問題。

陳述句 答案 (B)

這是提到預算報告上似乎有一些數字錯誤的陳述句。

(A) [╳] 題目提到預算報告中似乎有一些數字錯誤，這裡卻回答在藥廠工作，毫不相關，因此是錯誤選項。這裡利用發音相似單字 numerical – pharmaceutical 來造成混淆。

(B) [○] 這裡反問是否能幫自己把錯誤指出來，要求提供更多資訊，因此是正確答案。

(C) [╳] 這是利用 having 來重複使用題目中出現的 have，並透過與 errors（錯誤）有關的 problem（問題）來造成混淆的錯誤選項。

單字　budget [`bʌdʒɪt] 預算；預算案　numerical [nju`mɛrɪkḷ] 數值的；數字的　error [[美] `ɛrɚ [英] `erə] 錯誤
pharmaceutical [[美] ˏfɑrmə`sjutɪkḷ [英] ˏfɑ:mə`sju:tikl] 製藥的　point out 指出；提出

18 低

🔊 加拿大式發音 → 美式發音 Haven't you already thrown out the garbage? (A) An updated recycling policy. (B) Park it in the garage. (C) Only half of it.	你不是已經把垃圾丟掉了嗎？ (A) 一項最新的回收政策。 (B) 把它停在車庫裡。 (C) 只有一半。

否定疑問句 答案 (C)

這是詢問是不是已經把垃圾丟掉了的否定疑問句。

(A) [╳] 這是利用和 garbage（垃圾）相關的 recycling（回收）來造成混淆的錯誤選項。

(B) [╳] 題目詢問是不是已經把垃圾丟掉了，這裡卻回答把它停在車庫裡，毫不相關，因此是錯誤選項。這裡利用發音相似單字 garbage – garage 來造成混淆。

(C) [○] 這裡回答只有一半，表示只丟了一半，因此是正確答案。

單字　throw out 丟掉　garbage [`gɑrbɪdʒ] 垃圾　recycling [ˏri`saɪkḷɪŋ] 回收　policy [`pɑləsɪ] 政策
garage [gə`rɑʒ] 車庫

19 高

🔊 澳洲式發音 → 英式發音 The path to Mount Cape is this way. (A) He's heading our way. (B) With my hiking gear. (C) Are you positive about that?	往 Cape 山的路是這個方向。 (A) 他正往我們這裡來。 (B) 用我的健行裝備。 (C) 這你確定嗎？

陳述句 答案 (C)

這是表達往 Cape 山的路是這個方向的客觀事實陳述句。

(A) [╳] 題目中沒有可以用 He 代稱的對象，因此是錯誤選項。這裡利用題目中 way（方向）的另一字義「路」來造成混淆。

(B) [╳] 這是利用和 Mount（山）有關的 hiking gear（健行裝備）來造成混淆的錯誤選項。

(C) [○] 這裡反問對方是否確定這件事，要求提供更多資訊，因此是正確答案。

單字 head [hɛd] 往；朝向 gear [[美] gɪr [英] giə] 裝備 positive [[美] ˋpɑzətɪv [英] ˋpɔzitiv] 確定的

20 中

🔊 英式發音 → 澳洲式發音 What materials have been prepared for the trade fair? (A) Someone else is handling that. (B) The fares are reasonable. (C) Yes, a booth has been reserved.	已經為貿易展準備了什麼資料？ (A) 其他人正在處理這件事。 (B) 票價合理。 (C) 是，已經預約了一個攤位。

What 疑問句 答案 (A)

這是詢問為貿易展準備了什麼資料的 What 疑問句。這裡一定要聽到 What materials 才能順利作答。

(A) [○] 這裡回答其他人正在處理這件事，間接表示自己不清楚，因此是正確答案。

(B) [╳] 題目詢問為貿易展準備了什麼資料，這裡卻回答票價合理，毫不相關，因此是錯誤選項。這裡利用發音相似單字 fair – fares 來造成混淆。

(C) [╳] 這裡以 Yes 來回答疑問詞疑問句，因此是錯誤選項。這裡利用與 fair（展覽）相關的 booth（攤位）來造成混淆。

單字 trade [tred] 貿易 fair [[美] fɛr [英] fɛə] 展覽；公正的；尚可的 handle [ˋhændḷ] 處理
fare [[美] fɛr [英] fɛə]（交通工具的）票價 reasonable [ˋriznəbḷ] 合理的；（價錢）公道的

21 中

🔊 美式發音 → 加拿大式發音 How often are performance reviews held? (A) Hold on. I'll give you a tour. (B) The counters are washed every day. (C) Usually once per year.	績效評估多久進行一次？ (A) 等一下。我會帶你參觀。 (B) 每天都會洗流理台。 (C) 通常每年一次。

How 疑問句 答案 (C)

這是詢問績效評估多久進行一次的 How 疑問句。這裡必須知道 How often 是用來詢問頻率的表達。

(A) [╳] 這裡利用 hold 的另一字義「保持」來重複使用題目中的 held（舉辦），企圖造成混淆。

(B) [╳] 題目詢問績效評估多久進行一次，這裡卻回答每天都會洗流理台，毫不相關，因此是錯誤選項。這裡使用表示頻率的 every day（每天）來造成混淆。

(C) [○] 這裡回答每年一次，提到進行績效評估的頻率，因此是正確答案。

單字 performance review 績效評估 give a tour 帶～參觀 counter [ˋkaʊntɚ] 流理台；櫃台

22
●●●○○ 中

🔊 英式發音 → 美式發音

Which assignment should I prioritize next? (A) Before I get home. (B) I agree. You should. (C) Please edit this press release.	我接下來該優先處理的是哪項工作？ (A) 在我回到家之前。 (B) 我同意。你應該要的。 (C) 請編輯這篇新聞稿。

Which 疑問句 答案 (C)

這是詢問接下來該優先處理哪項工作的 Which 疑問句。這裡一定要聽到 Which assignment 才能順利作答。

(A) [╳] 題目詢問接下來該優先處理哪項工作，這裡卻回答時間點，因此是錯誤選項。這裡利用和 next（接下來）有關的 Before（在～之前）來造成混淆。

(B) [╳] 這裡以和 Yes 意思相同的 I agree 來回答疑問詞疑問句，因此是錯誤選項。這裡利用可以代稱題目中 I 的 you 及重複使用題目中出現的 should 來造成混淆。

(C) [○] 這裡要求編輯新聞稿，提到該優先處理的工作，因此是正確答案。

單字 assignment [əˋsaɪnmənt]（分派的）工作，任務 prioritize [美 praɪˋɔrəˏtaɪz 英 praiˋɔriˏtaiz] 按優先順序處理 edit [ˋɛdɪt] 編輯 press release 新聞稿

23
●●●○○ 中

🔊 加拿大式發音 → 澳洲式發音

The lounge area is located on the ground floor, isn't it? (A) Yes, down the hall from the elevator. (B) No, the floors have been mopped. (C) The lounge is spacious.	休息區位在一樓，不是嗎？ (A) 是的，從電梯出來順著走廊走到底。 (B) 不，地板已經拖過了。 (C) 休息室很寬敞。

附加問句 答案 (A)

這是確認休息區是否在一樓的附加問句。

(A) [○] 這裡以 Yes 來肯定休息區是在一樓，並說從電梯出來順著走廊走到底，提供更多資訊，因此是正確答案。

(B) [╳] 這是使用題目中 floor（樓層）的另一字義 floors（地板）來造成混淆的錯誤選項。注意不要聽到 No 就選擇這個答案。

(C) [╳] 這是藉由重複題目中出現的 lounge 來造成混淆的錯誤選項。

單字 lounge area 休息區 ground floor 一樓 mop [美 mɑp 英 mɔp]（用拖把）拖擦 spacious [ˋspeʃəs] 寬敞的

24
●○○○○ 低

🔊 加拿大式發音 → 英式發音

Why are you returning this monitor? (A) Keep monitoring the situation. (B) I'm interested in something larger. (C) Whenever you get back.	你為什麼要退這個螢幕？ (A) 繼續監控狀況。 (B) 我想要比較大的。 (C) 每當你回來的時候。

Why 疑問句 答案 (B)

這是詢問對方為什麼要把螢幕退回的 Why 疑問句。

(A) [╳] 題目詢問對方為什麼要把螢幕退回，這裡卻回答繼續監控狀況，毫不相關，因此是錯誤選項。這裡以動詞「監控」之意的 monitoring 來重複使用題目中的 monitor（螢幕），企圖造成混淆。

(B) [○] 這裡回答自己想要比較大的，提到退回的原因，因此是正確答案。

(C) [╳] 這是使用和題目中 returning（退回）的另一字義「返回」意義相近的 get back（回來）來造成混淆的錯誤選項。

單字 monitor [美 ˋmɑnətɚ 英 ˋmɔnitə] 螢幕；監控 situation [ˏsɪtʃʊˋeʃən] 狀況 get back 回來

25 ●●○○ 中

澳洲式發音 → 美式發音 When will the company merger be officially announced? (A) I have a question about the new regulation. (B) With another manufacturing firm. (C) At the shareholder meeting.	什麼時候會正式宣布公司合併？ (A) 我對這個新規定有疑問。 (B) 和另一間製造公司。 (C) 在股東會上。

When 疑問句 答案 (C)

這是詢問什麼時候會正式宣布公司合併的 When 疑問句。

(A) [╳] 這是利用和 merger（合併）相關的 new regulation（新規定）來造成混淆的錯誤選項。

(B) [╳] 這是利用能夠從 merger（合併）聯想到的合併對象 another manufacturing firm（另一間製造公司）來造成混淆的錯誤選項。

(C) [○] 這裡回答在股東會上，間接表達了正式宣布公司合併的時間點，因此是正確答案。

單字 merger [[美] mɝdʒɚ [英] mə:dʒə] 合併 officially [əˋfɪʃəlɪ] 正式地 announce [əˋnaʊns] 宣布
regulation [ˏrɛgjəˋleʃən] 法規，規定 manufacturing [ˏmænjəˋfæktʃərɪŋ] 製造的；製造業
shareholder [ˋʃɛrˏholdɚ] 股東

26 ●●○○ 中

英式發音 → 澳洲式發音 Does this cruise ship feature live entertainment? (A) It's an entertaining radio program. (B) This pamphlet should say. (C) Passengers require boarding passes.	這艘郵輪有特別提供現場表演嗎？ (A) 它是一個娛樂性廣播節目。 (B) 這本小冊子上應該有寫。 (C) 乘客需要登機證。

助動詞疑問句 答案 (B)

這是確認郵輪是否有特別提供現場表演的助動詞（Do）疑問句。

(A) [╳] 題目詢問郵輪是否有特別提供現場表演，這裡卻回答它是一個娛樂性廣播節目，毫不相關，因此是錯誤選項。這裡利用發音相似單字 entertainment – entertaining 來造成混淆。

(B) [○] 這裡回答這本小冊子上應該有寫，間接表示自己不知道，因此是正確答案。

(C) [╳] 這是利用和 cruise ship（遊輪）相關的 Passengers（乘客）來造成混淆的錯誤選項。

單字 cruise ship 郵輪 feature [[美] fitʃɚ [英] fi:tʃə] 特別提供～（以做為特色）；特載
entertaining [[美] ˏɛntɚˋtenɪŋ [英] ˏentəˋteiniŋ] 娛樂性的 pamphlet [ˋpæmflɪt] 小冊子
passenger [[美] ˋpæsndʒɚ [英] ˋpæsindʒə] 乘客 boarding pass 登機證

27 ●●●○ 高

加拿大式發音 → 英式發音 The spare bedroom needs to be cleaned out. (A) Have James give you a hand. (B) A double mattress. (C) The kitchen looks clean to me.	那間閒置的臥室需要打掃乾淨。 (A) 請 James 幫你。 (B) 一張雙人床墊。 (C) 我覺得這廚房看起來很乾淨。

陳述句 答案 (A)

這是表達閒置的臥室需要打掃乾淨的客觀事實陳述句。

(A) [○] 這裡回答要對方去請 James 幫忙，提出自己的意見，因此是正確答案。

(B) [╳] 這是利用和 bedroom（臥室）相關的 double mattress（雙人床墊）來造成混淆的錯誤選項。

(C) [╳] 這是利用可以透過 bedroom（臥室）聯想到居家空間功能配置的 kitchen（廚房），並以 clean 的形容詞字義「乾淨的」重複使用題目中的 cleaned（打掃）來造成混淆的錯誤選項。注意不要聽到 looks clean to me 就選擇這個選項。

單字 spare [spɛr] 閒置的；多餘的 clean out 打掃乾淨 give a hand 提供協助
double [ˋdʌbl] 兩人用的；雙倍的

28 ●●●○ 高

澳洲式發音 → 美式發音 Would you rather keep your reward points, or use them for a room upgrade? (A) Well, the banquet was rather long. (B) Both resorts have views of the mountains. (C) I'll save them for my next visit.	你比較想要留著你的回饋點數，還是把它們用來做房間升等？ (A) 這個嘛，這場宴會滿久的。 (B) 兩間渡假村都有山景。 (C) 我留到下次來再用吧。

選擇疑問句 答案 (C)

這是詢問要保留回饋點數還是用來做房間升等的選擇疑問句。

(A) [╳] 題目詢問要保留回饋點數還是用來做房間升等，這裡回答宴會滿久的，毫不相關，因此是錯誤選項。這裡利用重複題目中出現的 rather 來造成混淆。

(B) [╳] 這是利用和 room（房間）相關的 resorts（渡假村）來造成混淆的錯誤選項。

(C) [○] 這裡回答要留到下次來再用，表示要保留回饋點數，因此是正確答案。

單字 reward [美 rɪ`wɔrd 英 ri`wɔ:d] 回饋；獎勵 banquet [`bæŋkwɪt] 宴會 save [sev] 保留；儲蓄

29 ●●●○ 高

加拿大式發音 → 英式發音 I can put in some overtime this evening. (A) Go ahead and set them here. (B) Patrick offered to make some desserts. (C) Let's discuss the matter later this afternoon.	我今晚可以加一下班。 (A) 去吧，然後把它們架在這裡。 (B) Patrick 願意去做些甜點。 (C) 我們今天下午晚點來討論這件事。

陳述句 答案 (C)

這是說明自己今晚可以加班的提議陳述句。

(A) [╳] 這是利用與題目中 put in（加進）的另一字義「安裝」相關的 set（架設）來造成混淆的錯誤選項。

(B) [╳] 題目說自己今晚可以加一下班，這裡卻回答 Patrick 願意去做些甜點，毫不相關，因此是錯誤選項。注意不要聽到 Patrick offered to 就選擇這個選項。

(C) [○] 這裡回答今天下午晚點來討論這件事，間接表示接受這項提議，因此是正確答案。

單字 put in 加進（工作等）；安裝 overtime [`ovɚ͵taɪm] 加班（時間） matter [美 `mætɚ 英 `mætə] 事項

30 ●●●● 難

英式發音 → 加拿大式發音 Would you like some milk in your tea as well? (A) I ordered coffee. (B) We provide tea and snacks to clients. (C) I don't like the new menus.	你的茶裡也要加點牛奶嗎？ (A) 我點了咖啡。 (B) 我們會提供茶和點心給客戶。 (C) 我不喜歡新的菜單。

提供疑問句 答案 (A)

這是詢問對方是否也要在茶裡加點牛奶的提供疑問句。這裡必須知道 Would you like 是提供的表達。

(A) [○] 這裡回答自己點了咖啡，間接表示拒絕，因此是正確答案。

(B) [╳] 題目詢問是否也要在茶裡加點牛奶，這裡卻回答會提供茶和點心給客戶，毫不相關，因此是錯誤選項。這裡透過重複使用題目中出現的 tea 來造成混淆。

(C) [╳] 這是利用能夠從 tea（茶）聯想到、且和食物有關的 menus（菜單）來造成混淆的錯誤選項。注意不要聽到 I don't like 就選擇這個選項。

單字 as well 也 client [`klaɪənt] 客戶

31 ○●●● 高		
	🔊 美式發音 → 澳洲式發音 How will we transport the furniture to the new office? (A) Let's meet near the exit. (B) They tested out the same chairs. (C) It comes fully furnished.	我們要怎樣把家具運到新的辦公室？ (A) 我們在出口附近碰面吧。 (B) 他們測試過一樣的椅子了。 (C) 那裡附有完備的家具。

How 疑問句 答案 (C)

這是詢問要怎樣把家具運到新辦公室的 How 疑問句。

(A) [╳] 題目詢問要怎樣把家具運到新的辦公室，這裡卻回答在出口附近碰面，毫不相關，因此是錯誤選項。

(B) [╳] 這是利用和 furniture（家具）相關的 chairs（椅子）來造成混淆的錯誤選項。

(C) [○] 這裡回答那裡附有完備的家具，間接表示不需要運家具到新的辦公室，因此是正確答案。

單字 transport [`træns͵pɔrt] 運送 exit [美] `ɛksɪt [英] `eksit] 出口 test out 檢驗，測試 come [kʌm] 有供應；存在 furnished [[美] `fɝnɪʃt [英] `fə:niʃt] 備有家具的

32
33
34

Questions 32-34 refer to the following conversation.

美式發音 → 澳洲式發音

W: By the way, [32]**an employee from the state sanitation department will be coming here to our electronics production facility** tomorrow. He will inspect the waste management equipment. It'd be nice if you could give me a hand making sure there aren't any known issues with the machinery.
M: Yeah, but [33]**I'm busy at the moment with repairing our conveyor belt, as you told me to do this morning.**
W: Just let me know as soon as you're free. I want to take care of everything today since [34]**we won't have much time to get ready tomorrow morning.**

第 32-34 題請參考下列對話。

女：對了，明天 [32] 會有一個州立衛生部的員工來我們電子產品生產設施這裡。他會檢查廢棄物處理設備。如果你能幫我確定那台裝置沒有任何已知問題，那就太好了。
男：好啊，但 [33] 我現在忙著修我們的輸送帶，就妳今天早上跟我說要修的。
女：等你一有空就跟我說。我想要在今天把所有事情都處理完，因為 [34] 我們明天早上不會有太多時間來做好準備。

32 Where most likely is the conversation taking place?
(A) At a government office
(B) At a manufacturing plant
(C) At an accommodation facility
(D) At a convention center

32. 這段對話最有可能發生在哪裡？
(A) 政府辦公室
(B) 製造工廠
(C) 住宿設施
(D) 會議中心

33 According to the man, what did the speakers discuss this morning?
(A) Schedule changes
(B) Machinery prices
(C) Building renovations
(D) Malfunctioning equipment

33. 根據男子所說，說話者們今天早上討論了什麼？
(A) 行程的更動
(B) 裝置的價格
(C) 建築物的整修
(D) 故障的設備

34 What problem does the woman mention?
(A) There is not much preparation time.
(B) An evaluation went poorly.
(C) There are not enough employees.
(D) A regulation has been altered.

34. 女子提到什麼問題？
(A) 準備時間不多。
(B) 評估進行得很糟。
(C) 員工不足。
(D) 規定被改動了。

題目 sanitation [ˌsænəˋteʃən] 衛生環境 inspect [ɪnˋspɛkt] 檢查 waste [west] 廢棄物 management [ˋmænɪdʒmənt] 處理；管理 at the moment 現在
32 government office 政府辦公室 accommodation [əˌkɑməˋdeʃən] 住宿
33 malfunction [mælˋfʌŋʃən] 故障
34 evaluation [ɪˌvæljʊˋeʃən] 評估 poorly [ˋpʊrlɪ] 糟糕地 alter [ˋɔltɚ] 改變；修改

32 低 **整體對話相關問題－地點** 答案 (B)

題目詢問對話的發生地點，因此必須注意聽和地點相關的表達。女子說：「an employee ~ will be coming here to our electronics production facility」，表示一名員工會來自己的電子產品生產設施這裡，由此可知對話的發生地點在工廠，因此正確答案是 (B) At a manufacturing plant。

換句話說

production facility 生產設施 → manufacturing plant 製造工廠

33 中 **細節事項相關問題－特定細項** 答案 (D)

題目詢問男子說今天早上討論了什麼，因此必須確認男子話中提及題目關鍵字（this morning）的前後部分。男子說：「I'm busy at the moment with repairing our conveyor belt, as you told me to do this morning」，表示女子今天早上跟男子說過要修輸送帶，所以男子現在正忙著修它，由此可知，說話者們早上在談論的是故障的設備，因此正確答案是 (D) Malfunctioning equipment。

34 中 **細節事項相關問題－問題點** 答案 (A)

題目詢問女子提到什麼問題，因此要注意聽女子話中出現負面表達之後的內容。女子說：「we won't have much time to get ready tomorrow morning」，表示明天早上不會有太多時間來做好準備，因此正確答案是 (A) There is not much preparation time.。

35 36 37 新

Questions 35-37 refer to the following conversation.

加拿大式發音 → 英式發音

M: Hey, Soojin. [35]**I'm about to head to Forest Café to buy coffee for our team. Would you like something, too?**
W: Yes. I love the seasonal espresso drink sold there . . . the pumpkin latte.
M: I think that one was discontinued. [36]**It was being offered in the fall only. The café is advertising winter drinks now.**
W: Too bad. Well, I'll just have a cappuccino, then.
M: All right. And [37]**you recently mentioned you're on a diet, so should I ask if they can use low-fat milk instead of regular milk?**
W: That'd be great. Thanks so much.

35 What does the man offer to do?
(A) Give the woman a menu
(B) Purchase a beverage
(C) Make a pot of coffee
(D) Contact a café manager

36 新 What does the man mean when he says, "I think that one was discontinued"?
(A) A seasonal promotion was changed.
(B) A flavor was unsuccessful.
(C) Some merchandise will be refunded.
(D) Some new items have been reordered.

37 Why must a special request be made?
(A) The woman is in a rush.
(B) The woman is on a diet.
(C) The man has a coupon.
(D) The man has an allergy.

第 35-37 題請參考下列對話。

男：嘿，Soojin。[35] 我要去 Forest 咖啡廳幫我們組買咖啡。妳也想要來點什麼嗎？
女：要。我熱愛那裡賣的季節限定濃縮咖啡飲品……那個南瓜拿鐵。
男：我想那個沒在賣了。[36] 它只在秋天有賣而已。那間咖啡廳現在在廣告冬季飲品了。
女：太可惜了。嗯，那我就來杯卡布奇諾好了。
男：好。還有 [37] 妳最近有說過妳在飲食控制，那我要不要問問看他們可不可以用低脂鮮奶取代一般鮮奶？
女：能的話就太好了。太感謝了。

35. 男子願意做什麼？
(A) 給女子菜單
(B) 買飲料
(C) 沖一壺咖啡
(D) 聯絡咖啡廳經理

36. 當男子說：「我想那個沒在賣了」，意思是什麼？
(A) 一個季節性宣傳活動已經改了。
(B) 一款口味不成功。
(C) 會退一些商品的錢。
(D) 已再次訂購一些新品了。

37. 為什麼必須提出特殊要求？
(A) 女子很急。
(B) 女子在飲食控制。
(C) 男子有優惠券。
(D) 男子有過敏。

題目 be about to 正要做　seasonal [`siznəl] 季節限定的；季節性的　discontinue [ˏdɪskən`tɪnju] 中斷　advertise [`ædvɚˏtaɪz] 廣告；宣傳　low-fat 低脂的　regular [`rɛgjəlɚ] 一般的；正常的
35 purchase [`pɝtʃəs] 購買　beverage [`bɛvərɪdʒ] 飲料　pot [pɑt] 壺；一壺的量
36 promotion [prə`moʃən] 促銷；宣傳活動　flavor [`flevɚ] 口味　merchandise [`mɝtʃənˏdaɪz] 商品，貨物　reorder [ri`ɔrdɚ] 再次訂購
37 in a rush 匆忙地；緊急地　allergy [`ælɚdʒɪ] 過敏

35 細節事項相關問題－提議　中　答案 (B)

題目詢問男子願意做什麼，因此要注意聽男子話中提到要為女子做事的內容。男子對女子說：「I'm about to head to ~ Café to buy coffee for our team. Would you like something, too?」，表示自己正準備去咖啡店買咖啡，並詢問女子要不要買點什麼，因此正確答案是 (B) Purchase a beverage。

新 **36** 細節事項相關問題－掌握意圖　高　答案 (A)

題目詢問男子的說話意圖，因此要注意題目引用句（I think that one was discontinued）的前後部分。男子說：「It[pumpkin latte] was being offered in the fall only. The café is advertising winter drinks now.」，表示南瓜拿鐵只在秋天有賣，且該咖啡店現在在廣告冬天飲品了，由此可知，季節性宣傳活動已經改了，因此正確答案是 (A) A seasonal promotion was changed.。

37 細節事項相關問題－理由　低　答案 (B)

題目詢問提出特別要求的理由，因此要注意和題目關鍵字（special request）相關的內容。男子對女子說：「you recently mentioned you're on a diet, so should I ask if they can use low-fat milk instead of regular milk?」，男子先表示最近有聽女子說過她在飲食控制，接著詢問要不要自己替她問問看咖啡廳能否用低脂鮮奶取代一般鮮奶，因此正確答案是 (B) The woman is on a diet.。

Questions 38-40 refer to the following conversation.

澳洲式發音 → 美式發音

M: [38]**Our department is struggling to finalize the necessary financial reports** for the upcoming shareholders' meeting. I'm sorry to ask on short notice, but [38]**can you work on them over the weekend?**

W: [39]**I'll be out of town from Saturday through next Tuesday. I'm visiting Charleston for my sister's birthday party.** You approved my leave last month.

M: Oh, that's right. We've been so busy lately that I completely forgot. In that case, I'll have to ask someone else from your team to do it.

W: Try checking with Catherine Dawkins. Just last week, [40]**she said that she'd be open to working more overtime**, as she's saving money to go to Europe.

38 What does the man ask the woman to do?

(A) Scan some documents
(B) Postpone a departure date
(C) Come up with an agenda
(D) Complete some reports

39 Why is the woman going out of town?

(A) To attend a shareholders' meeting
(B) To sign a sales contract
(C) To speak at a team seminar
(D) To participate in a celebration

40 According to the woman, what is Catherine Dawkins willing to do?

(A) Switch divisions
(B) Work additional hours
(C) Lead an accounting team
(D) Increase a budget

第 38-40 題請參考下列對話。

男：[38] 我們部門正在努力完成在即將到來的股東會上所必需的財務報告。我很抱歉這麼臨時問妳，不過 [38] 妳這週末可以處理它們嗎？

女：[39] 我從週六到下週二都不會在鎮上。我要去 Charleston 參加我妹妹的生日派對。你上個月准我的假了。

男：噢，對耶。我們最近忙到讓我完全忘了這件事。這樣的話，我得去請妳們團隊裡的其他人來做這件事了。

女：試試看去問 Catherine Dawkins 吧。她上週才 [40] 說她願意加更多班，因為她在存錢要去歐洲。

38. 男子要求女子做什麼？

(A) 掃描一些文件
(B) 延後出發日期
(C) 制定議程
(D) 完成一些報告

39. 女子為何會不在鎮上？

(A) 為了出席股東會
(B) 為了簽署銷售合約
(C) 為了在團隊研討會上發言
(D) 為了參加慶祝活動

40. 根據女子所說，Catherine Dawkins 願意做什麼？

(A) 調換部門
(B) 加班
(C) 領導會計團隊
(D) 增加預算

題目 struggle [ˋstrʌgl] 奮鬥；努力　upcoming [ˋʌpˏkʌmɪŋ] 即將到來的　on short notice 臨時　leave [liv] 休假　check with 詢問～

38 scan [skæn] 掃描　come up with 制定～；想出～　agenda [əˋdʒɛndə] 議程；代辦事項　complete [kəmˋplit] 完成；結束

40 switch [swɪtʃ] 調換；轉移

38 細節事項相關問題－要求　答案 (D)

中

題目詢問男子要求女子做什麼，因此必須注意聽男子話中出現要求表達之後的內容。男子對女子說：「Our department is struggling to finalize the necessary financial reports」，表示自己部門正在努力完成財務報告，接著說：「can you work on them over the weekend?」，要求女子在週末做這些報告，因此正確答案是 (D) Complete some reports。

39 細節事項相關問題－理由　答案 (D)

中

題目詢問女子不在鎮上的原因，因此要注意提到題目關鍵字（out of town）的前後部分。女子說：「I'll be out of town ~. I'm visiting Charleston for my sister's birthday party.」，表示自己要出鎮去參加妹妹的生日派對，因此正確答案是 (D) To participate in a celebration。

40 細節事項相關問題－特定細項　答案 (B)

低

題目詢問女子說 Catherine Dawkins 願意做什麼，因此必須確認女子話中提到題目關鍵字（Catherine Dawkins）的前後部分。女子說：「she[Catherine Dawkins] said that she'd be open to working more overtime」，表示 Catherine Dawkins 說她願意加更多班，因此正確答案是 (B) Work additional hours。

41 42 43

Questions 41-43 refer to the following conversation.

加拿大式發音 → 英式發音

M: Hi. This is Larry Bates. [41]**I ordered a textbook from your store two weeks ago**, but it still hasn't arrived at my apartment. My order confirmation number is 42345.

W: According to the tracking information, your book was delivered almost three days ago. However, the courier must not have brought it directly to your door, since [42]**you didn't include a specific apartment number with the shipping information**.

M: Hmm . . . But I never saw the item by my complex's main door either.

W: [43]**Why don't you talk to your building manager** to find out whether the package is being held for you? Otherwise, you can get in touch with the courier service, Package Express. They may be able to help you.

第 41-43 題請參考下列對話。

男：嗨。我是 Larry Bates。[41] 我兩個星期前從你們店裡訂了一本課本，但到現在都沒送到我公寓裡。我的訂單確認編號是 42345。

女：根據追蹤資訊，你的書在快三天前送到了。不過，快遞人員一定是沒有把它直接送到你家，因為 [42] 你沒有在寄件資訊裡加上明確的公寓編號。

男：嗯……但我在我們社區大門旁也從沒看到過它。

女：[43] 你要不要問問你們的大樓管理員，看看是不是有幫你把這件包裹收起來了？除此之外，你可以聯絡快遞公司 Package Express。他們也許能協助你。

41 What did the man do two weeks ago?

(A) Returned a book to a store
(B) Sent a package overseas
(C) Bought an item
(D) Enrolled in a course

41. 男子兩星期前做了什麼？

(A) 將一本書退回了店裡
(B) 寄了一個包裹到海外
(C) 買了一件商品
(D) 報名了一個課程

42 What does the woman say the man failed to provide?

(A) A book title
(B) A recipient name
(C) An e-mail address
(D) A unit number

42. 女子說男子沒有提供什麼？

(A) 書名
(B) 收受人姓名
(C) 電子郵件地址
(D) 公寓編號

43 What does the woman recommend?

(A) Talking to a property manager
(B) Using another courier service
(C) Correcting some billing information
(D) Placing an order through a Web site

43. 女子建議什麼？

(A) 和物業管理人談談
(B) 使用另一家快遞公司
(C) 更正一些請款資訊
(D) 透過網站下訂

題目 track [træk] 追蹤　courier [(美) `kʊrɪɚ (英) `kuriə] 快遞人員；信使　specific [(美) spɪ`sɪfɪk (英) spi`sifik] 具體的；明確的　package [`pækɪdʒ] 包裹

41 overseas [`ovɚ`siz] 向海外　enroll [ɪn`rol] 報名；註冊

42 recipient [rɪ`sɪpɪənt] 收受人

43 property [`prɑpɚtɪ] 不動產；物業　correct [kə`rɛkt] 更正　billing [`bɪlɪŋ] 請款；開具發票　place an order 下訂

41 細節事項相關問題－特定細項　答案 (C)

低

題目詢問男子在兩星期前做了什麼，因此要注意提到題目關鍵字（two weeks ago）的前後部分。男子說：「I ordered a textbook ~ two weeks ago」，表示在兩星期前買了一本課本，因此正確答案是 (C) Bought an item。

42 細節事項相關問題－特定細項　答案 (D)

中

題目詢問女子說男子沒有提供什麼，因此要注意和題目關鍵字（man failed to provide）相關的內容。女子對男子說：「you didn't include a specific apartment number with the shipping information」，表示男子沒有在寄件資訊裡加上明確的公寓編號，因此正確答案是 (D) A unit number。

43 細節事項相關問題－提議　答案 (A)

低

題目詢問女子建議什麼，因此必須注意聽女子話中出現的提議相關表達。女子對男子說：「Why don't you talk to your building manager」，提議讓男子去問問大樓管理員，因此正確答案是 (A) Talking to a property manager。

44 45 46

Questions 44-46 refer to the following conversation.

美式發音 → 澳洲式發音

W: Hello. I have a mobile service plan through your organization, and [44]**I want to buy a new cell phone. I'd like to know if I qualify for any discounts.**

M: This month, customers can sell their phones to the store and put that money towards an upgrade. [45]**The deal applies to any newly released devices, including the Verso X3** and the Blade 4S. However, should you take advantage of this offer, [46]**the amount that you can receive depends on the condition of the phone you sell us**.

W: What a wonderful deal! Oh, and I was considering buying the Verso X3 anyway. [46]**Here's my device. I'm curious to know how much I can get for it.**

44 What is the conversation mainly about?

(A) A cell phone plan
(B) A new product model
(C) A special promotional offer
(D) A business's warranty policy

45 What is mentioned about the Verso X3?

(A) It was recently released.
(B) It was recalled by the manufacturer.
(C) It can be ordered online.
(D) It can be upgraded for free.

46 What will most likely happen next?

(A) The man will give a demonstration.
(B) The man will explain some options.
(C) The woman's profile will be updated.
(D) The woman's device will be examined.

第 44-46 題請參考下列對話。

女：哈囉。我有你們公司的手機門號，然後 [44] 我想要買一支新手機。我想知道我有沒有什麼折扣優惠可以用。

男：這個月客人可以把他們的手機賣給我們店，再拿這筆錢來升級。[45] 這個方案適用於所有新推出的手機，包括 Verso X3 及 Blade 4S。不過，妳用這個方案的話，[46] 能拿到多少錢要看妳賣給我們的手機狀態怎麼樣。

女：這方案真棒！噢，而且我本來就在考慮要買 Verso X3 了。[46] 這是我的手機，我很好奇我可以用它換到多少錢。

44. 這段對話主要與什麼有關？

(A) 手機方案
(B) 新產品型號
(C) 特殊促銷優惠
(D) 公司的保固政策

45. 關於 Verso X3，提到了什麼？

(A) 它剛推出。
(B) 它被製造商召回了。
(C) 它可以在網路上訂購。
(D) 它可以免費升級。

46. 接下來最有可能會發生什麼？

(A) 男子會進行示範。
(B) 男子會說明一些選項。
(C) 女子的簡介會被更新
(D) 女子的裝置會被檢查。

題目 qualify [`kwɑlə͵faɪ] 符合資格　put towards 用（一筆錢）補貼購買～　deal [dil] 交易　apply to 適用於～　release [rɪ`lis] 推出　take advantage of 利用～　depend on 取決於～　condition [kən`dɪʃən] 狀態

44 promotional [prə`moʃənl] 促銷的　warranty [`wɔrəntɪ] 保固；保證書

45 recall [rɪ`kɔl] 召回

46 demonstration [͵dɛmən`streʃən] 示範　option [`ɑpʃən] 選項　profile [`profaɪl] 檔案；人物簡介　examine [ɪg`zæmɪn] 檢查

44 中 **整體對話相關問題－主題** 答案 (C)

題目詢問對話主題，因此要注意對話的開頭，並掌握整體對話脈絡。女子說：「I want to buy a new cell phone. I'd like to know if I qualify for any discounts.」，表示自己想買一支手機，且想知道有什麼折扣可以用，男子則接著說明買手機可用的特別方案內容，因此正確答案是 (C) A special promotional offer。

45 高 **細節事項相關問題－提及** 答案 (A)

題目詢問提到什麼與 Verso X3 有關的事，因此要注意提到題目關鍵字（Verso X3）的前後部分。男子說：「The deal applies to any newly released devices, including the Verso X3」，表示這個方案適用於包含 Verso X3 在內的新機，因此正確答案是 (A) It was recently released.。

46 高 **細節事項相關問題－接下來要做的事** 答案 (D)

題目詢問接下來最有可能會發生什麼，因此要注意對話的最後部分。男子對女子說：「the amount that you can receive depends on the condition of the phone you sell us」，表示女子能拿到多少錢要看她的手機狀態怎樣，接著女子說：「Here's my device. I'm curious to know how much I can get for it.」，可以知道她拿出了自己的手機，且很好奇可以用手機換到多少錢，由此可知，女子為了知道自己能換到多少錢，會把手機交給男子檢查，因此正確答案是 (D) The woman's device will be examined.。

Questions 47-49 refer to the following conversation.

加拿大式發音 → 英式發音

M: [47]**You're in charge of organizing tomorrow's architecture team gathering, correct?**

W: [47]**Yeah.** I've finalized all the activities that are gonna take place. Those details will be included in the reminder e-mail that I'll be sending to attendees before lunch. But why do you ask? Does anything need to be changed?

M: Yes, actually. [48]**Helen's presentation on modern design is going to be longer than originally expected, so please allow her an extra 15 minutes.** Also, Oliver will be unable to attend. He must give a consultation to an important client instead. So, [49]**we should remove him from the agenda entirely.**

W: No problem. [49]**I'll take care of those updates right now.**

47 What is the woman in charge of?

(A) Hiring new architects
(B) Correcting an e-mail error
(C) Planning a meeting
(D) Gathering some files

48 Why will more time be allowed for Helen?

(A) She lives far away from a building.
(B) She has not finished a design.
(C) She will be showing a visitor around.
(D) She needs more time for a presentation.

49 What will the woman most likely do next?

(A) Photocopy some printouts
(B) Revise an agenda
(C) Reserve a conference room
(D) Take a lunch break

第 47-49 題請參考下列對話。

男：[47] 妳負責籌辦明天的建築團隊聚會，對嗎？

女：[47] 是啊。我已經確定所有要進行的活動了。細節會寫在我午餐前會寄給參加者的提醒電子郵件裡。但你為什麼要問？有什麼必須要改的嗎？

男：事實上是的。[48]Helen 的現代設計簡報會比原本預期的要長，所以請多給她 15 分鐘。還有，Oliver 不能參加了。他必須改去為一位重要的客戶做諮詢。所以 [49] 我們應該要把他從議程裡整個去掉。

女：沒問題。[49] 我現在立刻來處理這些更新事項。

47. 女子負責什麼？

(A) 招聘新的建築師
(B) 修正一個電子郵件的錯誤
(C) 規劃一場集會
(D) 收集一些檔案

48. 為什麼會給 Helen 更多時間？

(A) 她住得離一棟大樓很遠。
(B) 她還沒有完成一項設計。
(C) 她會帶一個來訪者參觀。
(D) 她需要更多時間做簡報。

49. 女子接下來最有可能會做什麼？

(A) 影印一些資料文件
(B) 修訂一份議程
(C) 預約一個會議室
(D) 去午休

題目 in charge of 負責～　organize [`ɔrgə͵naɪz] 籌辦　architecture [`ɑrkə͵tɛktʃɚ] 建築
finalize [`faɪnḷ͵aɪz] 最終確定；完成　attendee [ə`tɛndi] 參加者　modern [`mɑdɚn] 現代的　allow [ə`laʊ] 給予；容許
consultation [͵kɑnsəl`teʃən] 諮詢；商議　agenda [ə`dʒɛndə] 議程
47 architect [`ɑrkə͵tɛkt] 建築師　gather [`gæðɚ] 收集　**48** show around 參觀
49 photocopy [`fotə͵kɑpɪ] 影印　printout [`prɪnt͵aʊt]（印出來的）資料文件　revise [rɪ`vaɪz] 修正
conference room 會議室

47 中 **細節事項相關問題－特定細項** 答案 (C)

題目詢問女子負責什麼，因此要注意提到題目關鍵字（in charge of）的前後部分。男子對女子說：「You're in charge of organizing tomorrow's architecture team gathering, correct?」，詢問女子是不是負責籌辦明天的建築團隊聚會，女子說：「Yeah.」，表示是她沒錯，因此正確答案是 (C) Planning a meeting。

換句話說

organizing ~ gathering 籌辦聚會 → Planning a meeting 規劃集會

48 中 **細節事項相關問題－理由** 答案 (D)

題目詢問給 Helen 更多時間的原因，因此要注意提到題目關鍵字（Helen）的前後部分。男子說：「Helen's presentation ~ is going to be longer than originally expected, so please allow her an extra 15 minutes.」，表示 Helen 的簡報時間會比原本預期的更長，所以要求女子多給她 15 分鐘，因此正確答案是 (D) She needs more time for a presentation.。

49 高 **細節事項相關問題－接下來要做的事** 答案 (B)

題目詢問女子接下來最有可能會做什麼，因此要注意對話的最後部分。男子說：「we should remove him[Oliver] from the agenda entirely」，表示應該將 Oliver 從議程裡整個去掉，接著女子說：「I'll take care of those updates right now.」，表示會立刻處理，因此正確答案是 (B) Revise an agenda。

50
51
52

Questions 50-52 refer to the following conversation.

加拿大式發音 → 美式發音

M: Hi, Sophia. [50]**Do you know what the procedure for securing vacation time at our company is?**
W: It was changed not too long ago . . . Let me check my manual. Are you hoping to take some days off?
M: Yes—February 21 to 25.
W: OK. Well, the handbook says [50]**you have to fill in a form on the human resources Web page**. Two days later, you'll receive a notification indicating whether your supervisor has approved the request.
M: Where exactly is the form posted on the page?
W: Just click on the Scheduling tab, and you'll see it. However, [51]**several employees have already applied for time off toward the end of February, so it might not be approved.** [52]**You should talk to your manager** about this.
M: OK, [52]**I'll do that now**. Thanks for your help.

第 50-52 題請參考下列對話。

男：嗨，Sophia。[50] 妳知道在我們公司要拿到休假的程序是什麼嗎？
女：那個不久前改過了……讓我確認一下我的手冊。你是想要請幾天假嗎？
男：沒錯——2 月 21 到 25 日。
女：好。嗯，這本手冊上說 [50] 你得到人資的網頁上填寫一張表單。兩天後你會收到通知說你主管有沒有准假。
男：那個表單究竟是放在網頁的哪裡啊？
女：你只要點排程這個標籤就會看到了。不過，[51] 有幾位員工已經申請要在二月底休假了，所以你的可能不會被批准。[52] 你應該和你經理談談這件事。
男：好，[52] 我現在就去。謝謝妳的幫忙。

50 How can employees secure time off?
(A) By completing the necessary form
(B) By calling the human resources department
(C) By sending an e-mail to a director
(D) By placing paperwork in a mailbox

50. 員工要如何拿到休假？
(A) 完成必要表單
(B) 致電人資部
(C) 寄一封電子郵件給主任
(D) 將文件放進信箱裡

51 According to the woman, why might the man's request be denied?
(A) A colleague is not in the office.
(B) Some teams are understaffed.
(C) A manager was not notified in advance.
(D) Other people have submitted applications.

51. 根據女子所說，為什麼男子的申請可能會被拒絕？
(A) 一位同事不在辦公室。
(B) 一些團隊人手不足。
(C) 沒有事先通知一位經理。
(D) 其他人已經提交了申請。

52 What will the man probably do next?
(A) Review some instructions
(B) Share notes with a coworker
(C) Speak with a supervisor
(D) Change some travel arrangements

52. 男子接下來可能會做什麼？
(A) 檢視一些指示
(B) 與一位同事共用筆記
(C) 和一位主管談談
(D) 更改一些旅行安排

題目 procedure [prə`sidʒɚ] 程序　secure [sɪ`kjʊr] 獲得　fill in 填寫～　apply for 申請～　time off 休假
51 understaffed [ˌʌndɚ`stæft] 人手不足的
52 instruction [ɪn`strʌkʃən] 指示　arrangement [ə`rendʒmənt] 安排；準備工作

50 細節事項相關問題－方法　　答案 (A)
中
題目詢問員工要怎麼拿到休假，因此要注意和題目關鍵字（secure time off）相關的內容。男子說：「Do you know what the procedure for securing vacation time at our company is?」，表示自己想要知道公司的請假程序，女子說：「you have to fill in a form on the human resources Web page」，表示男子必須到人資的網頁上填寫表單，因此正確答案是 (A) By completing the necessary form。

51 細節事項相關問題－理由　　答案 (D)
中
題目詢問女子說男子的申請可能會被拒絕的原因，因此必須確認女子話中和題目關鍵字（man's request ~ denied）相關的內容。女子對男子說：「several employees have already applied for time off ~, so it[request] might not be approved」，表示因為有幾位員工已提出休假申請，所以男子的申請可能不會獲准，因此正確答案是 (D) Other people have submitted applications.。

52 細節事項相關問題－接下來要做的事　　答案 (C)
高
題目詢問男子接下來可能會做什麼，因此必須注意對話的最後部分。女子對男子說：「You should talk to your manager」，表示男子應該去和經理談談，接著男子說：「I'll do that now」，表示自己現在就去，因此正確答案是 (C) Speak with a supervisor。

新

53
54
55

Questions 53-55 refer to the following conversation with three speakers.

澳洲式發音 → 美式發音 → 英式發音

M: Excuse me. [53]**I'm hoping to learn more about your Chinese language classes**, since many of my clients are based in China.

W1: Our course of business Chinese should be perfect for you. Oh, the instructor is coming down the hallway now. [54]**Jenny, can you provide some details about your class?**

W2: Sure. We focus on expressions used in corporate settings. We meet twice weekly for two months. And [54]**the next course starts on June 2**—this Friday.

M: Hmm . . . Two months? That'll be difficult for me, as I'm traveling to Hong Kong in July.

W2: In that case, there's another one starting in August.

W1: Yes, and [55]**you'll also be eligible for an advance registration discount if you enroll at our institute before July 10**.

M: Great. [55]**I'll sign up for it now.**

53 What are the speakers mainly discussing?

(A) International travel plans
(B) Foreign language lessons
(C) An overseas branch opening
(D) An educational publication

54 What information does Jenny provide?

(A) The costs of enrollment
(B) The number of students
(C) The start date of a course
(D) The material list for a class

55 What is the man eligible to receive?

(A) A special fee reduction
(B) A free online lecture
(C) A membership upgrade
(D) A complimentary handout

第 53-55 題請參考下列三人對話。

男： 不好意思。[53] 我想要更了解你們的中文課程，因為我有很多客戶的總部都設在中國。

女 1： 我們的商業中文課程應該非常適合你。噢，那門課的講師正從走廊走過來。[54]Jenny，妳能提供一些與妳課程相關的細節資訊嗎？

女 2： 當然。我們把重點放在企業環境下會用到的表達方式。我們每週上兩次課，為期兩個月。而[54] 下一次課程在 6 月 2 日——這星期五開始。

男： 嗯⋯⋯兩個月？這對我來說會有困難，因為我七月要去香港。

女 2： 這樣的話，還有一次是在八月開始。

女 1： 沒錯，而且[55] 如果你在 7 月 10 日前報名我們學院，還有資格獲得早鳥報名折扣。

男： 太棒了。[55] 我現在就報名。

53. 說話者們主要在討論什麼？

(A) 海外旅行計畫
(B) 外語課程
(C) 海外分公司開幕
(D) 教育性的刊物

54. Jenny 提供什麼資訊？

(A) 報名費用
(B) 學生數量
(C) 課程的開始日期
(D) 一堂課的教材清單

55. 男子有資格獲得什麼？

(A) 特別的折扣
(B) 免費的線上講座
(C) 會員資格升級
(D) 免費的講義

題目 based in 總部設在～ instructor [ɪnˋstrʌktɚ] 講師 eligible [ˋɛlɪdʒəbl] 有資格的 institute [ˋɪnstətjut] 學院
53 publication [ˌpʌblɪˋkeʃən] 刊物；出版品
55 reduction [rɪˋdʌkʃən] 削減 complimentary [ˌkɑmpləˋmɛntərɪ] 免費的 handout [ˋhændaʊt] 講義

53 整體對話相關問題－主題 答案 (B)

低

題目詢問對話主題，因此必須注意對話的開頭，並掌握整體對話脈絡。男子說：「I'm hoping to learn more about your Chinese language classes」，表示想要更了解中文課程，接著對話繼續談論與中文課程相關的資訊，因此正確答案是 (B) Foreign language lessons。

54 細節事項相關問題－特定細項 答案 (C)

中

題目詢問女 2 的 Jenny 提供了什麼資訊，因此必須注意和題目關鍵字（information ~ Jenny provide）相關的內容。女 1 說：「Jenny, can you provide some details about your class?」，詢問 Jenny 是否能提供課程相關細節資訊，接著女 2[Jenny] 說：「the next course starts on June 2」，表示下一次課程在 6 月 2 日開始，因此正確答案是 (C) The start date of a course。

55 細節事項相關問題－特定細項 答案 (A)

低

題目詢問男子有資格獲得什麼，因此要注意提到題目關鍵字（eligible）的前後部分。女 1 對男子說：「you'll also be eligible for an advance registration discount if you enroll ~ before July 10」，表示如果男子在 7 月 10 日前報名，就有資格獲得早鳥折扣，接著男子說：「I'll sign up for it now.」，表示要現在報名，由此可知，男子有資格獲得特別的折扣，因此正確答案是 (A) A special fee reduction。

56
57
58

新

Questions 56-58 refer to the following conversation.

英式發音 → 加拿大式發音

W: Now that the Evergreen Project is over, [56]**let's begin our next assignment.**
M: [56]**You mean creating the advertisement for the furniture shop . . . ah . . . Redwood Home, right?**
W: Exactly. We first need to plan the concept for the TV commercial.
M: Maybe [57]**we should concentrate on the business's selection of outdoor furniture.**
W: That's a good suggestion. [58]**Can you collaborate with Alyssa to put together a storyboard with that focus?**
M: Oh, Alyssa's at an off-site training session all day today about . . . um . . . digital media. So, [58]**I'll get started on that by myself and continue with her when she returns to the office tomorrow.**

第 56-58 題請參考下列對話。

女：既然 Evergreen 專案結束了，[56] 我們開始做下一項工作吧。
男：[56] 妳是指為家具店……呃……Redwood Home 製作廣告，對嗎？
女：沒錯。我們必須先規劃那支電視廣告的概念。
男：或許 [57] 我們應該專注於這間公司的戶外家具系列。
女：這是個好建議。[58] 你可以和 Alyssa 合作整理出以那為重點的分鏡腳本嗎？
男：噢，Alyssa 今天一整天都在上……嗯……數位媒體的外部培訓課程。所以，[58] 我會先自己開始做，然後等她明天回辦公室再一起繼續。

56 What type of business do the speakers most likely work for?
(A) A television station
(B) An advertising firm
(C) A furniture retailer
(D) A fashion design company

56. 說話者最有可能在什麼類型的公司裡工作？
(A) 電視台
(B) 廣告公司
(C) 家具零售商
(D) 時裝設計公司

57 What does the man suggest?
(A) Forwarding a staff memo
(B) Passing out some surveys
(C) Promoting outdoor merchandise
(D) Turning in an assignment

57. 男子建議什麼？
(A) 轉寄一則員工備忘錄
(B) 分發一些調查表
(C) 宣傳戶外商品
(D) 繳交一份作業

58 新 Why does the man say, "Alyssa's at an off-site training session all day today"?
(A) To express concern about a deadline
(B) To explain why he will work alone
(C) To clarify who will miss an orientation
(D) To ask for help from other team members

58. 男子為什麼說：「Alyssa 今天一整天都在上外部培訓課程」？
(A) 表達對一個截止日期的擔憂
(B) 解釋他為何會獨自作業
(C) 釐清誰會錯過說明會
(D) 向其他團隊成員尋求協助

題目 now that 既然　concept [美 `kɑnsɛpt 英 `kɔnsept] 概念，想法
commercial [美 kə`mɝʃəl 英 kə`mə:ʃəl]（電視或廣播中的）商業廣告
put together（收集意見或資料後）整理並做出～
storyboard [美 `storɪˌbord 英 `stɔ:riˌbɔ:d] 分鏡腳本（電影或電視的影像配置順序規劃）

56 ■ **整體對話相關問題－說話者** 答案 (B)
中
題目詢問說話者們最有可能在什麼類型的公司裡工作，因此要注意聽和身分、職業相關的表達。女子說：「let's begin our next assignment」，表示要開始做下一項工作，接著男子說：「You mean creating the advertisement for the furniture shop ~, right?」，詢問下一項工作是不是指要為家具店製作廣告，由此可知，說話者們在廣告公司工作，因此正確答案是 (B) An advertising firm。

57 ■ **細節事項相關問題－提議** 答案 (C)
中
題目詢問男子建議什麼，因此要注意聽男子話中出現的提議相關表達。男子說：「we should concentrate on the business's selection of outdoor furniture」，建議專注在這間公司的戶外家具系列，因此正確答案是 (C) Promoting outdoor merchandise。

新 **58** ■ **細節事項相關問題－掌握意圖** 答案 (B)
高
題目詢問男子的說話意圖，因此要注意題目引用句（Alyssa's at an off-site training session all day today）的前後部分。女子在前面對男子說：「Can you collaborate with Alyssa ~?」，詢問男子是否可以和 Alyssa 合作，而男子在引用句之後說：「I'll get started on that by myself and continue with her when she returns to the office tomorrow」，表示會自己先開始做，然後等 Alyssa 明天回辦公室再一起繼續，由此可知，男子是想解釋他為何會獨自作業，因此正確答案是 (B) To explain why he will work alone。

59 60 61

Questions 59-61 refer to the following conversation.

🔊 加拿大式發音 → 英式發音

M: Ms. Martinez, it's Phillip Gray calling from Kerman and Associates. [59]**Have you had a chance to review the revised contract we sent you last week?**

W: [60]**Our legal team is taking a look at it now**, Mr. Gray. They've told me most of the contract looks satisfactory, but some small changes will need to be made to the section on licensing fees.

M: That sounds great. By the way, [61]**I heard that your corporation's soft drink Orange Lite has become quite popular in Mexico ever since it was introduced this spring. Congratulations on the success thus far.**

W: Thank you. Yes, sales have definitely outperformed our expectations. We hope to make the most of the drink's popularity by continuing to expand distribution in the coming quarters.

第 59-61 題請參考下列對話。

男：Martinez 小姐，我是從 Kerman and Associates 打來的 Phillip Gray。[59] 也許您已經查看過我們上週寄給您的修改版合約了嗎？

女：[60] 我們的法律團隊現在正在看，Gray 先生。他們曾跟我說過，合約的大部分內容看起來都很令人滿意，不過在授權金條款方面得做些小修改。

男：聽起來很棒。對了，[61] 我聽說您公司的無酒精飲料 Orange Lite，自今年春天引進墨西哥後便大受歡迎。恭喜您至今為止獲得的成功。

女：謝謝你。沒錯，銷售額的表現絕對已超出了我們的預期。我們希望藉著在下一季持續擴大銷路來充分利用這款飲料的受歡迎程度。

59 Why does the man call the woman?

(A) To follow up on an agreement
(B) To discuss unpaid charges
(C) To describe service coverage
(D) To encourage an expansion

59. 男子為什麼打電話給女子？

(A) 追蹤一份合約
(B) 討論未繳納的費用
(C) 詳述服務涵蓋範圍
(D) 鼓勵擴張

60 What does the woman say about the legal team?

(A) It has been downsized.
(B) It is checking a document.
(C) It has acquired a license.
(D) It is being evaluated.

60. 關於法律團隊，女子說什麼？

(A) 已縮減人數了。
(B) 正在查看一份文件。
(C) 已取得了一張許可證。
(D) 正在接受評估。

61 Why does the man congratulate the woman?

(A) A firm has received an award.
(B) A safety inspection was passed.
(C) A distributor has been contracted.
(D) A product has attracted attention.

61. 男子為何恭喜女子？

(A) 一間公司得到了一個獎項。
(B) 通過了一項安全稽查。
(C) 已和一家分銷商簽約。
(D) 一項產品已獲得了關注。

題目 satisfactory [ˌsætɪsˋfæktərɪ] 令人滿意的　licensing fee 授權費　corporation [ˌkɔrpəˋreʃən] 公司
introduce [ˌɪntrəˋdjus] 引進　outperform [[美] ˌaʊtpɚˋfɔrm [英] ˌautpəˋfɔ:m] 超過；做得比～更好
make the most of 充分利用～　expand [ɪkˋspænd] 擴張
distribution [[美] ˌdɪstrəˋbjuʃən [英] ˌdistriˋbju:ʃən]（貨物等的）銷路，分銷　quarter [[美] ˋkwɔrtɚ [英] ˋkwɔ:tə] 季度

59 follow up 跟進；追蹤　unpaid [ʌnˋped] 未繳納的　coverage [ˋkʌvərɪdʒ] 涵蓋範圍　encourage [ɪnˋkɝɪdʒ] 鼓勵

60 downsize [ˋdaʊnˋsaɪz] 縮減（員工）人數　acquire [əˋkwaɪr] 獲得

61 inspection [ɪnˋspɛkʃən] 檢查；稽查　distributor [dɪˋstrɪbjətɚ] 分銷商　attract [əˋtrækt] 引起；吸引
attention [əˋtɛnʃən] 關注；專心

59 ■ 整體對話相關問題－目的 答案 (A)

高

題目詢問男子打電話給女子的目的，因此必須注意對話的開頭。男子對女子說：「Have you had a chance to review the revised contract we sent you last week?」，詢問女子是否已經看過修改版合約了，由此可知，男子是為了追蹤一份合約而打電話給女子，因此正確答案是 (A) To follow up on an agreement。

60 ■ 細節事項相關問題－提及 答案 (B)

中

題目詢問女子提到什麼與法律團隊有關的事，因此必須確認女子話中提到題目關鍵字（legal team）的前後部分。女子說：「Our legal team is taking a look at it[contract] now」，表示現在法律團隊正在看合約，因此正確答案是 (B) It is checking a document.。

換句話說

taking a look at 正在看 → checking 正在查看

61 ■ 細節事項相關問題－理由 答案 (D)

中

題目詢問男子為什麼要祝賀女子，因此要注意和題目關鍵字（congratulate）相關的內容。男子說：「I heard that your corporation's soft drink ~ has become quite popular ~. Congratulations on the success thus far.」，表示自己聽說了女子公司的無酒精飲料大受歡迎，並接著祝賀其至今獲得的成功，因此正確答案是 (D) A product has attracted attention.。

62
63
64

Questions 62-64 refer to the following conversation and table.

澳洲式發音 → 美式發音

M: Ms. Lynch, [62]**I just checked the pharmacy's inventory, and [63]we're running low on cough medicine.**
W: I'm not surprised. [63]**We're entering the flu season, and we've already had many people coming in to buy that.**
M: Should I contact the pharmaceutical manufacturers and place additional orders?
W: Please do. Also, let's get extra pain relief drugs, since our supply of that needs to be replenished, too. I meant to order more last week but forgot to.
M: I'll do that. And [64]**as for the pain relief medicine, I'll get the one with the lowest per-pill cost**, as customers seem to prefer that brand.

Pain Relief Medication	Price Per Box	Price Per Pill
UltraMed	$3.50	10¢
[64]**NoAche**	$4.50	**8¢**
HealFast	$5.50	12¢
SootheNow	$7.50	9¢

62 What did the man already do?
(A) Cleared products from the shelves
(B) Contacted a drug manufacturer
(C) Assisted some customers
(D) Reviewed stock levels

63 Why is cough medicine in short supply?
(A) An illness is common at the moment.
(B) A delivery has not arrived on schedule.
(C) A firm has stopped producing goods.
(D) A new brand was recently released.

64 Look at the graphic. Which item will the man order?

(A) UltraMed
(B) NoAche
(C) HealFast
(D) SootheNow

第 62-64 題請參考下列對話及表格。

男：Lynch 小姐，[62] 我剛確認過藥房的庫存，結果 [63] 我們的咳嗽藥快要沒有了。
女：我不意外。[63] 我們要進入流感季節了，所以已經有很多人來我們這裡要買咳嗽藥了。
男：我要聯絡藥廠追加下訂嗎？
女：請去聯絡吧。還有，我們還要多訂止痛藥，因為我們那個的庫存也需要補了。我本來打算上禮拜要再訂，但卻忘了。
男：我會去處理這件事。另外 [64] 關於止痛藥，我會訂單顆售價最低的那款，因為客人們似乎比較喜歡那個牌子。

止痛藥	單盒售價	單顆售價
UltraMed	3.50 美金	10 美分
[64]NoAche	4.50 美金	8 美分
HealFast	5.50 美金	12 美分
SootheNow	7.50 美金	9 美分

62. 男子已經做了什麼？
(A) 清除架上商品
(B) 聯絡藥廠
(C) 協助一些客人
(D) 檢查了庫存量

63. 為什麼咳嗽藥庫存不足？
(A) 現在正流行一種病。
(B) 一批貨沒有按預定送達。
(C) 一間公司已停止生產商品。
(D) 最近推出了一個新品牌。

64. 請看圖表。男子會訂哪一個品項？
(A) UltraMed
(B) NoAche
(C) HealFast
(D) SootheNow

題目 pharmacy [美 \`fɑrməsɪ 英 \`fɑ:məsi] 藥局 inventory [美 \`ɪnvən͵torɪ 英 \`invəntri] 庫存 run low on 即將耗盡～ cough [美 kɑf 英 kɔf] 咳嗽 enter [\`ɛntɚ] 進入 supply [sə\`plaɪ] 庫存品；供給 replenish [rɪ\`plɛnɪʃ] 補充 mean to 打算～ as for 關於～
62 clear [klɪr] 清除 shelf [ʃɛlf] 層架 stock [stɑk] 庫存
63 illness [\`ɪlnɪs] 疾病 on schedule 按照預定 produce [prə\`djus] 生產

62 細節事項相關問題－特定細項 答案 (D)

高

題目詢問男子已經做了什麼，因此必須注意和題目關鍵字（man already do）相關的內容。男子說：「I just checked the pharmacy's inventory」，表示自己剛剛確認了藥局的庫存，因此正確答案是 (D) Reviewed stock levels。

換句話說

checked ~ inventory 確認過庫存 → Reviewed stock levels 檢查了庫存量

63 細節事項相關問題－理由 答案 (A)

中

題目詢問為什麼咳嗽藥的庫存會不足，因此要注意提到題目關鍵字（cough medicine）的部分。男子說：「we're running low on cough medicine」，表示咳嗽藥要沒有了，接著女子說：「We're entering the flu season, and we've already had many people coming in to buy that.」，表示因為要進入流感季節了，所以已經有很多人來自己藥房這裡要買咳嗽藥了，因此正確答案是 (A) An illness is common at the moment.。

換句話說

in short supply 庫存不足 → running low 快要沒有了

新 64 細節事項相關問題－圖表資料 答案 (B)

高

題目詢問男子會訂哪個品項，因此必須確認題目提供的表格內容，並注意和題目關鍵字（item ~ man order）相關的內容。男子說：「as for the pain relief medicine, I'll get the one with the lowest per-pill cost」，表示止痛藥會買單顆售價最低的，透過表格可知，單顆售價最低的是 NoAche，因此正確答案是 (B) NoAche。

65 66 67 新

Questions 65-67 refer to the following conversation and map.

加拿大式發音 → 英式發音

M: Thanks for calling Tuscan Sun Excursions. What can I help you with today?

W: Do you offer guided tours of art galleries around the area? I'm hoping to view some during my four-day trip here.

M: Absolutely. [65]**Our art tour stops by the city's three major museums. It takes place twice daily** and begins right outside our office on Truro Avenue.

W: Oh, [66]**I'm actually hoping to browse smaller galleries. There's one at the intersection of Riviera Street and Fresco Road . . . umm . . . just opposite the theater downtown.**

M: Hmm . . . Our company doesn't provide tours there, unfortunately. But [67]**I can give you the phone number of Complete Activities—another tourism firm in the area.** They offer tours of those locations.

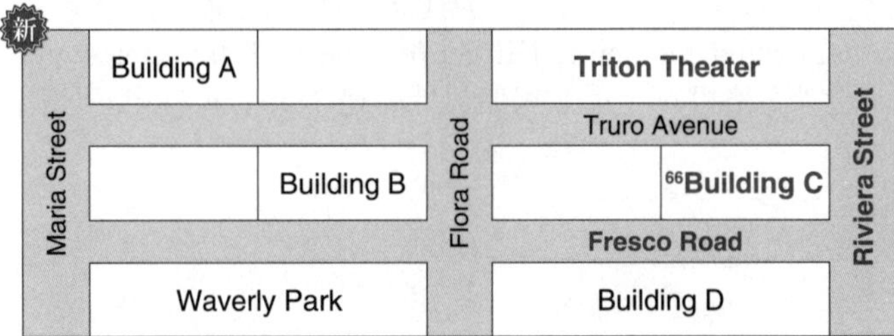

65 According to the man, how many art tours does Tuscan Sun Excursions operate daily?

(A) 1
(B) 2
(C) 3
(D) 4

66 Look at the graphic. Where most likely does the woman want to go? 新

(A) To Building A
(B) To Building B
(C) To Building C
(D) To Building D

67 What does the man offer to do?

(A) Provide contact information
(B) Make some reservations
(C) Get a map of a downtown area
(D) Telephone a local gallery

第 65-67 題請參考下列對話及地圖。

男：感謝來電 Tuscan Sun Excursions。今天有什麼能為您服務的？

女：你們有這區附近美術館的導覽行程嗎？我想要在我在這裡旅遊的四天裡去參觀幾間。

男：當然有。[65] 我們的藝術之旅會造訪市內的三大博物館。一天有兩場，且就從我們辦公室外面的 Truro 大道開始。

女：噢，[66] 我其實想要參觀比較小的美術館。在 Riviera 街與 Fresco 路的交叉口有一間……嗯……就在市中心劇院的對面。

男：嗯……我們公司不巧沒有去那裡的行程。不過 [67] 我可以給你這區裡另一間旅行社 Complete Activities 的電話號碼。他們有去那些地方的行程。

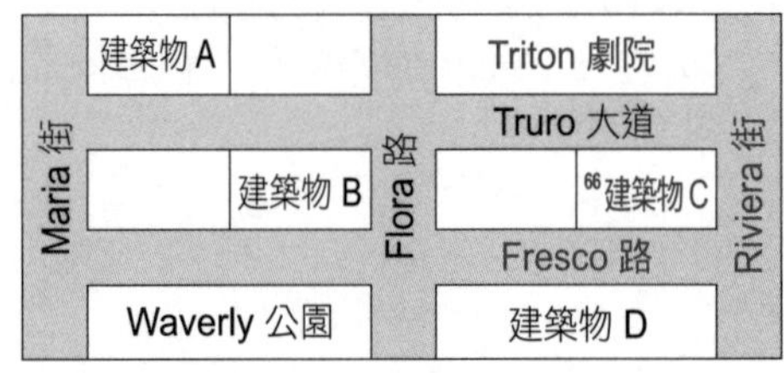

65. 根據男子所說，Tuscan Sun Excursions 每天進行多少場藝術之旅？

(A) 1
(B) 2
(C) 3
(D) 4

66. 請看圖表。女子最有可能想去哪裡？

(A) 建築物 A
(B) 建築物 B
(C) 建築物 C
(D) 建築物 D

67. 男子願意做什麼？

(A) 提供聯絡資訊
(B) 進行一些預約
(C) 取得一張市區地圖
(D) 致電一家當地美術館

題目 art gallery 美術館 view [vju] 觀賞；看 browse [braʊz] 瀏覽 intersection [美 ˌɪntɚˋsɛkʃən 英 ˌintəˋsekʃən] 交叉路口 opposite [美 ˋɑpəzɪt 英 ˋɔpəzit] 在對面 tourism [ˋtʊrɪzəm] 旅遊，觀光

65 operate [ˋɑpəˌret] 經營；運行

67 telephone [ˋtɛləˌfon] 打電話

65 低 ■ 細節事項相關問題－程度　答案 (B)

題目詢問男子說 Tuscan Sun Excursions 每天進行多少場藝術之旅，因此要確認男子話中和題目關鍵字（art tours ~ Tuscan Sun Excursions operate daily）相關的內容。男子說：「Our[Tuscan Sun Excursions's] art tour stops by the city's three major museums. It takes place twice daily」，表示 Tuscan Sun Excursions 的藝術之旅會去市內的三大博物館，每天有兩場，因此正確答案是 (B) 2。

新 **66** 中 ■ 細節事項相關問題－圖表資料　答案 (C)

題目詢問女子想去的地點是哪裡，因此要確認題目提供的地圖，並注意和題目關鍵字（woman want to go）相關的內容。女子說：「I'm actually hoping to browse smaller galleries. There's one at the intersection of Riviera Street and Fresco Road ~ just opposite the theater downtown.」，表示自己想要參觀比較小的美術館，而那間美術館位在 Riviera 街與 Fresco 路的交叉口、市中心劇院的對面。透過地圖可知，女子想去的是建築物 C，因此正確答案是 (C) To Building C。

67 低 ■ 細節事項相關問題－提議　答案 (A)

題目詢問男子願意做什麼，因此必須注意聽男子話中提到要為女子做什麼的內容。男子說：「I can give you the phone number of ~ another tourism firm in the area」，表示可以給女子這區裡另一間旅行社的電話號碼，因此正確答案是 (A) Provide contact information。

換句話說

give ~ phone number 給電話號碼 → Provide contact information 提供聯絡資訊

68
69
70

Questions 68-70 refer to the following conversation and label.

美式發音 → 澳洲式發音

W: This vending machine sells Dalton Pretzels. They contain very little sugar and a lot of carbohydrates, so they're a great way to get a boost of energy. [68]**I'm gonna buy some here in the terminal before we board our plane.** Do you want a bag of them too?

M: Although I'm getting a bit hungry, I'll pass. I've had those pretzels before. They're really tasty, but [69]**they include too much fat**. I'm trying to be careful about what I eat at the moment.

W: Oh, no worries. There're other options if you're interested—nuts and dried fruit snacks.

M: That's OK. [70]**We'll be receiving lunch once we take off, so I should be fine until then.**

新

Nutrition Facts

Serving Size: 10 pretzels
Servings per Pack: 3

Ingredient	Amount per Serving
Sugar	6g
Carbohydrates	32g
Fat	[69]**22g**
Cholesterol	20mg

68 Where is the conversation most likely taking place?

(A) At a restaurant
(B) At an office building
(C) At a convenience store
(D) At an airport

69 新 Look at the graphic. Which ingredient amount is too high for the man?

(A) 6g
(B) 32g
(C) 22g
(D) 20mg

70 What does the man say he will do?

(A) Pick another snack
(B) Wait for a meal
(C) Read a product label
(D) Inquire about a lunch menu

第 68-70 題請參考下列對話及標籤。

女：這台販賣機有賣 Dalton 椒鹽捲餅。它的糖分非常少，且有大量碳水化合物，所以它們是補充能量的絕佳管道。[68] 我要在我們登機前在航廈這裡買一些。你要也買一包嗎？

男：雖然我有點餓了，不過不用了。我之前吃過這種椒鹽捲餅。它們真的很好吃，可是 [69] 脂肪含量太高了。我現在正在試著要對我吃的東西多注意一點。

女：噢，沒關係。如果你有興趣的話，這裡有其他選項——堅果和果乾的點心。

男：沒關係。[70] 等我們起飛就會拿到午餐了，所以我應該可以撐到那時候沒問題。

營養成份表

一份：10 個椒鹽捲餅
每包含：3 份

成份	每份含量
糖	6g
碳水化合物	32g
脂肪	[69]22g
膽固醇	20mg

68. 這段對話最有可能在哪裡發生？

(A) 餐廳
(B) 辦公大樓
(C) 便利商店
(D) 機場

69. 請看圖表。哪個成份含量對男子來說太高？

(A) 6g
(B) 32g
(C) 22g
(D) 20mg

70. 男子說他會做什麼？

(A) 選擇另一個點心
(B) 等著用餐
(C) 閱讀產品標籤
(D) 詢問午餐菜單

題目 vending machine 自動販賣機 contain [kən`ten] 包含 carbohydrate [ˌkarbə`haɪdret] 碳水化合物 boost [bust] 促進；提升 energy [`ɛnədʒɪ] 能量；精力 board [bord] 登上（船、飛機等交通工具）pass [美 pæs 英 pɑːs] 跳過（輪到自己的這一輪或他人的提議等） once [wʌns] 一～就～ take off 起飛

70 inquire [ɪn`kwaɪr] 詢問

68 整體對話相關問題－地點 答案 (D)

高

題目詢問對話發生地點，因此必須注意聽和地點相關的表達。女子說：「I'm gonna buy some[Dalton Pretzels] here in the terminal before we board our plane.」，表示登機前要在航廈裡買一些 Dalton 椒鹽捲餅，由此可知，對話發生地點在機場，因此正確答案是 (D) At an airport。

新 69 細節事項相關問題－圖表資料 答案 (C)

低

題目詢問哪個成份含量對男子來說太高，因此必須確認題目提供的營養成份標籤，並注意和題目關鍵字（ingredient amount ~ too high）相關的內容。男子說：「they[pretzels] include too much fat」，表示椒鹽捲餅的脂肪含量太高。透過圖表可知，脂肪含量 22g 對男子來說太高，因此正確答案是 (C) 22g。

70 細節事項相關問題－接下來要做的事 答案 (B)

高

題目詢問男子說他會做什麼，因此必須確認男子話中和題目關鍵字（will do）相關的內容。男子說：「We'll be receiving lunch once we take off, so I should be fine until then.」，表示因為等起飛就會拿到午餐了，所以自己應該可以撐到那時候沒問題，由此可知，男子會等著用午餐，因此正確答案是 (B) Wait for a meal。

71
72
73

Questions 71-73 refer to the following talk.

🔊 澳洲式發音

[71]**We've now reached what's probably the most famous painting in this museum's collection,** ***The Flames of Clouds***. It was created by Guido Mariano and is believed to date back to 1821. As you can see, [72]**the picture uses a combination of bright orange and yellow paint, which was quite uncommon at the time it was made.** This innovative technique gained Mariano a lot of praise from fellow painters and art critics of his era. OK, [73]**let's move on and view some of our 20th century artworks. They're located in the next gallery at the end of the hallway.** Please follow me.

71 Where most likely are the listeners?

(A) At a museum
(B) At an art school
(C) At a public library
(D) At a painting studio

72 According to the speaker, what is unusual about *The Flames of Clouds*?

(A) Its size
(B) Its use of color
(C) Its date of origin
(D) Its name

73 What will listeners most likely do next?

(A) Read about some artwork
(B) Visit a gift shop
(C) Watch a brief video
(D) Go to another gallery

第 71-73 題請參考下列談話。

[71] 我們現在已經抵達可能是這間博物館收藏中最知名的畫作《The Flames of Clouds》。它是由 Guido Mariano 創作的，且一般認為可追溯至 1821 年。如各位所見，[72] 這幅畫混合使用了亮橘色及黃色顏料，這點在其創作當時是相當不尋常的。這項創新技術使 Mariano 獲得許多來自與他同一時期的畫家同儕及藝術評論家的讚賞。好，[73] 讓我們繼續往前去看一些我們的 20 世紀藝術品。它們被放在這條走廊盡頭的下一個陳列廳裡。請跟我來。

71. 聽者們最有可能在哪裡？

(A) 在博物館
(B) 在藝術學校
(C) 在公共圖書館
(D) 在繪畫工作室

72. 根據說話者所說，《The Flames of Clouds》有什麼不尋常的？

(A) 尺寸
(B) 用色
(C) 起源日期
(D) 名稱

73. 聽者們接下來最有可能會做什麼？

(A) 閱讀與一些藝術品有關的內容
(B) 去禮品店
(C) 看短片
(D) 去另一間陳列廳

題目 reach [ritʃ] 抵達　collection [kə`lɛkʃən] 收藏品　date back to 追溯到～
combination [[美] ˌkɑmbə`neʃən [英] ˌkɔmbi`neiʃən] 混合；組合　uncommon [[美] ʌn`kɑmən [英] ʌn`kɔmən] 不尋常的
innovative [[美] `ɪnoˌvetɪv [英] `inəuveitiv] 創新的　gain [gen] 獲得　praise [prez] 讚賞
fellow [[美] `fɛlo [英] `feləu] 夥伴；同儕　critic [`krɪtɪk] 評論家　era [`ɪrə] 時期；年代　artwork [`ɑrtˌwɝk] 藝術品
71 studio [`stjudɪˌo] 工作室
72 unusual [ʌn`juʒʊəl] 不尋常的
73 brief [brif] 簡短的

71 整體內容相關問題－地點 答案 (A)

低

題目詢問聽者們身在何處，因此必須注意聽獨白中和地點有關的表達。獨白說：「We've now reached what's probably the most famous painting in this museum's collection」，表示現在已經抵達在這座博物館的收藏中最知名的畫作這裡，由此可知，聽者們的所在地點是博物館，因此正確答案是 (A) At a museum。

72 細節事項相關問題－特定細項 答案 (B)

中

題目詢問《The Flames of Clouds》有什麼不尋常的，因此必須注意和題目關鍵字（*The Flames of Clouds*）相關的內容。獨白說：「the picture[*The Flames of Clouds*] uses a combination of bright orange and yellow paint, which was quite uncommon at the time it was made」，表示《The Flames of Clouds》混合使用了亮橘色及黃色顏料，這點在其創作當時是相當不尋常的，因此正確答案是 (B) Its use of color。

73 細節事項相關問題－接下來要做的事 答案 (D)

中

題目詢問聽者們接下來最可能會做什麼，因此必須注意聽獨白的最後部分。獨白說：「let's move on and view some of our 20th century artworks. They're located in the next gallery at the end of the hallway.」，表示要繼續往前去看 20 世紀的藝術品，而這些藝術品被放在走廊盡頭的下一個陳列廳裡，因此正確答案是 (D) Go to another gallery。

74
75
76

Questions 74-76 refer to the following advertisement.	第 74-76 題請參考下列廣告。
加拿大式發音	
Want to beat the hot weather? [74]**Stop by Stevie's Frozen Yogurt for a cold, refreshing treat!** We offer 22 flavors, such as vanilla, chocolate, peanut butter, and coffee. Moreover, [75]**we're the only frozen yogurt shop in town that allows customers to add as many toppings as they'd like for no additional charge.** [76]**Be sure to check out our social media page, where we'll be holding promotions throughout July. There, you'll find a new deal featured daily**, including amazing discounts and free items. You won't want to miss out on our incredible offers!	想要擊敗炎熱的天氣嗎？[74] 來 Stevie's 冷凍優格吃冰涼消暑的點心吧！我們有 22 種口味，例如香草、巧克力、花生醬及咖啡。除此之外，[75] 我們是鎮上唯一一家讓客人們可以免費想加多少配料就加多少的冷凍優格店。[75] 請一定要到我們的社群媒體頁面上看看，我們整個七月都會在上面舉辦促銷活動。在那裡，你會找到每日主打的新優惠，包括超棒折扣及免費商品。你不會想要錯過我們的絕佳優惠的！
74 What type of business is being advertised? (A) An online retailer (B) A catering company (C) A food outlet (D) A department store	74. 正在廣告的是哪一種公司？ (A) 線上零售商 (B) 外燴公司 (C) 食品商店 (D) 百貨公司
75 According to the speaker, what distinguishes the company from its competitors? (A) Reasonable prices (B) Unlimited toppings (C) Unique flavors (D) Natural ingredients	75. 根據說話者所說，是什麼使這間公司能從其競爭者間脫穎而出？ (A) 價格合理 (B) 配料沒有限制 (C) 口味獨特 (D) 材料天然
76 Why should listeners visit the business's social media page? (A) Some deals are available. (B) A newsletter was published. (C) A menu can be downloaded. (D) Some reviews have been posted.	76. 聽者們為什麼應該要上該公司的社群媒體頁面？ (A) 可以拿到一些優惠。 (B) 刊出了一份業務通訊。 (C) 可以下載一份菜單。 (D) 張貼了一些評論

題目 beat [bit] 擊敗　refreshing [rɪˋfrɛʃɪŋ] 提神醒腦的；（心情）耳目一新的　topping [ˋtɑpɪŋ]（加在食物上的）配料　throughout [θruˋaʊt] 從頭到尾　miss out 錯過　incredible [ɪnˋkrɛdəbl̩] 絕佳的；令人難以置信的
74 catering [ˋketərɪŋ] 提供外燴服務；承辦宴席　outlet [ˋaʊtˏlɛt] 通路；商店
75 reasonable [ˋriznəbl] 合理的　unlimited [ʌnˋlɪmɪtɪd] 無限制的　unique [juˋnik] 獨特的　natural [ˋnætʃərəl] 天然的　ingredient [ɪnˋgridɪənt] 材料
76 newsletter [ˋnjuzˋlɛtɚ] 業務通訊；商業通訊　publish [ˋpʌblɪʃ] 刊出；發行

74 中 整體內容相關問題－主題　答案 (C)

題目詢問廣告的主題是什麼，因此必須仔細聽廣告的開頭。獨白說：「Stop by Stevie's Frozen Yogurt ~!」，請聽者到 Stevie's 冷凍優格店，接著繼續介紹這間販售冷凍優格的食品商店，因此正確答案是 (C) A food outlet。

75 中 細節事項相關問題－特定細項　答案 (B)

題目詢問說話者說能讓這間公司從其競爭者間脫穎而出的是什麼，因此要注意和題目關鍵字（distinguishes ~ company from ~ competitors）相關的內容。獨白說：「we're the only frozen yogurt shop in town that allows customers to add as many toppings as they'd like for no additional charge」，表示自己這家店是鎮上唯一一家讓客人們可以免費想加多少配料就加多少的冷凍優格店，因此正確答案是 (B) Unlimited toppings。

76 中 細節事項相關問題－理由　答案 (A)

題目詢問聽者們應該要上該公司社群媒體頁面的理由，因此必須注意提到題目關鍵字（social media page）的前後部分。獨白說：「Be sure to check out our social media page, where we'll be holding promotions throughout July. There, you'll find a new deal featured daily」，表示整個七月都會在社群媒體頁面上舉辦促銷活動，而且會在那裡找到每日主打的新優惠，因此正確答案是 (A) Some deals are available.。

TEST 1 2 3 4 5 6 7 8 9 10

77
78
79

Questions 77-79 refer to the following announcement.	第 77-79 題請參考下列公告。
澳洲式發音	
May I have your attention, please? Tonight's performance of the award-winning play *Miles to Home* will begin in half an hour. I have some unfortunate news, though. [77]**Roberta Mendez was injured in rehearsal and therefore won't be performing tonight. She has been replaced by Tanya Wilkins.** Information about this talented young actor is in the play's program. [78]**Just ask an usher for one of these booklets.** And please note that [79]**snacks are no longer permitted in the auditorium during the performance. We received complaints about people eating during our last production, so we had to make some changes.** Thank you for your cooperation.	可以請大家注意我這裡嗎？今晚要演出的獲獎劇《Miles to Home》將會在半小時後開始。不過我有一些不幸的消息。[77]Roberta Mendez 在彩排中受了傷，因此今晚無法演出。已由 Tanya Wilkins 代替她。在這齣劇的節目表中有這位才華洋溢的年輕演員的相關資訊。[78] 請直接向帶位人員拿一本小冊子吧。另外請注意，[79] 演出期間，不再允許帶零食進入表演廳。我們在上一場演出時接到了有人在吃東西的投訴，因此我們得做出一些更動。謝謝各位的合作。
77 Why is the speaker addressing the audience? (A) To apologize for a delay (B) To introduce a director (C) To announce a change (D) To discuss an actor's role	77. 說話者為何要對聽眾說話？ (A) 要為一次延誤道歉 (B) 要介紹一位導演 (C) 為了宣布一項更動 (D) 為了討論一位演員的角色
78 What can listeners obtain from a staff member? (A) Photos of cast members (B) Gift certificates (C) Programs for the event (D) Complimentary tickets	78. 聽者們可以從員工那裡取得什麼？ (A) 演出陣容的照片 (B) 禮券 (C) 活動節目表 (D) 免費票券
79 新 What does the speaker imply when he says, "We received complaints about people eating during our last production"? (A) A regulation was no longer followed. (B) A problem is difficult to resolve. (C) A decision will be made soon. (D) A policy was recently altered.	79. 當說話者說：「我們在上一場演出時接到了有人在吃東西的投訴」，是在暗示什麼？ (A) 一項規定不再被遵守了。 (B) 一個問題難以解決。 (C) 很快會做出一項決定。 (D) 一項政策最近變更了。

題目 award-winning 獲獎的 injure [美 `ɪndʒɚ 英 `indʒə] 使受傷 talented [`tæləntɪd] 才華洋溢的
usher [美 `ʌʃɚ 英 `ʌʃə] 帶位人員 auditorium [ˌɔdə`torɪəm] 表演廳；禮堂 production [prə`dʌkʃən]（戲劇等）演出
cooperation [美 koˌɑpə`reʃən 英 kəuˌɔpə`reiʃən] 合作，協力
78 obtain [əb`ten] 獲得 cast member 演出陣容
79 resolve [rɪ`zɑlv] 解決

77 中 ■ 整體內容相關問題－目的 答案 (C)

題目詢問說話者對聽眾發言的目的，因此必須注意聽獨白的開頭部分。獨白說：「Roberta Mendez was injured in rehearsal and therefore won't be performing tonight. She has been replaced by Tanya Wilkins.」，表示 Roberta Mendez 在彩排時受傷，因此無法參與晚上的演出，故已由 Tanya Wilkins 代替她了，由此可知，說話者是在對聽眾公告變更事項，因此正確答案是 (C) To announce a change。

78 中 ■ 細節事項相關問題－特定細項 答案 (C)

題目詢問聽者們可以從員工那裡得到什麼，因此要注意和題目關鍵字（obtain from ~ staff member）相關的內容。獨白說：「Just ask an usher for one of these booklets[play's program].」，表示聽者們可以直接跟帶位人員拿一本小冊子，因此正確答案是 (C) Programs for the event。

新 **79** 高 ■ 細節事項相關問題－掌握意圖 答案 (D)

題目詢問說話者的說話意圖，因此必須注意題目引用句（We received complaints about people eating during our last production）的前後部分。獨白先說：「snacks are no longer permitted in the auditorium during the performance」，表示不再允許在演出期間帶零食進入表演廳，接著說：「We received complaints about people eating during our last production, so we had to make some changes.」，表示是因為在上一場演出時接到了有人在吃東西的投訴，所以才做出更動，由此可知，說話者是想要解釋政策變更的背景原因，因此正確答案是 (D) A policy was recently altered.。

Questions 80-82 refer to the following radio broadcast.

英式發音

Welcome to *Top Science* on WRP 101.5. I'm your host, Nina Esteban. As part of our ongoing podcast series on the impact of climate change, I've invited Dr. Luis Mattson from Fillmore College to the show. [80]**Dr. Mattson teaches in the school's ecology department** and, just [81]**this Monday, published a paper in a respected journal. The paper examines the rise of sea levels along the United States coastline as a result of melting glaciers.** Throughout today's program, [82]**our guest is going to discuss his findings and respond to a few critiques that his research has received.** Dr. Mattson, do you mind starting by outlining the results of your research?

第 80-82 題請參考下列電台廣播。

歡迎收聽 WRP 101.5 的《Top Science》。我是你們的主持人 Nina Esteban。做為我們針對氣候變遷影響所正在進行的 podcast 系列節目的一部分，我邀請了 Fillmore 學院的 Luis Mattson 博士來到了節目之中。[80]Mattson 博士在該所學校的生態學系中任教，而就在 [81] 這個星期一，他在一本備受推崇的期刊上刊出了一篇論文。這篇論文檢視了因冰河融化而造成的美國海岸線沿線海平面上升。在今天的節目之中，[82] 我們的來賓將會詳敘他的發現，並針對他的研究所收到的一些批評做出回應。Mattson 博士，您介意先從大略說明您的研究成果開始嗎？

80 What is Dr. Mattson's area of expertise?

(A) Economics
(B) Journalism
(C) Statistics
(D) Ecology

80. Mattson 博士的專業領域是什麼？

(A) 經濟學
(B) 新聞學
(C) 統計學
(D) 生態學

81 According to the speaker, what was released on Monday?

(A) An academic publication
(B) A podcast series
(C) A policy review
(D) A list of keynote speakers

81. 根據說話者所說，在星期一發表了什麼？

(A) 學術刊物
(B) podcast 系列節目
(C) 政策評論
(D) 專題演講者的名單

82 What is mentioned about Dr. Mattson?

(A) He will address some criticisms.
(B) He will take calls from listeners.
(C) He will talk about a course curriculum.
(D) He will submit a research proposal.

82. 關於 Mattson 博士，提到了什麼？

(A) 他會對一些批評發表意見。
(B) 他會接聽聽眾來電。
(C) 他會談論課程大綱。
(D) 他會提交研究提案。

題目 podcast [美 `pɑdˏkæst 英 `pɔdˏkɑ:st] 事先錄製並以網路發布的音訊節目（由 iPod 和 broadcast 兩字所結合而成的字）
climate [美 `klaɪmɪt 英 `klaimit] 氣候 ecology [美 ɪ`kɑlədʒɪ 英 i:`kɔlədʒi] 生態學；生態
paper [美 `pepɚ 英 `peipə] 論文 respected [rɪ`spɛktɪd] 備受推崇的

80 area of expertise 專業領域 journalism [`dʒɝnḷˏɪzm] 新聞學 statistics [stə`tɪstɪks] 統計學

81 keynote speaker 專題演講者

82 address [ə`drɛs] 對～發表言論 criticism [`krɪtəˏsɪzəm] 批評

80 低 細節事項相關問題－特定細項 答案 (D)

題目詢問 Mattson 博士的專業領域是什麼，因此必須注意和題目關鍵字（Dr. Mattson's area of expertise）相關的內容。獨白說：「Dr. Mattson teaches in ~ ecology department」，表示 Mattson 博士在生態學系任教，因此正確答案是 (D) Ecology。

81 中 細節事項相關問題－特定細項 答案 (A)

題目詢問星期一發表了什麼，因此必須注意和題目關鍵字（released on Monday）相關的內容。獨白說：「this Monday, published a paper in a respected journal. The paper examines the rise of sea levels ~ as a result of melting glaciers.」，表示這個星期一在備受推崇的期刊上刊出了一篇論文，因此正確答案是 (A) An academic publication。

82 高 細節事項相關問題－提及 答案 (A)

題目詢問獨白中提到什麼與 Mattson 博士有關的事，因此要注意和題目關鍵字（Dr. Mattson）相關的內容。獨白說：「our guest [Dr. Mattson] is going to ~ respond to a few critiques that his research has received」，表示 Mattson 博士將針對批評做出回應，因此正確答案是 (A) He will address some criticisms.。

換句話說

respond to a few critiques 回應一些批評 → address some criticisms 對一些批評發表意見

83
84
85

Questions 83-85 refer to the following excerpt from a meeting.

美式發音

One last thing . . . [83]**I want to discuss the product testing for our upcoming lipstick line.** We posted an advertisement seeking paid test subjects to participate in the research, and . . . well, now we've got a problem. [84]**A lot more people than we need signed up.** I don't want to turn anyone away, though. [84]**Instead, let's see if they'd be willing to take part in other studies.** I just spoke to our research manager Beth Meyers, and she told me that more people are needed to test some eye makeup that we're developing. [85]**She's going to reach out to those who applied** to see whether they'd be open to trying those products instead.

第 83-85 題請參考下列會議節錄。

最後一件事……[83] 我想就我們即將推出的唇膏系列產品的產品測試進行討論。我們貼出了一則尋求付費受試者來參與研究的廣告，而……嗯，現在我們有個麻煩了。[84] 報名的人比我們需要的人要多很多。不過我不想要拒絕任何人。[84] 反倒是想看看他們是否會願意參加其他的研究。我剛和我們的研究經理 Beth Meyers 談過，她跟我說我們正在開發的一些眼妝產品需要更多人來測試。[85] 她會去聯繫那些來報名的人，看看他們會不會願意改去試用那些產品。

83 Where do the listeners most likely work?

(A) At an educational institution
(B) At a cosmetics firm
(C) At an advertising company
(D) At an electronics manufacturer

83. 聽者們最有可能在哪裡工作？

(A) 教育機構
(B) 化妝品公司
(C) 廣告公司
(D) 電子產品製造商

84 新 Why does the speaker say, "I don't want to turn anyone away, though"?

(A) She will provide a solution.
(B) She will reconsider a decision.
(C) She will approve a plan.
(D) She will reject a request.

84. 說話者為什麼說：「不過我不想要拒絕任何人」？

(A) 她會提供一個解決方案。
(B) 她會重新考慮一項決策。
(C) 她會批准一個計畫。
(D) 她會拒絕一項請求。

85 What will Beth Meyers most likely do?

(A) Try out some products
(B) Organize an activity
(C) Attend a meeting
(D) Contact applicants

85. Beth Meyers 最有可能會做什麼？

(A) 試用一些產品
(B) 籌辦一項活動
(C) 出席一場會議
(D) 聯絡報名者

題目 paid [ped] 付費的　test subject 受試者　turn away 轉過臉去；拒絕　reach out 聯繫
83 educational [ˌɛdʒʊˋkeʃənl̩] 教育的　cosmetic [kɑzˋmɛtɪk] 化妝品　electronics [ɪlɛkˋtrɑnɪks] 電子產品　manufacturer [ˌmænjəˋfæktʃərə] 製造商
84 reconsider [ˌrikənˋsɪdə] 重新考慮　approve [əˋpruv] 批准　reject [rɪˋdʒɛkt] 拒絕
85 try out 試用　applicant [ˋæpləkənt] 申請者；應徵者

83 低 **整體內容相關問題－聽者** 答案 (B)

題目詢問聽者們的身分，因此要注意聽和身分、職業相關的表達。獨白說：「I want to discuss the product testing for our upcoming lipstick line.」，表示想要就即將推出的唇膏系列產品的產品測試進行討論，由此可知，聽者們是在化妝品公司內任職，因此正確答案是 (B) At a cosmetics firm。

新 **84** 高 **細節事項相關問題－掌握意圖** 答案 (A)

題目詢問說話者的說話意圖，因此要注意題目引用句（I don't want to turn anyone away, though）的前後部分。獨白先說：「A lot more people than we need signed up.」，表示報名的人比所需的人要多很多，接著說：「Instead, let's see if they'd be willing to take part in other studies.」，表示反倒是想看看報名的人是否會願意參加其他研究，由此可知，說話者想要解決報名的人比所需的人多很多的這個問題，因此正確答案是 (A) She will provide a solution.。

85 中 **細節事項相關問題－接下來要做的事** 答案 (D)

題目詢問 Beth Meyers 最有可能會做什麼，因此要注意和題目關鍵字（Beth Meyers ~ do）相關的內容。獨白說：「She[Beth Meyers]'s going to reach out to those who applied」，表示 Beth Meyers 會和報名的人聯繫，因此正確答案是 (D) Contact applicants。

換句話說
reach out to those who applied 聯繫那些來報名的人 → Contact applicants 聯絡報名者

86
87
88

Questions 86-88 refer to the following introduction.

英式發音

I'd like you all to meet Ivan Schwartz. [86]**Mr. Schwartz is the head application developer at our company's Vienna branch**, and he has traveled to Liverpool to undergo training with our IT department. [87]**While here, he will be shown how to operate the data collection program that we will be rolling out across all of our branches in March.** As you all know, the program is quite complicated, which is why [88]**we've asked Mr. Schwartz to travel here and work with our staff in person rather than virtually. Please be sure to make him feel welcome over the next five days and answer any questions that he may have.** OK, that's all for now.

86 What is Ivan Schwartz's occupation?

(A) Consultant
(B) Travel agent
(C) Programmer
(D) Instructor

87 According to the speaker, what will Ivan Schwartz do?

(A) Install some equipment
(B) Oversee an ongoing project
(C) Create a computer application
(D) Learn about new software

88 What are listeners asked to do?

(A) Undergo some training
(B) Welcome a colleague
(C) Set up an office for a manager
(D) Prepare for a business trip

第 86-88 題請參考下列介紹。

我想要你們大家都見見 Ivan Schwartz。[86]Schwartz 先生是我們公司維也納分公司的首席應用程式開發人員，而且他曾到利物浦和我們的資訊科技部門一起接受培訓。[87] 在他在這裡時，我們將會為他示範要怎麼執行我們將在三月於所有分公司中推出的資料收集程式。如你們大家所知，這個程式相當複雜，這也就是為什麼 [88] 我們會請 Schwartz 先生親自來到這裡與我們員工一起工作，而不是透過電腦。請務必在接下來的五天間讓他覺得賓至如歸，並回答任何他可能會有的疑問。好，現在就先這樣。

86. Ivan Schwartz 的職業是什麼？

(A) 顧問
(B) 旅行專員
(C) 程式設計師
(D) 講師

87. 根據說話者所說，Ivan Schwartz 會做什麼？

(A) 安裝一些設備
(B) 監督一個進行中的計畫
(C) 製作一個電腦應用程式
(D) 學習新軟體

88. 聽者們被要求做什麼？

(A) 接受一些培訓
(B) 歡迎一位同事
(C) 為一位經理設置辦公室
(D) 為出差做準備

題目 head [hɛd] 首席；首長 undergo [美 ˌʌndɚˋgo 英 ˌʌndəˋgəu] 接受；歷經 show [美 ʃo 英 ʃəu] 示範（做某事的方法）
roll out 推出 complicated [美 ˋkɑmpləˌketɪd 英 ˋkɔmplikeitid] 複雜的 in person 親自
virtually [美 ˋvɝtʃʊəlɪ 英 ˋvə:tjuəli] 透過電腦地；虛擬地

87 oversee [ˋovɚˋsi] 監督 ongoing [ˋɑnˌgoɪŋ] 進行中的

86 細節事項相關問題－特定細項 答案 (C)

中

題目詢問 Ivan Schwartz 的職業，因此要注意聽和提問對象（Ivan Schwartz）的身分、職業相關的表達。獨白說：「Mr. Schwartz is the head application developer ~」，表示 Schwartz 是首席應用程式開發人員，由此可知，Ivan Schwartz 是程式設計師，因此正確答案是 (C) Programmer。

87 細節事項相關問題－接下來要做的事 答案 (D)

高

題目詢問 Ivan Schwartz 會做什麼，因此必須注意和題目關鍵字（Ivan Schwartz do）相關的內容。獨白說：「While here, he[Ivan Schwartz] will be shown how to operate the data collection program that we will be rolling out ~ in March.」，表示在 Ivan Schwartz 在這裡時，會為他示範如何執行資料收集程式，因此正確答案是 (D) Learn about new software。

88 細節事項相關問題－要求 答案 (B)

中

題目詢問聽者被要求做什麼，因此要注意聽在獨白的中後半部分裡出現要求相關表達的句子。獨白說：「we've asked Mr. Schwartz to ~ work with our staff in person ~. Please be sure to make him feel welcome ~ and answer any questions that he may have.」，表示 Schwartz 先生會和大家一起工作，並要求聽者們要讓他覺得賓至如歸，並回答任何他可能會有的疑問，因此正確答案是 (B) Welcome a colleague。

89
90
91

Questions 89-91 refer to the following telephone message.	第 89-91 題請參考下列電話留言。
美式發音	
Hi, Carol. [89]**I just called to thank you for asking me to attend your dinner party on Saturday.** It was great to see you and some of the other people from our neighborhood. Um, [90]**one of your guests mentioned that she ran an interior design firm.** If I remember correctly, her name was, uh, Kathy Turner. Could you give me her contact information? [90]**I'm going to remodel my kitchen, and I'll need the services of a professional designer.** Also, before I forget . . . [91]**I just received word that the community center will no longer provide transportation for its summer program.** Your children are enrolled in classes there as well, right? Maybe we can take turns driving them each day. Let me know if you're interested in doing that.	嗨，Carol。[89] 我打來只是想謝謝妳邀請我參加妳星期六的晚餐派對。我很高興看到妳和我們社區裡的其他一些人。嗯，[90] 妳其中一位客人提到她開了一間室內設計公司。如果我記得沒錯的話，她的名字是，呃，Kathy Turner。可以請妳給我她的聯絡資訊嗎？[90] 我打算整修我的廚房，所以我會需要專業設計師的服務。還有，在我忘記之前……[91] 我剛收到消息說社區中心不會再為暑期課程提供載送服務了。妳的孩子們也報了那邊的課程，對吧？也許我們可以每天輪流開車載他們。請讓我知道妳有沒有興趣這樣做。
89 Why does the speaker thank the listener? (A) For making a restaurant reservation (B) For inviting her to a social gathering (C) For supporting a local charity (D) For providing her with class information	89. 說話者為何感謝聽者？ (A) 因為她預訂了餐廳 (B) 因為她邀請自己參加社交聚會 (C) 因為她支持一個當地的慈善事業 (D) 因為她提供自己課程資訊
90 (新) What does the speaker imply when she says, "Could you give me her contact information"? (A) She was contacted by a neighbor. (B) She wants to apply to a firm. (C) She may hire a designer. (D) She will reschedule an appointment.	90. 當說話者說：「可以請妳給我她的聯絡資訊嗎？」，是在暗示什麼？ (A) 一位鄰居聯絡了她。 (B) 她想要應徵一間公司。 (C) 她可能會雇用一位設計師。 (D) 她會重新安排一次會面的時間。
91 What problem is mentioned? (A) A course was canceled. (B) A fee has been increased. (C) A facility will close down. (D) A service is no longer offered.	91. 提到了什麼問題？ (A) 一個課程取消了。 (B) 一筆費用增加了。 (C) 一間機構會關閉。 (D) 不再提供一項服務。

題目 ask [æsk] 邀請；詢問　neighborhood [`nebɚ͵hʊd] 鄰近地區；街坊鄰居　service [`sɝvɪs] 幫助；服務　professional [prə`fɛʃənl] 專業的　enroll [ɪn`rol] 登記（名字等）；註冊　take turns 輪流

89 gathering [`gæðərɪŋ] 聚會　support [sə`port] 支持　charity [`tʃærətɪ] 慈善事業

89 細節事項相關問題－理由 答案 (B)

低

題目詢問說話者對聽者表示感謝的原因，因此要注意提到題目關鍵字（thank）的前後部分。獨白說：「I just called to thank you for asking me to attend your dinner party on Saturday.」，表示打這通電話是為了感謝對方邀請自己參加星期六的晚餐派對，因此正確答案是 (B) For inviting her to a social gathering。

換句話說

asking ~ to attend ~ dinner party 邀請參加晚餐派對 → inviting ~ to a social gathering 邀請參加社交聚會

(新) 90 細節事項相關問題－掌握意圖 答案 (C)

中

題目詢問說話者的說話意圖，因此要注意題目引用句（Could you give me her contact information）的前後部分。獨白說：「one of your guests mentioned that she ran an interior design firm」，表示聽者的其中一位客人提過她開了一間室內設計公司，接著說：「I'm going to remodel my kitchen, and I'll need the services of a professional designer.」，表示自己打算整修廚房，所以會需要專業設計師的服務，由此可知，說話者可能會雇用設計師，因此正確答案是 (C) She may hire a designer.。

91 細節事項相關問題－特定細項 答案 (D)

中

題目詢問提到了什麼問題，因此要注意和題目關鍵字（problem）相關的內容。獨白說：「I just received word that the community center will no longer provide transportation for its summer program.」，表示聽到消息說社區中心不會再為暑期課程提供載送服務了，因此正確答案是 (D) A service is no longer offered.。

92
93
94

Questions 92-94 refer to the following radio broadcast.	第 92-94 題請參考下列電台廣播。
加拿大式發音	
According to a recent press conference held by the city's mayor, [92]**Shenzhen will be launching a major campaign to attract foreign businesses**. A local publicity firm has created the campaign, which focuses on [93]**the city's low corporate tax rates** and large labor market. Moreover, it draws attention to how Shenzhen's growing population offers an excellent consumer base for multiple enterprises. Although Shenzhen is already well known among Chinese entrepreneurs, [94]**officials feel the city has yet to reach its full business potential. They are optimistic that the campaign will generate more attention from international companies, as well as increase tourism in the region.** For further information about the campaign or to view any of its promotional materials, you can visit www.shenzhenbusiness.gov.cn.	根據市長最近舉行的一場記者會，[92] 深圳將著手進行一項大型宣傳活動以吸引外國企業。一間本地的公關公司已規劃了本次的宣傳活動，活動將聚焦於 [93] 本市的低公司稅率及龐大的勞動市場。此外，深圳成長中的人口能如何為多家企業提供絕佳客群的這件事引起了關注。儘管深圳在中國企業家間已具知名度，[94] 但官方仍認為這座城市尚未發揮其最大商業潛能。他們對於這次宣傳活動將引起更多來自國際企業的關注並提升區域內觀光產業感到樂觀。若想取得更多有關這次宣傳活動的消息，或瀏覽所有活動宣傳資料，您可以上 www.shenzhenbusiness.gov.cn。
92 What is the purpose of the report? (A) To describe promotional efforts (B) To discuss an upcoming election (C) To explain tour restrictions (D) To outline a construction project	92. 這篇報導的目的是什麼？ (A) 描述為宣傳所做的努力 (B) 討論即將來到的一次選舉 (C) 說明旅遊限制 (D) 概述一項建築計畫
93 According to the speaker, what does Shenzhen possess? (A) A world-renowned shopping complex (B) Favorable tax rates (C) An international airport (D) Numerous vacant retail spaces	93. 根據說話者所說，深圳擁有什麼？ (A) 世界知名的購物園區 (B) 有利的稅率 (C) 國際機場 (D) 許多閒置的零售空間
94 What do officials think about Shenzhen? (A) It currently has a high population. (B) It is experiencing increases in tourism. (C) It can achieve further economic success. (D) It is a safe place for travelers from abroad.	94. 官方認為深圳如何？ (A) 目前人口很多。 (B) 正經歷觀光產業的成長。 (C) 可以達成更高的經濟成就。 (D) 對國外旅客來說是個安全的地方。

題目 mayor [`meɚ] 市長　publicity [pʌb`lɪsətɪ] 公關；宣傳　corporate tax rate 公司稅率　population [͵pɑpjə`leʃən] 人口　enterprise [`ɛntɚ͵praɪz] 企業　entrepreneur [͵ɑntrəprə`nɝ] 企業家　potential [pə`tɛnʃəl] 有潛力的　optimistic [͵ɑptə`mɪstɪk] 樂觀的

92 effort [`ɛfɚt] 努力做出來的成果；努力　election [ɪ`lɛkʃən] 選舉　restriction [rɪ`strɪkʃən] 限制

93 world-renowned 世界知名的　favorable [`fevərəbḷ] 有利的；有幫助的　numerous [`njumərəs] 許多的

92 ○●●● 高　**整體內容相關問題－目的**　答案 (A)

題目詢問這篇報導的目的是什麼，因此必須注意獨白的開頭部分，並掌握整體脈絡。獨白開頭說：「Shenzhen will be launching a major campaign to attract foreign businesses」，表示深圳將著手進行大型宣傳活動以吸引外國企業，接著繼續說明相關資訊，因此正確答案是 (A) To describe promotional efforts。

93 ○●●● 高　**細節事項相關問題－特定細項**　答案 (B)

題目詢問深圳擁有什麼，因此要注意和題目關鍵字（Shenzhen possess）相關的內容。獨白說：「the city[Shenzhen]'s low corporate tax rates」，表示深圳的公司稅率低，因此正確答案是 (B) Favorable tax rates。

94 ●●●● 難　**細節事項相關問題－特定細項**　答案 (C)

題目詢問官方如何看待深圳，因此要注意和題目關鍵字（officials think）相關的內容。獨白說：「officials feel the city[Shenzhen] has yet to reach its full business potential. They are optimistic that the campaign will generate more attention from international companies, as well as increase tourism in the region.」，表示官方仍認為深圳尚未發揮其最大商業潛能，且對於這次宣傳活動將引起更多來自國際企業的關注並提升區域內觀光產業感到樂觀，由此可知，官方認為深圳在經濟上還可以更加成功，因此正確答案是 (C) It can achieve further economic success.。

95
96
97

Questions 95-97 refer to the following telephone message and form.

第 95-97 題請參考下列電話留言及表單。

美式發音

My name is Miranda Cruz, and I'm calling regarding *Elegant Fashion Magazine*. About a week ago, I was e-mailed a subscription renewal form for the publication. At the time, I signed up for a year-and-a-half subscription. However, [95]**I learned yesterday that I'll be traveling to France in December for a work project**. Since the length of my stay in the country is open-ended, I . . . uh . . . [96]**I can only commit to a one-year subscription to the magazine**. Of course, [97]**I would like the amount I overpaid to be returned to me**. If you have any questions, you can reach me at 555-2197.

我的名字是 Miranda Cruz，我打來是要說和《Elegant Fashion 雜誌》有關的事。大概一個禮拜前，我的電子郵件收到了這本雜誌的續訂表。那個時候我登記了要訂一年半。但是，[95] 我昨天得知我在十二月要前往法國進行一項工作專案。因為不確定我要待在那個國家多久，所以我……呃……[96] 這本雜誌我只能確定訂一年。當然，[97] 我想要拿回我多付的那筆錢。如果有任何問題，你可以打 555-2197 聯絡我。

Subscription Renewal Form

Subscription Period	Fee	Selection
6 months	$30	
12 months	[96]**$50**	
18 months	$70	√
24 months	$100	

續訂表

訂閱期間	費用	選擇
6 個月	30 美金	
12 個月	[96]50 美金	
18 個月	70 美金	√
24 個月	100 美金	

95 What does the speaker plan to do in December?

(A) Update her mailing address
(B) Make a subscription payment
(C) Submit a magazine article
(D) Travel overseas for work

95. 說話者計畫在十二月做什麼？

(A) 更新她的郵寄地址
(B) 支付訂閱費用
(C) 提交雜誌報導
(D) 前往海外工作

96 Look at the graphic. How much does the subscription the speaker is interested in cost?

(A) $30
(B) $50
(C) $70
(D) $100

96. 請看圖表。說話者有興趣的訂閱方案要花多少錢？

(A) 30 美金
(B) 50 美金
(C) 70 美金
(D) 100 美金

97 What does the speaker request?

(A) A partial refund
(B) A contract extension
(C) An account closure
(D) An e-mail confirmation

97. 說話者要求什麼？

(A) 部分退款
(B) 合約延長
(C) 終止帳戶
(D) 以電子郵件確認

題目 regarding [rɪˋgɑrdɪŋ] 關於 subscription [səbˋskrɪpʃən] 訂閱 renewal [rɪˋnjuəl]（合約等）展延；換新 length [lɛŋθ] 期間 open-ended 開放性的；無限制的 commit [kəˋmɪt] 承諾，保證 overpay [ˋovəˋpe] 多付

95 article [ˋɑrtɪkḷ] 報導；文章

97 partial [ˋpɑrʃəl] 部分的 contract [ˋkɑntrækt] 合約 extension [ɪkˋstɛnʃən] 延長 confirmation [ˌkɑnfəˋmeʃən] 確認；確定

95 ■ 細節事項相關問題－特定細項　　答案 (D)

中

題目詢問說話者計畫在十二月要做什麼，因此要注意提到題目關鍵字（December）的前後部分。獨白說：「I learned yesterday that I'll be traveling to France in December for a work project」，表示自己在十二月要前往法國工作，因此正確答案是 (D) Travel overseas for work。

換句話說

traveling to France ~ for a work project 前往法國進行一項工作專案 → Travel overseas for work 前往海外工作

新 **96** ■ 細節事項相關問題－圖表資料　　答案 (B)

高

題目詢問說話者有興趣的訂閱方案要花多少錢，因此必須確認題目提供的表格，並注意和題目關鍵字（subscription ~ interested in）相關的內容。獨白說：「I can only commit to a one-year subscription to the magazine」，表示自己只能確定會訂一年，透過題目所附的表格可知，說話者有興趣要訂的一年方案，也就是 12 個月的訂閱費用是 50 美金，因此正確答案是 (B) $50。

97 ■ 細節事項相關問題－要求　　答案 (A)

中

題目詢問說話者提出了什麼要求，因此必須注意聽獨白的中後半部出現要求相關表達的句子。獨白說：「I would like the amount I overpaid to be returned to me」，表示想要拿回多付的錢，因此正確答案是 (A) A partial refund。

98
99
100

Questions 98-100 refer to the following announcement and graph.

澳洲式發音

May I have everyone's attention? I've got a quick announcement to make before the Eastern Hills National Park opens today. [98]**The number of shuttle buses will increase next month. Specifically, buses will run from the main parking lot to the Cold Bridge National Monument every 20 minutes** instead of every 30. [99]**We will resume our regular schedule at the end of the peak season . . . uh, the month in which we usually receive less than 10,000 visitors.** I also wanted to remind you about [100]**the special lectures that will be held at the information center**. Each week, a different expert will discuss an aspect of the park's history. Um, [100]**Brenda Kirk did a great job of organizing this program,** so make sure to tell visitors about it.

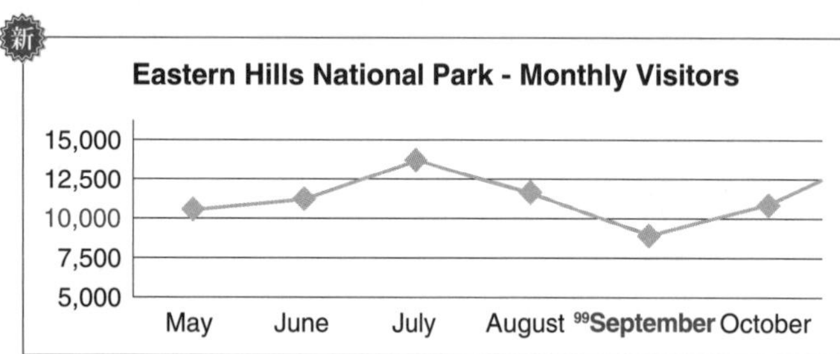

98 How often will buses run beginning next month?

(A) Every 20 minutes
(B) Every 30 minutes
(C) Every 40 minutes
(D) Every 60 minutes

99 新 Look at the graphic. When will the regular shuttle bus service most likely resume?

(A) In July
(B) In August
(C) In September
(D) In October

100 What is mentioned about Brenda Kirk?

(A) She manages the information center.
(B) She has arranged a lecture series.
(C) She will participate in a training program.
(D) She gave a presentation on the park's history.

第 98-100 題請參考下列公告及圖表。

可以請大家注意我這裡嗎？在今天 Eastern Hills 國家公園開幕前，我有一件事要很快宣布一下。[98] 接駁巴士的數量會在下個月增加。具體來說，巴士會改為每 20 分鐘從大停車場出發前往 Cold Bridge 國家紀念碑，而不是每 30 分鐘。[99] 我們在旺季結束後就會恢復成正常的時刻表……呃，也就是在我們一般要接待的遊客少於 10,000 名的那個月。我也想要提醒你們有關 [100] 將在服務中心舉辦的特別講座的事。每週都會有一位不同的專家來講述這座公園歷史的某一面向。嗯，[100]Brenda Kirk 在這項計畫的籌備上做得很好，所以請務必要告訴遊客們有關這個講座的事。

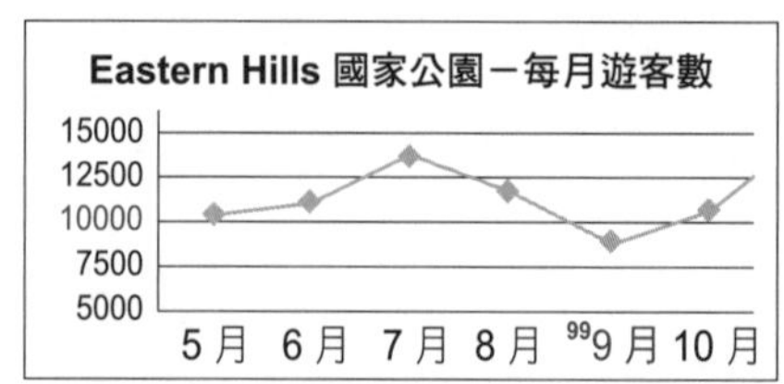

98. 巴士從下個月開始多久發一班車？

(A) 每 20 分鐘
(B) 每 30 分鐘
(C) 每 40 分鐘
(D) 每 60 分鐘

99. 請看圖表。最有可能會在什麼時候恢復成正常的接駁巴士服務？

(A) 七月
(B) 八月
(C) 九月
(D) 十月

100. 關於 Brenda Kirk，提到了什麼？

(A) 她管理服務中心。
(B) 她安排了系列講座。
(C) 她會參與一個培訓課程。
(D) 她就這座公園的歷史進行了簡報。

題目 specifically [美 spɪˋsɪfɪkḷɪ 英 spiˋsifikəli] 具體來說 run [rʌn] 運行；（車等）行駛
monument [美 ˋmɑnjəmənt 英 ˋmɔnjumənt] 紀念碑 resume [美 rɪˋzjum 英 riˋzju:m] 繼續；恢復
peak season 旺季 expert [美 ˋɛkspɚt 英 ˋekspə:t] 專家 aspect [ˋæspɛkt] 面相，觀點
100 arrange [əˋrendʒ] 安排；籌備

98 ■ 細節事項相關問題－程度 答案 (A)

中

題目詢問下個月開始巴士多久發一班車，因此要注意提到題目關鍵字（next month）的前後部分。獨白說：「The number of shuttle buses will increase next month. ~, buses will run ~ every 20 minutes」，表示下個月開始接駁巴士的數量會增加，改成每 20 分鐘發一班車，因此正確答案是 (A) Every 20 minutes。

新 **99** ■ 細節事項相關問題－圖表資料 答案 (C)

高

題目詢問正常接駁巴士服務的恢復時間點，因此必須確認題目提供的圖表內容，並注意和題目關鍵字（regular shuttle bus service ~ resume）相關的內容。獨白說：「We will resume our regular schedule at the end of the peak season ~, the month in which we usually receive less than 10,000 visitors.」，表示在旺季結束後，也就是在一般要接待的遊客少於 10,000 名的那個月，就會恢復成正常的時刻表，透過圖表可知，一般要接待的遊客少於 10,000 名的那個月是九月，因此正確答案是 (C) In September。

100 ■ 細節事項相關問題－提及 答案 (B)

中

題目詢問提到什麼與 Brenda Kirk 有關的事，因此必須注意提到題目關鍵字（Brenda Kirk）的前後部分。獨白說：「the special lectures that will be held at the information center」，提到將在服務中心舉辦特別講座，並說：「Brenda Kirk did a great job of organizing this program」，表示 Brenda Kirk 在這項計畫的籌備上做得很好，因此正確答案是 (B) She has arranged a lecture series.。

換句話說

did a great job of organizing ~ program 在計畫的籌備上做得很好
→ arranged a lecture series 安排了系列講座

TEST 07

Part 1 原文・翻譯・解析

Part 2 原文・翻譯・解析

Part 3 原文・翻譯・解析 新

Part 4 原文・翻譯・解析 新

MP3 收錄於 TEST 07.mp3。

進行深入練習或複習時，可以一邊多聽幾次收錄各國口音的試題 MP3，一邊搭配解答中的中英對照翻譯和解析，以及單字記憶表和多元口音單字記憶 MP3，達到事半功倍的效果。

1
○○●
低

澳洲式發音

(A) People are pouring some beverages.
(B) People are spreading out platters.
(C) People are holding wine glasses.
(D) People are sitting across from each other.

(A) 人們正在倒一些飲料。
(B) 人們正在把大淺盤分出去。
(C) 人們正拿著紅酒杯。
(D) 人們正面對面坐著。

兩人以上的照片

答案 (C)

仔細觀察照片中一對男女並肩坐著且拿著酒杯的模樣。

(A) [╳] pouring（正在倒）和照片中的人物動作無關，因此是錯誤選項。這裡使用照片中有出現的飲料（beverages）來造成混淆。

(B) [╳] spreading out（正在分出去）和照片中的人物動作無關，因此是錯誤選項。這裡使用照片中有出現的大淺盤（platters）來造成混淆。

(C) [○] 這裡正確描述拿著紅酒杯的模樣，所以是正確答案。

(D) [╳] 照片中的人並肩坐著，這裡卻描述成面對面坐著（across from each other），因此是錯誤選項。注意不要聽到 People are sitting（人們正坐著）就選擇這個選項。

單字　pour [㊊ por ㊇ pɔː] 傾倒　beverage [ˋbɛvərɪdʒ] 飲料　spread out 分散開來；攤開
platter [㊊ ˋplætɚ ㊇ ˋplætə] 大淺盤

2
○○●
中

英式發音

(A) She's removing fabric from a machine.
(B) She's connecting a pipe to a device.
(C) She's pulling a laundry cart.
(D) She's laying a sheet on the floor.

(A) 她正從機器裡把布料拿走。
(B) 她正在把管子連上裝置。
(C) 她正拉著洗衣籃推車。
(D) 她正把床單放在地板上。

單人照片

答案 (A)

仔細觀察照片中一名女子正從洗衣機中把布拿出來的模樣。

(A) [○] 這裡正確描述女子正從洗衣機中把布拿出來的模樣，所以是正確答案。

(B) [╳] connecting（正在連接）和女子的動作無關，因此是錯誤選項。這裡使用照片中出現的管子（pipe）和裝置（device）來造成混淆。

(C) [╳] pulling a laundry cart（正拉著洗衣籃推車）和女子的動作無關，因此是錯誤選項。這裡使用照片中出現的洗衣籃推車（laundry cart）來造成混淆。

(D) [╳] 透過照片無法確認女子是否正在把床單放到地板上，因此是錯誤選項。這裡使用和照片中出現的布料相關的 sheet（床單）來造成混淆。

單字　remove [rɪˋmuv] 移開；去除　fabric [ˋfæbrɪk] 布料；織物　connect [kəˋnɛkt] 連接
device [dɪˋvaɪs] 裝置，儀器　pull [pʊl] 拉　laundry [ˋlɔndrɪ] 待洗（或剛洗好的）衣物　lay [le] 放置
sheet [ʃit] 床單

3
○○●
中

加拿大式發音

(A) A woman is waving at a group.
(B) A woman is photographing a tree.
(C) The men are setting up a camera.
(D) The men are posing for a picture.

(A) 一名女子正朝一群人揮手。
(B) 一名女子正在拍一棵樹的照片。
(C) 男子們正在架設相機。
(D) 男子們正在擺姿勢拍照。

■ 兩人以上的照片 答案 (D)

仔細觀察照片中一名女子正在幫幾位擺好姿勢的男子照相的模樣。

(A) [╳] waving（正在揮手）和女子的動作無關，因此是錯誤選項。這裡使用照片中有出現的一群人（group）來造成混淆。

(B) [╳] 女子不是在拍樹（tree）的照片，而是在拍幾名男子，因此是錯誤選項。注意不要聽到 A woman is photographing（一名女子正在拍照）就選擇這個選項。

(C) [╳] setting up（正在架設）和男子的動作無關，因此是錯誤選項。這裡使用照片中有出現的相機（camera）來造成混淆。

(D) [○] 這裡正確描述幾名男子正擺出姿勢拍照的模樣，所以是正確答案。

單字 wave [wev] 揮（手、腳等） photograph [ˋfotəˏgræf] 為～拍照 set up 架設 pose for 為～擺姿勢

4 高

美式發音

(A) A power tool has been left in a case.
(B) An electrical cord is being coiled.
(C) A worker is cutting the base of a pole.
(D) A ladder has been propped against a wall.

(A) 一個電動工具被放在了箱子裡。
(B) 正在把一條電線捲成圈狀。
(C) 一名工人正在切割柱子的基座。
(D) 一道梯子靠在了牆上。

■ 單人照片 答案 (D)

仔細觀察照片中一名男子正在戶外使用工具工作的模樣，以及周遭事物的狀態。

(A) [╳] 男子正在使用電動工具，但這裡卻描述成工具被放在了箱子裡（has been left in a case），因此是錯誤選項。這裡使用照片中有出現的電動工具（power tool）來造成混淆。

(B) [╳] 照片中雖然有出現電線，但沒有正在把它捲成圈狀（is being coiled），因此是錯誤選項。

(C) [╳] 工人正在切割板子，但這裡卻描述為在切割柱子的基座（base of a pole），因此是錯誤選項。注意不要聽到 A worker is cutting（工人正在切割）就選擇這個答案。

(D) [○] 這裡正確描述梯子靠在牆上的狀態，所以是正確答案。

單字 power tool 電動工具 coil [kɔɪl] 把～捲成圈狀；盤繞 base [bes] 基座 pole [pol] 柱子
ladder [ˋlædɚ] 梯子 prop against 靠在～

5 高

英式發音

(A) A frame has been hung near a lamp.
(B) Windows are on both sides of a room.
(C) Some diners are having a meal at a table.
(D) A flowerpot is situated next to a carpet.

(A) 靠近檯燈的地方掛了一個相框。
(B) 房間的兩側都有窗戶。
(C) 一些用餐的人正在桌前用餐。
(D) 一個花盆放在了地毯旁邊。

■ 事物及風景照片 答案 (A)

仔細觀察照片中房間物品的狀態和位置。

(A) [○] 這裡正確描述相框掛在檯燈附近的樣子，所以是正確答案。

(B) [╳] 透過照片無法確認房間兩側是否有窗戶，因此是錯誤選項。注意不要聽到 Windows（窗戶）就選擇這個選項。

(C) [╳] 照片中沒有用餐的人（diners），因此是錯誤選項。這裡使用照片中有出現的桌子（table）來造成混淆。

(D) [╳] 花盆不在地毯旁邊（next to a carpet），而是在桌上，因此是錯誤選項。注意不要聽到 A flowerpot is situated（花盆放在）就選擇這個選項。

單字 frame [frem] 相框 hang [hæŋ] 懸掛 diner [美 ˋdaɪnɚ 英 ˋdainə] 用餐的人
flowerpot [美 ˋflaʊɚˏpɑt 英 ˋflauəpɔt] 花盆 situate [ˋsɪtʃʊˏet] 使位於

6 ●●●● 高

加拿大式發音

(A) Some equipment is being carried indoors. (B) A monitor is mounted on the wall. (C) A room has been decorated with patterned paper. (D) Some weights have been stored in a box.	(A) 正在把一些設備搬進室內。 (B) 一個螢幕被固定在牆上。 (C) 一個房間貼了有圖案的壁紙。 (D) 一些重物被存放在箱子裡了。

事物及風景照片

答案 (B)

仔細觀察照片中室內物品的狀態和位置。

(A) [╳] 照片中雖然出現了設備，但沒有正在搬（is being carried）它們，因此是錯誤選項。注意不要聽到 Some equipment（一些設備）就選擇這個選項。

(B) [〇] 這裡正確描述螢幕被固定在牆上的樣子，所以是正確答案。

(C) [╳] 房間裡貼的壁紙沒有圖案，這裡卻描述成貼了有圖案的壁紙，因此是錯誤選項。這裡利用照片拍攝地點的「房間（room）」來造成混淆。

(D) [╳] 重物沒有被存放在箱子裡，因此是錯誤選項。注意不要聽到 Some weights（一些重物）就選擇這個答案。

單字 equipment [ɪ`kwɪpmənt] 器具；設備　carry [`kærɪ] 搬運　indoors [`ɪn`dorz] 往室內
mount [maʊnt] 固定；安裝　decorate [`dɛkəˌret] 裝飾；為～貼壁紙　patterned [`pætɚnd] 有圖案的
weight [wet] 重物　store [stor] 存放

7 低

美式發音 → 澳洲式發音

When can I buy tickets for a semi-final game?

(A) No, I'm fine.
(B) Right now, the score is tied.
(C) The first week of June.

我什麼時候可以買準決賽的門票？

(A) 不用，我很好。
(B) 現在，分數追平了。
(C) 六月的第一週。

When 疑問句 答案 (C)

這是詢問什麼時候可以買準決賽門票的 When 疑問句。

(A) [╳] 這裡以 No 來回答疑問詞疑問句，因此是錯誤選項。這裡利用發音相似單字 final – fine 來造成混淆。

(B) [╳] 這裡使用和 game（比賽）相關的 score（分數）來造成混淆。注意不要聽到 Right now（現在）就選擇這個選項。

(C) [○] 這裡提到六月的第一週，也就是能買準決賽門票的時間點，因此是正確答案。

單字 semi-final 準決賽的 score [美 skor 英 skɔː] 分數 tie [taɪ] 同分，平手

8 中

加拿大式發音 → 英式發音

What's included in the gift bag for visitors?

(A) Thank you for the present.
(B) Items displaying our company's name.
(C) Give Kevin a few more plates.

給訪客的禮物袋裡有什麼？

(A) 謝謝你的禮物。
(B) 上面有我們公司名字的東西。
(C) 再多給 Kevin 幾個盤子。

What 疑問句 答案 (B)

這是詢問送給訪客的禮物袋裡有什麼的 What 疑問句。

(A) [╳] 這是利用和題目中 gift（禮物）字義相同的 present（禮物）來混淆的錯誤選項。

(B) [○] 這裡表示是上面有公司名稱的東西，提到送給訪客的禮物袋內容物，因此是正確答案。

(C) [╳] 這是使用可以透過 gift bag（禮物袋）聯想到的相關動作 Give（給）來混淆的錯誤選項。

單字 include [ɪn`klud] 包含 visitor [`vɪzɪtɚ] 訪客 display [dɪ`sple] 顯示；陳列 plate [plet] 盤子

9 低

美式發音 → 加拿大式發音

How long will it take to reach the ski resort?

(A) About four hours.
(B) My winter break is almost over.
(C) Take the next freeway exit.

到滑雪度假村要花多久時間？

(A) 大概四個小時。
(B) 我的寒假差不多結束了。
(C) 走下一個高速公路出口。

How 疑問句 答案 (A)

這是詢問要花多久時間才會到滑雪度假村的 How 疑問句。這裡必須知道 How long 在詢問期間。

(A) [○] 這裡表示大概四個小時，也就是到滑雪度假村的所需時間，因此是正確答案。

(B) [╳] 這是利用和 ski（滑雪）相關的 winter（冬天）來造成混淆的錯誤選項。

(C) [╳] 題目詢問要花多久時間才會到滑雪度假村，這裡卻回答要走下一個高速公路出口，毫不相關，因此是錯誤選項。這裡以另一字義「使用」來重複使用題目中出現的 take（花費），企圖造成混淆。

單字 take [tek] 花費（時間等）；使用（交通方式、道路等）；搭乘 reach [ritʃ] 到達 freeway [`frɪˌwe] 高速公路 exit [`ɛksɪt] 出口

10 ○●●● 中

澳洲式發音 → 美式發音	
Who is going to talk first at the economics forum?	誰要在經濟論壇上第一個發言？
(A) It begins at 9:30 tomorrow morning. (B) The president of the research firm. (C) Yes, I've got the transcript here.	(A) 它在明天早上 9 點 30 分開始。 (B) 研究公司的總裁。 (C) 是的，我這裡有文字記錄。

Who 疑問句 答案 (B)

這是詢問誰要在經濟論壇上第一個發言的 Who 疑問句。

(A) [╳] 題目詢問誰要在經濟論壇上第一個發言，這裡卻回答在明天早上 9 點 30 分開始，毫不相關，因此是錯誤選項。這裡利用可以代稱題目中 economics forum（經濟論壇）的 It 來造成混淆。

(B) [○] 這裡回答研究公司的總裁，提到要在經濟論壇上第一個發言的人是誰，因此是正確答案。

(C) [╳] 這裡以 Yes 來回答疑問詞疑問句，因此是錯誤選項。這裡使用和 talk（發言）相關的 transcript（文字記錄）來造成混淆。

單字 economics [美 ˌikəˋnɑmɪks 英 ˌi:kəˋnɔmiks] 經濟學 forum [ˋforəm] 論壇，討論會
president [ˋprɛzədənt] 總裁；會長 transcript [ˋtrænˌskrɪpt]（演講等的）文字記錄

11 ○●●● 高

英式發音 → 澳洲式發音	
Can't we go to the theater later in the week?	我們不能這週晚點再去劇院嗎？
(A) It's not my second visit. (B) A new play by a local writer. (C) No, we reserved seats for this evening.	(A) 這不是我第二次去。 (B) 一齣當地作家寫的新戲。 (C) 不行，我們預訂了今晚的位子。

否定疑問句 答案 (C)

這是詢問能不能這週晚點再去劇院的否定疑問句。

(A) [╳] 這是利用和 go（去）相關的 visit（造訪）來造成混淆的錯誤選項。

(B) [╳] 這是利用和 theater（劇院）相關的 play（戲劇）來造成混淆的錯誤選項。

(C) [○] 這裡用 No 表示不能這週晚點再去，並附加說明已預訂了今晚的位子，因此是正確答案。

單字 visit [ˋvɪzɪt] 造訪；參觀 play [ple] 戲劇 reserve [美 rɪˋzɝv 英 riˋzə:v] 預約，預訂 seat [sit] 座位

12 ○●●● 中

美式發音 → 加拿大式發音	
Has the package been delivered yet?	那件包裹送到了嗎？
(A) There is no charge for delivery. (B) Check with the other receptionist. (C) I ordered it online.	(A) 沒有運費。 (B) 問問另一位接待人員。 (C) 我在網路上訂購的。

助動詞疑問句 答案 (B)

這是確認包裹是否已送達的助動詞（Have）疑問句。

(A) [╳] 題目詢問包裹是否已送達，這裡卻回答沒有運費，毫不相關，因此是錯誤選項。這裡利用發音相似單字 delivered – delivery 來造成混淆。

(B) [○] 這裡回答去問問另一位接待人員，間接表示自己不知道是否已送達，因此是正確答案。

(C) [╳] 這是利用可以代稱題目中 package（包裹）的 it 及和 delivered（送達）相關的 ordered（訂購）來造成混淆的錯誤選項。

單字 package [ˋpækɪdʒ] 包裹；包裝 deliver [dɪˋlɪvɚ] 運送；投遞 charge [tʃɑrdʒ] 費用 check with 詢問～
receptionist [rɪˋsɛpʃənɪst] 接待人員

13 ○○●● 中

🔊 英式發音 → 加拿大式發音	
What's the matter with your briefcase?	你的公事包發生什麼事了？
(A) That's very interesting.	(A) 那非常有趣。
(B) Juice was spilled on it.	(B) 果汁灑在上面了。
(C) My car is fine.	(C) 我的車沒事。

■ **What 疑問句** 答案 (B)

這是詢問對方的公事包發生了什麼事的 What 疑問句。

(A) [╳] 這是使用可以代稱題目中 briefcase（公事包）的 That 來造成混淆的錯誤選項。

(B) [○] 這裡說果汁灑在了上面，提到公事包發生了什麼事，因此是正確答案。

(C) [╳] 題目詢問對方的公事包發生了什麼事，這裡卻回答自己的車沒事，毫不相關，因此是錯誤選項。注意不要聽到 fine（好的）就選擇這個選項。

單字　matter [[美] `mætɚ [英] `mætə] 事情；重要性　briefcase [`brif͵kes] 公事包　spill [spɪl] 灑出；溢出

14 ○○●● 中

🔊 英式發音 → 澳洲式發音	
How would you like to spend the afternoon?	你下午想做什麼？
(A) If you'd like to.	(A) 如果你想的話。
(B) Because I spent too much money.	(B) 因為我花了太多錢。
(C) I haven't given it much thought.	(C) 我還沒怎麼去想這件事。

■ **How 疑問句** 答案 (C)

這是詢問對方下午想做什麼的 How 疑問句。這裡必須知道 How 詢問的是方法，才能順利作答。

(A) [╳] 題目詢問下午想做什麼，這裡卻回答如果你想的話，毫不相關，因此是錯誤選項。這裡利用與題目的 would you like to 發音相似的 you'd like to 來造成混淆。

(B) [╳] 這是利用題目中 spend（花費）的另一字義「花錢」來造成混淆的錯誤選項。

(C) [○] 這裡說還沒怎麼去想這件事，間接表示不知道，因此是正確答案。

單字　spend [spɛnd] 花費（時間或精力等）；花錢

15 ○●●● 高

🔊 英式發音 → 美式發音	
Should we distribute awards to staff now or after dinner?	我們要現在還是在晚餐之後把獎品發給員工？
(A) Not everyone has arrived yet.	(A) 還有人沒到。
(B) I'll have the tomato soup.	(B) 我要番茄湯。
(C) Our main distribution center.	(C) 我們主要的配送中心。

■ **選擇疑問句** 答案 (A)

這是詢問要現在還是在晚餐之後把獎品發給員工的選擇疑問句。

(A) [○] 這裡回答還有人沒到，間接選擇要在晚餐後發，因此是正確答案。

(B) [╳] 這是使用可以透過 dinner（晚餐）的餐點而聯想到的 tomato soup（番茄湯）來造成混淆的錯誤選項。

(C) [╳] 題目詢問要現在還是在晚餐之後把獎品發給員工，這裡卻回答我們主要的配送中心，毫不相關，因此是錯誤選項。這裡利用發音相似單字 distribute – distribution 來造成混淆。

單字　distribute [dɪ`strɪbjʊt] 分發；分銷　award [[美] ə`wɔrd [英] ə`wɔ:d] 獎品；獎項
distribution [͵dɪstrə`bjuʃən] 分發；分銷

16 ○●●● 中

🔊 美式發音 → 加拿大式發音 Mr. Willis from the payroll department called for me, right? (A) All the supplies have been paid for. (B) Here's my extension number. (C) No, he was looking for Andrea.	薪資部的 Willis 先生有打給我，對嗎？ (A) 所有備品都已付過款了。 (B) 這是我的分機號碼。 (C) 沒有，他找的是 Andrea。

附加問句 答案 (C)

這是確認薪資部的 Willis 先生是否有打電話給自己的附加問句。

(A) [╳] 題目詢問薪資部的 Willis 先生是否有打電話給自己，這裡卻回答所有備品都已付過款了，毫不相關，因此是錯誤選項。這裡利用發音相似單字 payroll – paid for 來造成混淆。

(B) [╳] 這是使用和 called（打電話）相關的 extension number（分機號碼）來造成混淆的錯誤選項。

(C) [○] 這裡以 No 表示薪資部的 Willis 先生沒有打電話給對方，並附加說明他找的是 Andrea，因此是正確答案。

單字 payroll department 薪資部 supply [sə`plaɪ] 備品；生活用品 pay for 支付～的費用
extension number 分機號碼 look for 尋找～；期待～

17 ○●●● 高

🔊 加拿大式發音 → 英式發音 Are employees cataloging complaints that we receive from customers? (A) It's the product catalog. (B) That's what I've been told. (C) Only a few workers were disappointed.	員工們是在記錄我們從客人那裡接到的投訴嗎？ (A) 這是產品型錄。 (B) 我是這麼聽說的。 (C) 只有幾個員工很失望。

Be 動詞疑問句 答案 (B)

這是詢問員工們是否在記錄從客人那裡接到的投訴的 Be 動詞疑問句。

(A) [╳] 題目詢問員工們是否在記錄從客人那裡接到的投訴，這裡卻回答這是產品型錄，毫不相關，因此是錯誤選項。這裡以名詞「型錄」之意重複使用題目中做為動詞的 cataloging（記錄）來造成混淆。

(B) [○] 這裡回答自己是這麼聽說的，表示員工們的確正在記錄從客人那裡接到的投訴，因此是正確答案。

(C) [╳] 這是使用和 employees（員工們）相關的 workers（工人們）及與 complaints（投訴）相關的 disappointed（失望的）來造成混淆的錯誤選項。

單字 catalog [[美] `kætəlɔg [英] `kætəlɔ:g] 型錄；記錄（成清單） disappoint [͵dɪsə`pɔɪnt] 使失望

18 ○●●● 高

🔊 美式發音 → 澳洲式發音 Don't purchases over €75 qualify for free shipping? (A) Payments can be made over the phone. (B) Take these parcels as well. (C) We no longer offer that service.	消費超過 75 歐元不是符合免運資格嗎？ (A) 可以透過電話付款。 (B) 也把這些包裹拿走吧。 (C) 我們不再提供這項服務了。

否定疑問句 答案 (C)

這是確認消費超過 75 歐元是否符合免運資格的否定疑問句。

(A) [╳] 這是利用和 purchases（消費）相關的 Payments（付款）來造成混淆的錯誤選項。

(B) [╳] 這是利用和 shipping（運送）相關的 parcels（包裹）來造成混淆的錯誤選項。

(C) [○] 這裡回答不再提供該服務，間接表示消費超過 75 歐元仍然沒有免運，因此是正確答案。

單字 purchase [`pɝtʃəs] 消費；購買 qualify for 符合～的資格 payment [`pemənt] 付款；支付款項
parcel [[美] `pɑrsl̩ [英] `pɑ:sl] 包裹

19 ●●●○ 高

澳洲式發音 → 英式發音 When can you update the bulletin board? (A) Generally, Steven takes care of it. (B) The most up-to-date medications. (C) We upgraded the network last month.	你什麼時候可以更新布告欄？ (A) 一般 Steven 會處理這件事。 (B) 最新的藥物。 (C) 我們上個月升級了網路。

When 疑問句 答案 (A)

這是詢問對方什麼時候可以更新布告欄的 When 疑問句。

(A) [○] 這裡回答一般 Steven 會處理這件事，間接表示自己不會去更新，因此是正確答案。

(B) [╳] 題目詢問對方什麼時候可以更新布告欄，這裡卻回答最新的藥物，毫不相關，因此是錯誤選項。這裡利用發音相似單字 update – up-to-date 來造成混淆。

(C) [╳] 這是使用發音相似單字 update – upgraded 及時間點 last month 來造成混淆的錯誤選項。

單字 bulletin board 布告欄 generally [ˋdʒɛnərəlɪ] 通常，一般地 take care of 處理～；負責～
up-to-date 最新的 medication [美 ˌmɛdɪˋkeʃən 英 ˌmediˋkeiʃən] 藥物

20 ●●●● 難

英式發音 → 加拿大式發音 Mr. Adams, where should we discuss the Ford Project? (A) As soon as I return from my meeting. (B) The second-floor conference room isn't being used. (C) Everyone is pleased with the project.	Adams 先生，我們該在哪裡討論 Ford 專案？ (A) 一等我開完會回來。 (B) 二樓的會議室現在沒人用。 (C) 大家都對這個專案很滿意。

Where 疑問句 答案 (B)

這是詢問 Adams 先生該在哪裡討論專案的 Where 疑問句。

(A) [╳] 題目詢問該在哪裡討論專案，這裡卻回答時間點，因此是錯誤選項。這裡利用與題目的 where 發音相似的 when 來造成混淆，請注意不要聽成 when should we discuss the Ford Project（我們什麼時候該討論 Ford 專案）而選擇這個選項。

(B) [○] 這裡回答二樓的會議室現在沒人用，間接表示要在二樓的會議室討論專案，因此是正確答案。

(C) [╳] 這是透過重複題目中出現的 Project 來造成混淆的錯誤選項。

單字 pleased [plizd] 滿意的；高興的

21 ●●●○ 高

美式發音 → 加拿大式發音 Supervisors must strictly adhere to established regulations. (A) The store was established a decade ago. (B) What about in special circumstances? (C) Management provided lunch.	管理者必須嚴守既定規範。 (A) 這間店在十年前創立。 (B) 那在特殊情況下呢？ (C) 管理階層提供了午餐。

陳述句 答案 (B)

這是陳述管理者必須嚴守既定規範的客觀事實陳述句。

(A) [╳] 題目陳述管理者必須嚴守既定規範，這裡卻回答這間店在十年前創立，毫不相關，因此是錯誤選項。這裡以動詞字義「創立」來重複使用題目中的 established（既定的），企圖造成混淆。

(B) [○] 這裡反問在特殊情況下會如何，要求對方提供更多資訊，因此是正確答案。

(C) [╳] 這是使用和 Supervisors（管理者）相關的 Management（管理階層）來造成混淆的錯誤選項。

單字 supervisor [ˌsupəˋvaɪzə] 管理者；監督人 strictly [ˋstrɪktlɪ] 嚴格地 adhere to 遵守～
established [əsˋtæblɪʃt] 既有的；已確立的 establish [əˋstæblɪʃ] 創立；建立 decade [ˋdɛked] 十年
circumstance [ˋsɝkəmˌstæns] 情況；情勢 management [ˋmænɪdʒmənt] 管理階層；管理

TEST 1 2 3 4 5 6 7 8 9 10

22 ○○●●● 中

[🔊] 英式發音 → 澳洲式發音

Did Ms. LaPlante request extra towels and pillows, or just pillows?

(A) Because I'm going to the pool.
(B) Additional interns.
(C) She'd like both.

LaPlante 小姐是要求要額外的毛巾和枕頭嗎？還是只要枕頭而已？

(A) 因為我要去游泳池。
(B) 額外的實習生。
(C) 她兩個都要。

選擇疑問句 答案 (C)

這是詢問 LaPlante 小姐是要求要額外的毛巾和枕頭，還是只要枕頭而已的選擇疑問句。

(A) [╳] 題目詢問 LaPlante 小姐是要求要額外的毛巾和枕頭，還是只要枕頭而已，這裡卻回答理由，因此是錯誤選項。這裡使用可以透過 towels（毛巾）的使用地點而聯想到的 pool（游泳池）來造成混淆。

(B) [╳] 這是使用和題目中 extra（額外的）意義相同的 Additional（額外的）來造成混淆的錯誤選項。

(C) [○] 這裡回答她兩個都要，表示 LaPlante 要求要額外的毛巾和枕頭，因此是正確答案。

單字 extra [`ɛkstrə] 額外的；附加的 pillow [[美] `pɪlo [英] `piləu] 枕頭 additional [ə`dɪʃənl] 額外的；附加的

23 ○○●●● 中

[🔊] 加拿大式發音 → 美式發音

Have you had a chance to train the new waitress?

(A) Not as of yet.
(B) No, we'd better head to Platform 2.
(C) There's a chance it might snow.

你有機會訓練新的女服務生了嗎？

(A) 目前還沒有。
(B) 不是，我們最好去第二月台。
(C) 有機會可能會下雪。

助動詞疑問句 答案 (A)

這是詢問對方是否有機會訓練新的女服務生的助動詞（Have）疑問句。

(A) [○] 這裡回答目前還沒有，表示還沒機會訓練她們，因此是正確答案。

(B) [╳] 這裡利用與題目中 train（訓練）的另一字義「火車」相關的 Platform（月台）來造成混淆。注意不要聽到 No 就選擇這個選項。

(C) [╳] 題目詢問是否有機會訓練新的女服務生，這裡卻回答有機會可能會下雪，毫不相關，因此是錯誤選項。這裡透過題目中 chance（機會）的另一字義「可能性」來造成混淆。

單字 chance [tʃæns] 機會；可能性 train [tren] 訓練；火車 platform [`plæt͵fɔrm] 月台

24 ○○●●● 中

[🔊] 英式發音 → 加拿大式發音

Are you aware that we can't use our normal route to work?

(A) There's a way to fix the device.
(B) You'll find them quite useful.
(C) Yes, a lane is being added to Highway 43.

你有發覺我們無法走一般路線來上班了嗎？

(A) 有個方法可以修好這個裝置。
(B) 你會發現它們相當有用。
(C) 有，43 號公路上正在增加一個車道。

Be 動詞疑問句 答案 (C)

這是確認對方是否有發覺無法走一般路線來上班的 Be 動詞疑問句。

(A) [╳] 這是利用和 route（路線）相關的 way（路）的另一字義「方法」來造成混淆的錯誤選項。注意不要聽到 There's a way 就選擇這個選項。

(B) [╳] 題目詢問對方是否有發覺無法走一般路線來上班，這裡卻回答對方會發現它們相當有用，毫不相關，因此是錯誤選項。這裡利用發音相似單字 use – useful 來造成混淆。

(C) [○] 這裡以 Yes 表示自己有發覺無法走一般路線來上班，並附加說明 43 號公路上正在增加一個車道，提供更多資訊，因此是正確答案。

單字 aware [[美] ə`wɛr [英] ə`wɛə] 察覺的 normal [[美] `nɔrml̩ [英] `nɔ:məl] 一般的；普通的 route [rut] 路線；路程 lane [len] 車道；巷道 highway [`haɪ͵we] 公路

25 ○○●●● 中

美式發音 → 澳洲式發音 Which of these printers has wireless capabilities? (A) As far as I know, that's right. (B) A small section of wire. (C) They all do.	這些印表機裡哪台有無線功能？ (A) 就我所知，沒錯。 (B) 一小段的電線。 (C) 它們全都有。

Which 疑問句 答案 (C)

這是詢問哪台印表機具有無線功能的 Which 疑問句。這裡一定要聽到 Which of these printers 才能順利作答。

(A) [╳] 這裡以和 Yes 意思相同的 that's right 來回答疑問詞疑問句，因此是錯誤選項。這裡利用與題目的 Which of these printers has 發音相似的 Do these printers have 來造成混淆，請小心不要誤聽成 Do these printers have wireless capabilities（這些印表機有無線功能嗎）而選擇這個答案。

(B) [╳] 題目詢問哪台印表機具有無線功能，這裡回答一小段的電線，毫不相關，因此是錯誤選項。這裡利用發音相似單字 wireless – wire 來造成混淆。

(C) [○] 這裡回答它們全都有，表示所有印表機都有無線功能，因此是正確答案。

單字 wireless [`waɪrlɪs] 無線的 capability [ˌkepə`bɪlətɪ] 性能；能力 section [`sɛkʃən] 部分；（切下的）段，塊 wire [美 waɪr 英 `waiə] 金屬線；電線

26 ○○●●● 中

澳洲式發音 → 英式發音 None of our guests have dietary restrictions, do they? (A) We've been granted restricted access. (B) Those details are written on this sheet. (C) None of the vehicles.	我們的來賓之中沒有人有飲食禁忌，對嗎？ (A) 我們已經獲得有限度的使用權了。 (B) 那些細節都寫在這張紙上了。 (C) 這些車輛都不是。

附加問句 答案 (B)

這是確認來賓是不是都沒有飲食禁忌的附加問句。

(A) [╳] 這是利用發音相似單字 restrictions – restricted 來造成混淆的錯誤選項。

(B) [○] 這裡回答細節都寫在這張紙上了，間接表示不清楚，因此是正確答案。

(C) [╳] 題目詢問來賓是不是都沒有飲食禁忌，這裡回答這些車輛都不是，毫不相關，因此是錯誤選項。這裡藉著重複題目中出現的 None of 來造成混淆。

單字 dietary [美 `daɪəˌtɛrɪ 英 `daiəteri] 飲食的 restriction [rɪ`strɪkʃən] 限制 grant [美 grænt 英 grɑ:nt] 准予；給予 restricted [rɪ`strɪktɪd] 有限度的；受限的 access [`æksɛs] 使用權 vehicle [美 `viɪkḷ 英 `vi:ikl] 車輛；搭載工具

27 ○○○●● 低

加拿大式發音 → 美式發音 Some of this produce is beginning to spoil. (A) I just started this week. (B) Factory production levels. (C) Please replace it with fresh vegetables.	這些農產品裡有一些開始壞了。 (A) 我這週剛開始。 (B) 工廠的生產水準。 (C) 請將其更換成新鮮蔬菜。

陳述句 答案 (C)

這是指出有部分農產品開始壞了的問題點的陳述句。

(A) [╳] 這是利用和題目中 beginning（開始）意義相同的 started（開始）來造成混淆的錯誤選項。

(B) [╳] 題目指出有部分農產品開始壞了，這裡卻回答工廠的生產水準，毫不相關，因此是錯誤選項。這裡利用發音相似單字 produce – production 來造成混淆。

(C) [○] 這裡要求把壞掉的農產品更換成新鮮蔬菜，提出解決問題點的方法，因此是正確答案。

單字 produce [`prɑdjus] 農產品 spoil [spɔɪl]（食物等）腐壞 factory [`fæktərɪ] 工廠 production [prə`dʌkʃən] 生產；產量 replace [rɪ`ples] 替換；取代 vegetable [`vɛdʒətəbl] 蔬菜

28
●●●○ 高

加拿大式發音 → 英式發音	
Why didn't you ask me for a ride from the airport?	你為什麼不叫我去機場載你？
(A) I made other arrangements. (B) I asked for a window seat. (C) At the international airport.	(A) 我另有安排了。 (B) 我要了靠窗的位子。 (C) 在國際機場。

Why 疑問句

答案 (A)

這是詢問對方為什麼不叫自己去機場載他的 Why 疑問句。

(A) [○] 這裡回答另有安排了，直接回答原因，因此是正確答案。

(B) [╳] 這是以 asked 來重複題目中出現的 ask，且利用可以透過 airport（機場）聯想到的與飛機相關的 window seat（靠窗的位子）來造成混淆的錯誤選項。請注意不要一聽到 I asked for 就選擇這個答案。

(C) [╳] 題目詢問對方為什麼不叫自己去機場載他，這裡卻回答地點，因此是錯誤選項。這裡藉重複題目中出現的 airport 來造成混淆。

單字　ride [raɪd] 搭載；搭乘　arrangement [ə`rendʒmənt] 安排；準備工作

29
●●○○ 中

澳洲式發音 → 美式發音	
This wristwatch has to be engraved with a client's name.	這支腕錶必須刻上客人的名字。
(A) My wrist still hurts. (B) OK, but it can't be done until tomorrow. (C) Yes, watch out for the beam.	(A) 我的手腕還在痛。 (B) 好，但這要到明天才會弄好。 (C) 沒錯，注意光線。

陳述句

答案 (B)

這是提出必須在腕錶上刻上客人名字的要求陳述句。

(A) [╳] 題目陳述要在腕錶上刻上客人名字的要求，這裡卻回答自己的手腕還在痛，毫不相關，因此是錯誤選項。這裡以 wrist 來重複題目中出現的 wristwatch（腕錶）來造成混淆。

(B) [○] 這裡以 OK 來答應要求，並附加說明要到明天才會完成，因此是正確答案。

(C) [╳] 這裡將題目中 wristwatch（腕錶）一字裡的 watch 以動詞字義的「注意」來重複使用，企圖造成混淆。注意不要聽到 Yes 就選擇這個答案。

單字　engrave [ɪn`grev] 雕刻；銘記　wrist [rɪst] 手腕　beam [bim] 光線

30
●●●○ 高

加拿大式發音 → 英式發音	
Why don't I ask the engineers to improve this prototype?	要不要我去請工程師們改善這個原型？
(A) No, we don't own any. (B) Tell them to apply our feedback. (C) Research and development costs.	(A) 不，我們一個都沒有。 (B) 告訴他們要運用我們的回饋意見。 (C) 研發成本。

提供疑問句

答案 (B)

這是表示自己要去請工程師們改善原型的提供疑問句。這裡必須知道 Why don't I 是提供的表達。

(A) [╳] 這裡透過重複題目中出現的 don't 來造成混淆。注意不要聽到 No 就選擇這個答案。

(B) [○] 這裡回答告訴他們要運用回饋意見，間接表示答應，因此是正確答案。

(C) [╳] 這是利用和 improve（改善）相關的 development（開發）來造成混淆的錯誤選項。

單字　engineer [͵ɛndʒə`nɪr] 工程師　improve [ɪm`pruv] 改善；提升　prototype [`protə͵taɪp] 原型；樣品
apply [ə`plaɪ] 使用，運用　feedback [`fid͵bæk] 回饋意見　development [dɪ`vɛləpmənt] 開發

31 ○●●●● 高

美式發音 → 澳洲式發音 These machines ought to be unloaded immediately. (A) We should order them soon. (B) Do you mean the dishwashers? (C) All downloads are free of charge.	應該立刻卸下這些機器。 (A) 我們應該快點訂購它們。 (B) 你是指洗碗機嗎？ (C) 所有下載都免費。

陳述句　　答案 (B)

這是表示應該立刻卸下這些機器的客觀事實陳述句。

(A) [╳] 這是使用與題目中 ought to（應該～）意義相近的 should（應該～），且以 them 來代稱題目中出現的 These machines（這些機器）來造成混淆的錯誤選項。

(B) [○] 這裡反問是不是在指洗碗機，要求提供更多資訊，因此是正確答案。

(C) [╳] 題目表示應該立刻卸下這些機器，這裡卻回答所有下載都免費，毫不相關，因此是錯誤選項。這裡利用發音相似單字 unloaded – downloads 來造成混淆。

單字　ought to 應該～　unload [ʌnˋlod] 卸下（貨物等）　immediately [ɪˋmidɪɪtlɪ] 立刻
dishwasher [㊤ ˋdɪʃˏwɑʃɚ ㊥ ˋdiʃˏwɔʃə] 洗碗機　free of charge 免費的

TEST 1 2 3 4 5 6 7 8 9 10

32
33
34

Questions 32-34 refer to the following conversation.

英式發音 → 加拿大式發音

W: Hi, Mark. [32]**Our department head wants me to arrange the corporation's year-end party.** However, I'm not sure when it should be hosted. How about December 21?

M: [33]**Could you think about choosing another day?** The 21st is when the Tampa Bay Hurricanes plays in the championship ice hockey game, and I know a lot of staff plan to watch that.

W: Thanks for reminding me. Would December 22 be better, then?

M: Definitely. Also, [34]**I can help out by sending a notice to fellow employees.** So, let me know once you settle on a specific time and the other details.

第 32-34 題請參考下列對話。

女：嗨，Mark。[32] 我們部門主管想要我來安排公司的尾牙。不過，我不確定應該要辦在什麼時候。12 月 21 日怎麼樣？

男：[33] 妳可以考慮選別天嗎？21 日是坦帕灣 Hurricanes 隊要進行冰球冠軍賽的日子，我知道很多員工都打算要看那場比賽。

女：謝謝你提醒我。那 12 月 22 日會比較好嗎？

男：一定會。還有，[34] 我可以幫忙寄通知給同事們。所以，等妳搞定具體時間和其他細節就跟我說吧。

32 What task has the woman been assigned?

(A) Planning an event
(B) Revising an annual report
(C) Arranging rides for staff
(D) Promoting a competition

33 What does the man request the woman do?

(A) Lead a team-building exercise
(B) Consider a different date
(C) Speak to a department head
(D) Announce the results of a match

34 What does the man offer to do?

(A) Get passes for a game
(B) Write down some directions
(C) Search for a local business
(D) Message some colleagues

32 女子被分派到什麼任務？

(A) 策劃一個活動
(B) 修改一份年報
(C) 為員工安排交通工具
(D) 宣傳一項競賽

33 男子要求女子做什麼？

(A) 主持團隊建立的活動
(B) 考慮不同的日期
(C) 和部門主管談談
(D) 宣布比賽的結果

34 男子願意做什麼？

(A) 取得一場比賽的通行證
(B) 寫下一些指示
(C) 尋找一間當地企業
(D) 傳遞訊息給一些同事

題目 year-end party 尾牙　championship [ˋtʃæmpɪən͵ʃɪp] 冠軍資格　fellow [ˋfɛlo] 同事的；同事　settle on 搞定～；決定～　specific [spɪˋsɪfɪk] 具體的；明確的

32 revise [rɪˋvaɪz] 修改　annual [ˋænjʊəl] 年度的　competition [͵kɑmpəˋtɪʃən] 比賽；賽會

33 consider [kənˋsɪdɚ] 考慮　announce [əˋnaʊns] 宣布　match [mætʃ]（一場）比賽

34 pass [pæs] 通行證　direction [dəˋrɛkʃən] 指示　search for 搜尋～　message [ˋmɛsɪdʒ] 傳遞訊息　colleague [ˋkɑlig] 同事

32 細節事項相關問題－特定細項 答案 (A)

中

題目詢問女子被分配到什麼任務，因此要注意聽和題目關鍵字（task ~ woman ~ assigned）相關的內容。女子說：「Our department head wants me to arrange the corporation's year-end party.」，表示部門主管想要自己來安排公司的尾牙，因此正確答案是 (A) Planning an event。

33 細節事項相關問題－要求 答案 (B)

低

題目詢問男子要求女子做什麼，因此必須注意聽男子話中提到與要求女子做事相關的內容。男子對女子說：「Could you think about choosing another day?」，詢問女子可否考慮選別天，因此正確答案是 (B) Consider a different date。

換句話說

think about choosing another day 考慮選別天 → Consider a different date 考慮不同的日期

34 細節事項相關問題－提議 答案 (D)

中

題目詢問男子願意做什麼，因此要注意聽男子話中出現的提議相關表達。男子說：「I can help out by sending a notice to fellow employees」，表示可以幫忙寄通知給同事們，因此正確答案是 (D) Message some colleagues。

換句話說

sending a notice to fellow employees 寄通知給同事們 → Message some colleagues 傳遞訊息給一些同事

Questions 35-37 refer to the following conversation.

英式發音 → 澳洲式發音

W: Excuse me, [35]**I'd like to see the 8:00 P.M. screening** of *Voyage Across Australia*.

M: I'm sorry. But [35]**tickets for that and all other show times tonight have been sold out**. You may book a seat for tomorrow night, however.

W: I didn't realize the movie was that popular. I have to be at the office tomorrow night. [36]**Will the film still be playing at the theater next week?**

M: Yes. In fact, [37]**Andy Baker, the director, will be present for a question and answer session** following the screening next Wednesday at 3:30 P.M. You can find out more information about that by reading the flyer posted behind you.

35 Who most likely is the man?

(A) A film editor
(B) A television program host
(C) A box office attendant
(D) A movie critic

36 What does the woman ask the man about?

(A) The name of an actor
(B) The availability of a showing
(C) The length of a performance
(D) The price of a ticket

37 What does the man say about Andy Baker?

(A) He will meet with investors.
(B) He attended a cinema opening.
(C) He will respond to some inquiries.
(D) He released a production last year.

第 35-37 題請參考下列對話。

女：不好意思，[35] 我想看晚上 8 點那場的《Voyage Across Australia》。

男：我很抱歉。但 [35] 那場和今晚其他所有場次的票都已經賣完了。不過妳可以預訂明天晚上的位子。

女：我沒想到這部電影有這麼受歡迎。我明天晚上得上班。[36] 這部電影下星期還會在電影院播放嗎？

男：會。事實上，[37] 導演 Andy Baker 在下星期三下午 3 點 30 分那場放映結束之後會現身進行問答時間。妳可以看貼在妳身後的那張傳單來了解更多相關資訊。

35 男子最有可能是誰？

(A) 影片剪輯師
(B) 電視節目主持人
(C) 售票人員
(D) 電影評論家

36 女子詢問男子什麼？

(A) 一位演員的名字
(B) 一部電影能不能看得到
(C) 一場表演的長度
(D) 一張門票的價格

37 關於 Andy Baker，男子說什麼？

(A) 他會和投資人見面。
(B) 他出席了電影院的開幕式。
(C) 他會回應一些問題。
(D) 他去年推出了一部作品。

題目 screening [ˋskrinɪŋ]（電影等）放映　sell out 賣完　director [㊊ dəˋrɛktɚ ㊇ diˋrektə] 導演　present [ˋprɛznṭ] 出席的　flyer [㊊ ˋflaɪɚ ㊇ ˋflaiə] 傳單

35 editor [ˋɛdɪtɚ] 編輯　host [host] 主持人　box office 售票處　attendant [əˋtɛndənt] 服務人員　critic [ˋkrɪtɪk] 評論家

37 investor [ɪnˋvɛstɚ] 投資者　cinema [ˋsɪnəmə] 電影院　opening [ˋopənɪŋ] 開幕式　inquiry [ɪnˋkwaɪrɪ] 問題　release [rɪˋlis] 推出；發行　production [prəˋdʌkʃən]（戲劇、電影等的）作品；（戲劇、電影等的）製作

35 中 **整體對話相關問題－說話者** 答案 (C)

題目詢問男子的身分，因此要注意聽和身分、職業相關的表達。女子說：「I'd like to see the 8:00 P.M. screening」，表示想看 8 點那場的電影，男子回答：「tickets for that and all other show times tonight have been sold out」，表示該場和今天晚上全部場次的票都賣完了，由此可知，男子是賣票處的服務人員，因此正確答案是 (C) A box office attendant。

36 中 **細節事項相關問題－特定細項** 答案 (B)

題目詢問女子問男子什麼，因此要注意聽女子說的話。女子對男子說：「Will the film still be playing at the theater next week?」，詢問該電影下星期是否還會在電影院播放，因此正確答案是 (B) The availability of a showing。

37 高 **細節事項相關問題－提及** 答案 (C)

題目詢問男子提到什麼與 Andy Baker 有關的事，因此要注意聽男子話中和題目關鍵字（Andy Baker）相關及前後的內容。男子說：「Andy Baker, the director, will be present for a question and answer session」，表示導演 Andy Baker 會現身進行問答時間，因此正確答案是 (C) He will respond to some inquiries.。

38 39 40 新

Questions 38-40 refer to the following conversation.

美式發音 → 加拿大式發音

W: Good morning. This is Clara Davis, and [38]**I'm having trouble with my laptop. Your shop did a fantastic job fixing it previously, so I'd like to hire you again.**
M: What's the issue this time, Ms. Davis?
W: The screen keeps freezing, and the computer often restarts automatically.
M: Well, that sounds like a software error, which isn't my area of expertise. My associate Robert specializes in those types of repairs. [39]**Would it be possible to bring your laptop to our office next Monday?** He can work on it then.
W: I'm going abroad for a real estate workshop on Sunday. I'd really like it running properly before then.
M: Hmm . . . let me transfer you to Robert now. [40]**I can't say whether he'll be able to fit you into his schedule sometime today.** One moment, please.

第 38-40 題請參考下列對話。

女：早安。我是 Clara Davis，[38] 我的筆記型電腦出問題了。你們店之前修它的時候處理得非常好，所以我想再請你們修。
男：這次的問題是什麼？Davis 小姐？
女：畫面一直不會動，而且這台電腦常常會自動重開機。
男：嗯，聽起來像是軟體故障，這部分不是我的專長。我同事 Robert 專門做這類型的維修。[39] 您下星期一能把您的筆記型電腦帶來我們辦公室嗎？他那個時候可以處理。
女：我星期日要出國參加一場房地產的工作坊。我真的很希望它能在那之前正常運作。
男：嗯……我現在把您的電話轉給 Robert 吧。[40] 我沒有把握他會不會有辦法把您安插進他今天的行程裡。請稍等。

38 Where does the man most likely work?

(A) At a travel agency
(B) At a repair shop
(C) At a real estate office
(D) At shopping center

38 男子最有可能在哪裡工作？

(A) 旅行社
(B) 維修行
(C) 不動產公司
(D) 購物中心

39 What does the man suggest the woman do?

(A) Bring a device to a business
(B) Restart a machine
(C) Install some software
(D) Replace a laptop component

39 男子建議女子做什麼？

(A) 把裝置帶到店裡
(B) 重新啟動裝置
(C) 安裝一些軟體
(D) 更換筆記型電腦的零件

40 新 What does the man mean when he says, "let me transfer you to Robert now"?

(A) He has to get approval from a superior.
(B) He is unfamiliar with a product model.
(C) He has to leave for a workshop.
(D) He is unable to set up an appointment.

40 當男子說：「我現在把您的電話轉給 Robert 吧」，意思是什麼？

(A) 他必須獲得上級同意。
(B) 他對一款產品不熟悉。
(C) 他必須出發前往一個工作坊。
(D) 他無法安排一個會面。

題目 freeze [friz] 停住　associate [əˋsoʃɪɪt] 同事　specialize in 專門做～　properly [ˋprɑpəlɪ] 正確地
39 component [kəmˋponənt] 零件

38 整體對話相關問題－說話者　答案 (B)
中
題目詢問男子的工作地點，因此要注意聽和身分、職業相關的表達。女子說：「I'm having trouble with my laptop. Your shop did a fantastic job fixing it previously, so I'd like to hire you again.」，表示自己的筆記型電腦出了問題，因為之前男子他們店把它修得很好，所以想再請他們修，由此可知，男子的工作地點是維修行，因此正確答案是 (B) At a repair shop。

39 細節事項相關問題－提議　答案 (A)
中
題目詢問男子建議女子做什麼，因此要注意聽男子話中出現的提議相關表達。男子對女子說：「Would it be possible to bring your laptop to our office next Monday?」，詢問下星期一女子能否把筆記型電腦帶來自己辦公室，因此正確答案是 (A) Bring a device to a business。

新 **40** 細節事項相關問題－掌握意圖　答案 (D)
高
題目詢問男子的說話意圖，因此要注意與題目引用句（let me transfer you to Robert now）相關及前後的內容。男子說：「I can't say whether he[Robert]'ll be able to fit you into his schedule sometime today.」，表示自己沒有把握 Robert 會不會有辦法把女子安插進他今天的行程裡，由此可知，男子無法安排會面，因此正確答案是 (D) He is unable to set up an appointment.。

新

Questions 41-43 refer to the following conversation.

澳洲式發音 → 英式發音

M: [41]**Did you hear about the policy change for business travel expenses?** Employees will have to submit relevant receipts within at least three days following the end date of a trip.

W: But that means I'll need to get the paperwork from my recent visit to our warehouse in Dubai in order by today. I won't have time for that.

M: Don't worry. The rule doesn't take effect until the end of next month.

W: That's a relief. [42]**Why is the policy being modified?**

M: The goal is to improve efficiency within the financial department.

W: Makes sense. [43]**Last week, the head of the division was actually telling me how hard it is to track costs when people aren't timely about turning in their receipts.**

第 41-43 題請參考下列對話。

男：[41] 妳有聽說差旅支出的政策改了嗎？員工將必須在出差結束那天後的最慢三天內提交相關收據。

女：但這代表我必須要在今天整理好我最近去我們在杜拜的倉庫出差的那些書面文件。我不會有時間做這件事的。

男：別擔心。這項規定要到下個月底才會生效。

女：真是好險。[42] 這個政策為什麼要修改？

男：目標是要提升財務部門的效率。

女：有道理。[43] 上個星期，那個部門的主管其實才在跟我說，要在有人不及時繳交收據的情況下追蹤開支有多麼困難。

41 What are the speakers mainly discussing?
(A) A coworker's vacation
(B) A corporate regulation
(C) An overseas investment
(D) A supervisor's promotion

41 說話者們主要在討論什麼？
(A) 同事的假期
(B) 公司規定
(C) 海外投資
(D) 主管的晉升

42 What does the woman ask the man about?
(A) The reason for a change
(B) The duration of a trip
(C) The cost of a renovation
(D) The size of a warehouse

42 女子詢問男子什麼？
(A) 更改的理由
(B) 旅行持續的時間
(C) 整修的成本
(D) 倉庫的大小

43 What did the woman do last week?
(A) Talked with a manager
(B) Applied for a transfer
(C) Edited a policy manual
(D) Submitted a written complaint

43 女子上星期做了什麼？
(A) 和一位主管說話
(B) 申請調任
(C) 編輯政策手冊
(D) 提交書面申訴

題目 expense [ɪk`spɛns] 開支　relevant [`rɛləvənt] 相關的　paperwork [(美) `pepɚ͵wɝk (英) `peipə͵wəːk] 書面資料；文書工作　warehouse [(美) `wɛr͵haʊs (英) `wɛəhaus] 倉庫　take effect 生效　improve [ɪm`pruv] 提升　efficiency [ɪ`fɪʃənsɪ] 效率　track [træk] 追蹤　timely [`taɪmlɪ] 及時地；適時地　turn in 繳交～

41 corporate [`kɔrpərɪt] 公司的　promotion [prə`moʃən] 晉升

42 duration [djʊ`reʃən]（時間的持續）期間

43 manual [`mænjʊəl]（說明或宣傳用的）手冊　written [`rɪtn̩] 書面的　complaint [kəm`plent] 申訴

41 整體對話相關問題－主題　低　答案 (B)

題目詢問對話主題，因此要注意對話的開頭。男子對女子說：「Did you hear about the policy change for business travel expenses?」，詢問對方是否有聽說差旅支出的政策改了，由此可知，接下來要討論與差旅支出的政策更改有關的事，因此正確答案是 (B) A corporate regulation。

42 細節事項相關問題－特定細項　低　答案 (A)

題目詢問女子問男子什麼，因此要注意聽女子說的話。女子對男子說：「Why is the policy being modified?」，詢問政策為什麼要修改，因此正確答案是 (A) The reason for a change。

43 細節事項相關問題－特定細項　高　答案 (A)

題目詢問女子上星期做了什麼，因此要注意聽和題目關鍵字（last week）相關的內容。女子說：「Last week, the head of the division was actually telling me how hard it is to track costs when people aren't timely about turning in their receipts.」，表示上星期該部門主管和自己說過，要在有人不及時繳交收據的情況下追蹤開支有多麼困難，因此正確答案是 (A) Talked with a manager。

44
45
46

Questions 44-46 refer to the following conversation.

第 44-46 題請參考下列對話。

美式發音 → 澳洲式發音

W: Excuse me. [44]**I checked out some novels here earlier today, and I may have left my wallet somewhere near this circulation desk.** Has one been found recently?

M: Not to my knowledge. However, [45]**I think you'd better visit our lost-and-found center just one floor up.** Someone could have possibly picked it up and brought it there.

W: I see. Also, I'm wondering if it's possible to borrow these DVDs without my library card. Unfortunately, my card was also in my wallet.

M: Certainly. We have your account in our system, so I can go ahead and do that for you. [46]**May I ask for your account number?**

女：不好意思。[44] 我今天稍早在這裡借了一些小說，而我可能把我的皮夾留在這個流通櫃台附近了。最近有發現皮夾嗎？

男：就我所知沒有。不過，[45] 我想妳最好到我們就在樓上一層的遺失物中心看看。可能會有人撿到並把它送去那裡。

女：我知道了。此外，我想知道有沒有可能在沒有借書證的情況下借走這些DVD？不幸我的卡也在我的皮夾裡。

男：當然。我們系統裡有妳的帳號，所以我可以直接幫妳辦理。[46] 可以告訴我妳的帳號編號嗎？

44 Where does the conversation probably take place?

(A) At a department store
(B) At a library
(C) At an accounting office
(D) At a bookstore

44 這段對話可能發生在哪裡？

(A) 百貨公司
(B) 圖書館
(C) 會計室
(D) 書店

45 What suggestion does the man make?

(A) Contacting an organization again
(B) Borrowing a specific book
(C) Going to another area
(D) Ordering a replacement card

45 男子做了什麼建議？

(A) 再次聯繫一間機構
(B) 借走一本特定的書
(C) 去另一個地方
(D) 訂購一張替換用的卡片

46 What information does the man need?

(A) An account holder's name
(B) A publication title
(C) An e-mail address
(D) An identification number

46 男子需要什麼資訊？

(A) 一個帳號持有者的名字
(B) 一本刊物名稱
(C) 一個電子郵件地址
(D) 一個識別編號

題目 check out 借出（書籍等） circulation desk 流通櫃台 lost-and-found center 遺失物中心
possibly [美 `pɑsəblɪ 英 `pɔsəbli] 也許，可能 unfortunately [ʌn`fɔrtʃənɪtlɪ] 不幸地；遺憾地 account [ə`kaʊnt] 帳號

45 organization [ˌɔrgənə`zeʃən] 機構，團體 replacement [rɪ`plesmənt] 替換用的人事物；代替

46 holder [`holdɚ] 持有者 publication [ˌpʌblɪ`keʃən] 刊物；出版品 identification [aɪˌdɛntəfə`keʃən] 識別

44 整體對話相關問題－地點 答案 (B)

中

題目詢問對話發生的地點，因此要注意聽和地點相關的表達。女子說：「I checked out some novels here ~, and I may have left my wallet somewhere near this circulation desk.」，表示自己在這裡借了一些小說，且可能把皮夾留在流通櫃台附近了，由此可知，對話發生的地點是在圖書館，因此正確答案是 (B) At a library。

45 細節事項相關問題－提議 答案 (C)

中

題目詢問男子提了什麼建議，因此必須注意聽男子話中出現的提議相關表達。男子對女子說：「I think you'd better visit our lost-and-found center just one floor up」，建議女子到就在樓上一層的遺失物中心看看，因此正確答案是 (C) Going to another area。

46 細節事項相關問題－特定細項 答案 (D)

中

題目詢問男子需要什麼資訊，因此要注意聽和題目關鍵字（information ~ man need）相關的內容。男子對女子說：「May I ask for your account number?」，詢問對方的帳號編號，因此正確答案是 (D) An identification number。

換句話說

account number 帳號編號 → identification number 識別編號

47
48
49

Questions 47-49 refer to the following conversation.	第 47-49 題請參考下列對話。
英式發音 → 加拿大式發音	
W: The Sporting Supplier. This is Wanda. What can I help you with?	女：The Sporting Supplier。我是 Wanda。有什麼能協助您的嗎？
M: [47]**I'd like to ask about a tennis racquet** I found on your homepage—the Kendell Swift XE. I'm wondering if these racquets come with spare grips for the handle or if those would need to be purchased separately.	男：[47] 我想問一款我在你們首頁上看到的網球拍—Kendell Swift XE 那款。我想知道這款球拍是否附有備用的握把布，還是要另外購買？
W: All tennis racquets come with just one standard grip. But [48]**we offer a variety of other grips that absorb shock and reduce hand strain**. Those can be added on for an extra charge.	女：所有網球拍都只會附一卷標準型握把布。但 [48] 我們提供其他各式各樣可以吸震並減輕手部負擔的握把布。這些都可以加購。
M: OK. I'm interested in the shock-absorbing types, so [49]**I'll take another look online this afternoon and see what specific options are available**. Thanks.	男：好。因為我對吸震型的有興趣，所以 [49] 我今天下午會再上網看看具體有什麼選項可以買。謝謝。
47 Why did the man call the woman? (A) To provide payment details (B) To reserve some merchandise (C) To inquire about a piece of gear (D) To learn about an upcoming launch	47 男子為何打電話給女子？ (A) 提供付款細節資訊 (B) 預訂一些商品 (C) 詢問有關一件裝備的事 (D) 了解即將到來的發表會相關事項
48 What does the woman mention about racquet grips? (A) They are currently out of stock. (B) They are made with quality materials. (C) They come in various types. (D) They have been used by sports stars.	48 關於球拍握把布，女子提到什麼？ (A) 目前缺貨。 (B) 以高級材料製成。 (C) 有各式各樣的類型。 (D) 被運動明星們使用。
49 What will the man probably do this afternoon? (A) Attend a tennis class (B) Browse some items (C) Call a sales associate (D) Return some racquets	49 男子今天下午可能會做什麼？ (A) 出席網球課 (B) 瀏覽一些品項 (C) 致電一位銷售助理 (D) 退回一些球拍

題目 come with 附有～　spare [spɛr] 備用的　grip [grɪp] 緊握；（網球或羽球拍的）握把布　separately [ˋsɛpərɪtlɪ] 分別地　standard [美 ˋstændɚd 英 ˋstændəd] 標準的　absorb [美 əbˋsɔrb 英 əbˋsɔːb] 吸收　shock [美 ʃɑk 英 ʃɔk] 震動　strain [stren] 負擔

47 gear [gɪr] 裝備

48 out of stock 無庫存的　quality [ˋkwɑlətɪ] 高級的；品質　material [məˋtɪrɪəl] 材料

49 browse [braʊz] 瀏覽　sales associate 銷售助理

47 整體對話相關問題－目的　中　答案 (C)

題目詢問男子打電話給女子的目的，因此必須注意對話開頭。男子說：「I'd like to ask about a tennis racquet」，表示想詢問關於網球拍的事，因此正確答案是 (C) To inquire about a piece of gear。

48 細節事項相關問題－提及　高　答案 (C)

題目詢問女子提到什麼與球拍握把布有關的事，因此要注意聽女子話中和題目關鍵字（racquet grips）相關的內容。女子說：「we offer a variety of other grips that absorb shock and reduce hand strain」，表示店裡提供各式各樣可以吸震並減輕手部負擔的握把布，因此正確答案是 (C) They come in various types.。

49 細節事項相關問題－接下來要做的事　中　答案 (B)

題目詢問男子今天下午可能會做什麼，因此要注意聽和題目關鍵字（this afternoon）相關的內容。男子說：「I'll take another look online this afternoon and see what specific options are available」，表示自己今天下午會再上網看看具體有什麼選項可以買，因此正確答案是 (B) Browse some items。

50
51
52

Questions 50-52 refer to the following conversation.

美式發音 → 澳洲式發音

W: Hi, Charlie. I'm having dinner with our investment consultant in Brownville in 30 minutes, but [50]**I forgot my day planner at the office**. It contains the name and address of the restaurant we agreed to meet at, which I need.

M: Yes, it's right here on your desk. [51]**Is it OK if I open it and find those details?**

W: [51]**Please do.** Is there a sticky note attached to the page with the information for the meeting with Charles Grand?

M: Indeed. [52]**It says that you have a table booked at El Toro Bistro on 45 Weston Avenue.**

50 What problem does the woman describe?

(A) She visited the incorrect office.
(B) She lost a financial document.
(C) She does not have a day planner.
(D) She is late for a consultation.

51 What does the woman allow the man to do?

(A) Participate in a conference call
(B) Remove equipment from an office
(C) Send notes to an advisor
(D) Review her personal belongings

52 What detail does the man provide?

(A) A meeting location
(B) A reservation time
(C) A client's name
(D) A coworker's address

第 50-52 題請參考下列對話。

女：嗨，Charlie。我 30 分鐘後要在 Brownville 和我們的投資顧問吃晚餐，但 [50] 我把我的行事曆忘在辦公室了。裡面有我們約好要在那裡見面的餐廳名稱和地址，我需要這些資訊。

男：好，它就在妳桌上這裡。[51] 我可以把它打開來找這些細節資訊嗎？

女：[51] 拜託你了。有和 Charles Grand 見面這件事的那頁上有貼著一張便利貼嗎？

男：沒錯。[52] 上面說妳在 Weston 大道 45 號的 El Toro 餐酒館訂了位子。

50 女子描述了什麼問題？

(A) 她去錯辦公室了。
(B) 她弄丟了財務文件。
(C) 她沒有行事曆。
(D) 她諮商遲到了。

51 女子允許男子做什麼？

(A) 參加電話會議
(B) 移除辦公室設備
(C) 把記錄寄給顧問
(D) 檢視她的個人物品

52 男子提供什麼細節資訊？

(A) 會面的地點
(B) 預約的時間
(C) 客戶的名字
(D) 同事的地址

題目 investment [ɪnˋvɛstmənt] 投資 consultant [kənˋsʌltənt] 顧問 contain [kənˋten]（裡面）有；包含 sticky [ˋstɪkɪ] 黏的 attach [əˋtætʃ] 貼上

51 conference call 電話會議 remove [rɪˋmuv] 移除 advisor [ədˋvaɪzɚ] 顧問 personal [ˋpɝsn̩l] 個人的 belongings [bəˋlɔŋɪŋz]（隨身攜帶的）擁有物

50 細節事項相關問題－問題點 低 答案 (C)

題目詢問女子描述了什麼問題，因此要注意聽女子說的話中出現負面表達之後的內容。女子說：「I forgot my day planner at the office」，表示自己將行事曆忘在辦公室了，因此正確答案是 (C) She does not have a day planner.。

51 細節事項相關問題－特定細項 高 答案 (D)

題目詢問女子允許男子做什麼，因此要注意聽和題目關鍵字（allow ~ man to do）相關的內容。男子說：「Is it OK if I open it[day planner] and find those details?」，詢問自己是否能打開行事曆來找所需的細節資訊，女子說：「Please do.」，拜託男子這樣做，因此正確答案是 (D) Review her personal belongings。

52 細節事項相關問題－特定細項 低 答案 (A)

題目詢問男子提供什麼細節資訊，因此要注意聽和題目關鍵字（detail ~ man provide）相關的內容。男子說：「It[sticky note] says that you have a table booked at El Toro Bistro on 45 Weston Avenue.」，表示女子在 Weston 大道 45 號的 El Toro 餐酒館訂了位子，因此正確答案是 (A) A meeting location。

新 53 54 55

Questions 53-55 refer to the following conversation.	第 53-55 題請參考下列對話。
加拿大式發音 → 英式發音	
M: [53]**Thanks for joining me as a special guest on my cooking show here at our broadcasting studio** today, Wendy. [53]**I'm sure many of my TV viewers have been looking forward to this.**	男：[53] 謝謝妳今天到我們攝影棚這裡擔任我料理節目的特別來賓，Wendy。[53] 我相信我的電視觀眾裡有很多人都一直期待著這件事。
W: No problem, Chef Hammond. So, what will you be creating with these ingredients?	女：這沒什麼，Hammond 主廚。那麼，你會用這些材料做出什麼呢？
M: Well, since the theme of our program is Italian dishes, I'll demonstrate how to make spaghetti with cream sauce.	男：這個嘛，既然我們節目的主題是義大利料理，那麼我會示範要怎麼做白醬義大利麵。
W: Sounds delicious. Um, [54]**there are eggs mixed into the sauce, right?**	女：聽起來很好吃。嗯，[54] 這個醬裡面會混入雞蛋，對嗎？
M: Oh, you're familiar with this dish? [54]**The recipe calls for two eggs.** And here's something to keep in mind. It's important to lower the heat on the stovetop when adding the eggs so that they don't become scrambled.	男：噢，妳對這道料理很熟嗎？[54] 這道食譜會用到兩顆蛋。然後這裡還有一件事要記得。在把蛋加進去的時候，很重要的是要把爐子上的火關小，這樣蛋才不會變成炒蛋。
W: That's a fantastic tip! Should I add the cheese now?	女：這訣竅真棒！我現在要加起司了嗎？
M: Yes, please. Meanwhile, [55]**I'll show our audience the differences between Italian- and American-style bacon.**	男：沒錯，請加。在此同時，[55] 我要告訴我們的觀眾義式和美式培根有什麼不同。

53 Where is the conversation most likely taking place?
(A) In a grocery store
(B) In a private residence
(C) In a television studio
(D) In a dining establishment

54 Why does the man say, "you're familiar with this dish"? 新
(A) To accept a recommendation about a recipe
(B) To show appreciation for a cooking tip
(C) To request assistance with a demonstration
(D) To express agreement regarding an ingredient

55 What will the man most likely do next?
(A) Explain food differences
(B) Read over menu options
(C) Consult with a culinary expert
(D) Put away some utensils

53 這段對話最有可能發生在哪裡？
(A) 食品雜貨店
(B) 私人住宅
(C) 電視攝影棚
(D) 餐廳

54 男子為什麼說：「妳對這道料理很熟嗎」？
(A) 為了接受關於食譜的一項建議
(B) 為了表示對一個料理訣竅的欣賞
(C) 為了要求協助一次示範
(D) 為了表達對一項材料的贊同

55 男子接下來最有可能做什麼？
(A) 說明食物的差異
(B) 仔細看過菜單選項
(C) 諮詢一位料理專家
(D) 收起一些用具

題目 call for 需要～ stovetop [ˋstovtɑp] 爐子上方 scramble [ˋskræmbl] 炒（蛋） difference [ˋdɪfərəns] 差異
55 culinary [ˋkjulɪˌnɛrɪ] 料理的；廚房的 expert [ˋɛkspɝt] 專家 utensil [juˋtɛnsl] 用具；器皿

53 整體對話相關問題－地點 答案 (C)
中

題目詢問對話的發生地點，因此要注意聽對話中與地點相關的表達。男子對女子說：「Thanks for joining me ~ on my cooking show here at our broadcasting studio」，表示感謝女子來當自己料理節目的來賓，接著說：「I'm sure many of my TV viewers have been looking forward to this.」，表示相信自己的電視觀眾裡有很多人都一直期待著這件事，由此可知，對話的發生地點是在電視攝影棚裡，因此正確答案是 (C) In a television studio。

新 54 細節事項相關問題－掌握意圖 答案 (D)
難

題目詢問男子的說話意圖，因此要注意與題目引用句（you're familiar with this dish）相關及前後的對話內容。女子先說：「there are eggs mixed into the sauce, right?」，詢問醬裡面是否會混入雞蛋，男子之後說：「The recipe calls for two eggs.」，表示這道食譜會用到兩顆蛋，由此可知，男子想要對女子提出的材料表達贊同，因此正確答案是 (D) To express agreement regarding an ingredient。

55 細節事項相關問題－接下來要做的事 答案 (A)
中

題目詢問男子接下來會做什麼，因此必須注意對話的最後部分。男子說：「I'll show our audience the differences between Italian- and American-style bacon」，表示自己要告訴觀眾義式和美式培根之間有何不同，因此正確答案是 (A) Explain food differences。

56 57 58

Questions 56-58 refer to the following conversation.

澳洲式發音 → 美式發音

M: Kumiko, [56]**do you know where I can find a copy of the study our research department conducted on health care devices?** I need data from it to make another report.

W: I've got a printout of that in my file cabinet right here. By the way, [57]**are you going to the Heart and Lung Foundation's annual charity fundraiser on May 4?** Or will you be too busy working on this project?

M: I requested a deadline extension. [57]**I heard that there will be many industry professionals attending the fundraiser, so I don't want to miss it.** It would be a great opportunity to network with them.

W: Definitely . . . [58]**If you haven't registered yet, I can do it for you.**

第 56-58 題請參考下列對話。

男：Kumiko，[56] 妳知道我可以在哪裡找到我們研究部門對健康照護裝置所做的研究副本嗎？我需要裡面的資料來做另一份報告。

女：我的檔案櫃這裡就有一份已經印出來的。對了，[57] 你要去 Heart and Lung 基金會在 5 月 4 日辦的年度慈善募款活動嗎？還是你會因為太忙著處理這個專案而不能去？

男：我要求延長截止期限了。[57] 我聽說會有很多業界專業人士出席這場募款活動，所以我不想錯過。這會是個和他們建立關係的絕佳機會。

女：當然……[58] 如果你還沒報名，我可以幫你報。

56 What department does the man work in?

(A) Administration
(B) Marketing
(C) Finance
(D) Research

57 新 What does the man imply when he says, "I requested a deadline extension"?

(A) He will reschedule a business meeting.
(B) He will deal with other problems.
(C) He will appear at a gathering.
(D) He will expand a work project.

58 What does the woman offer to do?

(A) Give some notes to a superior
(B) Sign a colleague up for an event
(C) Make a personal donation
(D) Revise some reports

56 男子在什麼部門裡工作？

(A) 行政
(B) 行銷
(C) 財務
(D) 研究

57 當男子說：「我要求延長截止期限了」時，是在暗示什麼？

(A) 他會重新安排商業會議的時間。
(B) 他會處理其他問題。
(C) 他會出現在聚會上。
(D) 他會擴大工作專案。

58 女子願意做什麼？

(A) 把一些記錄拿給上級
(B) 替同事報名一場活動
(C) 捐出一筆個人捐款
(D) 修改一些報告

題目 conduct [kən`dʌkt] 實施 foundation [faʊn`deʃən] 基金會
network [美 `nɛt͵wɝk 英 `net͵wəːk] 建立關係網絡，建立人脈
56 administration [əd͵mɪnə`streʃən] 行政
57 expand [ɪk`spænd] 擴大 **58** donation [do`neʃən] 捐款

56 整體對話相關問題－說話者 答案 (D)

中

題目詢問男子在什麼部門工作，因此要注意聽和身分、職業相關的表達。男子對女子說：「do you know where I can find a copy of the study our research department conducted ~?」，詢問女子是否知道自己研究部門所做的研究副本在哪裡，由此可知，男子是在研究部門工作，因此正確答案是 (D) Research。

新 **57** 細節事項相關問題－掌握意圖 答案 (C)

高

題目詢問男子的說話意圖，因此要注意與題目引用句（I requested a deadline extension）相關及前後的對話內容。女子先說：「are you going to the ~ annual charity fundraiser ~?」，詢問男子是否要去年度募款活動，後面男子說：「I heard that there will be many industry professionals attending the fundraiser, so I don't want to miss it.」，表示聽說會有很多業界專業人士出席這場募款活動，所以自己不想錯過，由此可知，男子會出席這次聚會，因此正確答案是 (C) He will appear at a gathering.。

58 細節事項相關問題－提議 答案 (B)

中

題目詢問女子願意做什麼，因此要注意聽女子話中提到要為男子做事的內容。女子對男子說：「If you haven't registered yet, I can do it for you.」，表示如果男子還沒完成報名，那自己可以替他報，因此正確答案是 (B) Sign a colleague up for an event。

59
60
61

Questions 59-61 refer to the following conversation.

美式發音 → 澳洲式發音

W: You did a great job creating these charts about our export trends. [59]**Our team leader wants you to make a presentation on them at the Manila branch next week.**

M: That's great. But [60]**will I have enough time to secure a visa for business travel before then? It took longer than I anticipated to get one the last time I went abroad.**

W: I've already spoken with the head of human resources about that. He was informed by the embassy that the visa approval process can be completed in under a week.

M: OK. Then, [61]**could you e-mail me the presentation template you made for last week's audit meeting?** I liked the design of it and want to use it.

59 What does the team leader want the man to do?

(A) Hire a branch manager
(B) Give an award to a top performer
(C) Present some diagrams
(D) Choose a representative

60 Why is the man worried?

(A) A process may take too long.
(B) A presentation did not go well.
(C) A chart has been misplaced.
(D) An audit is approaching.

61 What does the man ask the woman to do?

(A) Update a mailing list
(B) Turn in an application
(C) Share a template
(D) Meet with a designer

第 59-61 題請參考下列對話。

女：你針對我們外銷趨勢所製作的這些圖表做得真棒。[59] 我們組長想要你下星期在馬尼拉分公司就這些圖表進行簡報。

男：太好了。但 [60] 我在那之前會有足夠時間取得出差用的簽證嗎？我上次出國時花了比我預期要久的時間才拿到。

女：我已經和人力資源部的主管談過這件事了。大使館告訴他，這個簽證批准的程序可以在一週內完成。

男：好。那麼，[61] 妳可以把妳為上週的審計會議所製作的簡報範本用電子郵件寄給我嗎？我喜歡那個設計，所以想要用它。

59 組長想要男子做什麼？

(A) 僱用一位分公司經理
(B) 頒獎給表現最佳者
(C) 簡報一些圖表
(D) 選擇一位代表

60 男子為什麼擔心？

(A) 一個流程可能會花太長時間。
(B) 一個簡報進行得不順利。
(C) 一個圖表被放錯位置了。
(D) 快要進行一次審計了。

61 男子要求女子做什麼？

(A) 更新郵寄名單
(B) 繳交申請表
(C) 分享範本
(D) 和設計師碰面

題目 export [`ɛksport] 出口 trend [trɛnd] 趨勢 secure [[美] sɪ`kjʊr [英] si`kjuə] 取得
anticipate [[美] æn`tɪsə͵pet [英] æn`tisipeit] 預期 human resources 人力資源部 inform [ɪn`fɔrm] 告知；通知
embassy [`ɛmbəsɪ] 大使館 audit [`ɔdɪt] 審計

59 performer [pɚ`fɔrmɚ] 執行者 diagram [`daɪə͵græm] 圖表 representative [rɛprɪ`zɛntətɪv] 代表

60 misplace [mɪs`ples] 錯置 approach [ə`protʃ] 接近

61 mailing list 郵寄名單 share [ʃɛr] 分享

59 細節事項相關問題－特定細項 答案 (C)

中

題目詢問組長想要男子做什麼，因此要確認和題目關鍵字（team leader want ~ man to do）相關的內容。女子說：「Our team leader wants you to make a presentation on them[charts] at the Manila branch next week.」，表示組長想要男子下星期在馬尼拉分公司就這些圖表進行簡報，因此正確答案是 (C) Present some diagrams。

60 細節事項相關問題－問題點 答案 (A)

中

題目詢問男子擔心的是什麼，因此要注意聽男子話中出現負面表達之後的內容。男子說：「will I have enough time to secure a visa for business travel before then[next week]? It took longer than I anticipated to get one the last time I went abroad.」，詢問自己是否會有足夠的時間來拿到簽證，並說自己上次出國時花了比預期要久的時間才拿到，因此正確答案是 (A) A process may take too long.。

61 細節事項相關問題－要求 答案 (C)

低

題目詢問男子要求女子做什麼，因此必須注意聽男子話中提到要請女子做事的內容。男子對女子說：「could you e-mail me the presentation template you made for last week's audit meeting?」，要求女子把她為上週的審計會議所製作的簡報範本用電子郵件寄給自己，因此正確答案是 (C) Share a template。

新

62 63 64

Questions 62-64 refer to the following conversation with three speakers.	第 62-64 題請參考下列三人對話。
美式發音 → 英式發音 → 加拿大式發音	
W1: This has been an excellent year for our company.	女 1：今年對我們公司來說是很棒的一年。
W2: Without a doubt. [62]**We've increased the number of jobseekers who we have helped find work** by almost 25 percent.	女 2：毫無疑問是這樣。[62] 透過我們協助而找到工作的求職者人數已經增加了快 25%。
M: What's more, [62]**we've established strong relationships with major employers.**	男：還有，[62] 我們已和主要雇主建立了穩固的關係。
W2: Yeah. Consistent dealings with enterprises such as South Bend Corporation will be central to our success moving forward.	女 2：是啊。持續和像 South Bend 公司這樣的企業來往，會是我們邁向成功的關鍵。
W1: [63]**Is it true that South Bend has contracted us again to find more engineering interns?**	女 1：[63]South Bend 是真的又和我們簽約要找更多工程實習生了嗎？
M: [63]**That's right.**	男：[63] 沒錯。
W2: Do you know the number of positions they need filled?	女 2：你知道他們要補的缺有多少嗎？
M: Not exactly. I'm guessing five or six. What I do know is that [64]**the contract we signed gives us four weeks to find suitable applicants.**	男：不清楚。我在猜是五到六個。我確切知道的是，[64] 我們簽的這份合約給我們四個禮拜來找到適合的應徵者。
W1: That should be a comfortable amount of time to work with.	女 1：這時間要找應該滿充裕的。
62 Where most likely do the speakers work? (A) At an advertising company (B) At an educational institution (C) At an engineering firm (D) At a staffing agency	62 說話者們最有可能在哪裡工作？ (A) 廣告公司 (B) 教育機構 (C) 工程公司 (D) 人力仲介
63 What is implied about South Bend Corporation? (A) It is unsatisfied with a candidate. (B) It wants to negotiate some prices. (C) It terminated some employees. (D) It hired a business in the past.	63 關於 South Bend 公司，暗示了什麼？ (A) 對一位人選不滿意。 (B) 想要協商一些價格。 (C) 解雇了一些員工。 (D) 過去有聘請過一間公司。
64 How long will the speakers have to complete a task? (A) Three weeks (B) Four weeks (C) Five weeks (D) Six weeks	64 說話者們會有多長時間來完成一項任務？ (A) 三個禮拜 (B) 四個禮拜 (C) 五個禮拜 (D) 六個禮拜

題目 consistent [kən`sɪstənt] 持續的 comfortable [`kʌmfətəbl] 寬裕的 **63** terminate [`tɝmə͵net] 解雇

62 ■ 整體對話相關問題－說話者 答案 (D)

高

題目詢問說話者們的工作地點在哪裡，因此要注意聽和身分、職業相關的表達。女 2 說：「We[our company]'ve increased the number of jobseekers who we have helped find work」，表示求職者會透過自己公司協助來找到工作，接著男子說：「we've established strong relationships with major employers」，表示公司已和主要雇主建立了穩固的關係，由此可知，說話者們的工作地點是人力仲介，因此正確答案是 (D) At a staffing agency。

63 ■ 細節事項相關問題－推論 答案 (D)

難

題目詢問對話中暗示了什麼關於 South Bend 公司的事，因此要注意聽和題目關鍵字（South Bend Corporation）有關及前後的對話內容。女 1 說：「Is it true that South Bend has contracted us again ~?」，確認 South Bend 是否真的又和公司簽約了，男子說：「That's right.」，表示沒錯，由此可知，South Bend 公司過去有聘請過說話者們的公司，因此正確答案是 (D) It hired a business in the past.。

64 ■ 細節事項相關問題－程度 答案 (B)

低

題目詢問說話者們會有多少時間來完成任務，因此要注意聽和題目關鍵字（complete a task）相關的內容。男子說：「the contract we signed gives us four weeks to find suitable applicants」，表示公司簽的這份合約給了四個禮拜來找到適合的應徵者，因此正確答案是 (B) Four weeks。

65
66
67

Questions 65-67 refer to the following conversation and coupon.

英式發音 → 加拿大式發音

W: Shane, [65]**the IT team was supposed to update the Web site yesterday to include information about our new Oceans Alive line of soap, but it hasn't been done yet.**

M: I forgot to tell you. They're gonna finish this afternoon, by . . . um . . . 3:00 P.M. at the latest.

W: OK, I'll check it then. Is there anything that needs to be done for [66]**the product release event being held at SuperSmart at the end of next month?**

M: Of our new products, [67]**the shampoo, hand soap, and face cleanser are made of organic ingredients, but the body wash isn't.** The current coupon must be modified to ensure it's valid for the entire line.

Oceans Alive

Buy one, get one free
([67]**Good for all organic merchandise**)
Sold at SuperSmart
Valid until March 31

65 What problem does the woman mention?

(A) A manager is not available.
(B) A soap line received poor reviews.
(C) A team is understaffed.
(D) An assignment has not been finished.

66 What kind of event will be held next month?

(A) A product release
(B) A trade show
(C) A yearly sale
(D) An awards ceremony

67 新 Look at the graphic. Which product is not covered by the coupon?

(A) Shampoo
(B) Hand soap
(C) Face cleanser
(D) Body wash

第 65-67 題請參考下列對話及優惠券。

女：Shane，[65] 資訊科技團隊原本應該要在昨天更新網站，把我們新的 Oceans Alive 肥皂系列產品的相關資訊加進去，但這到現在都還沒完成。

男：我忘了告訴妳。他們會在今天下午……嗯……最晚 3 點前完成。

女：好吧，我到時候再看看。針對 [66] 下個月底要辦在 SuperSmart 的產品發表活動，有什麼必須要做的事情嗎？

男：在我們的新產品之中，[67] 洗髮精、洗手皂和洗面乳都是以有機原料製成，但沐浴乳不是。現在的優惠券必須修改以確保它適用於全系列產品。

Oceans Alive

買一送一
（[67] 所有有機商品皆適用）
於 SuperSmart 販售
3 月 31 日以前有效

65 女子提到什麼問題？

(A) 一位經理沒空。
(B) 一個肥皂系列產品獲得了糟糕的評價。
(C) 一個團隊人手不足。
(D) 一項工作還沒完成。

66 下個月會舉行什麼種類的活動？

(A) 產品發表
(B) 貿易展
(C) 年度特賣
(D) 頒獎典禮

67 請看圖表。哪項產品不適用這張優惠券？

(A) 洗髮精
(B) 洗手皂
(C) 洗面乳
(D) 沐浴乳

題目 be supposed to 應該要做～　at the latest 最遲　organic [ɔr`gænɪk] 有機的　ingredient [ɪn`gridɪənt] 成分；原料　modify [`mɑdə͵faɪ] 修改　valid [`vælɪd] 有效的　good [gʊd] 有效的

65 available [ə`veləbl] 有空的　poor [pʊr] 糟糕的　review [rɪ`vju] 評價　understaffed [͵ʌndɚ`stæft] 人手不足的

66 trade show 貿易展　yearly [`jɪrlɪ] 一年一度的　awards ceremony 頒獎典禮

67 cover [`kʌvɚ] 涵蓋；適用於

65 細節事項相關問題－問題點 答案 (D)

中

題目詢問女子提到什麼問題，因此必須注意聽女子說的話中出現負面表達之後的內容。女子說：「the IT team was supposed to update the Web site yesterday ~, but it hasn't been done yet.」，表示資訊科技團隊原本應該要在昨天更新網站，但到現在都還沒完成，因此正確答案是 (D) An assignment has not been finished.。

66 細節事項相關問題－特定細項 答案 (A)

中

題目詢問下個月會舉辦什麼種類的活動，因此要注意聽和題目關鍵字（event ~ next month）相關及前後的對話內容。女子對男子說：「the product release event being held at SuperSmart at the end of next month」，表示下個月底會舉辦產品發表活動，因此正確答案是 (A) A product release。

新 **67** 細節事項相關問題－圖表資料 答案 (D)

難

題目詢問哪項產品不適用這張優惠券，因此必須確認題目提供的優惠券，並注意和題目關鍵字（not covered by the coupon）相關的內容。男子說：「the shampoo, hand soap, and face cleanser are made of organic ingredients, but the body wash isn't」，表示洗髮精、洗手皂和洗面乳都是以有機原料製成，但沐浴乳不是，由此可知，沐浴乳不適用這張優惠券，因此正確答案是 (D) Body wash。

68
69
70

新

Questions 68-70 refer to the following conversation and graph.

澳洲式發音 → 美式發音

M: Gina, [68/69]**has the environmental assessment that Skylark Incorporated commissioned our research firm to conduct been completed?**

W: It has. [69]**I was in charge of carrying it out**, and everything went smoothly.

M: Good. If I remember correctly, the company is concerned with rainfall levels.

W: That's right—in four counties that it's considering constructing an amusement park.

M: So, [70]**I assume you recommend that the firm build at the driest location of the ones analyzed.**

W: No, actually. [70]**That one isn't suitable, since land costs there exceed Skylark's budget. As a result, we recommended the next best option.**

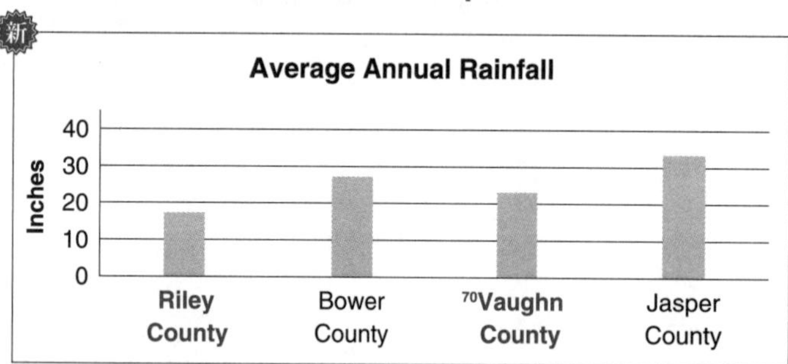

第 68-70 題請參考下列對話及圖表。

男：Gina，[68/69]Skylark 企業委託我們研究公司進行的環境評估已經完成了嗎？

女：已經完成了。[69] 我負責執行了這項工作，一切都進行得很順利。

男：很好。如果我記得沒錯，這間公司很關注降雨量。

女：沒錯——在它考慮要興建遊樂園的那四個郡裡。

男：那麼，[70] 我想妳會建議這間公司蓋在分析地點中最乾燥的地方。

女：其實不是。[70] 那個地點不適合，因為那裡的土地成本超過了 Skylark 的預算。因此，我們建議了次佳的選項。

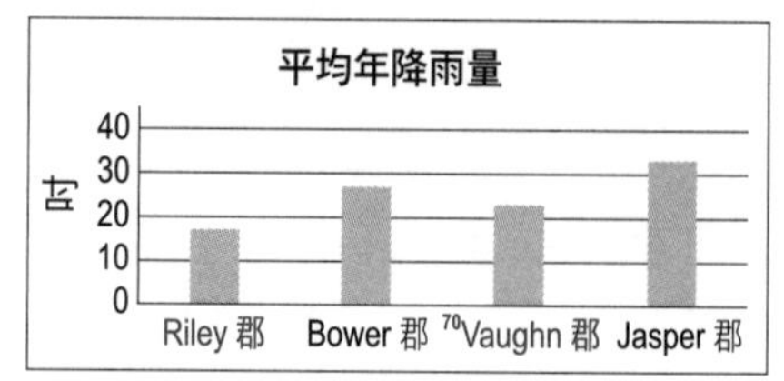

68 What does the man ask the woman about?

(A) Why an analysis was performed
(B) When construction will begin
(C) Whether an assessment is finished
(D) If an amusement park has opened

69 What was the woman responsible for?

(A) Conducting an examination
(B) Selecting a meeting place
(C) Printing a map of a region
(D) Securing a business contract

70 新 Look at the graphic. Which county has been recommended?

(A) Riley County
(B) Bower County
(C) Vaughn County
(D) Jasper County

68 男子問女子什麼？

(A) 為何進行一項分析
(B) 工程將於何時開始
(C) 一項評估是否已完成
(D) 一間遊樂園是否已開幕

69 女子負責了什麼？

(A) 進行一次調查
(B) 挑選一個會面地點
(C) 印一個區域的地圖
(D) 取得一張商業合約

70 請看圖表。被建議的是哪個郡？

(A) Riley 郡
(B) Bower 郡
(C) Vaughn 郡
(D) Jasper 郡

題目 environmental [㊊ ɪnˌvaɪrən`mɛntḷ ㊇ inˌvaiərən`mentl] 環境的　assessment [ə`sɛsmənt] 評估
commission [kə`mɪʃən] 委託　in charge of 負責～　smoothly [smuðlɪ] 順利地　rainfall [`renˌfɔl] 降雨；降雨量
county [`kaʊntɪ] 郡　analyze [`ænḷˌaɪz] 分析　exceed [ɪk`sid] 超過

69 examination [ɪgˌzæmə`neʃən] 檢查；調查　contract [`kɑntrækt] 合約

68 細節事項相關問題－特定細項 答案 (C)

高

題目詢問男子問女子什麼事情，因此要注意聽男子說的話。男子對女子說：「has the environmental assessment that Skylark Incorporated commissioned our research firm to conduct been completed?」，詢問 Skylark 企業委託進行的環境評估是否已經完成，因此正確答案是 (C) Whether an assessment is finished。

69 細節事項相關問題－特定細項 答案 (A)

中

題目詢問女子負責了什麼，因此要注意聽和題目關鍵字（woman responsible for）相關的內容。男子對女子說：「has the environmental assessment that Skylark Incorporated commissioned our research firm to conduct been completed?」，詢問 Skylark 企業委託進行的環境評估是否已經完成，女子回答：「I was in charge of carrying it out」，表示自己負責執行了這項工作，也就是環境評估的工作，因此正確答案是 (A) Conducting an examination。

新 70 細節事項相關問題－圖表資料 答案 (C)

難

題目詢問被建議的是哪個郡，因此必須確認題目提供的圖表上的資訊，並注意和題目關鍵字（county ~ recommended）相關的內容。男子說：「I assume you recommend that the firm build at the driest location of the ones analyzed」，表示自己推測女子會建議這間公司蓋在這些分析地點中最乾燥的地方，但女子回答：「That one isn't suitable, since land costs there exceed Skylark's budget. As a result, we recommended the next best option.」，表示因為最乾燥那裡的土地成本超過了 Skylark 的預算，所以不適合，並因此建議了次佳的選項，由此可知，被建議的是平均年降雨量第二低的 Vaughn 郡，因此正確答案是 (C) Vaughn County。

PART 4

71
72
73

Questions 71-73 refer to the following telephone message.

美式發音

Cynthia, it's Haley Vincent. [71]**I know you're busy preparing for the convention in Orlando you'll be attending on behalf of our investment company**, but I could really use your help. [72]**I'm presenting some information about a couple of stocks to a client on Monday.** I'm a little nervous because I've never done that before. It'd be great if you could go over my notes and visual materials with me beforehand. I want to make sure everything is in order. Oh, also, [73]**do you happen to know of any good vegetarian places in town?** I might go for lunch with the client after the meeting, and he doesn't eat meat. Thanks in advance, and I'll talk to you soon.

第 71-73 題請參考下列電話留言。

Cynthia，我是 Haley Vincent。[71] 我知道妳正在忙著準備要代表我們投資公司參加的那場在奧蘭多的大會，但我真的需要妳的幫忙。[72] 我週一要向客戶簡報有關幾檔股票的一些資訊。我有點緊張，因為我之前從來沒做過這件事。如果妳能事先和我一起仔細看過我的筆記和圖表資料的話，那就太好了。我想確保一切都準備就緒了。噢，還有，[73] 妳會不會剛好知道鎮上有什麼可以吃素食的好地方啊？我開完會後可能會和客戶去吃午餐，但他不吃肉。先謝謝妳了，我很快會去找妳。

71 Where does the listener probably work?
(A) At a travel agency
(B) At a media company
(C) At a financial firm
(D) At a law office

71 聽者可能在哪裡工作？
(A) 旅行社
(B) 媒體公司
(C) 金融公司
(D) 法律事務所

72 What will the speaker do on Monday?
(A) Prepare a report
(B) Go to the airport
(C) Attend a convention
(D) Give a presentation

72 說話者在週一會做什麼？
(A) 準備報告
(B) 前往機場
(C) 參加會議
(D) 進行簡報

73 What information does the speaker ask for?
(A) Restaurant recommendations
(B) Clients' names
(C) A meeting agenda
(D) An order number

73 說話者要求取得什麼資訊？
(A) 推薦的餐廳
(B) 客戶的名字
(C) 會議的議程
(D) 訂單的編號

題目 on behalf of 代表～ could use 需要 stock [stɑk] 股票 nervous [`nɝvəs] 緊張不安的 go over 仔細看過；檢討 visual material 圖表（或其他視覺化的）資料 in order 就緒的 vegetarian [͵vɛdʒə`tɛrɪən] 素食的

71 整體內容相關問題－聽者 答案 (C)

中

題目詢問聽者的身分，因此要注意聽和身分、職業相關的表達。獨白說：「I know you're busy preparing for the convention ~ you'll be attending on behalf of our investment company」，表示知道對方正忙著準備要代表投資公司參加大會，由此可知，聽者在金融公司裡工作，因此正確答案是 (C) At a financial firm。

換句話說

investment company 投資公司 → financial firm 金融公司

72 細節事項相關問題－接下來要做的事 答案 (D)

中

題目詢問說話者週一會做什麼，因此必須注意聽提到題目關鍵字（Monday）的部分。獨白說：「I'm presenting some information about a couple of stocks to a client on Monday.」，表示週一要和客戶簡報幾檔股票的相關資訊，因此正確答案是 (D) Give a presentation。

73 細節事項相關問題－要求 答案 (A)

中

題目詢問說話者要求取得什麼資訊，因此要注意聽獨白中後半部分出現要求相關表達的句子。獨白說：「do you happen to know of any good vegetarian places in town?」，詢問對方是否知道有什麼可以吃素食的好地方，因此正確答案是 (A) Restaurant recommendations。

74 75 76

Questions 74-76 refer to the following speech.

澳洲式發音

[74]**Thank you all very much for being here to celebrate the release of our company's latest device**, the Access Portable Charger. [75]**I would like to give Patricia Sanderson from the design team special praise today. She came up with the idea to include a flashlight function in the charger.** This feature has proven popular with online reviewers who were given the device in advance. They say it makes this the perfect charger for a camping trip, which should result in more sales. Now, please turn your attention to the screen at the front of the room . . . [76]**A commercial for the Access Portable Charger will air on several major TV networks starting tomorrow, and I'd like to give you a sneak preview.**

74 At what event is the speech being given?

(A) A service center opening
(B) A product launch party
(C) A monthly shareholders meeting
(D) A company anniversary celebration

75 Why does the speaker praise Patricia Sanderson?

(A) She altered a logo design.
(B) She designed a popular Web site.
(C) She suggested a device feature.
(D) She signed an important client.

76 What will most likely happen next?

(A) An employee will be introduced.
(B) A device will be demonstrated.
(C) A speech will be given.
(D) A video will be played.

第 74-76 題請參考下列致詞。

[74] 非常感謝各位來到這裡慶祝我們公司的最新裝置 Access 攜帶式充電器的發表。[75] 我今天想要特別稱讚設計團隊的 Patricia Sanderson。她想到了在充電器裡加進手電筒功能的這個構想。這項特別功能已證實在事先拿到這件裝置的網路評論家間大受歡迎。他們說這項功能使這款充電器非常適合在露營之旅時使用，這點應該能帶來更多銷售量。現在請把你們的注意力放到這個場地前方的螢幕上……[76]Access 攜帶式充電器的廣告將從明天起於幾個主要電視網播送，我想讓大家先睹為快。

74 這段致詞是在什麼場合進行的？

(A) 服務中心開幕
(B) 產品發表派對
(C) 每月股東會議
(D) 公司年度慶祝活動

75 說話者為何稱讚 Patricia Sanderson？

(A) 她更改了一個標誌的設計。
(B) 她設計了一個受歡迎的網站。
(C) 她建議了一項裝置的特別功能。
(D) 她簽下了一個重要的客戶。

76 接下來最有可能會發生什麼？

(A) 會介紹一位員工。
(B) 會示範一項裝置。
(C) 會進行一場演講。
(D) 會播放一支影片。

題目 portable [美 `portəbl̩ 英 `pɔ:təbl] 攜帶式的　charger [美 `tʃɑrdʒɚ 英 `tʃɑ:dʒə] 充電器　praise [prez] 稱讚
come up with 想出～　flashlight [`flæʃ͵laɪt] 手電筒　function [`fʌŋkʃən] 功能
feature [美 fitʃɚ 英 fi:tʃə]（可以做為特色的）特別功能；特色
commercial [美 kə`mɝʃəl 英 kə`mə:ʃəl]（電視或廣播裡的）廣告　air [美 ɛr 英 ɛə] 播送　TV network 電視網
sneak preview 影片在公開前的試看

74 整體內容相關問題－地點　　答案 (B)

中

題目詢問致詞進行的場合，因此要注意聽和地點相關的表達。獨白說：「Thank you all very much for being here to celebrate the release of our company's latest device」，表示感謝聽者們前來一同慶祝公司最新裝置的發表，由此可知，致詞進行的場合是產品發表派對，因此正確答案是 (B) A product launch party。

75 細節事項相關問題－理由　　答案 (C)

高

題目詢問說話者稱讚 Patricia Sanderson 的原因，因此要注意聽提到題目關鍵字（Patricia Sanderson）的部分。獨白說：「I would like to give Patricia Sanderson ~ special praise today. She came up with the idea to include a flashlight function in the charger.」，表示自己想要特別稱讚 Patricia Sanderson，因為她想到了在充電器裡加進手電筒功能的這個構想，因此正確答案是 (C) She suggested a device feature.。

換句話說

came up with the idea to include a ~ function in the charger 想到了在充電器裡加進一個功能的這個構想
→ suggested a device feature 建議了一項裝置的特別功能

76 細節事項相關問題－接下來要做的事　　答案 (D)

中

題目詢問接下來會發生什麼，因此要注意聽獨白的最後部分。獨白說：「A commercial ~ will air on several major TV networks starting tomorrow, and I'd like to give you a sneak preview.」，表示廣告將從明天起於幾個主要電視網播送，所以想讓大家先睹為快，由此可知，接下來將會播放影片，因此正確答案是 (D) A video will be played.。

TEST 1 2 3 4 5 6 7 8 9 10

新

77
78
79

Questions 77-79 refer to the following telephone message.

英式發音

Hello, Mr. Holster. This is Julie Thompson from Beaumont Industries. [77]**You did very well during the interview on Thursday.** [78]**Our CEO was impressed with your idea about how to sell more of our products in the Chinese home appliance market.** As a result, I'm pleased to inform you that you've been selected to take over as manager of our Beijing branch. I'll e-mail you the contract today. [79]**If you decide to accept the terms, please sign it and bring it to my office.** I don't want to rush you, but . . . um, the current manager will be retiring in three weeks. Obviously, [79]**we'd like you to spend a few weeks working with him.** Call me back at 555-0393 if you have any questions.

第 77-79 題請參考下列電話留言。

哈囉，Holster 先生。我是 Beaumont 工業的 Julie Thompson。[77] 您在星期四的面試表現得非常好。[78] 我們的執行長對於您就如何在中國家電用品市場賣出更多我們產品的構想感到印象深刻。因此，我很高興通知您，我們已選擇您接任我們北京分公司的經理一職。我今天會以電子郵件將合約寄給您。[79] 若您決定接受這些條件，請在簽名後把它帶到我的辦公室。我不想要催促您，不過⋯⋯嗯，現任經理將在三個星期後退休。當然，[79] 我們會希望您能與他共事幾個星期。若您有任何問題，請回撥 555-0393 給我。

77 What did the listener do on Thursday?
(A) Submitted an application
(B) E-mailed a manager
(C) Participated in an interview
(D) Revised a contract

77 聽者在星期四做了什麼？
(A) 提交一份申請書
(B) 寄電子郵件給一位經理
(C) 參加一場面試
(D) 修改一份合約

78 What was the CEO impressed with?
(A) A proposal to boost sales
(B) A plan to train new employees
(C) A design for a home appliance
(D) A suggestion for a brochure

78 執行長對什麼感到印象深刻？
(A) 提高銷量的一項提議
(B) 訓練新員工的一個計畫
(C) 一項家電用品的一個設計
(D) 對一本小冊子的一個建議

79 新 What does the speaker mean when she says, "the current manager will be retiring in three weeks"?
(A) A schedule will likely be updated.
(B) A decision must be made quickly.
(C) An employee will be promoted soon.
(D) A position has just become available.

79 當說話者說：「現任經理將在三個星期後退休」，意思是什麼？
(A) 一份時間表很可能會更新。
(B) 必須快點做出一項決定。
(C) 一位員工很快會升職。
(D) 一個職位剛開缺。

題目 home appliance **家電用品** take over **接任** term [美 tɝm 英 tɜ:m] **條件** rush [rʌʃ] **催促；匆忙地做** obviously [美 ˋɑbvɪəslɪ 英 ˋɔbviəsli] **當然；顯然** **78** proposal [prəˋpozl] **提議** boost [bust] **提高**

77 中 **細節事項相關問題－特定細項** 答案 (C)

題目詢問聽者在星期四做了什麼，因此要注意聽和題目關鍵字（Thursday）相關的內容。獨白說：「You did ~ during the interview on Thursday.」，提到聽者在星期四參加了面試，因此正確答案是 (C) Participated in an interview。

78 高 **細節事項相關問題－特定細項** 答案 (A)

題目詢問執行長對什麼感到印象深刻，因此要注意聽和題目關鍵字（CEO impressed with）相關的內容。獨白說：「Our CEO was impressed with your idea about how to sell more of our products in the Chinese home appliance market.」，表示執行長對於如何賣出更多產品的構想感到印象深刻，因此正確答案是 (A) A proposal to boost sales。

換句話說

idea about how to sell more of ~ products **如何賣出更多產品的構想**
→ A proposal to boost sales **提高銷量的一項提議**

新 **79** 高 **細節事項相關問題－掌握意圖** 答案 (B)

題目詢問說話者的說話意圖，因此要注意與題目引用句（the current manager will be retiring in three weeks）相關的內容。獨白先說：「If you decide to accept the terms, please sign it[contract] and bring it to my office.」，表示若聽者決定接受條件，則請將合約簽名後帶到自己的辦公室來，後面說：「we'd like you to spend a few weeks working with him[current manager]」，希望聽者能和現任經理共事幾個星期，由此可知，聽者必須快點做決定，因此正確答案是 (B) A decision must be made quickly.。

80
81
82

Questions 80-82 refer to the following talk.

美式發音

OK . . . My name is Sarah Edwards, and [80]**I'll be showing you around our tire manufacturing facility today**. As new employees, it's important that you be familiar with the various sections. Now, [81]**we usually visit the tire testing laboratory first during these orientation tours**. But, since researchers are currently wrapping up an urgent study, [81]**I've been asked to do the tour in reverse order today. So, we'll start by heading to the viewing deck of our assembly line room.** Throughout the tour, [82]**please refrain from placing your hands or fingers on any of the machines**. Are there any questions before we begin?

80 Where most likely are the listeners?

(A) At a construction site
(B) At a medical clinic
(C) At a manufacturing plant
(D) At a car dealership

81 According to the speaker, what has been changed?

(A) The price of some merchandise
(B) The order of a tour
(C) The type of machines used
(D) The operational hours of a facility

82 What are listeners instructed to do?

(A) Avoid touching equipment
(B) Read an instruction manual
(C) Wear protective gear
(D) Enroll in a class

第 80-82 題請參考下列談話。

好……我的名字是 Sarah Edwards，而 [80] 我今天會帶你們參觀我們的輪胎製造廠。做為新進員工，熟悉各個不同區塊對你們來說是很重要的。那麼，[81] 在進行這種新進人員導覽時，我們第一個通常會參觀輪胎測試實驗室。不過，因為研究人員目前正在收尾一項緊急研究，所以 [81] 我被要求今天要按相反順序進行導覽。那麼，我們會從前往我們組裝生產線室的觀景台開始。在整場導覽之中，[82] 請不要將你們的手掌或手指放在任何裝置上。在我們開始之前，有任何問題嗎？

80 聽者們最有可能在哪裡？

(A) 工地
(B) 診所
(C) 製造工廠
(D) 汽車經銷商

81 根據說話者所說，什麼已經被變更了？

(A) 一些商品的價格
(B) 導覽的順序
(C) 使用裝置的類型
(D) 設施的營運時間

82 聽者們被指示做什麼？

(A) 避免觸碰設備
(B) 閱讀使用說明手冊
(C) 穿戴防護裝備
(D) 報名課程

題目 wrap up 收尾　urgent [ˋɝdʒənt] 緊急的　reverse order 相反順序　viewing deck 觀景台　assembly [əˋsɛmblɪ] 組裝　refrain [rɪˋfren] 克制；忍住

80 construction [kənˋstrʌkʃən] 建設；工程

81 operational [ˌɑpəˋreʃənl] 營運的

82 protective [prəˋtɛktɪv] 防護用的　gear [gɪr] 裝備　enroll in 報名～

80 低 **整體內容相關問題－地點** 答案 (C)

題目詢問聽者們的所在地點，因此要注意聽和地點相關的表達。獨白說：「I'll be showing you around our tire manufacturing facility today」，表示今天要帶聽者們參觀輪胎製造廠，由此可知，聽者們身在製造工廠，因此正確答案是 (C) At a manufacturing plant。

81 中 **細節事項相關問題－特定細項** 答案 (B)

題目詢問變更了什麼，因此要注意聽和題目關鍵字（changed）相關的內容。獨白說：「we usually visit the tire testing laboratory first during these orientation tours」，表示導覽通常會從參觀輪胎測試實驗室開始，接著說：「I've been asked to do the tour in reverse order today. So, we'll start by heading to the viewing deck of our assembly line room.」，表示自己今天被要求按相反順序進行導覽，因此要從去組裝生產線室的觀景台開始，由此可知，導覽的路線順序變更了，因此正確答案是 (B) The order of a tour。

82 高 **細節事項相關問題－特定細項** 答案 (A)

題目詢問聽者們被指示做什麼，因此要注意聽和題目關鍵字（instructed to do）相關的內容。獨白說：「please refrain from placing your hands or fingers on any of the machines」，要求聽者們不要將手掌或手指放在任何裝置上，因此正確答案是 (A) Avoid touching equipment。

83
84
85

Questions 83-85 refer to the following telephone message.

澳洲式發音

Felicity, this is Pedro. [83]**Have you seen today's edition of the *Santa Cruise Herald*? It features an article about our bistro! The popular food critic Rebecca Clay wrote the piece.** Overall, her review was very positive! Although she stated that our chocolate cake was a bit too sweet, [84]**she said the steak and appetizer she ordered were cooked to perfection.** You know, Ms. Clay has very high standards. [84]**It will probably result in a lot more customers for us.** [85]**Could you add this review to our social media page today?** I want as many people as possible to read it. Thanks!

第 83-85 題請參考下列電話留言。

Felicity，我是 Pedro。[83] 你看到今天出的那份《Santa Cruise Herald》了嗎？它特別刊了一篇和我們餐酒館有關的報導！這篇報導是那個很受歡迎的美食評論家 Rebecca Clay 寫的。整體來說，她的評論非常正面！儘管她指出我們的巧克力蛋糕有點太甜了，[84] 但她說她點的牛排和開胃菜都烹調得恰到好處。你知道的，Clay 小姐的標準非常高。[84] 這篇報導可能會為我們帶來多很多的客人。[85] 可以請你在今天把這篇評論放到我們社群媒體的頁面上嗎？我希望越多人看到它越好。謝謝！

83 What is the message mainly about?

(A) A new menu
(B) A recent critique
(C) A facility reopening
(D) A catering inquiry

83 這則留言主要與什麼有關？

(A) 新菜單
(B) 最近的評論
(C) 設施的重新開幕
(D) 關於外燴的疑問

84 Why does the speaker say, "Ms. Clay has very high standards"?

新

(A) To indicate regret
(B) To express anticipation
(C) To explain a recurring request
(D) To complain about a coworker

84 為何說話者說：「Clay 小姐的標準非常高」？

(A) 表示遺憾
(B) 傳達期待
(C) 說明一個一再出現的要求
(D) 抱怨一位同事

85 What does the speaker ask the listener to do?

(A) Adjust a recipe
(B) Organize a party
(C) Post a review online
(D) Visit a newspaper office

85 說話者要求聽者做什麼？

(A) 調整食譜
(B) 籌辦派對
(C) 把評論張貼到網路上
(D) 造訪報社

題目 feature [美 fitʃɚ 英 fiːtʃə] 特載；以～為特色 bistro [美 `bistro 英 `biːstrəu] 餐酒館 piece [pis]（一則）報導 state [stet]（正式）陳述；說明 to perfection 恰到好處 standard [美 `stændɚd 英 `stændəd] 標準

83 critique [krɪ`tik] 評論；批評

84 regret [rɪ`grɛt] 遺憾 anticipation [æn͵tɪsə`peʃən] 期待 recurring [rɪ`kɝɪŋ] 一再發生的

83 整體內容相關問題－主題 答案 (B)

中

題目詢問留言的主題，因此要注意聽獨白的開頭部分。獨白說：「Have you seen today's edition of the *Santa Cruise Herald*? It features an article about our bistro! The popular food critic Rebecca Clay wrote the piece.」，詢問對方是否已看到今天出的《Santa Cruise Herald》了，並說上面特別刊了一篇和自己餐酒館有關的報導，接著說報導是那個很受歡迎的美食評論家 Rebecca Clay 寫的，提及最近刊出的評論報導，因此正確答案是 (B) A recent critique。

新 **84 細節事項相關問題－掌握意圖** 答案 (B)

高

題目詢問說話者的說話意圖，因此要注意與題目引用句（Ms. Clay has very high standards）相關的內容。引用句之前說：「she[Ms. Clay] said the steak and appetizer she ordered were cooked to perfection」，表示 Clay 小姐點的牛排和開胃菜都烹調得恰到好處，引用句之後則說：「It will probably result in a lot more customers for us.」，表示這篇報導可能會為餐廳帶來多很多的客人，由此可知，說話者說這句話是想傳達對 Clay 小姐的這篇評論可能會帶來更多生意的期待，因此正確答案是 (B) To express anticipation。

85 細節事項相關問題－要求 答案 (C)

中

題目詢問說話者要求聽者做什麼，因此要注意聽獨白的後半部分中，有出現要求相關表達的句子。獨白說：「Could you add this review to our social media page today?」，要求聽者將這則評論放到社群媒體的頁面上，因此正確答案是 (C) Post a review online。

86
87
88

Questions 86-88 refer to the following advertisement.

加拿大式發音

Are you a singer or musician looking for your first big break? Then [86]**Star Broadcast Network's newest program is for you! *Music Icon* is a talent competition** that will end with one participant receiving a contract with a major entertainment company. [87]**On the show, a panel of celebrity judges—which varies every week—will eliminate one contestant.** And once there are only three participants left, the viewers alone will get to select the winner. We'll be holding auditions across the country from May 11 until June 15 to select our competitors. So sign up for the one in the city closest to you today! [88]**Visit our Web site for a list of audition sites.**

86 What is the advertisement mainly about?

(A) A radio program
(B) An awards ceremony
(C) An acting audition
(D) A musical contest

87 What does the speaker say about the judges?

(A) They will be former contestants.
(B) They will choose the final winner.
(C) They will be changed each week.
(D) They will consider viewer feedback.

88 What does the speaker say is available on the Web site?

(A) An audio recording
(B) A venue list
(C) A performance schedule
(D) A film trailer

第 86-88 題請參考下列廣告。

你是正在尋求第一個重大機會的歌手或音樂家嗎？那麼 [86]Star Broadcast Network 的最新節目就是你的機會！《Music Icon》是一個選秀節目，節目最終會有一名參賽者可以獲得一紙大型娛樂公司的合約。[87] 在這個節目之中，名人評審團——評審團每週都不同——會淘汰一名參賽者。而當只剩下三名參賽者時，將交由觀眾們獨力選出優勝者。我們將從 5 月 11 日到 6 月 15 日於全國各地進行海選來選出我們的參賽者。所以今天就報名離你最近的城市裡的那場吧！[88] 請上我們的網站取得海選地點的清單。

86 這則廣告主要與什麼有關？

(A) 電台節目
(B) 頒獎典禮
(C) 表演試鏡
(D) 音樂競賽

87 關於評審，說話者說什麼？

(A) 他們會是之前的參賽者。
(B) 他們會選出最終優勝者。
(C) 他們會每週變動。
(D) 他們會考慮觀眾的回饋意見。

88 說話者說在網站上可以取得什麼？

(A) 錄音音檔
(B) 場地清單
(C) 表演時間表
(D) 電影預告片

題目 big break 重大機會　eliminate [ɪˋlɪməˌnet] 淘汰　contestant [kənˋtɛstənt] 參賽者　alone [əˋlon] 單獨；單單　competitor [kəmˋpɛtətɚ] 參賽者；競爭者　sign up for 報名～
86 awards ceremony 頒獎典禮　acting [ˋæktɪŋ] 演戲，表演
87 former [ˋfɔrmɚ] 以前的，過去的
88 recording [rɪˋkɔrdɪŋ] 錄音　trailer [ˋtrelɚ]（電影等的）預告片

86 整體內容相關問題－主題 答案 (D)
高
題目詢問廣告的主題是什麼，因此要注意聽獨白的開頭部分。獨白說：「Star Broadcast Network's newest program is for you[singer or musician]! *Music Icon* is a talent competition」，表示 Star Broadcast Network 的最新節目《Music Icon》是給歌手或音樂家參加的一個選秀節目，因此正確答案是 (D) A musical contest。

87 細節事項相關問題－提及 答案 (C)
難
題目詢問說話者提到什麼與評審有關的事，因此要注意聽和題目關鍵字（judges）相關的內容。獨白說：「On the show, a panel of celebrity judges—which varies every week—will eliminate one contestant.」，表示每週都會是不同的名人評審團來淘汰一名參賽者，因此正確答案是 (C) They will be changed each week.。

88 細節事項相關問題－特定細項 答案 (B)
低
題目詢問說話者說可以在網站上取得什麼，因此要注意聽和題目關鍵字（Web site）相關的內容。獨白說：「Visit our Web site for a list of audition sites.」，表示網站上可以取得海選地點的清單，因此正確答案是 (B) A venue list。
換句話說
a list of ~ sites 地點的清單 → A venue list 場地清單

Questions 89-91 refer to the following talk.

澳洲式發音

I'd like to start by saying that it's a great honor to be able to participate in this lecture series at James College. [89]**Several speakers have already given excellent talks, and I hope that you'll find mine as engaging as theirs.** Now . . . [90]**the focus of my lecture is the impact that fiction has on society**. Specifically, I'm going to look at how [91]**one popular novel . . . um, *The Looking Glass* by Jack Coyle** . . . led to several reforms to the legal system. If you haven't read Coyle's book, don't panic. I'll hand out the relevant excerpts from it now, so you can refer to them during my lecture.

89 What is mentioned about the previous speakers?

(A) They worked for major publications.
(B) They graduated from James College.
(C) They gave stimulating lectures.
(D) They received writing prizes.

90 What will the speaker talk about?

(A) The importance of reading
(B) The influence of literature
(C) The value of higher education
(D) The effects of legal reform

91 Who is Jack Coyle?

(A) An author
(B) A college lecturer
(C) A public official
(D) A lawyer

第 89-91 題請參考下列談話。

我一開始想先說，能參加這次在 James 學院的系列講座真的非常榮幸。[89] 幾位演講人都講得非常精采，我希望你們也會覺得我的演講和他們的一樣吸引人。那麼……[90] 我的講座會聚焦於小說對於社會所造成的影響。具體來說，我打算要來看 [91] 一本很受歡迎的小說……嗯，Jack Coyle 寫的《The Looking Glass》……是如何造成法律制度的幾項變革。如果你還沒有看過 Coyle 的書，不用驚慌。我現在會發下書中相關的節錄內容，讓你們可以在我進行講座時參考。

89 關於之前的演講人，提到了什麼？

(A) 他們製作過重要的出版品。
(B) 他們畢業於 James 學院。
(C) 他們進行了具有啟發性的講座。
(D) 他們得過寫作獎。

90 說話者將討論什麼？

(A) 閱讀的重要性
(B) 文學的影響力
(C) 高等教育的價值
(D) 法律改革的影響

91 Jack Coyle 是誰？

(A) 一位作家
(B) 一位學院講師
(C) 一位公職人員
(D) 一位律師

題目 honor [美 `ɑnɚ 英 `ɔnə] 榮耀 engaging [ɪn`gedʒɪŋ] 有吸引力的；迷人的 fiction [`fɪkʃən] 小說
reform [美 ˌrɪ`fɔrm 英 ri`fɔ:rm] 改革 legal [`ligḷ] 法律的 panic [`pænɪk] 驚慌的 relevant [`rɛləvənt] 相關的
excerpt [美 ɪk`sɝpt 英 ek`sə:pt] 節錄（的內容）

89 stimulating [`stɪmjəˌletɪŋ] 具有啟發性的

90 influence [`ɪnflʊəns] 影響（力） literature [`lɪtərətʃɚ] 文學 value [`vælju] 價值

91 author [`ɔθɚ] 作家 public official 公職人員 lawyer [`lɔjɚ] 律師

89 細節事項相關問題－提及 答案 (C)

高

題目詢問提到了什麼與之前的演講人有關的事，因此要注意聽和題目關鍵字（previous speakers）相關的內容。獨白說：「Several speakers have already given excellent talks, and I hope that you'll find mine as engaging as theirs.」，說話者表示幾位演講人都講得非常精采，並希望聽眾能覺得自己的演講和前面演講人的一樣吸引人，由此可知，之前的演講人所進行的講座內容都非常精采，因此正確答案是 (C) They gave stimulating lectures.。

90 細節事項相關問題－特定細項 答案 (B)

高

題目詢問說話者會討論什麼內容，因此要注意聽和題目關鍵字（speaker talk about）相關的內容。獨白說：「the focus of my lecture is the impact that fiction has on society」，表示自己會聚焦於小說對於社會所造成的影響，因此正確答案是 (B) The influence of literature。

換句話說

the impact that fiction has on society 小說對於社會所造成的影響 → The influence of literature 文學的影響力

91 細節事項相關問題－特定細項 答案 (A)

中

題目詢問 Jack Coyle 的身分，因此要注意聽和提問對象（Jack Coyle）的身分、職業相關的表達。獨白說：「one popular novel ~ *The Looking Glass* by Jack Coyle」，表示一本很受歡迎的小說《The Looking Glass》是由 Jack Coyle 寫的，由此可知，Jack Coyle 是作家，因此正確答案是 (A) An author。

92
93
94

Questions 92-94 refer to the following announcement and floor plan.

英式發音

Attention, everyone. Before we open today, I just want to remind you that our clothing store is having a sale this week in honor of the holidays. [92]**Make sure to tell customers that over 20 of our best-selling sportswear items are marked down.** [93]**The display has been set up in the aisle closest to the main entrance**, so it will be the first thing people see when they enter the store. Oh . . . one more thing. [94]**We're going to close down for two days toward the end of the month so that our checkout area can be expanded. I'll announce the dates tomorrow** after I have met with a representative of the interior design firm doing the work.

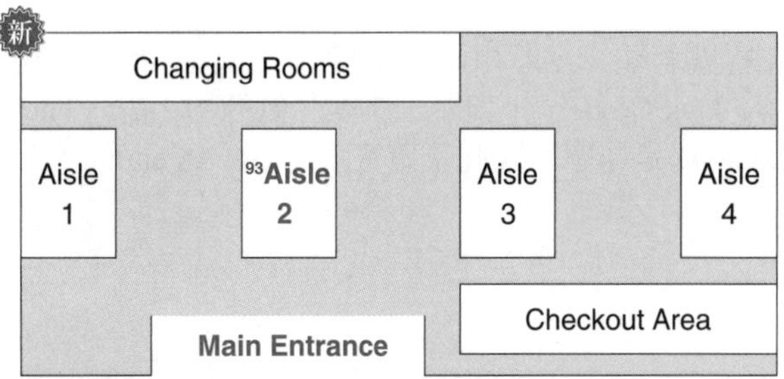

92 Who is the speaker most likely addressing?

(A) Store customers
(B) Marketing consultants
(C) Shop employees
(D) Construction workers

93 Look at the graphic. Where has the display been set up?

(A) In Aisle 1
(B) In Aisle 2
(C) In Aisle 3
(D) In Aisle 4

94 According to the speaker, what will be announced tomorrow?

(A) The dates of a renovation project
(B) The name of a design firm
(C) The details of a sportswear production
(D) The location of a new branch

第 92-94 題請參考下列公告與樓層平面圖。

大家請注意。在我們今天開門之前，我想提醒一下你們，我們服飾店要在這週進行特賣來慶祝假期。[92] 一定要告訴客人，在我們最熱賣的運動服飾商品中，有超過 20 款降價了。[93] 這個展示區設置在最靠近大門的走道上，所以當人們進到店裡，他們會最先看到這個展示區。噢……還有一件事。[94] 我們在這個月要月底的時候會休息兩天，讓我們可以把結帳區擴大。在和做這項工程的室內設計公司的代表見面之後，我會在明天宣布日期。

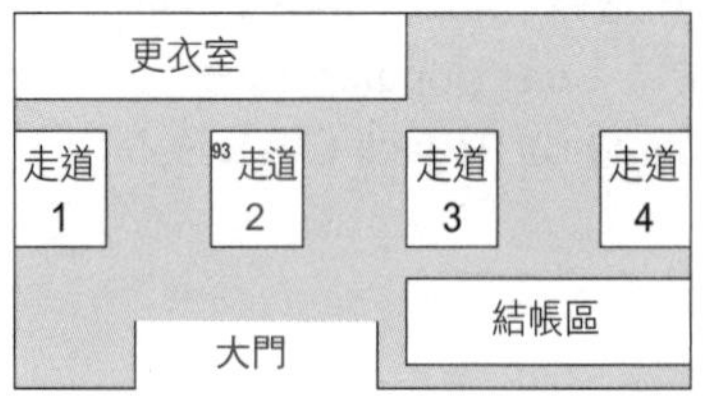

92 說話者最有可能在對誰說話？

(A) 店內客人
(B) 行銷顧問
(C) 商店員工
(D) 建築工人

93 請看圖表。展示區設置在哪裡？

(A) 走道 1
(B) 走道 2
(C) 走道 3
(D) 走道 4

94 根據說話者所說，明天會宣布什麼？

(A) 整修計畫的日期
(B) 設計公司的名字
(C) 運動服飾生產的細節資訊
(D) 新分店的位置

題目 remind [rɪˋmaɪnd] 提醒　in honor of 為慶祝～；為表對～的尊敬　mark down 調降價格
toward [美 təˋwɔrd 英 təˋwɔːd] 接近　checkout [ˋtʃɛkˌaʊt] 收銀台　representative [rɛprɪˋzɛntətɪv] 代表
94 renovation [ˌrɛnəˋveʃən] 整修　production [prəˋdʌkʃən] 產量；生產

92 整體內容相關問題－聽者 答案 (C)

中

題目詢問說話者的說話對象是誰，因此要注意聽和身分、職業相關的表達。獨白說：「Make sure to tell customers that over 20 of our best-selling sportswear items are marked down.」，表示一定要告訴客人，在最熱賣的運動服飾商品中，有超過 20 款降價了，由此可知，聽者們是販售運動服飾店家的員工，因此正確答案是 (C) Shop employees。

新 93 細節事項相關問題－圖表資料 答案 (B)

中

題目詢問展示區的設置地點，因此要確認題目提供的樓層平面圖，並注意和題目關鍵字（display ~ set up）相關的內容。獨白說：「The display has been set up in the aisle closest to the main entrance」，表示展示區設置在最靠近大門的走道上，透過樓層平面圖可知，最靠近大門的走道是走道 2，所以展示區會設置在走道 2 上，因此正確答案是 (B) In Aisle 2。

94 細節事項相關問題－特定細項 答案 (A)

中

題目詢問明天會宣布什麼，因此要注意聽和題目關鍵字（announced tomorrow）相關的內容。獨白說：「We're going to close down for two days toward the end of the month so that our checkout area can be expanded. I'll announce the dates tomorrow」，表示要月底的時候會休息兩天，因為要把結帳區擴大，並說明天會宣布工程進行的日期，因此正確答案是 (A) The dates of a renovation project。

95
96
97

Questions 95-97 refer to the following excerpt from a meeting and graph.

美式發音

Before we wrap up, I'd like to talk about how our four stores are doing. [95]**I went through the figures in our quarterly sales report yesterday**, and . . . well, there's good news and bad news. The Kingston branch continues to do well. It exceeded $30,000 in revenue every month last quarter. In addition, [96]**the Albany branch has improved. Sales have increased each month since Harry Ferguson took over as manager in June.** I'm concerned about the Bethany and Newark locations, though, because sales have declined since they opened in August. [97]**I'm going to pass out the report now.** Please look through it and then come up with some suggestions for our next meeting on how to turn things around.

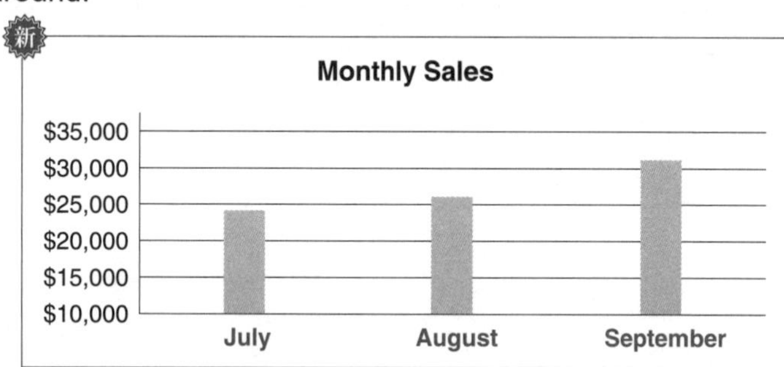

95 What did the speaker do yesterday?

(A) Visited a business
(B) Looked at some data
(C) Went to a sales conference
(D) Gave a presentation

96 Look at the graphic. Which branch does the graph refer to?

(A) Kingston
(B) Albany
(C) Bethany
(D) Newark

97 What will most likely happen next?

(A) A report will be revised.
(B) A manager will be introduced.
(C) A document will be distributed.
(D) A store will be contacted.

第 95-97 題請參考下列會議節錄與圖表。

在我們結束之前，我想談談我們四間店的表現如何。[95] 我昨天仔細看過我們季銷售報告裡的數字了，然後……嗯，有好消息，也有壞消息。Kingston 分店的表現依然很好。它上一季的每月收益都超過 30,000 美金。此外，[96]Albany 分店的表現進步了。從 Harry Ferguson 在六月接任經理開始，每個月的銷售額都增加了。不過，在 Bethany 及 Newark 的據點則讓我擔心，因為它們自八月開幕以來銷售額都在減少。[97] 我現在會把報告發下去。請先看過這份報告，然後就要如何翻轉這個局面，在我們下次會議上提出一些建議。

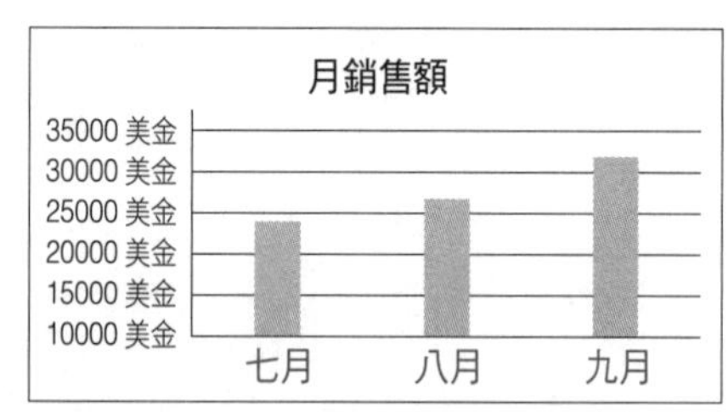

95 說話者昨天做了什麼？

(A) 拜訪了一間公司
(B) 檢視了一些數據
(C) 去了一場銷售會議
(D) 做了一場簡報

96 請看圖表。這張圖表與哪一間分店有關？

(A) Kingston
(B) Albany
(C) Bethany
(D) Newark

97 接下來最有可能會發生什麼？

(A) 會修改一份報告。
(B) 會介紹一位經理。
(C) 會分發一份文件。
(D) 會聯絡一間店。

題目 go through 仔細看過 figure [ˋfɪgjɚ] 數量；數字 quarterly [ˋkwɔrtɚlɪ] 季度的 revenue [ˋrɛvəˏnju] 收益 take over as 接任～ pass out 分發 look through 瀏覽 turn around 翻轉

97 distribute [dɪˋstrɪbjʊt] 分發

95 ○○●●●中 **細節事項相關問題－特定細項** 答案 (B)

題目詢問說話者昨天做了什麼，因此要注意聽和題目關鍵字（yesterday）相關的內容。獨白說：「I went through the figures in our quarterly sales report yesterday」，表示自己昨天仔細看過季銷售報告裡的數字了，因此正確答案是 (B) Looked at some data。

換句話說

went through the figures in ~ report 仔細看過報告裡的數字了 → Looked at some data 檢視了一些數據

新 **96** ●●●●●難 **細節事項相關問題－圖表資料** 答案 (B)

題目詢問這張圖表與哪一間分店有關，因此必須確認題目提供的圖表內容資訊，並注意和題目關鍵字（branch ~ refer to）有關的內容。獨白說：「the Albany branch has improved. Sales have increased each month since Harry Ferguson took over as manager in June」，表示 Albany 分店的表現進步了，且從六月開始，每個月的銷售額都增加，透過圖表可知，七月以來每個月的銷售額都是增加的，因此這是 Albany 店的月銷售額圖表，正確答案是 (B) Albany。

97 ○○●●●中 **細節事項相關問題－接下來要做的事** 答案 (C)

題目詢問接下來最有可能會發生什麼，因此要注意聽獨白的最後部分。獨白說：「I'm going to pass out the report now.」，表示現在會把報告發下去，因此正確答案是 (C) A document will be distributed.。

98
99
100

Questions 98-100 refer to the following announcement and chart.

加拿大式發音

Ever since [98]**we started working on the Raymon Arena Project last month**, things have been very busy. [99]**The tight deadlines have created problems for some of you architects, which we need to address.** If you look at this flow chart, you'll see that our normal work process for drafting blueprints includes five steps. However, for the rest of this project, [100]**I want you to draft blueprints right after meeting with clients.** [99]**I think eliminating one step will expedite the work process.** Now, I want to say a few things about a new city regulation that we need to take into account when designing the stadium. It'll only take a few minutes.

新

STEP 1	Meet with clients
STEP 2	[100]Discuss plan with team leader
STEP 3	Draft blueprints
STEP 4	Modify plans based on feedback
STEP 5	Submit for approval

98 What happened last month?

(A) A permit application was rejected.
(B) A structure was inspected.
(C) A project was started.
(D) A sports arena was completed.

99 Why is a change being made?

(A) To reduce some expenses
(B) To reflect client requests
(C) To improve communication
(D) To accommodate time constraints

100 新 Look at the graphic. Which step was removed from a work process?

(A) Meet with clients
(B) Discuss plan with team leader
(C) Modify plans based on feedback
(D) Submit for approval

第 98-100 題請參考下列公告與圖表。

自從 [98] 我們上個月開始進行 Raymon 競技場的計畫以來，工作就一直非常忙碌。[99] 緊湊的截止期限已經對你們建築師中的一些人造成了困難，而我們必須處理這件事。如果你們看看這張流程圖，就會看到我們在畫藍圖的草圖時，正常的工作流程包含了五個步驟。不過，在這項計畫的剩餘部分，[100] 我想要你們在與客戶會面後就立刻畫藍圖的草圖。[99] 我認為刪除一個步驟會加快工作流程。現在，我想要針對一項我們在設計這座體育場時必須納入考量的新市內法規說幾件事。這只會花幾分鐘。

步驟 1	和客戶會面
步驟 2	[100] 和組長討論平面圖
步驟 3	畫藍圖的草圖
步驟 4	根據回饋意見修改平面圖
步驟 5	提交以供批准

98 上個月發生了什麼？

(A) 許可證申請遭到駁回。
(B) 視察建築物。
(C) 開始計畫。
(D) 完成運動競技場。

99 為什麼要做出一項變更？

(A) 減少一些支出
(B) 反映客戶要求
(C) 改善溝通
(D) 配合時間限制

100 請看圖表。從工作流程中移除了哪一個步驟？

(A) 和客戶會面
(B) 和組長討論平面圖
(C) 根據回饋意見修改平面圖
(D) 提交以供批准

題目 arena [əˋrinə] 競技場　address [əˋdrɛs] 處理（問題等）　flow chart 流程圖　draft [dræft] 起草；畫草圖
blueprint [ˋbluˋprɪnt] 設計圖；藍圖　eliminate [ɪˋlɪmə͵net] 刪除；消除　expedite [ˋɛkspɪ͵daɪt] 加快；迅速完成
take into account 把～列入考量　stadium [ˋstedɪəm] 體育場

98 permit [ˋpɝmɪt] 許可證　structure [ˋstrʌktʃɚ] 建築物；構造　inspect [ɪnˋspɛkt] 視察；檢查；審查

99 accommodate [əˋkɑmə͵det] 配合　constraint [kənˋstrent] 限制

98 ■ 細節事項相關問題－特定細項　答案 (C)

中

題目詢問上個月發生了什麼，因此要注意聽和題目關鍵字（last month）相關的內容。獨白說：「we started working on the Raymon Arena Project last month」，表示上個月開始進行 Raymon 競技場的計畫，因此正確答案是 (C) A project was started.。

99 ■ 細節事項相關問題－理由　答案 (D)

高

題目詢問做出一項變更的理由，因此要注意聽和題目關鍵字（change ~ made）相關的內容。獨白說：「The tight deadlines have created problems for some of you architects, which we need to address.」，表示緊湊的截止期限已經對一些建築師造成了困難，而這件事必須要處理，接著說：「I think eliminating one step will expedite the work process.」，表示自己認為刪除一個步驟後可以加快工作流程，由此可知，是為了配合時間限制才會做出變更，因此正確答案是 (D) To accommodate time constraints。

新 **100** ■ 細節事項相關問題－圖表資料　答案 (B)

難

題目詢問被移除的是哪一個步驟，因此必須確認題目提供的圖表，並注意和題目關鍵字（step ~ removed）相關的內容。獨白說：「I want you to draft blueprints right after meeting with clients」，表示想要聽者們在與客戶會面後立刻畫藍圖的草圖，透過圖表可知，被移除的是在「和客戶會面」和「畫藍圖的草圖」之間的「和組長討論平面圖」這一個步驟，因此正確答案是 (B) Discuss plan with team leader。

TEST 08

Part 1 原文・翻譯・解析

Part 2 原文・翻譯・解析

Part 3 原文・翻譯・解析 新

Part 4 原文・翻譯・解析 新

MP3 收錄於 TEST 08.mp3。

進行深入練習或複習時，可以一邊多聽幾次收錄各國口音的試題 MP3，一邊搭配解答中的中英對照翻譯和解析，以及單字記憶表和多元口音單字記憶 MP3，達到事半功倍的效果。

PART 1

1 ○○○● 低

🔊 加拿大式發音

(A) The man is wiping a fan.
(B) The man is twisting a metal knob.
(C) The man is washing a cup.
(D) The man is drinking water.

(A) 男子正在擦電扇。
(B) 男子正在轉金屬把手。
(C) 男子正在洗杯子。
(D) 男子正在喝水。

單人照片 答案 (C)

仔細確認一名男子正在擦洗杯子的模樣。

(A) [╳] 男子不是在擦電扇（fan），而是在擦洗杯子，因此是錯誤選項。注意不要聽到 The man is wiping（男子正在擦）就選擇這個選項。

(B) [╳] twisting（正在轉）和男子的動作無關，因此是錯誤選項。這裡使用照片中有出現的金屬把手（metal knob）來造成混淆。

(C) [○] 這裡正確描述男子正在擦洗杯子的模樣，所以是正確答案。

(D) [╳] drinking（正在喝）和男子的動作無關，因此是錯誤選項。這裡利用照片中有出現的水（water）來造成混淆。

單字　wipe [waɪp] 擦乾淨　twist [twɪst] 扭轉　metal [`mɛtl] 金屬的　knob [nɑb]（球狀的）把手

2 ○○●● 中

🔊 英式發音

(A) The woman is dressing a mannequin.
(B) The woman is looking at her reflection.
(C) The woman is collecting some hangers.
(D) The woman is putting away some merchandise.

(A) 女子正在幫假人模特兒穿衣服。
(B) 女子正看著她的倒影。
(C) 女子正在把一些衣架收集起來。
(D) 女子正在收拾一些商品。

單人照片 答案 (B)

仔細觀察照片中一名女子正在照鏡子的模樣，以及周遭事物的狀態。

(A) [╳] dressing（正在幫～穿衣服）和女子的動作無關，因此是錯誤選項。這裡使用照片中有出現的假人模特兒（mannequin）來造成混淆。

(B) [○] 這裡正確描述女子正在照鏡子的模樣，所以是正確答案。

(C) [╳] collecting（正在收集）和女子的動作無關，因此是錯誤選項。這裡使用照片中有出現的衣架（hangers）來造成混淆。

(D) [╳] putting away（正在收拾）和女子的動作無關，因此是錯誤選項。這裡使用照片中有出現的商品（merchandise）來造成混淆。

單字　mannequin [`mænəkɪn] 假人模特兒　reflection [rɪ`flɛkʃən] 倒影　collect [kə`lɛkt] 收集
hanger [[美] `hæŋɚ [英] `hæŋə] 衣架

3 ○○●● 中

🔊 澳洲式發音

(A) One of the women is wearing a headset.
(B) One of the women is shaking hands with the man.
(C) They are posting a document on a notice board.
(D) They are working at different stations.

(A) 其中一名女子戴著耳機麥克風。
(B) 其中一名女子正在和男子握手。
(C) 他們正在公告欄上張貼一份文件。
(D) 他們正在不同的站工作。

兩人以上的照片 答案 (A)

仔細確認照片中眾人一起在看文件的模樣。

(A) [○] 這裡正確描述其中一名女子戴著耳機麥克風的樣子，所以是正確答案。請注意可以用現在進行式（is wearing）來描述人的狀態。

(B) [╳] 照片中沒有正在和男子握手（shaking hands with the man）的女子，因此是錯誤選項。

(C) [╳] 照片中沒有公告欄（notice board），照片中的人物也沒有做 posting（正在張貼）的動作，因此是錯誤選項。這裡使用照片中有出現的文件（document）來造成混淆。

(D) [╳] 照片中的人在同個地方工作，這裡卻描述為在不同的站（at different stations），因此是錯誤選項。

單字 headset [ˋhɛdˏsɛt] 耳機麥克風 shake hands 握手 notice board 公告欄
station [ˋsteʃən]（車站等機構的）站；駐地

4 高

美式發音

(A) Textbooks are being distributed in a lecture hall.
(B) Some people are giving a presentation.
(C) Some people are leaving an auditorium.
(D) A pen is being pointed at a page.

(A) 演講廳裡正在發課本。
(B) 一些人正在進行簡報。
(C) 一些人正在離開禮堂。
(D) 正在用一枝筆指著一頁。

兩人以上的照片 答案 (D)

仔細確認一名女子正用筆指著男子的書且人們都坐著的樣子。

(A) [╳] 照片中出現了課本，但不是正在發（are being distributed）課本，因此是錯誤選項。注意不要聽到 Textbooks（課本）和 in a lecture hall（演講廳裡）就選擇這個選項。

(B) [╳] 透過照片無法確認是否正在進行簡報，因此是錯誤選項。

(C) [╳] 照片中的人們都坐著，這裡卻描述成正在離開（leaving），因此是錯誤選項。這裡使用照片的可能拍攝地點「禮堂（auditorium）」來造成混淆。

(D) [○] 這裡正確描述用筆指著書裡其中一頁的模樣，所以是正確答案。

單字 distribute [dɪˋstrɪbjʊt] 分發 lecture hall 演講廳 auditorium [ˏɔdəˋtorɪəm] 禮堂 point [pɔɪnt] 指；指向

5 高

澳洲式發音

(A) Some umbrellas are lined up side by side.
(B) The grass is being cut in a field.
(C) Some trees are growing between two seating areas.
(D) A tent is being broken down beside the woods.

(A) 一些傘被並排擺放。
(B) 正在割原野上的草。
(C) 在兩個座位區之間長著一些樹。
(D) 正在森林旁拆解一座帳篷。

兩人以上的照片 答案 (A)

仔細觀察照片中森林前方有著一排陽傘座位區的模樣，以及周遭的整體風景。

(A) [○] 這裡正確描述陽傘被並排擺放的模樣，所以是正確答案。記住陽傘可以用 umbrella 表達。

(B) [╳] 照片拍攝地點是有長草的原野，但不是正在割（is being cut）草，因此是錯誤選項。

(C) [╳] 照片中的樹不是長在在兩個座位區之間（between two seating areas），而是在座位區的後面，因此是錯誤選項。注意不要聽到 Some trees are growing（長著一些樹）就選擇這個選項。

(D) [╳] 帳篷是打開的狀態，這裡卻用現在進行式被動語態（is being broken down）描述成正在拆解帳篷，因此是錯誤選項。

單字 umbrella [ʌmˋbrɛlə] 陽傘；雨傘 line up 排列 side by side 肩並肩地；在彼此旁邊地 break down 拆解

6
難

美式發音

(A) A window frame of a house is being painted.
(B) A mailbox has fallen on the ground.
(C) A residential garage door has been raised.
(D) A railing has been erected near an entrance.

(A) 正在粉刷房子的窗框。
(B) 郵箱掉到了地上。
(C) 住宅的車庫門被打開了。
(D) 靠近入口處豎立著欄杆。

事物及風景照片 答案 (D)

仔細觀察照片中在房屋門口之前有欄杆的模樣，以及周遭的整體景色。

(A) [╳] 照片中雖出現窗框，但不是正在粉刷（is being painted）窗框，因此是錯誤選項。注意不要聽到 A window frame of a house（房子的窗框）就選擇這個答案。

(B) [╳] 郵箱是豎立著的狀態，但這裡卻描述成掉到了地上（fallen on the ground），因此是錯誤選項。

(C) [╳] 車庫門是關著的狀態，這裡卻描述成被打開了（raised），因此是錯誤選項。注意不要聽到 A residential garage door（住宅的車庫門）就選擇這個答案。

(D) [○] 這裡正確描述靠近入口處豎立著欄杆的模樣，所以是正確答案。

單字　window frame 窗框　residential [ˌrɛzəˋdɛnʃəl] 住宅的；居住的　railing [ˋrelɪŋ] 欄杆　erect [ɪˋrɛkt] 使豎立

7 低

🔊 加拿大式發音 → 美式發音

When would it be convenient for you to have dinner? (A) I can meet at 7 o'clock. (B) Yes, we definitely have. (C) At the new sushi restaurant.	你什麼時候方便吃晚餐？ (A) 我可以在 7 點鐘見面。 (B) 是的，我們一定有過。 (C) 在新的壽司餐廳。

When 疑問句 答案 (A)

這是詢問什麼時候方便吃晚餐的 When 疑問句。

(A) [○] 這裡回答可以在 7 點鐘見面，提到吃晚餐的時間點，因此是正確答案。

(B) [╳] 這裡以 Yes 來回答疑問詞疑問句，因此是錯誤選項。這裡透過重複題目中出現的 have 來造成混淆。

(C) [╳] 題目詢問什麼時候方便吃晚餐，這裡卻回答地點，因此是錯誤選項。這裡使用和 have dinner（吃晚餐）相關的 restaurant（餐廳）來造成混淆。

單字 convenient [kən`vinjənt] 合宜的；便利的 definitely [`dɛfənɪtlɪ] 一定；絕對

8 中

🔊 英式發音 → 澳洲式發音

Hasn't Ms. Kramer's plane already landed? (A) Her passport hasn't expired. (B) It gets in soon. (C) She has plain black luggage.	Kramer 小姐的飛機不是已經降落了嗎？ (A) 她的護照還沒到期。 (B) 它很快就會到了。 (C) 她有素面的黑色行李箱。

否定疑問句 答案 (B)

這是詢問 Kramer 小姐的飛機是否已經降落的否定疑問句。

(A) [╳] 這是利用可以代稱題目中 Kramer 小姐的 Her 及與 plane（飛機）相關的 passport（護照）來造成混淆的錯誤選項。

(B) [○] 這裡回答很快就會到了，間接表示飛機還沒降落，因此是正確答案。

(C) [╳] 這是利用可以代稱題目中 Kramer 小姐的 She 及發音相似單字 plane – plain 來造成混淆的錯誤選項。

單字 land [lænd] 降落 expire [㊈ ɪk`spaɪr ㊇ iks`paiə] 到期 get in 到達 plain [plen] 沒有花樣的；平凡的

9 高

🔊 加拿大式發音 → 英式發音

Why am I getting so many advertisements in my e-mail? (A) We get a lot of packages too. (B) I prefer the other commercial. (C) Have you tried unsubscribing from mailing lists?	為什麼我的電子郵件會收到這麼多廣告？ (A) 我們也收到很多包裹。 (B) 我比較喜歡另一支廣告。 (C) 你有試過從郵寄名單裡取消訂閱嗎？

Why 疑問句 答案 (C)

這是詢問為何自己的電子郵件會收到這麼多廣告的 Why 疑問句。

(A) [╳] 這是以 get 重複使用題目中的 getting，並利用與題目中 many（許多的）字義相近的 a lot of（許多的）來造成混淆的錯誤選項。

(B) [╳] 這是使用和 advertisements（廣告）相關的 commercial（廣告）來造成混淆的錯誤選項。

(C) [○] 這裡反問對方是否有試過從郵寄名單裡取消訂閱，提到解決收到很多廣告的方法，因此是正確答案。

單字 advertisement [ˌædvɚ`taɪzmənt] 廣告 commercial [㊈ kə`mɝʃəl ㊇ kə`mə:ʃəl]（廣播或電視裡的）商業廣告
unsubscribe [ˌʌnsəb`skraɪb]（從名單中）取消訂閱；解除訂閱資格 mailing list 郵寄名單

10
●●○○
中

☊ 澳洲式發音 → 英式發音 What's the price of bananas at the grocery store? (A) A worker will restock the store shelves. (B) According to this flyer, 50¢ each. (C) Most of this fruit is still not ripe.	食品雜貨店裡的香蕉多少錢？ (A) 一位員工會把店裡的架子補滿。 (B) 根據這張傳單，每根 50 美分。 (C) 這種水果大部分都還沒熟。

What 疑問句 答案 (B)

這是詢問食品雜貨店裡的香蕉多少錢的 What 疑問句。

(A) [╳] 題目詢問食品雜貨店裡的香蕉多少錢，這裡卻回答員工會把店裡的架子補滿，毫不相關，因此是錯誤選項。這裡利用重複題目中的 store 來造成混淆。

(B) [○] 這裡回答根據傳單上的內容，一根是 50 美分，提到了香蕉價格，因此是正確答案。

(C) [╳] 這是利用和 bananas（香蕉）相關的 fruit（水果）來造成混淆的錯誤選項。

單字 grocery store 食品雜貨店，雜貨店 restock [[美] ri`stɑk [英] ri:`stɔk] 補滿存貨；為～補貨
ripe [raɪp]（水果等）成熟的

11
●○○○
低

☊ 美式發音 → 澳洲式發音 You can join us on the corporate retreat, can't you? (A) I may. (B) I joined the gym as well. (C) We were treated to cocktails.	你可以和我們一起參加員工旅遊，不是嗎？ (A) 我也許可以。 (B) 我也加入了健身房。 (C) 我們被招待了雞尾酒。

附加問句 答案 (A)

這是詢問對方是否可以參加員工旅遊的附加問句。

(A) [○] 這裡回答也許可以，表示也許會參加員工旅遊，因此是正確答案。

(B) [╳] 這是利用可以代稱題目中 you 的 I，並以「加入」之意的 joined 來重複使用題目裡出現的 join（和～一起做），企圖造成混淆的錯誤選項。

(C) [╳] 題目詢問對方是否可以參加員工旅遊，這裡卻回答被招待了雞尾酒，毫不相關，因此是錯誤選項。這裡利用發音相似單字 retreat – treated 來造成混淆。

單字 treat [trit] 招待

12
●●○○
中

☊ 加拿大式發音 → 美式發音 Where did you work during the first half of your career? (A) Primarily at Champlain Law Office. (B) Throughout most of the last decade. (C) My superior makes the hiring decisions.	你的職業生涯前半在哪裡工作？ (A) 主要在 Champlain 法律事務所。 (B) 過去十年的大部分時間。 (C) 我的上級會決定是否任用。

Where 疑問句 答案 (A)

這是詢問對方的職業生涯前半在哪裡工作的 Where 疑問句。

(A) [○] 這裡回答主要在 Champlain 法律事務所，提到了工作地點，因此是正確答案。

(B) [╳] 題目詢問職業生涯前半在哪裡工作，這裡卻回答了一段期間，因此是錯誤選項。這裡利用與題目中 during（在～期間）字義相近的 Throughout（在～整段期間）來造成混淆。

(C) [╳] 這是透過可藉 career（職業生涯）聯想到的雇用相關詞彙 hiring decisions（決定是否任用）來造成混淆的錯誤選項。

單字 first half 前半段，上半段 career [kə`rɪr] 職業生涯；經歷 primarily [praɪ`mɛrəlɪ] 主要地；首先
throughout [θru`aʊt] 在～整段期間 decade [`dɛked] 十年

13 ○○●低

美式發音 → 加拿大式發音 Who is getting beverages for the social gathering? (A) This drink is quite delicious. (B) Sorry, but how do I get there? (C) Nancy and Ben will bring something.	誰會為這場社交聚會準備飲料？ (A) 這款飲料很好喝。 (B) 抱歉，但我要怎麼到那裡？ (C) Nancy 和 Ben 會帶東西來。

Who 疑問句 答案 (C)

這是詢問誰會準備飲料的 Who 疑問句。

(A) [╳] 這是利用和題目中 beverages（飲料）意義相近的 drink（飲料）來造成混淆的錯誤選項。

(B) [╳] 題目詢問誰會準備飲料，這裡反問要怎麼到那裡，毫不相關，因此是錯誤選項。這裡利用字義是「到達」的 get 來重複使用題目中的 getting（準備），企圖造成混淆。

(C) [○] 這裡回答 Nancy 和 Ben 會帶東西來，提及會準備飲料的人，因此是正確答案。

單字 social gathering 社交聚會

14 ○○●中

英式發音 → 澳洲式發音 Should we try to renegotiate the price or switch suppliers? (A) Give him the lease agreement. (B) Our supply is low. (C) I'm fine with either strategy.	我們應該去試著重談價格還是換供應商？ (A) 給他租賃契約吧。 (B) 我們的供應量很低。 (C) 這兩個策略我都可以。

選擇疑問句 答案 (C)

這是詢問對方想要重談價格還是換供應商的選擇疑問句。

(A) [╳] 題目中沒有可以用 him 代稱的對象，且這是利用可以透過 renegotiate（重新商議）聯想到的 agreement（協議）來造成混淆的錯誤選項。

(B) [╳] 題目詢問對方想要重談價格還是換供應商，這裡卻回答自己的供應量很低，毫不相關，因此是錯誤選項。這裡利用發音相似單字 suppliers – supply 來造成混淆。

(C) [○] 這裡回答兩個策略都可以，表示兩者都選擇，因此是正確答案。

單字 renegotiate [美 ˌrinɪ`goʃɪˌet 英 ˌri:ni`gəuʃi:eit] 重新商議 switch [swɪtʃ] 更換
supplier [美 sə`plaɪɚ 英 sə`plaiə] 供應商 agreement [ə`grimənt] 協議
supply [sə`plaɪ] 供應量；庫存品；用品 strategy [`strætədʒɪ] 策略

15 ○○●中

加拿大式發音 → 美式發音 Has a band been booked for the event? (A) Concert tickets are $20 each. (B) At a nearby venue. (C) A jazz group is going to perform.	有為活動預約樂團嗎？ (A) 演唱會門票每張 20 美金。 (B) 在附近的場地。 (C) 一個爵士團體會來表演。

助動詞疑問句 答案 (C)

這是確認是否有為活動預約樂團的助動詞（Have）疑問句。

(A) [╳] 這是利用和 band（樂團）相關的 Concert（演唱會）來造成混淆的錯誤選項。

(B) [╳] 題目詢問是否有為活動預約樂團，這裡卻回答地點，因此是錯誤選項。這裡利用可以透過 event（活動）聯想到與活動地點相關的 At a nearby venue（在附近的場地）來造成混淆。

(C) [○] 這裡回答爵士團體會來表演，間接表示已經為活動預約了樂團，因此是正確答案。

單字 nearby [`nɪrˌbaɪ] 附近的 perform [pɚ`fɔrm] 表演

16 ○○○● 低

英式發音 → 澳洲式發音	
Which products have been discounted?	哪些商品有打折？
(A) Everything in Aisle 4. (B) A special promotion. (C) Yes, I have an account.	(A) 4 號走道的所有東西。 (B) 一個特別的促銷活動。 (C) 是的，我有一個帳號。

Which 疑問句 答案 (A)

這是詢問哪些商品有打折的 Which 疑問句。這裡一定要聽到 Which products 才能順利作答。

(A) [○] 這裡回答 4 號走道的所有東西，提到有打折的商品是什麼，因此是正確答案。

(B) [╳] 這是利用和 discounted（打折）相關的 promotion（促銷活動）來造成混淆的錯誤選項。

(C) [╳] 這裡以 Yes 來回答疑問詞疑問句，因此是錯誤選項。這裡利用發音相似單字 discounted – account 來造成混淆。

單字 aisle [aɪl] 走道

17 ○●●● 高

加拿大式發音 → 美式發音	
When should we inform the audience about upcoming shows?	我們該什麼時候告訴觀眾與接下來的表演有關的事？
(A) There's an intermission in 30 minutes. (B) In the main auditorium. (C) Over 30 of the people here.	(A) 30 分鐘後有中場休息時間。 (B) 在主禮堂裡。 (C) 在這裡的人之中有超過 30 個。

When 疑問句 答案 (A)

這是詢問該什麼時候告訴觀眾與接下來的表演有關的事的 When 疑問句。

(A) [○] 這裡回答 30 分鐘後有中場休息時間，提到要告訴觀眾與接下來的表演有關的事的時間點，因此是正確答案。

(B) [╳] 題目詢問該什麼時候告訴觀眾與接下來的表演有關的事，這裡卻回答地點，因此是錯誤選項。這裡利用與題目的 When 發音相似的 Where 來造成混淆，注意不要因為聽成 Where should we inform the audience about upcoming shows（我們該在哪裡告訴觀眾與接下來的表演有關的事）而選錯答案。

(C) [╳] 題目詢問該什麼時候告訴觀眾與接下來的表演有關的事，這裡卻回答對象，因此是錯誤選項。這裡使用可以代稱題目中 audience（觀眾）的 people（人們）來造成混淆。

單字 inform [ɪn`fɔrm] 告知 intermission [ˏɪntɚ`mɪʃən] 中場休息時間

18 ○○●● 中

澳洲式發音 → 美式發音	
Why haven't you ever owned a vehicle?	為什麼你一直都沒有車？
(A) Bring it to the automotive shop. (B) My city has a great public transit system. (C) I guess we can drive.	(A) 把它帶去修車行。 (B) 我的城市有很棒的大眾運輸系統。 (C) 我猜我們可以開車。

Why 疑問句 答案 (B)

這是詢問對方為何一直都沒有車的 Why 疑問句。

(A) [╳] 這是利用和 vehicle（車輛）相關的 automotive shop（修車行）來造成混淆的錯誤選項。

(B) [○] 這裡回答自己的城市有很棒的大眾運輸系統，提到沒有車的原因，因此是正確答案。

(C) [╳] 這是利用和 vehicle（車輛）相關的 drive（開車）來造成混淆的錯誤選項。

單字 automotive [ˏɔtə`motɪv] 汽車的 public transit 大眾運輸

19 ●●● 高

[音] 英式發音 → 澳洲式發音

Please don't forget to give me the files I requested.

(A) Don't worry about the ticket.
(B) You should pile the supplies in the corner.
(C) I wrote myself a reminder.

請不要忘記給我我要的檔案。
(A) 別擔心票的事。
(B) 你應該把補給品堆在那個角落裡。
(C) 我給自己寫了一張提醒字條。

陳述句 答案 (C)

這是要求對方不要忘記給自己檔案的陳述句。

(A) [╳] 題目要求對方不要忘記給自己檔案，這裡卻回答別擔心票的事，毫不相關，因此是錯誤選項。注意不要聽到 Don't worry about 就選擇這個選項。
(B) [╳] 這是利用可以代稱題目中 I 的 you，並利用發音相似單字 files – pile 來造成混淆的錯誤選項。
(C) [○] 這裡回答已經給自己寫了一張提醒字條，表示不會忘記，因此是正確答案。

單字　pile [paɪl] 堆疊　in the corner 在角落裡　reminder [[美] rɪ`maɪndɚ [英] ri`maində] 提醒用的事物

20 ●●● 中

[音] 加拿大式發音 → 英式發音

How did the conference attendees like your lecture about social media?

(A) Their Web site is due for upgrades.
(B) By heading to Conference Room 1.
(C) Overall, it was a success.

參加會議的人喜歡你的社群媒體講座嗎？
(A) 他們的網站應該要升級了。
(B) 藉由前往會議室 1。
(C) 整體來說很成功。

How 疑問句 答案 (C)

這是詢問參加會議的人是否喜歡對方的社群媒體講座的 How 疑問句。這裡必須知道 How did ~ like 是用來詢問意見的表達。

(A) [╳] 這是利用和 social media（社群媒體）有關的 Web site（網站）來造成混淆的錯誤選項。
(B) [╳] 題目詢問參加會議的人是否喜歡對方的講座，這裡卻回答方法，因此是錯誤選項。這裡藉重複題目中出現的 conference 來造成混淆。
(C) [○] 這裡回答整體來說很成功，間接表示參加會議的人喜歡自己的講座，因此是正確答案。

單字　attendee [ə`tɛndi] 出席者，參加者　due for 應該得到～　overall [`ovɚ͵ɔl] 整體的

21 ●●● 高

[音] 美式發音 → 加拿大式發音

Are all the servers required to wear a uniform?

(A) They served snacks this afternoon.
(B) It is standard procedure.
(C) I think your outfit looks very nice.

所有服務人員都被要求穿制服嗎？
(A) 他們今天下午上了點心。
(B) 這是標準程序。
(C) 我覺得你這套衣服看起來非常棒。

Be 動詞疑問句 答案 (B)

這是確認是否所有服務人員都被要求穿制服的 Be 動詞疑問句。

(A) [╳] 這是利用可以代稱題目中 servers（服務人員）的 They，並使用發音相似單字 servers – served 來造成混淆的錯誤選項。
(B) [○] 這裡回答這是標準程序，表示所有服務人員都被要求穿制服，因此是正確答案。
(C) [╳] 這是利用和 uniform（制服）相關的 outfit（全套服裝）來造成混淆的錯誤選項。

單字　server [`sɝvɚ] 服務人員　serve [sɝv] 上（菜等）　standard [`stændɚd] 標準的
procedure [prə`sidʒɚ] 程序；手續　outfit [`aʊt͵fɪt]（特定情境下穿的）全套服裝

22 ○○●● 中

🔊 美式發音 → 澳洲式發音 Should we order one or two desks for the office? (A) I'm undecided. (B) I will wait in the office. (C) There are three lamps.	我們該訂一張還是兩張桌子放在辦公室？ (A) 我還沒決定。 (B) 我會在辦公室裡等。 (C) 有三盞檯燈。

助動詞疑問句 答案 (A)

這是確認要放辦公室的桌子要訂一張還是兩張的助動詞（Should）疑問句。

(A) [○] 這裡回答還沒決定，表示不確定要訂一張還是兩張，因此是正確答案。

(B) [╳] 題目詢問要放辦公室的桌子要訂一張還是兩張，這裡卻回答在辦公室裡等，毫不相關，因此是錯誤選項。這裡透過重複題目中出現的 office 來造成混淆。

(C) [╳] 這是利用和 one or two（一或二）相關的 three（三）來造成混淆的錯誤選項。

單字 undecided [ˌʌndɪˋsaɪdɪd] 未決定的

23 ○●●●● 高

🔊 英式發音 → 加拿大式發音 Wouldn't you rather share a taxi to save money? (A) We only accept cash. (B) I'm riding with some friends. (C) Taxes are going to increase.	你不會比較想要共乘計程車來省錢嗎？ (A) 我們只收現金。 (B) 我會和一些朋友一起搭車。 (C) 稅金要增加了。

提議疑問句 答案 (B)

這是提出共乘計程車來省錢的提議疑問句。這裡必須知道 Wouldn't you rather 是用來表示提議的表達。

(A) [╳] 這是利用和 money（錢）有關的 cash（現金）來造成混淆的錯誤選項。

(B) [○] 這裡回答會和一些朋友一起搭車，表示同意這項提議的內容，因此是正確答案。

(C) [╳] 題目提議共乘計程車來省錢，這裡卻回答稅金要增加了，毫不相關，因此是錯誤選項。這裡利用發音相似單字 taxi – Taxes 來造成混淆。

單字 share a taxi 共乘計程車 accept [əkˋsɛpt] 接受

24 ○●●● 中

🔊 澳洲式發音 → 英式發音 We're not sure how to make copies on this odd paper size. (A) The tray has to be adjusted. (B) You have a good idea. (C) Our hats come in one size.	我們不確定要怎麼用這種奇怪尺寸的紙來影印。 (A) 得要調整紙盤。 (B) 你這主意很好。 (C) 我們的帽子都是單一尺寸。

陳述句 答案 (A)

這是表達不確定要怎麼用奇怪尺寸的紙來影印的陳述句。

(A) [○] 這裡回答得要調整紙盤，提到解決方法，因此是正確答案。

(B) [╳] 這是利用和 not sure（不確定）相反的 have a good idea（有好主意）來造成混淆的錯誤選項。

(C) [╳] 題目表示不確定要怎麼用奇怪尺寸的紙來影印，這裡卻回答自己的帽子都是單一尺寸，毫不相關，因此是錯誤選項。這裡藉重複題目中出現的 size 來造成混淆。

單字 odd [[美] ɑd [英] ɔd] 奇怪的，奇特的 tray [tre] 托盤；文件盤 adjust [əˋdʒʌst] 調整
come in 有（種類）；可以買到（商品等）

25 ○○●●● 中

加拿大式發音 → 美式發音	
A representative must inspect our factory in China, right? (A) Some of the labor regulations. (B) That won't be necessary. (C) Yes, across from the plant.	必須要有一位代表去視察我們在中國的工廠，對嗎？ (A) 部分勞動法規。 (B) 沒有這個必要。 (C) 沒錯，在工廠對面。

附加問句 答案 (B)

這是確認是否必須要有代表去視察中國廠的附加問句。

(A) [╳] 這是利用可以透過 inspect（視察）聯想到的相關視察標的 labor regulations（勞動法規）來造成混淆的錯誤選項。

(B) [○] 這裡回答沒有這個必要，表示沒有必要去視察中國廠，因此是正確答案。

(C) [╳] 這是利用可以用來回答附加問句的 Yes 及和題目中 factory（工廠）意義相近的 plant（工廠）來造成混淆的錯誤選項。

單字 representative [rɛprɪˋzɛntətɪv] 代表，代理人 regulation [ˌrɛgjəˋleʃən] 法規；規定

26 ○○●●● 中

澳洲式發音 → 英式發音	
Do you know what the fastest route downtown is? (A) Take Sonny Street. (B) Oh, just set them down. (C) I know how they feel.	你知道去市中心最快的路是哪條嗎？ (A) 走 Sonny 街。 (B) 噢，只要放他們下來就好。 (C) 我知道他們的感受。

包含疑問詞的一般疑問句 答案 (A)

這是詢問去市中心最快的路是哪條的包含疑問詞 what 的一般疑問句。

(A) [○] 這裡回答走 Sonny 街，提到最快那條路的名稱，因此是正確答案。

(B) [╳] 題目詢問去市中心最快的路是哪條，這裡卻回答只要放他們下來就好，毫不相關，因此是錯誤選項。這裡利用發音相似單字 downtown – down 來造成混淆。

(C) [╳] 這裡藉重複題目中出現的 know 來造成混淆。注意不要聽到 I know（我知道）就選擇這個選項。

單字 route 路；路線 downtown 市中心 set down 放（乘客等）下（車）

27 ○○○●● 高

美式發音 → 加拿大式發音	
Will the architect be able to stop by for a consultation today? (A) Well, the building has modern furnishings. (B) A tour of the architecture in Delaware. (C) Her assistant made an appointment for 3 P.M.	那位建築師今天能順道過來做諮詢嗎？ (A) 嗯，那棟建築物有著現代的室內陳設。 (B) 在德拉威爾的建築之旅。 (C) 她的助理約了下午 3 點。

助動詞疑問句 答案 (C)

這是確認建築師今天是否能來做諮詢的助動詞（Will）疑問句。

(A) [╳] 這是利用和 architect（建築師）相關的 building（建築物）來造成混淆的錯誤選項。

(B) [╳] 題目詢問建築師今天是否能來做諮詢，這裡卻回答建築之旅，毫不相關，因此是錯誤選項。這裡利用發音相似單字 architect – architecture 來造成混淆。

(C) [○] 這裡回答她的助理約了下午 3 點，間接表示建築師今天能來做諮詢，因此是正確答案。

單字 architect [ˋɑrkəˌtɛkt] 建築師 consultation [ˌkɑnsəlˋteʃən] 諮詢 furnishing [ˋfɝnɪʃɪŋ] 室內陳設
architecture [ˋɑrkəˌtɛktʃɚ] 建築物

28 中

🎧 英式發音 → 澳洲式發音

How can I access my online bank account while I'm overseas?

(A) Our financial institution has expanded.
(B) Just log in using your normal information.
(C) You'll thoroughly enjoy traveling abroad.

我在國外的時候要怎麼使用我的網路銀行帳戶？

(A) 我們金融機構已經擴大了。
(B) 只要用你平常的資料登入就行了。
(C) 你會徹底享受在國外旅遊。

How 疑問句 答案 (B)

這是詢問在國外時要怎麼使用網路銀行帳戶的 How 疑問句。這裡必須知道 How 是詢問方法的表達。

(A) [╳] 這是利用和 bank account（銀行帳戶）相關的 financial institution（金融機構）來造成混淆的錯誤選項。

(B) [○] 這裡回答用平常的資料登入就行了，提到在國外使用網路銀行帳戶的方法，因此是正確答案。

(C) [╳] 這是使用可以代稱題目中 I 的 you 及和 overseas（在國外）意義相近的 abroad（在國外）來造成混淆的錯誤選項。

單字　institution [[美] ͵ɪnstəˋtjuʃən [英] ͵instiˋtju:ʃən] 機構　thoroughly [ˋθɝolɪ] 徹底地；非常

29 高

🎧 美式發音 → 加拿大式發音

What is the plan for replacing Ms. Jenkins after her retirement?

(A) We're hoping to hire internally.
(B) Formal attire is required at the party.
(C) She's been with us for 30 years.

在 Jenkins 小姐退休後，頂替她的計畫是什麼？

(A) 我們會希望內部聘任。
(B) 這場派對要求穿著正式服裝。
(C) 她和我們一起已經 30 年了。

What 疑問句 答案 (A)

這是詢問要頂替 Jenkins 小姐的計畫是什麼的 What 疑問句。

(A) [○] 這裡回答希望內部聘任，提到頂替 Jenkins 小姐的計畫，因此是正確答案。

(B) [╳] 題目詢問要頂替 Jenkins 小姐的計畫是什麼，這裡卻回答派對要求穿著正式服裝，毫不相關，因此是錯誤選項。這裡利用發音相似單字 retirement – required 來造成混淆。

(C) [╳] 這是利用可以代稱題目中 Ms. Jenkins 的 She 及可透過 retirement（退休）聯想到的工作期間 for 30 years （30 年）來造成混淆的錯誤選項。

單字　retirement [rɪˋtaɪrmənt] 退休　internally [ɪnˋtɝnəlɪ] 內部地　formal attire 正式服裝

30 高

🎧 澳洲式發音 → 美式發音

This rental space is very conveniently located.

(A) It's on top of the microwave.
(B) I have a feeling it's overpriced.
(C) No, another parking space.

這個租賃空間在非常方便的地方。

(A) 它在微波爐的上方。
(B) 我覺得它的定價太高了。
(C) 不是，另一個停車位。

陳述句 答案 (B)

這是表達該租賃空間的所在地點非常便利的意見陳述句。

(A) [╳] 這是利用和 located（位在）相關的 on top of（在～的上方）來造成混淆的錯誤選項。

(B) [○] 這裡回答覺得定價太高，提出自己對該租賃空間的意見，因此是正確答案。

(C) [╳] 題目說租賃空間在非常方便的地方，這裡卻回答另一個停車位，毫不相關，因此是錯誤選項。這裡藉重複題目中出現的 space 來造成混淆。

單字　microwave [ˋmaɪkro͵wev] 微波爐　overpriced [͵ovəˋpraɪst] 定價過高的

31 ○●●● 高

英式發音 → 加拿大式發音 Are you willing to write a reference letter on my behalf? (A) All the résumés were left in that folder. (B) If you don't need one until next week. (C) Yes, both reference manuals.	你願意替我寫一封推薦信嗎？ (A) 所有履歷表都放進那個資料夾裡了。 (B) 如果你到下星期才需要的話。 (C) 是的，兩個參考手冊都是。

Be 動詞疑問句 答案 (B)

這是詢問對方是否願意替自己寫推薦信的 Be 動詞疑問句。

(A) [╳] 這是利用和 reference letter（推薦信）有關的 résumés（履歷表）來造成混淆的錯誤選項。

(B) [○] 這裡回答如果到下星期才需要的話，間接表示願意，因此是正確答案。

(C) [╳] 這裡以字義「參考」來重複使用題目裡 reference letter（推薦信）中的 reference，企圖造成混淆。注意不要聽到 Yes 就選擇這個選項。

單字 be willing to 願意～ reference letter 推薦信 on one's behalf 代替～；代表～
reference manual 參考手冊

32
33
34

Questions 32-34 refer to the following conversation.

英式發音 → 澳洲式發音

W: [32]**Now that we've finished weeding the existing flowerbed, the new rose bushes must be planted along the front of the customer's house.** This task will take us a couple of hours at most to complete, so we'll be done with it by lunchtime.

M: OK, but [33]**before we unload the plants, holes need to be dug for the bushes.** I'll pull our shovels and work gloves out of the truck.

W: [34]**Could you also bring over the small cart?** We'll use it to carry away the excess dirt.

M: Oh! [34]**I didn't remember to pack that this morning.** I'd better go get it from our company's shed. Sorry about that.

第 32-34 題請參考下列對話。

女：[32] 既然我們已經把現有花圃的草給除好了，那麼現在就得沿著客人家前面來栽種新的玫瑰花叢了。這項工作最多會花上我們兩個小時來完成，所以我們在午餐時間之前就會做完了。

男：好，但 [33] 在我們把那些植物卸下來之前，我們得先挖要給玫瑰花叢用的洞。我去把我們的鏟子和工作手套從卡車上拿下來。

女：[34] 你可以把小推車也帶過來嗎？我們要用它來把多餘的土搬走。

男：噢！[34] 我今天早上收拾的時候忘了那個。我最好去把它從我們公司的棚子拿過來。抱歉。

32 Who most likely are the speakers?

(A) Park rangers
(B) Construction workers
(C) Florists
(D) Landscapers

32 說話者們最有可能是誰？

(A) 公園巡警
(B) 建築工人
(C) 花商
(D) 景觀設計師

33 What does the man want to do first?

(A) Prepare the ground for plants
(B) Fill in holes with dirt
(C) Go on an early lunch break
(D) Clean out the back of a truck

33 男子想要先做什麼？

(A) 準備植物要用的地
(B) 用土把洞填滿
(C) 提早去休午休
(D) 把卡車後面清空

34 What problem does the man mention?

(A) A cart was left behind.
(B) A bush cannot be removed.
(C) A glove was damaged.
(D) A shovel is not large enough.

34 男子提到什麼問題？

(A) 沒帶到推車。
(B) 無法移除樹叢。
(C) 手套破損了。
(D) 鏟子不夠大。

題目 weed [wid] 除草　flowerbed [㊕ `flaʊɚ͵bɛd ㊥ `flauə͵bed] 花圃　at most 最多　carry away 搬走
excess [ɪk`sɛs] 多餘的；過量的　pack [pæk] 收拾（行李等）　shed [ʃɛd]（儲物用的）棚子；小屋

32 park ranger 公園巡警　florist [`florɪst] 花商　landscaper [`lænd͵skepɚ] 景觀設計師

34 leave behind 遺留

32 ■ **整體對話相關問題—說話者** 答案 (D)

中

題目詢問說話者們的身分，因此要注意聽和身分、職業相關的表達。女子對男子說：「Now that we've finished weeding the existing flowerbed, the new rose bushes must be planted along the front of the customer's house.」，表示已經把花圃的草給除好了，所以要開始栽種新的玫瑰花叢了，由此可知，說話者們是景觀設計師，因此正確答案是 (D) Landscapers。

33 ■ **細節事項相關問題—特定細項** 答案 (A)

高

題目詢問男子想先做什麼，因此要注意聽和題目關鍵字（do first）相關的內容。男子說：「before we unload the plants, holes need to be dug for the bushes」，表示在把植物卸下來之前，得先挖要給玫瑰花叢用的洞，因此正確答案是 (A) Prepare the ground for plants。

換句話說

holes need to be dug for the bushes 需要挖給花叢用的洞 → Prepare the ground for plants 準備植物要用的地

34 ■ **細節事項相關問題—問題點** 答案 (A)

中

題目詢問男子提到什麼問題，因此要注意聽男子話中出現負面表達之後的內容。女子對男子說：「Could you also bring over the small cart?」，詢問是否可以把小推車也帶過來，男子說：「I didn't remember to pack that this morning.」，表示今天早上收拾的時候忘了要帶小推車，因此正確答案是 (A) A cart was left behind.。

35 36 37 新

Questions 35-37 refer to the following conversation.

第 35-37 題請參考下列對話。

加拿大式發音 → 美式發音

M: Welcome to Harvey Home Goods. How can I help you?
W: Yes. 35**I need hooks that adhere to the wall**—not ones that are drilled in—to hang paintings in my apartment.
M: Those are in Aisle 13, which is where we keep hardware and fixtures. 36**Is there anything else I can give you a hand locating?**
W: Thanks, but I'm pretty sure 36**I remember where the other products I need are located.**
M: All right. Just in case you have trouble finding other products, 37**there's a . . . um . . . computer that you can use to search for store merchandise. The machine indicates where specific goods are shelved as well as whether they're in stock.** It's situated near the front doors.

男：歡迎來到 Harvey 家居用品。有什麼我可以協助妳的嗎？
女：有。35 我需要黏在牆上的那種掛鉤——不是要鑽牆的那種——來把畫掛在我的公寓裡。
男：那種在 13 走道，我們的五金用品和固定裝置都放在那裡。36 還有什麼我能幫妳找的嗎？
女：謝謝，但我滿確定 36 我記得我需要的其他產品放在哪裡。
男：好吧。只是以防萬一妳找不到其他產品，37 有一台……嗯……妳可以用來搜尋店內商品的電腦。這台機器可以指出特定商品有沒有貨和放在哪裡。它在靠前門的地方。

35 What is the woman trying to find?
(A) A spray cleaner
(B) A power drill
(C) Some artwork
(D) Some hooks

35 女子試著要找到什麼？
(A) 噴霧清潔劑
(B) 電鑽
(C) 一些藝術品
(D) 一些掛鉤

36 Why does the woman reject an offer?
(A) She is being assisted by other staff.
(B) She is not interested in a promotion.
(C) She knows where some items are stocked.
(D) She knows why a product is sold out.

36 女子為什麼拒絕一項主動協助？
(A) 她正由其他工作人員協助中。
(B) 她對一項促銷活動不感興趣。
(C) 她知道一些商品的存放地點。
(D) 她知道一件產品售完的原因。

37 According to the man, how can the woman get more information?
(A) By downloading an application
(B) By picking up a shop directory
(C) By seeking out employees
(D) By using a device

37 根據男子所說，女子能如何獲得更多資訊？
(A) 下載一張申請表
(B) 拿一本商店指南
(C) 找員工
(D) 使用一個裝置

題目 adhere [əd`hɪr] 黏附　hardware [`hɑrd͵wɛr] 五金用品　fixture [`fɪkstʃɚ]（屋內的）固定裝置
shelve [ʃɛlv] 把～放在架上　situate [`sɪtʃʊ͵et] 使位於

35 細節事項相關問題—特定細項 　答案 (D)
低
題目詢問女子試著要找到什麼，因此要注意聽和題目關鍵字（trying to find）相關的內容。女子說：「I need hooks that adhere to the wall」，表示需要黏在牆上的那種掛鉤，因此正確答案是 (D) Some hooks。

36 細節事項相關問題—理由 　答案 (C)
中
題目詢問女子拒絕一項主動協助的原因，因此要注意聽和題目關鍵字（reject an offer）相關的內容。男子說：「Is there anything else I can give you a hand locating?」，詢問是否還有什麼能幫女子找的，女子說：「I remember where the other products I need are located」，表示自己記得需要的其他產品放在哪裡，因此正確答案是 (C) She knows where some items are stocked.。

換句話說
remember where ~ products ~ are located 記得產品放在哪裡
→ knows where ~ items are stocked 知道商品的存放地點

37 細節事項相關問題—方法 　答案 (D)
中
題目詢問男子說女子可以如何獲得更多資訊，因此要注意聽男子話中提到與題目關鍵字（get more information）相關的內容。男子說：「there's a ~ computer that you can use to search for store merchandise. The machine indicates where specific goods are shelved as well as whether they're in stock.」，表示店裡有一台可以搜尋商品、確定有沒有貨和商品放在哪裡的電腦，因此正確答案是 (D) By using a device。

38
39
40

Questions 38-40 refer to the following conversation.

英式發音 → 澳洲式發音

W: OK, Mr. Mattson, you've now seen our renovated locker rooms, lobby, and concession area. What do you think so far?

M: I must say, [38/39]**I'm glad I came here today to check out the renovations that were made to the stadium**. It looks like the money I invested in this facility has been put to good use. The new court is especially impressive. The Hawks' players must be very pleased with the results.

W: Absolutely. In fact, many commented on how nice the court is after practicing on it two days ago. Now, if you follow me this way, I'll show you around [40]**the new luxury seating area, which only VIP guests will be able to use for our home games**.

第 38-40 題請參考下列對話。

女：好了，Mattson 先生，您現在已經看過我們整修過的更衣室、大廳和販賣區了。您目前為止覺得怎麼樣？

男：我必須說，[38/39] 我很高興我今天有來這裡看看體育場所做的這些整修。看起來我投資在這座設施上的錢有獲得妥善利用。那座新球場特別令人印象深刻。Hawks 隊的球員一定會對這個成果非常滿意。

女：當然。事實上，兩天前在那裡練習之後，有很多人表示那座球場真的很棒。那麼，如果您跟著我往這邊走，我會帶您去參觀 [40] 新的豪華座位區，那裡只有 VIP 貴賓能在我們主場比賽時使用。

38 Where does the conversation take place?

(A) At a company gym
(B) At a sports arena
(C) At a luxury resort
(D) At an architectural studio

38 這段對話發生在哪裡？

(A) 公司健身房
(B) 運動競技場
(C) 豪華度假村
(D) 建築工作室

39 What is the purpose of the man's visit?

(A) To view changes to a facility
(B) To watch an athletic event
(C) To recommend building improvements
(D) To submit blueprints for a structure

39 男子的來訪目的是什麼？

(A) 看設施的改變
(B) 觀看體育賽事
(C) 建議建築物的改進事項
(D) 提交建築物藍圖

40 What does the woman say about VIP guests?

(A) They can receive a price reduction.
(B) They are waiting in a seating area.
(C) They are pleased with the modifications.
(D) They will have access to a special section.

40 關於 VIP 貴賓，女子說什麼？

(A) 他們可以獲得折價。
(B) 他們正在座位區等候。
(C) 他們對修改處感到滿意。
(D) 他們會擁有進入特別區域的權利。

題目 locker room 更衣室 concession [kən`sɛʃən]（在特定區域）銷售商品的權利 put to good use 妥善利用
comment [美 `kɑmɛnt 英 `kɔment] 表示（意見） luxury [`lʌkʃərɪ] 豪華的
38 arena [ə`rinə] 競技場 studio [`stjudɪˌo] 工作室
39 athletic [æθ`lɛtɪk] 體育的 improvement [ɪm`pruvmənt] 改進事項 blueprint [`blu`prɪnt] 藍圖

38 整體對話相關問題—地點 答案 (B)
中
題目詢問對話發生地點，因此要注意聽和地點相關的表達。男子說：「I'm glad I came here today to check out the renovations that were made to the stadium」，表示很高興今天有到體育場來看整修狀況，由此可知，對話發生地點是在體育場，因此正確答案是 (B) At a sports arena。

換句話說
stadium 體育場 → sports arena 運動競技場

39 整體對話相關問題—目的 答案 (A)
中
題目詢問男子的造訪目的，因此必須注意對話的開頭部分。男子說：「I'm glad I came here today to check out the renovations that were made to the stadium」，表示很高興自己今天有來看體育場所做的整修，因此正確答案是 (A) To view changes to a facility。

40 細節事項相關問題—提及 答案 (D)
高
題目詢問女子說了什麼與 VIP 貴賓有關的事，因此要注意聽女子話中和題目關鍵字（VIP guests）有關及前後的內容。女子說：「the new luxury seating area, which only VIP guests will be able to use for our home games」，說明只有 VIP 貴賓能在主場比賽時使用新的豪華座位區，由此可知，VIP 貴賓會擁有進入特別區域的權利，因此正確答案是 (D) They will have access to a special section.。

41 42 43 新

Questions 41-43 refer to the following conversation.

加拿大式發音 → 英式發音

M: Jackie, [41]**do you have a comprehensive list of our clients' e-mail addresses? I seem to have lost mine.**

W: Not on hand, but [42]**why don't you look them up on our new online marketing database?**

M: Oh . . . I didn't realize that was possible.

W: It is. A trainer from the IT department taught our team members how to get those types of details from the database during last Tuesday's workshop.

M: [43]**The session sounds like it was very helpful. I wish I had made it**, but I was in Richmond for the International Advertising Conference.

W: Yeah, it was quite educational. If you want, I can tell you more about it during our break.

第 41-43 題請參考下列對話。

男：Jackie，[41] 妳有我們客戶的電子郵件地址的完整清單嗎？我的似乎不見了。

女：我手邊沒有，但 [42] 你要不要在我們新的網路行銷資料庫裡查查看？

男：噢……我不知道可以這樣做。

女：可以。在上星期二的工作坊中，來自資訊科技部門的培訓師教了我們的團隊成員要如何從資料庫中獲取這種類型的詳細資料。

男：[43] 這講習聽起來好像非常有用。真希望我能參加，但我那時在里奇蒙參加國際廣告會議。

女：是啊，講習滿有教育意義的。如果你想的話，我可以在我們休息的時候再告訴你一些和講習有關的事。

41 What problem does the man mention?

(A) A list has been misplaced.
(B) A software program has errors.
(C) A conference has been postponed.
(D) A department member is late.

41 男子提到什麼問題？

(A) 忘記清單放在哪裡。
(B) 軟體程式有錯。
(C) 會議被延期了。
(D) 部門成員遲到了。

42 What does the woman suggest?

(A) Registering for a workshop
(B) Speaking with a technician
(C) Using a database
(D) Taking some notes

42 女子建議什麼？

(A) 報名工作坊
(B) 和技術人員談談
(C) 使用資料庫
(D) 做一些筆記

43 Why does the man say, "I was in Richmond"?

新 (A) To apologize for a mistake
(B) To clarify a decision
(C) To explain his absence
(D) To describe his vacation

43 為什麼男子說：「我那時在里奇蒙」？

(A) 為一項錯誤道歉
(B) 為澄清一項決定
(C) 為解釋他的缺席
(D) 為描述他的假期

題目 comprehensive [ˌkɑmprɪ`hɛnsɪv] 完整的　on hand 在手邊　make it 及時趕到（聚會等）
41 misplace [mɪs`ples] 錯置；忘記放在哪裡（而暫時找不到）
43 apologize [ə`pɑləˌdʒaɪz] 道歉　clarify [`klærəˌfaɪ] 澄清；闡明　absence [`æbsn̩s] 缺席

41 細節事項相關問題—問題點　答案 (A)

中

題目詢問男子提到什麼問題，因此要注意聽男子話中出現負面表達之後的內容。男子對女子說：「do you have a comprehensive list of our clients' e-mail addresses? I seem to have lost mine.」，詢問女子是否有客戶的電子郵件地址的完整清單，並說自己的似乎不見了，因此正確答案是 (A) A list has been misplaced.。

42 細節事項相關問題—提議　答案 (C)

中

題目詢問女子建議什麼，因此要注意聽女子話中出現提議相關表達的句子。女子對男子說：「why don't you look them[e-mail addresses] up on our new online marketing database?」，建議男子可以在新的網路行銷資料庫裡查電子郵件地址，因此正確答案是 (C) Using a database。

新 **43** 細節事項相關問題—掌握意圖　答案 (C)

高

題目詢問男子的說話意圖，因此要注意與題目引用句（I was in Richmond）有關及前後的內容。男子說：「The session sounds like it was very helpful. I wish I had made it」，表示這場講習聽起來好像非常有用，並說真希望自己能參加，由此可知，男子是想說明自己沒有參加的原因，因此正確答案是 (C) To explain his absence。

44 45 46

Questions 44-46 refer to the following conversation.

第 44-46 題請參考下列對話。

美式發音 → 澳洲式發音

W: Thank you for setting aside some time to talk with me, Mr. Gabo. Now, [44]**I'll explain why your retail outlet should stock the DirtDuster vacuum cleaner**. First, [45]**the DirtDuster has a motor attached to the wheels, making it self-propelled**. Plus, it can be used on hard surfaces as well as carpets.

M: I don't know. We already have the SwiftClean, which works well on wood floors.

W: But unlike the SwiftClean, the DirtDuster is guaranteed not to leave scratches on any surfaces. Consumer polls indicate that people really appreciate this aspect of the vacuum.

M: Well, [46]**I'd like you to demonstrate how the machine operates before I decide. You can use it on the floor in our staff kitchen**, just down the hall.

女：謝謝您留了一些時間和我談談，Gabo 先生。那麼，[44] 我會說明為什麼您的零售店應該要進 DirtDuster 吸塵器。首先，[45]DirtDuster 有一個連接到輪子上的馬達，讓它能自行前進。此外，它可在地毯及硬地板上使用。

男：我不知道。我們已經有進 SwiftClean 了，它在木頭地板上運作得很好。

女：但與 SwiftClean 不同，DirtDuster 保證不會在任何地板上留下刮痕。消費者意見調查顯示人們真的很欣賞這台吸塵器的這點。

男：嗯，[46] 在我決定之前，我想請妳示範這台裝置是怎麼運作的。妳可以在我們員工廚房的地板上使用它，走廊走到底就是了。

44 Who most likely is the woman?

(A) A repairperson
(B) A salesperson
(C) A janitor
(D) A maintenance worker

44 女子最有可能是誰？

(A) 維修人員
(B) 銷售人員
(C) 管理員
(D) 養護工人

45 According to the woman, what is a feature of the product?

(A) It can move itself.
(B) It can be cleaned easily.
(C) It is environmentally friendly.
(D) It comes in various sizes.

45 根據女子所說，這款產品的一項特色是什麼？

(A) 它可以自己移動。
(B) 它很好清理。
(C) 它很環保。
(D) 它有多種尺寸。

46 What will most likely happen next?

(A) A floor will be blocked off.
(B) A store will be restocked.
(C) A device will be used.
(D) An item will be put on sale.

46 接下來最有可能會發生什麼？

(A) 會封鎖一層樓。
(B) 會補一間店的貨。
(C) 會使用一項裝置。
(D) 會出售一個品項。

題目 set aside 留出　guarantee [ˌgærən`ti] 保證　scratch [skrætʃ] 刮痕　poll [pol]（對群眾進行的）意見調查　appreciate [ə`priʃɪˌet] 欣賞　aspect [`æspɛkt] 方面

44 janitor [`dʒænɪtɚ]（大型建築物的）管理人員　maintenance [`mentənəns] 養護　**46** put on sale 出售

44 整體對話相關問題—說話者　答案 (B)

中

題目詢問女子的身分，因此要注意聽和身分、職業相關的表達。女子說：「I'll explain why your retail outlet should stock the DirtDuster vacuum cleaner」，表示將說明為什麼男子的零售店應該要進 DirtDuster 吸塵器，由此可知，女子是銷售人員，由此可知，因此正確答案是 (B) A salesperson。

45 細節事項相關問題—特定細項　答案 (A)

高

題目詢問女子說產品有什麼特色，因此要注意聽女子說的話中和題目關鍵字（feature of the product）有關的內容。女子說：「the DirtDuster has a motor attached to the wheels, making it self-propelled」，表示 DirtDuster 有一個連接到輪子上的馬達，讓它能自行前進，因此正確答案是 (A) It can move itself.。

換句話說

self-propelled 自行前進 → move itself 自己移動

46 細節事項相關問題—接下來要做的事　答案 (C)

低

題目詢問接下來會發生什麼，因此要注意對話的最後部分。男子對女子說：「I'd like you to demonstrate how the machine operates ~. You can use it on the floor in our staff kitchen」，表示想看女子示範操作這台裝置，並說她可以在員工廚房的地板上使用，由此可知，接下來會示範這台吸塵器要怎麼用，因此正確答案是 (C) A device will be used.。

47 48 49 新

Questions 47-49 refer to the following conversation with three speakers.	第 47-49 題請參考下列三人對話。
加拿大式發音 → 澳洲式發音 → 美式發音	
M1: Look at this. [47]**Someone must have accidentally poured a beverage on the lobby sofa.**	男 1： 看看這個。[47] 一定是有人不小心把飲料打翻在大廳沙發上了。
M2: Yeah, I see what you mean. It still looks pretty wet, so it probably happened recently.	男 2： 是啊，我知道你在說什麼。它看起來還很濕，所以可能剛發生沒多久。
W: [48]**We should let the hotel receptionist know, so it can be dealt with.**	女： [48] 我們應該跟飯店的接待人員說，這樣就能有人來處理它了。
M2: OK. I'll tell them about it now while we wait for our rooms to be prepared for us.	男 2： 好。在我們等房間準備好的時候，我去跟他們說這件事。
W: And could you ask them when the pool closes? [49]**I'd like to swim this evening before I head out for the music festival.**	女： 還有你能問他們游泳池什麼時候關嗎？[49] 我今天晚上在去音樂節之前想先去游泳。
M1: Unfortunately, [49]**the singer we want to see starts performing at 8:30 P.M.—just an hour from now. So, I don't think we'll have time.**	男 1： 不巧的是，[49] 我們想看的那個歌手會在晚上 8 點 30 分開始表演——離現在只有一個小時。所以我不覺得我們會有時間。
47 What is the problem? (A) A lobby is crowded. (B) A drink has been spilled. (C) A hotel has no vacancies. (D) A room is too small.	47 問題是什麼？ (A) 大廳很擁擠。 (B) 飲料灑出來了。 (C) 飯店沒有空房了。 (D) 房間太小了。
48 What solution does the woman suggest? (A) Talking to a personnel member (B) Canceling hotel reservations (C) Finding some other chairs (D) Modifying an itinerary	48 女子建議了什麼解決方案？ (A) 和員工說 (B) 取消飯店預訂 (C) 找一些其他的椅子 (D) 修改旅行行程
49 Why will the woman be unable to use the swimming pool? (A) A check-in process was delayed. (B) A performance has been scheduled. (C) The facility is being remodeled. (D) The water is being tested.	49 女子為什麼會無法使用游泳池？ (A) 入住程序延遲了。 (B) 已經排定了表演。 (C) 該設施正在整修中。 (D) 水正在受檢。

47 crowded [`kraʊdɪd] 擁擠的 spill [spɪl] 灑出 vacancy [`vekənsɪ] 空房

48 personnel [ˌpɝsn̩`ɛl]（總稱）人員，員工 modify [`mɑdəˌfaɪ] 修改 itinerary [aɪ`tɪnəˌrɛrɪ] 旅行行程

47 細節事項相關問題—問題點 答案 (B)
低

題目詢問問題是什麼，因此要注意聽出現負面表達之後的內容。男 1 說：「Someone must have accidentally poured a beverage on the lobby sofa.」，表示一定是有人不小心把飲料打翻在大廳沙發上了，因此正確答案是 (B) A drink has been spilled.。

48 細節事項相關問題—提議 答案 (A)
中

題目詢問女子建議了什麼解決方法，因此要注意聽女子話中出現提議相關表達的句子。女子說：「We should let the hotel receptionist know, so it can be dealt with.」，表示應該去跟飯店的接待人員說這件事，這樣就能有人來處理了，因此正確答案是 (A) Talking to a personnel member。

換句話說

let the hotel receptionist know 跟飯店的接待人員說 → Talking to a personnel member 和員工說

49 細節事項相關問題—理由 答案 (B)
中

題目詢問女子無法使用游泳池的原因，因此要注意聽和題目關鍵字（unable to use the swimming pool）相關的內容。女子說：「I'd like to swim this evening before I head out for the music festival.」，表示自己今晚在去音樂節前想先去游泳，男 1 說：「the singer we want to see starts performing at 8:30 P.M.—just an hour from now. So, I don't think we'll have time.」，表示想看的歌手要在晚上 8 點 30 分開始表演，距離現在只有一個小時，所以認為女子不會有時間在看表演前先去游泳，因此正確答案是 (B) A performance has been scheduled.。

Questions 50-52 refer to the following conversation.

加拿大式發音 → 英式發音

M: Good morning, Michaela. [50]**Do you have all the information you'll need to make a notice for passengers about the subway system's new transit cards?**

W: I think so. But just to confirm, the cards will be able to hold up to $500 worth of credit, right?

M: Correct. And funds can be added to them at the automated machines in each station. [51]**Riders can also put money on their cards by making an account on the transportation authority's Web site.**

W: Great. [52]**Is there anything else that we need to tell people about?**

M: [52]**The upcoming closure of Line 5 tomorrow, from 10 A.M. until noon.**

W: Oh, yeah. [52]**I forgot all about that.** I'll be sure to note it too.

50 According to the man, why does the woman require some information?

(A) To prepare a notification
(B) To propose an idea to a supervisor
(C) To respond to client inquiries
(D) To complete a questionnaire

51 What does the man say riders can do online?

(A) Sign up for a newsletter
(B) Request fare reductions
(C) Read about subway routes
(D) Add money to a card

52 What did the woman forget about?

(A) A new fee
(B) A special giveaway
(C) A temporary closure
(D) A station remodel

第 50-52 題請參考下列對話。

男：早安，Michaela。[50] 妳有製作地鐵系統新交通卡的乘客通知所需要的所有資訊了嗎？

女：我想是有。但還是確認一下，這張卡最高能存 500 美金在裡面，對吧？

男：沒錯。而且可以在各站的自動裝置做卡片加值。[51] 乘客也可以透過在交通局網站上辦帳號來把錢存進他們的卡片裡。

女：太好了。[52] 還有什麼是我們需要告訴民眾的嗎？

男：[52]5 號線即將在明天早上的 10 點到中午停駛。

女：噢，對。[52] 我完全忘了這件事。我會確定也提到這件事的。

50 根據男子所說，女子為什麼需要一些資訊？

(A) 為了準備一份通知
(B) 為了向主管提出一個構想
(C) 為了回應客戶的疑問
(D) 為了完成一份問卷

51 男子說乘客能在線上做什麼？

(A) 登記取得業務通訊
(B) 要求車資減價
(C) 看有關地鐵路線的資訊
(D) 替卡片加值

52 女子忘記了什麼？

(A) 新的費用
(B) 特別贈品
(C) 暫時的停駛
(D) 車站整修

題目 worth [(美) wɝθ (英) wɜ:θ] 值一定金額的數量；價值 credit [ˋkrɛdɪt] 信用；（帳戶裡的）餘額 transportation authority 交通局 **52** giveaway [ˋgɪvə͵we] 贈品

50 低 細節事項相關問題—理由 答案 (A)

題目詢問男子說女子需要資訊的理由，因此要注意聽男子話中和題目關鍵字（information）相關及前後的內容。男子對女子說：「Do you have all the information you'll need to make a notice for passengers about the subway system's new transit cards?」，詢問女子是否有製作地鐵系統新交通卡的乘客通知所需要的所有資訊，因此正確答案是 (A) To prepare a notification。

51 高 細節事項相關問題—特定細項 答案 (D)

題目詢問男子說乘客可以在線上做什麼，因此要注意聽男子話中和題目關鍵字（riders can do online）相關的內容。男子說：「Riders can also put money on their cards by making an account on the transportation authority's Web site.」，表示乘客可以在交通局網站上辦帳號，再把錢存進他們的卡片裡，因此正確答案是 (D) Add money to a card。

52 低 細節事項相關問題—特定細項 答案 (C)

題目詢問女子忘記了什麼，因此要注意聽和題目關鍵字（woman forget）相關的內容。女子對男子說：「Is there anything else that we need to tell people about?」，詢問是否還有什麼需要告訴民眾的事，男子說：「The upcoming closure of Line 5 tomorrow, from 10 A.M. until noon.」，表示 5 號線會在明天早上的 10 點到中午停駛，接著女子說：「I forgot all about that.」，表示自己完全忘了這件事，因此正確答案是 (C) A temporary closure。

53
54
55

Questions 53-55 refer to the following conversation.	第 53-55 題請參考下列對話。
英式發音 → 澳洲式發音	
W: Good afternoon, Vincent. I want to let you know that [53]**Martin Marquez, the recently appointed manager of the Northeast district, is expected to come to our headquarters**. The visit will give him an opportunity to acquaint himself with our CEO. [54]**He'll arrive on November 3**—one month from now.	女：午安，Vincent。我想告訴你，[53] 預期最近被指派的東北區經理 Martin Marquez 會來我們總公司。這次來訪會給他機會讓他認識一下我們執行長。[54] 他會在 11 月 3 日抵達——從現在算起的一個月後。
M: [54]**Hasn't a consultant been hired to give a talk about productivity to some of our staff on that date?** If so, [55]**it might be hard to fit everything into the schedule, as there will be many activities going on**.	男：[54] 那一天不是已經請了一位顧問要來對我們一些員工進行有關生產力的演講嗎？如果是這樣的話，[55] 可能會很難把所有事情都排進時間表裡，因為會有很多活動要進行。
W: I've actually requested that Mr. Marquez stop by on the same day so he can attend the lecture. I think he'd benefit from it because it will be targeted at middle management.	女：我其實要求 Marquez 先生要在那同一天過來，以便他可以參加這場講座。我認為他會從講座中受益，因為這場講座會是以中間管理階層為對象。
53 What is mentioned about Mr. Marquez? (A) He requested a transfer. (B) He moved to a new position. (C) He hired a consultant. (D) He organized a staff activity.	53 關於 Marquez 先生，提到了什麼？ (A) 他要求了轉調。 (B) 他調到了新的職位。 (C) 他聘了顧問。 (D) 他籌辦了員工活動。
54 What will most likely happen on November third? (A) Some invitations will be mailed out. (B) Some employees will listen to a lecture. (C) A safety procedure will be implemented. (D) A director will announce a fundraiser date.	54 在 11 月 3 日最有可能會發生什麼？ (A) 會郵寄一些邀請函。 (B) 一些員工會聽一場講座。 (C) 會實行一項安全程序。 (D) 一位董事會宣布募款活動的日期。
55 What is the man concerned about? (A) A failed inspection (B) A frequent complaint (C) A scheduling conflict (D) An unsuccessful workshop	55 男子擔心什麼？ (A) 檢查不通過 (B) 經常性的投訴 (C) 排程上的衝突 (D) 不成功的工作坊

題目 appoint [ə`pɔɪnt] 指派　headquarters [[美] `hɛd`kwɔrtɚz [英] `hed`kwɔ:təz] 總公司　acquaint with 使熟悉～
fit into 排進（做某事或見某人的時間）　target [[美] `tɑrgɪt [英] `tɑ:git] 以～為對象　middle management 中間管理階層
53 transfer [træns`fɝ] 轉調；轉移
54 mail out 郵寄　implement [`ɪmplə͵mɛnt] 實行
55 conflict [kən`flɪkt] 衝突

53 ■ 細節事項相關問題—提及　答案 (B)
中
題目詢問提到 Marquez 先生的什麼事，因此要注意聽和題目關鍵字（Mr. Marquez）有關及前後的內容。女子說：「Martin Marquez, the recently appointed manager of the Northeast district, is expected to come to our headquarters.」，表示 Martin Marquez 是最近被指派的東北區經理，因此正確答案是 (B) He moved to a new position.。

54 ■ 細節事項相關問題—接下來要做的事　答案 (B)
高
題目詢問 11 月 3 日會發生什麼事，因此要注意聽和題目關鍵字（November third）有關及前後的內容。女子說：「He[Martin Marquez]'ll arrive on November 3」，表示 Martin Marquez 會在 11 月 3 日抵達，接著男子說：「Hasn't a consultant been hired to give a talk ~ to some of our staff on that date?」，反問那一天不是已請了一位顧問要來進行演講，因此正確答案是 (B) Some employees will listen to a lecture.。

55 ■ 細節事項相關問題—問題點　答案 (C)
中
題目詢問男子擔心什麼，因此必須注意聽男子話中出現負面表達之後的內容。男子說：「it might be hard to fit everything into the schedule, as there will be many activities going on」，表示很難把所有事情都排進時間表裡，因為會有很多活動要進行，因此正確答案是 (C) A scheduling conflict。

56 57 58

Questions 56-58 refer to the following conversation.

美式發音 → 澳洲式發音

W: Jake and [56]**I have been asked to take five workers who are visiting from our partner corporation in Japan out next week.** And we're struggling to think of something fun to do with them rather than simply dining at a fancy restaurant.

M: [57]**How about renting a boat and taking them sailing for an evening?** If you go around sunset, you can enjoy views of the Miami cityscape.

W: That's a wonderful suggestion, but would our boss approve something so costly?

M: [58]**It's more affordable than you'd expect. Boats can be rented from local businesses for as little as $1,200 a day.** Our company has spent more than that on expensive meals for similarly sized groups.

56 What is the woman planning to do next week?

(A) Entertain some visitors
(B) Book a table at a restaurant
(C) Organize a tour of a factory
(D) Travel to Japan for work

57 What does the man recommend the woman do?

(A) Ask about a down payment
(B) Contact an agent in advance
(C) Place a meal order
(D) Arrange for a boat ride

58 What does the man mention about some local businesses?

(A) They specialize in cruise packages.
(B) They offer reasonably priced rentals.
(C) They will send some representatives.
(D) They will provide area guidebooks.

第 56-58 題請參考下列對話。

女：Jake 和 [56] 我被要求在下星期帶五位從我們在日本的合夥公司來訪的員工出去。所以我們正在努力想出有什麼有趣的事能和他們一起做，而不只是帶他們去高級餐廳吃飯。

男：[57] 晚上租條船帶他們坐怎麼樣？如果你們在日落時分去，就能欣賞到邁阿密的城市風景。

女：這個建議很棒，但我們老闆會批准做這麼花錢的事嗎？

男：[58] 這比妳預期的要經濟實惠。船可以跟本地公司租，一天只需 1,200 美金。我們公司曾為差不多人數的團體花過比這更多的錢在昂貴的餐點上。

56 女子下星期計劃要做什麼？

(A) 招待一些訪客
(B) 在餐廳訂位
(C) 安排參觀工廠
(D) 前往日本工作

57 男子建議女子做什麼？

(A) 詢問有關頭期款的事
(B) 事先聯繫代理商
(C) 訂餐
(D) 安排遊船

58 關於一些本地公司，男子提到什麼？

(A) 他們專做乘船遊覽的套裝方案。
(B) 他們的租金開價合理。
(C) 他們會派出一些代表。
(D) 他們會提供地區旅遊指南。

題目 take out 帶出去 struggle [ˋstrʌgl] 努力 cityscape [ˋsɪtɪˏskep] 城市風景
56 entertain [ˏɛntɚˋten] 招待
57 down payment 頭期款 agent [ˋedʒənt] 代理商；代理人
58 cruise [kruz] 乘船遊覽 reasonably [ˋriznəblɪ] 適當地；合理地

56 高 細節事項相關問題—特定細項 答案 (A)

題目詢問女子下星期計劃要做什麼，因此要注意聽和題目關鍵字（next week）相關及前後的內容。女子說：「I have been asked to take five workers who are visiting from our partner corporation ~ out next week」，表示自己被要求在下星期帶五位從合夥公司來訪的員工出去，因此正確答案是 (A) Entertain some visitors。

57 中 細節事項相關問題—提議 答案 (D)

題目詢問男子建議女子做什麼，因此要注意聽男子話中出現提議相關表達的句子。男子對女子說：「How about renting a boat and taking them[workers] sailing for an evening?」，提議女子去租條船帶來訪的員工坐，因此正確答案是 (D) Arrange for a boat ride。

58 中 細節事項相關問題—提及 答案 (B)

題目詢問男子提到什麼與本地公司有關的事，因此要注意聽男子話中和題目關鍵字（local businesses）有關及前後的內容。男子說：「It's more affordable than you'd expect. Boats can be rented from local businesses for as little as $1,200 a day.」，表示租船的價格比女子預期的要經濟實惠，一天只需 1,200 美金就能和當地公司租到船，因此正確答案是 (B) They offer reasonably priced rentals.。

換句話說

affordable 經濟實惠的 → reasonably priced 開價合理的

59 60 61 新

Questions 59-61 refer to the following conversation.

美式發音 → 加拿大式發音

W: This is Grace from Yellowstone Apartments' management office. May I speak to Jim Risen?

M: This is Jim.

W: Mr. Risen, you own a blue Dent Razor with the license plate number 124FGA, right? If so, [59]**your car is blocking the garbage bins in the parking lot, which is an issue.**

M: I'm sorry about that. There were no vacant spaces in the lot when I returned home last night.

W: I see. Well, since that isn't an authorized spot, [60/61]**I'll need you to move the car immediately**, especially since trash is being collected today.

M: Ah . . . I apologize. I'll be at work until 5 P.M. But [61]**I can move it afterward**.

W: In that case, I'm sorry to inform you that your car will have to be towed. That's the building policy.

第 59-61 題請參考下列對話。

女：我是 Yellowstone 公寓管理室的 Grace。我可以找一下 Jim Risen 嗎？

男：我是 Jim。

女：Risen 先生，您有一台車牌號碼是 124FGA 的藍色 Dent Razor，對嗎？如果是的話，[59] 您的車現在擋住了停車場的垃圾桶，這造成了問題。

男：我很抱歉。我昨晚回家的時候，停車場裡沒有空位了。

女：我知道了。嗯，因為那裡不開放停車，[60/61] 所以我得請您立刻去移車，尤其因為今天要收垃圾。

男：啊……我很抱歉。我要工作到下午 5 點。但 [61] 我在那之後就可以把它移走了。

女：這樣的話，我很抱歉要告訴您，我們必須把您的車拖走。這是這棟大樓的政策。

59 Why is the woman calling?

(A) To alert a colleague of a mistake
(B) To notify the man of a problem
(C) To inform a tenant of a policy change
(D) To tell the man about an accident

59 女子為何打電話？

(A) 為了提醒同事一項錯誤
(B) 為了通知男子一個問題
(C) 為了通知房客一項政策變更
(D) 為了告訴男子一項意外事件

60 What does the woman want the man to do?

(A) Return a signed document
(B) Remove a waste container
(C) Relocate a vehicle
(D) Clean an apartment unit

60 女子想要男子做什麼？

(A) 交回一份簽好名字的文件
(B) 移走一個垃圾桶
(C) 把車移到別的地方
(D) 清理一間公寓

61 Why does the man say, "I'll be at work until 5 P.M."?

新 (A) He is planning to end his shift early.
(B) He is able to attend a session.
(C) He can meet a deadline.
(D) He cannot carry out a task immediately.

61 男子為什麼說：「我要工作到下午 5 點」？

(A) 他打算要提早結束他的班。
(B) 他能夠出席一場講習。
(C) 他可以趕上一個截止期限。
(D) 他無法立刻執行一項作業。

題目 own [on] 擁有 license plate number 車牌號碼 authorized [ˋɔθəˏraɪzd] 經授權的；經批准的 tow [to] 拖（車）
59 alert [əˋlɝt] 警告 notify [ˋnotəˏfaɪ] 通知 tenant [ˋtɛnənt] 承租人
61 shift [ʃɪft] 輪班 session [ˋsɛʃən] 講習 carry out 執行

59 ■ 整體對話相關問題—目的 答案 (B)

高

題目詢問女子為什麼要打電話，因此必須注意聽對話的開頭。女子對男子說：「your car is blocking the garbage bins in the parking lot, which is an issue」，表示男子的車擋住了停車場的垃圾桶，造成了問題，由此可知，女子是為了告知問題而打電話給男子，因此正確答案是 (B) To notify the man of a problem。

60 ■ 細節事項相關問題—特定細項 答案 (C)

低

題目詢問女子希望男子做什麼，因此要注意聽和題目關鍵字（want the man to do）相關的內容。女子對男子說：「I'll need you to move the car immediately」，表示需要男子立刻去移車，因此正確答案是 (C) Relocate a vehicle。

換句話說

move ~ car 移車 → Relocate a vehicle 把車移到別的地方

新 **61** ■ 細節事項相關問題—掌握意圖 答案 (D)

中

題目詢問男子的說話意圖，因此要注意題目引用句（I'll be at work until 5 P.M.）相關及前後的內容。女子先說：「I'll need you to move the car immediately」，表示需要男子立刻去移車，後面男子則說：「I can move it afterward」，表示要在之後才能去移車，由此可知，男子無法立刻去移車，因此正確答案是 (D) He cannot carry out a task immediately.。

62
63
64

新

Questions 62-64 refer to the following conversation and table.

加拿大式發音 → 英式發音

M: You've reached Frost Beauty. Adrian speaking.
W: Hello. Will your salon's current special offer on beauty treatments continue throughout this month?
M: We actually have sales on two services each month. [62]**For this month . . . ah . . . April, we'll be discounting nail art and hair dyeing.**
W: Perfect. [62]**I bought a box of brown dye in March**, but it didn't work well. So now [63]**I need my hair to be recolored. Can I make an appointment for 4 P.M. today?**
M: [63]**Yes.** I should also mention that [64]**we'll have a booth at Denver's Professional Salon Expo on April 20.** There will be promotions on various hair and nail products that day, so you should come by.

第 62-64 題請參考下列對話。

男：這裡是 Frost Beauty。我是 Adrian。
女：哈囉。你們沙龍現在的美容療程特別優惠，這整個月都一直會有嗎？
男：我們其實每個月都會有兩項服務做優惠。[62] 這個月是……呃……四月，我們的美甲和染髮會打折。
女：太棒了。[62] 我三月時買了一盒棕色染劑，但效果不好。所以現在 [63] 我得重新再染一次我的頭髮。我可以約今天下午 4 點嗎？
男：[63] 可以。我應該也要提一下，[64] 我們 4 月 20 日在丹佛的專業沙龍博覽會裡會有一個攤位。那天會有各種髮類和指甲的產品做促銷活動，所以妳應該去看看。

新

Service	Discount	Sale Month
Facial	20% off	March
Haircut	25% off	March
Nail Art	15% off	April
Hair Dyeing	**[63]10% off**	April

服務	折扣	優惠月分
臉部美容	八折	三月
剪髮	七五折	三月
美甲	八五折	四月
染髮	[63] 九折	四月

62 What did the woman do last month?
(A) Stopped by an expo center
(B) Bought a hair product
(C) Applied for a salon membership
(D) Made an appointment

62 女子上個月做了什麼？
(A) 去了一個博覽中心
(B) 購買了一個髮類產品
(C) 申請了一個沙龍的會員
(D) 做了一個預約

63 新 Look at the graphic. What discount will the woman most likely receive today?
(A) 20 percent off
(B) 25 percent off
(C) 15 percent off
(D) 10 percent off

63 請看圖表。女子今天最有可能會獲得什麼折扣？
(A) 八折
(B) 七五折
(C) 八五折
(D) 九折

64 According to the man, what will happen on April 20?
(A) An exhibition will be held.
(B) A new service will be offered.
(C) A discount amount will be increased.
(D) A beauty treatment will be introduced.

64 根據男子所說，4 月 20 日會發生什麼？
(A) 會舉行一場展覽。
(B) 會提供一項新服務。
(C) 會提高一項折扣的金額。
(D) 會引進一項美容療程。

題目 reach [ritʃ] 與～聯絡；抵達 dyeing [ˋdaɪɪŋ] 染色 appointment [əˋpɔɪntmənt]（會面的）約定 expo [ˋɛkspo] 博覽會 come by（到某地點）短暫停留；順道前往（某地點） facial [ˋfeʃəl] 臉部美容
64 exhibition [ˌɛksəˋbɪʃən] 展覽

62 細節事項相關問題—特定細項 答案 (B)

中

題目詢問女子上個月做了什麼，因此要注意聽和題目關鍵字（last month）相關的內容。男子說：「For this month ~ April, we'll be discounting nail art and hair dyeing.」，表示這個四月美甲和染髮有打折，接著女子說：「I bought a box of brown dye in March」，表示自己在三月買了一盒棕色染劑，由此可知，女子在三月時買了髮類產品，因此正確答案是 (B) Bought a hair product。

新 63 細節事項相關問題—圖表資料 答案 (D)

中

題目詢問女子今天會得到什麼折扣，因此要確認題目提供的圖表，並注意和題目關鍵字（discount ~ receive today）相關的內容。女子說：「I need my hair to be recolored. Can I make an appointment for 4 P.M. today?」，表示自己得重新再染一次頭髮，並詢問是否可以約在今天下午 4 點，男子說：「Yes.」，表示可以，透過圖表可知，女子今天染髮可以打九折，因此正確答案是 (D) 10 percent off。

64 細節事項相關問題—接下來要做的事 答案 (A)

中

題目詢問男子說 4 月 20 日會發生什麼，因此必須注意聽男子話中和題目關鍵字（April 20）相關及前後的內容。男子說：「we'll have a booth at Denver's Professional Salon Expo on April 20」，表示 4 月 20 日自己店在丹佛的專業沙龍博覽會裡會有一個攤位，由此可知，在 4 月 20 日會舉行一場展覽，因此正確答案是 (A) An exhibition will be held.。

65
66
67

Questions 65-67 refer to the following conversation and map.

澳洲式發音 → 美式發音

M: During Wednesday's hiking trip, let's rest and have a picnic lunch before reaching the observation point on Mt. Evans.

W: Great suggestion. [65]**I can swing by a convenience store and buy some snacks and soft drinks for us.** I'll just do that on my way to meet you at Grove Station on Wednesday morning.

M: Sounds good. I'll pack sandwiches too. [66/67]**How about having our picnic at a waterfall alongside Ridge Road?**

W: I recently heard that path is blocked off. Apparently, [66/67]**last week's storm knocked down some large trees on it that have yet to be cleared away.** [67]**But there's another spot at the intersection of Breeze Road and Peak Road. I think it'll be comfortable there.**

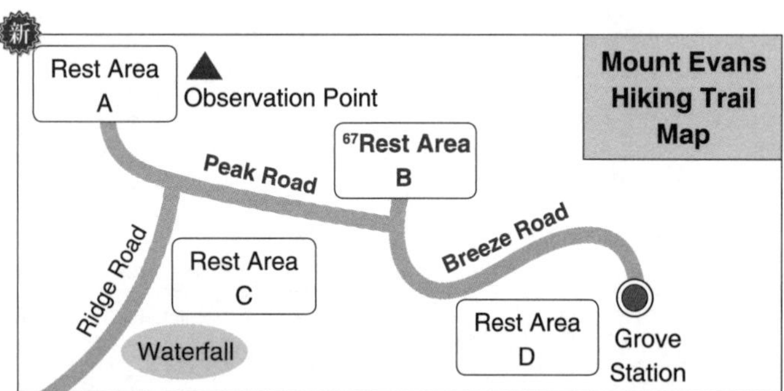

第 65-67 題請參考下列對話及地圖。

男：星期三去健行之旅的時候，我們在抵達 Evans 山的觀測點之前，先休息和野餐當午餐吧。

女：好建議。[65] 我可以順便去一下便利商店幫我們買些零食和無酒精飲料。我會在星期三早上要去 Grove 站和你碰面的路上去買。

男：聽起來很棒。我也會帶些三明治。[66/67] 我們在 Ridge 路旁的瀑布野餐怎麼樣？

女：我最近聽說那條路被封起來了。顯然 [66/67] 上星期的暴風雨吹倒了一些那條路上的大樹，而且到現在都還沒清除。[67] 不過在 Breeze 路和 Peak 路的交叉口那裡有另一個地方。我覺得那裡會是個舒服的地方。

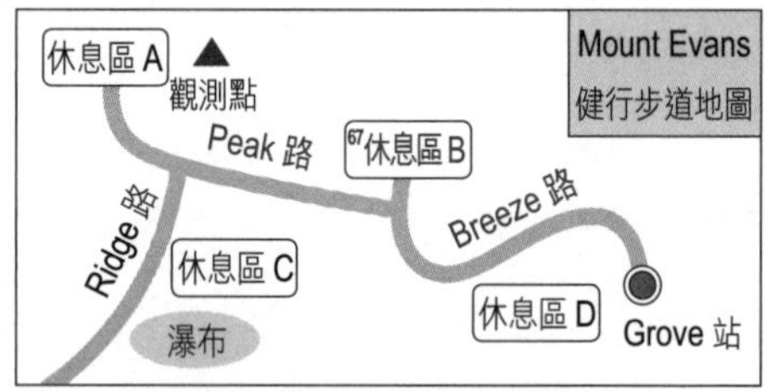

65 What does the woman offer to do?

(A) Borrow some hiking gear
(B) Take pictures of a landscape
(C) Purchase some refreshments
(D) Contact a station official

66 According to the woman, what happened last week?

(A) A path was officially opened.
(B) A picnic area was used for an event.
(C) A hike had to be postponed.
(D) A storm created poor conditions.

67 Look at the graphic. Where does the woman suggest taking a break?

新

(A) At Rest Area A
(B) At Rest Area B
(C) At Rest Area C
(D) At Rest Area D

65 女子願意去做什麼？

(A) 借一些健行裝備
(B) 拍風景照片
(C) 買一些茶點
(D) 聯絡站務人員

66 根據女子所說，上星期發生了什麼？

(A) 一條小徑正式開放了。
(B) 一個野餐區被用來辦了一場活動。
(C) 一次健行不得不延期了。
(D) 一場暴風雨造成了糟糕的情形。

67 請看圖表。女子建議在哪裡休息一下？

(A) 休息區 A
(B) 休息區 B
(C) 休息區 C
(D) 休息區 D

題目 swing by 順便去一下～　soft drink 無酒精飲料　alongside [美 ə`lɔŋ`saɪd 英 ə`lɔŋ`said] 在～旁邊　block off 封閉　apparently [ə`pærəntlɪ] 顯然地　knock down 擊倒　clear away 清除　intersection [ˌɪntɚ`sɛkʃən] 交叉口　comfortable [`kʌmfɚtəbl] 舒適的

65 gear [gɪr] 裝備　landscape [`lændˌskep] 風景　refreshment [rɪ`frɛʃmənt] 茶點，輕食

66 officially [ə`fɪʃəlɪ] 正式地　condition [kən`dɪʃən]（周遭）環境；情形

65 細節事項相關問題—提議 答案 (C)

中

題目詢問女子願意做什麼，因此要注意聽女子話中提到要為男子做事的相關內容。女子說：「I can swing by a convenience store and buy some snacks and soft drinks for us.」，表示自己可以順便去一下便利商店買些零食和無酒精飲料，因此正確答案是 (C) Purchase some refreshments。

換句話說

buy ~ snacks and soft drinks 買零食和無酒精飲料 → Purchase some refreshments 買茶點

66 細節事項相關問題—特定細項 答案 (D)

中

題目詢問女子說上星期發生了什麼事，因此要注意聽女子話中和題目關鍵字（last week）相關及前後的內容。男子說：「How about having our picnic at a waterfall alongside Ridge Road?」，提議在 Ridge 路旁邊的瀑布野餐，接著女子說：「last week's storm knocked down some large trees on it that have yet to be cleared away」，表示上星期那裡因為暴風雨而有大樹被吹倒且尚未清除，因此正確答案是 (D) A storm created poor conditions.。

換句話說

storm knocked down some large trees 暴風雨吹倒了一些大樹
→ A storm created poor conditions 一場暴風雨造成了糟糕的情形

新 67 細節事項相關問題—圖表資料 答案 (B)

高

題目詢問女子建議在哪裡休息，因此要確認題目提供的地圖，並注意和題目關鍵字（taking a break）相關的內容。男子說：「How about having our picnic at a waterfall alongside Ridge Road?」，提議在 Ridge 路旁邊的瀑布野餐，女子說：「last week's storm knocked down some large trees on it that have yet to be cleared away. But there's another spot at the intersection of Breeze Road and Peak Road. I think it'll be comfortable there.」，表示上星期的暴風雨造成了 Ridge 路上有大樹被吹倒，而且到現在都還沒清除。又說在 Breeze 路和 Peak 路的交叉口那裡有另一個地方，並表示自己覺得那裡會是個舒服的地方，透過地圖可知，女子建議的地點是位在 Breeze 路和 Peak 路交叉口的休息區 B，因此正確答案是 (B) At Rest Area B。

68
69
70

Questions 68-70 refer to the following conversation and e-mail inbox.

加拿大式發音 → 英式發音

M: Hannah, [68]**did you end up ordering new jackets to be used in the photo shoot for our magazine's October issue?**

W: Yes, Raymond. They'll be delivered on August 16. [69]**I also submitted a complaint about the shirts that arrived on August 9. I mentioned that they had tears in them in an e-mail to Nextwear's manager, Ken Powers. He responded a few days later and attached a discount coupon.**

M: Nicely done. Oh, by the way, have you received an e-mail from the photographer, Linda Wright? She had a question about whether she can be compensated for the cost of her taxi ride to the shoot location.

W: [70]**I replied to that right after this morning's press conference** regarding our October edition.

新

From	Subject	Date
Ken Powers	Thanks for Your Order	August 6
Ken Powers	**RE: Complaint about Order #4991**	[69]**August 12**
Raymond Liu	RE: Coupon Specifications	August 13
Linda Wright	Question about Taxi Cost	August 15

68 What does the man imply about the jackets?

(A) They will be featured in a publication.
(B) They will be kept at an art studio.
(C) They were paid for with a gift card.
(D) They were imported from overseas.

69 Look at the graphic. When did the woman receive a discount coupon?

新

(A) On August 6
(B) On August 12
(C) On August 13
(D) On August 15

70 According to the woman, what happened earlier today?

(A) A consultation with a photographer
(B) A launch for a clothing line
(C) A show for fashion designers
(D) A gathering with the media

第 68-70 題請參考下列對話及電子郵件收件匣。

男： Hannah，[68] 妳最後有訂要用來拍我們十月號雜誌上照片的新夾克嗎？

女： 有的，Raymond。它們會在 8 月 16 日送到。[69] 我也針對 8 月 9 日到貨的襯衫提出申訴了。我在寄給 Nextwear 經理 Ken Powers 的電子郵件裡有提到它們上面有裂縫。他幾天後回了信並附上了一張折價券。

男： 做得好。噢，對了，妳有收到攝影師 Linda Wright 的電子郵件嗎？她對於她搭計程車到拍攝地點的車資能不能報帳有疑問。

女： [70] 我在今天早上那場和我們十月號有關的記者會後就立刻回信了。

來自	主旨	日期
Ken Powers	感謝訂購	8 月 6 日
Ken Powers	回覆：關於訂單 #4991 的申訴	[69]8 月 12 日
Raymond Liu	回覆：優惠券詳細說明	8 月 13 日
Linda Wright	關於計程車車資的問題	8 月 15 日

68 關於夾克，男子暗示什麼？

(A) 它們會特別出現在一本刊物中。
(B) 它們會被存放在一間藝術工作室中。
(C) 它們的錢是用禮物卡付的。
(D) 它們是從國外進口的。

69 請看圖表。女子是在何時收到折價券的？

(A) 8 月 6 日
(B) 8 月 12 日
(C) 8 月 13 日
(D) 8 月 15 日

70 根據女子所說，今天稍早發生了什麼？

(A) 和一位攝影師做了諮詢
(B) 一個服裝系列的發表會
(C) 一場時裝設計師的秀
(D) 一場與媒體的聚會

題目 end up 最後～ shoot [ʃut] 拍攝 tear [㊚ tɛr ㊛ tɛə] 被扯破的裂縫 compensate [ˋkɑmpən͵set] 補償；抵銷 press conference 記者會

68 gift card 禮物卡 import [ɪmˋport] 進口

68 中 **細節事項相關問題—推論** 答案 (A)

題目詢問男子暗示了什麼與夾克有關的事，因此要注意聽和題目關鍵字（jackets）相關及前後的內容。男子說：「did you end up ordering new jackets to be used in the photo shoot for our magazine's October issue?」，詢問女子是否有訂要用來拍雜誌上照片的新夾克，由此可知，夾克將會出現在雜誌上，因此正確答案是 (A) They will be featured in a publication.。

新 **69** 難 **細節事項相關問題—圖表資料** 答案 (B)

題目詢問女子是何時收到折價券的，因此必須確認題目所附的電子郵件收件匣的內容，並注意和題目關鍵字（receive a discount coupon）相關的內容。女子說：「I also submitted a complaint about the shirts that arrived on August 9. I mentioned that they had tears in them in an e-mail to ~ Ken Powers. He responded a few days later and attached a discount coupon.」，表示自己已經針對 8 月 9 日到貨的襯衫提出申訴了，並說在寄給 Nextwear 經理 Ken Powers 的電子郵件裡有提到襯衫上有裂縫，而 Ken Powers 在幾天後回了信並附上了一張折價券，透過題目所附的收件匣內容可知，女子在 8 月 9 日之後的 8 月 12 日收到了 Ken Powers 的回信並取得折價券，因此正確答案是 (B) On August 12。

70 中 **細節事項相關問題—特定細項** 答案 (D)

題目詢問女子說今天稍早發生了什麼，因此要注意聽女子話中和題目關鍵字（earlier today）相關的內容。女子說：「I replied to that[e-mail] right after this morning's press conference」，表示自己在今天早上記者會結束後就立刻回了電子郵件，由此可知今天稍早辦了記者會，因此正確答案是 (D) A gathering with the media。

換句話說

press conference 記者會 → A gathering with the media 一場與媒體的聚會

71
72
73

Questions 71-73 refer to the following telephone message.

英式發音

Hello, Ms. Han. This is Sunmi Park calling from Edge Designs. [71]**I want to inform you about an issue regarding the project you commissioned us to do.** Although the T-shirts that my firm is designing for your organization are supposed to be ready by this Thursday, they will not be done by then. One of our staff members was sick the last two days, so the work is taking longer than expected to finish. As a result, [72]**we won't be able to send the completed products to you until Friday.** I'm very sorry, and [73]**we intend to take 10 percent off your final bill to make up for the delay.** If you have any inquiries, please reach out to me. I'd be happy to answer them.

71 Why is the speaker calling?
(A) To request a payment
(B) To answer a question
(C) To ask for additional shirts
(D) To report a problem

72 What will most likely happen on Friday?
(A) An order will be sent.
(B) Staff members will receive training.
(C) A project will get underway.
(D) T-shirt designs will be changed.

73 What does the speaker offer to do?
(A) Contact a designer
(B) Exchange a product
(C) Reduce a charge
(D) Provide a work sample

第 71-73 題請參考下列電話留言。

哈囉，Han 小姐。我是從 Edge 設計打來的 Sunmi Park。[71] 我想要通知您一個與您委託我們做的專案有關的問題。儘管我們公司應該是要在這星期四前，做好正在為您機構設計的 T 恤，但這些 T 恤無法在那時完成了。因為我們一位員工在過去的兩天生病了，所以這項作業將會花上比預期要久的時間來完成。因此，[72] 我們要到星期五才能將成品寄給您。我感到非常抱歉，所以 [73] 我們想要為您的尾款帳單打九折來彌補這次的延誤。如果您有任何問題，請和我聯繫。我很樂意回答您的問題。

71 說話者為什麼打電話？
(A) 為了索取一筆款項
(B) 為了回答一個問題
(C) 為了要求取得額外的襯衫
(D) 為了回報一個問題

72 星期五最有可能會發生什麼？
(A) 寄出一筆訂單的貨。
(B) 員工會接受訓練。
(C) 一項專案會開始進行。
(D) 會更改 T 恤的設計。

73 說話者願意做什麼？
(A) 聯繫設計師
(B) 更換產品
(C) 減少收費
(D) 提供作品範本

題目 issue [`ɪʃjʊ] 問題　commission [kə`mɪʃən] 委託　intend [ɪn`tɛnd] 想要；打算　bill [bɪl] 帳單　make up for 彌補～　inquiry [ɪn`kwaɪrɪ] 問題

72 order [`ɔrdɚ] 訂購的物品；訂購　get underway 開始進行

71 整體內容相關問題—目的　答案 (D)
中

題目詢問打電話的目的，因此要注意聽獨白的開頭部分。獨白說：「I want to inform you about an issue regarding the project you commissioned us to do.」，表示想要通知對方與委託專案有關的問題，因此正確答案是 (D) To report a problem。

換句話說

inform ~ about an issue 通知一個問題 → report a problem 回報一個問題

72 細節事項相關問題—接下來要做的事　答案 (A)
中

題目詢問星期五最有可能會發生什麼，因此要注意聽和題目關鍵字（Friday）相關的內容。獨白說：「we won't be able to send the completed products to you until Friday」，表示要到星期五才能將成品寄出，因此正確答案是 (A) An order will be sent.。

73 細節事項相關問題—提議　答案 (C)
低

題目詢問說話者願意做什麼，因此必須注意聽獨白後半部中出現提議相關表達的句子。獨白說：「we intend to take 10 percent off your final bill to make up for the delay」，表示想要以尾款打九折的方式來彌補這次的延誤，因此正確答案是 (C) Reduce a charge。

74
75
76

Questions 74-76 refer to the following announcement.

加拿大式發音

I have an important announcement for all administrative staff. Over the weekend, [74]**a technician installed a new operating system on all of the computers in our clinic.** Unfortunately, some data was lost in the process. Patient medical records were not affected, but the schedule for the upcoming week was accidentally deleted. So, [75]**we have to contact our patients immediately to find out the dates and times of their appointments. This is currently our top priority**, as we don't know who has an appointment tomorrow. Our lead receptionist—[76]**Janet Lee—will now hand out a list of patients and their contact information**. You each will be assigned 70 of them to call.

第 74-76 題請參考下列公告。

我有一件重要的事要對全體行政人員宣布。在週末的時候，[74] 技術人員替我們診所的所有電腦都安裝了新的作業系統。不幸的是，有些資料在這過程中遺失了。雖然病患的病歷未受影響，但接下來這禮拜的時間表都被意外刪除了。因此，[75] 我們必須立刻聯繫病患以查明他們約診的日期和時間。這是我們目前的首要任務，因為我們不知道明天約診的有誰。我們的接待長——[76]Janet Lee——現在會把患者和他們聯絡資料的名單分發下去。你們每個人都會分配到 70 個要打電話的病患。

74 Where do the listeners most likely work?

(A) At a research facility
(B) At a medical clinic
(C) At a service center
(D) At a staffing agency

74 聽者們最有可能在哪裡工作？

(A) 研究設施
(B) 醫療診所
(C) 服務中心
(D) 人力仲介

75 新 Why does the speaker say, "we don't know who has an appointment tomorrow"?

(A) To complain about an event program
(B) To indicate the need for more staff
(C) To emphasize the urgency of a task
(D) To address a recent question

75 說話者為什麼說：「我們不知道明天約診的有誰」？

(A) 為了抱怨一場活動的節目
(B) 為了表明需要更多人手
(C) 為了強調一項任務的迫切
(D) 為了應對一個最近的疑問

76 What does the speaker mention about Janet Lee?

(A) She is currently on leave.
(B) She has contacted some customers.
(C) She will distribute a document.
(D) She was recently promoted.

76 關於 Janet Lee，說話者提到什麼？

(A) 她現在在休假。
(B) 她聯絡了一些客人。
(C) 她會分發一份文件。
(D) 她最近升職了。

題目 administrative [ədˋmɪnəˌstretɪv] 行政的　install [ɪnˋstɔl] 安裝　operating system 作業系統　top priority 首要任務
75 indicate [ˋɪndəˌket] 表明　emphasize [ˋɛmfəˌsaɪz] 強調　urgency [ˋɝdʒənsɪ] 迫切　address [əˋdrɛs] 應對
76 on leave 在休假中　promote [prəˋmot] 使升職

74 整體內容相關問題—聽者 (低) 答案 (B)

題目詢問聽者們的工作地點，因此必須注意聽和身分、職業相關的表達。獨白說：「a technician installed a new operating system on all of the computers in our clinic」，表示技術人員替他們診所的所有電腦都安裝了新的作業系統，因此可以知道聽者們是在診所裡工作，正確答案是 (B) At a medical clinic。

新 **75** 細節事項相關問題—掌握意圖 (中) 答案 (C)

題目詢問說話者的說話意圖，因此要注意與題目引用句（we don't know who has an appointment tomorrow）相關的內容。獨白說：「we have to contact our patients immediately to find out the dates and times of their appointments. This is currently our top priority」，表示必須立刻聯繫病患以查明約診日期和時間，並說這件事是目前的首要任務，由此可知，說話者是想要強調這項任務很迫切，因此正確答案是 (C) To emphasize the urgency of a task。

76 細節事項相關問題—提及 (中) 答案 (C)

題目詢問說話者提到什麼與 Janet Lee 有關的事，因此要注意聽和題目關鍵字（Janet Lee）有關的內容。獨白說：「Janet Lee—will now hand out a list of patients and their contact information」，表示 Janet Lee 將會把患者和他們聯絡資料的名單分發下去，因此正確答案是 (C) She will distribute a document。

換句話說

hand out 分發 → distribute 分發

77 78 79

Questions 77-79 refer to the following telephone message.

美式發音

Hello, Mr. Hong. It's Denise Reynolds. [77]**I may have found a suitable tenant for the apartment you are trying to sublease through my firm.** A visiting researcher at Forest University named Brad Patterson contacted me about it. [78]**He wants to rent your home until September 1. Um, you asked me to find someone to take the apartment until the end of September**, but . . . um, few people have shown interest. [78]**This is the best I can do.** Mr. Patterson would like to visit your unit this week. I know you work on Thursday and Friday, so how about on the weekend? [79]**He mentioned that he was free on Saturday afternoon.** Call me at 555-0394 to let me know what time would be best.

第 77-79 題請參考下列電話留言。

哈囉，Hong 先生。我是 Denise Reynolds。[77] 我也許為您試著要透過我們公司轉租的公寓找到了適合的房客。一位 Forest 大學叫做 Brad Patterson 的訪問研究員為了這件事和我聯絡了。[78] 他想要租您的房子租到 9 月 1 日。嗯，您要求我找可以租這間公寓租到九月底的人，但……嗯，幾乎沒有人感興趣。[78] 這是我能找到最好的了。Patterson 先生想要在這星期去看看您的公寓。我知道您在星期四和星期五要工作，那麼約週末怎麼樣？[79] 他提過他星期六下午有空。請打 555-0394 跟我說什麼時候最方便。

77 Who most likely is the speaker?
(A) An accountant
(B) A researcher
(C) A lawyer
(D) A realtor

77 說話者最有可能是誰？
(A) 會計師
(B) 研究員
(C) 律師
(D) 房地產經紀人

78 新 What does the speaker imply when she says, "few people have shown interest"?
(A) A request cannot be granted.
(B) A deadline may be extended.
(C) A fee cannot be reduced.
(D) A contract may be revised.

78 當說話者說：「幾乎沒有人感興趣」，是暗示什麼？
(A) 無法應允一項要求。
(B) 一個截止期限可能會延長。
(C) 一筆費用無法減少。
(D) 一份合約可能會修改。

79 When will the listener most likely meet Mr. Patterson?
(A) On Thursday
(B) On Friday
(C) On Saturday
(D) On Sunday

79 聽者最有可能會在什麼時候與 Patterson 先生見面？
(A) 星期四
(B) 星期五
(C) 星期六
(D) 星期日

題目 suitable [ˋsutəbl̩] 適合的 sublease [ˋsʌbˏlis] 轉租；分租 rent [rɛnt] 租用；出租
77 accountant [əˋkaʊntənt] 會計師 realtor [ˋriəltɚ] 房地產經紀人
78 grant [grænt] 應允，同意

77 ■ 整體內容相關問題—說話者 答案 (D)
中
題目詢問說話者的身分，因此要注意聽和身分、職業相關的表達。獨白說：「I may have found a suitable tenant for the apartment you are trying to sublease through my firm.」，表示自己也許已經找到了適合的承租人，由此可知，說話者是房地產經紀人，因此正確答案是 (D) A realtor。

新 **78** ■ 細節事項相關問題—掌握意圖 答案 (A)
中
題目詢問說話者意圖，因此要注意與題目引用句（few people have shown interest）相關的內容。獨白說：「He[Brad Patterson] wants to rent your home until September 1. ~ you asked me to find someone to take the apartment until the end of September」，表示 Brad Patterson 希望租到 9 月 1 日，但聽者要求說話者要找可以租到九月底的人，而說話者之後說：「This is the best I can do.」，表示這是自己能找到最好的了，由此可知，「找可以租到九月底的人」這個要求無法實現，因此正確答案是 (A) A request cannot be granted.。

79 ■ 細節事項相關問題—特定細項 答案 (C)
低
題目詢問說話者和 Patterson 先生什麼時候會見面，因此必須注意聽和題目關鍵字（meet Mr. Patterson）相關的內容。獨白說：「He[Mr. Patterson] mentioned that he was free on Saturday afternoon.」，表示 Patterson 先生說過他在星期六下午有空，因此正確答案是 (C) On Saturday。

80
81
82

Questions 80-82 refer to the following talk.	第 80-82 題請參考下列談話。
澳洲式發音	
[80]**Our CEO organized this four-day retreat for managers** in order to express gratitude for the hard work you have done. She recognizes that you all strive to perform at a high level and wants you to know that you are essential to the firm's success. Now, in addition to relaxing and enjoying this beautiful resort, [81]**we're going to carry out a few team-building exercises together over the next few days**. While the exercises are designed to be lighthearted and fun, they will also give you a chance to enhance your communication abilities. One more thing . . . [82]**The CEO would like a picture of everyone together. So, please meet in the resort's main event room at 4 P.M.**	[80] 我們執行長為經理們籌辦了這次為期四天的員工旅遊，以對各位的辛勤工作表達感謝。她認為你們大家都努力達成了高水準的表現，並希望各位知道你們對公司的成功來說是不可或缺的。那麼，除了放鬆並享受這個美麗的度假村之外，[81] 我們在接下來的幾天間會一起進行一些團隊建立的活動。儘管這些活動都設計得輕鬆愉快又有趣，但它們也會給大家增進溝通能力的機會。還有一件事……[82] 執行長想要大家一起拍張照。因此，請在下午 4 點到度假村的大活動室集合。
80 According to the speaker, what type of event did the CEO arrange? (A) An industry convention (B) A company orientation (C) A fund-raising dinner (D) A corporate retreat	80 根據說話者所說，執行長安排了什麼類型的活動？ (A) 產業大會 (B) 公司說明會 (C) 募款晚宴 (D) 公司員工旅遊
81 What are listeners expected to do over the next few days? (A) Watch some instructional videos (B) Participate in group activities (C) Discuss potential trip destinations (D) Share updates with a board member	81 預期聽者們在接下來的幾天間會做什麼？ (A) 看一些教學影片 (B) 參加團體活動 (C) 討論可能的旅行目的地 (D) 和董事會成員分享最新消息
82 Why must listeners meet at 4 P.M.? (A) To pose for a photograph (B) To take a tour of a resort (C) To make decisions about an event (D) To listen to a talk from an executive	82 聽者們為何必須在下午 4 點集合？ (A) 為了擺姿勢照相 (B) 為了參觀度假村 (C) 為了做出有關一項活動的決定 (D) 為了聽一位主管的演講

題目 gratitude [美 `grætə,tjud 英 `grætitju:d] 感謝　strive [straɪv] 努力
lighthearted [美 `laɪt`hartɪd 英 `lait`ha:tid] 輕鬆愉快的　enhance [美 ɪn`hæns 英 in`ha:ns] 提升
81 potential [pə`tɛnʃəl] 可能的　board member 董事會成員
82 executive [ɪg`zɛkjʊtɪv] 執行者；主管

80 細節事項相關問題—特定細項　答案 (D)
中
題目詢問執行長安排的活動類型是什麼，因此必須注意聽和題目關鍵字（CEO arrange）相關的內容。獨白說：「Our CEO organized this four-day retreat for managers」，表示執行長籌辦了員工旅遊，因此正確答案是 (D) A corporate retreat。

81 細節事項相關問題—特定細項　答案 (B)
高
題目詢問聽者們在接下來的幾天間預計會做什麼，因此要注意聽和題目關鍵字（over the next few days）相關的內容。獨白說：「we're going to carry out a few team-building exercises together over the next few days」，表示接下來的幾天間會一起進行一些團隊建立的活動，因此正確答案是 (B) Participate in group activities。
換句話說
carry out ~ team-building exercises 進行團隊建立的活動 → Participate in group activities 參加團體活動

82 細節事項相關問題—理由　答案 (A)
中
題目詢問聽者們為什麼必須在下午 4 點集合，因此要注意聽和題目關鍵字（4 P.M.）相關的內容。獨白說：「The CEO would like a picture of everyone together. So, please meet in the resort's main event room at 4 P.M.」，表示因為執行長想要大家一起拍張照，所以要在下午 4 點到度假村的大活動室集合，因此正確答案是 (A) To pose for a photograph。

83
84
85

Questions 83-85 refer to the following telephone message.

美式發音

This message is for Richard Brendholt. My name is Emma Compton, and [83]**I'm the principal at Charleston Elementary School**. I'm calling because [84]**we're hosting a Career Day early next month as a way of introducing students to different vocations** that they could possibly pursue in the future. It would be wonderful if you could send a representative from your fire station to the event. Many of our pupils find your line of work fascinating. I'm certain that they'd appreciate hearing about the duties and responsibilities that emergency personnel deal with on a daily basis. [85]**The person you send will need to give a 10-minute talk about a firefighter's job and demonstrate the gear that is used.** If you're interested in participating, please let me know by Monday, March 23. Thanks.

83 What sector does the speaker represent?

(A) Emergency services
(B) Transportation
(C) Education
(D) Health care

84 What is scheduled to take place next month?

(A) A training workshop
(B) A career information session
(C) A building safety inspection
(D) A student performance

85 According to the speaker, what would a representative need to do?

(A) Describe the nature of a position
(B) Explain the flaws in some gear
(C) Provide advice on public speaking
(D) Show participants around a facility

第 83-85 題請參考下列電話留言。

這是給 Richard Brendholt 的留言。我的名字是 Emma Compton，[83] 我是 Charleston 小學的校長。我打來是因為 [84] 我們下個月初要舉辦職業體驗日，以向學生介紹他們未來可能會想從事的不同職業。若您可以派一位您消防局的代表來參加這次活動的話，那就太棒了。我們很多學生都認為你們的這份工作非常吸引人。我有把握他們會很高興聽到與應急人員每天在處理的職責內容有關的事。[85] 您派來的代表將必須就消防員的工作進行 10 分鐘的演講，並展示使用的裝備。若您有興趣參與，請在 3 月 23 日星期一前告訴我。謝謝。

83 說話者代表什麼領域？

(A) 應急服務
(B) 交通
(C) 教育
(D) 衛生保健

84 下個月預定要舉行什麼？

(A) 訓練工作坊
(B) 職業說明會
(C) 建築安全檢查
(D) 學生表演

85 根據說話者所說，代表必須做什麼？

(A) 描述一項職務的本質
(B) 說明一些裝備的缺點
(C) 就公開發言提供建議
(D) 帶參加者參觀設施

題目 vocation [voˋkeʃən] 職業 pursue [pɚˋsu] 從事 fire station 消防局 pupil [ˋpjupl]（小）學生 emergency personnel 應急人員

83 sector [ˋsɛktɚ]（社會、產業等的）領域，部門

85 nature [ˋnetʃɚ] 本質 flaw [flɔ] 缺點

83 ■ 整體內容相關問題—說話者 答案 (C)

中

題目詢問說話者所代表的領域是什麼，因此要注意聽和身分、職業相關的表達。獨白說：「I'm the principal at Charleston Elementary School」，表示自己是 Charleston 小學的校長，因此正確答案是 (C) Education。

84 ■ 細節事項相關問題—接下來要做的事 答案 (B)

高

題目詢問下個月預定要舉辦什麼，因此要注意聽和題目關鍵字（next month）相關的內容。獨白說：「we're hosting a Career Day early next month as a way of introducing students to different vocations」，表示學校下個月初要舉辦職業體驗日，用來向學生介紹不同的職業，因此正確答案是 (B) A career information session。

85 ■ 細節事項相關問題—特定細項 答案 (A)

高

題目詢問代表必須要做什麼，因此要注意聽和題目關鍵字（representative need to do）相關的內容。獨白說：「The person[representative] you send will need to give a 10-minute talk about a firefighter's job and demonstrate the gear that is used.」，表示聽者派的代表必須就消防員的工作進行 10 分鐘的演講，並展示使用的裝備，因此正確答案是 (A) Describe the nature of a position。

86
87
88

Questions 86-88 refer to the following broadcast.

澳洲式發音

In local news, [86]**the Meyerville city council voted to tear down the historic city hall building** on July 12. The decision comes after an inspection last year uncovered cracks in the foundation. For months, the government debated whether to undertake costly renovations or simply demolish the facility. [87]**Mayor John Hamilton** held a press conference this morning, during which he announced plans to build a public park in the building's lot. [88]**The city council will hold a special session to discuss the design of the new park this Friday** at 7 P.M. at Fairview High School. Residents are encouraged to attend and share their ideas.

86 What did the city council do?

(A) Voted to change a tax code
(B) Updated an outdated policy
(C) Decided to demolish a building
(D) Held a debate on safety standards

87 Who is John Hamilton?

(A) A government official
(B) A historian
(C) An architect
(D) A park employee

88 What will happen on Friday?

(A) A plan will be announced.
(B) An inspection will take place.
(C) A meeting will be held.
(D) A facility will open.

第 86-88 題請參考下列廣播。

在地方新聞部分，[86]Meyerville 市議會在 7 月 12 日投票決定拆除具重要歷史意義的市政府大樓。這項決定是在去年一次檢查時於地基上發現裂縫之後所做的。市政府就是要進行所費不貲的整修還是逕行拆除爭論了數個月。[87] 市長 John Hamilton 今天早上舉行了記者會，在記者會中宣布於該大樓所在地興建公共公園的計畫。[88] 市議會將於本週五晚上 7 點在 Fairview 高中舉行一場特別座談會來討論新公園的設計。歡迎居民們參加並分享自己的想法。

86 市議會做了什麼？

(A) 投票變更一條稅法
(B) 更新一項過時的政策
(C) 決定拆除一棟大樓
(D) 就安全標準舉行一場辯論會

87 誰是 John Hamilton？

(A) 政府官員
(B) 歷史學家
(C) 建築師
(D) 公園的員工

88 週五會發生什麼？

(A) 會宣布一項計畫。
(B) 會舉行一次檢查。
(C) 會舉辦一次聚會。
(D) 一座設施會開放。

題目 city council 市議會　vote [美 vot 英 vəut] 投票決定　tear down 拆除　crack [kræk] 裂痕
foundation [faʊnˋdeʃən]（建築的）地基；基礎　debate [dɪˋbet] 辯論；爭辯
undertake [美 ˌʌndɚˋtek 英 ˌʌndəˋteik] 進行　demolish [美 dɪˋmɑlɪʃ 英 diˋmɔliʃ] 拆除
lot [美 lɑt 英 lɔt]（有特定用途的）一塊地　resident [美 ˋrɛzədənt 英 ˋrezidənt] 居民
86 tax code 稅法　outdated [ˌaʊtˋdetɪd] 過時的

86 細節事項相關問題—特定細項　答案 (C)

高

題目詢問市議會做了什麼，因此必須注意聽和題目關鍵字（city council）相關的內容。獨白說：「the Meyerville city council voted to tear down the historic city hall building」，表示 Meyerville 市議會投票決定拆除具重要歷史意義的市政府大樓，因此正確答案是 (C) Decided to demolish a building。

換句話說

voted to tear down the ~ building 投票決定拆除大樓 → Decided to demolish a building 決定拆除一棟大樓

87 細節事項相關問題—特定細項　答案 (A)

中

題目詢問 John Hamilton 的身分，因此要注意聽和提問對象（John Hamilton）的身分、職業相關的表達。獨白說：「Mayor John Hamilton」，表示 John Hamilton 是市長，由此可知，John Hamilton 是政府官員，因此正確答案是 (A) A government official。

換句話說

Mayor 市長 → government official 政府官員

88 細節事項相關問題—接下來要做的事　答案 (C)

中

題目詢問週五會發生什麼，因此要注意聽和題目關鍵字（Friday）相關的內容。獨白說：「The city council will hold a special session to discuss the design of the new park this Friday」，表示市議會本週五會舉行一場特別座談會來討論新公園的設計，因此正確答案是 (C) A meeting will be held.。

89 90 91

Questions 89-91 refer to the following speech.

英式發音

The Snow and Ice Festival has grown considerably in recent years, and it now attracts many visitors from overseas. This increase in the number of international travelers has a very positive impact on Brenton City's economy. [89]**Your goal for today is to figure out how to promote the festival to foreign tourists and continue this trend.** Just keep in mind that [90]**most guests find the snow sculptures and ice palace to be the two most impressive features of the festival**. So, those attractions should be emphasized in our campaign. All right, I'd now like everyone to split up into small groups and brainstorm ideas. Then, [91]**in about half an hour, break for lunch**.

89 What task have the listeners been assigned?

(A) Developing an event for local tourists
(B) Determining how to target foreign visitors
(C) Creating a new attraction
(D) Planning an international fund-raiser

90 What does the speaker say about the snow sculptures?

(A) They are at risk of melting.
(B) They take a long time to construct.
(C) They are popular among attendees.
(D) They were previously featured in flyers.

91 What will the listeners do in 30 minutes?

(A) Take a break
(B) Listen to a speech
(C) Watch a presentation
(D) Discuss some ideas

第 89-91 題請參考下列致詞。

Snow and Ice 節近年來大幅成長，且現在吸引許多來自海外的人造訪。國際旅客數量的這種成長為 Brenton 市的經濟帶來了非常正面的影響。[89] 各位今天的目標是想出要如何向外國遊客推廣這個節並延續這項風潮。只是務必要記得，[90] 大部分來賓都認為雪雕與冰宮是這個節裡最令人印象深刻的兩項特色。因此，在我們的宣傳活動裡應該要強調這些景點。好了，現在我想要大家分成小組並腦力激盪出點子來。接著，[91] 大概在半小時後，休息吃午餐。

89 聽者們被指派了什麼任務？

(A) 為當地觀光客開發一項活動
(B) 決定要如何鎖定外國訪客
(C) 打造一個新的景點
(D) 規劃一場國際募款活動

90 關於雪雕，說話者說什麼？

(A) 它們有融化的危險。
(B) 建造它們要花很長的時間。
(C) 它們在參加者之間很受歡迎。
(D) 之前在傳單裡特別介紹了它們。

91 聽者們在 30 分鐘後會做什麼？

(A) 休息一下
(B) 聽演講
(C) 看簡報
(D) 討論一些點子

題目 considerably [kən`sɪdərəblɪ] 大幅地；相當地　attract [ə`trækt] 吸引　figure out 想出
sculpture [(美) `skʌlptʃɚ (英) `skʌlptʃə] 雕像　palace [`pælɪs] 宮殿　feature [(美) fitʃɚ (英) fi:tʃə] 特色；特別提供
attraction [ə`trækʃən]（吸引人的）景點　emphasize [`ɛmfə͵saɪz] 強調　split up 分開

89 target [`tɑrgɪt] 鎖定

90 at risk of ~ 有～的危險

89 細節事項相關問題—特定細項　答案 (B)

高

題目詢問聽者們被指派了什麼任務，因此要注意聽和題目關鍵字（task ~ assigned）相關的內容。獨白說：「Your goal for today is to figure out how to promote the festival to foreign tourists and continue this trend.」，表示今天聽者們的目標是要想出該如何向外國遊客推廣這個節並延續這項風潮，因此正確答案是 (B) Determining how to target foreign visitors。

90 細節事項相關問題—提及　答案 (C)

中

題目詢問說話者提到什麼和雪雕有關的事，因此要注意聽和題目關鍵字（snow sculptures）相關的內容。獨白說：「most guests find the snow sculptures and ice palace to be the two most impressive features of the festival」，表示大部分來賓都認為雪雕與冰宮是最令人印象深刻的兩項特色，由此可知，雪雕很受參加者們的歡迎，因此正確答案是 (C) They are popular among attendees.。

91 細節事項相關問題—接下來要做的事　答案 (A)

中

題目詢問聽者們在 30 分鐘後會做什麼，因此要注意聽和題目關鍵字（in 30 minutes）相關的內容。獨白說：「in about half an hour, break for lunch」，表示大概在半小時、也就是 30 分鐘後會去休息吃午餐，因此正確答案是 (A) Take a break。

92
93
94

Questions 92-94 refer to the following excerpt from a workshop. 加拿大式發音	第 92-94 題請參考下列工作坊節錄。
I'm Milo Forsythe, and I was hired to provide training on how to manage complaints. [92]**As new employees of the customer service department, it's important that you know how to effectively respond when someone is unhappy with one of the company's products.** This is because handling a complaint well can actually lead to increased customer satisfaction and loyalty. [93]**To better demonstrate this point, I'd like to do a simple role-play exercise. One of you will be an upset customer, and I'll be the company representative.** [94]**Pay close attention to how I deal with the situation by validating the other person's experience.** You may be surprised by the results. [94]**Hopefully, you will use this technique when interacting with customers.**	我是 Milo Forsythe，我被請來就要如何處理申訴進行培訓。[92] 身為顧客服務部門的新員工，知道如何在有人對公司的某項產品不滿時有效回應是很重要的。這是因為申訴處理得當其實可以使顧客滿意度及忠誠度都獲得提升。[93] 為了更清楚說明這項論點，我想要做一次簡單的角色扮演演練。你們其中一個人當不滿的顧客，我則當公司代表。[94] 請仔細注意我是如何藉著認可對方經歷來處理這個情況。你們可能會對結果感到驚訝。[94] 但願各位在與顧客互動時會把這項技巧用上。
92 Who most likely are the listeners? (A) Personnel managers (B) Sales representatives (C) Administrative assistants (D) Customer service agents	92 聽者們最有可能是誰？ (A) 人事經理 (B) 業務代表 (C) 行政助理 (D) 顧客服務專員
93 What will most likely happen next? (A) A demonstration will be given. (B) A manual will be handed out. (C) Job duties will be explained. (D) Evaluations will be conducted.	93 接下來最有可能會發生什麼？ (A) 會進行一次示範。 (B) 會發放一本手冊。 (C) 會說明職務內容。 (D) 會進行評估。
94 新 Why does the speaker say, "You may be surprised by the results"? (A) To suggest that a product is popular (B) To point out the disadvantages of a plan (C) To indicate that a method is effective (D) To show the accuracy of some data	94 說話者為什麼說：「你們可能會對結果感到驚訝」？ (A) 為了暗示一項產品很受歡迎 (B) 為了指出一個計畫的缺點 (C) 為了指出一個方法很有效 (D) 為了顯示一些數據的準確性

題目 handle [ˋhændl] 處理 demonstrate [ˋdɛmənˏstret]（用實例或示範等方式）說明 role-play 角色扮演 validate [ˋvæləˏdet] 認可 hopefully [ˋhopfəlɪ] 但願
92 agent [ˋedʒənt] 專員；代理人 **94** accuracy [ˋækjərəsɪ] 準確性

92 ■ **整體內容相關問題—聽者** 答案 (D)
低
題目詢問聽者的身分，因此要注意聽和身分、職業相關的表達。獨白說：「As new employees of the customer service department, it's important that you know how to ~ respond when someone is unhappy with ~ company's products.」，表示身為顧客服務部門的新員工，知道如何在有人對公司的某項產品不滿時有效回應是很重要的，由此可知，聽者們是顧客服務專員，因此正確答案是 (D) Customer service agents。

93 ■ **細節事項相關問題—接下來要做的事** 答案 (A)
高
題目詢問接下來會發生什麼，因此要注意聽和題目關鍵字（happen next）相關的內容。獨白說：「To better demonstrate this point, I'd like to do a simple role-play exercise. One of you will be an upset customer, and I'll be the company representative.」，表示為了說明得更清楚，所以會做一次角色扮演演練，讓其中一個聽者當顧客，說話者則當公司代表，因此正確答案是 (A) A demonstration will be given.。

新 **94** ■ **細節事項相關問題—掌握意圖** 答案 (C)
中
題目詢問說話者的說話意圖，因此要注意和題目引用句（You may be surprised by the results）相關的內容。獨白說：「Pay close attention to how I deal with the situation by validating the other person's experience.」，表示請聽者們注意自己是如何藉著認可對方經歷來處理這個情況，接著說：「Hopefully, you will use this technique when interacting with customers.」，表示希望聽者們在與顧客互動時會把這項技巧用上，由此可知，說話者是想指出自己要使用的這個方法能有效處理申訴，因此正確答案是 (C) To indicate that a method is effective。

95
96
97

Questions 95-97 refer to the following advertisement and schedule.

澳洲式發音

Are you looking for ways to save money on airfare and accommodations? Then be sure to tune in to 108.6 FM's newest program, *The Frugal Traveler*. Hosted by [95]**Jeff Wallace, who ran his own travel agency for 25 years** before retiring, the program will provide tips on how to stretch your budget while on vacation. Jeff will set aside time each day to respond to questions from listeners, and [96]**callers will have their names entered into a monthly draw to win a flight to any major city in Europe with Omega Air**. *The Frugal Traveler* will air Wednesday afternoons, starting May 2. [97]**It will fill the time slot immediately after our local traffic update.** Make sure to check it out!

Broadcast Schedule Wednesday Afternoons (April)	
12:00-2:00	*Health Check*
2:00-2:20	**Traffic Report**
2:20-3:30	[97]***Culture Break***
3:30-5:00	*Investment Strategies*
5:00-5:10	Weather Update
5:10-6:00	*Gourmet Cooking*

95 What does the speaker mention about Jeff Wallace?

(A) He has hosted other radio programs.
(B) He travels often for his job.
(C) He was the owner of a company.
(D) He is planning to retire soon.

96 According to the speaker, what might some callers receive?

(A) A bus pass
(B) A hotel voucher
(C) An airline ticket
(D) A guidebook

97 Look at the graphic. Which show will be replaced?

(A) *Health Check*
(B) *Culture Break*
(C) *Investment Strategies*
(D) *Gourmet Cooking*

第 95-97 題請參考下列廣告及時間表。

你正在尋找節省機票及住宿費用的方法嗎？那麼一定要收聽 FM 108.6 的最新節目《The Frugal Traveler》。由在退休前 [95] 經營自己的旅行社經營了 25 年的 Jeff Wallace 所主持，這個節目會就如何在度假時把你的預算運用到最大限度上提供訣竅。Jeff 每次節目都會留時間回應聽眾提問，且 [96] 打電話進來的人將可參加每月抽獎，以贏得 Omega 航空飛往歐洲任何主要城市的機票。《The Frugal Traveler》將從 5 月 2 日起於每星期三下午播送。[97] 它會在我們的地方路況最新報導之後的時段立刻播出。一定要來聽看看！

廣播時間表 每星期三下午（四月）	
12:00-2:00	*Health Check*
2:00-2:20	路況報導
2:20-3:30	[97]*Culture Break*
3:30-5:00	*Investment Strategies*
5:00-5:10	最新氣象報告
5:10-6:00	*Gourmet Cooking*

95 關於 Jeff Wallace，說話者提到什麼？

(A) 他曾主持過其他廣播節目。
(B) 他因為工作時常旅行。
(C) 他以前是一間公司的老闆。
(D) 他打算很快退休。

96 根據說話者所說，某些打電話進來的人可能會獲得什麼？

(A) 公車乘車券
(B) 飯店抵用券
(C) 機票
(D) 旅遊指南

97 請看圖表。哪一個節目將被取代？

(A) *Health Check*
(B) *Culture Break*
(C) *Investment Strategies*
(D) *Gourmet Cooking*

題目 airfare [美 ˋɛrfɛr 英 ˋeəfeə] 機票費用　accommodation [美 əˌkɑməˋdeʃən 英 əˌkɔməˋdeiʃn] 住宿
tune in（調整頻率或頻道等）收看；收聽　stretch [strɛtʃ] 到～的最大限度；竭盡　set aside 留出　draw [drɔ] 抽籤
time slot 時段

95 高 ■ 細節事項相關問題—提及　　答案 (C)

題目詢問說話者提到什麼與 Jeff Wallace 有關的事，因此要注意聽和題目關鍵字（Jeff Wallace）相關的內容。獨白說：「Jeff Wallace, who ran his own travel agency for 25 years」，表示 Jeff Wallace 經營自己的旅行社經營了 25 年，因此正確答案是 (C) He was the owner of a company.。

換句話說

ran his own travel agency 經營自己的旅行社 → was the owner of a company 以前是一間公司的老闆

96 中 ■ 細節事項相關問題—特定細項　　答案 (C)

題目詢問打電話進來的人可能會獲得什麼，因此要注意聽和題目關鍵字（callers receive）相關的內容。獨白說：「callers will have their names entered into a monthly draw to win a flight to any major city in Europe with Omega Air」，表示打電話進來的人將可參加每月抽獎，以贏得 Omega 航空飛往歐洲任何主要城市的機票，因此正確答案是 (C) An airline ticket。

新 **97** 高 ■ 細節事項相關問題—圖表資料　　答案 (B)

題目詢問哪一個節目會被取代，因此要確認題目提供的時間表，並注意和題目關鍵字（show ~ replaced）相關的內容。獨白說：「It[*The Frugal Traveler*]will fill the time slot immediately after our local traffic update.」，表示《The Frugal Traveler》會在路況報導之後的時段立刻播出，透過時間表可知，會被取代掉的是路況報導之後的《Culture Break》，因此正確答案是 (B) *Culture Break*。

98
99
100

Questions 98-100 refer to the following telephone message and receipt.

第 98-100 題請參考下列電話留言及收據。

英式發音

My name is Janis Lyle, and I rented a car from your company when [98]**I visited a client in Manchester last week.** While filling out an application for reimbursement from my company, I noticed an error on my receipt. [99]**I was told that if I upgraded to a larger vehicle, I would receive the navigation system for free, but I realize now that I was charged for it. I'd like to have that amount refunded** to my credit card. In addition, I . . . ah . . . I've got one more request. Your Web site mentions that your company has a rewards program. [100]**Could you send me a brochure that describes the benefits of membership?** I'm going to be taking a lot of business trips this year, so I might sign up. Thanks.

我的名字是 Janis Lyle，[98] 我上週在曼徹斯特拜訪客戶時向你們公司租了一輛車。在填寫我公司的核銷申請表時，我注意到我收據上有一個錯誤。[99] 我當時被告知，如果我升級成比較大的車，那就可以免費使用導航系統，但我現在發現我那時被收了這個的錢。我想刷退這筆錢（到我的信用卡）。此外，我……啊……我還有一個要求。你們網站提到你們公司有回饋計畫。[100] 可以請你寄一本說明會員福利的小冊子給我嗎？我今年會出差很多次，所以我可能會申請。謝謝。

新

EZ Auto Rentals

Customer: Janis Lyle
Rental Period: October 12-19
Branch: Manchester, England
Receipt #: 84758

Vehicle Rental:	£125.00
Fuel:	£45.00
Collision Insurance:	£75.00
Navigation System:	[99]**£25.00**
Total:	£270.00

EZ 租車

顧客：Janis Lyle
租用期間：10 月 12-19 日
分店：曼徹斯特，英格蘭
收據編號：84758

車輛租金：	125.00 英鎊
燃料：	45.00 英鎊
碰撞險：	75.00 英鎊
導航系統：	[99]25.00 英鎊
總計：	270.00 英鎊

98 What did the speaker do last week?
(A) Visited some relatives
(B) Met with a customer
(C) Attended a convention
(D) Toured an overseas branch

98 說話者上週做了什麼？
(A) 拜訪了一些親戚
(B) 與一位客人見了面
(C) 參加了一場大會
(D) 參觀了一間海外分公司

99 新 Look at the graphic. How much will the woman be refunded?
(A) £125.00
(B) £45.00
(C) £75.00
(D) £25.00

99 請看圖表。女子會可以退回多少錢？
(A) 125.00 英鎊
(B) 45.00 英鎊
(C) 75.00 英鎊
(D) 25.00 英鎊

100 What does the speaker request be sent to her?
(A) Promotional materials
(B) A customer satisfaction survey
(C) Insurance documents
(D) An updated invoice

100 說話者要求要寄什麼給她？
(A) 宣傳資料
(B) 顧客滿意度調查
(C) 保險文件
(D) 更新後的發票

題目 reimbursement [美 ˌriɪm`bɝsmənt 英 ˌri:im`bə:smənt] 核銷　sign up 登記～　insurance [ɪn`ʃʊrəns] 保險
98 relative [`rɛlətɪv] 親戚
100 invoice [`ɪnvɔɪs] 發票，發貨單

98 細節事項相關問題—特定細項 答案 (B)

低

題目詢問說話者上週做了什麼，因此要注意聽和題目關鍵字（last week）相關的內容。獨白說：「I visited a client in Manchester last week」，表示自己上週在曼徹斯特拜訪客戶，因此正確答案是 (B) Met with a customer。

換句話說

visited a client 拜訪了客戶 → Met with a customer 與一位客人見了面

新 99 細節事項相關問題—圖表資料 答案 (D)

中

題目詢問女子會可以退回多少錢，因此要確認題目提供的收據內容，並注意和題目關鍵字（How much ~ refunded）相關的內容。獨白說：「I was told that if I upgraded to a larger vehicle, I would receive the navigation system for free, but I realize now that I was charged for it. I'd like to have that amount refunded」，表示自己當時被告知，如果升級成比較大的車，就可以免費使用導航系統，但後來卻被收了導航系統的錢，因此想刷退這筆錢，透過收據可知，將會退回使用導航系統的 25 英鎊給女子，因此正確答案是 (D) ￡25.00。

100 細節事項相關問題—要求 答案 (A)

高

題目詢問說話者要求聽者寄給自己什麼，因此要注意聽獨白的後半部中出現要求相關表達的句子。獨白說：「Could you send me a brochure that describes the benefits of membership?」，要求聽者寄說明會員福利的小冊子給自己，因此正確答案是 (A) Promotional materials。

換句話說

brochure that describes the benefits of membership 說明會員福利的小冊子
→ Promotional materials 宣傳資料

TEST 09

Part 1 原文・翻譯・解析

Part 2 原文・翻譯・解析

Part 3 原文・翻譯・解析 新

Part 4 原文・翻譯・解析 新

MP3 收錄於 TEST 09.mp3。

進行深入練習或複習時，可以一邊多聽幾次收錄各國口音的試題 MP3，一邊搭配解答中的中英對照翻譯和解析，以及單字記憶表和多元口音單字記憶 MP3，達到事半功倍的效果。

1 ○○●● 中

澳洲式發音

(A) He's carrying some jackets.
(B) He's riding an escalator.
(C) He's weighing a suitcase.
(D) He's waiting for an elevator.

(A) 他正拿著一些夾克 。
(B) 他正在搭乘手扶梯。
(C) 他正在秤行李箱的重量。
(D) 他正在等電梯。

單人照片 答案 (B)

仔細觀察照片中一名男子拉著行李箱搭手扶梯的模樣。

(A) [╳] 男子拉著行李箱，但這裡卻描述成拿著夾克（jackets），因此是錯誤選項。注意不要聽到 He's carrying（他正拿著）就選擇這個答案。

(B) [○] 這裡正確描述男子搭乘手扶梯的樣子，所以是正確答案。

(C) [╳] weighing（正在秤重）和男子的動作無關，因此是錯誤選項。這裡使用照片中有出現的行李箱（suitcase）來造成混淆。

(D) [╳] 照片中沒有電梯（elevator），因此是錯誤選項。這裡使用和照片中手扶梯相關的 elevator（電梯）來造成混淆

單字　weigh [we] 秤重　suitcase [ˋsut͵kes] 行李箱

2 ○○○● 低

英式發音

(A) Some men are operating devices.
(B) Some men are moving a couch.
(C) Some men are clearing a table.
(D) Some men are setting up a computer.

(A) 一些男子正在操作裝置。
(B) 一些男子正在搬沙發。
(C) 一些男子正在清理桌子。
(D) 一些男子正在設置電腦。

兩人以上的照片 答案 (A)

仔細觀察照片中兩名男子正坐著在使用裝置的模樣。

(A) [○] 這裡正確描述男子正在使用裝置的模樣，所以是正確答案。

(B) [╳] moving（正在搬）和男子的動作無關，因此是錯誤選項。這裡使用照片中有出現的沙發（couch）來造成混淆。

(C) [╳] clearing（正在清理）和男子的動作無關，因此是錯誤選項。這裡使用照片中有出現的桌子（table）來造成混淆。

(D) [╳] setting up（正在設置）和男子的動作無關，因此是錯誤選項。這裡使用和照片中的筆記型電腦有關的 computer（電腦）來造成混淆

單字　operate [㊊ ˋɑpə͵ret ㊋ ˋɔpəreit] 操作（機器等）；營運　couch [kaʊtʃ] 沙發　clear [㊊ klɪr ㊋ kliə] 清理　set up 設置（機器等）

3 ○○●● 中

加拿大式發音

(A) She is plugging a cable into a printer.
(B) She is copying some pages.
(C) She is placing a book on a shelf.
(D) She is sliding paper into a tray.

(A) 她正在把傳輸線插到印表機上。
(B) 她正在影印一些頁面。
(C) 她正在把書放到架上。
(D) 她正在把紙放進紙盤裡。

■ 單人照片 答案 (B)

仔細觀察照片中一名女子正在影印書本的樣子。

(A) [╳] plugging（正在插）和女子的動作無關，因此是錯誤選項。這裡使用和照片中的影印機相關的 printer（印表機）來造成混淆。

(B) [○] 這裡正確描述女子正在影印書本內頁的樣子，所以是正確答案。

(C) [╳] 女子不是正在把書放到架上，而是放在了影印機上，因此是錯誤選項。注意不要聽到 She is placing a book（她正在放書）就選擇這個答案。

(D) [╳] sliding（正在放進）和女子的動作無關，因此是錯誤選項。這裡使用和照片中的書有關的 paper（紙）來造成混淆。

單字 plug [plʌg] 插 cable [ˋkebl] 傳輸線 slide [slaɪd]（滑動）放進 tray [tre] 托盤

4 中

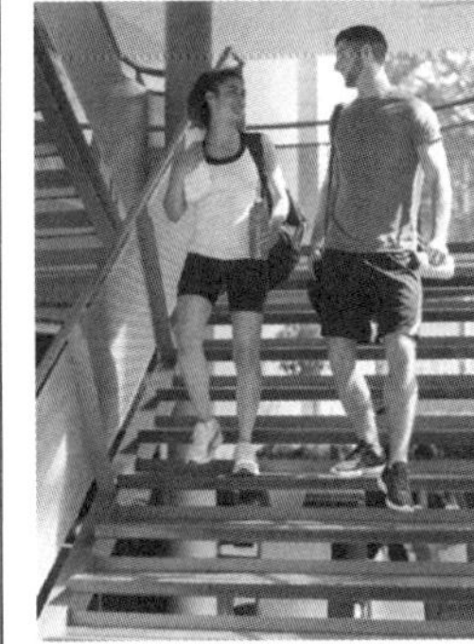

英式發音

(A) They are stepping down from a curb.
(B) They are tying their shoelaces.
(C) They are lifting bags with their hands.
(D) They are walking next to each other.

(A) 他們正踏下路緣。
(B) 他們正在綁鞋帶。
(C) 他們正在用手提起包包。
(D) 他們正並肩走在一起。

■ 兩人以上的照片 答案 (D)

仔細觀察照片中一對男女正在下樓梯的模樣。

(A) [╳] 照片中沒有出現路緣（curb），因此是錯誤選項。注意不要聽到 They are stepping down（他們正踏下）就選擇這個答案。

(B) [╳] tying（正在綁）和照片中的人物動作無關，因此是錯誤選項。這裡使用照片中有出現的鞋帶（shoelaces）來造成混淆。

(C) [╳] 照片中的人背著包包，這裡卻描述成用手提，因此是錯誤選項。

(D) [○] 這裡正確描述並肩行走的模樣 ，所以是正確答案。

單字 curb [美 kɝb 英 kə:b]（街道的）路緣 tie [taɪ] 綁 shoelace [ˋʃuˏles] 鞋帶 lift [lɪft] 提起

5 高

加拿大式發音

(A) An advertisement is being taken down.
(B) Shoppers are paying for sweaters.
(C) Some clothing has been put on display.
(D) A scarf has been draped over a rack.

(A) 正在撤下一則廣告。
(B) 購物者正在付錢買毛衣。
(C) 一些衣服被陳列著。
(D) 一條圍巾垂掛在架子上。

■ 事物及風景照片 答案 (C)

仔細觀察照片中購物中心陳列著假人模特兒的模樣，以及周遭事物的狀態。

(A) [╳] 透過照片無法得知是否正在撤下廣告，因此是錯誤選項。這裡使用和照片拍攝地點的購物中心有關的 advertisement（廣告）來造成混淆

(B) [╳] 照片中沒有人，選項中卻出現 Shoppers（購物者），因此是錯誤選項。

(C) [○] 這裡正確描述衣服被擺出來陳列的模樣，所以是正確答案。這裡必須知道 put on display 是指「陳列的狀態」。

(D) [╳] 圍巾圍在假人模特兒身上，這裡卻描述成垂掛在架子上，因此是錯誤選項。注意不要聽到 A scarf has been draped（一條圍巾垂掛著）就選擇這個選項。

單字 take down 拿下，撤下 be put on display（擺出來）陳列，展示 drape [drep] 垂掛；裝飾 rack [ræk] 架子

6 ○●●●● 高

	美式發音 (A) Containers are being piled up on a deck. (B) Passengers are disembarking from a ship. (C) A vessel is sailing through the water. (D) Storage crates are being unloaded from a boat.	(A) 正在把貨櫃堆上甲板。 (B) 乘客正在從船上下來。 (C) 一艘船正在水上航行。 (D) 正在從船上卸下儲存箱。

事物及風景照片 答案 (C)

仔細觀察照片中的船在水上航行的模樣，以及周遭事物的狀態。

(A) [╳] 貨櫃已經在甲板上了，這裡卻使用現在進行式被動語態（are being piled up）描述為正在堆，因此是錯誤選項。這裡使用照片中有出現的貨櫃（Containers）和甲板（deck）來造成混淆。

(B) [╳] 透過照片無法確認乘客（Passengers）的存在，因此是錯誤選項。這裡使用照片中有出現的船（ship）來造成混淆。

(C) [○] 這裡正確描述船在水上航行的模樣 ，所以是正確答案。

(D) [╳] 照片中雖然有箱子，但沒有正在從船上卸下（are being unloaded）箱子，因此是錯誤選項。這裡使用照片中有出現的儲存箱（Storage crates）和船（boat）來造成混淆。

單字 deck [dɛk] 甲板 disembark [ˌdɪsɪm`bɑrk] 下（車、船、飛機等交通工具） vessel [`vɛsl̩] 船 sail [sel] 航行 crate 條板箱；（分格而用來運送瓶裝物的）貨箱

7 低

澳洲式發音 → 美式發音

When did you start seeking another job?

(A) A few days ago.
(B) It's a good start.
(C) At the employment agency.

你什麼時候開始找其他工作的？

(A) 幾天前。
(B) 這是一個好的開始。
(C) 在就業服務處。

When 疑問句 答案 (A)

這是詢問對方在什麼時候開始找其他工作的 When 疑問句。

(A) [○] 這裡回答幾天前，提到開始找其他工作的時間點，因此是正確答案。

(B) [╳] 題目詢問什麼時候開始找其他工作，這裡卻回答是一個好的開始，毫不相關，因此是錯誤選項。這裡以名詞字義「開始」來重複使用題目中的動詞 start（開始），企圖造成混淆。

(C) [╳] 題目詢問什麼時候開始找其他工作，這裡卻回答地點，因此是錯誤選項。這裡利用與題目的 When 發音相似的 Where 來造成混淆，注意不要因為聽成 Where did you start seeking another job（你在哪裡開始找其他工作的）而選錯答案。

單字　seek [sik] 尋求　employment agency 就業服務處

8 低

英式發音 → 加拿大式發音

How long did medical school take for you to complete?

(A) I'm glad they're finally done.
(B) Dr. Robinson is my physician.
(C) Almost six years.

你花了多長時間讀完醫學院？

(A) 我很高興他們終於結束了。
(B) Robinson 醫生是我的醫生。
(C) 將近六年。

How 疑問句 答案 (C)

這是詢問讀完醫學院花了多長時間的 How 疑問句。這裡必須知道 How long 是在詢問期間。

(A) [╳] 這是利用和題目中 complete（完成）意義相近的 done（結束）來造成混淆的錯誤選項。

(B) [╳] 這是利用和 medical school（醫學院）相關的 physician（醫生）來造成混淆的錯誤選項。

(C) [○] 這裡回答將近六年，提到讀完醫學院所需的時間，因此是正確答案。

單字　medical school 醫學院　complete [kəm`plit] 完成　physician [fɪ`zɪʃən] 醫生；內科醫生

9 中

加拿大式發音 → 美式發音

What date should we get together?

(A) Let me get a table.
(B) We left on July 21.
(C) I'm not really sure.

我們應該要在哪天相聚？

(A) 讓我去訂個位子。
(B) 我們在 7 月 21 日離開了。
(C) 我不太確定。

What 疑問句 答案 (C)

這是詢問應該要在哪天相聚的 What 疑問句。這裡一定要聽到 What date 才能順利作答。

(A) [╳] 題目詢問要在哪天相聚，這裡卻回答自己要去訂位，毫不相關，因此是錯誤選項。這裡利用題目 get together（相聚）中 get 的另一字義「取得」來造成混淆。

(B) [╳] 這是藉重複使用題目中出現的 we 及表示日期的 July 21（7 月 21 日）來造成混淆的錯誤選項。

(C) [○] 這裡回答不太確定，間接表示不知道要在哪天相聚，因此是正確答案。

單字　get together 相聚

10 ○○●低

英式發音 → 澳洲式發音	
Who left these tools out all night?	是誰把這些工具留在外面一整晚的？
(A) Yes, put them in here. (B) The entire evening. (C) I did.	(A) 是的，把它們放在這裡面。 (B) 整個晚上。 (C) 是我。

Who 疑問句 答案 (C)

這是詢問是誰把工具留在外面一整晚的 Who 疑問句。

(A) [╳] 這裡以 Yes 來回答疑問詞疑問句，因此是錯誤選項。這裡以可以代稱題目中 tools（工具）的 them 來造成混淆。

(B) [╳] 題目詢問是誰把工具留在外面一整晚，這裡卻回答一段期間，因此是錯誤選項。這裡利用和 all night（一整晚）相關的時間表達 entire evening（整個晚上）來造成混淆。

(C) [○] 這裡回答是自己，提到把工具留在外面一整晚的人，因此是正確答案。

單字 all night 一整晚

11 ○●●中

美式發音 → 英式發音	
Was the moving company willing to reschedule on short notice?	搬家公司願意臨時改期嗎？
(A) I appreciate your being so flexible. (B) It fortunately was. (C) By moving the furniture.	(A) 感謝你這麼有彈性。 (B) 很幸運它願意。 (C) 透過移動家具。

Be 動詞疑問句 答案 (B)

這是確認搬家公司是否願意臨時改期的 Be 動詞疑問句。

(A) [╳] 這是利用和 reschedule（重新安排時間）相關的 flexible（有彈性的）來造成混淆的錯誤選項。

(B) [○] 這裡回答很幸運它願意，表示搬家公司願意臨時改期，因此是正確答案。

(C) [╳] 題目確認搬家公司是否願意臨時改期，這裡卻回答方法，因此是錯誤選項。這裡利用重複題目中出現的 moving 來造成混淆。

單字 moving company 搬家公司 flexible [`flɛksəbl] 有彈性的 fortunately [[美] `fɔrtʃənɪtlɪ [英] `fɔ:tʃənitli] 幸運地

12 ○●●中

澳洲式發音 → 美式發音	
Don't you want to apply to become the department head?	你不想申請成為部門主管嗎？
(A) Toward the head of the line. (B) A late departure time. (C) I don't feel ready for it.	(A) 朝著隊伍的最前頭。 (B) 晚了的出發時間。 (C) 我覺得我還沒準備好。

否定疑問句 答案 (C)

這是詢問對方是否想申請成為部門主管的否定疑問句。

(A) [╳] 這裡利用題目中 head（主管）的另一字義「最前頭」來造成混淆。

(B) [╳] 題目詢問是否想申請成為部門主管，這裡卻回答晚了的出發時間，毫不相關，因此是錯誤選項。這裡利用發音相似單字 department – departure 來造成混淆。

(C) [○] 這裡回答覺得自己還沒準備好，間接表示不會申請成為部門主管，因此是正確答案。

單字 apply [ə`plaɪ] 申請 departure [dɪ`pɑrtʃɚ] 出發

13 ○○●●● 中

🔊 加拿大式發音 → 英式發音 How did tennis with Mitch go on Monday? (A) Youth tennis courses are popular. (B) We both enjoyed it. (C) Can he drive on Tuesday instead?	星期一和 Mitch 打網球打得怎麼樣？ (A) 青年網球課程很受歡迎。 (B) 我們都很享受。 (C) 他能改在星期二開車嗎？

How 疑問句 答案 (B)

這是詢問對方星期一和 Mitch 打網球打得如何的 How 疑問句。

(A) [╳] 題目詢問星期一和 Mitch 打網球打得如何，這裡卻回答青年網球課程很受歡迎，毫不相關，因此是錯誤選項。這裡利用重複題目中出現的 tennis 來造成混淆。

(B) [○] 這裡回答自己和 Mitch 都很享受，表示星期一和 Mitch 打網球打得很開心，因此是正確答案。

(C) [╳] 這是使用可以代稱題目中 Mitch 的 he 及和 Monday（星期一）相關的 Tuesday（星期二）來造成混淆的錯誤選項。

單字 youth [juθ] 青年；年輕 course [[美] kors [英] kɔ:s] 課程

14 ○○○●● 低

🔊 澳洲式發音 → 英式發音 Why is the CEO leaving early? (A) He has to take part in a workshop. (B) Probably around 8:30. (C) His name is Steve Erickson.	執行長為什麼提早離開了？ (A) 他必須參加一個工作坊。 (B) 大概 8 點 30 分左右。 (C) 他的名字是 Steve Erickson。

Why 疑問句 答案 (A)

這是詢問執行長為什麼提早離開的 Why 疑問句。

(A) [○] 這裡回答他必須參加一個工作坊，提到提早離開的原因，因此是正確答案。

(B) [╳] 題目詢問執行長為什麼提早離開，這裡卻回答時間，因此是錯誤選項。

(C) [╳] 題目詢問執行長為什麼提早離開，這裡卻回答他的名字是 Steve Erickson，毫不相關，因此是錯誤選項。這裡利用可以代稱 CEO（執行長）的 His 來造成混淆。

單字 take part in 參加～ probably [`prɑbəblɪ] 大概

15 ○○●●● 中

🔊 美式發音 → 加拿大式發音 I plan to purchase a house later this fall. (A) I want to see your place once you move. (B) In the bedroom. (C) The blueprints have gone missing.	我計畫在今年秋天晚一點買間房子。 (A) 等你搬了我想去看看你家。 (B) 在臥室裡。 (C) 藍圖已經不見了。

陳述句 答案 (A)

這是表達自己計畫在今年秋天晚一點買間房子的客觀事實陳述句。

(A) [○] 這裡回答等對方搬家想去看房子，表達自己對這件事的期待，因此是正確答案。

(B) [╳] 這是利用和 house（房子）有關的 bedroom（臥室）來造成混淆的錯誤選項。

(C) [╳] 這是利用可以透過 house（房子）聯想到的建築物 blueprints（藍圖）來造成混淆的錯誤選項。

單字 purchase [`pɝtʃəs] 購買 blueprint [`blu`prɪnt] 藍圖 missing [`mɪsɪŋ] 遺失的

16 ○○●● 中

加拿大式發音 → 美式發音	
What event did you and Jonas go to last weekend? (A) There's a fashion show tomorrow. (B) We saw a concert in New Jersey. (C) He decided to.	你和 Jonas 上週末去了什麼活動？ (A) 明天有一場時裝秀。 (B) 我們在紐澤西看了一場演唱會。 (C) 他決定要做。

What 疑問句 答案 (B)

這是詢問對方和 Jonas 上週末去了什麼活動的 What 疑問句。這裡一定要聽到 What event 才能順利作答。

(A) [╳] 題目詢問對方和 Jonas 上週末去了什麼活動，這裡卻以現在式回答明天有時裝秀，因此是錯誤選項。這裡利用和 event（活動）有關的 fashion show（時裝秀）來造成混淆。

(B) [○] 這裡回答在紐澤西看了一場演唱會，提到自己和 Jonas 上週末去了什麼活動，因此是正確答案。

(C) [╳] 題目詢問對方和 Jonas 上週末去了什麼活動，這裡卻回答他決定要去，毫不相關，因此是錯誤選項。這裡使用可以代稱題目中 Jonas 的 He 來造成混淆。

單字 decide [dɪˋsaɪd] 決定

17 ○●●● 高

澳洲式發音 → 英式發音	
Aren't we operating a booth at the agricultural convention? (A) Our overseas operations. (B) There weren't any spaces available. (C) Driving would be more convenient.	我們在農業大會上不是要擺一個攤位嗎？ (A) 我們的海外事業。 (B) 沒有能用的地方了。 (C) 開車會更方便。

否定疑問句 答案 (B)

這是確認是否要在農業大會上擺一個攤位的否定疑問句。

(A) [╳] 這是利用發音相似單字 operating – operations 來造成混淆的錯誤選項。

(B) [○] 這裡回答沒有能用的地方了，間接表示不會在農業大會上擺攤，因此是正確答案。

(C) [╳] 題目詢問是否要在農業大會上擺攤，這裡卻回答開車會更方便，毫不相關，因此是錯誤選項。這裡利用發音相似單字 convention – convenient 來造成混淆。

單字 agricultural [͵ægrɪˋkʌltʃərəl] 農業的 operation [㊡ ͵ɑpəˋreʃən ㊣ ͵ɔpəˋreiʃən] 事業；營運
convenient [㊡ kənˋvinjənt ㊣ kənˋvi:njənt] 方便的

18 ○○○● 低

加拿大式發音 → 美式發音	
Have you enrolled in a photography class yet? (A) Glass items should be recycled. (B) He takes nice pictures. (C) Yes, it begins tomorrow.	你報名攝影課了嗎？ (A) 玻璃製品應該要回收。 (B) 他很會拍照。 (C) 是的，課明天開始。

助動詞疑問句 答案 (C)

這是確認對方是否已報名攝影課的助動詞（Have）疑問句。

(A) [╳] 題目詢問是否已報名攝影課，這裡卻回答玻璃製品應該要回收，毫不相關，因此是錯誤選項。這裡利用發音相似單字 class – Glass 來造成混淆。

(B) [╳] 題目中沒有 He 能代稱的對象，因此是錯誤選項。這裡利用和 photography（攝影）相關的 takes ~ pictures（拍照）來造成混淆。

(C) [○] 這裡回答 Yes 表示自己已報名攝影課，並附加說明課明天開始，提供更多資訊，因此是正確答案。

單字 enroll [ɪnˋrol] 報名 photography [fəˋtɑgrəfɪ] 攝影 recycle [riˋsaɪkl] 回收

19 ●●● 高

澳洲式發音 → 英式發音 I'm supposed to film a video of the guest speaker, right? (A) You can use this equipment. (B) The video was very well produced. (C) I suppose we'll require a vehicle.	我應該要拍一支客座講者的影片，對嗎？ (A) 你可以用這個設備。 (B) 這支影片製作得非常好。 (C) 我猜我們會需要一台車。

附加問句 答案 (A)

這是確認自己是否應該要拍一支客座講者的影片的附加問句。

(A) [○] 這裡回答可以用這個設備，間接肯定對方是應該要拍客座講者的影片沒錯，因此是正確答案。

(B) [╳] 題目詢問自己是否應該要拍一支客座講者的影片，這裡卻回答影片製作得非常好，毫不相關，因此是錯誤選項。這裡透過重複使用題目中出現的 video 來造成混淆。

(C) [╳] 這是利用字義是「猜想」的 suppose 來重複使用題目中的 supposed（應該～），企圖造成混淆的錯誤選項。

單字 be supposed to 應該～ guest speaker 客座講者 equipment [ɪ`kwɪpmənt] 設備
produce [prə`djus] 製作 suppose [㊈ sə`poz ㊇ sə`pəuz] 猜想；假定 require [rɪ`kwaɪr] 需要

20 ●●○ 中

英式發音 → 加拿大式發音 The gym on Halifax Road is now open. (A) Just close the door. (B) I'll stop by later today. (C) No, I canceled my membership.	Halifax 路上的健身房現在開了。 (A) 把門關上就對了。 (B) 我今天晚點會過去一趟。 (C) 不，我取消我的會員資格了。

陳述句 答案 (B)

這是表達 Halifax 路上的健身房現在開了的客觀事實陳述句。

(A) [╳] 題目說 Halifax 路上的健身房現在開了，這裡卻回答把門關上，毫不相關，因此是錯誤選項。這裡利用和題目中 open（開放的）意義上相反的 close（關閉）來造成混淆。

(B) [○] 這裡回答自己今天晚點會過去一趟，表示會去 Halifax 路上的健身房，因此是正確答案。

(C) [╳] 這是利用和 gym（健身房）相關的 membership（會員資格）來造成混淆的錯誤選項。

單字 stop by 短暫停留；順道拜訪

21 ●●● 高

美式發音 → 澳洲式發音 Why don't we update the information on our Web site? (A) You can order it online. (B) The site on Oak Street. (C) Yes, that's long overdue.	我們要不要更新我們網站上的資訊啊？ (A) 你可以在網路上訂購它。 (B) 在 Oak 街上的那個地方。 (C) 好，早該做這件事了。

提議疑問句 答案 (C)

這是提議要更新網站資訊的提議疑問句。這裡必須知道 Why don't we 是用來表示提議的表達。

(A) [╳] 這是利用與 Web site（網站）相關的 online（在網路上）來造成混淆的錯誤選項。

(B) [╳] 題目提議要更新網站資訊，這裡卻回答地點，毫不相關，因此是錯誤選項。這裡透過重複使用題目中出現的 site 來造成混淆。

(C) [○] 這裡以 Yes 表示同意提議，並附加說明早該做這件事了，因此是正確答案。

單字 long [㊈ lɔŋ ㊇ lɔŋ] 長久的 overdue [㊈ `ovə`dju ㊇ `əuvə`dju:] 延誤的；過期的

22 ○○●● 中

加拿大式發音 → 英式發音	
The fabric for the new curtain will arrive very soon.	新窗簾的布料會非常快送到。
(A) That's good to know. (B) The window in the kitchen. (C) The shuttle bus hasn't arrived.	(A) 太好了。 (B) 廚房的窗戶。 (C) 接駁車還沒到。

陳述句 答案 (A)

這是表達新窗簾的布料會非常快送到的客觀事實陳述句。

(A) [○] 這裡回答太好了，提出自己對這件事實的意見，因此是正確答案。

(B) [╳] 這是透過可以從 curtain（窗簾）聯想到的地點 window in the kitchen（廚房的窗戶）來造成混淆的是錯誤選項。

(C) [╳] 題目說新窗簾的布料會非常快送到，這裡卻回答接駁車還沒到，毫不相關，因此是錯誤選項。這裡以 arrived 來重複使用題目中出現的 arrive，企圖造成混淆。

單字 fabric [ˋfæbrɪk] 布料；織物

23 ○○●● 中

澳洲式發音 → 美式發音	
When must my existing credit card balance be paid?	我現在剩下的信用卡費必須要在什麼時候付？
(A) I believe I've been overcharged. (B) You gave me those cards. (C) By the end of the month.	(A) 我認為我被超收了費用。 (B) 你給了我那些卡片。 (C) 在這個月底之前。

When 疑問句 答案 (C)

這是詢問自己現在剩下的信用卡費必須要在什麼時候付的 When 疑問句。

(A) [╳] 這是利用和 credit card（信用卡）相關的 overcharged（超收了費用）來造成混淆的錯誤選項。

(B) [╳] 題目詢問自己現在剩下的信用卡費必須要在什麼時候付，這裡卻回答對方給了自己那些卡片，毫不相關，因此是錯誤選項。這裡以 cards 重複使用題目中出現的 card 來造成混淆。

(C) [○] 這裡回答在這個月底之前，表示在這個月底之前必須支付剩下的信用卡費，因此是正確答案。

單字 existing [ɪgˋzɪstɪŋ] 現有的 credit card 信用卡 balance [ˋbæləns] 餘額
overcharge [ˋovɚˋtʃɑrdʒ] 超收費用

24 ○●●● 高

英式發音 → 加拿大式發音	
Is Brandon still taking his break, or did he return to work?	Brandon 是還在休息還是已經回來工作了？
(A) We took Flight 362. (B) I still need supplies. (C) He's at his desk right now.	(A) 我們搭了 362 號航班。 (B) 我還是需要補給品。 (C) 他現在正在他的座位上。

選擇疑問句 答案 (C)

這是詢問 Brandon 是還在休息還是已經回來工作了的選擇疑問句。

(A) [╳] 這是以字義是「搭乘」的 took 重複使用題目中出現的 taking（採用）來造成混淆的錯誤選項。

(B) [╳] 題目詢問 Brandon 是還在休息還是已經回來工作了，這裡卻回答自己還是需要補給品，毫不相關，因此是錯誤選項。這裡透過重複題目中出現的 still 來造成混淆。

(C) [○] 這裡回答他現在正在他的座位上，間接表示 Brandon 已經回來工作了，因此是正確答案。

單字 take a break（短暫）休息 flight [flaɪt] 航班；班機 supply [səˋplaɪ] 補給品

25 ○●●中

澳洲式發音 → 英式發音	
We should hold a training session for new employees.	我們應該為新員工舉辦培訓課程。
(A) All former personnel. (B) I've already organized one. (C) Basic software skills.	(A) 所有之前的員工。 (B) 我已經籌劃了一堂。 (C) 基礎的軟體技巧。

陳述句 答案 (B)

這是表示應該為新員工舉辦培訓課程的陳述句。

(A) [╳] 這是透過和 employees（員工）意思相近的 personnel（員工）來造成混淆的錯誤選項。

(B) [○] 這裡回答已經籌劃了一堂，表示將會為新員工舉辦培訓課程，因此是正確答案。

(C) [╳] 這是利用可以透過 training session（培訓課程）聯想到的課程相關內容 Basic software skills（基礎的軟體技巧）來造成混淆的錯誤選項。

單字 former [㊥ ˋfɔrmɚ ㊕ ˋfɔ:mə] 之前的 personnel [㊥ ˌpɝsn̩ˋɛl ㊕ ˌpə:səˋnel]（總稱）員工
organize [㊥ ˋɔrgəˌnaɪz ㊕ ˋɔ:gənaiz] 籌劃，籌辦 basic [ˋbesɪk] 基礎的，基本的 skill [ˋskɪl] 技巧

26 ●●●高

英式發音 → 澳洲式發音	
Is the marketing presentation going to be completed by Friday?	行銷簡報會在星期五前完成嗎？
(A) We're actually ahead of schedule. (B) I didn't attend the seminar. (C) Wilbur's Supermarket has specials every day.	(A) 我們其實超前進度了。 (B) 我沒有參加那場研討會。 (C) Wilbur's 超市每天都有特價商品。

Be 動詞疑問句 答案 (A)

這是確認行銷簡報是否會在星期五前完成的 Be 動詞疑問句。

(A) [○] 這裡回答其實超前進度了，間接表示可以在星期五前完成，因此是正確答案。

(B) [╳] 這是利用和 presentation（簡報）相關的 seminar（研討會）來造成混淆的錯誤選項。

(C) [╳] 題目詢問行銷簡報是否會在星期五前完成，這裡卻回答 Wilbur's 超市每天都有特價商品，毫不相關，因此是錯誤選項。這裡利用發音相似單字 Friday – every day 來造成混淆。

單字 ahead of schedule 超前進度

27 ○●●中

加拿大式發音 → 美式發音	
Will you take care of the office plants or should I ask Karen to do it?	你會照顧辦公室裡的植物嗎？還是我應該請 Karen 來照顧？
(A) A pot of flowers. (B) I'd be happy to help. (C) I'll be more careful next time.	(A) 一盆花。 (B) 我很樂意幫忙。 (C) 下次我會更小心。

選擇疑問句 答案 (B)

這是詢問對方是否會照顧辦公室裡的植物，還是自己應該要請 Karen 來照顧的選擇疑問句。

(A) [╳] 這是利用和 plants（植物）相關的 pot of flowers（～盆花）來造成混淆的錯誤選項。

(B) [○] 這裡回答很樂意幫忙，表示自己會照顧辦公室裡的植物，因此是正確答案。

(C) [╳] 題目詢問對方是否會照顧辦公室裡的植物，還是自己應該要請 Karen 來照顧，這裡卻回答下次會更小心，毫不相關，因此是錯誤選項。這裡利用發音相似單字 care – careful 來造成混淆。

單字 take care of 照顧～；處理～ happy [ˋhæpɪ] 高興的；滿意的 careful [ˋkɛrfəl] 小心的；仔細的

28 ●●●●● 難

澳洲式發音 → 美式發音 Where can I set up a workstation? (A) The statue has been erected. (B) I thought you were assigned to another division. (C) Anytime after lunch.	我可以在哪裡設置工作站？ (A) 已經豎立了雕像。 (B) 我以為你被分派到其他部門了。 (C) 午餐之後的時間都可以。

Where 疑問句 答案 (B)

這是詢問自己可以在哪裡設置工作站的 Where 疑問句。

(A) [╳] 這是使用和題目中 set up（設置）意思相近的 erect（豎立）的過去式 erected 來造成混淆的錯誤選項。

(B) [○] 這裡回答以為對方被分派到其他部門了，間接表示自己不知道對方可以在哪裡設置工作站，因此是正確答案。

(C) [╳] 題目詢問自己可以在哪裡設置工作站，這裡卻回答時間點，因此是錯誤選項。這裡利用與題目的 Where 發音相似的 When 來造成混淆，注意不要因為聽成 When can I set up a workstation（我什麼時候可以設置工作站）而選擇這個選項。

單字 statue [ˋstætʃʊ] 雕像 erect [ɪˋrɛkt] 豎立 assign [əˋsaɪn] 分派 division [dəˋvɪʒən] 部門

29 ●●●○○ 中

英式發音 → 加拿大式發音 The sales forecast has changed due to the shortage of raw materials. (A) It's a pretty short documentary. (B) I just heard the weather forecast. (C) By how much?	銷售預測因為原物料短缺而更改了。 (A) 這是一部滿短的紀錄片。 (B) 我剛剛聽了氣象預報。 (C) 改了多少？

陳述句 答案 (C)

這是表示銷售預測因為原物料短缺而更改的客觀事實陳述句。

(A) [╳] 這是利用發音相似單字 shortage – short 來造成混淆的錯誤選項。

(B) [╳] 題目說銷售預測因為原物料短缺而更改，這裡卻回答自己剛剛聽了氣象預報，毫不相關，因此是錯誤選項。這裡利用重複使用題目中出現的 forecast 來造成混淆。

(C) [○] 這裡反問改了多少，要求提供銷售預測更改幅度的更多資訊，因此是正確答案。

單字 forecast [美 ˋforˏkæst 英 ˋfɔ:kɑ:st] 預測，預報 shortage [美 ˋʃɔrtɪdʒ 英 ˋʃɔ:tidʒ] 不足，短缺
raw material 原物料

30 ●●●○○ 中

加拿大式發音 → 英式發音 Are your current sneakers as comfortable as your previous pair? (A) I'd say they're fairly similar. (B) This color suits you better. (C) She bought them yesterday.	你現在的運動鞋和你以前的那雙一樣舒服嗎？ (A) 我覺得它們相當類似。 (B) 這顏色比較適合你。 (C) 她昨天買了它們。

Be 動詞疑問句 答案 (A)

這是確認對方現在的運動鞋是否和以前的那雙一樣舒服的 Be 動詞疑問句。

(A) [○] 這裡回答覺得它們相當類似，表示新運動鞋和以前的那雙一樣舒服，因此是正確答案。

(B) [╳] 這是利用能夠從 sneakers（運動鞋）聯想到的 color suits（顏色適合）來造成混淆的錯誤選項。

(C) [╳] 題目中沒有能用 She 代稱的對象，因此是錯誤選項。這裡透過可以代稱題目中 sneakers（運動鞋）的 them 來造成混淆。

單字 current [ˋkɝənt] 當前的，現在的 comfortable [ˋkʌmfɚtəbl̩] 舒服的 previous [ˋpriviəs] 以前的
fairly [美 ˋfɛrlɪ 英 ˋfɛəli] 相當，非常 suit [sut] 適合

31 ●●●●● 難

🔊 澳洲式發音 → 美式發音 Which type of cake should we bring to Louis's birthday party? (A) He was very pleased with the gift. (B) Yes, try the ice cream too. (C) I had to choose last time.	我們該帶哪種蛋糕去 Louis 的生日派對？ (A) 他那時對這個禮物非常滿意。 (B) 沒錯，也試試這個冰淇淋吧。 (C) 上次我不得不選過了。

Which 疑問句 答案 (C)

這是詢問該帶哪種蛋糕去 Louis 的生日派對的 Which 疑問句。這裡一定要聽到 Which type of cake 才能順利作答。

(A) [╳] 這是利用和 birthday party（生日派對）相關的 gift（禮物）來造成混淆的錯誤選項。

(B) [╳] 這裡以 Yes 來回答疑問詞疑問句，因此是錯誤選項。這裡利用能夠從 cake（蛋糕）聯想到的 ice cream（冰淇淋）來造成混淆。

(C) [○] 這裡回答上次自己不得不選過了，間接表示自己這次不想再選要帶哪種蛋糕去 Louis 的生日派對，因此是正確答案。

單字 pleased with 對～滿意

32
33
34

Questions 32-34 refer to the following conversation.

美式發音 → 加拿大式發音

W: [32]**I just heard that Malinda can't stay until 5 P.M. Her son isn't feeling well, so she has to leave work early in order to get him from school.** [33]**Would you be able to cover her duties?**

M: [33]**Sure.** But can you be more specific about what I'll need to do?

W: She's currently checking in gym members and answering phone calls at the main desk, so I'd like you to do that. Seeing as [34]**you used to be a receptionist at an advertising company**, you should be able to handle everything.

M: Well, I'm not very familiar with our registration system, but I'm sure I'll manage.

第 32-34 題請參考下列對話。

女：[32] 我剛聽說 Malinda 無法待到下午 5 點。她兒子身體不舒服，所以她得早點下班好去學校接他。[33] 你能幫她代班嗎？

男：[33] 當然。但妳能再具體一點跟我説我得做什麼嗎？

女：她現在在主櫃台替健身房會員報到和接電話，我想要你去做這些事。既然 [34] 你曾當過廣告公司的接待人員，你應該能處理所有事情。

男：這個嘛，我對我們的登記系統不是很熟，不過我一定會設法處理好的。

32 Why is Malinda unable to stay until 5 P.M.?

(A) She is not feeling very well.
(B) She must get a family member.
(C) She has to drop off some supplies.
(D) She will go to a school function.

32 Malinda 為什麼無法待到下午 5 點？

(A) 她身體不太舒服。
(B) 她必須去接一個家人。
(C) 她得去送一些補給品。
(D) 她會去一場學校的活動。

33 What does the man agree to do?

(A) Call a receptionist
(B) Interview an applicant
(C) Show people around a gym
(D) Fill in for a colleague

33 男子同意做什麼？

(A) 致電一位接待人員
(B) 面試一位應徵者
(C) 帶人參觀健身房
(D) 替一位同事代班

34 According to the woman, where did the man previously work?

(A) At a fitness center
(B) At an advertising firm
(C) At a construction company
(D) At a recruitment agency

34 根據女子所説，男子之前在哪裡工作？

(A) 健身中心
(B) 廣告公司
(C) 建築公司
(D) 人力仲介

題目 leave work 下班　cover [ˋkʌvɚ] 頂替　duty [ˋdjutɪ] 職務　receptionist [rɪˋsɛpʃənɪst] 接待人員　handle [ˋhændl̩] 處理　manage [ˋmænɪdʒ] 設法做到

32 drop off 帶去（某地點）　function [ˋfʌŋkʃən] 盛大的集會活動

33 interview [ˋɪntɚˏvju] 面試　applicant [ˋæpləkənt] 應徵者　show around 帶～參觀　fill in for 臨時頂替～

32 低 細節事項相關問題—理由 答案 (B)

題目詢問 Malinda 無法待到下午 5 點的理由，因此要注意聽和題目關鍵字（unable to stay until 5 P.M.）相關的內容。女子說：「I just heard that Malinda can't stay until 5 P.M. Her son isn't feeling well, so she has to leave work early in order to get him from school.」，表示剛剛聽說 Malinda 無法待到下午 5 點，因為她兒子身體不舒服，所以她得提早下班去接他，因此正確答案是 (B) She must get a family member.。

33 中 細節事項相關問題—特定細項 答案 (D)

題目詢問男子同意做什麼，因此要注意聽和題目關鍵字（agree to do）相關的內容。女子對男子說：「Would you be able to cover her[Malinda's] duties?」，詢問男子是否可以替 Malinda 代班，男子說：「Sure.」，表示可以，因此正確答案是 (D) Fill in for a colleague。

換句話說

cover ~ duties 代～的班 → Fill in for ~ 替～代班

34 低 細節事項相關問題—特定細項 答案 (B)

題目詢問女子說男子以前在哪裡工作，因此要注意聽女子話中和題目關鍵字（man previously work）相關的內容。女子對男子說：「you used to be a receptionist at an advertising company」，表示男子曾當過廣告公司的接待人員，因此正確答案是 (B) At an advertising firm。

35
36
37

Questions 35-37 refer to the following conversation.

英式發音 → 澳洲式發音

W: It seems as if more people have been stopping by our store in recent weeks. That's probably because [35]**we've started selling albums that are hard to find on the Internet.**

M: Yes, I think you're right. But [35]**we're still losing a lot of customers to online music retailers.** To ensure that people keep coming, [36]**we should ask some regional bands and singers to appear here at our business.**

W: Funny you should suggest that. [37]**I've already reached out to several jazz and blues musicians in the area to see if they could come and sign autographs here. That's what many customers indicated they want in our satisfaction survey.**

35 Where do the speakers most likely work?

(A) At a concert hall
(B) At a clothing retail outlet
(C) At a record store
(D) At an electronics repair shop

36 What does the man recommend?

(A) Selling merchandise online
(B) Contacting local performers
(C) Organizing jazz concerts
(D) Giving away prizes

37 According to the woman, what do some customers want?

(A) Artists' signatures
(B) Musical instruments
(C) Limited edition posters
(D) New albums

第 35-37 題請參考下列對話。

女：最近幾週好像有比較多人來我們店裡。這可能是因為 [35] 我們開始賣那些很難在網路上找到的專輯了。

男：沒錯，我想妳是對的。但 [35] 我們還是因為線上音樂零售商而流失了很多客人。為了確保人會一直來，[36] 我們應該要請一些地區樂團和歌手到我們店這裡露面。

女：這麼巧你提了這個建議。[37] 我已經聯繫了這區裡的幾位爵士和藍調音樂家，看看他們能不能來這裡進行簽名。這是很多客人在我們的滿意度調查裡提到想要的。

35 說話者們最有可能在哪裡工作？

(A) 演奏廳
(B) 服裝零售商店
(C) 唱片行
(D) 電子產品維修行

36 男子建議什麼？

(A) 線上販售商品
(B) 聯繫地方的表演者
(C) 籌劃爵士音樂會
(D) 送出獎品

37 根據女子所說，有些客人想要什麼？

(A) 藝人的簽名
(B) 樂器
(C) 限量版海報
(D) 新專輯

題目 lose [luz] 失去　retailer [美 rɪ`telɚ 英 ri`teilə] 零售商　ensure [美 ɪn`ʃʊr 英 in`ʃuə] 確保　regional [`ridʒənḷ] 地區的　sign an autograph（親筆）簽名　satisfaction [͵sætɪs`fækʃən] 滿意度

35 retail outlet 零售商店　electronics [ɪlɛk`trɑnɪks] 電子產品

36 give away 送出；發放　prize [praɪz] 獎品

37 signature [`sɪgnətʃɚ] 簽名

35 高　**整體對話相關問題—說話者**　答案 (C)

題目詢問說話者的工作地點，因此要注意聽和身分、職業相關的表達。女子說：「we've started selling albums that are hard to find on the Internet」，表示店內開始賣在網路難尋的專輯，接著說：「we're still losing a lot of customers to online music retailers」，表示這間店因為線上音樂零售商而流失了很多客人，由此可知，說話者是在唱片行工作，因此正確答案是 (C) At a record store。

36 中　**細節事項相關問題—提議**　答案 (B)

題目詢問男子建議什麼，因此必須注意聽男子話中出現提議相關表達的句子。男子說：「we should ask some regional bands and singers to appear here at our business」，建議應該要請一些地區樂團和歌手到店裡露面，因此正確答案是 (B) Contacting local performers。

換句話說

regional bands and singers 地區樂團和歌手 → local performers 地方的表演者

37 中　**細節事項相關問題—特定細項**　答案 (A)

題目詢問女子說客人想要什麼，因此要注意聽女子說的話中和題目關鍵字（customers want）相關及前後的內容。女子說：「I've already reached out to several ~ musicians ~ to see if they could come and sign autographs here. That's what many customers indicated they want in our satisfaction survey.」，表示自己已經聯繫了幾位音樂家，看看他們能不能來唱片行進行簽名，而請藝人來簽名這件事是很多客人想要的，因此正確答案是 (A) Artists' signatures。

Questions 38-40 refer to the following conversation.

英式發音 → 加拿大式發音

W: Excuse me. [38]**I'd like to leave my car in this indoor parking lot for a couple of hours** while I run some errands. [39]**My husband works at a dental clinic down the street**, and he gave me his parking pass. Can I use it here?

M: Unfortunately, it looks like your husband's pass expired two days ago. You'll have to pay to use our space.

W: Oh, OK. How does the payment process work?

M: The fee for parking is $3.50 an hour. Here . . . I'll print a new ticket for you. [40]**When you leave, you can insert it into the machine located near the exit and pay using cash or credit card.**

38 Where most likely does the conversation take place?

(A) At a bus terminal
(B) At a park
(C) At a garage
(D) At a car dealership

39 What does the woman say about her husband?

(A) He forgot to print a document.
(B) He wants to buy a monthly pass.
(C) He is employed by a nearby business.
(D) He is running some errands.

40 What should the woman do when she leaves?

(A) Make a payment
(B) Speak with an attendant
(C) Ask for a ticket
(D) Confirm an appointment

第 38-40 題請參考下列對話。

女：不好意思。[38] 我想在我去辦一些雜事的時候，把我的車停在這間室內停車場裡幾個小時。[39] 我先生在這條街上的一間牙醫診所工作，所以他把他的停車證給了我。我可以在這裡用嗎？

男：真不巧，看起來妳先生的停車證在兩天前到期了。妳必須付錢才能停我們這裡。

女：噢，好。這個錢要怎麼付？

男：停車費是一小時 3.50 美金。這裡⋯⋯我會印一張新的票給妳。[40] 妳離開的時候可以把它插到在出口附近的那台機器裡，然後用現金或信用卡付錢。

38 這段對話最有可能發生在哪裡？

(A) 公車總站
(B) 公園
(C) 停車場
(D) 汽車經銷商

39 關於她的先生，女子說什麼？

(A) 他忘了列印一份文件。
(B) 他想要買月票。
(C) 他受雇於附近的一家業者。
(D) 他正在辦一些雜事。

40 女子在離開時應該要做什麼？

(A) 付款
(B) 和服務人員說話
(C) 索取票券
(D) 確定預約

題目 indoor [(美) `ɪn͵dor (英) `ɪndɔ:] 室內的　errand [`ɛrənd] 雜事　parking pass 停車證　expire [ɪk`spaɪr] 到期
payment [`pemənt] 支付；支付款項　insert [ɪn`sɝt] 放入；插入　exit [`ɛksɪt] 出口

38 dealership [`dilɚ͵ʃɪp] 經銷商

40 attendant [ə`tɛndənt] 服務人員　confirm [kən`fɝm] 確定

38 ■ 整體對話相關問題—地點　答案 (C)

中

題目詢問對話的發生地點，因此要注意聽和地點相關的表達。女子說：「I'd like to leave my car in this indoor parking lot for a couple of hours」，表示想把車停在這間停車場幾個小時，由此可知，對話的發生地點在停車場，因此正確答案是 (C) At a garage。

換句話說

parking lot 停車場 → garage 停車場

39 ■ 細節事項相關問題—提及　答案 (C)

中

題目詢問女子提到什麼和自己先生有關的事，因此要注意聽和題目關鍵字（husband）相關及前後的內容。女子說：「My husband works at a dental clinic down the street」，表示自己先生在這條街上的牙醫診所內工作，因此正確答案是 (C) He is employed by a nearby business.。

40 ■ 細節事項相關問題—特定細項　答案 (A)

低

題目詢問女子離開時應該要做什麼，因此要注意聽和題目關鍵字（do when she leaves）相關的內容。男子對女子說：「When you leave, you can insert it[ticket] into the machine ~ and pay using cash or credit card.」，表示女子在離開時要把票插到出口附近的機器裡，然後用現金或信用卡付錢，因此正確答案是 (A) Make a payment。

41
42
43

Questions 41-43 refer to the following conversation.

美式發音 → 澳洲式發音

W: Tyler, have you read the quarterly sales report yet?
M: No. I'm planning to look through it on Thursday. [41]**I have to fly to Seattle this afternoon for . . . um . . . a trade exhibition, and I won't be back until Wednesday evening.** Why? Is there a problem?
W: Actually, there is. Sales of the company's latest dishwasher model are much lower than expected. [42]**The CEO wants our team to develop some new marketing strategies and present them tomorrow morning.** We don't have much time to prepare, so [43]**I could really use your assistance.**
M: I'll take a later flight, then. [43]**This sounds important, and I don't want to let the team down.**

第 41-43 題請參考下列對話。

女：Tyler，你看過季度銷售報告了嗎？
男：沒有，我打算星期四再來看。[41] 我今天下午必須飛去西雅圖參加……嗯……一場貿易展，而且我要到星期三晚上才會回來。怎麼了？有什麼問題嗎？
女：事實上是有。公司最新那款洗碗機的銷售量遠低預期。[42] 執行長要我們團隊制定一些新的行銷策略並在明天早上報告。我們沒多少時間能準備，所以 [43] 我真的很需要你的幫忙。
男：那我就搭晚一點的飛機吧。[43] 這聽起來很重要，而且我不想讓團隊失望。

41 When is the man planning to return from Seattle?
(A) On Tuesday
(B) On Wednesday
(C) On Thursday
(D) On Friday

41 男子打算什麼時候從西雅圖回來？
(A) 星期二
(B) 星期三
(C) 星期四
(D) 星期五

42 What will probably take place tomorrow morning?
(A) A product demonstration
(B) A sales workshop
(C) A marketing presentation
(D) A shareholders' meeting

42 明天早上可能會舉行什麼？
(A) 產品展示會
(B) 銷售工作坊
(C) 行銷報告
(D) 股東會議

43 Why does the man say, "I'll take a later flight, then"?
新
(A) To accept an upgrade
(B) To turn down a proposal
(C) To confirm a departure time
(D) To agree to a request

43 男子為什麼說：「那我就搭晚一點的飛機吧」？
(A) 為了接受升等
(B) 為了拒絕提議
(C) 為了確定出發時間
(D) 為了同意請求

題目 look through 瀏覽 exhibition [美 ˌɛksəˋbɪʃən 英 ˌeksiˋbiʃən] 展覽 latest [ˋletɪst] 最新的 strategy [ˋstrætədʒɪ] 策略 assistance [əˋsɪstəns] 幫助，協助 let down 使～失望
43 turn down 拒絕 proposal [prəˋpozl] 提議

41 細節事項相關問題—特定細項 答案 (B)
中
題目詢問男子打算什麼時候從西雅圖回來，因此要注意聽和題目關鍵字（return from Seattle）相關的內容。男子說：「I have to fly to Seattle this afternoon ~, and I won't be back until Wednesday evening.」，表示自己今天下午飛去西雅圖之後，要到星期三晚上才會回來，因此正確答案是 (B) On Wednesday。

42 細節事項相關問題—接下來要做的事 答案 (C)
中
題目詢問明天早上會舉行什麼，因此要注意聽和題目關鍵字（tomorrow morning）相關及前後的內容。女子說：「The CEO wants our team to develop some new marketing strategies and present them tomorrow morning.」，表示執行長要自己團隊制定一些新的行銷策略並在明天早上報告，因此正確答案是 (C) A marketing presentation。

新 **43** 細節事項相關問題—掌握意圖 答案 (D)
高
題目詢問男子說這句話的意圖，因此要注意聽與題目引用句（I'll take a later flight, then）相關及前後的內容。女子對男子說：「I could really use your assistance」，表示自己真的很需要男子的幫忙，後面男子則說：「This sounds important, and I don't want to let the team down.」，表示這個報告聽起來很重要，而且自己不想讓團隊失望，由此可知，男子說這句話是想要答應女子提出的請求，因此正確答案是 (D) To agree to a request。

44
45
46

Questions 44-46 refer to the following conversation.

英式發音 → 加拿大式發音

W: [44]**I'm thinking of getting lunch at the cafeteria in our office building today.** Do you want to join me?

M: No, thanks. I ate there when I started working here, and the food wasn't very good. I would prefer to dine at a restaurant.

W: Did you know that [45]**the food service company at our facility was changed last month in response to feedback from staff**? Beatrice Dining now provides meals. I find their dishes to be delicious.

M: I probably missed that piece of news while I was on vacation three weeks ago. In that case, [46]**I'd be happy to come along. Just let me finish writing this e-mail message first.**

44 What is the conversation mainly about?

(A) Hiring a personal chef
(B) Postponing a luncheon
(C) Eating at an on-site facility
(D) Extending a break period

45 According to the woman, why has there been a change?

(A) To respond to worker comments
(B) To improve safety measures
(C) To reduce company expenses
(D) To accommodate staff schedules

46 When will the man most likely join the woman?

(A) When a restaurant opens
(B) When a work trip ends
(C) When a menu is changed
(D) When a task is completed

第 44-46 題請參考下列對話。

女：[44] 我今天想在我們辦公大樓的自助餐廳吃午餐。你想要一起嗎？

男：不，謝了。我開始在這裡上班的時候去那裡吃過，那裡的食物不怎麼好吃。我比較喜歡去餐廳吃飯。

女：你知道 [45] 我們機構為了回應員工的回饋意見而在上個月更換了餐飲公司嗎？現在由 Beatrice Dining 供餐。我覺得他們的菜很好吃。

男：可能我在三個星期前去度假的時候錯過了這個消息。這樣的話，[46] 我很樂意一起去。只是要讓我先把這封電子郵件寫完。

44 這段對話主要與什麼有關？

(A) 聘用私人廚師
(B) 延後午餐餐會
(C) 在工作地點的設施裡吃飯
(D) 延長休息時間

45 根據女子所說，為什麼發生了改變？

(A) 為回應員工的意見
(B) 為改善安全措施
(C) 為減少公司開支
(D) 為配合員工的行程表

46 男子最有可能會在什麼時候和女子一起去？

(A) 當一間餐廳營業時
(B) 當一次出差結束時
(C) 當一份菜單變更時
(D) 當一項工作完成時

題目 dine [daɪn] 用餐　in response to 回應～　dish [dɪʃ] 菜餚　come along 一起去～
44 luncheon [ˋlʌntʃən] 午餐餐會　on-site 工作（進行）地點的
45 measure [ˋmɛʒɚ] 措施　expense [ɪkˋspɛns] 開支　accommodate [əˋkɑməˏdet] 配合

44 ■ **整體對話相關問題—主題**　答案 (C)
中

題目詢問對話主題，因此必須注意聽對話的開頭。女子對男子說：「I'm thinking of getting lunch at the cafeteria in our office building today. Do you want to join me?」，表示自己今天想在辦公大樓的自助餐廳吃午餐，並詢問男子是否要一起去，接著繼續談論與在餐廳吃飯有關的事，因此正確答案是 (C) Eating at an on-site facility。

換句話說
the cafeteria in ~ office building 辦公大樓的自助餐廳 → an on-site facility 工作地點的設施

45 ■ **細節事項相關問題—理由**　答案 (A)
高

題目詢問女子說發生改變的原因是什麼，因此要注意聽女子說的話中和題目關鍵字（change）相關的內容。女子說：「the food service company at our facility was changed ~ in response to feedback from staff」，表示公司為了回應員工的回饋意見而在上個月更換了餐飲公司，因此正確答案是 (A) To respond to worker comments。

46 ■ **細節事項相關問題—特定細項**　答案 (D)
中

題目詢問男子會在什麼時候和女子一起去，因此要注意聽和題目關鍵字（join the woman）相關的內容。男子對女子說：「I'd be happy to come along. Just let me finish writing this e-mail message first.」，表示很樂意一起去，並說自己要先寫完電子郵件再去，因此正確答案是 (D) When a task is completed。

換句話說
finish writing ~ e-mail message 寫完電子郵件 → a task is completed 一項工作完成

47
48
49

Questions 47-49 refer to the following conversation.

🔊 美式發音 → 澳洲式發音

W: Walter, [47]**I need you to update the staff manual for our investment bank's stock market research software.** Here's a copy of the current handbook.

M: Thanks. But . . . ah . . . [48]**when does the document need to be completed?**

W: You'll have three days to work on it. Also, you should make revisions based on the version of the software that our IT workers are developing now. I asked the team to provide you with a list of changes to the program.

M: Got it. But [49]**can I look at the manual in an electronic format instead of this printout?** It will be easier for me to refer to that.

第 47-49 題請參考下列對話。

女：Walter，[47] 我需要你去更新我們投資銀行的股市研究軟體的員工手冊。這裡有一本現行的手冊。

男：謝謝。不過……呃……[48] 這份文件需要在什麼時候完成？

女：你會有三天來處理這件事。此外，你應該要根據我們資訊科技人員現在正在開發的這個版本的軟體來進行修訂。

男：了解。但是 [49] 我可以看電子版的手冊而不是這種印出來的嗎？這樣對我來說要參考會比較簡單。

47 Where most likely do the speakers work?

(A) At a financial firm
(B) At a print shop
(C) At a research institute
(D) At an appliance manufacturer

44 說話者們最有可能在哪裡工作？

(A) 金融公司
(B) 影印店
(C) 研究機構
(D) 電器製造商

48 What does the man ask the woman about?

(A) A team's research results
(B) A document's size specifications
(C) An order's delivery date
(D) An assignment's deadline

45 男子詢問女子什麼？

(A) 團隊的研究成果
(B) 文件的大小規格
(C) 訂單的到貨日期
(D) 工作的截止期限

49 新 What does the man mean when he says, "It will be easier for me to refer to that"?

(A) He wants to use updated software.
(B) He would rather print a brochure.
(C) He wants to view an electronic file.
(D) He would like to reference a memo.

46 當男子說：「這樣對我來說要參考會比較簡單」，是什麼意思？

(A) 他想要使用更新後的軟體。
(B) 他比較想要把小冊子印出來。
(C) 他想要看電子檔。
(D) 他想要引用備忘錄。

題目 handbook [ˋhændˏbʊk] 手冊　make a revision 做修訂　based on 根據～
electronic [㊤ ɪlɛkˋtrɑnɪk ㊥ ilekˋtrɔnik] 電子的　format [㊤ ˋfɔrmæt ㊥ ˋfɔ:mæt] 型式　easy [ˋizɪ] 簡單的
refer [㊤ rɪˋfɝ ㊥ riˋfə:] 參考

48 specification [ˏspɛsəfəˋkeʃən] 規格　assignment [əˋsaɪnmənt] 工作；指派

47 中 **整體對話相關問題—說話者** 答案 (A)

題目詢問說話者的工作地點，因此要注意聽和身分、職業相關的表達。女子對男子說：「I need you to update the staff manual for our investment bank's stock market research software」，表示需要男子去更新他們自己投資銀行的股市研究軟體的員工手冊，由此可知，說話者們的工作地點是金融公司，因此正確答案是 (A) At a financial firm。

換句話說

investment bank 投資銀行 → financial firm 金融公司

48 中 **細節事項相關問題—特定細項** 答案 (D)

題目詢問男子問了女子什麼，因此要注意聽男子說的話。男子對女子說：「when does the document[staff manual] need to be completed?」，詢問自己什麼時候要完成員工手冊的更新，因此正確答案是 (D) An assignment's deadline。

新 **49** 高 **細節事項相關問題—掌握意圖** 答案 (C)

題目詢問男子的說話意圖，因此要注意題目引用句（It will be easier for me to refer to that）相關及前後的內容。男子前面先說：「can I look at the manual in an electronic format instead of this printout?」，詢問是否能看電子版本的手冊，由此可知，他想看手冊的電子檔，因此正確答案是 (C) He wants to view an electronic file.。

Questions 50-52 refer to the following conversation.

加拿大式發音 → 英式發音

M: My name is Stanley Coburn. [50]**When I logged in to my library account today, I saw that I have an overdue book. But I never received a voice mail reminder about this. I'm a little upset about the situation.**

W: [51]**We switched to sending notices by e-mail last month,** Mr. Coburn. You should've received a message about the development.

M: Really? I check my e-mails regularly, and I never received one. Maybe the library hasn't been using my correct e-mail address.

W: I apologize for the inconvenience. Umm . . . [52]**here's what I can do . . . If you return the book today, you won't have to pay a late fee.**

50 Why is the man calling?

(A) To reserve an item
(B) To cancel an account
(C) To request an extension
(D) To make a complaint

51 According to the woman, what did the library do last month?

(A) Launched a Web site
(B) Changed a notification procedure
(C) Increased fines for overdue materials
(D) Ordered new books

52 What does the woman say she can do?

(A) Return a book
(B) Pass on a message
(C) Send an e-mail
(D) Waive a charge

第 50-52 題請參考下列對話。

男：我的名字是 Stanley Coburn。[50] 我今天登入我的圖書館帳號時，我看到我有一本書逾期了。但我從來沒有收到關於這件事的語音信箱提醒。我對這個情形感到有點不高興。

女：[51] 我們上個月換成用電子郵件寄送通知了，Coburn 先生。您應該有收到過關於這項新消息的訊息。

男：真的嗎？我定期會檢查我的電子郵件，但我從來沒有收到過。也許圖書館用的不是我正確的電子郵件地址。

女：我為造成您的不便道歉。嗯……[52] 我可以這樣處理……若您在今天歸還那本書，那麼您就不必支付滯還金。

50 男子為什麼打電話？

(A) 為了保留一個品項
(B) 為了取消一個帳號
(C) 為了要求一次延期
(D) 為了提出一項申訴

51 根據女子所說，圖書館上個月做了什麼？

(A) 啟用一個網站
(B) 變更一項通知程序
(C) 提高逾期資料的罰款
(D) 訂購新書

52 女子說她可以做什麼？

(A) 歸還一本書
(B) 傳遞一則訊息
(C) 寄出一封電子郵件
(D) 免除一筆費用

題目 switch [swɪtʃ] 轉換　notice [[美] `notɪs [英] `nəutis] 通知　development [dɪ`vɛləpmənt] 新消息；發展
regularly [`rɛgjələ·lɪ] 定期地　correct [kə`rɛkt] 正確的
inconvenience [[美] ˌɪnkən`vinjəns [英] ˌinkən`vi:njəns] 不方便；麻煩　late fee 滯還金

51 launch [lɔntʃ] 啟用　notification [ˌnotəfə`keʃən] 通知　procedure [prə`sidʒɚ] 程序　fine [faɪn] 罰款
material [mə`tɪrɪəl] 資料

52 pass on 傳遞　waive [wev] 免除　charge [tʃɑrdʒ] 費用

50 整體對話相關問題—目的　答案 (D)

中

題目詢問男子打電話的目的，因此必須注意聽對話的開頭。男子說：「When I logged in to my library account today, I saw that I have an overdue book. But I never received a voice mail reminder about this. I'm a little upset about the situation.」，表示自己今天登入圖書館帳號時，看到有一本書逾期，但卻從來沒有收到過語音信箱提醒，因而對這種情形感到有點不高興，由此可知，男子是為了提出申訴而打電話，因此正確答案是 (D) To make a complaint。

51 細節事項相關問題—特定細項　答案 (B)

中

題目詢問女子說圖書館上個月做了什麼，因此要注意聽女子話中和題目關鍵字（library do last month）相關的內容。女子說：「We[library] switched to sending notices by e-mail last month」，表示圖書館上個月換成用電子郵件寄送通知了，因此正確答案是 (B) Changed a notification procedure。

52 細節事項相關問題—特定細項　答案 (D)

高

題目詢問女子說自己可以做什麼，因此要注意聽和題目關鍵字（can do）相關及前後的內容。女子說：「here's what I can do ~. If you return the book today, you won't have to pay a late fee.」，表示若男子在今天歸還那本書，則自己可以免除男子原本必須支付的滯還金，因此正確答案是 (D) Waive a charge。

53 54 55 新

Questions 53-55 refer to the following conversation with three speakers.

美式發音 → 加拿大式發音 → 澳洲式發音

W: Before we wrap up this meeting, let's talk about the position we need to fill in the bookkeeping department. After going through the applications, I think Sheryl Johnson looks promising.
M1: I agree. [53]**I was really impressed by her responses during the interview on Monday.** What do you think, Dave?
M2: I don't know. [54]**She doesn't have much experience working in the financial field.**
W: It shouldn't be an issue, though. It's an entry-level position.
M1: Right. She'll receive on-the-job training.
M2: That's a good point. I don't have any objections to hiring her, then.
W: OK. But [55]**I should talk to the department head before making a final decision. I'll do that now.**

第 53-55 題請參考下列三人對話。

女： 在我們結束這次會議之前，我們來談談有關我們在記帳部門裡必須要補的那個位置的事。在仔細看過應徵資料後，我認為 Sheryl Johnson 看起來大有可為。
男 1： 我同意。[53] 她在星期一面試時的應對真的很讓我印象深刻。你覺得呢？Dave ？
男 2： 我不知道。[54] 她沒有什麼在金融領域工作的經驗。
女： 不過這應該不是問題。這是個低階的工作。
男 1： 沒錯。她會有在職訓練。
男 2： 這倒沒錯。那我沒什麼好反對雇用她的了。
女： 好。不過 [55] 在做最終決定之前，我應該去和那個部門的主管談談。我現在就去。

53 What was held on Monday?
(A) An employee orientation
(B) A job interview
(C) A staff meeting
(D) A training session

53 在星期一舉行了什麼？
(A) 員工說明會
(B) 工作面試
(C) 員工會議
(D) 培訓課程

54 What is mentioned about Sheryl Johnson?
(A) She lacks relevant experience.
(B) She will provide a work sample.
(C) She has requested a transfer.
(D) She will lead a seminar.

54 關於 Sheryl Johnson，提到了什麼？
(A) 她缺乏相關經驗。
(B) 她會提供作品範本。
(C) 她已申請轉調。
(D) 她會主持一場研討會。

55 What will the woman probably do next?
(A) Visit another company
(B) Contact an applicant
(C) Discuss a matter with a superior
(D) Place résumés in a filing cabinet

55 女子接下來可能會做什麼？
(A) 去其他公司
(B) 聯絡一位應徵者
(C) 和一位上司討論一件事
(D) 把履歷表放進檔案櫃裡

題目 wrap up 完成，結束 go through 仔細查看 application [ˌæplə`keʃən] 申請（書） promising [`prɑmɪsɪŋ] 大有可為的 on-the-job training 在職訓練 objection [əb`dʒɛkʃən] 異議；反對
54 lack [læk] 缺乏 relevant [`rɛləvənt] 相關的 transfer [`trænsfɝ] 轉調
55 matter [`mætɚ] 事項；問題 superior [sə`pɪrɪɚ] 上司；長官 filing cabinet 檔案櫃

53 細節事項相關問題—特定細項 低 答案 (B)

題目詢問星期一舉行了什麼，因此要注意聽和題目關鍵字（Monday）相關及前後的內容。男 1 說：「I was really impressed by her[Sheryl Johnson's] responses during the interview on Monday.」，表示 Sheryl Johnson 在星期一面試時的應對真的很讓自己印象深刻，由此可知，星期一舉行了工作面試，因此正確答案是 (B) A job interview。

54 細節事項相關問題—提及 中 答案 (A)

題目詢問提到什麼與 Sheryl Johnson 有關的事，因此要注意聽和題目關鍵字（Sheryl Johnson）相關的內容。男 2 說：「She[Sheryl Johnson] doesn't have much experience working in the financial field.」，表示 Sheryl Johnson 在金融領域沒有什麼工作經驗，因此正確答案是 (A) She lacks relevant experience.。

55 細節事項相關問題—接下來要做的事 中 答案 (C)

題目詢問女子接下來可能會做什麼，因此必須注意對話的最後部分。女子說：「I should talk to the department head before making a final decision. I'll do that now.」，表示在做最終決定之前，應該要去和該部門主管談談，並說自己現在就去，因此正確答案是 (C) Discuss a matter with a superior。

56
57
58

Questions 56-58 refer to the following conversation.

澳洲式發音 → 美式發音

M: Jasmine, [56]**did you hear that loud party in the apartment upstairs last night?**
W: [56]**Yeah. I had trouble sleeping because of it.** [57]**I'm going to complain to the building management office.**
M: [57]**It's a national holiday, so the office is closed today.**
W: Are you serious? [57]**That means I'm going to lose more sleep this weekend.**
M: Well, you could put a note on the door of the apartment upstairs.
W: I suppose I can try that first. [58]**Unit 74 is the one right above us, isn't it?** I wanna be sure I put the note on the proper door.

第 53-55 題請參考下列對話。

男：Jasmine，[56] 妳昨晚有聽到樓上公寓的那場很吵的派對嗎？
女：[56] 有啊，我因為這個睡得很差。[57] 我打算去大樓管理室申訴。
男：[57] 今天是國定假日，所以管理室沒開。
女：真的假的？[57] 這就代表我這週末能睡的時間變得更少了。
男：這個嘛，妳可以貼張字條在樓上公寓的門上。
女：我想我可以先試試看這樣做。[58] 我們正上方那間是 74 室，對吧？我想確定我會把字條貼在正確的門上。

56 What is the problem?
(A) A gathering was noisy.
(B) An alarm failed to go off.
(C) A heating system malfunctioned.
(D) A piece of furniture is uncomfortable.

56 問題是什麼？
(A) 一場聚會很吵。
(B) 一個警報器沒有響。
(C) 一個暖氣系統故障了。
(D) 一件家具不舒適。

57 新 What does the woman imply when she says, "Are you serious"?
(A) She missed an appointment.
(B) She has plans for a holiday.
(C) She is frustrated by a closure.
(D) She is disappointed with a unit.

57 當女子說：「真的假的」時，是暗示什麼？
(A) 她錯過了預約。
(B) 她假日有計畫。
(C) 她對沒開這件事感到喪氣。
(D) 她對於一組裝置感到失望。

58 What does the woman ask the man about?
(A) The number of an apartment
(B) The length of a holiday
(C) The location of some stationery
(D) The address of a landlord

58 女子問男子什麼？
(A) 公寓的編號
(B) 假日的長度
(C) 一些文具的位置
(D) 房東的地址

題目 national holiday 國定假日 unit [`junɪt]（全體之中的一個）單位；（裝置等的）一組 proper [`prɑpɚ] 正確的
56 alarm [ə`lɑrm] 警報器 fail [fel] 失去作用 go off（警報等）響起 malfunction [mæl`fʌŋʃən] 故障
57 miss [mɪs] 未履行（約定等）；錯過 frustrate [`frʌs͵tret] 使喪氣 closure [`kloʒɚ] 關閉；打烊
58 stationery [`steʃən͵ɛrɪ] 文具 landlord [`lænd͵lɔrd] 房東

56 細節事項相關問題—問題點 答案 (A)
低
題目詢問發生了什麼問題，因此必須注意聽對話中出現負面表達之後的內容。男子對女子說：「did you hear that loud party in the apartment upstairs last night?」，詢問女子昨晚是否有聽到樓上公寓的那場很吵的派對，女子說：「Yeah. I had trouble sleeping because of it.」，表示自己有聽到且因為這樣而睡得很差，因此正確答案是 (A) A gathering was noisy.。

新 **57** 細節事項相關問題—掌握意圖 答案 (C)
高
題目詢問女子的說話意圖，因此要確認和題目關鍵字（Are you serious）相關及前後的內容。女子說：「I'm going to complain to the building management office.」，表示自己要到管理室申訴，接著男子說：「It's a national holiday, so the office is closed today.」，表示今天是國定假日，所以管理室沒開。接著女子說：「That means I'm going to lose more sleep this weekend.」，表示這樣就是說自己週末能睡的時間變得更少了，由此可知，女子因為大樓管理室沒開而覺得喪氣，因此正確答案是 (C) She is frustrated by a closure.。

58 細節事項相關問題—特定細項 答案 (A)
中
題目詢問女子問男子什麼，因此要注意聽女子說的話。女子對男子說：「Unit 74 is the one right above us, isn't it?」，詢問正上方那間公寓是否是 74 室，因此正確答案是 (A) The number of an apartment。

59 60 61 新

Questions 59-61 refer to the following conversation.	第 59-61 題請參考下列對話。
美式發音 → 加拿大式發音	
W: Hi. [59]**I'd like to buy a watch as a gift for my assistant,** since he was really helpful while I was creating my latest clothing line.	女：嗨，[59] 我想買一支手錶當禮物送我助理，因為他在我之前做我最新的服裝系列時真的幫了很多忙。
M: Certainly. [59]**Our store has a number of great choices.** For instance, this piece has a leather band and costs $145.	男：沒問題。[59] 我們店裡有一些很棒的選擇。舉例來說，這支有皮革錶帶，價格是 145 美金。
W: I really like that. But . . . [60]**It looks like the face on it is cracked.** See here? Do you have any others in stock? If so, I'll take it.	女：我真的很喜歡這支。但是……[60] 它錶面看起來裂開了。你有看到這裡嗎？你們還有其他庫存的嗎？如果有我就買。
M: My apologies. Yes, let me grab another from our back room.	男：抱歉。有的，讓我去後面再拿一支來。
W: By the way, [61]**I'd appreciate it if you could gift-wrap it too.** That'll save me the hassle of doing it myself.	女：對了，[61] 如果你也能把它包成禮物的樣子，那我會很感謝。這樣我就省去要自己包的麻煩了。
59 Who most likely is the man? (A) A craftsman (B) A personal assistant (C) A salesperson (D) A fashion designer	59 男子最有可能是誰？ (A) 一位工匠 (B) 一位個人助理 (C) 一位銷售員 (D) 一位時裝設計師
60 What problem does the woman mention? (A) An order arrived late. (B) A stock room is messy. (C) A price tag is incorrect. (D) A product is damaged.	60 女子提到什麼問題？ (A) 一筆訂單晚到了。 (B) 一間倉庫很亂。 (C) 一個標價不正確。 (D) 一件產品受損了。
61 What does the woman ask the man to do? (A) Supply a receipt (B) Wrap a purchase (C) Repair an item (D) Provide a discount	61 女子要求男子做什麼？ (A) 提供收據 (B) 把買的東西包起來 (C) 修理物品 (D) 提供折扣

題目 assistant [ə`sɪstənt] 助理，助手　helpful [`hɛlpfəl] 有幫助的　leather [`lɛðɚ] 皮革製的　face [fes] 表面　crack [kræk] 裂開　in stock 有庫存　gift-wrap 包成禮物的樣子　save [sev] 省去（勞力等）　hassle [`hæsl] 麻煩的事情

59 craftsman [`kræftsmən] 工匠　salesperson [`selz͵pɝsn̩] 銷售員

60 order [`ɔrdɚ] 訂單　stock room 倉庫　messy [`mɛsɪ] 雜亂的　price tag 標價

61 supply [sə`plaɪ] 提供

59 整體對話相關問題—說話者　答案 (C)

高

題目詢問男子的身分，因此必須注意聽和身分、職業相關的表達。女子對男子說：「I'd like to buy a watch as a gift for my assistant」，表示想買手錶當禮物送助理，而男子接著說：「Our store has a number of great choices.」，表示自己店裡有一些很棒的選擇，由此可知，男子是銷售員，因此正確答案是 (C) A salesperson。

60 細節事項相關問題—問題點　答案 (D)

中

題目詢問女子提到什麼問題，因此要注意聽女子話中出現負面表達之後的內容。女子對男子說：「It looks like the face on it[watch] is cracked.」，表示錶面看起來裂開了，因此正確答案是 (D) A product is damaged.。

換句話說

cracked 裂開的 → damaged 受損的

61 細節事項相關問題—要求　答案 (B)

中

題目詢問女子要求男子做什麼，因此必須注意聽女子話中提到要請男子做事的內容。女子說：「I'd appreciate it if you could gift-wrap it[watch] too」，表示如果男子能把手錶包成禮物的樣子，她會很感謝，因此正確答案是 (B) Wrap a purchase。

62
63
64

新

Questions 62-64 refer to the following conversation with three speakers.	第 62-64 題請參考下列三人對話。
加拿大式發音 → 英式發音 → 美式發音	
M: [62]**Do you know why we're shutting down rides in the park an hour early tonight?**	男：[62] 你們知道我們為什麼今晚要提早一個小時關閉園區裡的遊樂設施嗎？
W1: There will be fireworks in the main plaza this evening.	女 1：今天晚上在主廣場會有煙火。
M: I didn't know about that. Did you, Amy?	男：我不知道有這件事。妳知道嗎？Amy?
W2: Sure did. [63]**This month, we're celebrating the first anniversary of our opening. As a result,** [64]**there's a special event each week. The schedule is posted in the staff break room.**	女 2：當然知道。[63] 這個月我們要慶祝開幕一周年。因此，[64] 每星期都有特別活動。時間表貼在員工休息室裡了。
M: Oh, odd. [64]**I never saw that throughout the week.**	男：噢，真奇怪。[64] 我這整個禮拜都沒有看到時間表。
W1: I see. Well, [64]**it's in there. OK,** [62]**we'd better get back to work. Don't forget to place closing signs near the ride entrances in 20 minutes.**	女 1：這樣啊。嗯，[64] 時間表在那裡。好了，[62] 我們最好回去工作了。別忘了在 20 分鐘後把關閉標示放在遊樂設施的入口附近。
62 Where is the conversation most likely taking place? (A) At a performance venue (B) At an amusement park (C) At a science museum (D) At a shopping mall	62 這段對話最有可能發生在哪裡？ (A) 表演場地 (B) 遊樂園 (C) 科學博物館 (D) 購物中心
63 According to Amy, how long has the facility been in operation? (A) For one month (B) For two months (C) For one year (D) For two years	63 根據 Amy 所說，這間設施已經營運多久了？ (A) 一個月 (B) 兩個月 (C) 一年 (D) 兩年
64 Why was the man unaware of an event? (A) He is not on a mailing list. (B) He could not attend a conference. (C) He did not notice a schedule. (D) He was given inaccurate information.	64 男子為什麼不知道有活動？ (A) 他不在郵寄名單上。 (B) 他無法參加會議。 (C) 他沒有注意到時間表。 (D) 他得到了不正確的資訊。

題目 shut down 關閉 ride [raɪd] 遊樂設施 firework [美 `faɪr͵wɝk 英 `faiwəːk] 煙火 opening [`opənɪŋ] 開幕 odd [ɑd] 奇怪的 closing [美 `klozɪŋ 英 `kləuziŋ] 關閉 sign [saɪn] 標示 entrance [`ɛntrəns] 入口
64 mailing list 郵寄名單 inaccurate [ɪn`ækjərɪt] 不正確的

62 整體對話相關問題—地點 答案 (B)
高

題目詢問對話發生地點，因此要注意聽和地點相關的表達。男子對女子說：「Do you know why we're shutting down rides in the park an hour early tonight?」，詢問其他人是否知道為什麼今天晚上要提早一個小時關閉園區的遊樂設施，女 1 在最後說：「we'd better get back to work. Don't forget to place closing signs near the ride entrances in 20 minutes.」，表示大家最好要回去工作了。並提醒要在 20 分鐘後擺放關閉標示在遊樂設施的入口附近，由此可知，這段對話發生的地點在遊樂園，因此正確答案是 (B) At an amusement park。

63 細節事項相關問題—程度 答案 (C)
中

題目詢問女 2 的 Amy 說這座設施已經營運多久了，因此必須注意聽女 2 所說的話中和題目關鍵字（facility ~ in operation）有關的內容。女 2[Amy] 說：「This month, we're celebrating the first anniversary of our opening.」，表示這個月要慶祝開幕一周年，由此可知，這座設施已營運了一年，因此正確答案是 (C) For one year。

64 細節事項相關問題—理由 答案 (C)
高

題目詢問男子為什麼不知道有活動，因此要注意聽和題目關鍵字（unaware of an event）相關的內容。女 2 說：「there's a special event each week. The schedule is posted in the staff break room.」，表示每星期都有特別活動，且時間表貼在員工休息室裡了，男子則說：「I never saw that throughout the week.」，表示自己整個禮拜都沒有看到時間表，因此正確答案是 (C) He did not notice a schedule.。

65 66 67 新

Questions 65-67 refer to the following conversation and employee directory.

第 65-67 題請參考下列對話與員工通訊錄。

美式發音 → 澳洲式發音

W: Josh, [65]**I heard you're staying late tonight to help with the marketing department's relocation to the fifth floor.**

M: [65]**Yeah.** I'm setting up the computers. [66]**I was given this list detailing which desks I'm supposed to set up. However, it includes only 25 staff members despite there being 30 in the department.** I need the rest of the information to finish the job.

W: Why don't you call the five employees who aren't included in the list and ask which workstations they're moving to?

M: I don't know their names, and our online directory doesn't include employees' departments.

W: Well, [67]**everyone in marketing has an extension starting with nine.** Just sort by extension number, and you'll be able to see everyone in that department.

女：Josh，[65] 我聽說你今天晚上會待到很晚去幫忙行銷部搬到五樓。

男：[65] 是啊。我要架電腦。[66] 我拿到了這張詳細說明我應該要架哪些位子的名單。可是，儘管這個部門裡有 30 個人，名單上卻只有 25 個員工。我需要剩下的那些資訊來完成這項工作。

女：你要不要打給沒在名單上的那五個員工，問他們要搬到哪個工作站？

男：我不知道他們的名字，而且我們的線上通訊錄裡沒有員工的部門。

女：這個嘛，[67] 行銷部裡所有人的分機開頭都是九。你就用分機號碼來分，就能找到那部門裡的所有人了。

新

Employee Name	Extension Number
[67]**Monica Pearce**	**9087**
Josh Han	1099
Valarie Dupree	4419
Will Garcia	7893

員工姓名	分機號碼
[67] Monica Pearce	9087
Josh Han	1099
Valarie Dupree	4419
Will Garcia	7893

65 What will the man do tonight?

(A) Upgrade computer software
(B) Assist with a move
(C) Get in touch with a client
(D) Participate in a meeting

65 男子今晚會做什麼？

(A) 升級電腦軟體
(B) 協助搬遷
(C) 與客戶取得聯絡
(D) 參加會議

66 What problem does the man mention?

(A) A goal was missed.
(B) A list is incomplete.
(C) A directory is inaccessible.
(D) A desk can no longer be used.

66 男子提到什麼問題？

(A) 沒有達成一個目標。
(B) 一份名單不完整。
(C) 無法取得一份通訊錄。
(D) 一張桌子不能再用了。

67 新 Look at the graphic. Who works in the marketing department?

(A) Monica Pearce
(B) Josh Han
(C) Valarie Dupree
(D) Will Garcia

67 請看圖表。誰在行銷部裡工作？

(A) Monica Pearce
(B) Josh Han
(C) Valarie Dupree
(D) Will Garcia

題目 relocation [rilo`keʃən] 搬遷；重新安置 detail [(美) `ditel (英) `di:teil] 詳細說明 despite [dɪ`spaɪt] 儘管 rest [rɛst] 剩餘部分 sort [sɔrt] 區分

65 assist with 協助～ get in touch with 與～取得聯絡

66 missed [mɪst] 未達成的；錯過的 incomplete [ˌɪnkəm`plit] 不完整的 inaccessible [ˌɪnæk`sɛsəbl] 無法取得的

65 中 ■ **細節事項相關問題—接下來要做的事** 答案 (B)

題目詢問男子今天晚上會做什麼，因此要注意聽和題目關鍵字（tonight）相關及前後的內容。女子說：「I heard you're staying late tonight to help with the marketing department's relocation to the fifth floor」，表示聽說男子今天晚上會待到很晚去幫忙行銷部搬到五樓，接著男子說：「Yeah.」，表示沒錯，由此可知，男子今天晚上會去幫行銷部搬遷，因此正確答案是 (B) Assist with a move。

換句話說

help with ~ relocation 幫忙搬遷 → Assist with a move 協助搬遷

66 高 ■ **細節事項相關問題—問題點** 答案 (B)

題目詢問男子提到什麼問題，因此要注意聽男子話中出現負面表達之後的內容。男子說：「I was given this list detailing which desks I'm supposed to set up. However, it includes only 25 staff members despite there being 30 in the department.」，先說自己拿到了詳細說明要架哪些位子的名單，再說雖然整個部門裡有 30 個人，但是名單上卻只有 25 個人，由此可知，男子收到的名單不完整，因此正確答案是 (B) A list is incomplete.。

新 **67** 高 ■ **細節事項相關問題—圖表資料** 答案 (A)

題目詢問是誰在行銷部裡工作，因此必須確認題目提供的員工通訊錄上的資訊，並注意和題目關鍵字（works in the marketing department）有關的內容。女子說：「everyone in marketing has an extension starting with nine」，表示行銷部所有人的分機都是九開頭，透過通訊錄可知，分機號碼以九開頭的 Monica Pearce 是行銷部員工，因此正確答案是 (A) Monica Pearce。

68
69
70

Questions 68-70 refer to the following conversation and ticket.

澳洲式發音 → 英式發音

M: Are you going to the Eastville Food Festival, Priscilla?

W: You bet! I bought my ticket today. I'm surprised they raised the prices this year, though.

M: Fortunately, [68]**I belong to the World Culinary Organization, so I got a $5 discount. Members pay $10 for a one-day pass** and $15 for a two-day pass.

W: Lucky you. Did you hear that they will be holding a cooking competition on Sunday afternoon? [69]**An announcement was added to the Web site yesterday.** Apparently, several international chefs will be participating.

M: Really? I'd love to watch that, but [70]**my parents are staying at my house from Sunday to Monday, and we already have arrangements then.** So I'll have to skip it.

Eastville Food Festival

Saturday, Aug 20 – Sunday, Aug 21
11 A.M. – 8 P.M.

[68]**One-Day Pass** Valid for Aug 20
World Culinary Organization Member

68 Look at the graphic. How much did the man pay for the ticket?

(A) $5
(B) $10
(C) $15
(D) $20

69 What happened yesterday?

(A) A discount was offered.
(B) A competition was held.
(C) A notice was posted online.
(D) A class was canceled.

70 Why is the man unable to attend the festival on Sunday?

(A) He is going to meet with family.
(B) He has to go on a business trip.
(C) He has to prepare for a contest.
(D) He is going to conduct a workshop.

第 65-67 題請參考下列對話與票券。

男：妳要去 Eastville 食品節嗎？Priscilla？

女：沒錯！我今天買了我的票。不過我很驚訝他們今年調漲了票價。

男：幸運的是，[68] 我是世界烹飪組織的成員，所以我可以折價 5 美金。會員買一日券是 10 美金，兩日券則是 15 美金。

女：你真幸運。你有聽說他們會在週日下午舉辦烹飪競賽嗎？[69] 昨天網站上貼出了一篇公告。顯然有幾位國際主廚會參加。

男：真的嗎？我很想去看那場比賽，但 [70] 我爸媽要在我家從週日待到週一，而且我們那個時間已經有安排了。所以我得跳過這場比賽了。

Eastville 食品節

8 月 20 日週六—8 月 21 日週日
上午 11 點—晚上 8 點

[69] 一日券 8 月 20 日有效
世界烹飪組織成員

68 請看圖表。男子付了多少錢買這張票？

(A) 5 美金
(B) 10 美金
(C) 15 美金
(D) 20 美金

69 昨天發生了什麼？

(A) 提供了一項折扣。
(B) 舉行了一場比賽。
(C) 網路上發布了一則公告。
(D) 取消了一門課。

70 男子為何無法在週日參加這個節？

(A) 他要和家人見面。
(B) 他必須去出差。
(C) 他得為比賽做準備。
(D) 他要舉辦工作坊。

題目 raise [rez] 提高　belong to 屬於～　culinary [(美) `kjulɪˌnɛrɪ (英) `kju:lineri] 烹飪的；烹飪用的
organization [(美) ˌɔrgənə`zeʃən (英) ˌɔ:gənai`zeiʃən] 組織，團體　announcement [ə`naʊnsmənt] 公告
apparently [ə`pærəntlɪ] 顯然地　arrangement [ə`rendʒmənt] 安排；準備工作

70 conduct [kən`dʌkt] 實施；舉辦

新 68 ●●● 高　細節事項相關問題—圖表資料　答案 (B)

題目詢問男子付了多少錢買題目附上的這張票，因此必須確認題目提供的票券資訊，並注意和題目關鍵字（pay for the ticket）相關的內容。男子說：「I belong to the World Culinary Organization ~. Members pay $10 for a one-day pass」，表示自己是世界烹飪組織的成員，而會員買一日券是 10 美金，因此正確答案是 (B) $10。

69 ●● 中　細節事項相關問題—特定細項　答案 (C)

題目詢問昨天發生了什麼，因此要注意聽和題目關鍵字（yesterday）相關及前後的內容。女子說：「An announcement was added to the Web site yesterday.」，表示昨天網站上貼出了一篇公告，因此正確答案是 (C) A notice was posted online.。

換句話說

An announcement was added to the Web site 網站上貼出了一篇公告

→ A notice was posted online 網路上發布了一則公告

70 ●● 中　細節事項相關問題—理由　答案 (A)

題目詢問男子為何無法在週日參加這個節，因此要注意聽和題目關鍵字（unable to attend the festival on Sunday）相關的內容。男子說：「my parents are staying at my house from Sunday to Monday, and we already have arrangements then」，表示自己的爸媽要從週日待到週一，而且週日的那個時間已經有安排了，因此正確答案是 (A) He is going to meet with family.。

71 72 73

Questions 71-73 refer to the following announcement.

美式發音

[71]**Attention, Flight 876 passengers. This is your captain speaking.** Thanks to some favorable air currents, [72]**we will reach Los Angeles approximately 20 minutes ahead of schedule. So we will arrive at 5:20 P.M. local time** instead of 5:40 P.M. The weather at our destination is partly cloudy and is expected to stay that way for the rest of the day. Since this is an international flight, [73]**many of you will need to submit an immigration form upon arrival, so I suggest filling it out now.** The seatbelt sign will be turned on in 10 minutes, at which time you will need to return to your seats and remain there until we land.

71 Who is the speaker?

(A) A flight attendant
(B) A ticket agent
(C) An airline pilot
(D) A security guard

72 When will Flight 876 reach its destination?

(A) At 5:10 P.M.
(B) At 5:20 P.M.
(C) At 5:30 P.M.
(D) At 5:40 P.M.

73 What does the speaker suggest listeners do?

(A) Complete a document
(B) Choose an in-flight meal
(C) Report to an information desk
(D) Confirm a flight time

第 71-73 題請參考下列公告。

[71] 876 號航班乘客請注意。這裡是機長廣播。多虧了有利的氣流，[72] 我們會比預定提早約 20 分鐘抵達洛杉磯。所以我們會在當地時間下午 5 點 20 分抵達，而不是下午 5 點 40 分。我們目的地的天氣是部分多雲，預期今天剩下的時間也都會維持這種狀態。由於本航班為國際航班，[73] 各位之中有許多人將需要在抵達後立刻提交入境卡，因此我建議現在填寫。安全帶燈號將於 10 分鐘後亮起，屆時各位須返回座位並留在座位上直到降落。

71 說話者是誰？

(A) 空服員
(B) 票務人員
(C) 航空公司飛行員
(D) 警衛

72 876 航班何時會抵達目的地？

(A) 下午 5 點 10 分
(B) 下午 5 點 20 分
(C) 下午 5 點 30 分
(D) 下午 5 點 40 分

73 說話者建議聽者們做什麼？

(A) 填寫一份文件
(B) 選擇一份飛機餐
(C) 向服務台回報
(D) 確認航班時間

題目 passenger [`pæsəndʒɚ] 乘客　captain [`kæptɪn] 機長　favorable [`fevərəbl] 有利的；贊同的　air current 氣流　approximately [ə`prɑksəmɪtlɪ] 大約　partly [`pɑrtlɪ] 部分地，不完全地　immigration form 入境卡　upon [ə`pɑn] 在～後立刻～　remain [rɪ`men] 留下
71 security guard 警衛
73 complete [kəm`plit] 填寫（文件等）　in-flight meal 飛機餐　report [rɪ`port] 回報；報導

71 整體內容相關問題—說話者　答案 (C)
中
題目詢問說話者的身分，因此要注意聽和身分、職業相關的表達。獨白說：「Attention, Flight 876 passengers. This is ~ captain speaking.」，要求 876 號航班的乘客注意，並表示自己是機長，因此正確答案是 (C) An airline pilot。

換句話說
captain 機長 → airline pilot 航空公司飛行員

72 細節事項相關問題—特定細項　答案 (B)
中
題目詢問 876 號航班抵達目的地的時間，因此要注意聽和題目關鍵字（reach ~ destination）相關的內容。獨白說：「we will reach Los Angeles approximately 20 minutes ahead of schedule. So we will arrive at 5:20 P.M. local time」，表示將提前 20 分鐘降落在洛杉磯，也就是在當地時間的下午 5 點 20 分，因此正確答案是 (B) At 5:20 P.M.。

73 細節事項相關問題—提議　答案 (A)
中
題目詢問說話者建議聽者們做什麼，因此要注意聽獨白的後半部分中出現提議相關表達的句子。獨白說：「many of you will need to submit an immigration form upon arrival, so I suggest filling it out now」，表示有許多人在抵達後必須立刻提交入境卡，所以自己會建議那些人現在開始填寫入境卡，因此正確答案是 (A) Complete a document。

74 75 76

Questions 74-76 refer to the following advertisement.	第 74-76 題請參考下列廣告。
美式發音	
At Durand Incorporated, we believe that cleaning supplies should not include harmful chemicals. That's why we created [74]**the LeMon line of environmentally friendly household cleaners**. Made from all-natural ingredients, these products will never damage countertops, stoves, or any other surfaces. [75]**Starting this March, LeMon brand items will be even easier to find, as they will be available in all Davis Market stores across the United States.** In the meantime, [76]**you can order any of our products at www.durandincorp.com**, where all of our goods are currently 5 percent off.	在 Durand 企業，我們相信清潔用品不應含有有害化學物質。這也就是為什麼我們打造了 [74]LeMon 環保家用清潔系列產品。以全天然成分製成，這些產品絕對不會對流理台、爐子或其他任何表面造成損害。[75] 從今年三月開始，就能更加輕鬆地找到 LeMon 牌產品了，因為它們將會在全美各地所有的 Davis Market 商店中販售。在此同時，[76] 您可以在 www.durandincorp.com 訂購我們的任何產品，我們的所有產品現在在那裡都打九五折。
74 What is being advertised? (A) A residential cleaning service (B) An eco-friendly product line (C) A new supermarket chain (D) An innovative home appliance	74 正在廣告什麼？ (A) 住家清潔服務 (B) 環保系列產品 (C) 新的連鎖超市 (D) 創新的家電產品
75 What is supposed to happen in March? (A) A marketing campaign will start. (B) Samples will be given to customers. (C) A product will be available in retail stores. (D) Existing models will be replaced.	75 在三月應該會發生什麼？ (A) 會展開一場行銷宣傳活動。 (B) 會給客人樣品。 (C) 在零售商店中將可買到一件產品。 (D) 現有的型號將會被取代。
76 According to the speaker, what can listeners do online? (A) Download a special coupon (B) Find a store location (C) Ask for a refund (D) Make a purchase	76 根據說話者所說，聽者們可以在網路上做什麼？ (A) 下載特別優惠券 (B) 找到商店的位置 (C) 要求退費 (D) 消費

題目 cleaning supply 清潔用品 harmful [ˋhɑrmfəl] 有害的 chemical [ˋkɛmɪkḷ] 化學物質 household [ˋhaʊsˏhold] 家用的 ingredient [ɪnˋgridɪənt] 成分 countertop [ˋkaʊntɚˏtɑp] 流理台 surface [ˋsɝfɪs] 表面 in the meantime 在此同時；同一期間 goods [gʊdz] 商品 currently [ˋkɝəntlɪ] 現在

74 residential [ˏrɛzəˋdɛnʃəl] 住宅的 eco-friendly 環保的 innovative [ˋɪnoˏvetɪv] 創新的 home appliance 家電產品

75 existing [ɪgˋzɪstɪŋ] 現有的 replace [rɪˋples] 取代

74 整體內容相關問題—主題 答案 (B)

中

題目詢問廣告的主題，因此要注意聽獨白的開頭部分。獨白說：「the LeMon line of environmentally friendly household cleaners」，表示這是在廣告 LeMon 環保家用清潔系列產品，並接著提及與該系列產品相關的內容，因此正確答案是 (B) An eco-friendly product line。

75 細節事項相關問題—特定細項 答案 (C)

中

題目詢問三月會發生什麼，因此要注意聽和題目關鍵字（March）相關的內容。獨白說：「Starting this March, LeMon brand items will be even easier to find, as they will be available in all Davis Market stores across the United States.」，表示從今年三月開始，LeMon 牌的產品將可在全美各地所有的 Davis Market 商店中買到，因此正確答案是 (C) A product will be available in retail stores.。

76 細節事項相關問題—特定細項 答案 (D)

低

題目詢問聽者們可以在網路上做什麼，因此要注意聽和題目關鍵字（online）相關的內容。獨白說：「you can order any of our products at www.durandincorp.com」，表示聽者們可以在該網站上訂購產品，因此正確答案是 (D) Make a purchase。

換句話說

order ~ products 訂購產品 → Make a purchase 消費

77
78
79

Questions 77-79 refer to the following telephone message.

澳洲式發音

[77]**This is Michael Danton calling from Harford Legal Services.** It's regarding the retirement party for another attorney at my firm that your company is catering tonight. I just spoke to one of your employees who is setting up at the banquet hall we rented, and [78]**she mentioned that there will be sufficient food for 50 people.** But over 75 guests will be attending this event. [78]**I'm not sure how this mistake happened** . . . I was very clear when I met with you to organize the party, and the contract I signed states the number of attendees. [79]**I expect to see you here at the hall within the hour with a plan to deal with this situation.**

第 77-79 題請參考下列電話留言。

[77] 這裡是 Harford 法律服務的 Michael Danton 來電。是關於你們公司今晚要承辦外燴的那場我們公司裡另一位律師的退休派對的事。我剛和你們一位正在布置我們租下的那個宴會廳的員工談過，而 [78] 她提到會有足夠給 50 人吃的食物。但這場活動將會有超過 75 名賓客出席。[78] 我不確定怎麼會發生這種錯誤……我當時在和你碰面籌劃這場派對的時候說得非常清楚，而且我簽署的合約上也載明了出席人數。[79] 我希望一個小時內能看到你帶著能夠處理這個狀況的計畫到宴會廳這裡來。

77 What type of business does the speaker work for?

(A) An accommodation facility
(B) A catering company
(C) A law firm
(D) A real estate agency

77 說話者在哪種公司裡工作？

(A) 住宿設施
(B) 外燴公司
(C) 法律事務所
(D) 房地產仲介

78 新 Why does the speaker say, "But over 75 guests will be attending this event"?

(A) To approve a request
(B) To confirm a plan
(C) To indicate a problem
(D) To show excitement

78 說話者為什麼說：「但這場活動將會有超過 75 名賓客出席」？

(A) 為了批准一項要求
(B) 為了確認一個計畫
(C) 為了指出一個問題
(D) 為了表示興奮

79 What does the speaker ask the listener to do?

(A) Print a revised contract
(B) Call a party planner
(C) Provide an attendee list
(D) Visit an event venue

79 說話者要求聽者做什麼？

(A) 列印修改過的合約
(B) 致電派對策劃者
(C) 提供出席名單
(D) 造訪活動場地

題目 legal [`ligl] 法律的 regarding [美 rɪ`gɑrdɪŋ 英 ri`gɑ:diŋ] 關於 retirement [美 rɪ`taɪrmənt 英 ri`taiəmənt] 退休 attorney [美 ə`tɝnɪ 英 ə`tə:ni] 律師 firm [美 fɝm 英 fə:m] 公司 cater [美 `ketɚ 英 `keitə] 提供飲食；承辦外燴 banquet hall 宴會廳 sufficient [sə`fɪʃənt] 足夠的 clear [美 klɪr 英 kliə] 清楚明白的 state [stet] 載明 attendee [ə`tɛndi] 出席者

77 accommodation facility 住宿設施

78 indicate [`ɪndəˌket] 指出

77 整體內容相關問題—說話者 答案 (C)

中

題目詢問說話者在哪種公司裡工作，因此必須注意聽和身分、職業相關的表達。獨白說：「This is Michael Danton calling from Harford Legal Services.」，表示自己是 Harford 法律服務的 Michael Danton，由此可知，說話者在法律事務所裡工作，因此正確答案是 (C) A law firm。

新 **78** 細節事項相關問題—掌握意圖 答案 (C)

高

題目詢問說話者的說話意圖，因此要注意題目引用句（But over 75 guests will be attending this event）相關的內容。獨白說：「she[one of your employees] mentioned that there will be sufficient food for 50 people」，表示聽者公司的一位員工說會有足夠給 50 人吃的食物，後面則說：「I'm not sure how this mistake happened」，表示不確定怎麼會發生這種錯誤，由此可知，說話者是想要指出食物在份量上有問題，因此正確答案是 (C) To indicate a problem。

79 細節事項相關問題—要求 答案 (D)

中

題目詢問說話者要求聽者做什麼，因此要注意聽獨白後半部分中出現要求相關表達的句子。獨白說：「I expect to see you here at the hall within the hour with a plan to deal with this situation.」，表示希望聽者在一個小時內帶著能夠處理這個狀況的計畫到宴會廳，因此正確答案是 (D) Visit an event venue。

80
81
82

Questions 80-82 refer to the following announcement.

加拿大式發音

This is an urgent announcement from the National Weather Bureau. Be advised [80]**the city of Toronto will experience a severe heat wave on August 6 and 7.** Daytime temperatures during this period are expected to exceed 36 degrees Celsius. [81]**Residents should avoid physically demanding activities, such as jogging or playing sports.** In addition, pets and young children should not be left unattended in parked vehicles. [82]**Information about the symptoms of heatstroke and methods of treatment is available on our Web site,** along with tips for coping with the heat. Rain is forecasted for the area on August 8, which will lead to a significant drop in temperature.

80 When will the heat wave begin?

(A) On August 5
(B) On August 6
(C) On August 7
(D) On August 8

81 What are listeners advised to do?

(A) Avoid exercise
(B) Park in designated areas
(C) Report health problems
(D) Contact an official

82 What does the speaker say is available on the Web site?

(A) Traffic updates
(B) Medical information
(C) Air quality data
(D) Nutrition tips

第 80-82 題請參考下列公告。

這是來自國家氣象局的緊急公告。請注意 [80] 多倫多市將在 8 月 6 日及 7 日遭受嚴重熱浪。這段期間的日間氣溫預期會超過攝氏 36 度。[81] 居民應避免太消耗體力的活動，如慢跑或體育活動。此外，不應於無人照料的狀況下將寵物與兒童留置於停放的車輛之中。[82] 中暑症狀的相關資訊及治療方法可在我們的網站上取得，亦提供應對高溫的訣竅。預期本區會在 8 月 8 日下雨，這將會導致氣溫明顯下降。

80 熱浪何時會開始？

(A) 8 月 5 日
(B) 8 月 6 日
(C) 8 月 7 日
(D) 8 月 8 日

81 聽者們被建議做什麼？

(A) 避免運動
(B) 在指定區域內停車
(C) 回報健康問題
(D) 聯繫一位官員

82 說話者說可以在網站上取得什麼？

(A) 最新路況
(B) 醫療資訊
(C) 空氣品質數據
(D) 有關營養的訣竅

題目 urgent [`ɝdʒənt] 緊急的　bureau [`bjʊro]（政府的）局，署　advise [əd`vaɪz] 告知；勸告　severe [sə`vɪr] 嚴重的　heat wave 熱浪　exceed [ɪk`sid] 超過；勝過　degree [dɪ`gri] 度　Celsius [`sɛlsɪəs] 攝氏的　physically [`fɪzɪkl̩ɪ] 身體地　demanding [dɪ`mændɪŋ] 吃力的　unattended [ˌʌnə`tɛndɪd] 無人照料的　symptom [`sɪmptəm] 症狀　heatstroke [`hitˌstrok] 中暑　treatment [`tritmənt] 治療；處置　along with 還有～　cope with 應對～　significant [sɪg`nɪfəkənt] 明顯的；重大的　drop [drɑp] 下降

81 designated [`dɛzɪgˌnetɪd] 指定的　official [ə`fɪʃəl] 官員

82 medical [`mɛdɪkl] 醫療的　nutrition [nju`trɪʃən] 營養

80 細節事項相關問題—特定細項　答案 (B)

低

題目詢問熱浪何時會開始，因此要注意聽和題目關鍵字（heat wave begin）相關的內容。獨白說：「the city of Toronto will experience a severe heat wave on August 6 and 7」，表示多倫多市在 8 月 6 日和 7 日會遭受嚴重的熱浪，因此正確答案是 (B) On August 6。

81 細節事項相關問題—提議　答案 (A)

中

題目詢問聽者們被建議做什麼，因此要注意聽獨白中後半部分出現提議相關表達的句子。獨白說：「Residents should avoid physically demanding activities, such as jogging or playing sports.」，表示居民應該要避免慢跑或體育活動等太消耗體力的活動，因此正確答案是 (A) Avoid exercise。

82 細節事項相關問題—特定細項　答案 (B)

中

題目詢問說話者說可以在網站上取得什麼，因此要注意聽和題目關鍵字（Web site）相關的內容。獨白說：「Information about the symptoms of heatstroke and methods of treatment is available on our Web site」，表示可以在網站上取得中暑症狀的相關資訊及治療方法，因此正確答案是 (B) Medical information。

83
84
85

Questions 83-85 refer to the following advertisement.

澳洲式發音

[83]**Are you confused by all the different types of investments?** Worried about making the wrong choices? [83]**Then contact Fieldstone Services, the largest wealth management firm in the country.** Established in 1945, our company is the nation's most popular source of investment advice, as demonstrated by [84]**our number one ranking in the National Brand Survey for seven consecutive years. This is because clients know that our employees can be trusted.** They do not receive commissions, so they never try to sell unnecessary products or services. [85]**If you would like to make an appointment with one of our trained professionals, call our 24-hour hotline.**

83 What type of business is being advertised?

(A) An advertising firm
(B) An educational institution
(C) A financial company
(D) A recruitment agency

84 According to the speaker, why is the company highly ranked in a survey?

(A) Its services are inexpensive.
(B) Its managers are experienced.
(C) Its products are reliable.
(D) Its employees are trustworthy.

85 Why should listeners contact the hotline?

(A) To verify a payment
(B) To arrange a consultation
(C) To cancel a service
(D) To participate in a survey

第 83-85 題請參考下列廣告。

[83] 你對各種不同類型的投資感到困惑嗎？擔心做出錯誤的選擇嗎？[83] 那就聯絡全國最大財富管理公司 Fieldstone 服務吧。創立於 1945 年，我們公司是國內最受歡迎的投資建議提供者，從 [84] 我們連續七年都在國家品牌調查中排名第一就可證實這點。這是因為客戶知道可以信賴我們的員工。他們不收取佣金，因此絕不會試圖銷售非必要的產品或服務。[85] 若您想與我們訓練有素的專業人員預約會面，請打我們的 24 小時熱線電話。

83 在廣告的是哪一類型的公司？

(A) 廣告公司
(B) 教育機構
(C) 金融公司
(D) 人力仲介

84 根據說話者所說，這間公司為何在一項調查中名列前茅？

(A) 它的服務不貴。
(B) 它的經理們很有經驗。
(C) 它的產品很可靠。
(D) 它的員工值得信賴。

85 為什麼聽者們要打熱線電話？

(A) 為確認一筆支付款項
(B) 為安排一次諮詢
(C) 為取消一項服務
(D) 為參與一項調查

題目 confused [kən`fjuzd] 困惑的　wealth [wɛlθ] 財富　establish [ə`stæblɪʃ] 創設　demonstrate [`dɛmən͵stret] 證實　consecutive [美 kən`sɛkjʊtɪv 英 kən`sekjutiv] 連續不斷的　commission [kə`mɪʃən] 佣金　unnecessary [ʌn`nɛsə͵sɛrɪ] 非必要的　trained [trend] 訓練有素的　professional [prə`fɛʃənl̩] 專業人員；職業的　hotline [美 `hɑtlaɪn 英 `hɔtlain] 熱線電話

84 inexpensive [͵ɪnɪk`spɛnsɪv] 不昂貴的　experienced [ɪk`spɪrɪənst] 有經驗的　reliable [rɪ`laɪəbl] 可靠的

85 verify [`vɛrə͵faɪ] 確認　arrange [ə`rendʒ] 安排；籌備

83 ■ **整體內容相關問題—主題** 答案 (C)

低

題目詢問廣告的主題，因此要注意聽獨白的開頭部分。獨白說：「Are you confused by all the different types of investments?」，詢問聽者們是否會對不同類型的投資感到困惑，並說：「Then contact Fieldstone Services, the largest wealth management firm in the country.」，表示如果會的話，就聯絡全國最大的財富管理公司 Fieldstone 服務，因此正確答案是 (C) A financial company。

84 ■ **細節事項相關問題—理由** 答案 (D)

高

題目詢問說話者說這間公司在一項調查中名列前茅的理由，因此必須注意聽和題目關鍵字（highly ranked in a survey）相關的內容。獨白說：「our number one ranking in the National Brand Survey ~. This is because clients know that our employees can be trusted.」，表示在國家品牌調查中排名第一，是因為客戶知道可以信賴這間公司的員工，因此正確答案是 (D) Its employees are trustworthy.。

85 ■ **細節事項相關問題—理由** 答案 (B)

中

題目詢問聽者們要打熱線電話的原因，因此要注意聽和題目關鍵字（hotline）相關的內容。獨白說：「If you would like to make an appointment with one of our trained professionals, call our 24-hour hotline.」，表示如果聽者們想和專業人員約時間，就打熱線電話，因此正確答案是 (B) To arrange a consultation。

換句話說

make an appointment with ~ trained professionals 與訓練有素的專業人員預約會面
→ arrange a consultation 安排一次諮詢

86
87
88

Questions 86-88 refer to the following telephone message.

第 86-88 題請參考下列電話留言。

加拿大式發音

Hello, Ms. Chen. It's Damien Marks from Vox Wireless. I have some bad news . . . [86]**I won't be able to repair your phone. I know I told you that it would be easy to replace the cracked screen.** However, the problem is more serious than I thought. [87]**When you dropped your phone, you broke several internal components. This means that it's going to cost more to fix your phone than to buy a new one.** Why don't you stop by the store to look at the models in stock? [88]**We'll even give you a $100 store credit for your broken phone to use on your purchase.** We're open from 8 A.M. to 10 P.M. each day, and I'm here from 9 A.M. to 6 P.M. on weekdays if you have any questions.

哈囉，Chen 小姐。我是 Vox 無線的 Damien Marks。我有些壞消息……[86] 我沒辦法把妳的電話修好了。我知道我跟妳說過要把裂掉的螢幕換掉很簡單。不過，問題比我原本以為的要嚴重。[87] 妳在摔到電話的時候，弄壞了幾個內部零件。這代表要把妳電話修好的費用會比買一支新的要高。妳要不要來店裡一趟看看有現貨的型號？[88] 我們還可以讓妳把壞掉的電話換成 100 美金的店內抵用金來折抵消費。我們每天從早上 8 點開到晚上 10 點，若妳有任何問題，我平日從早上 9 點到晚上 6 點都會在這裡。

86 Who most likely is the speaker?

(A) A technician
(B) A designer
(C) A secretary
(D) A telemarketer

86 說話者最有可能是誰？

(A) 技術人員
(B) 設計師
(C) 祕書
(D) 電話行銷人員

87 新 What does the speaker mean when he says, "the problem is more serious than I thought"?

(A) A screen cannot be ordered.
(B) A phone is an outdated model.
(C) A device is significantly damaged.
(D) A component needs to be upgraded.

87 當說話者說：「問題比我原本以為的要嚴重」是什麼意思？

(A) 無法訂購一款螢幕。
(B) 一支電話是過時的型號。
(C) 一個裝置嚴重受損。
(D) 一個零件需要升級。

88 What does the speaker offer?

(A) A store credit
(B) A special discount
(C) A free product
(D) A warranty extension

88 說話者提供什麼？

(A) 店內抵用金
(B) 特殊折扣
(C) 免費產品
(D) 延長保固

題目 internal [ɪnˋtɝnl̩] 內部的 component [kəmˋponənt] 零件 cost [kɔst] 花費（金錢等） fix [fɪks] 修理
86 secretary [ˋsɛkrə͵tɛrɪ] 祕書
87 outdated [͵aʊtˋdetɪd] 過時的
88 warranty [ˋwɔrəntɪ] 保固 extension [ɪkˋstɛnʃən] 延長

86 ■ 整體內容相關問題—說話者 答案 (A)

中

題目詢問說話者的身分，因此要注意聽和身分、職業相關的表達。獨白說：「I won't be able to repair your phone. ~ I told you that it would be easy to replace the cracked screen.」，表示雖然自己曾說過要把裂掉的螢幕換掉很簡單，但現在卻沒辦法把對方的電話修好了，由此可知，說話者是負責修理手機的技術人員，因此正確答案是 (A) A technician。

新 **87** ■ 細節事項相關問題—掌握意圖 答案 (C)

中

題目詢問說話者的說話意圖，因此要注意與題目引用句（the problem is more serious than I thought）相關的內容。獨白說：「When you dropped your phone, you broke several internal components. This means that it's going to cost more to fix your phone than to buy a new one.」，表示手機摔到的時候，內部有幾個零件壞了，因此修手機的費用會比買一支新的還要高，由此可知，這支手機嚴重受損，因此正確答案是 (C) A device is significantly damaged.。

88 ■ 細節事項相關問題—提議 答案 (A)

低

題目詢問說話者提供什麼，因此要注意聽獨白的後半部中出現提供相關表達的句子。獨白說：「We'll ~ give you a $100 store credit for your broken phone to use on your purchase.」，表示可以讓女子把壞掉的電話換成 100 美金的店內抵用金來折抵消費，因此正確答案是 (A) A store credit。

TEST 1 2 3 4 5 6 7 8 9 10

89
90
91

Questions 89-91 refer to the following instructions.

英式發音

[89]**Thank you for this opportunity to give a sales presentation on my company's newest application.** I think it'll be perfect for your insurance firm. Um, Scheduler 2.0 is an integrated online platform that makes it easy to manage client appointments. A customer who visits your Web site will be prompted to select an appointment time, and the program will then automatically assign an agent. Uh, the employee will be able to access the client's information to prepare for the meeting. [90]**For managers, this system can be used to see how many clients each team member is meeting and what products they have sold.** OK . . . [91]**let me show you how it works.** Then, I'll answer any questions you might have.

第 89-91 題請參考下列說明。

[89] 謝謝各位給我這個機會針對我公司最新的應用程式進行商品宣傳。我認為這個應用程式非常適合你們保險公司。嗯，Scheduler 2.0 是一個能使管理客戶預約變簡單的整合性線上平台。上你們網站的客戶會被引導選擇預約時間，而這個程式接著會自動指派專員。呃，員工將能取得客戶資料來為會面做準備。[90] 至於經理們，這個系統可以用來看每個組員將與多少客戶會面及他們賣出了什麼產品。好……[91] 讓我為各位示範它是如何運作的。接著我會回答各位可能會有的任何問題。

89 What is the main purpose of the talk?

(A) To explain a company regulation
(B) To introduce a software product
(C) To discuss an insurance plan
(D) To promote a Web site

89 這段話的主要目的是什麼？

(A) 說明公司規定
(B) 介紹軟體產品
(C) 討論保險方案
(D) 推銷網站

90 According to the speaker, what can managers do?

(A) Receive customer feedback
(B) Approve program updates
(C) Change staff assignments
(D) Track employee performance

90 根據說話者所說，經理們可以做什麼？

(A) 收到客人的回饋意見
(B) 同意程式更新
(C) 更改員工被指派的工作
(D) 追蹤員工績效

91 What will most likely happen next?

(A) A video will be played.
(B) A demonstration will be given.
(C) A supervisor will be introduced.
(D) A questionnaire will be distributed.

91 接下來最有可能會發生什麼？

(A) 會播放影片。
(B) 會進行示範。
(C) 會介紹主管。
(D) 會分發問卷。

題目 sales presentation 商品宣傳　insurance [(美) ɪn`ʃʊrəns (英) in`ʃuərəns] 保險
integrated [(美) `ɪntə͵gretɪd (英) `intigreitɪd] 整合性的　prompt [(美) prɑmpt (英) prɔmpt] 引導（做某事）；促使
select [sə`lɛkt] 選擇　automatically [͵ɔtə`mætɪkḷɪ] 自動地　access [`æksɛs] 存取（資料）

90 track [træk] 追蹤　performance [pɚ`fɔrməns] 績效；表現

91 questionnaire [͵kwɛstʃən`ɛr]（調查）問卷　distribute [dɪ`strɪbjʊt] 分發

89 整體內容相關問題—目的 答案 (B)

高

題目詢問這段話的目的是什麼，因此必須注意聽獨白的開頭部分。獨白說：「Thank you for this opportunity to give a sales presentation on my company's newest application.」，對聽者們給自己機會針對自己公司最新的應用程式進行商品宣傳表示感謝，並接著繼續介紹軟體程式，因此正確答案是 (B) To introduce a software product。

90 細節事項相關問題—特定細項 答案 (D)

高

題目詢問經理們可以做什麼，因此必須注意聽和題目關鍵字（managers）相關的內容。獨白說：「For managers, this system can be used to see how many clients each team member is meeting and what products they have sold.」，表示經理們可以用這個系統來看每個組員將與多少客戶會面以及賣出了什麼產品，因此正確答案是 (D) Track employee performance。

換句話說

see how many clients each team member is meeting and what products they have sold
看每個組員將與多少客戶會面及賣出了什麼產品
→ Track employee performance 追蹤員工的績效

91 細節事項相關問題—接下來要做的事 答案 (B)

中

題目詢問接下來最有可能會發生什麼，因此要注意聽獨白的最後部分。獨白說：「let me show you how it[application] works」，表示自己要示範這個應用程式是如何運作的，由此可知，接下來將會進行示範，因此正確答案是 (B) A demonstration will be given.。

換句話說

show ~ how it works 示範它是如何運作的 → A demonstration ~ be given 會進行示範

92
93
94

Questions 92-94 refer to the following telephone message and table.

第 92-94 題請參考下列電話留言及表格。

英式發音

Good morning, Mr. Davis. This is Marsha Foster. [92]**I'm calling about my interview on Tuesday.** Unfortunately, I have a family emergency to deal with, and I won't be available until the following week. [93]**Would it be possible to reschedule the interview?** Also, I received an e-mail from Aiden Parker asking me for another example of my work. Um, [94]**I dropped it off at the reception desk on Wednesday.** If he hasn't received the sample yet, it should be waiting for him there. Of course, should my application be missing anything else, I'll be happy to send it.

早安，Davis 先生。我是 Marsha Foster。[92] 我打來是想說和我星期二要進行的面試有關的事情。不幸的是，我家裡有急事要處理，而且要到下星期才會有時間。[93] 有沒有可能重新安排面試時間呢？此外，我收到了一封來自 Aiden Parker 的電子郵件，要求我再提供一件我的作品範例。嗯，[94] 我星期三把它帶去給接待櫃檯了。如果他還沒拿到那件範例，它應該就在那裡等著他。當然，如果我的應徵資料還有缺其他任何東西，我都很樂意寄過去。

新

Bretford Incorporated - Interview Dates	
Monday, May 2	Marketing Department
Tuesday, May 3	[92]**Design Department**
Wednesday, May 4	Sales Department
Thursday, May 5	Accounting Department
Friday, May 6	*No Interviews Scheduled*

Bretford 企業一面試日期	
5 月 2 日星期一	行銷部
5 月 3 日星期二	[92] 設計部
5 月 4 日星期三	銷售部
5 月 5 日星期四	會計部
5 月 6 日星期五	*未排定面試*

92 新 Look at the graphic. Which department is the woman applying to?
(A) Marketing
(B) Design
(C) Sales
(D) Accounting

92 請看圖表。女子應徵的是哪一個部門？
(A) 行銷
(B) 設計
(C) 銷售
(D) 會計

93 What does the speaker ask the listener to do?
(A) Provide a job description
(B) Check on a delivery
(C) Change a schedule
(D) Expedite a process

93 說話者要求聽者做什麼？
(A) 提供職務說明
(B) 檢查一批貨
(C) 更改時間安排
(D) 加快一個程序

94 What did the speaker do on Wednesday?
(A) Replied to an e-mail
(B) Submitted a sample
(C) Visited a family member
(D) Filled out an application

94 說話者星期三做了什麼？
(A) 回覆一封電子郵件
(B) 提交一件範例
(C) 拜訪一個家人
(D) 填寫一份申請書

題目 following [美 \`fɑləwɪŋ 英 \`fɔləuiŋ] 接下來的 reschedule [ri\`skɛdʒʊl] 重新安排時間 drop off at 帶～（到某地放下）
93 job description 職務說明 expedite [\`ɛkspɪˌdaɪt] 加快
94 reply [rɪ\`plaɪ] 回覆；回答

新 92 細節事項相關問題—圖表資料 答案 (B)
中

題目詢問女子應徵的是哪一個部門，因此要確認題目提供的圖表資訊，並注意和題目關鍵字（department ~ woman applying to）相關的內容。獨白說：「I'm calling about my interview on Tuesday.」，表示自己打來是想說和星期二要進行的面試有關的事情，透過圖表可知，星期二是設計部的面試，因此正確答案是 (B) Design。

93 細節事項相關問題—要求 答案 (C)
低

題目詢問說話者要求聽者做什麼，因此要注意聽獨白的中後半部分出現要求相關表達的句子。獨白說：「Would it be possible to reschedule the interview?」，詢問是否可能重新安排面試時間，因此正確答案是 (C) Change a schedule。

換句話說
reschedule 重新安排時間 → Change a schedule 更改時間安排

94 細節事項相關問題—特定細項 答案 (B)
中

題目詢問說話者星期三做了什麼，因此要注意聽和題目關鍵字（Wednesday）相關的內容。獨白說：「I dropped it[example of my work] off at the reception desk on Wednesday」，表示星期三把作品範例帶去給接待櫃檯了，因此正確答案是 (B) Submitted a sample。

95
96
97

Questions 95-97 refer to the following broadcast and map.

澳洲式發音

This is Colin Edwards reporting live from the 20th Annual Pottery Expo, which is being held in Canberra this year. [95]**Hundreds of people have gathered here at Melville Hall to see the work of artists from 12 different countries.** Today, I'll be interviewing Matthew Walsh, the owner of the popular local studio Rustic Ceramics. [96]**Be sure to check out his booth next to the stairway on the ground floor** to view some of his creations. Before I introduce him, though, I want to let you know that free pottery lessons are being offered to all attendees. If this interests you, [97]**just stop by the information desk to sign up for a session**. Now, let's meet Mr. Walsh . . .

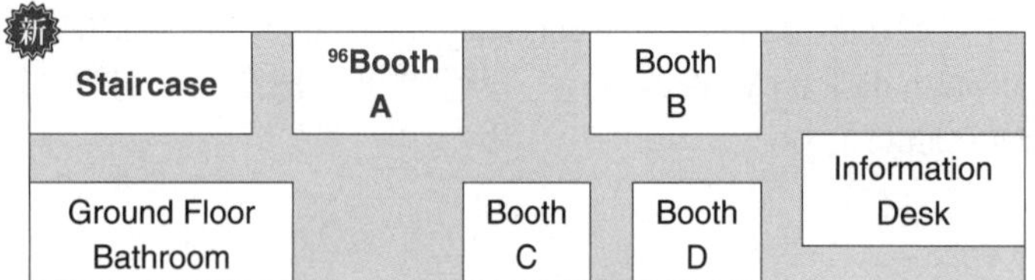

95 What is mentioned about the event?

(A) It has participants from many countries.
(B) It occurs in the same city every year.
(C) It is sponsored by local organizations.
(D) It will end later than expected.

96 新 Look at the graphic. Which booth is Matthew Walsh using?

(A) Booth A
(B) Booth B
(C) Booth C
(D) Booth D

97 According to the speaker, what can listeners do at the information desk?

(A) Pick up a brochure
(B) Buy a ticket
(C) Enter a contest
(D) Register for a class

第 95-97 題請參考下列廣播及地圖。

這裡是 Colin Edwards 於今年在坎培拉舉辦的第 20 屆年度陶藝博覽會進行實況報導。[95] 數百位民眾齊聚 Melville 廳這裡看來自 12 個不同國家的藝術家作品。今天我會訪問當地很受歡迎的工作室 Rustic Ceramics 的老闆 Matthew Walsh。[96] 請一定要去他在一樓樓梯旁的攤位上看看，欣賞一些他的作品。不過，在我介紹他之前，我想要告訴大家，所有來賓都可以參加免費的陶藝課。如果您對這有興趣，[97] 就到服務台去報名課程吧。那麼，讓我們歡迎 Walsh 先生……

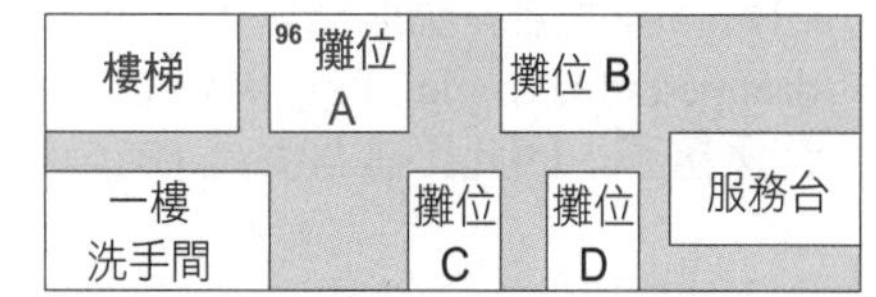

95 關於這個活動，提到了什麼？

(A) 它有來自很多國家的參加者。
(B) 它每年都在同一個城市舉行。
(C) 它由當地機構贊助。
(D) 它會比預期要晚結束。

96 請看圖表。Matthew Walsh 用的是哪一個攤位？

(A) 攤位 A
(B) 攤位 B
(C) 攤位 C
(D) 攤位 D

97 根據說話者所說，聽者們可以在服務台做什麼？

(A) 拿一本小冊子
(B) 買一張票
(C) 參加一場比賽
(D) 報名一門課

題目 pottery [美 `pɑtərɪ 英 `pɔtəri] 陶藝　gather [美 `gæðɚ 英 `gæðə] 聚集　check out 查看
stairway [美 `stɛr͵we 英 `stɛəwei] 樓梯　ground floor 一樓　creation [krɪ`eʃən] 作品；創造
interest [美 `ɪntərɪst 英 `intərist] 使產生興趣；引起～的關注

95 occur [ə`kɝ] 發生　sponsor [`spɑnsɚ] 贊助

97 register for 報名～

95 高 **細節事項相關問題—提及** 答案 (A)

題目詢問提到了什麼與活動有關的事，因此要注意聽和題目關鍵字（event）相關的內容。獨白說：「Hundreds of people have gathered here ~ to see the work of artists from 12 different countries.」，表示數百位民眾齊聚 Melville 廳這裡看來自 12 個不同國家的藝術家作品，因此正確答案是 (A) It has participants from many countries.。

新 **96** 低 **細節事項相關問題—圖表資料** 答案 (A)

題目詢問 Matthew Walsh 使用的攤位是哪一個，因此要確認題目提供的地圖，並注意和題目關鍵字（booth ~ Matthew Walsh using）相關的內容。獨白說：「Be sure to check out his[Matthew Walsh's] booth next to the stairway on the ground floor」，表示 Matthew Walsh 的攤位是在一樓的樓梯旁，透過地圖可知，Matthew Walsh 使用的攤位是在一樓樓梯旁的攤位 A，因此正確答案是 (A) Booth A。

97 中 **細節事項相關問題—特定細項** 答案 (D)

題目詢問聽者們可以在服務台做什麼，因此要注意聽和題目關鍵字（information desk）相關的內容。獨白說：「just stop by the information desk to sign up for a session」，表示可以在服務台報名陶藝課，因此正確答案是 (D) Register for a class。

換句話說

sign up for a session 報名課程 → Register for a class 報名一門課

Questions 98-100 refer to the following telephone message and coupon.

美式發音

Good afternoon, Mr. Choi. This is Emily O'Neil from marketing. My manager asked that I contact the accounting department about buying a piece of furniture. [98]**We were just notified that someone from sales will be joining our team on October 13, and we need another chair.** [99]**The model we would like to purchase is available at Dickson's Office Supply for $45.** I called the nearest branch, and the person I spoke to said it was in stock. She also mentioned that we could get a discount if we downloaded a coupon. [100]**I'll e-mail you the requisition form in a few minutes.** Please call me at extension 674 if you have any questions. Thank you.

Dickson's Office Supply

[99]**$10 off any purchase over $40 in value**
$20 off any purchase over $60 in value

Expires October 20

01234567890123

98 Why does the speaker need to purchase furniture?

(A) A manager is being promoted.
(B) A department is changing offices.
(C) An employee is being transferred.
(D) A team is starting a new project.

99 Look at the graphic. How much of a discount will the company most likely receive?

(A) $10
(B) $20
(C) $40
(D) $60

100 What does the speaker say she will do?

(A) Reply to an e-mail
(B) Send a form
(C) Contact a supplier
(D) Drop by a store

第 98-100 題請參考下列電話留言及優惠券。

午安，Choi 先生。我是行銷部的 Emily O'Neil。我們經理請我聯絡會計部說要買一件家具的事。[98] 我們剛剛接到了通知說銷售部有人會在 10 月 13 日加入我們團隊，所以我們需要多一張椅子。[99] 我們想要買的那款可以在 Dickson's 辦公用品以 45 美金買到。我打過電話給最近的分店，而和我說話的那個人說它有貨。她還提到如果我們下載優惠券，那就能拿到折扣。[100] 我等一下會用電子郵件把申請表寄給你。如果你有任何問題，請打分機 674 找我。謝謝你。

Dickson's 辦公用品

[99] 價值超過 40 美金的任何消費可折 10 美金
價值超過 60 美金的任何消費可折 20 美金

10 月 20 日到期

01234567890123

98 說話者為什麼需要買家具？

(A) 一位經理要被升職了。
(B) 一個部門要換辦公室了。
(C) 一個員工要轉調了。
(D) 一個團隊要開始一項新專案了。

99 請看圖表。這間公司最有可能會獲得多少折扣？

(A) 10 美金
(B) 20 美金
(C) 40 美金
(D) 60 美金

100 說話者說她會做什麼？

(A) 回一封電子郵件
(B) 寄出一張表格
(C) 聯絡一家供應商
(D) 前往一間店

題目 notify [ˋnotəˏfaɪ] 通知 requisition [ˏrɛkwəˋzɪʃən] 正式請求；（索取物資的）申請單 form [fɔrm] 表格 extension [ɪkˋstɛnʃən] 分機
98 promote [prəˋmot] 晉升 transfer [trænsˋfɝ] 轉調
100 supplier [səˋplaɪɚ] 供應商

98 細節事項相關問題—理由 答案 (C)

高

題目詢問說話者需要買家具的原因，因此要注意聽和題目關鍵字（purchase furniture）相關的內容。獨白說：「We were just notified that someone from sales will be joining our team ~, and we need another chair.」，表示剛剛收到通知，銷售部會有人要加入自己部門的團隊，因此需要多一張椅子，因此正確答案是 (C) An employee is being transferred.。

新 99 細節事項相關問題—圖表資料 答案 (A)

中

題目詢問這間公司會獲得多少折扣，因此必須確認題目提供的優惠券上的資訊，並注意和題目關鍵字（discount ~ receive）相關的內容。獨白說：「The model we would like to purchase is available at Dickson's Office Supply for $45.」，表示想要買的那款椅子可以在 Dickson's 辦公用品用 45 美金買到，透過優惠券上的資訊可知，價值超過 40 美金的消費可以折 10 美金，因此正確答案是 (A) $10。

100 細節事項相關問題—接下來要做的事 答案 (B)

低

題目詢問說話者說她會做什麼，因此要注意聽和題目關鍵字（will do）相關的內容。獨白說：「I'll e-mail you the requisition form in a few minutes.」，表示自己等一下會用電子郵件寄出申請表，因此正確答案是 (B) Send a form。

TEST 10

Part 1 原文・翻譯・解析

Part 2 原文・翻譯・解析

Part 3 原文・翻譯・解析 新

Part 4 原文・翻譯・解析 新

MP3 收錄於 TEST 10.mp3。

進行深入練習或複習時，可以一邊多聽幾次收錄各國口音的試題 MP3，一邊搭配解答中的中英對照翻譯和解析，以及單字記憶表和多元口音單字記憶 MP3，達到事半功倍的效果。

PART 1

1 低

🔊 加拿大式發音

(A) He is reading in a library.
(B) He is touching the spoke of a wheel.
(C) He is pulling out a book.
(D) He is dusting some shelves.

(A) 他正在圖書館裡看書。
(B) 他正摸著輪子的輪幅。
(C) 他正在抽出一本書。
(D) 他正在除去一些架子的灰塵。

單人照片 答案 (C)

仔細觀察照片中一名男子乘坐輪椅並正從書架上取書的樣子。

(A) [╳] reading（正在看書）和男子的動作無關，因此是錯誤選項。這裡使用照片可能的拍攝地點「圖書館（library）」來造成混淆。

(B) [╳] 男子並非正摸著輪子的輪幅（spoke of a wheel），而是摸著書，因此是錯誤選項。注意不要聽到 He is touching（他正摸著）就選擇這個選項。

(C) [○] 這裡正確描述男子正從書架上抽出一本書的樣子，所以是正確答案。

(D) [╳] dusting（正在除去～的灰塵）和男子的動作無關，因此是錯誤選項。這裡利用照片中有出現的架子（shelves）來造成混淆。

單字　spoke [spok] 輪輻　wheel [hwil] 輪子　pull out 抽出　dust [dʌst] 除去～的灰塵　shelf [ʃɛlf] 架子

2 中

🔊 英式發音

(A) A man is standing behind a counter.
(B) A man is holding a microphone.
(C) A man is collecting papers from some students.
(D) A man is addressing a group of people.

(A) 一名男子正站在櫃台後方。
(B) 一名男子正握著麥克風。
(C) 一名男子正從一些學生那裡收回紙張。
(D) 一名男子正對著一群人說話。

兩人以上的照片 答案 (D)

仔細觀察照片中有一名男子站在人們面前演說的模樣。

(A) [╳] 男子站在講桌旁，這裡卻描述成站在櫃台後方，因此是錯誤選項。注意不要聽到 A man is standing（一名男子站著）就選擇這個答案。

(B) [╳] 照片中沒有握著麥克風（holding a microphone）的男子，因此是錯誤選項。這裡使用照片中有出現的麥克風（microphone）來造成混淆。

(C) [╳] 照片中沒有正在收回紙張（collecting papers）的男子，因此是錯誤選項。這裡使用照片中有出現的學生（students）來造成混淆。

(D) [○] 這裡正確描述男子正對著一群人演說的模樣，所以是正確答案。

單字　hold [[美] hold [英] həuld] 握著　microphone [[美] `maɪkrə͵fon [英] `maikrəfəun] 麥克風
collect [kə`lɛkt] 收集；收回　address [ə`drɛs] 對～說話

3 高

🔊 澳洲式發音

(A) He is gazing toward the window.
(B) He has his arm on a surface.
(C) He has laid a device on a table.
(D) He is buttoning up his shirt.

(A) 他正凝視著窗戶。
(B) 他把手臂放在一個表面上。
(C) 他把一台裝置放在了桌上。
(D) 他正在扣他襯衫的釦子。

■ 單人照片 答案 (B)

仔細觀察照片中一名男子將手臂放在桌上、拿著裝置在看的模樣。

(A) [╳] 男子並非正凝視著窗戶（window），而是在看手中的裝置，因此是錯誤選項。注意不要聽到 He is gazing（他正凝視著）就選擇這個選項。

(B) [○] 這裡正確描述男子將手臂放在桌上的模樣，所以是正確答案。

(C) [╳] 男子把裝置拿在手中，這裡卻描述成放在了桌上，因此是錯誤選項。這裡使用照片中有出現的裝置（device）來造成混淆。

(D) [╳] buttoning up（正在扣鈕子）和男子的動作無關，因此是錯誤選項。這裡使用照片中有出現的襯衫（shirt）來造成混淆。

單字 gaze [gez] 凝視 lay [le] 放置，平放 button up 扣鈕子

4 高

美式發音

(A) A desk has been cleared of items.
(B) Light fixtures have been turned off.
(C) Some people are handing out writing utensils.
(D) Tiles cover the ceiling of an office.

(A) 一張桌子上的物品已被清空了。
(B) 燈具已經被關掉了。
(C) 一些人正在發放書寫工具。
(D) 一間辦公室的天花板上覆蓋著（天花板）磚。

■ 兩人以上的照片 答案 (D)

仔細觀察照片中人們在辦公室裡工作的模樣，以及周遭事物的狀態。

(A) [╳] 桌上擺放著物品，這裡卻描述成已被清空，因此是錯誤選項。這裡使用照片中有出現的桌子（desk）和物品（items）來造成混淆。

(B) [╳] 燈具是開著的狀態，這裡卻描述成已經關掉了，因此是錯誤選項。注意不要聽到 Light fixtures（燈具）就選擇這個答案。

(C) [╳] handing out（正在發放）和照片中的人物動作無關，因此是錯誤選項。這裡使用照片中有出現書寫工具（writing utensils）來造成混淆。

(D) [○] 這裡正確描述辦公室天花板上覆蓋著天花板磚的模樣，因此是正確答案。

單字 clear [klɪr] 清除 light fixture 燈具 hand out 分發 writing utensil 書寫工具 cover [ˋkʌvɚ] 覆蓋 ceiling [ˋsilɪŋ] 天花板

5 高

英式發音

(A) Food is being cooked at a campsite.
(B) An awning extends above some furniture.
(C) Part of a lawn is being watered.
(D) A cloth has been placed on the grass.

(A) 正在營地裡烹煮食物。
(B) 一個遮陽棚在一些家具上方展開。
(C) 正在澆灌部分的草坪。
(D) 草上鋪了一塊布。

■ 事物及風景照片 答案 (B)

仔細觀察照片中營地上的遮陽棚及周遭事物的狀態。

(A) [╳] 透過照片無法確認食物（Food）的存在，因此是錯誤選項。這裡使用照片可能的拍攝地點「營地（campsite）」來造成混淆。

(B) [○] 這裡正確描述遮陽棚所呈現的狀態，所以是正確答案。

(C) [╳] 照片中雖然有草坪，但不是正在澆灌（is being watered），因此是錯誤選項。注意不要聽到 Part of a lawn（部分的草坪）就選擇這個答案。

(D) [╳] 透過照片無法確認布（cloth）的存在，因此是錯誤選項。注意不要聽到 on the grass（草上）就選擇這個答案。

單字 campsite [ˋkæmp͵saɪt] 營地 awning[ˋɔnɪŋ] 遮陽篷 extend [ɪkˋstɛnd] 展開 water [㊤ ˋwɔtɚ ㊥ ˋwɔ:tə] 澆灌

加拿大式發音

(A) A motorcycle has been left under a roof.
(B) Vines are reaching to the ground.
(C) A door to a building is being opened.
(D) A vehicle is parked next to a wall.

(A) 一台機車被留在了屋頂之下。
(B) 藤蔓碰到了地面。
(C) 正在打開一扇通往建築物的門。
(D) 一台搭載工具停在了牆邊。

事物及風景照片

答案 (D)

仔細觀察照片中機車停在建築物旁的模樣，以及周遭事物的狀態。

(A) [╳] 透過照片無法確認屋頂（roof）的存在，因此是錯誤選項。注意不要聽到 A motorcycle has been left（機車被留在了）就選擇這個選項。

(B) [╳] 照片中的藤蔓沒有碰到地面（reaching to the ground），因此是錯誤選項。這裡使用照片中有出現的藤蔓（Vines）來造成混淆。

(C) [╳] 照片中雖然有門，但不是正在打開（is being opened）的狀態，因此是錯誤選項。注意不要聽到 A door to a building（一扇通往建築物的門）就選擇這個答案。

(D) [〇] 這裡正確描述可做為搭載工具的機車停在牆邊的樣子，所以是正確答案。注意這裡的機車以 vehicle（搭載工具）來表達。

單字　motorcycle [`motɚ͵saɪkl̩] 機車　vine [vaɪn] 藤蔓　reach [ritʃ] 碰觸到；延伸到　vehicle [`viɪkl̩] 搭載工具

7 低

澳洲式發音 → 英式發音	
Where can I find the milk and sugar?	我可以在哪裡找到牛奶和糖？
(A) Just behind you.	(A) 就在你後面。
(B) Low-fat milk, please.	(B) 低脂牛奶，謝謝。
(C) Let's find a hat for you.	(C) 我找頂帽子給你吧。

Where 疑問句 答案 (A)

這是詢問牛奶和糖在哪裡的 Where 疑問句。

(A) [○] 這裡回答就在對方的後面，提到牛奶和糖的所在地點，因此是正確答案。

(B) [╳] 題目詢問牛奶和糖在哪裡，這裡卻表示自己要低脂牛奶，毫不相關，因此是錯誤選項。這裡透過重複使用題目中出現的 milk 來造成混淆。

(C) [╳] 這裡透過重複使用題目中出現的 find 來造成混淆。注意不要聽到 Let's find 就選擇這個選項。

單字 low-fat 低脂的

8 低

美式發音 → 加拿大式發音	
When is the grant proposal due?	補助金提案在什麼時候到期？
(A) Yes, that's the deadline.	(A) 是的，那就是截止期限。
(B) I propose that we try.	(B) 我提議我們去試試。
(C) Not until next Tuesday.	(C) 下週二之前都不會。

When 疑問句 答案 (C)

這是詢問補助金提案在什麼時候到期的 When 疑問句。

(A) [╳] 這裡以 Yes 來回答疑問詞疑問句，因此是錯誤選項。這裡利用和 When is ~ due（～在什麼時候到期）相關的 deadline（截止期限）來造成混淆。

(B) [╳] 題目詢問補助金提案在什麼時候到期，這裡卻回答提議去試試，毫不相關，因此是錯誤選項。這裡利用發音相似單字 proposal – propose 來造成混淆。

(C) [○] 這裡回答下週二之前都不會，提到提案到期的時間點，因此是正確答案。

單字 grant [grænt] 補助金；同意 deadline [ˋdɛdˏlaɪn] 截止期限 propose [prəˋpoz] 提案

9 低

美式發音 → 澳洲式發音	
Who requested an adjustable computer chair?	誰申請了一張可調式電腦椅？
(A) The charts have been modified.	(A) 圖表已經修改過了。
(B) Kendra, the new bookkeeper.	(B) Kendra，新來的記帳人員。
(C) My laptop webcam.	(C) 我筆記型電腦的網路攝影機。

Who 疑問句 答案 (B)

這是詢問是誰申請了一張可調式電腦椅的 Who 疑問句。

(A) [╳] 這是利用和 adjustable（可調整的）相關的 modified（修改過的）來造成混淆的錯誤選項。

(B) [○] 這裡回答新來的記帳人員 Kendra，提到申請了可調式電腦椅的人，因此是正確答案。

(C) [╳] 這是利用和 computer（電腦）相關的 laptop（筆記型電腦）來造成混淆的錯誤選項。

單字 adjustable [əˋdʒʌstəbl̩] 可調整的 chart [美 tʃart 英 tʃɑːt] 圖表 modify [美 ˋmɑdəˏfaɪ 英 ˋmɔdifai] 修改 bookkeeper [美 ˋbʊkˏkipɚ 英 ˋbukˏkiːpə] 記帳人員 webcam [ˋwɛbˏkæm] 網路攝影機

10 ○○○● 低	英式發音 → 加拿大式發音 What are you conducting a study on? (A) Consumer spending. (B) In the research laboratory. (C) I could use an assistant.	你在進行什麼研究？ (A) 消費者支出。 (B) 在研究實驗室裡。 (C) 我想要一位助理。

What 疑問句 答案 (A)

這是詢問對方在進行什麼研究的 What 疑問句。

(A) [○] 這裡回答消費者支出，提到正在研究的主題，因此是正確答案。

(B) [╳] 題目詢問對方在進行什麼研究，這裡卻回答地點，因此是錯誤選項。這裡利用和題目中 study（研究）意思相近的 research（研究）來造成混淆。

(C) [╳] 這是利用和 conducting a study（進行研究）相關的 assistant（助理）來造成混淆的錯誤選項。

單字 conduct [kən`dʌkt] 經營；實施 spending [`spɛndɪŋ] 支出 research laboratory 研究實驗室
could use 想要～；需要～ assistant [ə`sɪstənt] 助理

11 ○○○● 低	英式發音 → 澳洲式發音 Which of the bicycles on the rack is yours? (A) They usually bike to work. (B) The purple one. (C) You can go for a ride.	架上的哪一台自行車是你的？ (A) 他們通常騎自行車上班。 (B) 紫色那台。 (C) 你可以去兜風。

Which 疑問句 答案 (B)

這是詢問對方的自行車是架上哪一台的 Which 疑問句。這裡一定要聽到 Which of the bicycles 才能順利作答。

(A) [╳] 這是利用和 bicycles（自行車）相關的 bike（騎自行車）來造成混淆的錯誤選項。

(B) [○] 這裡回答紫色那台，提到哪一台自行車是自己的，因此是正確答案。

(C) [╳] 這是利用和 bicycles（自行車）相關的 go for a ride（去兜風）來造成混淆的錯誤選項。

單字 rack [ræk] 架子

12 ○○○● 低	加拿大式發音 → 美式發音 Who is in charge of the division? (A) Divide the materials in half. (B) You'll be charged a small fee. (C) That would be Barney Richards.	誰負責這個部門？ (A) 把這些材料分成兩半。 (B) 你會被收取一小筆費用。 (C) 那會是 Barney Richards。

Who 疑問句 答案 (C)

這是詢問誰負責該部門的 Who 疑問句。

(A) [╳] 題目詢問誰負責該部門，這裡卻回答把材料分成兩半，毫不相關，因此是錯誤選項。這裡利用發音相似單字 division – Divide 來造成混淆。

(B) [╳] 這是利用字義為「索價」的動詞 charged 重複使用題目中的 charge（責任）來造成混淆的錯誤選項。

(C) [○] 這裡回答是 Barney Richards，提到負責人的名字，因此是正確答案。

單字 in charge of 負責～ divide [də`vaɪd] 分開 material [mə`tɪrɪəl] 材料 in half 分成兩半 fee [fi] 費用

13 高

澳洲式發音 → 英式發音

Ms. Moore's farewell celebration is coming up. (A) We are all going to miss you. (B) Yes. It's on Saturday. (C) She's doing well. Thanks for asking.	Moore 小姐的歡送會要到了。 (A) 我們都會想你的。 (B) 沒錯。在星期六。 (C) 她很好。謝謝關心。

陳述句 答案 (B)

這是表達 Moore 小姐的歡送會要到了的客觀事實陳述句。

(A) [╳] 這是使用可以從題目中 farewell celebration（歡送會）聯想到的 miss（思念）來造成混淆的錯誤選項。注意不要聽到 We are all going to miss 就選擇這個選項。

(B) [○] 這裡以 Yes 來回應 Moore 小姐的歡送會要到了的這件事，並附加說明歡送會是在星期六，因此是正確答案。

(C) [╳] 題目說 Moore 小姐的歡送會要到了，這裡卻回答她很好，並感謝對方關心，毫不相關，因此是錯誤選項。這裡使用可以代稱題目中 Ms. Moore 的 She 來造成混淆。

單字 farewell celebration 歡送會 come up 發生（某活動或事件）

14 中

美式發音 → 加拿大式發音

Which day do you want to depart for England? (A) Either May 17 or 18. (B) I want to leave from Incheon Airport. (C) It was quite a short trip.	你想在哪一天出發前往英國？ (A) 5 月 17 或 18 日。 (B) 我想從仁川機場出發。 (C) 那次旅行滿短的。

Which 疑問句 答案 (A)

這是詢問對方想在哪一天出發前往英國的 Which 疑問句。這裡一定要聽到 Which day 才能順利作答。

(A) [○] 這裡回答 5 月 17 或 18 日，提到出發前往英國的時間點，因此是正確答案。

(B) [╳] 這是利用和 depart for（出發前往～）相關的 leave from（從～出發）來造成混淆的錯誤選項。注意不要聽到 I want to leave 就選擇這個選項。

(C) [╳] 這是利用和 depart（出發）相關的 trip（旅行）來造成混淆的錯誤選項。

單字 depart [dɪˋpɑrt] 出發；離開

15 中

英式發音 → 澳洲式發音

How many company T-shirts have to be ordered? (A) Six or seven pencils. (B) Fill in this order form. (C) One for each team member.	公司的 T 恤必須要訂多少件？ (A) 六或七枝鉛筆。 (B) 填寫這張訂購單。 (C) 每位組員一件。

How 疑問句 答案 (C)

這是詢問公司的 T 恤必須要訂多少件的 How 疑問句。這裡必須知道 How many 是詢問數量的表達。

(A) [╳] 題目詢問公司的 T 恤必須要訂多少件，這裡卻回答六或七枝鉛筆，毫不相關，因此是錯誤選項。這裡使用表達數量的 Six or seven 來造成混淆。

(B) [╳] 這是利用字義為「訂購」的名詞 order 重複使用題目中的動詞 ordered（被訂購）來造成混淆的錯誤選項。

(C) [○] 這裡回答每位組員一件，提到必須訂購的數量，因此是正確答案。

單字 fill in 填寫 order form 訂購單

16 ○●● 中

澳洲式發音 → 美式發音	
We had to move the meal indoors because of the rainy weather.	我們因為下雨而得把餐點移到室內。
(A) This door leads to the staircase. (B) Oh, that's too bad. (C) That umbrella appears to be broken.	(A) 這扇門通往樓梯。 (B) 噢，這太糟了。 (C) 那把傘似乎壞了。

陳述句 答案 (B)

這是描述因為下雨而得把餐點移到室內的陳述句。

(A) [╳] 題目說因為下雨而得把餐點移到室內，這裡卻回答門通往樓梯，毫不相關，因此是錯誤選項。這裡利用發音相似單字 indoors – door 來造成混淆。

(B) [○] 這裡回答這太糟了，提出自己對這件事的意見，因此是正確答案。

(C) [╳] 這是利用和 rainy weather（下雨）相關的 umbrella（傘）來造成混淆的錯誤選項。

單字 indoors [美 `ɪn`dorz 英 `in`dɔ:z] 往室內 lead [lid] 通向 staircase [`stɛr͵kes] 樓梯 appear [ə`pɪr] 似乎 broken [`brokən] 損壞的

17 ○●● 中

加拿大式發音 → 美式發音	
Where did Andre get his camera lens?	Andre 是在哪裡買到他的相機鏡頭的？
(A) He's going to buy a digital camera. (B) Probably from an online seller. (C) It can take very sharp images.	(A) 他要去買一台數位相機。 (B) 可能是從網路賣家那裡吧。 (C) 它可以拍出非常鮮明的影像。

Where 疑問句 答案 (B)

這是詢問 Andre 的相機鏡頭是在哪裡買的 Where 疑問句。

(A) [╳] 這是利用可以代稱題目中 Andre 的 He 並重複題目中出現的 camera 來造成混淆的錯誤選項。

(B) [○] 這裡回答可能是從網路賣家那裡，間接提到 Andre 買到相機鏡頭的地點，因此是正確答案。

(C) [╳] 這是利用和 camera（相機）相關的 take ~ images（拍照）來造成混淆的錯誤選項。

單字 seller [`sɛlɚ] 銷售者 sharp [ʃarp]（輪廓等）鮮明的；銳利的

18 ○●● 中

英式發音 → 澳洲式發音	
Have the accountants been assigned tasks?	已經分派工作給會計師們了嗎？
(A) You'll have to ask Akiko. (B) We can't account for the decrease. (C) I have signed the contract.	(A) 你得去問 Akiko。 (B) 我們無法解釋這些減少的數量。 (C) 我已經簽下合約了。

助動詞疑問句 答案 (A)

這是確認是否已分派工作給會計師們了的助動詞（Have）疑問句。

(A) [○] 這裡回答得去問 Akiko，間接表示自己不知道，因此是正確答案。

(B) [╳] 題目詢問是否已分派工作給會計師們了，這裡卻回答無法解釋減少的數量，毫不相關，因此是錯誤選項。這裡利用發音相似單字 accountants – account 來造成混淆。

(C) [╳] 這是利用發音相似單字 assigned – signed 來造成混淆的錯誤選項。

單字 accountant [ə`kaʊntənt] 會計師 account for 解釋～ decrease [`dikris] 減少的數量 contract [美 `kɑntrækt 英 `kɔntrækt] 合約書

19 ○○●●● 中

[🔊] 加拿大式發音 → 英式發音

Some of the performers are in their dressing rooms, aren't they?	有一些表演者在他們的更衣室裡，不是嗎？
(A) The dressing isn't good.	(A) 這個醬料不好吃。
(B) That's what I heard.	(B) 我聽到的是那樣。
(C) They aren't on the shelf.	(C) 它們不在架上。

附加問句 答案 (B)

這是詢問是否有一些表演者在他們的更衣室裡的附加問句。

(A) [╳] 題目詢問是否有一些表演者在他們的更衣室裡，這裡卻回答醬料不好吃，毫不相關，因此是錯誤選項。這裡將題目中出現的 dressing rooms（更衣室）裡的 dressing 以另一字義「醬料」來重複使用，企圖造成混淆。

(B) [○] 這裡回答自己聽到的是那樣，表示的確有些表演者在他們的更衣室裡，因此是正確答案。

(C) [╳] 這是利用可以代稱題目中 performers（表演者）的 They 來造成混淆的錯誤選項。注意不要聽到 They aren't 就選擇這個選項。

單字 dressing room 更衣室 dressing [ˋdrɛsɪŋ]（調味食物用的）醬料；穿衣打扮

20 ○●●●● 高

[🔊] 美式發音 → 澳洲式發音

Our plant is experiencing some mechanical failures.	我們工廠正碰上一些機械故障。
(A) The applicant is very experienced.	(A) 應徵者非常有經驗。
(B) From a professional mechanic.	(B) 來自專業技師。
(C) That's the third time this year.	(C) 這是今年第三次了。

陳述句 答案 (C)

這是提到工廠正碰上一些機械故障的陳述句。

(A) [╳] 題目提到工廠正碰上一些機械故障，這裡卻回答應徵者非常有經驗，因此是錯誤選項。這裡利用發音相似單字 experiencing – experienced 來造成混淆。

(B) [╳] 這是利用和 mechanical failures（機械故障）相關的 mechanic（技師）來造成混淆的錯誤選項。

(C) [○] 這裡回答這是今年第三次了，提供更多與題目陳述相關的資訊，因此是正確答案。

單字 mechanical [məˋkænɪkl] 機械的 failure [ˋfeljɚ] 故障 experienced [ɪkˋspɪrɪənst] 有經驗的
mechanic [məˋkænɪk] 技師

21 ○●●●● 高

[🔊] 英式發音 → 加拿大式發音

When is the corporate fund-raising event?	公司的募款活動在什麼時候？
(A) Let me get back to you about that.	(A) 我晚點再回你這件事。
(B) The goal is to raise a lot of money.	(B) 目標是要募到很多錢。
(C) Volunteers must cooperate.	(C) 志工們必須配合。

When 疑問句 答案 (A)

這是詢問公司的募款活動在什麼時候的 When 疑問句。

(A) [○] 這裡回答晚點再回覆對方這件事，間接表示自己不知道，因此是正確答案。

(B) [╳] 這是利用和 fund-raising event（募款活動）相關的 raise ~ money（募到錢）來造成混淆的錯誤選項。

(C) [╳] 題目詢問公司的募款活動在什麼時候，這裡卻回答志工們必須配合，毫不相關，因此是錯誤選項。這裡利用發音相似單字 corporate – cooperate 來造成混淆。

單字 corporate [[美] ˋkɔrpərɪt [英] ˋkɔːpərit] 公司的 fund-raising event 募款活動 get back to 晚點再回覆
raise [rez] 募集（資金等）；提升 cooperate [koˋɑpəˌret] 配合

TEST 1 2 3 4 5 6 7 8 9 10

22 ●●●○ 高

澳洲式發音 → 美式發音	
Can I get a quote for having new windows installed? (A) Your home needs to be inspected first. (B) No, I'll print you a new receipt. (C) It was damaged during a storm.	可以給我安裝新窗戶的報價嗎？ (A) 得先看過你家才行。 (B) 不行，我會印一張新的收據給你。 (C) 它在暴風雨的時候受損了。

助動詞疑問句 答案 (A)

這是詢問自己能否拿到新窗戶的安裝報價的助動詞（Can）疑問句。

(A) [○] 這裡回答得先看過對方家才行，間接表示無法給出報價，因此是正確答案。

(B) [╳] 這是利用和 quote（報價）相關的 receipt（收據）來造成混淆的錯誤選項。注意不要聽到 No 就選擇這個選項。

(C) [╳] 這是利用可以透過 having new windows installed（安裝新窗戶）聯想到的安裝原因 damaged during a storm（在暴風雨的時候受損了）來造成混淆的錯誤選項。

單字 quote [美 kwot 英 kwəut] 報價 inspect [ɪn`spɛkt] 勘查（建築物等） storm [stɔrm] 暴風雨

23 ●●●○ 高

加拿大式發音 → 英式發音	
How about introducing yourself to our yoga instructor? (A) I met him earlier. (B) Our school is open throughout the year. (C) The introduction is being rewritten.	你要不要跟我們的瑜珈老師介紹一下你自己？ (A) 我之前見過他了。 (B) 我們學校全年開放。 (C) 正在重寫這篇緒論。

提議疑問句 答案 (A)

這是提議對方向瑜珈老師自我介紹的提議疑問句。這裡必須知道 How about 是表示提議的表達。

(A) [○] 這裡回答自己之前見過他了，間接表示拒絕，因此是正確答案。

(B) [╳] 這是利用和 instructor（教師）相關的 school（學校）來造成混淆的錯誤選項。

(C) [╳] 題目提議對方向瑜珈老師自我介紹，這裡卻回答正在重寫這篇緒論，毫不相關，因此是錯誤選項。這裡利用發音相似單字 introducing – introduction 來造成混淆。

單字 introduce oneself 自我介紹 instructor [ɪn`strʌktɚ] 教師 throughout [θru`aʊt] 從頭到尾
introduction [ˌɪntrə`dʌkʃən] 緒論；介紹

24 ●●○○ 中

英式發音 → 加拿大式發音	
Should I take the call from the client or the marketing director first? (A) OK, you talk to him. (B) I'm on call until 8 o'clock. (C) Answer the client on Line 3.	我該先接客戶的電話還是行銷總監的？ (A) 好，你跟他說。 (B) 我待命到 8 點。 (C) 接在 3 線的客戶。

選擇疑問句 答案 (C)

這是詢問自己該先接客戶還是行銷總監電話的選擇疑問句。

(A) [╳] 這裡以和 Yes 意義相近的 OK 來回答用 or 連接前後單字或片語的選擇疑問句，因此是錯誤選項。請一定要記得不能以 Yes/No 來回答用 or 連接前後單字或片語的選擇疑問句。

(B) [╳] 題目詢問該先接客戶還是行銷總監的電話，這裡卻回答自己待命到 8 點，毫不相關，因此是錯誤選項。這裡藉重複使用題目中出現的 call 來造成混淆。

(C) [○] 這裡回答接在 3 線的客戶，表示選擇先接客戶電話，因此是正確答案。

單字 on call 待命

25 ●●○ 中

美式發音 → 澳洲式發音 Do you want me to shovel the snow on the sidewalk? (A) If you can spare the time. (B) I guess it's snowing in Boston. (C) I just walked here.	你想要我去鏟人行道上的雪嗎？ (A) 如果你能騰出時間的話。 (B) 我猜波士頓正在下雪。 (C) 我剛走到這裡。

提供疑問句 答案 (A)

這是詢問對方是否想要自己去鏟人行道上的雪的提供疑問句。這裡必須知道 Do you want me to 是表示提供的表達。

(A) [○] 這裡回答如果對方能騰出時間的話，間接表示想要對方去鏟雪，因此是正確答案。

(B) [╳] 題目詢問對方是否想要自己去鏟人行道上的雪，這裡卻回答波士頓正在下雪，毫不相關，因此是錯誤選項。這裡以動詞字義「下雪」的 snowing 來重複使用題目中出現的 snow（雪），企圖造成混淆。

(C) [╳] 這是利用發音相似單字 sidewalk – walked 及可以代稱題目中 sidewalk（人行道）的 here（這裡）來造成混淆的錯誤選項。

單字 shovel the snow 鏟雪 sidewalk [ˋsaɪdˏwɔk] 人行道 spare [[美] spɛr [英] spɛə] 騰出（時間、金錢等）

26 ●●● 高

加拿大式發音 → 英式發音 Can't I get refreshments from this vending machine? (A) Most of the vendors have their own stalls. (B) Some of the guests are getting thirsty. (C) The last time I checked, it was out of order.	我不能用這台販賣機買飲料和點心嗎？ (A) 大部分的攤販有他們自己的攤位。 (B) 一些賓客漸漸覺得渴了。 (C) 我上次確認的時候，它故障了。

否定疑問句 答案 (C)

這是詢問是否能用這台販賣機買飲料和點心的否定疑問句。

(A) [╳] 題目詢問是否能用這台販賣機買飲料和點心，這裡卻回答大部分的攤販有他們自己的攤位，毫不相關，因此是錯誤選項。這裡利用發音相似單字 vending – vendors 來造成混淆。

(B) [╳] 這是利用和 refreshments（飲料和點心）相關的 thirsty（覺得渴的）來造成混淆的錯誤選項。

(C) [○] 這裡回答販賣機在自己上次確認的時候是故障的，間接表示不能用這台販賣機買飲料和點心，因此是正確答案。

單字 refreshment [rɪˋfrɛʃmənt] 茶點；飲料和點心 vending machine 販賣機 vendor [[美] ˋvɛndɚ [英] ˋvendə] 攤販 stall [stɔl] 攤位 out of order 故障

27 ●●○ 中

澳洲式發音 → 美式發音 My car has been fixed, so we can pick it up this afternoon. (A) My sedan has leather seats. (B) Let's go at around 1:30. (C) Apparently, we mixed up the files.	我的車已經修好了，所以我們今天下午可以去拿車。 (A) 我的轎車有皮革座椅。 (B) 我們在 1 點 30 分左右去吧。 (C) 顯然，我們把檔案搞混了。

陳述句 答案 (B)

這是表示車已經修好，所以今天下午可以去拿車的客觀事實陳述句。

(A) [╳] 這是利用和 car（車）相關的 sedan（轎車）來造成混淆的錯誤選項。

(B) [○] 這裡回答在 1 點 30 分左右去，表示今天下午會去拿車，因此是正確答案。

(C) [╳] 題目說車已經修好了，今天下午可以去拿，這裡卻回答把檔案搞混了，毫不相關，因此是錯誤選項。這裡利用發音相似單字 fixed – mixed 來造成混淆。

單字 sedan [sɪˋdæn] 轎車 leather [ˋlɛðɚ] 皮革製的 mix up 拌勻；混淆

28 ●○○○○ 高

🔊 美式發音 → 澳洲式發音	
The sink faucet in the staff room is leaking, isn't it?	員工休息室水槽的水龍頭在漏水，不是嗎？
(A) No, we haven't got any room. (B) Yes, there's ink all over the desk. (C) The problem has been resolved.	(A) 沒有，我們還沒得到任何機會。 (B) 是的，桌上到處都是墨水。 (C) 這個問題已經解決了。

附加問句 答案 (C)

這是詢問員工休息室水槽的水龍頭是否正在漏水的附加問句。

(A) [╳] 這是利用可以用來回答附加問句的 No，並將題目中的 room（房間）以另一字義「機會」來重複使用的錯誤答案。

(B) [╳] 這是使用可以用來回答附加問句的 Yes，並利用發音相似單字 sink – ink 來造成混淆的錯誤選項。

(C) [○] 這裡回答這個問題已經解決了，間接表示休息室水槽的水龍頭已經不會漏水了，因此是正確答案。

單字　faucet [`fɔsɪt] 水龍頭　leak [lik] 漏（水等）　all over 到處　resolve [[美] rɪ`zɑlv [英] ri`zɔlv] 解決

29 ●●●●● 難

🔊 英式發音 → 加拿大式發音	
Wendell, are you ready to assemble this bookshelf?	Wendell，你準備好要組裝這個書架了嗎？
(A) I'll grab the instruction manual. (B) Next to the door. (C) Once the game concluded.	(A) 我去拿說明手冊。 (B) 在門旁邊。 (C) 一旦當時的遊戲結束。

Be 動詞疑問句 答案 (A)

這是確認是否準備好要組裝書架了的 Be 動詞疑問句。

(A) [○] 這裡回答自己要去拿說明手冊，間接表示已經準備好要進行組裝了，因此是正確答案。

(B) [╳] 題目詢問是否準備好要組裝書架，這裡卻回答地點，因此是錯誤選項。

(C) [╳] 這是藉由能透過題目中 ready（準備好的）聯想到的時間點 once（一旦～）來造成混淆的錯誤選項。這裡使用可能會與 concludes 搞混的 concluded，注意不要聽成 Once the game concludes（一旦遊戲結束）而誤選成這個答案。

單字　assemble [ə`sɛmbl̩] 組裝；召集　instruction manual 說明手冊　once [wʌns] 一旦～；一等～就～
conclude [kən`klud] 結束

30 ●●○○○ 中

🔊 美式發音 → 加拿大式發音	
Would you rather sit here in the front row or further back?	你比較想要坐在前排這裡還是後面遠一點？
(A) It's a good fit. (B) I don't know where he is. (C) Let's sit close to the screen.	(A) 這很適合。 (B) 我不知道他在哪裡。 (C) 我們坐離銀幕近一點吧。

選擇疑問句 答案 (C)

這是詢問要坐前排還是後面遠一點的選擇疑問句。

(A) [╳] 題目詢問要坐前排還是後面遠一點，這裡卻回答這很適合，毫不相關，因此是錯誤選項。這裡利用發音相似單字 sit – fit 來造成混淆。

(B) [╳] 題目中沒有可以用 he 代稱的對象，因此是錯誤選項。這裡利用發音相似單字 row – know 來造成混淆。注意不要聽到 I don't know where 就選擇這個選項。

(C) [○] 這裡回答要坐離銀幕近一點，間接表示選擇坐前排，因此是正確答案。

單字　row [ro]（一排的）座位　further [`fɝðɚ] 進一步的；更遠的

31 ○●●● 高

[🔊] 澳洲式發音 → 英式發音

Why were you asked to revise the employee handbook?	為什麼你被要求去修改員工手冊？
(A) Because the train is at the platform.	(A) 因為火車在月台上。
(B) An explanation was missing from Section 24.	(B) 第 24 節有一段說明不見了。
(C) Give me the latest version.	(C) 給我最新的版本。

Why 疑問句 答案 (B)

這是詢問為什麼要修改員工手冊的 Why 疑問句。

(A) [╳] 題目詢問為什麼要修改員工手冊，這裡卻回答因為火車在月台上，毫不相關，因此是錯誤選項。注意不要聽到 Because 就選擇這個選項。

(B) [○] 這裡回答第 24 節有一段說明不見了，提到要修改員工手冊的原因，因此是正確答案。

(C) [╳] 這是利用可以透過 employee handbook（員工手冊）聯想到的手冊出版資訊 latest version（最新的版本）來造成混淆的錯誤選項。

單字 revise [rɪˋvaɪz] 修改 handbook [ˋhændˏbʊk] 手冊 platform [美] ˋplætˏfɔrm [英] ˋplætˏfɔ:m] 月台
explanation [ˏɛkspləˋneʃən] 說明 section [ˋsɛkʃən]（文章等的）節 latest version 最新的版本

32
33
34

Questions 32-34 refer to the following conversation.

澳洲式發音 → 美式發音

M: [32]**It's time that we seriously consider adding more tables to our café. Our location has become quite popular this summer thanks to many new businesses opening in the area. And we've often had to turn away patrons.**

W: Yes, it'd definitely be better to have another seating area. But where should we set it up? I feel as though we're already making good use of the space.

M: [33/34]**How do you feel about getting rid of one of the display cases and arranging tables to the left of the entrance?**

W: That might work. [34]**Let's try doing it tonight.** I think there are extra tables in the basement that we can use.

32 What problem are the speakers discussing?

(A) A restaurant's interior is outdated.
(B) A business is not attracting patrons.
(C) There is not enough seating.
(D) There are scratches on some tables.

33 What does the man suggest?

(A) Removing a display container
(B) Opening an outside seating area
(C) Leasing some new machinery
(D) Replacing some old chairs

34 What will the speakers most likely do this evening?

(A) Shop for additional furniture
(B) Put out some menus
(C) Reorganize a space
(D) Clean out a basement

第 32-34 題請參考下列對話。

男：[32] 我們是時候認真考慮增加我們咖啡廳的桌數了。多虧這一區裡新開了很多公司，我們店在今年夏天已經變得相當受歡迎了。但我們常常不得不把客人推掉。

女：沒錯，再多設一個座位區一定會比較好。但我們該設在哪裡？我覺得我們似乎已經充分運用這個空間了。

男：[33/34] 妳覺得把其中一個展示櫃撤掉，再把桌子擺在入口的左邊怎麼樣？

女：這樣可能行得通。[34] 我們今晚來試試看吧。我想地下室裡還有多的桌子可以給我們用。

32 說話者們在討論什麼問題？

(A) 一間餐廳的內部過時了。
(B) 一間公司不吸引顧客。
(C) 座位不夠。
(D) 一些桌子上有刮痕。

33 男子建議什麼？

(A) 移除一個展示用容器
(B) 開設一個戶外座位區
(C) 租用一些新的機器
(D) 換掉一些舊椅子

34 說話者們今天晚上最有可能會做什麼？

(A) 購買額外的家具
(B) 推出一些菜單
(C) 重新規劃一個空間
(D) 打掃一個地下室

題目 turn away 拒絕；臉轉開　patron [ˋpetrən] 顧客　definitely [ˋdɛfənɪtlɪ] 一定　make use of 運用～
arrange [əˋrendʒ] 擺放；安排　basement [ˋbesmənt] 地下室；地下層
32 attract [əˋtrækt] 吸引；引起　scratch [skrætʃ] 刮痕
33 lease [lis] 租用　machinery [məˋʃinərɪ] 機器
34 put out 推出；製作　reorganize [riˋɔrgəˌnaɪz] 重新規劃

32 細節事項相關問題—問題點 答案 (C)

中

題目詢問說話者們在討論的是什麼問題，因此要注意聽對話中出現負面表達之後的內容。男子說：「It's time that we seriously consider adding more tables to our café. Our location has become quite popular this summer ~. And we've often had to turn away patrons.」，表示是時候認真考慮增加桌數的事了，因為咖啡廳已經變得很受歡迎，但卻常常不得不把客人推掉，由此可知，問題在於咖啡廳裡的座位不夠，因此正確答案是 (C) There is not enough seating.。

33 細節事項相關問題—提議 答案 (A)

中

題目詢問男子建議什麼，因此要注意聽男子話中出現的提議表達。男子說：「How do you feel about getting rid of one of the display cases and arranging tables to the left of the entrance?」，建議把其中一個展示櫃撤掉，再把桌子擺在入口的左邊，因此正確答案是 (A) Removing a display container。

34 細節事項相關問題—接下來要做的事 答案 (C)

高

題目詢問說話者們今天晚上最有可能會做什麼，因此要注意聽和題目關鍵字（this evening）相關的內容。男子對女子說：「How do you feel about getting rid of one of the display cases and arranging tables to the left of the entrance?」，詢問女子覺得去掉一個展示櫃並把桌子擺在入口的左邊怎麼樣，女子則回答：「Let's try doing it tonight.」，表示今晚來試試看，因此正確答案是 (C) Reorganize a space。

35
36
37

Questions 35-37 refer to the following conversation.

美式發音 → 加拿大式發音

W: May I speak with Ludi Tan? [35]**I'm trying to contact him on behalf of Oakland Roofing about a voice mail he left for us an hour ago.**

M: This is he. Thanks for the quick response. As I mentioned in my message, [36]**a small spot on my roof was damaged** during last Friday's thunderstorm. One of your representatives came to my house yesterday. He said that [36]**the section near the chimney was in bad shape and would be costly to repair**. However, [37]**he never e-mailed me a final quote like he said he would**.

W: I apologize about that, Mr. Tan. I'll contact the person who visited your home, get the quote, and then call you back shortly.

第 35-37 題請參考下列對話。

女：我可以跟 Ludi Tan 說話嗎？[35] 我代表奧克蘭屋頂興建想就一小時前他留給我們的一段語音訊息和他聯繫。

男：我就是。謝謝你們這麼快就回覆我。如同我在訊息裡提到的，[36] 我的屋頂上有一小塊地方在上週五的大雷雨中壞了。一位你們的代表昨天來過我家了。他說 [36] 靠近煙囪的那區狀態很差，而且要修的話會很花錢。不過，[37] 他一直沒有像他說的那樣把最終報價用電子郵件寄給我。

女：我很抱歉發生這種事，Tan 先生。我會聯絡去你家的那個人，拿到報價，然後立刻回電給你。

35 Why is the woman calling the man?

(A) To cancel a gathering
(B) To ask about a service
(C) To report an emergency
(D) To respond to a message

35 女子為何打電話給男子？

(A) 為了取消一次聚會
(B) 為了詢問一項服務的事
(C) 為了回報一個緊急狀況
(D) 為了回覆一則訊息

36 What needs to be repaired?

(A) A sidewalk
(B) A road
(C) A store's window
(D) A building's roof

36 需要修理的是什麼？

(A) 人行道
(B) 道路
(C) 店鋪的窗戶
(D) 建築物的屋頂

37 According to the man, what did a representative fail to do?

(A) Fix part of a structure
(B) Provide an estimate
(C) Locate a property
(D) Process a payment

37 根據男子所說，一位代表沒有做什麼？

(A) 修理部分建築物
(B) 提供一個估價
(C) 確定一個物業的所在地點
(D) 處理一筆支付款項

題目 on behalf of 代表～；代替 thunderstorm [ˋθʌndɚˏstɔrm] 大雷雨 representative [rɛprɪˋzɛntətɪv] 代表人員；代表 chimney [ˋtʃɪmnɪ] 煙囪 costly [ˋkɔstlɪ] 代價高昂的 shortly [ˋʃɔrtlɪ] 立刻

37 structure [ˋstrʌktʃɚ] 建築物 estimate [ˋɛstəˏmet] 估價；估計值 locate [loˋket] 確定～的所在地點；找出 property [ˋprɑpɚtɪ] 物業；不動產

35 整體對話相關問題—目的 答案 (D)

中

題目詢問女子打電話的目的，因此要注意對話的開頭。女子說：「I'm trying to contact him[Ludi Tan] ~ about a voice mail he left for us an hour ago.」，表示 Ludi Tan 一個小時前留下了語音訊息，所以自己想要聯繫他，由此可知，女子是為了要回覆男子的語音訊息而打電話，因此正確答案是 (D) To respond to a message。

36 細節事項相關問題—特定細項 答案 (D)

低

題目詢問要修理的是什麼，因此要注意聽和題目關鍵字（repaired）相關的內容。男子說：「a small spot on my roof was damaged」，表示屋頂有一小塊壞了，接著說：「the section near the chimney was in bad shape and would be costly to repair」，表示煙囪附近的狀態很差，要修的話會花很多錢，由此可知，需要修理的是建築物的屋頂，因此正確答案是 (D) A building's roof。

37 細節事項相關問題—特定細項 答案 (B)

高

題目詢問男子說該公司的代表沒做什麼，因此必須注意聽男子話中和題目關鍵字（representative fail to do）相關的內容。男子說：「he[One of your representatives] never e-mailed me a final quote like he said he would」，表示女子公司的一位代表一直沒有把最終報價用電子郵件寄給自己，因此正確答案是 (B) Provide an estimate。

[新] 38 39 40

Questions 38-40 refer to the following conversation.

英式發音 → 澳洲式發音

W: Good morning. This is Christy from the administrative team. Seeing as [38]**you began working in a new position last Wednesday**, you should come to our office to replace your employee ID.

M: OK. However, I can't stop by tomorrow because I'm attending a convention in Baton Rouge. Would sometime next Monday be possible?

W: I'm afraid not. You're supposed to get a new ID before the end of the week according to company policy.

M: Hmm . . . I might be able to visit your office later this afternoon. Could I come at 4 P.M.?

W: That should work . . . [39]**I have a meeting at 3 P.M.**, but it shouldn't last long. [40]**Why don't you give me a call at around 3:30 P.M. to make sure I'm available?**

38 According to the woman, what happened last Wednesday?

(A) A team was assigned to a project.
(B) A job posting was uploaded.
(C) An administrator announced a policy change.
(D) A staff member started in a new role.

39 When will a meeting begin?

(A) At 3:00 P.M.
(B) At 3:30 P.M.
(C) At 4:00 P.M.
(D) At 4:30 P.M.

40 What does the woman suggest?

(A) Calling later
(B) Accepting a job offer
(C) Rescheduling an appointment
(D) Checking trip details again

第 38-40 題請參考下列對話。

女：早安。我是行政團隊的 Christy。既然 [38] 你上週三開始擔任新的職務了，你應該要來我們辦公室更換你的員工證。

男：好的。不過，我明天沒辦法過去，因為我要去 Baton Rouge 出席一場會議。可以在下週一再找個時間過去嗎？

女：恐怕不行。根據公司政策，你應該要在這週結束前拿到新的員工證。

男：嗯……我今天下午晚一點可能可以去你們辦公室。我可以在下午 4 點過去嗎？

女：應該可以……[39] 我下午 3 點有個會要開，不過應該不會開太久。[40] 不如你下午 3 點 30 分左右打個電話給我確認我有沒有空吧？

38 根據女子所說，上週三發生了什麼？

(A) 一個團隊被指派了一個專案。
(B) 上傳了一則徵才廣告。
(C) 一位管理人員宣布了一項政策變更。
(D) 一位員工開始了一個新的職務。

39 一場會議會在何時開始？

(A) 下午 3 點
(B) 下午 3 點 30 分
(C) 下午 4 點
(D) 下午 4 點 30 分

40 女子建議什麼？

(A) 晚點打電話
(B) 接受一個工作機會
(C) 重新安排一個預約的時間
(D) 再次確認旅行的細節資訊

題目 administrative [[美] əd`mɪnə͵stretɪv [英] əd`ministrətiv] 行政的 position [pə`zɪʃən] 職務；位置
38 job posting 徵人廣告 administrator [əd`mɪnə͵stretɚ] 管理人員
40 offer [`ɔfɚ] 提議；提供

38 細節事項相關問題—特定細項 答案 (D)
中

題目詢問女子說上週三發生了什麼，因此要注意聽女子話中和題目關鍵字（last Wednesday）相關及前後的內容。女子說：「you began working in a new position last Wednesday」，表示男子上週三開始擔任新的職務了，因此正確答案是 (D) A staff member started in a new role.。

換句話說

began working in a new position 開始擔任新的職務了 → started in a new role 開始了一個新的職務

39 細節事項相關問題—特定細項 答案 (A)
低

題目詢問會議會在什麼時候開始，因此要注意聽和題目關鍵字（meeting）相關及前後的內容。女子說：「I have a meeting at 3 P.M.」，表示下午 3 點有會要開，因此正確答案是 (A) At 3:00 P.M.。

40 細節事項相關問題—提議 答案 (A)
低

題目詢問女子建議什麼，因此要注意聽女子話中和提議相關的表達。女子對男子說：「Why don't you give me a call at around 3:30 P.M. to make sure I'm available?」，表示為確保自己那時有空，建議男子在下午 3 點 30 分左右打電話給自己，因此正確答案是 (A) Calling later。

新

Questions 41-43 refer to the following conversation with three speakers.

美式發音 → 加拿大式發音 → 澳洲式發音

W: [41]**We didn't order enough computers for the interns hired to work in the finance department.** As of now, only 15 of them will be delivered next Monday.

M1: [42]**Although we need 20 devices, we have five used ones in the storage closet** that we can reformat.

M2: Yeah. I thought we planned to use them, which is why I ordered as many as I did.

W: Unfortunately, [42]**the finance director said that he wants all interns to get brand-new devices**.

M2: Oh, I didn't realize that. I'll call our supplier now and see if the existing order can be updated to include the extra machines.

W: Thanks. And [43]**as we probably won't need those used computers anymore, please remove their serial numbers from the list of available devices** when you have a chance.

41 What concern does the woman mention?

(A) Some equipment was not repaired.
(B) A delivery did not arrive on schedule.
(C) Insufficient items were ordered.
(D) Workers were given faulty devices.

42 How many new computers are required for interns?

(A) 5
(B) 10
(C) 15
(D) 20

43 What task does the woman want carried out?

(A) Downloading some manuals
(B) Deleting some records
(C) Speaking with a supervisor
(D) Emptying out a storage closet

第 41-43 題請參考下列三人對話。

女：[41] 我們訂的電腦不夠給請來要在財務部裡工作的實習生們用。到目前為止，其中只有 15 台會在下星期一送到。

男 1：[42] 雖然我們需要 20 台裝置，不過我們在儲藏櫃裡有五台之前用過且可以重新設定格式的。

男 2：是啊。我以為我們打算要用那幾台，這也就是為什麼我之前會訂那個數量。

女：不巧的是，[42] 財務總監說過他希望所有實習生都拿到全新的裝置。

男 2：噢，我不知道這件事。我現在就打給我們的供應商，看看能不能更新現有的訂單，把要多訂的裝置加進去。

女：謝謝。還有 [43] 因為我們可能不會再需要那些用過的電腦了，所以請你們在有機會的時候把它們的序號從可用裝置清單裡移除。

41 女子提到擔心什麼？

(A) 一些設備沒有維修。
(B) 一批貨沒有按預定時間送到。
(C) 訂購的品項不足。
(D) 員工拿到了有瑕疵的裝置。

42 實習生們需要多少台新電腦？

(A) 5 台
(B) 10 台
(C) 15 台
(D) 20 台

43 女子想要進行什麼工作？

(A) 下載一些手冊
(B) 刪除一些記錄
(C) 和一位主管說話
(D) 清空一個儲藏櫃

題目 as of now 到目前為止　used [juzd] 用過的　reformat [ˌriˈfɔrmæt] 重新設定～的格式
41　insufficient [ˌɪnsəˈfɪʃənt] 不足的　faulty [ˈfɔltɪ] 有瑕疵的

41 中 **細節事項相關問題—問題點** 答案 (C)

題目詢問女子提到她在擔心什麼，因此要注意聽女子話中出現負面表達之後的內容。女子說：「We didn't order enough computers for the interns hired to work in the finance department.」，表示訂的電腦數量不夠實習生們用，因此正確答案是 (C) Insufficient items were ordered.。

42 高 **細節事項相關問題—程度** 答案 (D)

題目詢問實習生們需要的新電腦台數是多少，因此要注意聽和題目關鍵字（new computers ~ for interns）相關的內容。男 1 說：「Although we need 20 devices, we have five used ones in the storage closet」，表示共需要 20 台裝置，而儲藏櫃中有 5 台之前用過的電腦，但女子接著說：「the finance director said that he wants all interns to get brand-new devices」，表示財務總監希望所有實習生都有新電腦可用，由此可知，總共需要 20 台新電腦給實習生用，因此正確答案是 (D) 20。

43 高 **細節事項相關問題—特定細項** 答案 (B)

題目詢問女子想要進行的工作是什麼，因此要注意聽和題目關鍵字（task ~ woman want carried out）相關的內容。女子說：「as we probably won't need those used computers anymore, please remove their serial numbers from the list of available devices」，表示因為可能不會再需要那些用過的電腦了，所以要把它們的序號從可用裝置清單裡移除，因此正確答案是 (B) Deleting some records。

44
45
46

Questions 44-46 refer to the following conversation.

加拿大式發音 → 英式發音

M: There you are, Alice. An accident has apparently occurred in the waiting area for office visitors. Someone knocked over a vase, and [44]**pieces of glass are all over the floor. I've got to deal with a leaking pipe on the fourth floor, so [44/45]can you clean up that mess? [44]Just grab a broom and dustpan from our maintenance office.**

W: Actually, [45]**I'm on my way home. My shift ended 20 minutes ago.** Could you ask Ryan to do it instead?

M: [46]**He's helping set up for this afternoon's press conference.** The preparations are coming along slowly, so he probably can't break away from that now. I'll just take care of it myself.

44 Who most likely are the speakers?

(A) Seminar organizers
(B) Personal assistants
(C) Emergency personnel
(D) Maintenance staff

45 Why is the woman unable to help?

(A) She is training another colleague.
(B) She is no longer on duty.
(C) She has to meet a deadline.
(D) She is cleaning up a spill.

46 According to the man, what will happen this afternoon?

(A) A meeting with the press will be held.
(B) A lunch break will be postponed.
(C) An office tour will be planned.
(D) A lobby will undergo renovations.

第 44-46 題請參考下列對話。

男：妳在這裡啊，Alice。聽說辦公室訪客等候區裡發生了意外。有人撞倒了花瓶，所以 [44] 滿地都是玻璃碎片。我還得去處理四樓的水管漏水，所以 [44/45] 可以請妳去收拾殘局嗎？[44] 只要去我們維護處拿個掃把和畚箕就行了。

女：其實，[45] 我正要回家。我的班 20 分鐘前結束了。你可以改請 Ryan 去處理嗎？

男：[46] 他正在幫忙布置今天下午的記者會。準備工作進展緩慢，所以他現在可能無法從那裡抽身。我就自己去處理吧。

44 說話者最有可能是誰？

(A) 研討會籌辦人
(B) 個人助理
(C) 應急人員
(D) 維護人員

45 女子為什麼無法幫忙？

(A) 她正在訓練另一位同事。
(B) 她已經下班了。
(C) 她必須趕上一個截止日期。
(D) 她正在清理灑出的東西。

46 根據男子所說，今天下午會發生什麼？

(A) 會舉行一場和媒體的聚會。
(B) 一次午休會被延後。
(C) 會規劃一次到辦公室參觀。
(D) 一個大廳會進行整修。

題目 apparently [əˋpærəntlɪ] 顯然地；聽說　waiting area 等候區　leak [lik] 漏（水等）　mess [mɛs] 凌亂的狀態；雜亂　dustpan [ˋdʌst͵pæn] 畚箕　maintenance [ˋmentənəns] 維護；維修　shift [ʃɪft]（輪班的）工作時間　press conference 記者會　come along 進展　take care of 處理～

45 on duty 工作中　spill [spɪl] 灑出；灑出的東西

44 ○●●● 高　整體對話相關問題—說話者　答案 (D)

題目詢問說話者的身分，因此要注意聽和身分、職業相關的表達。男子對女子說：「pieces of glass are all over the floor. I've got to deal with a leaking pipe on the fourth floor, so can you clean up that mess? Just grab a broom and dustpan from our maintenance office.」，表示地上到處都是玻璃碎片，但自己必須去處理四樓的漏水，詢問女子是否能去收拾殘局，並說只要去拿我們自己維護處的掃把和畚箕就可以了，由此可知，說話者是維護人員，因此正確答案是 (D) Maintenance staff。

45 ○○●● 中　細節事項相關問題—理由　答案 (B)

題目詢問女子無法提供協助的原因，因此必須注意聽和題目關鍵字（unable to help）相關的內容。男子對女子說：「can you clean up that mess?」，詢問對方是否可以去收拾殘局，女子說：「I'm on my way home. My shift ended 20 minutes ago.」，表示自己的班在 20 分鐘前結束，而且正要回家，因此正確答案是 (B) She is no longer on duty.。

46 ○○●● 中　細節事項相關問題—接下來要做的事　答案 (A)

題目詢問男子說今天下午會發生什麼，因此要注意聽男子話中和題目關鍵字（this afternoon）相關的內容。獨白說：「He[Ryan]'s helping set up for this afternoon's press conference.」，表示 Ryan 正在幫忙布置今天下午的記者會，由此可知，今天下午會舉行記者會，因此正確答案是 (A) A meeting with the press will be held.。

47 48 49

新

Questions 47-49 refer to the following conversation.

美式發音 → 加拿大式發音

W: Hi. [47]**I'd like to book one of the barbecue areas near the community center's outdoor swimming pool.** I want to use it for a party next Sunday.
M: All right. You'll need to fill this out and pay a $100 security deposit.
W: Umm . . . sorry, but can I ask what the deposit is for?
M: We need it in case you damage any of the equipment. [48]**It should be given back to you following an inspection of the area after your party.**
W: That's understandable. Oh, also . . . [49]**Do you provide charcoal for the grill?**
M: We don't. There's a convenience store one block down Harvest Street. [49]**It should have some for sale.**

第 47-49 題請參考下列對話。

女：嗨。[47] 我想預訂靠近社區中心室外泳池的其中一個烤肉區。下星期日我想要用那裡辦派對。
男：好的。妳得把這個填好，並支付 100 美金的保證金。
女：嗯……不好意思，但我可以問一下這筆保證金是要用來做什麼嗎？
男：如果你們弄壞了任何設備，我們就需要這筆錢。[48] 這筆錢應該會在你們派對結束並完成那區的檢查後還給你們。
女：這樣可以理解。噢，還有……[49] 你們有提供烤肉用的木炭嗎？
男：我們沒有。沿 Harvest 街過一個街區有一間便利商店。[49] 那裡應該有賣一些。

47 What does the woman want to do?
(A) Park at a residential complex
(B) Purchase some equipment
(C) Reserve a venue
(D) Sign up for swimming lessons

47 女子想要做什麼？
(A) 在一個社區住宅停車
(B) 購買一些設備
(C) 預訂一個場地
(D) 報名游泳課

48 What is mentioned about the facilities?
(A) They will be cleaned in advance.
(B) They are being redeveloped.
(C) They are booked for a weekend.
(D) They will be examined after use.

48 關於這個設施，提到了什麼？
(A) 會事先清潔。
(B) 正在重新開發。
(C) 有一個週末被預訂下來了
(D) 在使用後會進行檢查。

49 新 What does the man mean when he says, "There's a convenience store one block down Harvest Street"?
(A) A shop offers competitive prices.
(B) A retailer sells required supplies.
(C) A building is easy to find.
(D) A store branch has been moved.

49 當男子說：「沿 Harvest 街過一個街區有一間便利商店」，意思是什麼？
(A) 一間店提供具競爭力的價格。
(B) 一家零售店販售所需用品。
(C) 一棟大樓很容易找。
(D) 一間店的分店已經搬遷了。

題目 community center 社區中心　fill out 填寫　security deposit 保證金　inspection [ɪn`spɛkʃən] 檢查　charcoal [`tʃɑr͵kol] 木炭
48 in advance 事先，事前　redevelop [͵ridɪ`vɛləp] 重新開發　examine [ɪg`zæmɪn] 檢查
49 competitive [kəm`pɛtətɪv] 具競爭力的　supply [sə`plaɪ]（生活）用品

47 細節事項相關問題—特定細項 答案 (C)
中
題目詢問女子想做什麼，因此要注意聽和題目關鍵字（woman want to do）相關的內容。女子說：「I'd like to book one of the barbecue areas near the community center's outdoor swimming pool.」，表示自己想預訂靠近社區中心室外泳池的其中一個烤肉區，因此正確答案是 (C) Reserve a venue。

48 細節事項相關問題—提及 答案 (D)
高
題目詢問提及什麼與設施有關的事，因此要注意聽和題目關鍵字（facilities）相關的內容。男子說：「It[deposit] should be given back to you following an inspection of the area after your party.」，表示保證金會在派對結束並完成檢查後歸還，因此正確答案是 (D) They will be examined after use.。

新 **49 細節事項相關問題—掌握意圖** 答案 (B)
中
題目詢問男子的說話意圖，因此要注意與題目引用句（There's a convenience store one block down Harvest Street）相關及前後的內容。女子對男子說：「Do you provide charcoal for the grill?」，詢問是否有提供木炭，男子之後則回答：「It[convenience store] should have some for sale.」，表示便利商店有賣木炭，由此可知，店內有賣所需用品，因此正確答案是 (B) A retailer sells required supplies.。

50 51 52

Questions 50-52 refer to the following conversation.

澳洲式發音 → 英式發音

M: Hello. [50]**I'm here to inquire about traveler's insurance for college students.**

W: I'm sorry. Our location doesn't offer insurance plans for students. Ah . . . did you mean to visit our branch near Northside Park? It's closer to Gregtown University, so they offer plans for students.

M: I just got the address for your travel agency from a flyer. [51]**I found it at a local study abroad fair I attended recently.** So, I wasn't aware you have multiple locations. Anyway, if you could give me the other branch's address, I'd appreciate it.

W: Certainly. I'll write it down for you. Um, [52]**that branch is about a mile away, so you might want to get a taxi.**

50 Why has the man visited the woman's office?

(A) To change an itinerary
(B) To request a pamphlet
(C) To pay some fees
(D) To ask about insurance

51 What did the man recently do?

(A) Visited a foreign country
(B) Met with an adviser
(C) Went to an event
(D) Enrolled in a membership

52 What does the woman encourage the man to do?

(A) Pay with a credit card
(B) Call a different employee
(C) Use a taxi service
(D) Check nearby branch hours

第 50-52 題請參考下列對話。

男：哈囉。[50] 我來這裡是想問和大學生旅遊險有關的事。

女：我很抱歉。我們店沒有給學生的保險方案。啊……你想去的是不是我們在 Northside 公園附近的分店？它離 Gregtown 大學比較近，所以他們有給學生的方案。

男：我只是從傳單上知道了你們旅行社的地址。[51] 我在最近去的一場本地的海外留遊學展拿到的。所以我沒注意到你們有多間據點。總之，如果妳能給我另一間分店的地址，我會很感謝。

女：當然。我會寫下來給你。嗯，[52] 那間分店大概有一哩遠，所以你可能會想要搭計程車。

50 男子為何造訪了女子的辦公室？

(A) 為了變更旅行行程
(B) 為了索取小冊子
(C) 為了支付一些費用
(D) 為了詢問有關保險的事

51 男子最近做了什麼？

(A) 去了國外
(B) 和顧問碰面了
(C) 去了活動
(D) 註冊了會員資格

52 女子鼓勵男子做什麼？

(A) 用信用卡付款
(B) 致電其他員工
(C) 使用計程車服務
(D) 確認附近分店的營業時間

題目 inquire [美 ɪn`kwaɪr 英 in`kwaiə] 詢問　insurance [美 ɪn`ʃʊrəns 英 in`ʃuərəns] 保險　flyer [美 `flaɪɚ 英 `flaiə] 傳單
fair [美 fɛr 英 fɛə] 展覽　multiple [美 `mʌltəpl̩ 英 `mʌltipl] 多個的

50 itinerary [aɪ`tɪnəˌrɛrɪ] 旅行行程　pamphlet [`pæmflɪt] 小冊子

51 adviser [əd`vaɪzɚ] 顧問；指導教授

52 encourage [ɪn`kɝɪdʒ] 促進；鼓勵　nearby [`nɪrˌbaɪ] 附近的　hour [aʊr] 營業時間

50 整體對話相關問題—目的 — 低　答案 (D)

題目詢問男子造訪女子辦公室的原因，因此要注意對話的開頭。男子說：「I'm here to inquire about traveler's insurance for college students.」，表示自己要詢問和大學生旅遊險有關的事，因此正確答案是 (D) To ask about insurance。

51 細節事項相關問題—特定細項 — 高　答案 (C)

題目詢問男子最近做了什麼，因此要注意聽和題目關鍵字（recently）相關及前後的內容。男子說：「I found it[flyer] at a local study abroad fair I attended recently.」，表示自己在最近去的一場本地的海外留遊學展拿到了傳單，由此可知，男子最近去參加了活動，因此正確答案是 (C) Went to an event。

52 細節事項相關問題—提議 — 中　答案 (C)

題目詢問女子鼓勵男子做什麼，因此要注意聽女子話中出現提議相關表達的句子。女子對男子說：「that branch is about a mile away, so you might want to get a taxi」，表示分店大概有一哩遠，所以男子可能會想要搭計程車，因此正確答案是 (C) Use a taxi service。

換句話說

get a taxi 搭計程車 → Use a taxi service 使用計程車服務

53
54
55

Questions 53-55 refer to the following conversation.

第 53-55 題請參考下列對話。

美式發音 → 加拿大式發音

W: I connected with a factory in India that can manufacture our copiers affordably. The plant's owner has a strong relationship with a shipping company. [53]**He said he could get us a cost-effective rate to transport our goods to the United States.**

M: Excellent. And did you explain that [54]**I'd want to come to India to inspect the facility in person** prior to making a decision? I'll need to evaluate its quality control process as I've done for our partners in Mexico and Thailand in the past.

W: [55]**I spoke with him about that via videoconference yesterday**, and it won't be an issue. He said you're welcome to travel there at your convenience.

M: OK. I'll have my assistant coordinate with him about dates.

女：我聯絡上了一間能用經濟實惠的價格製造我們影印機的印度工廠。這間工廠的老闆和一家運輸公司的關係很好。[53] 他說他可以替我們爭取到用划算的價格把我們的商品運送到美國。

男：太棒了。那妳有說明 [54] 我想在做決定前親自去印度視察廠房嗎？我會需要評估他們的品質管制程序，就像我以前對在墨西哥及泰國的夥伴們所做的那樣。

女：[55] 我昨天透過視訊會議和他說過這件事了，而這沒有問題。他說歡迎你找方便的時間過去那裡。

男：好。我會請我助理去和他協調日期的事。

53 What is the factory owner able to do?

(A) Renew an annual contract
(B) Arrange reasonable shipping rates
(C) Increase a facility's output
(D) Send sample products for free

53 工廠老闆能夠做什麼？

(A) 續年度合約
(B) 談成合理的運費
(C) 提高一座設施的產出
(D) 免費寄送產品的樣品

54 Where will the man most likely conduct an inspection?

(A) In India
(B) In the United States
(C) In Mexico
(D) In Thailand

54 男子最有可能會在哪裡進行視察？

(A) 印度
(B) 美國
(C) 墨西哥
(D) 泰國

55 What did the woman do yesterday?

(A) Revised a quality control report
(B) Discovered a manufacturing defect
(C) Participated in a videoconference
(D) Approved a partnership agreement

55 女子昨天做了什麼？

(A) 修改了品質管制報告
(B) 發現了製造上的缺陷
(C) 參加了視訊會議
(D) 批准了合作協議

題目 connect with 聯絡上～ cost-effective 划算的 in person 親自 evaluate [ɪ`væljʊˌet] 鑑定；評估 via [`vaɪə] 透過 videoconference [`vɪdɪoˌkɑnfərəns] 視訊會議 coordinate [ko`ɔrdənet] 協調

53 renew [rɪ`nju] 更新；續（合約等） reasonable [`rizənəbḷ] 合理的 output [`aʊtˌpʊt] 產出

55 defect [dɪ`fɛkt] 缺陷 partnership [`pɑrtnɚˌʃɪp] 合作關係 agreement [ə`grimənt] 協議

53 細節事項相關問題—特定細項 高　　答案 (B)

題目詢問工廠老闆能夠做什麼，因此要注意聽和題目關鍵字（factory owner able to do）相關的內容。女子說：「He[plant's owner] said he could get us a cost-effective rate to transport our goods to the United States.」，表示工廠老闆說可以替說話者的公司爭取到用划算的價格把商品運送到美國，因此正確答案是 (B) Arrange reasonable shipping rates。

換句話說

cost-effective rate to transport ~ goods 用划算的價格運送商品 → reasonable shipping rates 合理的運費

54 細節事項相關問題—特定細項 低　　答案 (A)

題目詢問男子進行視察的地點，因此要注意聽和題目關鍵字（conduct an inspection）相關的內容。男子說：「I'd want to come to India to inspect the facility in person」，表示想要親自到印度視察廠房，因此正確答案是 (A) In India。

55 細節事項相關問題—特定細項 中　　答案 (C)

題目詢問女子昨天做了什麼，因此要注意聽和題目關鍵字（yesterday）相關及前後的內容。女子說：「I spoke with him[plant's owner] ~ via videoconference yesterday」，表示昨天透過視訊會議和工廠老闆說過了，因此正確答案是 (C) Participated in a videoconference。

56
57
58

Questions 56-58 refer to the following conversation.

[🔊] 美式發音 → 澳洲式發音

W: Good afternoon. [57]**I just opened an office for my accounting firm at 209 Randall Drive in Kingfield.** And [56]**I need my business's garbage and recycling to be picked up weekly.** [56/57]**I'm contacting your trash collection company because it's very well reviewed on blogs.**

M: Thank you for your interest in TriStar Collection. [57]**Due to city zoning laws, however, we are prohibited from operating in the Kingfield neighborhood.** My apologies for the inconvenience. I recommend that you get in touch with Henderson Garbage, as they are contracted to serve Kingfield.

W: I recall reading positive comments about that business too, so [58]**I'll definitely contact them right away.**

56 What is the woman trying to do?

(A) Hire an accountant
(B) Submit a review
(C) Set up a service
(D) Relocate an office

57 Why does the man mention city zoning laws?

(A) To report a new regulation
(B) To justify denying a request
(C) To collect survey feedback
(D) To identify renovation costs

58 What will the woman most likely do next?

(A) Speak with a city official
(B) Read about a contractor
(C) Attend a neighborhood meeting
(D) Contact another company

第 56-58 題請參考下列對話。

女：午安。[56] 我剛為我的會計事務所在 Kingfield 的 Randall 路 209 號開了一間辦公室。所以 [56] 我需要有人每週來收我們公司的垃圾與資源回收。[56/57] 我會聯絡你們這間垃圾清運公司，是因為你們在部落格上的評價非常好。

男：謝謝您對 TriStar Collection 有興趣。[57] 不過，由於城市區劃條例，我們被禁止在 Kingfield 區執業。我很抱歉造成您的不便。我建議您和 Henderson Garbage 聯繫，因為他們承包了 Kingfield 的業務。

女：我記得也有看到那間公司的正面評價，那麼 [58] 我一定會立刻聯絡他們。

56 女子試圖做什麼？

(A) 聘請一位會計
(B) 提交一則評論
(C) 申辦一項服務
(D) 搬遷一間辦公室

57 男子為何提到城市區劃條例？

(A) 為了回報一項新規定
(B) 為了正當化拒絕一項要求的事
(C) 為了收集調查回饋意見
(D) 為了確定整修成本

58 女子接下來最有可能會做什麼？

(A) 和市府官員談話
(B) 看承包商的相關資訊
(C) 參加鄰里會議
(D) 聯繫另一間公司

題目 collection [kəˋlɛkʃən] 收取；收藏品　review [rɪˋvju] 寫評論；評論　due to 由於
zoning [美] ˋzonɪŋ [英] ˋzəuniŋ]（都市土地使用的）區劃　prohibit [[美] prəˋhɪbɪt [英] prəˋhibit] 禁止；使不可能
get in touch with 和～聯絡　recall [rɪˋkɔl] 記得

57 justify [ˋdʒʌstəˏfaɪ] 為～辯解；正當化　identify [aɪˋdɛntəˏfaɪ] 確定

58 contractor [ˋkɑntræktɚ] 承包商；立契約人　neighborhood meeting 鄰里會議

56 ■ 細節事項相關問題─特定細項 　　答案 (C)

中

題目詢問女子試圖要做什麼，因此要注意聽和題目關鍵字（woman trying to do）相關的內容。女子說：「I need my business's garbage and recycling to be picked up weekly. I'm contacting your trash collection company because it's very well reviewed on blogs.」，表示需要有人每週來收公司的垃圾與資源回收，並說因為男子的公司在部落格上的評價非常好而聯繫對方，因此正確答案是 (C) Set up a service。

57 ■ 細節事項相關問題─理由 　　答案 (B)

高

題目詢問男子提到城市區劃條例的原因，因此要注意聽和題目關鍵字（city zoning laws）相關及前後的內容。女子說：「I just opened an office ~ in Kingfield.」，表示自己剛在 Kingfield 開了一間辦公室，接著說：「I'm contacting your trash collection company because it's very well reviewed on blogs.」，表示因為男子的公司在部落格上的評價非常好而聯繫對方，接著男子說：「Due to city zoning laws ~, we are prohibited from operating in the Kingfield neighborhood.」，表示因為城市區劃條例，男子的公司在 Kingfield 無法執業，由此可知，男子在說明是因為城市區劃條例的規定而必須拒絕女子的要求，因此正確答案是 (B) To justify denying a request。

58 ■ 細節事項相關問題─接下來要做的事 　　答案 (D)

低

題目詢問女子接下來會做什麼，因此要注意聽對話的最後部分。女子說：「I'll definitely contact them[Henderson Garbage] right away」，表示自己會立刻聯繫 Henderson Garbage 公司，因此正確答案是 (D) Contact another company。

59 60 61 新

Questions 59-61 refer to the following conversation with three speakers.

第 59-61 題請參考下列三人對話。

澳洲式發音 → 美式發音 → 加拿大式發音

M1: [60]**Cathy, do you have any more questions for Mr. Williams before we conclude his interview?**
W: Just one. [59]**While you provided your résumé and cover letter, I didn't notice a letter of recommendation.** [60]**Do you have one?**
M2: Oh, yes. I thought I attached it to the other documents, but let me check my briefcase. Ah . . . [60]**here it is.**
W: I appreciate it. I think that will do it for me, Chris.
M1: In that case, [60]**we're done here**, Mr. Williams. [61]**We'll send you the interview results by e-mail no later than next Wednesday.** I can walk you back to the main lobby now.
M2: Wonderful. Thanks for your assistance, and I look forward to hearing back from you.

男 1：[60]Cathy，在我們結束 Williams 先生的面試前，妳還有任何問題要問他嗎？
女：只有一個。[59] 儘管你提供了履歷表和求職信，但我沒有看到推薦信。[60] 你有推薦信嗎？
男 2：噢，有的。我以為我把它附在其他文件上了，不過讓我確認一下我的公事包。啊……[60] 在這裡。
女：謝謝。我想我這樣就可以了，Chris。
男 1：這樣的話，[60] 我們就到這裡結束，Williams 先生。[61] 我們最晚會在下週三以電子郵件將面試結果寄給你。我現在可以帶你回主大廳。
男 2：太好了。謝謝你的幫忙，我很期待收到你們的回覆。

59 What problem does Cathy inform Mr. Williams about?
(A) A job is no longer available.
(B) A document is missing.
(C) An exam has been canceled.
(D) An interview has to be postponed.

59 Cathy 告知 Williams 先生什麼問題？
(A) 一份工作不再可得。
(B) 缺了一份文件。
(C) 一項考試被取消了。
(D) 一場面試必須延期。

60 新 What does the woman mean when she says, "I think that will do it for me, Chris"?
(A) She wants Chris to explain benefits.
(B) She wants Chris to address a concern.
(C) She is not able to assist Chris.
(D) She is ready for Chris to end a meeting.

60 當女子說：「我想我這樣就可以了，Chris」時，意思是什麼？
(A) 她想要 Chris 說明福利。
(B) 她想要 Chris 解決問題。
(C) 她無法協助 Chris。
(D) 她準備好讓 Chris 結束會面了。

61 What will be sent by next Wednesday?
(A) An updated résumé
(B) Interview results
(C) Evaluation scores
(D) A lobby blueprint

61 下週三以前會寄出什麼？
(A) 更新過的履歷表
(B) 面試的結果
(C) 評鑑的分數
(D) 大廳的藍圖

題目 conclude [kən`klud] 結束　résumé [ˌrɛzjʊ`me] 履歷表　cover letter 求職信　letter of recommendation 推薦信　briefcase [`brifˌkes] 公事包
59 available [ə`veləbl] 可得的

59 ■ 細節事項相關問題—問題點 答案 (B)

中

題目詢問 Cathy 告知 Williams 先生什麼問題，因此要注意聽女子話中出現負面表達之後的內容。女子 Cathy 說：「While you[Mr. Williams] provided your résumé and cover letter, I didn't notice a letter of recommendation.」，表示儘管 Williams 先生提供了履歷表和求職信，但她卻沒有看到推薦信，因此正確答案是 (B) A document is missing.。

新 60 ■ 細節事項相關問題—掌握意圖 答案 (D)

高

題目詢問女子的說話意圖，因此要確認女子說的話中和題目關鍵字（I think that will do it for me, Chris）相關及前後的內容。Chris 對女子說：「Cathy, do you have any more questions for Mr. Williams before we conclude his interview?」，詢問在 Williams 先生的面試結束前是否還有問題要問，女子回答：「Do you have one[letter of recommendation]?」，詢問他是否有推薦信。男 2 說：「here it is」，表示推薦信在這裡，男 1 後面則說：「we're done here」，表示面試到這裡結束了，由此可知，女子在拿到推薦信後就覺得可以結束面試了，因此正確答案是 (D) She is ready for Chris to end a meeting.。

61 ■ 細節事項相關問題—特定細項 答案 (B)

低

題目詢問下週三以前會寄出什麼，因此要注意聽對話中和題目關鍵字（next Wednesday）相關的內容。男 1 說：「We'll send you the interview results by e-mail no later than next Wednesday.」，表示最晚會在下週三以電子郵件寄出面試結果，因此正確答案是 (B) Interview results。

62
63
64

Questions 62-64 refer to the following conversation and pie chart.

英式發音 → 加拿大式發音

W: [62]**Do you have a list of the computer codes** associated with each color used in last month's flyer?

M: [62]**They all appear on our intranet page after you click on Designs**, so you can find them there. Are you working on a new membership advertisement?

W: Yes. Our airline's focus for the previous promotion was to attract more Basic Level members. But now, [63]**we want to promote the paid memberships, which provide better benefits to customers. Among those paid membership levels, we're specifically trying to improve the less popular of the two.**

M: I see. By the way, [64]**I developed a marketing research report on our competitors' paid membership programs. I can e-mail you a copy of that**, if you think it will be useful.

62 How can the woman find the codes?

(A) By looking through a manual
(B) By opening an e-mail attachment
(C) By accessing a Web site
(D) By checking a filing cabinet

63 Look at the graphic. Which level will the airline promote in the new advertisement?

(A) Basic Level
(B) Silver Level
(C) Gold Level
(D) Platinum Level

64 What does the man offer to do?

(A) Share a report
(B) E-mail some executives
(C) Duplicate some diagrams
(D) Analyze a marketing expense

第 62-64 題請參考下列對話及圓餅圖。

女：[62] 你有對應上個月傳單上所使用的每個顏色的電腦代碼清單嗎？

男：[62] 在你點選設計後，它們就全都會出現在我們的內網頁面上，所以妳可以在那裡找到它們。妳在處理新的會員廣告嗎？

女：沒錯。我們航空公司之前宣傳的重點是要吸引更多基本層級的會員。不過現在，[63] 我們想要推廣付費會員，這種會員資格會提供客人更好的福利。在這些付費會員的分級之中，我們特別試著要改善那兩個分級裡比較不受歡迎的那個。

男：我明白了。對了，[64] 我製作了一份我們競爭對手的付費會員計畫的行銷研究報告。如果妳覺得會有幫助的話，我可以用電子郵件寄一份給妳。

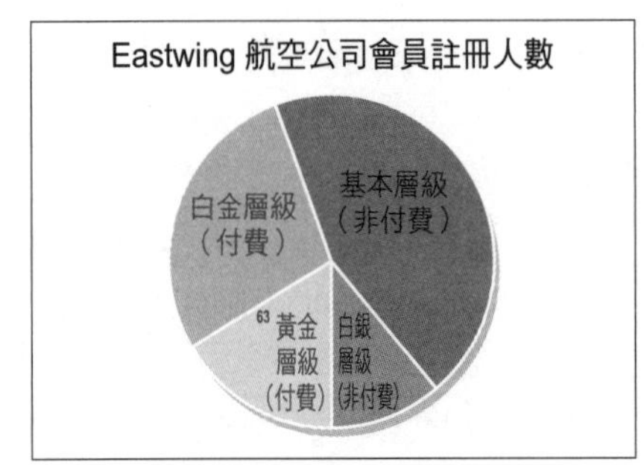

62 女子如何可以找到代碼？

(A) 瀏覽手冊
(B) 打開電子郵件的附檔
(C) 使用網站
(D) 查看檔案櫃

63 請看圖表。航空公司會在新的廣告裡推廣哪一個層級？

(A) 基本層級
(B) 白銀層級
(C) 黃金層級
(D) 白金層級

64 男子願意做什麼？

(A) 分享一份報告
(B) 寄電子郵件給一些主管
(C) 複製一些圖表
(D) 分析一筆行銷支出

題目 associated with 和～聯繫在一起 focus [美 `fokəs 英 `fəukəs] 重點 among [ə`mʌŋ] 在～之中 competitor [kəm`pɛtətɚ] 競爭對手

62 manual [`mænjʊəl] 手冊 attachment [ə`tætʃmənt]（電子郵件的）附檔 filing cabinet 檔案櫃

64 executive [ɪg`zɛkjʊtɪv] 主管 duplicate [`djupləˌket] 複製 analyze [`ænḷˌaɪz] 分析 expense [ɪk`spɛns] 支出

62 ●●● 中 **細節事項相關問題—方法** 答案 (C)

題目詢問女子如何可以找到代碼，因此要注意聽和題目關鍵字（find the codes）相關的內容。女子對男子說：「Do you have a list of the computer codes」，詢問男子是否有電腦代碼的清單，男子說：「They all appear on our intranet page after you click on Designs」，表示點選設計後代碼就都會出現在內網頁面上，因此正確答案是 (C) By accessing a Web site。

新 63 ●●● 高 **細節事項相關問題—圖表資料** 答案 (C)

題目詢問航空公司會在新的廣告裡推廣哪一個層級，因此必須確認題目提供的圓餅圖，並注意和題目關鍵字（level ~ promote）相關的內容。女子說：「we want to promote the paid memberships ~. Among those paid membership levels, we're specifically trying to improve the less popular ~.」，表示想要推廣付費會員，且特別試著要改善兩個付費會員分級裡比較不受歡迎的那個，透過圖表可知，新廣告要推廣的是黃金層級，因此正確答案是 (C) Gold Level。

64 ●●● 中 **細節事項相關問題—提議** 答案 (A)

題目詢問男子願意做什麼，因此要注意聽男子話中提到要為女子做事的內容。男子對女子說：「I developed a marketing research report on our competitors' paid membership programs. I can e-mail you a copy of that」，表示自己製作了一份行銷研究報告，並說自己可以用電子郵件把報告寄一份給女子，因此正確答案是 (A) Share a report。

[新] 65 66 67

Questions 65-67 refer to the following conversation and building directory.

第 65-67 題請參考下列對話及樓層指南。

澳洲式發音 → 美式發音

M: [65]**Thanks for showing me this laundry room.** The fact that it's so modern is one more great feature of the apartment building.

W: I'm glad you like it. [65]**I should also point out that the gym is just one floor above us now.**

M: Oh, could we take a look at it?

W: I'm sorry, but [66]**it's closed today because some new workout machines are being set up.**

M: Then what about the recreation room? I'm rather curious about that too.

W: I can take you there. But first, I need to run to my office quickly. [67]**My colleague just texted me saying he's having trouble printing out the application form** for you to review.

M: No problem. I'll wait here until you return.

男：[65] 謝謝妳帶我參觀這間洗衣房。它這麼現代化的這件事是這棟公寓大樓的又一個很棒的特色。

女：我很高興你喜歡它。[65] 我也應該提一下，健身房現在就在我們樓上一層。

男：噢，我們可以去看一下嗎？

女：我很抱歉，但 [66] 因為正在安裝一些新的健身器材，所以它今天沒有開。

男：那娛樂室呢？我也對那滿好奇的。

女：我可以帶你去那裡。但首先，我得趕緊回我辦公室一下。[67] 我同事剛剛傳訊息給我說，他在把要給你看的申請表印出來的時候碰到困難了。

男：沒問題。我會在這裡等妳回來。

[新]

Azalea Apartments Building Directory	
[65]**2nd Floor**	**Laundry Room**
3rd Floor	**Fitness Center**
4th Floor	Recreation Room
5th Floor	Management Office

Azalea 公寓樓層指南	
[65]2 樓	洗衣房
3 樓	健身中心
4 樓	娛樂室
5 樓	管理室

65 [新] Look at the graphic. Which floor are the speakers currently on?

(A) The 2nd Floor
(B) The 3rd Floor
(C) The 4th Floor
(D) The 5th Floor

65 請看圖表。說話者們目前在哪一層樓？

(A) 2 樓
(B) 3 樓
(C) 4 樓
(D) 5 樓

66 Why is the gym closed today?

(A) Flooring is being removed.
(B) New machines are being installed.
(C) A tour is being conducted.
(D) Some damage is being repaired.

66 健身房今天為什麼沒開？

(A) 正在移除地板。
(B) 正在安裝新的器材。
(C) 正在進行參觀。
(D) 正在修理一些損傷。

67 What does the woman imply about her colleague?

(A) He wants supplies for an office.
(B) He needs assistance with a device.
(C) He is having trouble locking a door.
(D) He will be late for an appointment.

67 關於她的同事，女子暗示什麼？

(A) 他想要一間辦公室的用品。
(B) 他在使用一項裝置上需要協助。
(C) 他在鎖門時碰到了困難。
(D) 他的一場會面會遲到。

題目 laundry room 洗衣房　modern [[美] `mɑdɚn [英] `mɔdən] 現代的　feature [[美] fitʃɚ [英] fi:tʃə] 特徵，特色　point out 提出，指出　workout [`wɝk͵aʊt] 健身　recreation room 娛樂室　curious [`kjʊrɪəs] 好奇的　text [tɛkst] 傳訊息　application form 申請表　review [rɪ`vju] 審視

66 flooring [`florɪŋ]（室內鋪設的）地板（材料）　tour [tʊr] 參觀

67 assistance [ə`sɪstəns] 協助　lock [lɑk] 鎖

新 **65** 低 **細節事項相關問題—圖表資料** 答案 (A)

題目詢問說話者們目前的所在樓層，因此必須確認題目提供的樓層指南資訊，並注意和題目關鍵字（floor ~ currently on）相關的內容。男子說：「Thanks for showing me this laundry room.」，感謝對方帶自己參觀洗衣房，接著女子說：「I should ~ point out that the gym is just one floor above us now.」，指出健身房現在就在樓上一層，透過圖表可知，說話者們目前人在洗衣房，也就是三樓健身中心樓下的二樓，因此正確答案是 (A) The 2nd Floor。

66 中 **細節事項相關問題—理由** 答案 (B)

題目詢問今天健身房沒開的原因，因此要注意聽和題目關鍵字（gym closed today）相關的內容。女子說：「it[gym]'s closed today because some new workout machines are being set up」，表示因為健身房正在安裝一些新的健身器材，所以今天沒開，因此正確答案是 (B) New machines are being installed.。

67 中 **細節事項相關問題—推論** 答案 (B)

題目詢問女子暗示了什麼與自己同事有關的事，因此要注意聽和題目關鍵字（her colleague）相關的內容。女子說：「My colleague just texted me saying he's having trouble printing out the application form」，表示自己同事傳訊息說在印申請表時碰到了困難，由此可知，女子的同事在使用裝置上需要協助，因此正確答案是 (B) He needs assistancc with a device.。

68
69
70

Questions 68-70 refer to the following conversation and sign.

加拿大式發音 → 英式發音

M: Anika, [68]**I just received a memo from Donald Powell . . . uh . . . the head of maintenance.** He said the parking areas in our industrial complex will be repainted.
W: OK. When will the work begin?
M: Well, [69]**each parking area will be closed for one day next month.** The research laboratory lot will be first, and then [69]**the factory lot will be painted on May 5. The next day, the workers will paint the administration office lot**, and they'll finish up with the warehouse lot on May 7. [69]**Signs will be posted in the respective buildings for each lot on the days when the work will be carried out.**
W: Where can staff park on those days?
M: [70]**Temporary passes for a nearby parking garage will be issued. I'll hand them out on May 1.**

Parking Lot Closed

[69]**May 6**

Parking is available
at the Dalton Center Garage.

68 Who is Donald Powell?

(A) A department manager
(B) A construction worker
(C) A human resources intern
(D) A company president

69 Look at the graphic. Where will the sign most likely be placed?

(A) In a research laboratory
(B) In a factory
(C) In an administration office
(D) In a warehouse

70 What will the man distribute on May 1?

(A) Employee handbooks
(B) Facility maps
(C) Work schedules
(D) Parking passes

第 68-70 題請參考下列對話及告示。

男：Anika，[68] 我剛從 Donald Powell……呃……維修部門的主管那裡收到一份備忘錄。他說我們工業園區裡的停車區將重新粉刷。
女：好。作業什麼時候會開始？
男：這個嘛，[69] 每個停車區在下個月都會有一天關閉。研究實驗室那區會最先，接著 [69] 工廠那區會在 5 月 5 日進行粉刷。隔天，工人們會去粉刷行政辦公室那區，然後他們會在 5 月 7 日完成倉庫那區。[69] 在作業進行的那天，各區內的個別建築物中都會張貼告示。
女：那幾天員工可以在哪裡停車？
男：[70] 會發放附近停車場的臨時停車證。我會在 5 月 1 日把它們發下去。

停車場關閉

[69]5 月 6 日

停車可至
Dalton 中心停車場。

68 誰是 Donald Powell？

(A) 部門經理
(B) 建築工人
(C) 人力資源部實習生
(D) 公司總裁

69 請看圖表。這則告示最有可能會放置在哪裡？

(A) 研究實驗室
(B) 工廠
(C) 行政辦公室
(D) 倉庫

70 男子在 5 月 1 日會發放什麼？

(A) 員工手冊
(B) 設施地圖
(C) 工作時間表
(D) 停車證

題目 industrial [ɪn`dʌstrɪəl] 產業的；工業的　research laboratory 研究實驗室　administration office 行政辦公室　warehouse [`wɛr͵haʊs] 倉庫　respective [rɪ`spɛktɪv] 個別的　parking garage 停車場
68 president [`prɛzədənt] 總裁

68 細節事項相關問題—特定細項 答案 (A)

中

題目詢問 Donald Powell 的身分，因此必須注意聽與提問對象（Donald Powell）相關的內容。男子說：「I just received a memo from Donald Powell ~ the head of maintenance」，表示自己剛剛收到維修部門主管 Donald Powell 的備忘錄，因此正確答案是 (A) A department manager。

新 69 細節事項相關問題—圖表資料 答案 (C)

難

題目詢問這則告示最有可能會放置在哪裡，因此要確認題目提供的告示上的資訊，並注意和題目關鍵字（sign ~ placed）相關的內容。男子說：「each parking area will be closed for one day next month」，表示各停車區在下個月都會關閉一天，接著說：「the factory lot will be painted on May 5. The next day, the workers will paint the administration office lot」，表示工廠那區會在 5 月 5 日進行粉刷，隔天則會粉刷行政辦公室那區，並說：「Signs will be posted in the respective buildings for each lot on the days when the work will be carried out.」，表示在作業進行的那天，各區內的個別建築物中都會張貼告示。由此可知，這則 5 月 6 日的告示會張貼在行政辦公室中，因此正確答案是 (C) In an administration office。

70 細節事項相關問題—特定細項 答案 (D)

低

題目詢問男子會在 5 月 1 日發放什麼，因此要注意聽和題目關鍵字（May 1）相關及前後的內容。男子說：「Temporary passes for a nearby parking garage will be issued. I'll hand them out on May 1.」，表示自己會在 5 月 1 日發放附近停車場的臨時停車證，因此正確答案是 (D) Parking passes。

71
72
73

Questions 71-73 refer to the following talk.

英式發音

As some of you already know, [71]**our firm has been asked to do a fashion show in February as part of the Rosebury Mall's Winter Fund-raiser. Eighty percent of the proceeds from the event will be donated to Power First, a local charity** that is dedicated to working with disadvantaged youth. As it is already mid-December, we need to start making preparations for the collection that we intend to present at the show. Following this meeting, [72/73]**I'd like each of you to submit your two favorite outfits** from our line that was released in November. Then, [73]**I'll look over your choices this afternoon** and decide whether they should be altered for the runway.

71 What type of event will take place in February?

(A) A design contest
(B) A product launch
(C) A store opening
(D) A charity event

72 What does the speaker ask the listeners to do?

(A) Purchase winter outfits
(B) Select clothing items
(C) Assist with staff training
(D) Choose meal options

73 What will the speaker probably do later today?

(A) Review submissions
(B) Return to a mall
(C) Attend a fashion show
(D) Make an announcement

第 71-73 題請參考下列談話。

如同各位之中部分人已經知道的那樣，[71] 我們公司已被要求在二月時舉行一場時裝秀，做為 Rosebury 購物中心的冬季募款活動的一部分。活動收益的百分之八十將捐給 Power First，它是一個本地致力於與弱勢青年合作的慈善團體。因為現在已經十二月中了，所以我們得開始為我們打算在這場秀裡呈現的服裝系列做準備了。在這次會議之後，[72/73] 我想要你們每個人都從我們在十一月發表的系列裡，提出自己最喜歡的兩套服裝。然後，[73] 我今天下午會看過各位的選擇並決定是否該為了伸展台修改它們。

71 二月會舉行哪種活動？

(A) 設計競賽
(B) 產品發表會
(C) 商店開幕式
(D) 慈善活動

72 說話者要求聽者們做什麼？

(A) 購買冬天的服裝
(B) 選擇服裝品項
(C) 協助員工訓練
(D) 選擇餐點選項

73 說話者今天晚點可能會做什麼？

(A) 檢視提交物
(B) 回到購物中心
(C) 參加時裝秀
(D) 宣布事項

題目 proceeds [(美) `prosidz (英) `prəusi:dz] 收益　donate [(美) `donet (英) `dəuneit] 捐贈　charity [`tʃærətɪ] 慈善團體；慈善
be dedicated to 致力於～　disadvantaged [(美) ˌdɪsəd`væntɪdʒd (英) ˌdisəd`vɑ:ntidʒd] 弱勢的
outfit [`aʊtˌfɪt]（一整套的）服裝　release [rɪ`lis] 發表　look over 快速看過
alter [(美) `ɔltɚ (英) `ɔ:ltə] 修改（衣服等）；變更　**73** submission [sʌb`mɪʃən] 提交；提交物

71 中 **細節事項相關問題—特定細項** 答案 (D)

題目詢問二月會舉辦何種活動，因此要注意聽和題目關鍵字（event ~ February）相關的內容。獨白說：「our firm has been asked to do a fashion show in February as part of the Rosebury Mall's Winter Fund-raiser. Eighty percent of the proceeds from the event will be donated to Power First, a local charity」，表示自己公司已被要求在二月時舉行時裝秀，且這場時裝秀會做為 Rosebury 購物中心的冬季募款活動的一部分，後面又提到這場活動收益的百分之八十會捐給本地的慈善團體 Power First，由此可知，二月將舉行的時裝秀是慈善活動，因此正確答案是 (D) A charity event。

72 中 **細節事項相關問題—要求** 答案 (B)

題目詢問說話者要求聽者們做什麼，因此必須注意聽獨白的中後半部分出現要求相關表達的句子。獨白說：「I'd like each of you to submit your two favorite outfits」，要求每個人都提出自己最喜歡的兩套服裝，因此正確答案是 (B) Select clothing items。

73 中 **細節事項相關問題—接下來要做的事** 答案 (A)

題目詢問說話者今天晚點可能會做什麼，因此要注意聽和題目關鍵字（later today）相關的內容。獨白說：「I'd like each of you to submit your two favorite outfits」，表示要求每個人都提出自己最喜歡的兩套服裝，接著說：「I'll look over your choices this afternoon」，表示自己今天下午會看過聽者們的選擇，因此正確答案是 (A) Review submissions。

換句話說

later today 今天晚點 → this afternoon 今天下午

74 75 76

Questions 74-76 refer to the following advertisement.

加拿大式發音

[74]Are you thinking about buying a new residential property? Then be sure to talk to Goldstein Real Estate first! We have decades of experience in helping people find properties that meet all their needs. **[75]Our specialty is locating beachfront properties along the Florida coast** and luxury condominiums throughout the state. Moreover, with our company's longstanding history in the industry, no other firm is in a better position than us to negotiate a fair property price. **[76]Contact our main office today at 555-8726 to get more information** about the amazing properties currently on the market. We look forward to working with you!

74 What is being advertised?
(A) A travel service
(B) A beach resort
(C) A residential remodeling company
(D) A real estate agency

75 What does the company specialize in?
(A) Hosting guests for long-term stays
(B) Providing housing loans
(C) Finding homes along a coastline
(D) Customizing interior designs

76 According to the speaker, how can listeners acquire more information?
(A) By calling a telephone number
(B) By sending an e-mail
(C) By filling in an online form
(D) By visiting an office

第 74-76 題請參考下列廣告。

[74] 你在考慮要買新的住宅物業嗎？那麼一定要先和 Goldstein 不動產談談！我們在協助人們找到符合他們所有需求的物業上有著數十年的經驗。[75] 我們的專長是位於佛羅里達沿岸的濱海物業以及州內各處的豪華公寓大樓。此外，我們公司在業界有著悠久歷史，沒有其他公司能比我們在協商公道的物業價格上更有優勢。[76] 今天就打 555-8726 和我們的總部聯絡來取得更多與目前市場上那些很棒的物業相關資訊吧。我們期待與你合作！

74 正在廣告什麼？
(A) 旅遊服務
(B) 海灘度假村
(C) 住宅整修公司
(D) 不動產仲介

75 這間公司專門做什麼？
(A) 接待長住的賓客
(B) 提供住宅貸款
(C) 尋找沿海住宅
(D) 客製化的室內設計

76 根據說話者所說，聽者們可以如何取得更多資訊？
(A) 打一個電話號碼
(B) 寄一封電子郵件
(C) 填寫一份線上表單
(D) 造訪一處辦公室

題目 residential [ˌrɛzəˋdɛnʃəl] 居住的；住宅的　specialty [ˋspɛʃəltɪ] 專長
condominium [ˋkandəˌmɪnɪəm] 產權獨立的公寓大樓　longstanding [ˋlɔŋˋstændɪŋ] 長時間的
negotiate [nɪˋgoʃɪˌet] 協商　fair [fɛr] 公道的；公正的
75 specialize in 專門做～　long-term 長期的　housing loan 住宅貸款

74 整體內容相關問題—主題 低　答案 (D)

題目詢問廣告的主題，因此要注意聽獨白的開頭部分。獨白說：「Are you thinking about buying a new residential property? Then be sure to talk to Goldstein Real Estate first!」，表示聽者們如果在考慮要買新的住宅物業，那就一定要先和 Goldstein 不動產談談，接著繼續說明該不動產仲介業者所提供的相關服務，因此正確答案是 (D) A real estate agency。

75 細節事項相關問題—特定細項 高　答案 (C)

題目詢問這間公司專門做什麼，因此要注意聽和題目關鍵字（specialize in）相關的內容。獨白說：「Our specialty is locating beachfront properties along the Florida coast」，表示公司的專長是位於佛羅里達沿岸的濱海物業，因此正確答案是 (C) Finding homes along a coastline。

換句話說

beachfront properties along ~ coast 沿岸的濱海物業 → homes along a coastline 沿海住宅

76 細節事項相關問題—方法 低　答案 (A)

題目詢問聽者們如何能獲得更多資訊，因此要注意聽和題目關鍵字（more information）相關的內容。獨白說：「Contact our main office today at 555-8726 to get more information」，表示想獲得更多資訊可以打 555-8726，因此正確答案是 (A) By calling a telephone number。

77 78 79	
Questions 77-79 refer to the following announcement. 澳洲式發音 Everyone, I have an announcement to make. Up until now, our yoga studio hasn't had a dress code. You've been able to wear whatever you like in the workplace. But [77]**starting next month, you'll be required to wear a uniform. It's a security issue . . . Some parts of the studio are off-limits to customers, and this policy change will make it easier to notice anyone who shouldn't be in these areas.** [78]**I know everyone enjoys dressing casually at work**, but you don't have anything to worry about. [78]**The uniform is simply a white polo shirt** with the company logo on it. I'll order these shirts from the supplier tomorrow, so [79]**please put your size on this chart**. Thanks.	第 77-79 題請參考下列公告。 各位，我有一件事要宣布。到目前為止，我們瑜珈工作室一直都沒有服裝規定。你們在工作地點能穿任何自己想穿的衣服。不過 [77] 從下個月開始，你們就會被要求穿制服了。這是個安全問題……這間工作室有些地方是不對客人開放的，而這項政策的改變會使我們更容易注意到任何不應該出現在這些區域裡的人。[78] 我知道大家都喜歡上班穿得輕鬆點，不過你們沒什麼好擔心的。[78] 制服只是一件上面有公司標誌的白色 polo 衫。我明天會跟供應商訂購這些衣服，所以 [79] 請把你們的尺寸填在這張表上。謝謝。
77 Why will a policy be changed? (A) To address customer complaints (B) To boost employee morale (C) To promote the company's brand (D) To improve workplace security	77 為什麼一項政策會變更？ (A) 為了處理顧客的投訴 (B) 為了提升員工士氣 (C) 為了推廣公司的品牌 (D) 為了改善工作地點的安全
78 新 What does the speaker imply when he says, "but you don't have anything to worry about"? (A) The yoga studio will reopen tomorrow. (B) The uniform will be informal. (C) The company logo will be popular. (D) The staff will receive a present.	78 當說話者說：「不過你們沒什麼好擔心的」，是暗示什麼？ (A) 瑜珈工作室明天會重新開幕。 (B) 制服會是日常款的。 (C) 公司的標誌會很受歡迎。 (D) 員工會得到禮物。
79 What does the speaker request that listeners do? (A) Examine some documents (B) Place an order with a supplier (C) Write down some information (D) Try on an outfit	79 說話者要求聽者們做什麼？ (A) 檢視一些文件 (B) 向供應商下訂 (C) 寫下一些資訊 (D) 試穿衣服

題目 studio [美 `stjudɪ͵o 英 `stju:diəu] 工作室；練習室　dress code 服裝規定
workplace [美 `wɝk͵ples 英 `wə:kpleis] 職場；工作地點　security [sɪ`kjʊrətɪ] 安全；保全　off-limits 禁止進入的
polo shirt（有領且可供運動用的）polo 衫

77 address [ə`drɛs] 處理；解決　boost [bust] 促進；提升　morale [mə`ræl] 士氣

78 informal [ɪn`fɔrml]（服裝等）日常使用的；非正式的

77 中 **細節事項相關問題—理由** 答案 (D)

題目詢問政策變更的原因，因此要注意聽和題目關鍵字（policy ~ changed）相關的內容。獨白說：「starting next month, you'll be required to wear a uniform. It's a security issue ~. Some parts of the studio are off-limits to customers, and this policy change will make it easier to notice anyone who shouldn't be in these areas.」，表示從下個月開始，會要求員工穿著制服，並說這是安全問題，接著說明因為工作室有些地方是不對客人開放的，而這項政策的改變可以讓員工更容易注意到任何不應出現在禁止進入區裡的人，因此正確答案是 (D) To improve workplace security。

新 **78** 高 **細節事項相關問題—掌握意圖** 答案 (B)

題目詢問說話者的說話意圖，因此要注意與題目引用句（but you don't have anything to worry about）相關的內容。獨白說：「I know everyone enjoys dressing casually at work」，表示自己知道大家喜歡工作時穿得輕鬆點，接著說：「The uniform is simply a white polo shirt」，表示制服只是一件白色 polo 衫，由此可知，制服是日常款的衣服，因此正確答案是 (B) The uniform will be informal.。

79 中 **細節事項相關問題—要求** 答案 (C)

題目詢問說話者要求聽者們做什麼，因此要注意聽獨白的後半部中出現要求相關表達的句子。獨白說：「please put your size on this chart」，要求聽者們在表上填入自己的尺寸，因此正確答案是 (C) Write down some information。

80
81
82

Questions 80-82 refer to the following talk.

美式發音

I'd like to go over a few basic payroll procedures with you all while I have your attention. To begin with, please make sure that you fill out your time sheets and send them to the accounting department every day. [80]**The departmental e-mail address is included on Page 12 of your employee handbook.** Staff members should also try to submit daily reports prior to the end of their shifts. [81]**It's OK if they're received by the next day on occasion, but turning them in any later will be reflected in your annual evaluations.** Also, be reminded that [82]**supervisors must formally agree to all overtime work** in order for employees to qualify for time and a half. Anyone who works overtime without the required approval will be paid their usual hourly wage.

80 According to the speaker, what can be found in the handbook?

(A) Some safety instructions
(B) A compensation policy
(C) Some contact information
(D) A list of work schedules

81 What will happen if staff submit daily reports more than a day late?

(A) They will have to write an explanatory note.
(B) They will have to resubmit some documentation.
(C) Their team leaders will notify them personally.
(D) Their yearly reviews will be affected.

82 According to the speaker, what should staff get permission for?

(A) Changing shifts with colleagues
(B) Working additional hours
(C) Accessing the accounting Web site
(D) Printing confidential records

第 80-82 題請參考下列談話。

趁大家的注意力還在我身上的時候，我想要和你們大家重申幾項基本的敘薪流程。首先，請你們每天務必填寫自己的工時表並把它們寄給會計部門。[80] **該部門的電子郵件地址在你們員工手冊的第 12 頁上有。**員工也應盡量在值班結束前繳交每日報告。[81] **偶爾隔天才交的話沒關係，不過再晚就會影響你們的年度評鑑了。**此外，請記得 [82] **主管必須正式批准所有的加班作業**，以讓員工符合取得 1.5 倍加班費的資格。任何人未經批准而加班都將以一般時薪計薪。

80 根據說話者所說，手冊中可以找到什麼？

(A) 一些安全指示
(B) 一項補償金政策
(C) 一些聯絡資訊
(D) 一張班表

81 若員工晚了超過一天繳交每日報告，會發生什麼？

(A) 他們會必須寫一條備註。
(B) 他們會必須重新提交一些文件。
(C) 他們的組長會親自通知他們。
(D) 他們的年度評鑑會受影響。

82 根據說話者所說，員工應該取得什麼的許可？

(A) 和同事換班
(B) 加班
(C) 使用會計網站
(D) 列印機密記錄

題目 go over 重申；重溫　procedure [prə`sidʒɚ] 流程　time sheet 工時表　on occasion 偶爾
reflect [rɪ`flɛkt] 反映；帶來影響　formally [`fɔrml̩ɪ] 正式地　time and a half（與正常工資相比）1.5 倍的加班費
approval [ə`pruvl̩] 批准　hourly wage 時薪
80 compensation [ˌkɑmpən`seʃən] 補償；補償金
82 confidential [ˌkɑnfə`dɛnʃəl] 機密的

80 細節事項相關問題—特定細節　答案 (C)
中

題目詢問在手冊內可以找到什麼，因此要注意聽和題目關鍵字（handbook）相關的內容。獨白說：「The departmental e-mail address is included on Page 12 of your employee handbook.」，表示該部門的電子郵件地址在員工手冊的第 12 頁上有，因此正確答案是 (C) Some contact information。

81 細節事項相關問題—特定細節　答案 (D)
高

題目詢問員工如果晚超過一天交報告會發生什麼，因此要注意聽和題目關鍵字（submit daily reports more than a day late）相關的內容。獨白說：「It's OK if they[daily reports]'re received by the next day on occasion, but turning them in any later will be reflected in your annual evaluations.」，表示偶爾隔天才交報告的話沒關係，不過再晚才交的話就會影響員工的年度評鑑，因此正確答案是 (D) Their yearly reviews will be affected.。

82 細節事項相關問題—特定細節　答案 (B)
中

題目詢問員工應該取得什麼的許可，因此要注意聽和題目關鍵字（get permission）相關的內容。獨白說：「supervisors must formally agree to all overtime work」，表示主管必須正式批准所有的加班作業，因此正確答案是 (B) Working additional hours。

83
84
85

Questions 83-85 refer to the following announcement.

🔊 澳洲式發音

Attention all visitors to the Greenford Botanical Gardens. [83]**It is now 10 P.M., and the facility will be closing in 30 minutes. The gift shop will cease operations ten minutes prior to this, at 10:20.** We encourage everyone to begin exiting the grounds now. Please take your belongings, including those stored in the lockers located near the visitors' center, with you when leaving. [84]**As a reminder, the South Gate has been temporarily blocked off for renovations.** Therefore, direct access to Parking Lot A is only available through the East Gate. [85]**I would also like to take this opportunity to invite you to come back next month. To celebrate our fifth anniversary, we will be hosting a special exhibition of roses and tulips from May 10 to 25.** We hope to see you then!

第 83-85 題請參考下列公告。

所有 Greenford 植物園的遊客請注意。[83] 現在是晚上 10 點，本園將在 30 分鐘後關閉。禮品店會在閉園前的十分鐘，於 10 點 20 分結束營業。我們建議各位現在開始離開園區。離開時請將您的隨身物品，包括放在遊客中心附近置物櫃裡的那些，一併帶走。[84] 提醒一下，南大門現因整修而暫時封閉。因此，要直接進入停車場 A 只能走東大門。[85] 我也想利用這個機會邀請各位於下個月再回來。為了慶祝我們的五週年，我們將於 5 月 10 日至 25 日舉辦玫瑰及鬱金香的特展。我們希望到時候能看到各位！

83 What does the speaker mention about the gift shop?
(A) It has been shut down for renovations.
(B) It is hosting a special event.
(C) It is located near the South Gate.
(D) It closes earlier than the main facility.

83 關於禮品店，說話者提到什麼？
(A) 因整修而關閉中。
(B) 正在舉行特別活動。
(C) 位在南大門附近。
(D) 比主園早關。

84 What does the speaker remind listeners about?
(A) An exit is inaccessible.
(B) A parking lot is full.
(C) A storage area is available.
(D) A center is open.

84 說話者提醒聽者們什麼？
(A) 一個出口不能用。
(B) 一個停車場滿了。
(C) 一個存放區可以用。
(D) 一個中心開著。

85 According to the speaker, what will happen next month?
(A) A performance will be given.
(B) A discount will be offered.
(C) A temporary exhibit will be displayed.
(D) An anniversary party will be held.

85 根據說話者所說，下個月會發生什麼？
(A) 會進行一場表演。
(B) 會提供一項折扣。
(C) 會展出一個臨時展。
(D) 會舉辦一個週年派對。

題目 botanical garden 植物園　cease [sis] 停止　exit [[美] `ɛksɪt [英] `eksit] 離開；出口
ground [graʊnd]（為某種目的而劃分出來的）場所　belongings [[美] bə`lɔŋɪŋz [英] bi`lɔːŋiŋz]（隨身攜帶的）財物
store [[美] stor [英] stɔː] 存放；商店　temporarily [[美] `tɛmpəˌrɛrəlɪ [英] `tempərerili] 暫時地，臨時地
access [`æksɛs] 進入；接近

83 shut down 關閉

84 inaccessible [ˌɪnæk`sɛsəbl] 無法去的；難以到達的　full [fʊl] 滿的　storage [`storɪdʒ] 保管，存放

83 ■ 細節事項相關問題—提及　答案 (D)

○●●● 高

題目詢問說話者提到什麼與禮品店有關的事，因此要注意聽和題目關鍵字（gift shop）相關的內容。獨白說：「It is now 10 P.M., and the facility will be closing in 30 minutes. The gift shop will cease operations ten minutes prior to this, at 10:20.」，表示晚上 10 點 30 分會閉園，而禮品店會提前 10 分鐘在 10 點 20 分結束營業，由此可知，禮品店會比主園早關，因此正確答案是 (D) It closes earlier than the main facility.。

84 ■ 細節事項相關問題—特定細項　答案 (A)

○○●● 中

題目詢問說話者提醒聽者們什麼，因此要注意聽和題目關鍵字（remind）相關的內容。獨白說：「As a reminder, the South Gate has been temporarily blocked off for renovations.」，提醒聽者們南門現因整修而關閉，因此正確答案是 (A) An exit is inaccessible.。

85 ■ 細節事項相關問題—接下來要做的事　答案 (C)

○○●● 中

題目詢問下個月會發生什麼，因此要注意聽和題目關鍵字（next month）相關的內容。獨白說：「I would ~ like to ~ invite you to come back next month. To celebrate our fifth anniversary, we will be hosting a special exhibition ~ from May 10 to 25.」，表示想邀請聽者們下個月再回來，參加為慶祝五週年而辦的玫瑰及鬱金香特展，因此正確答案是 (C) A temporary exhibit will be displayed.。

Questions 86-88 refer to the following news report.

英式發音

[86]**Thousands of people are expected to flock to Elk Lake this weekend for the first-ever Spencer Incorporated Fishing Tournament.** The contest begins tomorrow at 7 A.M. and is set to attract professional and amateur participants from around the country. [87]**Spencer Incorporated is the sponsor of the event and will donate the prizes.** The winner will receive a brand new Starline EZ fishing boat, while the contestants who come in second and third place will receive professional fishing poles and accessories. [88]**Anyone who intends to head to Elk Lake tomorrow is warned that the highway is being repaved.** So, event participants may experience traffic congestion.

86 What is the report mainly about?
(A) A public service
(B) A workshop
(C) A sponsorship program
(D) A competition

87 What has Spencer Incorporated agreed to do?
(A) Hire workers to clean the lake
(B) Pay for participants' hotel costs
(C) Supply awards for an event
(D) Host a celebratory lunch

88 What does the speaker warn listeners about?
(A) Weather complications
(B) Road construction
(C) Fishing permit modifications
(D) Contest entrance fees

第 86-88 題請參考下列新聞報導。

[86] 這個週末預計會有數千民眾聚集到 Elk 湖參加第一屆的 Spencer 企業釣魚錦標賽。這場比賽從明天早上 7 點開始，且預期會吸引來自全國各地的職業與業餘參賽者。[87]Spencer 企業是本活動的贊助商且將捐贈獎項。優勝者將獲得全新的 Starline EZ 釣魚小船，而第二及第三名的參賽者則會獲得專業釣竿及配件。[88] 提醒明天打算前往 Elk 湖的人，那條公路正在重新鋪設路面。因此，活動參加者可能會遇到塞車。

86 這則報導主要與什麼有關？
(A) 公共服務
(B) 工作坊
(C) 贊助計畫
(D) 比賽

87 Spencer 企業同意做什麼？
(A) 聘請工人清理湖泊
(B) 支付參賽者的飯店費用
(C) 提供活動獎項
(D) 主辦慶祝午宴

88 說話者提醒聽者們什麼？
(A) 天氣上的麻煩
(B) 道路工程
(C) 釣魚許可證的變更
(D) 比賽的入場費

題目 flock [美 flɑk 英 flɔk] 聚集　first-ever 最初的　tournament [美 `tɝnəmənt 英 `tuənəmənt] 錦標賽；比賽
be set to 預期～　sponsor [美 `spɑnsɚ 英 `spɔnsə] 贊助商　contestant [kən`tɛstənt] 參賽者　fishing pole 釣竿
warn [美 wɔrn 英 wɔ:n] 提醒；警告　repave [ri`pev] 重新鋪面　traffic congestion 塞車
86 sponsorship [`spɑnsɚ͵ʃɪp] 贊助　competition [͵kɑmpə`tɪʃən] 比賽；賽會
87 supply [sə`plaɪ] 提供；供給　award [ə`wɔrd] 獎品，獎項　celebratory [`sɛləbre͵torɪ] 慶祝的；祝賀的
88 complication [͵kɑmplə`keʃən]（使事情變複雜的）麻煩　permit [`pɝmɪt] 許可證
modification [͵mɑdəfə`keʃən] 變更；修改　entrance fee 入場費

86 整體內容相關問題—主題　答案 (D)
中
題目詢問報導的主題是什麼，因此要注意聽獨白的開頭部分。獨白說：「Thousands of people are expected to flock to Elk Lake this weekend for the first-ever Spencer Incorporated Fishing Tournament.」，表示這個週末預計會有數千民眾聚集到 Elk 湖參加釣魚錦標賽，接著說明這次比賽的相關資訊，因此正確答案是 (D) A competition。

87 細節事項相關問題—特定細項　答案 (C)
中
題目詢問 Spencer 企業同意做什麼，因此要注意聽和題目關鍵字（Spencer Incorporated ~ do）相關的內容。獨白說：「Spencer Incorporated is the sponsor of the event and will donate the prizes.」，表示 Spencer 企業是這場活動的贊助商且會捐贈獎項，因此正確答案是 (C) Supply awards for an event。

88 細節事項相關問題—特定細項　答案 (B)
中
題目詢問說話者提醒聽者們什麼，因此要注意聽和題目關鍵字（warn）相關的內容。獨白說：「Anyone who intends to head to Elk Lake tomorrow is warned that the highway is being repaved.」，提醒明天打算去 Elk 湖的人，那條公路正在重新鋪設路面，因此正確答案是 (B) Road construction。

89
90
91

Questions 89-91 refer to the following talk.

加拿大式發音

OK . . . I was just informed that [89]**we'll be participating in the Marketing Convention in Portland on August 17. This will be a great opportunity for us to introduce potential clients to the distinctive promotional campaigns we create.** [90]**Derek, I'd like you to contact the convention center to book a booth with the necessary audio-visual equipment.** You can use the company credit card to pay the deposit. We'll also require brochures to hand out at the convention. Document Express printed the materials for our previous event in Ottawa, and [91]**I was very pleased with their work. I'll contact that firm for this project as well.**

第 89-91 題請參考下列談話。

好的……我剛被通知 [89] 我們會去參加 8 月 17 日在波特蘭的行銷大會。這對我們來說是個向潛在客戶介紹我們所打造的獨特促銷宣傳活動的好機會。[90]Derek，我想要你去聯絡會議中心預訂一個有必需影音設備的攤位。你可以用公司信用卡付訂金。我們也需要小冊子來在大會上發放。Document Express 印了我們之前在渥太華那場活動的資料，而 [91] 我對他們的成果非常滿意。這次的案子我也會聯絡這間公司。

89 Where most likely do the listeners work?

(A) At an advertising agency
(B) At a convention center
(C) At a financial institution
(D) At a publishing firm

89 聽者們最有可能在哪裡工作？

(A) 廣告代理商
(B) 會議中心
(C) 金融機構
(D) 出版社

90 What does the man ask Derek to do?

(A) Purchase equipment
(B) Make a reservation
(C) Contact a client
(D) Distribute materials

90 男子要求 Derek 做什麼？

(A) 購買設備
(B) 進行預訂
(C) 聯絡客戶
(D) 分發資料

91 新 What does the speaker imply when he says, "Document Express printed the materials for our previous event in Ottawa"?

(A) A printer made an error.
(B) A promotion was successful.
(C) A company should be hired again.
(D) A brochure is not suitable for an event.

91 當說話者說：「Document Express 印了我們之前在渥太華那場活動的資料」，是暗示什麼？

(A) 一台表機出錯了。
(B) 一項促銷活動很成功。
(C) 應該再次聘請一間公司。
(D) 一本小冊子不適合一個活動。

題目 inform [ɪn`fɔrm] 通知 participate [pɑr`tɪsə͵pet] 參加 potential [pə`tɛnʃəl] 潛在的 distinctive [dɪ`stɪŋktɪv] 獨特的 audio-visual equipment 影音設備 require [rɪ`kwaɪr] 需要

91 suitable [`sutəbl̩] 適合的

89 高 **整體內容相關問題—聽者** 答案 (A)

題目詢問聽者們的工作地點，因此要注意聽和身分、職業相關的表達。獨白說：「we'll be participating in the Marketing Convention ~. This will be a great opportunity for us to introduce potential clients to the distinctive promotional campaigns we create.」，表示自己公司將會參加行銷大會，並認為這是向潛在客戶介紹公司打造的獨特促銷宣傳活動的好機會，由此可知，聽者們是在替客戶進行促銷宣傳活動的廣告代理商裡工作，因此正確答案是 (A) At an advertising agency。

90 中 **細節事項相關問題—要求** 答案 (B)

題目詢問男子要求 Derek 做什麼，因此要注意聽和題目關鍵字（Derek）相關的內容。獨白說：「Derek, I'd like you to contact the convention center to book a booth with the necessary audio-visual equipment.」，要求 Derek 聯繫會議中心預訂一個有必需影音設備的攤位，因此正確答案是 (B) Make a reservation。

新 **91** 高 **細節事項相關問題—掌握意圖** 答案 (C)

題目詢問說話者的說話意圖，因此要注意和題目引用句（Document Express printed the materials for our previous event in Ottawa）相關的內容。獨白說：「I was very pleased with their[Document Express's] work. I'll contact that firm for this project as well.」，表示自己對 Document Express 公司所達成的成果感到非常滿意，並說這次的案子自己也會聯絡這間公司，由此可知，說話者說這句話是要表達想再請 Document Express 公司來做這次案子的意圖，因此正確答案是 (C) A company should be hired again.。

92 93 94

Questions 92-94 refer to the following talk.

美式發音

[92]**I'd like to let you know about the company's latest wellness initiative.** Studies have shown that stretching on a regular basis can improve a person's health. So, beginning on Monday, all employees who are logged in to the company's Intranet system will receive a pop-up message twice a day. If you click it, a five-minute instructional video of various stretching exercises will play. Just follow along in your workspace. [93]**It's not mandatory but, um . . . why not give it a try?** You'll probably feel a lot better. I also wanted to mention that [94]**the fitness center in the building is holding a special promotion tomorrow. If you show your employee ID, you will receive a 15 percent discount on a membership. You should take advantage of this offer.**

第 92-94 題請參考下列談話。

[92] 我想讓各位知道公司最新的健康提案。研究顯示，定時伸展可以改善個人健康。因此，從週一開始，所有登入公司內網系統的員工都會收到一天兩次的彈出訊息。如果你們點下去，就會播放一段各種伸展運動的五分鐘教學影片。就在你們工作的地方跟著做吧。[93] 這沒有強制，不過，嗯……為什麼不試試看呢？你們可能會覺得舒服很多。我也想要提一下，[94] 這棟大樓裡的健身中心明天會舉行特別促銷活動。若出示你們的員工證，會員費就會打八五折。你們應該要利用這項優惠。

92 What is the speaker mainly discussing?

(A) An employee orientation
(B) A health program
(C) A research project
(D) An online discount

92 說話者主要在論述什麼？

(A) 員工說明會
(B) 健康計畫
(C) 研究計畫
(D) 線上折扣

93 新 Why does the speaker say, "You'll probably feel a lot better"?

(A) To show agreement
(B) To suggest a solution
(C) To encourage participation
(D) To confirm a decision

93 說話者為什麼說：「你們可能會覺得舒服很多」？

(A) 為了表示同意
(B) 為了建議一個解決方式
(C) 為了鼓勵參與
(D) 為了確認一項決策

94 What does the speaker recommend that listeners do tomorrow?

(A) Renew an identification card
(B) Go to another building
(C) Organize a workspace
(D) Sign up for a membership

94 說話者建議聽者們在明天做什麼？

(A) 換新身分證
(B) 去另一棟大樓
(C) 規劃一個工作地點
(D) 註冊會員

題目 wellness [ˋwɛlnɪs] 健康　on a regular basis 定時的　workspace [ˋwɝkˏspes] 工作地點
mandatory [ˋmændəˏtorɪ] 強制的

93 solution [səˋluʃən] 解決方式

92 中 **整體內容相關問題—主題** 答案 (B)

題目詢問這段談話的主題，因此要注意聽獨白的開頭部分。獨白說：「I'd like to let you know about the company's latest wellness initiative.」，表示自己想要讓聽者們知道公司最新的健康提案，接著繼續說明健康計畫的相關內容，因此正確答案是 (B) A health program。

換句話說

wellness initiative 健康提案 → health program 健康計畫

新 **93** 中 **細節事項相關問題—掌握意圖** 答案 (C)

題目詢問說話者的說話意圖，因此要注意與題目引用句（You'll probably feel a lot better）相關的內容。獨白說：「It's not mandatory but ~ why not give it a try?」，表示雖然這件事不是強制要做，不過聽者們不如試著做做看，由此可知，說話者想要鼓勵聽者們參加公司的健康提案，因此正確答案是 (C) To encourage participation。

94 中 **細節事項相關問題—提議** 答案 (D)

題目詢問說話者建議聽者們在明天做什麼，因此要注意聽獨白的後半部中出現提議相關表達的句子。獨白說：「the fitness center ~ is holding a special promotion tomorrow. If you show your employee ID, you will receive a 15 percent discount on a membership. You should take advantage of this offer.」，表示健身中心明天會舉行特別促銷活動，如果出示員工證，會員費就會打八五折，並建議聽者們應該要利用這項優惠，因此正確答案是 (D) Sign up for a membership。

95
96
97

Questions 95-97 refer to the following telephone message and list.

[🔊] 英式發音

Good afternoon. This is Jia Chen calling from Denver Flooring. [95]**I'd like to respond to the phone inquiry you made yesterday, when our business was closed . . . um, about our prices.** We generally charge $30 per hour for installation. Additionally, the flooring cost per square meter varies depending on the type of material you choose. [96]**Based on the flooring type you mentioned in your message, the amount we'd charge you per square meter is $35.** If you find this to be too expensive, please consider some of the other flooring options—our most popular one is $20 per square meter. [97]**You can find details about these materials at www.denfloor.com.** If you would like to schedule a consultation, you can reach me at 555-4988.

[新]

Flooring Type	Price per Square Meter
Tile	$20
Carpet	$25
Bamboo	$30
[97]**Hardwood**	**$35**

95 Why is the speaker calling?

(A) To accept an offer
(B) To answer a question
(C) To request assistance
(D) To arrange a consultation

96 [新] Look at the graphic. Which flooring type did the listener mention?

(A) Tile
(B) Carpet
(C) Bamboo
(D) Hardwood

97 According to the speaker, how can the listener get information about the materials?

(A) By going to a store
(B) By calling a hotline
(C) By visiting a Web site
(D) By sending an e-mail

第 95-97 題請參考下列電話留言及清單。

午安。我是 Denver 地板材料的 Jia Chen。[95] 我想要回覆您昨天在我們公司下班時打來詢問……嗯，和我們收費相關問題的電話。我們一般安裝是每小時收費 30 美金。此外，每平方公尺的地板材料費用會隨您選擇的材料種類而有所變動。[96] 就您在留言中提到的那種地板材料來說，我們每平方公尺會收您 35 美金。若您覺得這樣太貴，請考慮一些其他的地板材料選擇——我們最受歡迎的那種是每平方公尺 20 美金。[97] 您可以在 www.denfloor.com 上找到與這些材料有關的詳細資訊。若您想要安排時間做諮詢，可以打 555-4988 聯絡我。

地板材料種類	每平方公尺價格
磁磚	20 美金
地毯	25 美金
竹子	30 美金
[97] 硬木	35 美金

95 說話者為何打電話？

(A) 為了接受一項提議
(B) 為了回答一個問題
(C) 為了要求一項協助
(D) 為了安排一次諮詢

96 請看圖表。聽者提到過哪一種地板材料？

(A) 磁磚
(B) 地毯
(C) 竹子
(D) 硬木

97 根據說話者所說，聽者如何能取得關於這些材料的資訊？

(A) 去一間店
(B) 打一支熱線電話
(C) 上一個網站
(D) 寄送一封電子郵件

題目 generally [ˋdʒɛnərəlɪ] 一般地　charge [[美] tʃɑrdʒ [英] tʃɑ:dʒ] 收費　installation [ˌɪnstəˋleʃən] 安裝
square meter 平方公尺　vary [[美] ˋvɛrɪ [英] ˋvɛəri] 變動　material [məˋtɪrɪəl] 材料　consultation [ˌkɑnsəlˋteʃən] 諮詢

95 整體內容相關問題—目的 答案 (B)
中

題目詢問來電目的，因此要注意聽獨白的開頭部分。獨白說：「I'd like to respond to the phone inquiry you made ~ about our prices.」，表示想要回覆對方打來詢問收費相關問題的電話，因此正確答案是 (B) To answer a question。

新 96 細節事項相關問題—圖表資料 答案 (D)
中

題目詢問聽者提到過哪種地板材料，因此要確認題目提供的清單，並注意和題目關鍵字（flooring type）相關的內容。獨白說：「Based on the flooring type you mentioned ~, the amount we'd charge you per square meter is $35.」，表示聽者在留言中提到的那種地板材料，每平方公尺的收費是 35 美金，透過圖表可知，聽者提過的那種地板材料是硬木，因此正確答案是 (D) Hardwood。

97 細節事項相關問題—方法 答案 (C)
低

題目詢問聽者能如何取得材料的相關資訊，因此必須注意聽和題目關鍵字（get information about the materials）相關的內容。獨白說：「You can find details about these materials at www.denfloor.com.」，表示聽者可以在網站上找到與這些材料有關的詳細資訊，因此正確答案是 (C) By visiting a Web site。

98 99 100

Questions 98-100 refer to the following announcement and directory.

[3] 澳洲式發音

Attention, front desk staff. [98]**Tomorrow, the remodeled Presswood Hotel will be opened to the public.** Here are a few things to keep in mind . . . First, when guests check in, make sure they know that our room service hours have been extended. Um, they can place orders until midnight now. Also, there is a problem with the housekeeping office's extension. For the time being, [99]**guests should just contact the front desk if they need things like towels or pillows.** Finally, [100]**we will be offering a complimentary continental breakfast this week.** It will be served in the main dining room until 10 A.M. every day. OK. That's all.

[新]

Presswood Hotel Directory	
Housekeeping	5
Room Service	6
Front Desk	[99]**7**
Concierge	8

98 According to the speaker, what will happen tomorrow?

(A) A facility will reopen.
(B) A pamphlet will be printed.
(C) A workshop will be held.
(D) A room will be renovated.

99 [新] Look at the graphic. Which number should guests dial to request towels or pillows?

(A) 5
(B) 6
(C) 7
(D) 8

100 What will be offered to guests this week?

(A) Discounted tickets
(B) Free meals
(C) Gift bags
(D) Complimentary upgrades

第 98-100 題請參考下列公告及通訊錄。

前台員工請注意。[98] 明天，整修後的 Presswood 飯店將對外開放。這裡有幾件事要記得……首先，當客人入住時，請務必讓他們知道我們的客房服務提供時間已經延長了。嗯，他們現在直到午夜都可以點餐。還有，房務部的分機出了問題。暫時，[99] 客人如果需要像毛巾或枕頭等物品，應直接聯絡前台。最後，[100] 我們這星期會提供免費的歐陸早餐。每天會在主飯廳供應到早上 10 點。好。就這樣。

Presswood 飯店通訊錄	
房務	5
客房服務	6
前台	[99]7
門房	8

98 根據說話者所說，明天會發生什麼？

(A) 一座設施將重新開幕。
(B) 將印刷一本小冊子。
(C) 將舉辦一場工作坊。
(D) 會整修一個房間。

99 請看圖表。客人應撥打哪個號碼來索取毛巾或枕頭？

(A) 5
(B) 6
(C) 7
(D) 8

100 這星期會提供什麼給客人？

(A) 折扣後的票券
(B) 免費餐點
(C) 禮物袋
(D) 免費升等

題目 midnight [ˋmɪdˏnaɪt] 午夜，半夜 12 點鐘　housekeeping [ˋhaʊsˏkipɪŋ] 房務　pillow [美] ˋpɪlo [英] ˋpiləu] 枕頭
complimentary [[美] ˏkɑmpləˋmɛntərɪ [英] ˏkɔmpliˋmentəri] 免費的
continental [[美] ˏkɑntəˋnɛntḷ [英] ˏkɔntiˋnentl] 歐陸的；大陸的　concierge [[美] ˏkɑnsɪˋɛrʒ [英] ˏkɔnsiˋɛəʒ] 門房

98 中 **細節事項相關問題—接下來要做的事** 答案 (A)

題目詢問明天會發生什麼，因此必須注意聽和題目關鍵字（tomorrow）相關的內容。獨白說：「Tomorrow, the remodeled Presswood Hotel will be opened to the public.」，表示整修後的 Presswood 飯店明天將對外開放，因此正確答案是 (A) A facility will reopen.。

新 **99** 低 **細節事項相關問題—圖表資料** 答案 (C)

題目詢問客人應撥打哪個號碼來索取毛巾或枕頭，因此要確認題目提供的通訊錄資訊，並注意和題目關鍵字（towels or pillows）相關的內容。獨白說：「guests should just contact the front desk if they need things like towels or pillows」，表示客人如果需要像毛巾或枕頭等物品，應直接聯絡前台，透過通訊錄可知，客人應撥打分機 7 來索取毛巾或枕頭，因此正確答案是 (C) 7。

100 中 **細節事項相關問題—特定細項** 答案 (B)

題目詢問這星期會提供客人什麼，因此要注意聽和題目關鍵字（this week）相關的內容。獨白說：「we will be offering a complimentary continental breakfast this week」，表示這星期會提供免費的歐陸早餐，因此正確答案是 (B) Free meals。

換句話說

complimentary ~ breakfast 免費早餐 → Free meals 免費餐點

TEST 01_A

1	jog	v. 慢跑	26	shortly	adv. 很快，馬上
2	race	n.（賽跑）比賽	27	swimsuit	n. 泳衣
3	fasten	v. 扣緊；繫牢	28	deliver	v. 運送
4	get off	phr. 下（火車、飛機等交通工具）	29	pick up	phr. 購買；拿取
5	seat belt	phr. 安全帶	30	begin	v. 開始
6	aisle	n. 通道，走道	31	sail	n. 帆；v. 航行
7	label	v. 貼標籤；n. 標籤	32	tear	n. 扯破的裂縫，撕裂處；v. 撕開
8	look into	phr. 看～(的裡面)；調查	33	book	v. 預訂
9	microscope	n. 顯微鏡	34	passport	n. 護照
10	researcher	n. 研究員	35	plan	v. 計劃
11	in a row	phr. 一排	36	stay	v. 暫住；停留
12	overlook	v. 俯瞰	37	put in overtime	phr. 申請加班
13	patio	n. 露臺	38	time off	phr. 休息
14	stool	n. 凳子	39	rearrange	v. 重新布置；重新安排
15	reporter	n. 記者	40	a bit	phr. 一點，少許
16	shareholder	n. 股東	41	arrive	v. 抵達
17	presenter	n. 發表人	42	in a hurry	phr. 匆忙地；趕緊
18	topic	n. 主題	43	airline	n. 航空公司
19	luncheon	n. 午餐餐會	44	difference	n. 差異
20	mail	v. 郵寄	45	personally	adv. 個人地
21	manager	n. 經理，管理者	46	quite	adv. 相當
22	fill up	phr. 填滿	47	either	conj. 不是～就是～
23	gas station	phr. 加油站	48	task	n. 工作；任務
24	open	adj. 營業的	49	challenging	adj. 困難的，富挑戰性的
25	leave	v. 離開；n. 休假	50	faculty	n. 教職員

TEST 01_B

1	increase	v. 提高，增加	26	draft	v. 起草；n. 草稿，草圖
2	predict	v. 預料，預計	27	edition	n.（發行物的）版；版本
3	semester	n. 學期	28	review	n. 評論；v. 審閱；複審
4	surprisingly	adv. 意外地，出乎意料地	29	story	n. 報導；故事
5	tuition	n. 學費	30	submit	v. 提交；使服從；使經受
6	at least	phr. 至少	31	automotive	adj. 汽車的
7	last	v. 持續；維持	32	collision	n. 碰撞
8	print out	phr. 印出	33	dispatch	v. 派遣
9	private	adj. 隱密的；私人的	34	injure	v. 使受傷
10	seat	v. 使就座；n. 座位	35	public transportation	phr. 大眾運輸工具
11	spot	n. 地方，地點	36	tow	v. 拖
12	fluent in	phr. ～流利	37	appeal to	phr. 對～有吸引力；引起～的興趣
13	take a lesson	phr. 上課	38	aspiring	adj. 有抱負的；雄心勃勃的
14	accountant	n. 會計師	39	contact	v. 聯繫
15	conclude	v. 得出結論	40	meet-and-greet	n.（和群眾面對面的）見面會
16	hire	v. 聘僱	41	take pride in	phr. 對於～感到驕傲
17	process	n. 程序，流程；v. 處理；加工	42	complaint	n. 抗議；投訴
18	tax season	phr. 報稅季	43	crash	v.（程式等）突然停止運作
19	call back	phr. 回電	44	frustration	n.（因無法達成所想而）沮喪，挫敗感
20	instead	adv. 做為替代	45	install	v. 安裝，設置
21	recall	n. 召回；回想	46	multiple	adj. 多個的
22	show up	phr. 到來；出現	47	resolve	v. 解決
23	redecorate	v. 重新裝潢；重新布置	48	train	v. 訓練
24	avenue	n. 大街，大道	49	bedding	n. 寢具
25	approve	v. 批准；核可	50	look up	phr. 查詢

TEST 01_C

1	receipt	n. 收據	26	consultant	n. 顧問
2	refund	n. 退費	27	degree	n. 學位
3	request	v. 要求給予； n. 要求事項	28	executive	n. 主管；（公司或組織的）領導階層； adj. 執行的；行政上的
4	transaction	n. 交易	29	gathering	n. 聚會；聚集
5	look over	phr. 查看，仔細檢查	30	invest	v. 投資
6	complement	v. 與～相配	31	pursue	v. 進行，從事；追求
7	dress	v. 穿（衣物）	32	subsidize	v. 提供補助金
8	fashionable	adj. 時尚的	33	account	n. 帳號，帳戶
9	go with	phr. 與～相配	34	housewarming	n. 喬遷派對
10	make sure	phr. 確定	35	input	v.（將資料等）輸入（電腦等）
11	match	v. 適合；和～相配；n. 競賽	36	place an order	phr. 下訂
12	pattern	n. 花樣；圖案	37	pressure cooker	phr. 壓力鍋
13	put on	phr. 穿上	38	ship	v. 運送
14	recommendation	n. 推薦	39	take care of	phr. 處理～
15	try on	phr. 試（衣服等）	40	assist	v. 幫助
16	as planned	phr. 按照計畫的	41	attendance	n. 參加人數；出席
17	malfunction	n. 故障；失去功能	42	coworker	n. 同事
18	unexpectedly	adv. 未預料到地，意外地	43	funding	n. 資金
19	analyst	n. 分析師	44	pass out	phr. 分發
20	anxious	adj. 渴望的；焦慮不安的	45	registration	n. 報名；登記
21	approachable	adj. 待人友善的；易親近的	46	take over	phr. 接手
22	examine	v. 檢視；細查	47	work shift	phr. 輪班工作的班次
23	in charge of	phr. 負責～	48	celebration	n. 慶祝活動
24	trend	n. 趨勢	49	carpool	v. 共乘汽車
25	versatile	adj. 多種用途的；多才多藝的	50	come along	phr. 一起去

TEST 01_D

1	hold	v. 使發生；舉行；握著	26	witness	v. 目睹
2	come up with	phr. 想出～	27	further	adj. 進一步的；更遠的
3	doubtful	adj. 不確定的，懷疑的	28	measure	n. 措施；手段
4	personalize	v. 個人化	29	suspend	v. 暫停；中止
5	upset with	phr. 對～不滿的	30	suspicious	adj. 可疑的
6	absolutely	adv. 絕對地，一定地	31	temporarily	adv. 暫時地；臨時地
7	compatible	adj. 可相容的	32	unavailable	adj. 無法使用的
8	complimentary	adj. 免費贈送的	33	withdrawal	n. 提領（現金）
9	detector	n. 偵測器	34	alter	v. 更改；改變
10	keep track of	phr. 掌握～的狀態	35	at the latest	phr. 最晚
11	kitchen appliance	phr. 廚房電器	36	flextime	n. 彈性工作時間
12	similar	adj. 類似的	37	be aware of	phr. 注意～
13	take control of	phr. 控制～	38	part	n. 角色；部分
14	universal	adj. 萬用的，通用的	39	present	adj. 出席的
15	disappoint	v. 使失望	40	role	n. 角色；職責
16	glassware	n. 玻璃器皿	41	script	n. 劇本；文稿
17	overwhelm	v. 使難以承受；使不知所措	42	beginner	n. 初學者
18	poor	adj. 糟糕的	43	brief	adj. 簡短的；短暫的
19	supplier	n. 供應商	44	currently	adv. 現在
20	turnout	n.（聚會的）到場人數；投票人數	45	guideline	n. 指導方針
21	avoid	v. 避免	46	instructional	adj. 教學的
22	collapse	v. 倒場	47	suitable	adj. 適合的；適當的；恰當的
23	congestion	n. 壅塞	48	technique	n. 技巧；技術
24	identify	v. 確認；辨別	49	trail	n. 路徑；小道
25	injured	adj. 受傷的	50	discontinue	v. 停止；中斷（生產等）

TEST 02_A

1	decorate	v. 裝飾；布置	26	at the last minute	phr. 在最後一刻
2	light bulb	phr. 燈泡	27	refrigerator	n. 冰箱
3	replace	v. 替換	28	turn out	phr. 結果～
4	backpack	n. 後背包	29	clerk	n. 員工
5	face	v. 面向；面對； n. 表面；面孔	30	popular	adj. 受歡迎的
6	push	v. 推	31	boss	n. 老闆；長官
7	appliance	n.（尤指電器）設備，裝置	32	community service	phr. 社區服務
8	clothing	n. 衣物	33	major	adj. 重大的
9	exchange	v. 交換	34	success	n. 成功
10	pillar	n. 柱子	35	due	adj.（錢等）應支付的；到期的
11	shopper	n. 購物者	36	tax	n. 稅金
12	bowl	n. 碗	37	reasonable	adj. 適當的；合理的
13	container	n. 容器；貨櫃	38	candidate	n. 應徵者；候選人
14	corner	n. 角落	39	résumé	n. 履歷表
15	vase	n.（裝飾用的）瓶；花瓶	40	announce	v. 宣布；公告
16	mow	v. 割（草、穀物等）；修剪（草地等）	41	delay	n. 延誤；v. 延期
17	pathway	n. 路；小徑	42	press conference	phr. 記者會
18	pedestrian	n. 行人	43	reschedule	v. 重新排定時間
19	client	n. 客戶	44	brochure	n. 小冊子
20	no later than	phr. 最晚～；不晚於～	45	insufficient	adj. 不足的；不充分的
21	preference	n. 偏好	46	flight attendant	phr. 空服員
22	wrap	v. 包，裹	47	lot	n.（有特定用處的）一塊地
23	hand in	phr. 繳交	48	necessary	adj. 不可避免的；必需的
24	reimburse	v. 核銷；償付	49	outing	n. 郊遊
25	outside	adv. 在外面；n. 外面	50	organization	n. 組織，機構

TEST 02_B

1	partner with	phr. 和～合作	26	cover letter	phr. 求職信
2	establishment	n. 機構，設施	27	in regard to	phr. 關於～
3	celebrity	n. 名人；明星	28	inquire	v. 詢問
4	mention	v. 說起，提及	29	mark	v. 標記；標明；n. 記號
5	spokesperson	n. 發言人；代言人	30	blizzard	n. 暴風雪
6	form	n. 表格；表單	31	get in touch with	phr. 與～聯絡
7	low on	phr. ～快要沒有了	32	host	v. 主辦；以主人身分接待；n. 主持人
8	proper	adj. 適當的；正確的	33	unavoidable	adj. 無法避免的
9	choose	v. 選擇，挑選	34	accessible	adj. 可使用的；可接觸的
10	contract	v. 承包；締約；n. 合約	35	business trip	phr. 出差
11	bring	v. 帶來	36	entrance	n. 入口
12	join	v. 和～一起；加入	37	teller	n.（銀行窗口的）櫃員
13	snack	n. 點心；輕食	38	withdraw	v. 提領（錢）
14	discuss	v. 討論；詳述	39	acceptable	adj. 不錯的；可接受的
15	entire	adj. 全部的，整個的	40	distract	v. 使（注意力）不集中，使無法專心
16	cause	n. 理由，原因	41	lately	adv. 最近
17	drop	n. 下滑；v. 掉落	42	untidy	adj. 雜亂的
18	platter	n.（大而淺的）盤子	43	comparison	n. 比較
19	cost	v. 花費	44	consultancy	n. 顧問公司
20	outline	n. 大綱；概要	45	convert	v. 轉變
21	remodel	v. 整修；改建	46	landscaping	n. 景觀設計
22	limitation	n. 限制	47	property	n. 地產，不動產
23	restriction	n. 限制；限制規定	48	residential	adj. 居住用的；住宅的
24	appreciate	v. 欣賞；評鑑；感激	49	scale	n. 規模
25	blueprint	n. 藍圖	50	take on	phr. 承擔；接受（工作等）

TEST 02_C

1	flu shot	phr. 流感疫苗	26	debut	n. 初次登台
2	pharmacist	n. 藥師	27	frame	v. 裱框；n. 相框
3	prescribe	v. 開～處方	28	hand out	phr. 分發，發下
4	supervisor	n. 上司，主管	29	incoming	adj. 即將到來的；進來的
5	vaccination	n. 疫苗接種	30	program	n. 節目表，行程計畫表
6	device	n. 設備，裝置	31	accessory	n. 附件；配件
7	make sense	phr. 合理；講得通	32	availability	n. 可得性；可用性
8	rehearse	v. 演練，排練	33	checkout	n. 結帳台
9	storage	n. 儲存，保管	34	component	n. 零件；（機器、設備等的）構成要素
10	assure	v. 向～保證，擔保	35	durability	n. 耐用度；耐久性
11	come with	phr. 備有～，附有～	36	expiration date	phr. 截止日期
12	consult	v. 向～尋求意見	37	gear	n. 裝備
13	potential	adj. 潛在的；可能的	38	in stock	phr. 有庫存的
14	priority	n. 優先權；優先	39	on sale	phr. 特價
15	skyline	n. 天際線	40	pad	n.（座椅的）墊子
16	unit	n.（公寓大樓等的）一個單位	41	participate in	phr. 參加～
17	acquisition	n. 收購；獲得	42	promotion	n. 促銷活動；宣傳；升職
18	assessment	n. 評估	43	retail	adj. 零售的
19	be subject to	phr. 遭受～；須經～	44	valid	adj. 有效的；站得住腳的
20	dismiss	v. 解雇	45	weight	n. 重量
21	negotiation	n. 協商	46	block off	phr. 封閉（道路等）；封鎖（出入口等）
22	retention	n. 保持；保留	47	optometrist	n. 驗光師
23	term	n.（合約、協商等的）條件	48	outstanding	adj. 未結清的；未解決的
24	transfer	v. 調動；轉換	49	paperwork	n. 文書資料；文書工作
25	cast	n.（電影、戲劇或演出的）演員陣容	50	specialist	n. 專家

TEST 02_D

1	production	n.（戲劇、電影等）作品；製造；生產	26	noticeable	adj. 明顯的；值得注意的
2	range from ~ to ~	phr. 在～之間	27	spray	v. 噴灑
3	take advantage of	phr. 利用～	28	substance	n. 物質；實質
4	branch out	phr. 開始發展（新工作或新業務等）	29	a handful of	phr.（數量不多的）幾個～
5	brand recognition	phr. 品牌辨識度	30	breach	n. 違反；破壞
6	collaborate	v. 合作	31	case	n. 案例
7	credential	n. 資格證書；資歷	32	export	n. 出口
8	dozen	n. 數十；一打	33	independent	adj. 獨立的；獨自的
9	found	v. 建立	34	open forum	phr. 公開討論會，公開論壇
10	oversee	v. 監督	35	session	n. 集會；會議
11	amount	n. 數額	36	durable	adj. 耐用的；持久的
12	be accustomed to	phr. 慣於～	37	expensive	adj. 昂貴的
13	confidence	n. 信任；確信，把握	38	informal	adj. 非正式的
14	disposal	n. 處理	39	query	n. 疑問
15	take part in	phr. 參與～	40	questionnaire	n. 問卷；意見調查表
16	waste	n. 廢棄物	41	biologist	n. 生物學家
17	agency	n. 代理商；代理機構	42	enclosure	n. 圈地；圍場
18	certain	adj. 確信的；有把握的	43	inhabitant	n. 棲息動物；（某地區的）居住者
19	expert	n. 專家	44	inspector	n. 稽查人員，視察人員
20	renowned	adj. 有名的；有名聲的	45	medical	adj. 醫療的
21	trade show	phr. 貿易展	46	professor	n. 教授
22	useful	adj. 有用的	47	rely on	phr. 依賴～
23	application	n. 施用；申請	48	reserve	n. 保留區；v. 保存
24	chemical	n. 化學製品；化學藥劑	49	species	n. 物種
25	effective	adj. 有效的	50	wildlife	n. 野生動植物

TEST 03_A

1	power drill	phr. 電鑽	26	heavy traffic	phr. 交通繁忙；塞車
2	couch	n. 沙發；躺椅	27	highway	n. 公路；幹道
3	electronic device	phr. 電子設備	28	or so	phr. 大概～，～左右
4	reposition	v. 變換位置（到其他地點）；換～的位置	29	cab	n. 計程車
5	sewing machine	phr. 縫紉機	30	would rather	phr. 寧可～；比較想要～
6	tailor	n. 裁縫	31	binder	n.（用來整理紙類文書的）活頁夾
7	banner	n. 橫幅；旗幟	32	bookcase	n. 書架；書櫃
8	parking lot	phr. 停車場	33	mover	n. 搬家工人；搬家公司
9	display case	phr. 展示櫃	34	available	adj. 可以買到的；可使用的
10	put up	phr. 放上；設置	35	come in	phr.（商品等）有貨；可以買到
11	emerge	v. 出現；顯露	36	excellent	adj. 非常棒的，卓越的
12	platform	n. 月台	37	check	v. 確認；檢查；n. 支票
13	railroad track	phr. 鐵軌	38	quickly	adv. 快速地
14	depart	v. 離開；出發	39	assistant	n. 幫手，助理
15	downtown	n. 市中心；城市裡的商業區	40	expect	v. 預計；盼望
16	cooperate	v. 合作，協力	41	permanent	adj. 永久的；固定性的
17	director	n. 董事；主管	42	decide	v. 決定
18	manage	v. 處理；設法達成	43	mayor	n. 市長
19	exchange rate	phr. 匯率	44	square	n. 廣場
20	luggage	n. 行李	45	create	v. 製造；創造
21	separately	adv. 分別地	46	notice	n. 告示；通知；v. 注意到；通知
22	throughout	prep. 遍布～；從頭到尾～	47	sign	n. 告示牌；標示
23	quality control	phr. 品質管制	48	belongings	n. 隨身物品；擁有物
24	remote control	phr. 遙控器	49	unpack	v. 打開（行李或包裹等）把東西拿出來
25	delivery	n. 遞送的貨物或信件	50	donation	n. 捐款；捐獻

TEST 03_B

1	prefer	v. 偏好	26	competitive	adj. 有競爭力的；競爭的
2	sheet	n.（紙張）一張；床單；表單	27	courier company	phr. 快遞公司
3	ceremony	n. 典禮，儀式	28	home electronics	phr. 家電產品
4	fiancé	n. 未婚夫	29	investment	n. 投資；投資額
5	invitation	n. 邀請函；邀請	30	projection	n. 預測；估計
6	totally	adv. 完全地	31	template	n. 範本，樣板
7	flyer	n. 傳單	32	compile	v. 收集（資料等）；匯編
8	break room	phr. 休息室	33	decor	n.（室內）裝潢
9	current	adj. 現在的，當前的	34	facility	n.（有特定用途的）設施，場地
10	stove	n. 爐子	35	feedback	n. 回饋意見
11	document	n. 文件；公文	36	improve	v. 改善；提升
12	drawer	n. 抽屜	37	layout	n. 配置；版面設計
13	helpful	adj. 有用的，有幫助的	38	majority	n. 大多數
14	order	v. 訂購；n. 訂單	39	affect	v. 影響
15	single	adj. 一個的；個別的	40	alternative	n. 替代方案；adj. 替代的；兩者擇一的
16	edit	v. 編輯；校訂	41	figure out	phr. 理解；想出
17	editor	n. 編輯；（報章雜誌的）主編；校訂者	42	plumber	n. 水管工人
18	presentation	n. 簡報；發表	43	distribute	v. 分發
19	rest	n. 剩餘部分；休息	44	point out	phr. 指出，提到
20	advertising	n. 廣告業；（總稱）廣告	45	skylight	n.（屋頂、天花板等上方的）天窗
21	conference	n. 會談；會議	46	afford	v. 負擔得起
22	deal	n. 交易；方案	47	bring up	phr. 提出（話題等）
23	deluxe	adj. 豪華的	48	dramatically	adv. 劇烈地；大幅地
24	discount	n. 折價；折扣優惠	49	issue	n. 發行（刊物等）；（報刊等的）期號
25	renovate	v. 整修；翻新	50	junior	adj. 年輕的；資淺的

TEST 03_C

1	labor cost	phr. 人事費用	26	clearance sale	phr. 清倉特賣
2	of late	phr. 最近	27	double-check	v. 再次確認，再次檢查
3	raise	n.（費用等的）提升；加薪	28	formal	adj. 正式的
4	upper	adj. 上面的	29	inventory	n. 物品清單；存貨
5	boardroom	n. 會議室	30	on one's way to	phr. 在去～的途中
6	buzzing	adj. 嗡嗡聲	31	sufficient	adj. 充分的
7	demonstration	n. 示範；展示會	32	originally	adv. 原本
8	knock ~ off	phr. 撞掉；撞倒	33	damaged	adj. 受損的
9	projector	n. 投影機	34	exceptional	adj. 優秀的
10	reject	v. 拒絕	35	expire	v. 到期；（期限）截止
11	across the country	phr. 全國各地	36	fund-raiser	n. 募款活動
12	furnishing	n. 家具；室內陳設	37	garment	n. 衣服
13	manufacturer	n. 製造商	38	switch	v. 改變；轉換
14	out of stock	phr. 沒有庫存的；缺貨的	39	guidebook	n. 旅遊指南
15	remote	adj. 遠距的	40	loan	n. 借出
16	sell out	phr. 售完	41	search for	phr. 搜尋～，搜索～
17	ship out	phr. 發貨；（搭船）離開	42	shelf	n.（書架等的）架子
18	traffic	n.（客人的）來往量	43	typo	n. 打字錯誤
19	uncertain	adj. 不確定的	44	charitable	adj. 慈善的
20	collection	n. 收藏品；一堆（東西）	45	extension	n. 分機；延長
21	instrument	n. 儀器；設備	46	look forward to	phr. 期待～
22	interactive	adj. 互動的；交互作用的	47	needy	adj.（經濟上）有需要的；貧窮的
23	space exploration	phr. 太空探索	48	various	adj. 各式各樣的
24	space shuttle	phr. 太空梭	49	late fee	phr. 逾期罰款
25	cash register	phr. 收銀台	50	overdue	adj. 逾期的

TEST 03_D

1	owe	v. 積欠（債務等）	26	automatically	adv. 自動地
2	reservation	n. 預約	27	description	n. 描述
3	dock	n. 碼頭；v.（船等）停泊	28	detect	v. 偵測；察覺
4	perform	v. 演出；實行	29	promote	v. 宣傳
5	protective	adj. 防護的；保護用的	30	electronic	adj. 電子的
6	scene	n.（戲劇、電影的）場景	31	identification card	phr. 身分證
7	secure	v. 保管；確保； adj. 安全的	32	period	n. 期間
8	shoot	v. 拍攝；射擊	33	qualify	v. 符合～的資格
9	abroad	adv. 往海外	34	region	n. 地區
10	annual	adj. 年度的	35	risk	n. 風險；危險
11	debt	n. 債務	36	trial	n. 試用
12	generate	v. 產出	37	a number of	phr. 一些～
13	repayment	n. 償還	38	floor	n. 樓層
14	segment	n.（電視節目等的）單元	39	loading dock	phr. 裝卸碼頭；卸貨平台
15	square meter	phr. 平方公尺	40	outdated	adj. 過時的；老舊的
16	unemployment	n. 失業率；失業（狀態）	41	post	v. 張貼
17	a wide range of	phr. 各式各樣的；範圍廣泛的	42	testing	n. 測試；檢測
18	delighted	adj. 高興的	43	administration	n. 行政
19	dietary	adj. 飲食的	44	claim	v. 領取；主張
20	dish	n. 菜餚；盤碟	45	limited	adj. 有限的；受限的
21	graduation	n. 畢業	46	across from	phr. 在～的對面
22	respond	v. 回應；回答	47	dinner	n. 晚餐；晚宴
23	taste	v. 試吃；n. 味道	48	product launch	phr. 產品發表會
24	triumph	n. 大成功，勝利	49	push back	phr. 延後（時間、日期等）
25	vegan	adj. 全素食的；全素主義者	50	socialize	v. 交流；交際

TEST 04_A

1	reach for	phr. 把手伸向～	26	lower	v. 降下；降低
2	fuel	n. 燃料	27	volume	n. 總量；音量
3	mechanic	n. 技師；維修人員	28	vegetarian	adj. 素食的；素食主義者的
4	pump	v. 灌入	29	inspection	n. 視察
5	take off	phr. 脫去；除去	30	work	v. 工作；運作；n. 工作
6	bend	v. 彎曲（身體等）	31	clear	adj. 清楚的；易懂的
7	vacuum	v. 用吸塵器吸；n. 吸塵器	32	clear out	phr. 清空
8	cloth	n. 布；織品；衣料	33	explain	v. 說明
9	drawing	n. 圖畫	34	perfectly	adv. 正確地；完全地；完美地
10	hallway	n. 走廊；通道	35	take a measurement	phr. 測量
11	plant	n. 植物	36	amusement park	phr. 遊樂園
12	shut	v. 關上；封閉	37	ride	v. 搭（車等）；n. 搭乘；交通工具
13	editorial	n.（報刊等的）社論	38	belong in	phr. 應該在～
14	extremely	adv. 非常，極度	39	parcel	n. 包裹
15	impressive	adj. 令人印象深刻的	40	slightly	adv. 輕微地
16	cinema	n. 電影院；電影	41	building supplies	phr. 建築用品
17	star	v. 由～主演	42	floor plan	phr. 樓層平面圖
18	automatic	adj. 自動的	43	second	adj. 第二的
19	manual	n. 手冊；adj. 手動的	44	customs	n. 海關
20	read through	phr. 從頭到尾看一遍；快速看過（以找出錯誤）	45	check in	phr. 報到
21	refill	v. 再裝滿	46	otherwise	adv. 不同地；以其他方式
22	spill	v. 使溢出；使濺出	47	patient	n. 病人；adj. 有耐心的
23	communicate	v. 交流；溝通	48	reception desk	phr. 接待櫃台
24	run into	phr. 偶然碰到	49	typically	adv. 普通地，一般地
25	workflow	n. 工作流程	50	unless	conj. 除非

TEST 04_B

1	consumer	n. 消費者	26	as long as	phr. 只要～
2	survey	n.（意見）調查表	27	go for a walk	phr. 去散步
3	comparable	adj. 不相上下的；可比較的	28	busy signal	phr. 忙音
4	qualified	adj. 適任的；符合資格的	29	receiver	n. 話筒；接收者
5	attend	v. 出席，參加	30	repair	v. 修理
6	confused	adj. 混亂的；感到困惑的	31	unplug	v. 拔（電器的）插頭
7	follow	v. 按照；跟隨	32	accommodation	n. 住宿；住宿設施
8	launch	n. 發表會；v. 發表；開始	33	destination	n. 目的地
9	prepare	v. 準備	34	ruin	n. 遺跡；廢墟
10	press	n. 媒體；新聞界	35	site	n. 地點；場所
11	branch	n. 分公司；樹枝	36	transportation	n. 運輸工具
12	consider	v. 考慮	37	proceeds	n. 收益
13	possibility	n. 可能性；可能的選項	38	architectural	adj. 建築的
14	trim	v. 修剪	39	assign	v. 指派；選派
15	advice	n. 建議，勸告	40	capture	v.（以照片或文字）刻劃；拍攝
16	appoint	v. 指派，任命	41	interior	n. 內部；室內
17	booking	n. 預訂	42	subscription	n. 訂閱
18	council	n. 會議；理事會	43	agreement	n. 合約，協議；同意
19	name	v. 指名；選擇；n. 名字	44	demand	v. 要求；n. 需求
20	photography	n. 攝影	45	dissatisfied	adj. 不滿意的
21	portrait	n. 人物寫真；肖像	46	full refund	phr. 全額退費
22	specialize in	phr. 專門做～	47	partner	v. 與～合作；與～成為夥伴
23	place	v. 放置；擺放	48	reputable	adj. 聲譽良好的
24	storefront	n. 店鋪面向馬路的那個部分	49	shipment	n. 運輸；運輸的貨物
25	wonder	v. 納悶；覺得奇怪	50	billboard	n. 廣告看板

TEST 04_C

1	commercial	n.（電視或廣播中的）商業廣告；adj. 商業的	26	time sheet	phr. 工時表
2	delegate	v. 委派（某人）做；授權	27	activation	n. 啟動
3	evaluation	n. 評估	28	payment	n. 支付；支付款項
4	note	v. 提到	29	rate	n. 費用
5	periodic	adj. 定期的	30	business	n. 公司
6	rainforest	n. 雨林	31	complicated	adj. 複雜的
7	release	v. 發行，釋出	32	deal with	phr. 處理～
8	convince	v. 說服；使確信	33	frustrating	adj. 令人挫折的；令人洩氣的
9	recruit	v. 聘僱；招募；n. 新成員	34	missing	adj. 缺失的；不見的
10	advocate for	phr. 主張～；擁護～	35	straightforward	adj. 簡單的；易懂的
11	analysis	n. 分析	36	board of directors	phr. 董事會
12	extend	v. 延長	37	concerned	adj. 憂慮的，擔心的
13	financial	adj. 金融的；財務的	38	consecutive	adj. 連續的
14	necessity	n. 必要性；必需品	39	investor	n. 投資者
15	set up	phr. 設置（機器等）	40	responsibility	n. 責任；職責
16	advisor	n. 顧問	41	vice president	phr. 副總裁
17	customize	v. 客製化	42	welcome	v. 迎接，歡迎
18	forward	v. 傳送；轉發	43	cooperation	n. 合作，協力
19	properly	adv. 恰當地；正確地	44	detour	n. 繞道
20	refer to	phr. 參考～	45	fine	n. 罰金；罰鍰
21	tracking	n. 追蹤；跟蹤	46	in accordance with	phr. 根據～
22	against	prep. 對照	47	license plate number	phr. 車牌號碼
23	glitch	n. 小故障	48	tow truck	phr. 拖吊車
24	inaccuracy	n. 錯誤；不精確	49	content	n. 內容
25	payroll department	phr. 薪資管理部	50	familiar	adj. 熟悉的

TEST 04_D

1	massive	adj. 巨大的；嚴重的	26	access	v. 存取（資料等）； n. 進入的權利；使用
2	uncertainty	n. 不確定性	27	firm	n. 公司
3	construction	n. 工程；建設	28	keep in mind	phr. 記得
4	designate	v. 指定；指名	29	notify	v. 通知
5	make the best of	phr. 充分善用（不好的條件等）	30	postpone	v. 推遲
6	relocate	v. 重新安置；遷移	31	shut down	phr. 關閉
7	temporary	adj. 臨時的	32	technical	adj. 技術的
8	toward	prep. 朝向；接近	33	workload	n. 工作量
9	workstation	n. 工作站	34	bulk	adj. 大量的，大批的； n. 大部分
10	real estate	phr. 不動產	35	incorrect	adj. 不正確的
11	retrieve	v. 取回；重新得到	36	last-minute	adj. 在最後一刻的
12	signature	n. 簽名	37	partial	adj. 部分的
13	sorting	n. 分類；挑選	38	portable	adj. 可攜帶的；手提的
14	double	v. 使成兩倍；adj. 兩倍的	39	registration form	phr. 報名表
15	expansion	n. 擴張	40	statement	n. 明細表；聲明
16	gift certificate	phr. 禮券	41	confident	adj. 確信的；有信心的
17	incentive	n. 獎勵；動機	42	electric fan	phr. 電風扇
18	result	n. 成果；結果	43	focus group	phr. 焦點團體
19	revise	v. 修改，修正	44	next to	phr. 繼～之後；在～旁邊
20	still	adv. 仍然；儘管如此	45	percentage	n. 百分比
21	formalize	v. 正式確定	46	purifier	n. 淨化器
22	interface	n. 介面	47	respondent	n. 應答者
23	operation	n. 事業，活動；營運	48	affordable	adj.（價格）實惠的； 負擔得起的
24	stock price	phr. 股價	49	historical site	phr. 歷史景點
25	team up	phr. 合作	50	hop	v.（輕快地）跳上（交通工具）

TEST 05_A

1	adjust	v. 調整	26	dentist	n. 牙醫
2	coworker	n. 同事	27	permit	v. 允許；n. 許可（證）
3	chest	n. 胸膛	28	stage	n. 舞台
4	cross one's arms	phr. 交叉雙臂	29	accounting	n. 會計
5	stack	v. 堆疊；堆放； n. 一堆，一疊	30	employment	n. 受僱
6	windowsill	n. 窗台	31	training	n. 訓練，培訓
7	lean against	phr. 倚靠～	32	bulb	n. 燈泡
8	handrail	n. 欄杆；扶手	33	immediately	adv. 馬上，立刻
9	wharf	n. 碼頭	34	record	n. 記錄
10	jar	n. 罐；瓶	35	turn on	phr. 打開～
11	set out	phr. 擺放	36	manuscript	n. 原稿；手稿
12	damage	v. 損壞；毀損	37	recommend	v. 推薦；建議
13	paint	v. 畫；漆	38	shorten	v. 縮短；減少
14	pavement	n. 鋪設過的地面，路面；人行道	39	suggest	v. 建議
15	portion	n. 部分	40	conference call	phr. 電話會議
16	college	n. 大學；學院	41	campus	n.（大學等的）校園
17	wait in line	phr. 排隊等待	42	exhibit	n. 展覽；v. 展示
18	local	adj. 當地的	43	so long as	phr. 只要～
19	probably	adv. 也許	44	be open to	phr. 對～願意接受
20	row	n. 列，排	45	normally	adv. 通常，一般
21	boutique	n. 精品店	46	check on	phr. 確認（是否有異常）
22	lease	n. 租約；v. 租賃	47	instruction	n. 指示
23	compartment	n.（為特定目的而劃分的）隔間	48	receive	v. 接到，收到
24	voucher	n. 憑證；票券；保證人	49	status	n.（進行的）狀態
25	appointment	n. 會面；（會面的）約定	50	appealing	adj. 吸引人的

TEST 05_B

1	resign	v. 辭去	26	requirement	n. 要求；必要條件
2	proofread	v. 校對	27	selection	n. 選擇；可供選擇的東西
3	mistake	n. 錯誤	28	variety	n. 種類；各種
4	payroll	n. 薪資明細	29	venue	n. 場地
5	souvenir	n. 紀念品	30	adopt	v. 採用
6	executive officer	phr. 行政主管	31	by chance	phr. 剛好，偶然
7	step down	phr. 退位；卸任	32	in order	phr. 就緒
8	vacation	n. 度假；v. 度假	33	physical examination	phr. 健康檢查
9	merchandise	n. 貨物，商品	34	prescription	n. 處方箋
10	depend on	phr. 取決於～	35	register	v. 登記，註冊；n. 收銀機
11	trouble	n. 麻煩，困擾； v. 造成麻煩	36	capacity	n. 能力
12	troubleshoot	v. 分析並解決問題	37	craft	n. 工藝
13	appetizer	n. 開胃菜	38	decorative	adj. 裝飾性的
14	seem	v. 看起來好像	39	impressed	adj. 感到印象深刻的
15	undercooked	adj.（食物）沒有煮熟的	40	propose	v. 提議；提出
16	finance	n. 財務；財政	41	workforce	n.（特定企業、組織等的全部）員工；勞動力
17	function	n. 宴會；聚會；功能	42	workshop	n. 工作坊
18	update	v. 更新；為～提供最新消息	43	anticipate	v. 預期
19	chauffeur	n. 私人司機	44	close down	phr. 封閉
20	drop off	phr. 帶（到某地點）放下	45	concern	n. 憂慮
21	rental	n. 租賃	46	inspiration	n. 靈感
22	timetable	n. 行程表	47	new hire	phr. 新進人員
23	combination	n. 組合；混合	48	artwork	n. 藝術品
24	department	n. 部門	49	beforehand	adv. 事先
25	remaining	adj. 剩下的，剩餘的	50	display	v. 展示；n. 展示；展示品

TEST 05_C

1	enlarge	v. 擴大	26	volunteer	v. 自願做；自願提供
2	reference	v. 做為參考；提及	27	relaxing	adj. 悠閒的
3	room	n. 空間；位置	28	appropriate	adj. 適合的；恰當的
4	take down	phr. 將～拿下來；拆除（建物等）	29	dealership	n. 經銷商
5	tapestry	n. 掛毯	30	duplicate	n. 副本；v. 複製
6	tight	adj.（沒有餘裕時間而）緊湊的	31	minimum	adj. 最少的；最低限度的
7	vacant	adj. 空著的	32	notification	n. 通知；告示
8	administrator	n. 管理人員；行政人員	33	prepayment	n. 預付；提前支付
9	advanced	adj. 進階的；高級的；先進的	34	van	n. 廂型車
10	curriculum	n. 課程	35	be filled with	phr. 充滿～
11	gather	v. 收集；使聚集	36	boardwalk	n.（在海邊等地的）木棧道
12	institute	n. 學院；協會	37	fortunate	adj. 幸運的
13	participant	n. 參加者	38	harbor	n. 港口
14	accurate	adj. 精確的；正確的	39	kite-flying	n. 放風箏
15	look over	phr. 查看	40	observation deck	phr. 觀景台
16	produce	n. 農產品；v. 生產	41	resident	n. 居民
17	sample	n. 樣本；v. 品嘗	42	undergo	v. 進行
18	source	n. 來源	43	colleague	n. 同事
19	stall	n. 攤位	44	handout	n.（印製的）資料；講義
20	stand	n. 攤位	45	light fixture	phr. 燈具
21	stop by	phr. 順路造訪；短暫停留	46	mess	n. 髒亂的東西；亂七八糟的狀態
22	contribute	v. 貢獻；捐款	47	rug	n. 地毯
23	coordinate	v. 協調	48	section	n. 區塊；部分
24	engagement	n. 約會	49	stain	n. 汙漬
25	fill in for	phr. 頂替～	50	unoccupied	adj. 無人使用的

TEST 05_D

1	year-end	adj. 年終的	26	motivate	v. 激勵；賦予動機
2	accumulate	v. 累積	27	attorney	n. 律師；法定代理人
3	benefit	n. 利益，好處	28	cherish	v. 珍惜
4	frequent-flyer program	phr. 飛行常客計畫	29	gymnasium	n. 體育館
5	hotline	n. 熱線電話	30	janitorial staff	phr.（大樓等場地的）管理人員
6	recruitment	n. 招募	31	housing	n. 住宅
7	applause	n. 鼓掌	32	phase	n. 階段，時期
8	consequently	adv. 結果，因此	33	comment	n. 意見，評論；v. 發表意見
9	earning	n. 收入；利潤	34	division	n. 部門
10	implement	v. 實施，施行	35	help out	phr. 幫助～解決困難
11	meet	v. 達成（目標等）	36	lead	v. 領導；主持
12	profit	n. 利益；利潤	37	take charge of	phr. 負責～
13	publication	n. 刊物；出版品	38	bound for	phr. 前往～
14	run	v. 經營；管理	39	break down	phr. 故障
15	worth	n. 價值	40	disembark	v. 下（車、船或飛機等交通工具）
16	author	n. 作家	41	emergency procedure	phr. 緊急程序
17	give away	phr. 贈送	42	overbook	v. 超賣（機位、客房等）
18	installment	n.（連載中或系列中的）一集，一篇	43	travel	v. 移動（到另一地點）；旅行
19	newsletter	n. 業務通訊	44	vessel	n. 船
20	opportunity	n. 機會	45	existing	adj. 現有的；現行的
21	regarding	prep. 關於～	46	initial	adj. 最初的
22	commission	v. 委託；委託製作；n. 佣金	47	national holiday	phr. 國定假日
23	distribution	n. 分發；分銷	48	power generation	phr. 發電
24	high-end	adj. 高檔的	49	prototype	n. 樣品；原型
25	highlight	v. 強調；n. 最重要（或吸引人）的部分	50	solar panel	phr. 太陽能板

TEST 06_A

1	dig	v. 挖	26	costume	n. 服裝；戲服
2	grip	v. 抓； n. 緊握（球拍等）	27	informative	adj. 有用的；有教育意義的
3	kneel down	phr. 跪下	28	knowledgeable	adj. 知識淵博的；有見識的
4	raise	v. 舉起；提高	29	lecturer	n. 講者；講師
5	strap	n. 帶子	30	business card	phr. 名片
6	tighten	v. 使變緊	31	budget	n. 預算；預算案
7	baggage	n. 行李	32	numerical	adj. 數值的；數字的
8	load	v. 裝載（行李等）	33	pharmaceutical	adj. 製藥的
9	unzip	v. 拉開拉鍊	34	garage	n. 車庫
10	apparel	n. 衣物	35	garbage	n. 垃圾
11	courtyard	n. 庭院	36	policy	n. 政策
12	occupy	v. 占用；占據	37	recycling	n. 回收
13	position	v. 放置（在適當位置）；n. 位置	38	throw out	phr. 丟掉
14	border	v. 形成～的邊	39	head	v. 往；朝向；n. 首長
15	path	n. 道路；小徑	40	positive	adj. 確定的
16	racetrack	n. 賽道	41	fair	n. 展覽；adj. 公正的；尚可的
17	weekly	adv. 每週	42	fare	n.（交通工具的）票價
18	complex	n.（建築物等的）複合體	43	trade	n. 貿易
19	vacate	v. 清空	44	counter	n. 流理台；櫃台
20	bite	n.能快速食用的小份量食物	45	give a tour	phr. 帶～參觀
21	license	n. 執照；許可證	46	performance review	phr. 績效評估
22	tool	n. 工具	47	assignment	n.（分派的）工作，任務
23	autograph	n.（名人的）親筆簽名	48	press release	phr. 新聞稿
24	sign	v. 簽名	49	prioritize	v. 按優先順序處理
25	in a minute	phr. 立刻	50	lounge area	phr. 休息區

TEST 06_B

1	mop	v.（用拖把）拖擦	26	flavor	n. 口味
2	spacious	adj. 寬敞的	27	regular	adj. 一般的；正常的
3	monitor	n. 螢幕；v. 監控	28	reorder	v. 再次訂購
4	situation	n. 狀況	29	seasonal	adj. 季節限定的；季節性的
5	manufacturing	n. 製造的；製造業	30	agenda	n. 議程；代辦事項
6	merger	n. 合併	31	complete	v. 完成；結束
7	regulation	n. 法規，規定	32	on short notice	phr. 臨時
8	boarding pass	phr. 登機證	33	scan	v. 掃描
9	give a hand	phr. 提供協助	34	struggle	v. 奮鬥；努力
10	spare	adj. 閒置的；多餘的；v. 騰出（時間等）；分出（多餘的東西）	35	upcoming	adj. 即將到來的
11	banquet	n. 宴會	36	billing	n. 請款；開具發票
12	reward	n. 回饋；獎勵	37	recipient	n. 收受人
13	save	v. 保留；儲蓄	38	option	n. 選項
14	overtime	n. 加班（時間）	39	profile	n. 檔案；人物簡介
15	put in	phr. 加進（工作等）；安裝	40	promotional	adj. 促銷的
16	as well	phr. 也	41	put towards	phr. 用（一筆錢）補貼購買～
17	furnished	adj. 備有家具的	42	warranty	n. 保固；保證書
18	test out	phr. 檢驗，測試	43	allow	v. 給予；容許
19	transport	v. 運送	44	architecture	n. 建築師
20	at the moment	phr. 現在	45	consultation	n. 諮詢；商議
21	poorly	adv. 糟糕地	46	finalize	v. 最終確定；完成
22	sanitation	n. 衛生環境	47	printout	n.（印出來的）資料文件
23	advertise	v. 廣告；宣傳	48	arrangement	n. 安排；準備工作
24	allergy	n. 過敏	49	fill in	phr. 填寫～
25	be about to	phr. 正要做	50	based in	phr. 總部設在～

TEST 06_C

1	eligible	adj. 有資格的	26	replenish	v. 補充
2	instructor	n. 講師	27	run low on	phr. 即將耗盡～
3	reduction	n. 削減	28	stock	n. 庫存；v. 補貨；存有（商品等）
4	now that	phr. 既然	29	art gallery	phr. 美術館
5	put together	phr. 整理並做出～	30	opposite	adv. 在對面
6	storyboard	n. 分鏡腳本	31	tourism	n. 旅遊，觀光
7	acquire	v. 獲得	32	view	v. 觀賞；看
8	attention	n. 關注；專心	33	board	v. 登上（船、飛機等交通工具）
9	corporation	n. 公司	34	boost	n. 提升；v. 促進；提升
10	coverage	n. 涵蓋範圍	35	carbohydrate	n. 碳水化合物
11	distributor	n. 分銷商	36	contain	v. 包含
12	expand	v. 擴張	37	take off	phr. 起飛
13	follow up	phr. 跟進；追蹤	38	era	n. 時期；年代
14	licensing fee	phr. 授權費	39	gain	v. 獲得
15	make the most of	phr. 充分利用～	40	uncommon	adj. 不尋常的
16	outperform	v. 超過；做得比～更好	41	unusual	adj. 不尋常的
17	quarter	n. 季度	42	beat	v. 擊敗
18	satisfactory	adj. 令人滿意的	43	catering	n. 提供外燴服務；承辦宴席
19	unpaid	adj. 未繳納的	44	incredible	adj. 絕佳的；令人難以置信的
20	as for	phr. 關於～	45	miss out	phr. 錯過
21	cough	n. 咳嗽	46	natural	adj. 天然的
22	illness	n. 疾病	47	outlet	n. 通路；商店
23	mean to	phr. 打算	48	publish	v. 刊出；發行
24	on schedule	phr. 按照預定	49	refreshing	adj. 提神醒腦的；（心情）耳目一新的
25	pharmacy	n. 藥局	50	topping	n.（加在食物上的）配料

TEST 06_D

1	unlimited	adj. 無限制的	26	neighborhood	n. 鄰近地區；街坊鄰居
2	award-winning	adj. 獲獎的	27	support	v. 支持
3	obtain	v. 獲得	28	take turns	phr. 輪流
4	talented	adj. 才華洋溢的	29	effort	n. 努力做出來的成果；努力
5	usher	n. 帶位人員	30	election	n. 選舉
6	area of expertise	phr. 專業領域	31	enterprise	n. 企業
7	criticism	n. 批評	32	entrepreneur	n. 企業家
8	ecology	n. 生態學；生態	33	favorable	adj. 有利的；有幫助的
9	journalism	n. 新聞學	34	numerous	adj. 許多的
10	keynote speaker	phr. 專題演講者	35	optimistic	adj. 樂觀的
11	paper	n. 論文	36	population	n. 人口
12	respected	adj. 備受推崇的	37	publicity	n. 公關；宣傳
13	statistics	n. 統計學	38	world-renowned	adj. 世界知名的
14	applicant	n. 申請者；應徵者	39	article	n. 報導；文章
15	cosmetic	n. 化妝品	40	commit	v. 承諾，保證
16	electronics	n. 電子產品	41	confirmation	n. 確認；確定
17	paid	adj. 付費的	42	length	n. 期間
18	reconsider	v. 重新考慮	43	open-ended	adj. 開放性的；無限制的
19	test subject	phr. 受試者	44	overpay	v. 多付
20	try out	phr. 試用	45	renewal	n.（合約等）展延；換新
21	turn away	phr. 轉過臉去；拒絕	46	aspect	n. 面相，觀點
22	ongoing	adj. 進行中的	47	monument	n. 紀念碑
23	roll out	phr. 推出	48	peak season	phr. 旺季
24	virtually	adv. 透過電腦地；虛擬地	49	resume	v. 繼續；恢復
25	enroll	v. 登記（名字等）；註冊	50	specifically	adv. 具體來說

TEST 07_A

1	beverage	n. 飲料	26	semi-final	adj. 準決賽的
2	pour	v. 傾倒	27	tie	v. 同分，平手
3	spread out	phr. 分散開來；攤開	28	include	v. 包含
4	connect	v. 連接	29	plate	n. 盤子
5	laundry	n. 待洗（或剛洗好的）衣物	30	visitor	n. 訪客
6	pull	v. 拉	31	freeway	n. 高速公路
7	remove	v. 移開；去除	32	take	v. 花費（時間等）；使用（交通方式、道路等）；搭乘
8	photograph	v. 為～拍照	33	economics	n. 經濟學
9	pose for	phr. 為～擺姿勢	34	forum	n. 論壇，討論會
10	wave	v. 揮（手、腳等）	35	president	n. 總裁；會長
11	base	n. 基座	36	transcript	n.（演講等的）文字記錄
12	coil	v. 把～捲成圈狀；盤繞	37	play	n. 戲劇
13	ladder	n. 梯子	38	reserve	v. 預約，預訂
14	pole	n. 柱子	39	visit	n. 造訪；參觀；v. 造訪；參觀
15	power tool	phr. 電動工具	40	check with	phr. 詢問～
16	prop against	phr. 靠在～	41	deliver	v. 運送；投遞
17	diner	n. 用餐的人	42	package	n. 包裹；包裝
18	flowerpot	n. 花盆	43	spend	v. 花費（時間或精力等）；花錢
19	hang	v. 懸掛	44	extension number	phr. 分機號碼
20	carry	v. 搬運	45	look for	phr. 尋找～；期待～
21	equipment	n. 器具；設備	46	pay for	phr. 支付～的費用
22	indoors	adv. 往室內	47	catalog	v. 記錄（成清單）；n. 型錄
23	mount	v. 固定；安裝	48	purchase	n. 消費；v. 購買
24	patterned	adj. 有圖案的	49	bulletin board	phr. 布告欄
25	score	n. 分數	50	medication	n. 藥物

TEST 07_B

1	up-to-date	adj. 最新的	26	engineer	n. 工程師
2	pleased	adj. 滿意的；高興的	27	dishwasher	n. 洗碗機
3	circumstance	n. 情況；情勢	28	free of charge	phr. 免費的
4	establish	v. 創立；建立	29	ought to	phr. 應該～
5	established	adj. 既有的；已確立的	30	unload	v. 卸下（貨物等）
6	management	n. 管理階層；管理	31	championship	n. 冠軍資格
7	strictly	adv. 嚴格地	32	direction	n. 指示
8	additional	adj. 額外的；附加的	33	fellow	adj. 同事的；n. 同事
9	extra	adj. 額外的；附加的	34	message	v. 傳遞訊息
10	chance	n. 機會；可能性	35	pass	n. 通行證
11	aware	adj. 察覺的	36	settle on	phr. 搞定～；決定～
12	lane	n. 車道；巷道	37	specific	adj. 具體的；明確的
13	normal	adj. 一般的；普通的	38	year-end party	phr. 尾牙
14	route	n. 路線；路程	39	attendant	n. 服務人員
15	capability	n. 性能；能力	40	box office	phr. 售票處
16	wire	n. 金屬線；電線	41	critic	n. 評論家
17	wireless	adj. 無線的	42	screening	n.（電影等）放映
18	restricted	adj. 有限度的；受限的	43	associate	n. 同事
19	vehicle	n. 車輛；搭載工具	44	freeze	v. 停住
20	spoil	v.（食物等）腐壞	45	duration	n.（時間的持續）期間
21	vegetable	n. 蔬菜	46	efficiency	n. 效率
22	beam	n. 光線	47	take effect	phr. 生效
23	engrave	v. 雕刻；銘記	48	timely	adj. 及時的；適時的； adv. 及時地；適時地
24	wrist	n. 手腕	49	turn in	phr. 繳交～
25	apply	v. 使用，運用	50	written	adj. 書面的

TEST 07_C

1	check out	phr. 借出（書籍等）	26	human resources	phr. 人力資源部
2	circulation desk	phr. 流通櫃台	27	inform	v. 告知；通知
3	holder	n. 持有者	28	share	v. 分享
4	lost-and-found center	phr. 遺失物中心	29	consistent	adj. 持續的
5	possibly	adv. 也許，可能	30	terminate	v. 解雇
6	replacement	n. 替換用的人事物；代替	31	awards ceremony	phr. 頒獎典禮
7	unfortunately	adv. 不幸地；遺憾地	32	cover	v. 涵蓋；適用於
8	absorb	v. 吸收	33	ingredient	n. 成分；原料
9	browse	v. 瀏覽	34	organic	adj. 有機的
10	quality	adj. 高級的；n. 品質	35	review	n. 評價
11	sales associate	phr. 銷售助理	36	understaffed	adj. 人手不足的
12	shock	n. 震動	37	yearly	adj. 一年一度的
13	strain	n. 負擔	38	environmental	adj. 環境的
14	attach	v. 貼上	39	examination	n. 檢查；調查
15	personal	adj. 個人的	40	rainfall	n. 降雨；降雨量
16	sticky	adj. 黏的	41	smoothly	adv. 順利地
17	call for	phr. 需要～	42	go over	phr. 仔細看過；檢討
18	scramble	v. 炒（蛋）	43	nervous	adj. 緊張不安的
19	stovetop	n. 爐子上方	44	on behalf of	phr. 代表～
20	utensil	n. 用具；器皿	45	visual material	phr. 圖表（或其他視覺化的）資料
21	network	v. 建立關係網絡，建立人脈	46	air	v. 播送
22	approach	v. 接近	47	charger	n. 充電器
23	audit	n. 審計	48	feature	n. （可以做為特色的）特別功能；特色；v. 以～做為特色；給～特別重要的地位
24	diagram	n. 圖表	49	flashlight	n. 手電筒
25	embassy	n. 大使館	50	praise	n. 稱讚；v. 稱讚

TEST 07_D

1	sneak preview	phr. 影片在公開前的試看	26	fiction	n. 小說
2	TV network	phr. 電視網	27	influence	n. 影響（力）
3	obviously	adv. 當然；顯然	28	lawyer	n. 律師
4	rush	v. 催促；匆忙地做；adj. 緊急的	29	literature	n. 文學
5	assembly	n. 組裝	30	panic	v. 使驚慌；n. 驚慌
6	operational	adj. 營運的	31	public official	phr. 公職人員
7	refrain	v. 克制；忍住	32	reform	n. 改革；v. 改革
8	reverse order	phr. 相反順序	33	stimulating	adj. 具有啟發性的
9	viewing deck	phr. 觀景台	34	value	n. 價值
10	anticipation	n. 期待	35	in honor of	phr. 為慶祝～；為表對～的尊敬
11	bistro	n. 餐酒館	36	mark down	phr. 調降價格
12	critique	n. 評論；批評	37	remind	v. 提醒
13	piece	n.（一則）報導	38	renovation	n. 整修
14	recurring	adj. 一再發生的	39	figure	n. 數量；數字
15	regret	n. 遺憾	40	look through	phr. 瀏覽
16	to perfection	phr. 恰到好處	41	quarterly	adj. 季度的
17	acting	n. 演戲，表演	42	revenue	n. 收益
18	alone	adv. 單獨；單單	43	take over as	phr. 接任～
19	big break	phr. 重大機會	44	turn around	phr. 翻轉
20	eliminate	v. 淘汰	45	constraint	n. 限制
21	former	adj. 以前的，過去的	46	expedite	v. 加快；迅速完成
22	recording	n. 錄音	47	flow chart	phr. 流程圖
23	trailer	n.（電影等的）預告片	48	inspect	v. 視察；檢查；審查
24	engaging	adj. 有吸引力的；迷人的	49	stadium	n. 體育場
25	excerpt	n. 節錄（的內容）	50	take into account	phr. 把～列入考量

TEST 08_A

1	knob	n.（球狀的）把手	26	ripe	adj.（水果等）成熟的
2	metal	adj. 金屬的	27	treat	v. 招待
3	twist	v. 扭轉	28	career	n. 職業生涯；經歷
4	wipe	v. 擦乾淨	29	decade	n. 十年
5	collect	v. 收集	30	first half	phr. 前半段，上半段
6	hanger	n. 衣架	31	primarily	adv. 主要地；首先
7	mannequin	n. 假人模特兒	32	social gathering	phr. 社交聚會
8	reflection	n. 倒影	33	renegotiate	v. 重新商議
9	notice board	phr. 公告欄	34	strategy	n. 策略
10	station	n.（車站等機構的）站；駐地	35	nearby	adj. 附近的
11	auditorium	n. 禮堂	36	intermission	n. 中場休息時間
12	point	v. 指；指向	37	public transit	phr. 大眾運輸
13	line up	phr. 排列	38	in the corner	phr. 在角落裡
14	side by side	phr. 肩並肩地；在彼此旁邊地	39	pile	v. 堆疊；n. 堆
15	umbrella	n. 陽傘；雨傘	40	reminder	n. 提醒用的事物
16	erect	v. 使豎立	41	attendee	n. 出席者，參加者
17	railing	n. 欄杆	42	due for	phr. 應該得到～
18	window frame	phr. 窗框	43	overall	adv. 整體的
19	get in	phr. 到達	44	procedure	n. 程序；手續
20	land	v. 降落	45	serve	v. 上（菜等）
21	plain	adj. 沒有花樣的；平凡的	46	standard	adj. 標準的；n. 標準；規範
22	advertisement	n. 廣告	47	undecided	adj. 未決定的
23	unsubscribe	v.（從名單中）取消訂閱；解除訂閱資格	48	accept	v. 接受
24	grocery store	phr. 食品雜貨店，雜貨店	49	odd	adj. 奇怪的，奇特的
25	restock	v. 補滿存貨；為～補貨	50	tray	n. 托盤；文件盤

TEST 08_B

1	set down	phr. 放（乘客等）下（車）	26	shelve	v. 把～放在架上
2	architect	n. 建築師	27	situate	v. 使位於
3	institution	n. 機構	28	arena	n. 競技場
4	thoroughly	adv. 徹底地；非常	29	athletic	adj. 體育的
5	formal attire	phr. 正式服裝	30	blueprint	n. 藍圖
6	internally	adv. 內部地	31	concession	n.（在特定區域）銷售商品的權利
7	retirement	n. 退休	32	improvement	n. 改進事項
8	microwave	n. 微波爐	33	put to good use	phr. 妥善利用
9	overpriced	adj. 定價過高的	34	studio	n. 工作室
10	be willing to	phr. 願意～	35	absence	n. 缺席
11	on one’s behalf	phr. 代替～；代表～	36	apologize	v. 道歉
12	reference letter	phr. 推薦信	37	clarify	v. 澄清；闡明
13	reference manual	phr. 參考手冊	38	comprehensive	adj. 完整的
14	at most	phr. 最多	39	make it	phr. 及時趕到（聚會等）
15	carry away	phr. 搬走	40	misplace	v. 錯置；忘記放在哪裡（而暫時找不到）
16	excess	adj. 多餘的；過量的	41	on hand	phr. 在手邊
17	florist	n. 花匠	42	guarantee	v. 保證
18	flowerbed	n. 花圃	43	janitor	n.（大型建築物的）管理人員
19	landscaper	n. 景觀設計師	44	maintenance	n. 養護
20	park ranger	phr. 公園巡警	45	poll	n.（對群眾進行的）意見調查
21	shed	n.（儲物用的）棚子；小屋	46	put on sale	phr. 出售
22	weed	v. 除草；n. 雜草	47	scratch	n. 刮痕
23	adhere	v. 黏附	48	crowded	adj. 擁擠的
24	fixture	n.（屋內的）固定裝置	49	itinerary	n. 旅行行程
25	hardware	n. 五金用品	50	modify	v. 修改

TEST 08_C

1	vacancy	n. 空房	26	reach	v. 與～聯絡；抵達
2	credit	n. 信用；（帳戶裡的）餘額	27	alongside	prep. 在～旁邊
3	giveaway	n. 贈品	28	clear away	phr. 清除
4	transportation authority	phr. 交通局	29	comfortable	adj. 舒適的
5	acquaint with	phr. 使熟悉～	30	condition	n.（周遭）環境；情形
6	conflict	n. 衝突	31	intersection	n. 交叉口
7	fit into	phr. 排進（做某事或見某人的時間）	32	knock down	phr. 擊倒
8	headquarters	n. 總公司	33	landscape	n. 風景
9	middle management	phr. 中間管理階層	34	officially	adv. 正式地
10	target	v. 以～為對象	35	refreshment	n. 茶點，輕食
11	agent	n. 代理商；代理人	36	soft drink	phr. 無酒精飲料
12	cityscape	n. 城市風景	37	swing by	phr. 順便去一下～
13	cruise	n. 乘船遊覽	38	compensate	v. 補償；抵銷
14	down payment	phr. 頭期款	39	end up	phr. 最後～
15	entertain	v. 招待	40	gift card	phr. 禮物卡
16	reasonably	adv. 適當地；合理地	41	import	v. 進口；n. 進口
17	take out	phr. 帶出去	42	bill	n. 帳單
18	alert	v. 警告	43	fulfill	v. 達成；履行
19	authorized	adj. 經授權的；經批准的	44	get underway	phr. 開始進行
20	carry out	phr. 執行	45	inquiry	n. 問題
21	own	v. 擁有	46	intend	v. 想要；打算
22	tenant	n. 承租人	47	issue	n. 問題
23	come by	phr.（到某地點）短暫停留；順道前往（某地點）	48	make up for	phr. 彌補～
24	dyeing	n. 染色	49	administrative	adj. 行政的
25	expo	n. 博覽會	50	emphasize	v. 強調

TEST 08_D

1	indicate	v. 表明	26	foundation	n.（建築的）地基；基礎
2	on leave	phr. 在休假中	27	tax code	phr. 稅法
3	operating system	phr. 作業系統	28	tear down	phr. 拆除
4	top priority	phr. 首要任務	29	undertake	v. 進行
5	urgency	n. 迫切	30	vote	v. 投票決定
6	realtor	n. 房地產經紀人	31	at risk of	phr. 有～的危險
7	rent	v. 租用；出租	32	attraction	n.（吸引人的）景點
8	sublease	v. 轉租；分租	33	considerably	adv. 大幅地；相當地
9	board member	phr. 董事會成員	34	sculpture	n. 雕像
10	enhance	v. 提升	35	split up	phr. 分開
11	gratitude	n. 感謝	36	accuracy	n. 準確性
12	lighthearted	adj. 輕鬆愉快的	37	demonstrate	v.（用實例或示範等方式）說明
13	strive	v. 努力	38	hopefully	adv. 但願
14	emergency personnel	phr. 應急人員	39	role-play	n. 角色扮演
15	fire station	phr. 消防局	40	validate	v. 認可
16	flaw	n. 缺點	41	airfare	n. 機票費用
17	nature	n. 本質	42	draw	n. 抽籤
18	pupil	n.（小）學生	43	set aside	phr. 留出
19	pursue	v. 從事	44	stretch	v. 到～的最大限度；竭盡
20	sector	n.（社會、產業等的）領域，部門	45	time slot	phr. 時段
21	vocation	n. 職業	46	tune in	phr.（調整頻率或頻道等）收看；收聽
22	city council	phr. 市議會	47	invoice	n. 發票，發貨單
23	crack	n. 裂痕；v. 使破裂	48	reimbursement	n. 核銷
24	debate	v. 辯論；爭辯；n. 辯論會	49	relative	n. 親戚
25	demolish	v. 拆除	50	sign up	phr. 登記～

TEST 09_A

1	suitcase	n. 行李箱	26	course	n. 課程
2	weigh	v. 秤重	27	youth	n. 青年；年輕
3	operate	v. 操作（機器等）；營運	28	agricultural	adj. 農業的
4	cable	n. 傳輸線	29	convenient	adj. 方便的
5	plug	v. 插	30	recycle	v. 回收
6	slide	v.（滑動）放進	31	be supposed to	phr. 應該～
7	curb	n.（街道的）路緣	32	guest speaker	phr. 客座講者
8	lift	v. 提起	33	suppose	v. 猜想；假定
9	shoelace	n. 鞋帶	34	stop by	phr. 短暫停留；順道拜訪
10	be put on display	phr.（擺出來）陳列，展示	35	fabric	n. 布料；織物
11	drape	v. 垂掛；裝飾	36	balance	n. 餘額
12	rack	n. 架子	37	overcharge	v. 超收費用
13	take down	phr. 拿下，撤下	38	flight	n. 航班；班機
14	crate	n. 條板箱；（分格而用來運送瓶裝物的）貨箱	39	supply	n. 補給品；生活用品；v. 供給
15	deck	n. 甲板	40	take a break	phr.（短暫）休息
16	employment agency	phr. 就業服務處	41	organize	v. 籌劃，籌辦
17	seek	v. 尋求	42	personnel	n.（總稱）員工
18	medical school	phr. 醫學院	43	skill	n. 技巧
19	physician	n. 醫生；內科醫生	44	ahead of schedule	phr. 超前進度
20	get together	phr. 相聚	45	careful	adj. 小心的；仔細的
21	all night	phr. 一整晚	46	statue	n. 雕像
22	flexible	adj. 有彈性的	47	forecast	n. 預測，預報
23	fortunately	adv. 幸運地	48	raw material	phr. 原物料
24	moving company	phr. 搬家公司	49	shortage	n. 不足，短缺
25	departure	n. 出發	50	fairly	adv. 相當，非常

TEST 09_B

1	previous	adj. 以前的	26	accommodate	v. 配合；能容納
2	suit	v. 適合	27	dine	v. 用餐
3	pleased with	phr. 對～滿意	28	expense	n. 開支；支出
4	duty	n. 職務	29	in response to	phr. 回應～
5	handle	v. 處理	30	on-site	adj. 工作地點的
6	receptionist	n. 接待人員	31	based on	phr. 根據～
7	show around	phr. 帶～參觀	32	format	n. 型式
8	ensure	v. 確保	33	handbook	n. 手冊
9	lose	v. 失去	34	make a revision	phr. 做修訂
10	prize	n. 獎品	35	refer	v. 參考
11	regional	adj. 地區的	36	specification	n. 規格
12	retail outlet	phr. 零售商店	37	inconvenience	n. 不方便；麻煩
13	retailer	n. 零售商	38	pass on	phr. 傳遞
14	satisfaction	n. 滿意度	39	regularly	adv. 定期地
15	confirm	v. 確定	40	waive	v. 免除
16	errand	n. 雜事	41	filing cabinet	phr. 檔案櫃
17	indoor	adj. 室內的	42	go through	phr. 仔細查看
18	insert	v. 放入；插入	43	lack	v. 缺乏
19	parking pass	phr. 停車證	44	matter	n. 事項；問題；v. 要緊
20	assistance	n. 幫助，協助	45	objection	n. 異議；反對
21	exhibition	n. 展覽	46	on-the-job training	phr. 在職訓練
22	latest	adj. 最新的	47	promising	adj. 大有可為的
23	let down	phr. 使～失望	48	relevant	adj. 相關的
24	proposal	n. 提議	49	superior	n. 上司；長官
25	turn down	phr. 拒絕	50	transfer	n. 轉調

TEST 09_C

1	wrap up	phr. 完成，結束	26	incomplete	adj. 不完整的
2	alarm	n. 警報器	27	relocation	n. 搬遷；重新安置
3	closure	n. 關閉；打烊	28	sort	v. 區分
4	fail	v. 失去作用	29	announcement	n. 公告
5	frustrate	v. 使喪氣	30	belong to	phr. 屬於～
6	go off	phr.（警報等）響起	31	culinary	adj. 烹飪的；烹飪用的
7	landlord	n. 房東	32	air current	phr. 氣流
8	miss	v. 未履行（約定等）；錯過	33	approximately	adv. 大約
9	stationery	n. 文具	34	captain	n. 機長
10	craftsman	n. 工匠	35	immigration form	phr. 入境卡
11	gift-wrap	v. 包成禮物的樣子	36	in-flight meal	phr. 飛機餐
12	hassle	n. 麻煩的事情	37	partly	adv. 部分地，不完全地
13	leather	adj. 皮革製的；n. 皮革	38	passenger	n. 乘客
14	messy	adj. 雜亂的	39	remain	v. 留下
15	price tag	phr. 標價	40	report	v. 回報；報導
16	salesperson	n. 銷售員	41	security guard	phr. 警衛
17	stock room	phr. 倉庫	42	upon	conj. 在～之後立刻～
18	closing	n. 關閉	43	cleaning supply	phr. 清潔用品
19	firework	n. 煙火	44	countertop	n. 流理台
20	inaccurate	adj. 不正確的	45	eco-friendly	adj. 環保的
21	mailing list	phr. 郵寄名單	46	goods	n. 商品
22	opening	n. 開幕	47	harmful	adj. 有害的
23	ride	n. 遊樂設施	48	home appliance	phr. 家電產品
24	despite	prep. 儘管	49	household	adj. 家用的
25	detail	v. 詳細說明	50	in the meantime	phr. 在此同時；同一期間

TEST 09_D

1	innovative	adj. 創新的	26	inexpensive	adj. 不昂貴的
2	surface	n. 表面	27	professional	n. 專業人員； adj. 職業的
3	banquet hall	phr. 宴會廳	28	reliable	adj. 可靠的
4	cater	v. 提供飲食；承辦外燴	29	trained	adj. 訓練有素的
5	legal	adj. 法律的	30	unnecessary	adj. 非必要的
6	state	v. 載明	31	verify	v. 確認
7	advise	v. 告知；勸告	32	wealth	n. 財富
8	along with	phr. 還有～	33	internal	adj. 內部的
9	bureau	n.（政府的）局，署	34	secretary	n. 祕書
10	Celsius	n. 攝氏的	35	integrated	adj. 整合性的
11	cope with	phr. 應對～	36	performance	n. 績效；表現
12	demanding	adj. 吃力的	37	prompt	v. 引導（做某事）；促使
13	designated	adj. 指定的	38	select	v. 選擇
14	exceed	v. 超過；勝過	39	track	v. 追蹤
15	heat wave	phr. 熱浪	40	following	adj. 接下來的
16	heatstroke	n. 中暑	41	job description	phr. 職務說明
17	nutrition	n. 營養	42	reply	v. 回覆；回答
18	official	n. 官員	43	creation	n. 作品；創造
19	physically	adv. 身體地	44	ground floor	phr. 一樓
20	severe	adj. 嚴重的	45	occur	v. 發生
21	significant	adj. 明顯的；重大的	46	pottery	n. 陶藝
22	symptom	n. 症狀	47	register for	phr. 報名～
23	treatment	n. 治療；處置	48	sponsor	v. 贊助；n. 贊助者
24	unattended	adj. 無人照料的	49	stairway	n. 樓梯
25	urgent	adj. 緊急的	50	requisition	n. 正式請求；（索取物資的）申請單

TEST 10_A

1	dust	v. 除去～的灰塵	26	could use	phr. 想要～；需要～
2	pull out	phr. 抽出	27	research laboratory	phr. 研究實驗室
3	spoke	n. 輪輻	28	spending	n. 支出
4	wheel	n. 輪子	29	divide	v. 分開
5	address	v. 對～說話	30	fee	n. 費用
6	microphone	n. 麥克風	31	in half	phr. 分成兩半
7	button up	phr. 扣鈕子	32	come up	phr. 發生（某活動或事件）
8	gaze	v. 凝視	33	farewell celebration	phr. 歡送會
9	lay	v. 放置，平放	34	order form	phr. 訂購單
10	ceiling	n. 天花板	35	appear	v. 似乎
11	light fixture	phr. 燈具	36	broken	adj. 損壞的
12	writing utensil	phr. 書寫工具	37	staircase	n. 樓梯
13	awning	n. 遮陽篷	38	seller	n. 銷售者
14	campsite	n. 營地	39	sharp	adj.（輪廓等）鮮明的；銳利的
15	water	v. 澆灌	40	account for	phr. 解釋～
16	motorcycle	n. 機車	41	decrease	n. 減少的數量
17	vine	n. 藤蔓	42	dressing	n.（調味食物用的）醬料；穿衣打扮
18	low-fat	adj. 低脂的	43	dressing room	phr. 更衣室
19	deadline	n. 截止期限	44	experienced	adj. 有經驗的
20	grant	n. 補助金；v. 同意	45	failure	n. 故障
21	adjustable	adj. 可調整的	46	mechanical	adj. 機械的
22	bookkeeper	n. 記帳人員	47	corporate	adj. 公司的
23	chart	n. 圖表	48	quote	n. 報價
24	webcam	n. 網路攝影機	49	storm	n. 暴風雨
25	conduct	v. 經營；實施	50	introduction	n. 緒論；介紹

TEST 10_B

1	on call	phr. 待命	26	representative	n. 代表人員；代表
2	shovel the snow	phr. 鏟雪	27	structure	n. 建築物
3	sidewalk	n. 人行道	28	thunderstorm	n. 大雷雨
4	out of order	phr. 故障	29	offer	n. 提議；v. 提供
5	vending machine	phr. 販賣機	30	as of now	phr. 到目前為止
6	vendor	n. 攤販	31	faulty	adj. 有瑕疵的
7	mix up	phr. 拌勻；混淆	32	reformat	v. 重新設定～的格式
8	all over	phr. 到處	33	used	adj. 用過的
9	faucet	n. 水龍頭	34	apparently	adv. 顯然地；聽說
10	assemble	v. 組裝；召集	35	dustpan	n. 畚箕
11	once	conj. 一旦～；一等～就～	36	leak	v. 漏（水等）
12	explanation	n. 說明	37	on duty	phr. 工作中
13	arrange	v. 擺放；安排	38	shift	n.（輪班的）工作時間
14	attract	v. 吸引；引起	39	waiting area	phr. 等候區
15	basement	n. 地下室；地下層	40	charcoal	n. 木炭
16	definitely	adv. 一定	41	community center	phr. 社區中心
17	machinery	n. 機器	42	fill out	phr. 填寫
18	make use of	phr. 運用～	43	in advance	phr. 事先，事前
19	patron	n. 顧客	44	redevelop	v. 重新開發
20	put out	phr. 推出；製作	45	encourage	v. 促進；鼓勵
21	reorganize	v. 重新規劃	46	hour	n. 營業時間
22	chimney	n. 煙囪	47	insurance	n. 保險
23	costly	adj. 代價高昂的	48	pamphlet	n. 小冊子
24	estimate	n. 估價；估計值	49	cost-effective	adj. 划算的
25	locate	v. 確定～的所在地點；找出	50	defect	n. 缺陷

TEST 10_C

1	agreement	n. 協議	26	modern	adj. 現代的
2	evaluate	v. 鑑定；評估	27	recreation room	phr. 娛樂室
3	in person	phr. 親自	28	text	v. 傳訊息
4	output	n. 產出	29	tour	n. 參觀
5	partnership	n. 合作關係	30	workout	n. 健身
6	renew	v. 更新；續（合約等）	31	industrial	adj. 產業的；工業的
7	videoconference	n. 視訊會議	32	parking garage	phr. 停車場
8	contractor	n. 承包商；立契約人	33	respective	adj. 個別的
9	due to	phr. 由於	34	warehouse	n. 倉庫
10	justify	v. 為～辯解；正當化	35	be dedicated to	phr. 致力於～
11	prohibit	v. 禁止；使不可能	36	charity	n. 慈善團體；慈善
12	recall	v. 記得	37	disadvantaged	adj. 弱勢的
13	zoning	n.（都市土地使用的）區劃	38	donate	v. 捐贈
14	briefcase	n. 公事包	39	outfit	n.（一整套的）服裝
15	letter of recommendation	phr. 推薦信	40	submission	n. 提交；提交物
16	among	prep. 在～之中	41	condominium	n. 產權獨立的公寓大樓
17	analyze	v. 分析	42	longstanding	adj. 長時間的
18	associated with	phr. 和～聯繫在一起	43	long-term	adj. 長期的
19	attachment	n.（電子郵件的）附檔	44	negotiate	v. 協商
20	competitor	n. 競爭對手	45	specialty	n. 專長
21	focus	n. 重點	46	dress code	phr. 服裝規定
22	application form	phr. 申請表	47	morale	n. 士氣
23	curious	adj. 好奇的	48	off-limits	adj. 禁止進入的
24	flooring	n.（室內鋪設的）地板（材料）	49	polo shirt	phr. polo 衫
25	lock	v. 鎖	50	security	n. 安全；保全

台灣廣廈國際出版集團
Taiwan Mansion International Group

國家圖書館出版品預行編目（CIP）資料

全新！新制多益TOEIC聽力題庫解析 / Hackers Academia著；
Joung, 談采薇譯. -- 初版. -- 新北市：國際學村，2021.02
面；　公分
ISBN 978-986-454-144-7
1. 多益測驗

805.1895　　109018377

國際學村

全新！新制多益 TOEIC 聽力題庫解析

作　　者／Hackers Academia
譯　　者／Joung、談采薇
編輯中心編輯長／伍峻宏・**編輯**／徐淳輔
封面設計／何偉凱・**內頁排版**／菩薩蠻數位文化有限公司
製版・印刷・裝訂／東豪・弼聖・紘億・秉成

行企研發中心總監／陳冠蒨
媒體公關組／陳柔彣
綜合業務組／何欣穎

發 行 人／江媛珍
法律顧問／第一國際法律事務所 余淑杏律師・北辰著作權事務所 蕭雄淋律師
出　　版／國際學村
發　　行／台灣廣廈有聲圖書有限公司
地址：新北市235中和區中山路二段359巷7號2樓
電話：（886）2-2225-5777・傳真：（886）2-2225-8052
讀者服務信箱／cs@booknews.com.tw

代理印務・全球總經銷／知遠文化事業有限公司
地址：新北市222深坑區北深路三段155巷25號5樓
電話：（886）2-2664-8800・傳真：（886）2-2664-8801
郵政劃撥／劃撥帳號：18836722
劃撥戶名：知遠文化事業有限公司（※單次購書金額未滿1000元需另付郵資70元。）

■出版日期：2021年2月
2023年9月16刷
ISBN：978-986-454-144-7

TEST 10_D

1	workplace	n. 職場；工作地點	26	modification	n. 變更；修改
2	approval	n. 批准	27	repave	v. 重新鋪面
3	compensation	n. 補償；補償金	28	sponsorship	n. 贊助
4	confidential	adj. 機密的	29	tournament	n. 錦標賽；比賽
5	formally	adv. 正式地	30	traffic congestion	phr. 塞車
6	hourly wage	phr. 時薪	31	warn	v. 提醒；警告
7	on occasion	phr. 偶爾	32	audio-visual equipment	phr. 影音設備
8	reflect	v. 反映；帶來影響	33	distinctive	adj. 獨特的
9	time and a half	phr.（與正常工資相比）1.5 倍的加班費	34	participate	v. 參加
10	botanical garden	phr. 植物園	35	require	v. 需要
11	cease	v. 停止	36	mandatory	adj. 強制的
12	exit	v. 離開；n. 出口	37	on a regular basis	phr. 定時的
13	ground	n.（為某種目的而劃分出來的）場所	38	solution	n. 解決方式
14	inaccessible	adj. 無法去的；難以到達的	39	wellness	n. 健康
15	store	v. 存放；n. 商店	40	workspace	n. 工作地點
16	award	n.獎品，獎項	41	charge	n. 費用；v. 收費
17	be set to	phr. 預期～	42	generally	adv. 一般地
18	celebratory	adj. 慶祝的；祝賀的	43	installation	n. 安裝
19	competition	n. 比賽；賽會	44	material	n. 材料
20	complication	n.（使事情變複雜的）麻煩	45	vary	v. 變動
21	contestant	n. 參賽者	46	concierge	n. 門房
22	entrance fee	phr. 入場費	47	continental	adj. 歐陸的；大陸的
23	first-ever	adj. 最初的	48	housekeeping	n. 房務
24	fishing pole	phr. 釣竿	49	midnight	n. 午夜，半夜 12 點鐘
25	flock	v. 聚集	50	pillow	n. 枕頭